JOHN COLTER—experienced woodsman, resourceful, self-reliant. His prominent facial birthmark resembles a hawk in flight. His strict moral code compels him to keep his promises — often to his own detriment. He joins the Lewis and Clark Expedition to get away from one problem only to wind up teamed with the insufferable George Shannon and at the mercy of ruthless Sergeant John Ordway . . .

GEORGE SHANNON—naïve and inexperienced to a fault with an immobilizing fear of water and a penchant for taking the wrong fork in the trail. He joins the Expedition with dreams of glory that alienate the crew, including Colter, the man charged with keeping him out of trouble . . .

FRAGRANT GRASS—recently-widowed Mandan woman with a distinctive streak of white in her black hair. She overcomes Colter's hatred of Indians but ends up turning her own people against her . . .

JOSIAH HARTLEY—a deranged and unscrupulous preacher, driven by the promised rewards of riches, a permanent pulpit and the home he has always longed for, he tenaciously tracks John Colter and the Expedition up the uncharted Missouri only to get the one thing he had not counted on . . .

SERGEANT JOHN ORDWAY—determined to prove his worth to the leaders of the Expedition, he singles Colter out to use as a disciplinary example for the whole crew. Colter, however, has other ideas, resulting in a violent clash of wills . . .

McBAIN—a gambler and opportunist with no first name, a secretive past and a volatile disposition that is charming one minute and treacherous the next; he sees nothing wrong with using others to do the dirty work while he collects the spoils . . .

Also by Margaret Wyman

MISSION

The Birth of California, The Death of a Nation

(See Chapter 1 at the end of this book)

HARD MEN, HARD DECISIONS

"We need you with us, Colter," Clark said. "You have shown your mettle time and again."

He was too empty to speak or meet the captain's eyes. Whatever mettle he might have had left him, replaced by a numbing futility.

"Are you still with us?" Clark asked gently.

He swallowed. His spirit had already left this place to fly to Fragrant Grass ahead of his body. Now his body was trapped. There was no way to leave. Yet, here was the captain, asking him to call his spirit back, to force it to return to a place it did not want to be.

Clark's voice fell. "Colter, I need to hear your answer."

Colter lifted his eyes to the eastern horizon, to the direction he longed to go, the direction now blocked for him by circumstance. His words rang with all the bitterness he felt. "I'm here, ain't I?"

The captain's face softened. "Yes, thank God, you are."

What God? Colter thought. *Ain't no God. Ain't no hope. Ain't nothin' but this bloody river under a sky that gives a body blisters one minute, gooseflesh the next. I come all this way. For what? To get myself into a place I cain't never leave? To finally find a woman to love only to leave her behind? What kind of fool decision did I think I was makin' when I come on instead of waitin' for her? Why? Where's the sense in anythin'?*

SHINING MOUNTAINS, WESTERN SEA

The Untold Story of the Crewmen of the Lewis & Clark Expedition

MARGARET WYMAN

IDYLLWILD
PUBLISHING CO.
IDYLLWILD, CALIFORNIA

SHINING MOUNTAINS, WESTERN SEA

This is a work of fiction. Although certain historical characters and events serve as background, the characters and events in this novel are fictitious or are used fictitiously.

Book Design and Editing by Jerry Orton

Cover Design and Cover Art by Cathi A. Wong

First edition

Published by Idyllwild Publishing Co., a division of Wild Ink Productions,
P.O. Box 355, Idyllwild, CA 92549

IDYLLWILD PUBLISHING CO. and the accompanying logo are trademarks of Idyllwild Publishing Co., a division of Wild Ink Productions

Publisher's Cataloging-In-Publication
Wyman, Margaret
    Shining Mountains, Western Sea / by Margaret Wyman
        p. ;   cm.
    ISBN 1-931857-01-6
    1.   Historical Fiction–The Lewis and Clark Expediton
    2.   American Literature–The Early West
    3.   American Historical Literature–Westward Expansion
    I. Title

PS3573.Y58 S55 2003
813'.54 — dc21   LCCN: 2002111142

Printed in the United States of America

For Jerry, the blue-eyed, sweet-smilin'
Texan, mate of my soul
and
For Cheryl, whose love is as wide and
enfolding as a prairie sunset

Author's Notes

This is a work of fiction, the imagined tale of two of the enlisted men who made the Lewis and Clark Expedition a resounding success. The story is based on the historical accounts of that landmark journey, but it was never meant to be taken literally as fact.

There is no documentation (at least none that has been found) of Colter's unusual birthmark, Shannon's ineptness and liaisons, his return-trip amnesia or Ordway's dark secret. The famed journals of the expedition do not discuss the enmity between Colter and Ordway, or Shannon and Floyd. While all the Expedition members, Manuel Lisa, and many of the Indian leaders used in the story are real, other characters – Fragrant Grass, Josiah Hartley, McBain, Mint – were born of my imagination. These "not facts" are devices for creating what I hope is a compelling story of what the crewmen faced on their historic 8,000-mile, 29-month journey.

Why focus on the crewmen, instead of the captains?

It took the efforts of 35 men, not just two, to pull off the fantastic feat that was the Expedition. The experience of the crew would have been, by definition, different from that of the two captains. They were the ones who cordelled the boats and hunted the game, who endured rain, sleet, hail, snow and blazing sun day after wearying day, who kept going despite their doubts and aches, and yet they have faded into historic oblivion. To my mind, that's a wrong that needs righting, and it was that premise that guided my efforts over the fourteen years it took to research, write and edit this story.

The Expedition was documented in the journals of nine members, six of which have been found. These convey the details of the journey – the weather, miles traveled, latitude, longitude, descriptions of scenery and game, descriptions of the native peoples along the route, and the like. What they leave out are the reasons these brave souls joined the Corps of Discovery in the first place, their joys and sorrows, dreams and fears, friendships and frictions. In short, what is missing is the essence of the memories the crewmen carried with them to their graves. Those are the blanks that I attempted to fill in with this book. Only you, precious reader, can judge whether or not I succeeded.

Namasté,
Margaret Wyman
Idyllwild, California
August, 2002

Margaret (Peggy) Wyman

Margaret Wyman, author of **Mission**, **Talisman**, and **Shining Mountains, Western Sea**, has a degree in mathematics, but in her words, "I didn't let that stop me from writing!" She grew up in Idaho, where Lewis and Clark have the stature of demigods. This is one of the reasons she loves to write about historical characters and events. She now makes her home in the splendid San Jacinto Mountains of California, where she is currently writing the first book of a trilogy called **String of Pearls**. She is also a nationally recognized award-winning artist, having created a unique form of art, called *sculptural basketry* — sculptures woven with pine needles, waxed linen, beads, manzanita wood, and other combinations of natural components. She is represented by Songolo Gallery in Idyllwild, CA, one of the 100 best art destinations in the United States.

Acknowledgements

This book has been fourteen years in the making. Along the way, I have been blessed with the help, encouragement and love of many people.

This work of fiction would not have been possible without the scores of non-fiction works available on the subject of the Lewis and Clark Expedition. I am endebted to each and every researcher and writer whose work provided me with a solid base from which to imagine this story.

Most important, this book and all the others would never have been written were it not for the brave, hardy, persistent crewmen of the Lewis and Clark Expedition and the vision of Thomas Jefferson. Today, many of the members of the Corps of Discovery have been forgotten to the exclusion of the two expedition leaders. That is a situation I pray this book will remedy.

Ken Harris loaned me his Volkswagen camper van for a month-long trip along the Missouri, Kooskooskee, Snake and Columbia, tracing the route of the explorers. The trip is an experience I will never forget.

Ernie Walski cared enough about me to let me leave my job in order to pursue my dream.

My precious friend Cheryl Tellefson has been the cheerleader for this project from its beginning.

Sharer of dreams and ideas, gentle critic, PR guru, publisher, comedian, proofreader, accountant, the lovingest, handiest, most honest man I know – that's husband, friend and soul-mate, Jerry Orton,

My brother Jim Cuddihy and his wife Lorraine encouraged and accepted me even when they didn't have a clue why I was doing what I was doing.

To the thousands and thousands of people in this country who support the monuments and important sites along the Lewis and Clark Trail with their time, their energy, their money and their love, thanks from all of us who get to enjoy the product of your passion.

CORPS OF DISCOVERY
1803--1806

CAPTAINS

Meriwether Lewis   William Clark

SERGEANTS

Charles Floyd   Patrick Gass
John Ordway   Nathaniel Pryor

PRIVATES

William Bratton   John Collins
John Colter   Pierre Cruzatte
Joseph Field   Reuben Field
Robert Frazer   George Gibson
Silas Goodrich   Hugh Hall
Thomas Proctor Howard   Francois LaBiche
Jean Baptiste LePage   Hugh McNeal
John Potts   George Shannon
John Shields   John B. Thompson
Peter M. Weiser   William Werner
Joseph Whitehouse   Alex. Hamilton Willard
Richard Windsor

NON-MILITARY MEMBERS

Toussaint Charbonneau   Sacagawea
Jean Baptiste Charbonneau   Baptiste Deschamps
Pierre Dorion   George Drouillard
York

NON-HUMAN MEMBERS

Seaman

CONTENTS

Excerpt from **MISSION:** The Birth of California,
The Death of a Nation by Margaret Wyman

PART 1

BEGINNINGS

Fall, 1803

(They are) robust young Backwoodsmen of Character
helthy, hardy young men, recommended.
— William Clark

1. *Ma*

End of September, 1803 — Near Stuart's Draft, Virginia

J ohn Colter reined in his horse at the top of the lane leading down to the house and filled his lungs with the familiar scents of home. Ripening apples hung heavy on the trees in the little orchard, blocking his view of the house. Their perfume, mixed with the heavy pungency of the nearby privy and the mossy scent of the summer-sapped creek, drifted to him on the late-September breeze. Familiar smells that seemed sweeter to him now that he was on the verge of leaving them forever.

His hand moved automatically to the bulge in his saddlebag. His stake money, the result of ten years' hard work out on his trap lines in western Kentucky Territory. The last two winters since his partner Zoob died had been the worst, but now it was time to find new partners and a new life. In two weeks he would leave for Louisville to join Scratch Wilkes's outfit. That meant saying goodbye to Ma and Stuart's Draft for good. He had just two weeks to find the right moment to break the news, a task he dreaded like a child facing a whipping.

Blaze's nicker brought him out of his reverie. He patted her neck. "Yep. I see 'em."

He loosened the reins so she could feed on the fruit that had fallen from the apple trees. Apples were her favorite treat, one she had not tasted in months.

Looking about from his perch on Blaze's back, it struck Colter that his mother was finally relaxing her frugal ways now that Pa was gone. Windfall apples littered the orchard. It was not like her to not gather them up for cider or apple butter the minute they fell. He made a mental note to get out here early tomorrow to clean things up, then wheeled Blaze down the lane.

Approaching the house, he took note of the minor repairs he needed to see to before he left. He was almost at the porch before he noticed how quiet the place was. Where were the chickens? And Daisy, Ma's curious three-legged goat?

The door to the barn was shut so she was likely off visiting. Good. That gave him time to prepare for her reaction to his news.

He was about to step up to the porch when the barn door groaned open. Out came a man leading a horse. Enos Smoot, Farley Stuart's overseer.

Smoot stopped short as if startled to see Colter, then came forward with his hand outstretched. "You just get home, John?"

Colter shook the man's hand. "Just now."

Smoot nodded. "Be around long?"

Colter ignored the question to ask his own. "You got business with Ma?"

There was an awkward pause before Smoot said, "You haven't heard then."

"Heard what?"

"Your ma died. Two weeks back."

Colter flinched as if lashed by the words. "She what? How?"

"She took a fall in the spring house," Smoot continued. "Must have hit her head. She drowned in the spring pool."

Ma? Dead?

"I came by to see what repairs the place needs." Smoot glanced toward the barn, then back at Colter. "Suppose it falls to me to tell you that this place belongs to Mr. Stuart now. Your ma sold it to him before she died, but we been holding off doing any work till you got home. We did take the animals over to the big house though. Slaves're looking after them."

Colter pivoted slowly toward the little house that had long been his home. His mind rebelled at accepting what his ears had heard. Ma? Dead? No, it could not be. Surely this was some cruel joke.

The leather of Smoot's saddle complained as he climbed into it. "You got questions, best you go see Mr. Stuart."

Colter tried to imagine the kitchen without Ma, bustling to fix him some food, chattering all the news she had saved up for his return. He could not conjure such a picture.

"Sorry I had to be the one to break the bad news, Colter," Smoot said.

She can't be dead. I never said goodbye to her.

"Well, I got to get on back," said Smoot. "You need anything, you let us know. Hear?"

Colter was too numb to acknowledge Smoot's departure. He sank down on the porch and put his head in his hands.

The little slave boy lay curled in the corner of the church sound asleep. Except for the child's light breathing, the room was still as Josiah Hartley watched out the narrow window that looked onto the graveyard. Farley Stuart's orders had been specific: *The minute you see him, send Puddin back to let me know. Don't fail me now.*

Hartley was not about to fail Stuart. Not this close to fulfilling the vow he had made the day his boyhood had come to an abrupt end at the age of nine. He had been out hunting squirrels that afternoon and been unusually lucky. He had downed three and was carrying them back home when he stepped around the bushes at the edge of the clearing to a nightmare. Instead of the shanty cabin he had left, all that remained were blackened smoking ruins. He flung aside the squirrels and went looking for his family. What he found was five charred bodies: his parents and three sisters, all the blood kin he had in the world.

He would never know who had set the fire or what became of the squirrels. Suddenly he was homeless, penniless and all alone in the world. Frightened and crying, he wandered the forest for hours until exhaustion forced him to stop. Then he burrowed into a pile of leaves like an animal seeking warmth. He lay on the ground aching with sorrow until the discomfort of his body overcame the pain of his loss. As he got to his feet, he made himself a promise: No matter what it took, he would win a home for himself. A place no one could ever take away from him.

He took off walking, following the sun's course across the sky, and never looked back. Two weeks later, he stumbled onto a tent meeting. Never before had he seen such carryings-on. But it was the sight of hats being passed from hand to hand, brimming with contributions that captured and held his imagination. That night he plucked a leather-bound Bible from the hands of a snoring matron and helped himself to a horse from the picket line. Thus he began a career as a self-anointed man of the cloth.

Still, even though gifted with talents for oratory and manipulation, his life had not been an easy road. It had taken him twenty years to get to the Draft. Twenty years of scheming, of kow-towing to the right people, of wearing out his wits to bring him to this place, to this moment when the fulfillment of his dream was nearly in his grasp.

Just two more months. Sixty days, he told himself as he glanced around the little church. Daylight poured through the unrepaired chinks in the north wall. Streaks of sunlight fell across the rough plank benches and the hard-packed dirt floor. The only adorned wall had a simple cross nailed to it. An incongruously elegant lectern, a gift from Farley Stuart, rested a few paces from that cross. Stuart preferred to spend his money on things that stood out, whether or not they were necessary. To his mind, chinking and wood flooring were details for the rest of the congregation to see to.

The sound of an approaching horse checked Hartley's thoughts. A rider drew up at the entrance to the adjoining cemetery. Hartley pressed against the rough wall to keep the newcomer from spotting him through the window.

The slump of the man's shoulders attested to a deep weariness. He slid off his horse and stood for a moment facing the well-used saddle. When he turned, he moved woodenly.

Hartley held himself rigid. This could be the one he had been watching for, but he had to be sure before he made his move.

The horse was chestnut brown with a white star blaze between its eyes. It looked as weary as its rider. The man was a little less than six feet tall, in his late twenties, maybe twenty-eight or twenty-nine. His clothes were worn and trail-dirty. His legs had the outward bow of a man who spent long days in the saddle.

Pausing at the waist-high gate, the man made an attempt to brush some of the dirt off his clothes, then removed his hat and pushed straggling locks of light-brown hair out of his eyes before clapping the hat back into place.

Hartley sucked in a breath at the sight of the purplish mark spreading across the man's left cheek and temple. Ellen Colter, the dead woman whose grave this man had come to visit, had described that mark as the shadow of an angel flying across the face of God while the more cynical

Stuart claimed it looked like a crow circling a dead cow at high noon. To Hartley, it was his cue to move. This was the man he had been waiting for. "Puddin!"

The grave lay between Pa's and the three other children Ma had borne and buried. Colter walked slowly to the foot of the bare earthen mound. The grass trampled by his mother's mourners was just beginning to stand upright again. In two more weeks the little path around the grave would not be visible, and by next spring her burial mound would look like all the others, covered with gentians and spring lilies, as life — and death — marched on.

He drew out of his side pouch the wooden figure of a river otter poised to slide into a pool and placed it at the head of the grave. Ma had always treasured the carvings he made for her.

On the other side of Pa's marker stood another smaller stone. It marked the grave of Colter's boyhood friend and long-time trapping partner, Zoob, who had died in Colter's arms two years ago. Zoob, Pa, and now Ma. Three graves for the three people he had loved most. Three ragged holes in his heart.

As he stood among the dead, the numbness that had settled over him when he heard the news about his mother began to harden into the reality of loss. Then a footfall alerted him that he was not alone.

He turned to see a man coming toward him from the church. The man had the gangly body of an adolescent boy who had grown too tall to catch up to himself. His black shovel hat and frock coat seemed at once too small and too large, emphasizing a left shoulder that was decidedly higher than the right and a distinctive lopsided gait.

"Sorry to disturb you, friend. I'm the new preacher hereabouts. Name's Hartley. Josiah Hartley," said the stranger whose long narrow face was clean-shaven except for a thin mustache above a mouthful of uneven yellow teeth.

Colter shook the hand the man offered but did not feel inclined to introduce himself or to talk at all.

"You must be Ellen's son, John." Hartley nodded toward the grave. "It must be quite a shock for you to come home to this."

Colter offered no answer. He wanted to be left alone.

Hartley continued to prattle. "She was a fine woman. Upright, kind, God-fearing." He paused as if searching for words. "This isn't the best time to bring this up, but my conscience will not allow me to stay silent. We had to bury your mother without her Bible because your uncle insisted on keeping it for you. He would not listen to reason even though that Bible was as much a part of her as the wedding band she is still wearing. She was never without it in life and it isn't right for her to be without it in death. I hope you agree."

He cast an appealing glance at Colter who scarcely noticed. Grief had ripped apart the thin skin of his earlier denial and the pain oozing from that wound made it hard for him to care about anything else.

Hartley nodded sympathetically. "I understand. This is all so much to take in at one time." He laid a bony hand on Colter's forearm. "We'll talk again."

Colter shrugged away the hand. He wanted no sympathy, no talk. He wanted to be alone. Hartley seemed to get the message and hurried back to the church.

Colter knelt wearily at the foot of his mother's grave. He had spent weeks worrying about how she would take the news that he had decided to go west for good. Now his worries were over. She would never experience the pain of his leaving. She would never feel anything again. Ever.

The sun was past zenith when Colter finally left the cemetery. He knew he ought to go back to the farm, but he could not bring himself to face the empty house. Instead, he decided to go retrieve his mother's Bible.

Lorenzo Colter's house sat on top of a small hill with a patchwork of fields stretching between it and a spring-fed creek. A few years back his uncle had added a deep porch across the width of the house on the west. Hardly a day went by without Lorenzo and his wife Devonna watching the sun set from that porch.

As Colter rode up the sloping path to the house, his uncle walked out of the barn with a pitchfork slung over his shoulder. "Devonna. John's back," he called to his wife.

Lorenzo was of medium height and muscular. It took three grown men to knock him off a stance once he was set. For once he was without his favorite floppy-brimmed hat to cover up the widening streaks of gray in his dark brown hair. He took a long look at Colter. "You know then?"

Colter nodded and swung off Blaze's back. Grabbing the horse's reins, his uncle put a fatherly arm over his shoulders. "We didn't know when you'd get here. Only thing to do was wait."

Devonna came out of the house, wiping her hands on her apron. A shaft of sunlight fell on the thick braid that encircled her head, highlighting the red in her blonde hair. She hurried forward to embrace Colter. "What an awful homecoming for you, Johnny."

A little of Aunt Dev usually went a long way, but now he drew comfort from her arms. "Come on inside," she said, leading the way into the large warm kitchen. She poured cups of chickory coffee for the two men, then went back to the dough she had been kneading when Colter showed up, leaving them to talk.

"Was me found Ellen," Lorenzo said softly. "Either she tripped or she fainted. Found her face-down in that little pool in the spring house. Just that little bit of water's all it took."

Devonna cut in. "Go on, Lo. Tell him the rest."

Lorenzo threw her a warning look. "Not now. He's had enough of a shock."

"No, Uncle. Now's best. Might as well hear it all," Colter said.

His uncle's face and tone hardened. "It wasn't even a week later that Farley Stuart showed up with a bill of sale for your land, Johnny. Signed by your ma and dated a week before she died." He paused, his jaw working. "Now I don't know where Stuart got that paper, but I know — and you do, too — that your ma would never sell that land to Farley Stuart. She hated him worse than your pa did."

Aunt Dev chimed in. "If she needed to sell, she'd come to us first, but we never heard a word about it until Stuart showed up here pretending to be so concerned about you. Saying he wanted to do fair by you. Horse-feathers!"

Lorenzo waved for her to calm down before she worked herself into one of her spells. "And then there's the money. Stuart said he paid her in gold. Two hundred dollars. But we've searched your place top to bottom and found nary a plugged nickle."

"Stuart's been after that piece of land for years," Aunt Dev spat. "Now he has it, however he wangled it. And I do mean wangled. You mark my words."

The unspoken accusation hung in the air of the kitchen, souring the aroma of the baking biscuits. His aunt had put into words the doubts that had been niggling at Colter since he first heard the news about his mother.

Lorenzo reached for the leather-bound volume on the shelf behind him and slid it across the table to Colter. "Here's your ma's Bible. That new preacher wanted to bury it with her, but I figured you'd want it. I had to make one hell of a stink about it, too. That man didn't want to take 'no' for an answer."

Colter laid his hand on the cracked leather cover and harkened back to the many times he had seen his mother's hand resting on it just so. Opening it, he leafed through it until he came to the middle section where his mother had kept family records. Stuck between the pages listing births and deaths was a loose leaf. His parents' marriage contract.

He took the page in his hands and thought about his parents. Together they had devoted their lives to their land; first, scraping together the money to buy it, then clearing it, then planting it. Pa was always happiest with dirt — his own dirt — on his hands. Ma was always happiest when Pa was happy.

He slid the yellowed parchment back into the Bible and closed it. "I got to go."

"But you need to eat, Johnny," Aunt Dev insisted.

"Where you goin'?" Uncle Lorenzo asked.

"Farley Stuart's. He's got somethin' belongs to me," Colter said, shoving out the door.

◢

No one could accuse Farley Stuart of thinking small. "Enough" was not a word in his vocabulary. There was never enough for him, from the vast and growing acreage he controlled to the immense size of his fields; from the number of slaves he owned, to the dozens of outbuildings that seemed to spring out of the ground like weeds after a rain; from the elegant family cemetery with its many gaudy monuments, each competing for a viewer's attention, to the three ponds, each the size of a small lake.

Perched beside one of these latter stood the ramshackle house where Farley Stuart had been born. Stuart liked to tout his humble beginnings, but he was obviously unwilling to waste any effort or money to maintain the visible symbol of that start. For now, Enos Smoot, the overseer, and his family lived in the house, but doubtless one day soon, the dwelling would disappear, plowed under, Stuart's orders, to make way for a new field of sorghum. And soon as the first green shoots of that crop appeared, so too a new story would begin to circulate. A newly-created version of Stuart's birth and rearing would overlay the old one in the constantly reinvented tale of Farley Dumont Stuart's rise to the position of richest, most powerful man in this part of the Blue Ridge.

Colter slowed Blaze to a walk as they approached the two-story house. He had been inside, just inside the door once before, but he and everyone else in the Draft knew all about the ten rooms and their lavish furnishings, imported from Europe by Stuart's late wife. She had been a fussy little bird of a woman with a high-pitched voice, darting eyes and twitching hands who insisted on the very best of everything up to and including her overly elaborate burial seven years back. The money Stuart had spent on her funeral would have kept the average family of eight for four years.

A moon-faced groom scurried out of the nearby barn to take charge of Blaze. Colter waved him off. What he had to do here would not take long. He tied the reins to the iron hitching ring at the left of the steps, slid his saddlebags over his shoulder, and strode to the front door.

Stuart's daughter Fiona, instead of a slave, opened to his knock. Seeing Colter, she uttered a small cry and tried to slam the door. He proved quicker, wedging his boot into the opening.

Fiona had been a gaunt child who had lost all claim to beauty by the age of ten. Even her voice turned ugly. At fourteen when other girls were preparing for marriage, Fiona found religion. Over the years what had been an interest blossomed into a passion that bordered on obsession and caused her to act in odd ways.

"It's me, Fiona. John Colter," he said, gently but firmly pushing open the door and walking into the hallway.

With her eyes wide and bulging more than normal, Fiona raised a hand to her thin gray lips and shrank back against the opposite wall. Gray was Fiona's color. She had worn nothing else for years, and now even her hair and skin had taken on the color though she was not yet twenty-five.

Realizing that she might not recognize him since he still wore the dirt from his long journey, Colter took off his hat. "There. Know me now?"

She made a tiny panicked sound and shrank back even further. "Devil's spawn," she rasped in the voice of an aged crone.

It was the same nonsense she had been spouting for the last few years whenever she saw him. Somewhere she got the notion that birthmarks were the sign of the Devil. Colter was in no mood for such shenanigans now, but he did have to see this strange creature's father. "Is your pa here? I need to see him."

Before Fiona could answer, Farley Stuart himself appeared behind her. "Season!" he shouted.

A harried black woman issued out of a room at the rear of the house and bustled forward to take charge of Fiona. While Stuart watched the nurse shepherd his distraught daughter away, Colter watched him.

Farley Stuart was a small man, not much larger than his dead wife, but the impression he made was not that of a small man. From the studied cut of his clothes to the smallish people with whom he surrounded himself to the undersized furnishings of his home, he had made an art out of creating the illusion that he was tall and rugged. He wore his prematurely-white hair swept back from his forehead to give himself height. A stylish goatee lengthened his face and lent it an air of practiced sophistication.

Once the door closed on the women, Stuart turned his attention to Colter, extending a hand. "Welcome back, John."

Colter had never liked the man, and that feeling had deepened in the preceding moments. He pointedly ignored the offered hand. "I come to see the bill of sale for our land."

Stuart nodded cooperatively. "That's understandable. This way please." He led Colter into his office. From the size of the windows to the expensive leather-bound books on the shelves to the scaled-down chairs, everything helped to make Stuart look more substantial.

Stuart took a seat behind the mahogany desk inlaid with mother-of-pearl and motioned for Colter to sit as well. But Colter chose to remain standing. He took the document Stuart retrieved from the desk drawer and read it slowly, deliberately. He did not want to miss anything on the page.

The transaction was all there as his uncle had described it. The date, two weeks back. The sale price of two hundred dollars. And at the bottom, Ma's signature: Eleanor Susan Marie Shields Colter. The same signature that had stared up at him from the bottom of the marriage contract he had found in her Bible. There was no possibility of mistaking the writing. The three "l"'s all leaned left, opposite to the right-hand slant of the other letters. He gave the page back to Stuart.

"I realize what a shock this must be for you, John," Stuart said. "Of course you'll need time to go through the house and sort out what you want to keep."

Colter drew a lumpy sack out of his saddlebag and slapped it down on the desk. "Here's your money. I'm buyin' that there paper back."

Stuart placed the folded parchment into the drawer. "I'm afraid that's impossible."

Colter tossed a second bag atop the first, the sum total of his stake. "Four hundred then. Twice what you paid. Now give 'er here and we'll call it even."

Some of Stuart's vaunted composure slipped. He slammed the drawer shut. "That land belongs to me now, John. It is not for sale, at any price. In fact, it is my daughter's dowry."

The idea that anyone would be willing to marry Fiona even with all Stuart's money as incentive was beyond comprehension. "Who's she marryin'?"

"Perhaps you met the new preacher, Josiah Hartley. He and Fiona are to be married on November 15. I'm giving them the grandest wedding this region has ever seen. It's not every day a daughter of mine gets married."

Stuart rested his elbows on the carved arms of his chair and steepled his fingers. "A month ought to give you enough time to sort through what's left in the house and barn. I would give you longer, but there is a lot to be done to the place before Fiona can live there."

Before Colter could argue, Stuart pushed back his chair and stood up. "So you see, John. The matter's settled. Elijah, see Mr. Colter out."

Colter stared at the man for a long moment before picking up his money bags from the desk and following the hulking slave from the house.

It was full dark by the time Colter reached the farm that Farley Stuart now owned. With his feelings swinging between sadness and anger, he unsaddled Blaze, put her into a stall in the barn and fed her, all by rote. Then, taking his saddlebags and Ma's Bible, he walked up to the house and stepped onto the porch for the first time in nearly a year.

He stood there for a time taking in the unnatural quiet surrounding him. Ma had loved animals of all kinds. For as long as he could remember she had kept ducks and geese and chickens, pigs and goats. Their sounds had defined home for him as much as the people who lived there. Now only his own breathing challenged the silence.

The door's leather hinges creaked under his pull, a sound made louder and more penetrating by the stillness. He stepped into the kitchen to the smell of neglect overlaid with the powerful odor of rotting apples.

He located the lantern that hung on a nail inside the door, then dropped his saddlebags and the Bible on the table in order to light the wick. In the flaring flame the room appeared as his mother had left it. She must have been interrupted while peeling apples for one of her delicious pies. A bowl of rotting fruit, a pile of desiccated peels and her favorite knife rested on the floor next to her rocking chair. Behind the chair stood her butter churn, washed and ready to receive a fresh batch of milk. Milk that would never come.

Her spinning wheel had been pushed up against the opposite wall. Ma had loved to spin. She always sang when she did so, the haunting songs of her Scottish homeland whose words Colter did not need to know to understand. Songs she would sing no more. Death had silenced the whispery soprano that had given life to those mysterious melodies, the body that had given life to him.

A surge of sadness clumped in his throat. For comfort he picked up her Bible and brushed its leather cover with his fingertips in the same way Ma had always touched it every morning and every evening after she finished reading in it. That preacher Hartley was right. The Bible had been part of Ma in life and now it belonged with her in death. Tomorrow he would see to that.

He did not notice the fading lantern light until it guttered and died, leaving him in the dark in that now-lifeless room. He knew where the kerosene was. He could refill it. Then again, why bother? All the light did was bring up more memories of things he regretted never fully appreciating before.

He took the Bible and walked through the darkness to the barn. He could not stay in the house. Not tonight. Perhaps not ever again.

2. *Boy Soldier*
End of September - Belmont County, Ohio

O ne glance at his father's rigid posture told George Shannon he was in for a scolding. *Let it be something small,* he prayed silently. *That my uniform was not perfect last drill, or that there was an error in my Latin essay this morning. Let it be anything. Anything but my application to West Point.*

"Sit, George," ordered his father.

The air in the study weighed on Shannon's shoulders, but he knew better than to slump. Father valued discipline and obedience over everything. As commander of the local militia, he viewed the unit as an extension of himself, and he regularly humiliated men who failed to meet his lofty standards of perfection.

Those standards were even higher for his only son, a situation that had Shannon itching to be free of the yoke of parental expectation. West Point meant rebelling against his father's beliefs and spoiling his plans for shaping his son's life. But that was a risk Shannon was more than willing to take in order to have a life of his own.

His father picked methodically through the rack of his pipes, settling on the meerschaum. He then measured a precise amount of his special tobacco blend from its tin into the pipe's bowl before breaking the silence. "Let us see if these work."

Shannon had never seen the wooden box from which his father extracted a sliver of wood. The coated end of the stick made a rasping sound as it dragged across the sole of his father's boot, bursting into flames with an abruptness that made Shannon start.

Father held the flame to the pipe bowl and drew several puffs until the tobacco caught, then exhaled to snuff the flame. "Quite a useful new invention. Friction matches. A gift from Fergus O'Toole." He examined the used match. "Do you know how long O'Toole and I have known each other, George?"

Shannon knew the men's friendship stemmed from their youth. That was why he had written to O'Toole asking for a reference for the West Point application. Rather than answer the question, however, he held his breath in hopes that the conversation would veer toward a safer subject.

"Thirty-five years," his father said. "I met him the first day I went to school. Wheeling was the frontier then."

Shannon relaxed a bit. This was the way his father started philosophical talks, not reprimands.

"I miss O'Toole. Sometimes I wonder if we should have stayed in Wheeling.

Shannon decided it was safe to speak. "And miss your chance to get Ohio its statehood? Not you, Father. Besides, Wheeling is only a day's ride. You can see Mr. O'Toole whenever you want. You just have to make the time."

His father smoked in silence. Lulled, Shannon did not notice the flush spreading upward from Father's collar until too late. He had no time to steel himself for the explosion.

Father's fist came down on the desktop with a thud. "I can't believe you thought you could get away with it! No son of mine is going to make a career of war! No, sir. The one thing this country does not need is a standing army. God knows you have heard my views on that since you were in the cradle. The worst part is that you went behind my back. What do you have to say for yourself, young man?"

Shannon found it hard to swallow, even harder to find an answer. More than anything he wanted to be a hero like his father, and West Point seemed the best route to that goal. That, however, was the last thing the angry man in front of him wanted to hear.

"Speak up! Since you tried to fool me, I want to hear how you reached the outrageous conclusion that you might succeed."

Shannon had seldom seen his father so irate. He knew he needed to put some distance between himself and that empurpled face before he could figure out how to respond. He tried to be deliberate as he rose, but his feet seemed suddenly incapable of staying out of each other's way. He reached out for the edge of the mantel to steady himself.

He could not meet his father's glare. Instead, he focused on the fire irons on the hearth and decided to tell the truth. "I want to go to West Point. I knew you would never agree." He tried to shift his weight without appearing to squirm. "So I asked some other people to help me apply. Don't blame them, Father. It was my idea, and I asked them not to tell you. They all know how you feel."

He shut up and waited for a response. Yet nothing in his experience prepared him for what came.

His father's usual ramrod posture dissolved. His normal precise enunciation melted into slurred speech that Shannon had to strain to hear. "You had the best education I could afford. I sacrificed to raise you to be the kind of leader this country needs. I hoped you would follow in my footsteps. Hoped you would choose a life of public service to get this country off to the right start. Now this." The stem of the pipe traced in a listless arc.

Shannon hesitated, unsure whether to escape or offer comfort. To hide his uncertainty, he turned to face the hearth still heaped with last night's ashes.

The next thing he knew his father was standing behind him. "You are correct, Son. I ought to make time to see O'Toole more often. After all, if it had not been for him, I would not know about my own son's deceitfulness."

Shannon wanted to run out of the room, away from the menace in his father's voice.

"I want to be absolutely certain you understand me, George. I have withdrawn your West Point application. I will have no son of mine responsible for helping to create the pestilence of a professional military."

He marched to the desk. "Since you are so anxious to leave home, I am sending you to Philadelphia. There, my beloved son, you will study the law. Your tuition is paid. You will lodge with the Mallories. I do not have to remind you how much this is costing. Your mother and I, however, think of it as an investment in your future."

Frustration overwhelmed Shannon's fragile control. He whirled to face his father. "Your future, you mean. Not mine. You want me to be like you. But I'm not. No matter how much it costs, I will never be you. What's more, I don't want to be."

His father's slap caught Shannon across the mouth. Father had never hit him before. Ever. The shock of the blow hurt worse than the pain.

Stunned, Shannon bolted from the room, out of the house and straight into the woods.

"Is the parson here, ma'am?" Shannon asked. He was beyond caring how he looked after wandering for hours in the forest. He needed to unburden himself to someone who cared.

"Oh, George dearest, come inside right now." Sarah Cooper's arm snaked under Shannon's, and she supported him to the love seat in Parson Cooper's study. Though just five years older than Shannon, she seemed wiser, more mature than her age. Her presence calmed him.

She flung his hat onto the parson's desk, then sat down next to him and took his right hand in hers. "You poor boy, whatever happened?"

The concern in her eyes crumbled his shaky composure. He sought to hide his trembling lips behind his free hand. "Father knows about West Point. He's withdrawn my application. I came to ask Parson —"

"To see what he can do. There, there, you poor dear boy." Sarah gathered him to her and began to rock him, humming comforting sounds into his ear.

His initial upset subsided after a time. Still she continued to rock him against her attractive bosom, a motion that began to affect him in ways a gentleman did not admit to.

When he tried to push himself away, she tightened her embrace. "Poor, poor George. Such a handsome young man." Her fingers kneaded the tender skin at the back of his neck.

"Mrs. Cooper. . ."

"Sarah," she sighed into his ear.

The sound raced straight to his loins, the very place he was trying to ignore. The womanly scent of her filled his nostrils. Still she rocked him, every touch of her lush flesh heating his blood. He managed to twist his head to one side. "Mrs. Cooper."

"Sarah, George. Sarah."

"Sarah, Uh, I . . . This . . . We . . ."

"Hush, George. You've had an awful shock. What kind of friend would I be not to help you in your time of need?"

"But the Parson?"

"It's Tuesday, dearest. My husband is out on his circuit." Her fingers moved to caress his ear. "Until tomorrow."

Shannon shivered. His mind searched frantically for something to say. "I — I'll come back tomorrow, then."

"Nonsense. You will stay right here. You need a friend." As her other hand slowly kneaded his back through his shirt, he shivered again.

"Oh, you're cold. Here." She moved closer so that the front of her body pressed into his. The discovery that his chin rested on the swell of her breasts made him squirm.

"Ma'am, I —"

"Sarah, George. I want to hear you say it. Please."

"Sarah."

Her lips grazed his forehead, then moved to his eyelids.

"Ma'am, please. I ought to go. You've been —"

Warm lips on his choked off his words. "Kiss me back, George."

"But —" Again her lips smothered his protest. None of his imaginings about the mysteries of women had prepared him for his own reaction. Every nerve in his body seemed to come alive at once as he returned the kiss.

"Oh, my, that was nice," she murmured.

The warmth of her breath against his cheek raised gooseflesh on his arms.

"How old are you, George?"

Shannon had to swallow before he could speak. "Eighteen. Almost."

"Have you ever kissed a woman before?" she purred.

"N-no, ma'am."

"Sarah," she whispered, pressing harder against him. "Hard to believe." She sighed. "As handsome as you are." Another sigh. "When you smile, that gap between your teeth —"

Her tongue forced his lips apart. He felt its tip thrusting against the space between his front teeth, then engaging his tongue in a wet caress. He found that probing tongue impossible to resist.

Her hand left his neck and dropped onto his chest. Her fingers began to rub his skin through the muslin of his shirt front, gently at first, then with increasing pressure as she kissed him again and again.

Shannon moved her hand back to his shoulder, but it slipped down again with her next kiss.

Before he realized it, the buttons on his shirt were undone, leaving the front gaping open. Her hand massaged urgent circles into the skin of his chest. "Sarah, you have to stop."

She responded sucking his tongue into her mouth. One hand pulled the tail of his shirt free from his trousers. He jerked as her fingernails scraped across the bare skin of his back.

"You like that?"

"N-no." His voice shivered.

"You aren't telling the truth, George Shannon." As she breathed those words into his ear, her fingers brushed across the buttons of his trousers. That touch sent a shock through his system. Before he recovered, she had two of his trouser buttons undone.

"Please, stop!" he begged.

She licked him with her restless tongue. Working on the third button, her fingers grazed his stiffened member. He felt himself explode as he staggered to his feet. "No!" His cry bounced off the walls of the room.

"Don't go, George," she implored, extending the offending hand toward him. "Not now."

But Shannon was already out the door.

3. *Vengeance*

Morning light streaming through the seams between the planks of the barn walls woke Colter. He felt wool-headed from a stuporous sleep and did not register his surroundings until he saw the Bible on the straw beside his head. Then the events of the previous day flooded back to him.

He stepped out into an autumn morning that seemed to mock his grief. Plodding to the springhouse, he drew a bucket of icy water and dumped it over his head. He shook off the excess and made his slow way to the house to figure out what to do next.

The door stood wide open. "Durn you, Johnny. Where was your head last night?" he chastised himself. More than once skunks had sneaked into the house when he neglected to shut the door. One thing he did not need right now was a skunking.

Only, it was not a skunk that he saw when he entered the kitchen. Instead, the contents of his saddlebags lay strewn across the plank floor. "My stake," he gasped, launching a frenzied search for the two leather bags that represented so much hard work and sacrifice.

Searching did no good. The bags — and his money — were gone, and, with them, the future he had dreamed about for so long. A terrible ache settled over his already-hurting heart.

"Cousin!"

Colter started at the voice, then glanced out the door to see his cousin Quent riding up to the house. Quent was a youthful copy of his father

Lorenzo, but with Aunt Dev's strawberry blonde hair and the same scattering of freckles across his cheeks and nose. Today he sported a scrawny mustache and a patchy first-time beard that made his face look more dirty than mature. He swung off his horse, then stood awkwardly for a time as if trying to figure out what to say next. "Pa said you were out to our place yesterday. You just get back?"

"Yep. And just got robbed," Colter said furiously. "Some galoot helped hisself to my stake last night. Four hundred dollars."

Quent let out a low whistle. "Four hundred dollars? Dear God, that's a fortune!"

Colter did not bother to agree with the obvious. A gloomy silence followed until Quent cleared his throat. "You still headed to Louisville? If you are, I was wondering . . . I mean, could me and a friend tag along as far as Maysville? We're late startin' out, and we can't take a chance on getting' lost."

Scratch Wilkes ran the best outfit of trappers around. One of the reasons was the cost for joining up. That was what Colter's money had been for. With his stake gone, he now had no reason to go to Louisville. Wilkes never made exceptions. He didn't have to. Men fell all over themselves to join his crew. With the weight of his misfortunes mounting like blizzard snow driven against a fence, Colter sagged down on the porch steps.

"How 'bout we pay you to take us?" Quent asked. "I need to check with my friend first about that, but I'm sure he'll be up for it, seein' as how he's the one said we need us a guide. You heard about the expedition yet?"

Colter had no energy to answer but that did not stop Quent who went right on as if he had. "Congress is sendin' an expedition out to find the Northwest Passage once and for all. The man leadin' it is an Army Captain name of Lewis. Used to be the President's secretary. He's stoppin' at Maysville to take on recruits. Me and my friend mean to join up there."

Men had been talking about an all-water trade route from the Mississippi to the Western Sea since the first Europeans settled on the continent. Talk. That was all the Passage amounted to. That was what Colter believed. That was what he knew. If it had been any other time or place, he would have told Quent to forget such a wild goose chase. Instead, dejection held him mute and Quent rambled on.

"The way McBain sees it, the men who find the Passage have the inside track on makin' a fortune off it. Rich. That's what I want to be. Not stuck in this good-for-nothin' hole of a place, walkin' behind the butt-end of a plow horse my whole life. What do you say, Cousin? You willin' to guide us over there? We got to be there by October 15."

"Without a stake, I got no reason for goin', Quent."

Some of the eagerness fled the younger man's face. "This here land belongs to Stuart now, Johnny. What've you got to stay around for? Besides, you ain't no farmer. You told me so yourself at least a dozen times."

Quent was right, but Colter did not want to acknowledge that fact just now.

"How about I spot you a whiskey, Johnny? We can ride over to The Sisters and you can meet my friend McBain. What d'you say?"

A drink. Yes, that's what he needed. "I got some things to pack up first. Cain't stay here no more. Think your pa'd mind if'n I stayed over to your place for a time?"

Quent's face softened with sympathy. "Of course not. Pa'd love to have you. Ma, too. You know how she loves to cook. An extra mouth to feed's her idea of heaven. Come on. Let me help get you packed."

For what he had to do now, Colter did not need or want help. "Whyn't you saddle Blaze for me? That'd hurry things up."

Quent agreed and went off to the barn, leaving Colter to face the house and its memories alone. He stepped into the kitchen, moving slowly against an invisible weight that seemed attached to all his limbs. He stuffed his scattered belongings back into his saddlebags. Then he wrapped the Bible in a piece of fresh muslin and tucked it carefully into the top. Even moving his eyes took effort as he looked around the kitchen and made the decision to let Aunt Dev have everything.

The other room of the house had been his parents' bedroom. It was as strange to him as the kitchen was familiar. Ma had delivered him and his three now-dead siblings there, and Pa had died there, yet Colter had spent more time in church, though he had never been much on religion, than in that room.

The bed occupied most of the floor. The feather mattress sagged beneath his mother's prized Tree of Life quilt. The tree had twelve branches, one for each of the dozen children she had once dreamed of having. However, only four of the branches had names stitched along them. Four babies, all but one dead before the age of five.

Looking at it now made Colter wonder how many other unanswered dreams his mother had had that he never knew about. How many disappointments? How many sorrows? He would never know.

Aunt Dev had always admired the quilt. Folding it carefully, he decided to take it to her now, then turned to the little table laid with Ma's brushes. Hair still clung to the bristles. His mother had always been vain about her hair. Every night as a child, he used to press his eye to the crack in the wall that separated the kitchen, where he slept, from the bedroom and watch with fascination as she unpinned her hair and brushed it until it flowed and sparkled in the candlelight. Back then her hair had been a shade of rich brown, but the strands in her brushes now showed more gray than brown. The gray decided him. He would keep the brushes.

Two dresses and two aprons hung on a hook at the end of the bed. Well-worn, all four garments were spotless and crisply ironed and hung as if awaiting the woman to whom they belonged. Next to those garments was an empty hook where her good dress used to hang. That was the dress she wore to church and the one she now wore in her casket.

Used to hang. The thought brought him back to Quent's offer and the dilemma he now faced. With no money, no home and no prospects, where did he go from here?

The sounds of Quent's boots on the porch lifted him out of his reverie. He picked up the quilt and carried it into the kitchen in time to deliver it into his cousin's hands. "Think your ma'd like this?"

"Oh, my, yes. It's always been her favorite. You sure, though?"

He wasn't, but he also had no place to keep it. He nodded. "Now how about that drink?"

While Quent bounded out the door with a whoop, Colter paused to take in the kitchen one last time. The room had always meant home to him. The memory of its warmth and smells had sustained him through dozens of snow-bound days out on his trap lines, and images of it formed the backdrop of the best of his dreams. Now the room belonged to Fiona Stuart and her future husband, Josiah Hartley.

That thought hurt too much to hold for long. He closed the door behind him for the last time.

The two cabins stood side by side less than three paces apart. Identical twins had built them to be identical homes for the women each had married on the same day in identical ceremonies. Ten years later both men had died from falls within a week of each other. They left behind two childless widows with no means of support other than their wits and a knack for making good whiskey.

Where other wives sold their excess eggs, the widows, Petty and Hen, had always sold whatever home-made liquor their husbands did not consume. Since their product was excellent, they always had more customers than whiskey. After their widowing, the two women decided to trade upon their reputation and start a business. Hen moved in with Petty and they turned the vacant house into a tavern which they called The Sisters.

The business was a success from the day it opened not only because of the superior product they purveyed but also because of the unique way in which they ran their establishment. The rules were simple. They would tolerate no drunkenness, no cursing, no fighting, and no filth. The Sisters had clean lace curtains at the two windows, a white-washed door and a floor and three tables that were scrubbed down twice a week. And a piano which only the two women were allowed to touch, although only Hen knew how to play it. On the occasions when Hen sang to her own accompaniment, the women expected — and received — the undivided attention of their clientele.

Colter had never taken to the place. For one thing, it was entirely too clean. For another, the widows made unwelcome anyone who looked Indian, which was Zoob. Though as Irish as his father in every other way, Zoob had inherited his looks from his Shawnee mother, a fact that haunted him his whole life and sent him and Colter to less persnickety places for their liquor whenever they were back in the Draft.

Quent had none of Colter's compunctions. He bounced inside, leaving Colter to follow with his saddlebags.

A man Colter did not recognize sat on the piano stool facing an arc of five men he did know: the two Elwes brothers, Luke and Matt; the miller Nate Boggs; one-legged Zack Benton; and TG Guthrie. TG would have been Colter's father-in-law if Rachel Guthrie had not up and married before Colter could work up the courage to ask for her hand ten years ago.

Petty and Hen flanked the men, and everyone seemed engrossed by the stranger who was sitting where, according to the widows' rules, only they were allowed to sit. The author of this extraordinary breach of the rules appeared utterly ordinary except for his eyes. They were startlingly blue and riveting.

Quent nudged Colter and whispered pridefully toward the man, "That's my friend McBain."

The stranger held up his hands, fingers stretched wide. "It's the truth. I can play five C's on this piano simultaneously, and I'll be more than happy to show anyone who doubts that claim. For a price, of course."

Before the man finished speaking, Colter recognized Quent's friend for a gambler and opportunist. He had seen too many such smiles to be taken in. He watched the betting with a cynical eye, wishing he had never agreed to come along with Quent.

Even the normally-cautious widows bet against McBain though they did so with the giggling and preening women reserved for men they found attractive.

With theatrical flair, McBain handed the betting pot to Hen to hold. Colter's jaw tightened to see her blush when the man's hand brushed hers. She was a smart woman. Didn't she see through McBain's act?

McBain waved everyone back as if to give himself room to maneuver. Then he spent several minutes fussing with the position of the stool before he sat down facing the keyboard. He rotated his shoulders and crooked his head to the left and the right. Then, lifting his hands above the keys, he flexed his fingers. "Ready?"

The little group chorused an eager "yes" with the two female voices ringing clearly above the deeper tones of the five men. *Ready to get took*, Colter thought.

McBain spread his fingers wide and positioned them with his thumbs resting on the "C" notes above and below middle "C" and his little fingers spanning to the "C" an octave beyond those.

"Okay, let's see your other hand, Mac," said Matt Elwes. An angry scar ran from the corner of his nose to his left ear, witness to the man's penchant for trouble.

All the bettors and Quent laughed at the comment. Colter did not join them. McBain's type never bet unless they had all the angles figured.

"Here goes, all you doubters," McBain said, bending forward and pressing down middle "C" with his nose while striking the other four notes with his fingers at the same time.

The angry frown of a perennial loser quickly replaced the smile on Matt Elwes's face. "That's cheating!" he yelled, his voice resounding above the various groans and mutterings of the other bettors.

McBain popped to his feet, a satisfied smile on his fleshy mouth. He swept the money out of Hen's hand. "Thank you, gentlemen, ladies." His bow elicited another giggle from Hen and an uncertain half-smile from Petty. "Dear ladies, would you be so kind as to supply a round for everyone? On me, of course."

Colter decided he had had his fill when the two women fluttered off to do McBain's bidding. Not only had the man easily hoodwinked five men who ought to know better, he had also turned the hard-working widows into simpering fools.

Benton, Boggs and Guthrie followed the two women to the counter, but Matt and his brother Luke held their ground. "We don't take to bein' tricked, McBain," Matt growled.

"Give us our money back," Luke demanded.

McBain coolly pocketed the money in the face of the brothers' demands. "You've been bested, not tricked, gentlemen. Your drinks are waiting."

"We don't drink with the likes of you," Matt spit.

"Then you'll leave," declared Hen, stepping around the bar. "And you'll do so this instant."

The top of the widow's head barely reached to Matt's chin, but her stern schoolmarmish manner brooked no backtalk. The brothers did as they were told.

Seeming oblivious to the woman's intervention, McBain clapped Quent on the shoulder. "You're just in time for a free whiskey, my friend. Step right up."

Quent swept a hand toward Colter. "This here's my cousin Johnny, Mac. He's the one I been tellin' you about. He might be willin' to guide us over to —"

A warning frown from McBain dried up Quent's words. Quent lowered his voice to a whisper. "I told Johnny we'd pay him to take us."

"Did you now?" McBain said, then to Colter, "And how much would that cost?"

Colter had had enough of the man and everything he stood for. Without hesitation, he said, "Four hundred dollars."

"Johnny!" Quent gasped.

McBain reacted with an amused smile. "You must be quite a guide, Colter, if it takes a king's ransom to hire you."

Colter did not bat an eye. "I'm the best there is."

McBain tossed back the shot of whiskey and smoothed his sleek mustache. "Quent tells me you're quite a shot, too."

Colter had won the Draft's annual marksmanship title so many times that no one else bothered to enter the contest anymore.

"How about we make this interesting?" McBain asked. "With a shooting contest. If you win, I'll pay you your fee. If I win, you guide Quent and me for free."

McBain had tugged on the wrong string. "I ain't a wagerin' man. 'Sides I just quit the guide business."

"But Johnny, you can't," Quent pleaded. "We need you or we'll miss our chance for sure."

McBain slid a bemused look sideways at Quent. "I wouldn't be hasty, Colter. Four hundred dollars is a lot of money. What say I leave the offer open?"

"Don't bother. I ain't one to change my mind."

McBain picked up the tin cup that Petty had refilled. Raising it to his lips, he looked over the rim at Colter. "And I'm not one for choosing second best."

"Guess you'll have to. This time." Grabbing up his saddlebags, Colter strode out the door, all too aware of his cousin's disappointed eyes following him.

He was tying the bags onto the saddle and trying to figure out where he would spend the night now that he had let Quent down when a hatless Josiah Hartley rode up. Without the hat, the preacher looked unfinished and even more lopsided. "Oh, Colter. Glad to catch you here. Did you talk with your uncle? About your mother's Bible?"

The orneriness that McBain had raised in him was still running high. "Lorenzo did right, Preacher. Let it rest where it stands."

"Why, I'm sure if you thought about it some more —"

"Decision's made. Let 'er rest."

"But —"

"I said not, Preacher."

Hartley's mouth drew into a tight line. He nodded curtly and rode away.

With the need to sort things out strong upon him, Colter headed for the cemetery. He sat beside his mother's grave for a long time and stared out at the open field beyond the low fence. The field belonged to Stuart who had acquired it from Arch Campbell after Campbell dropped dead behind his plow one mild cloudless May day three years ago. Arch had been one of Pa's closest friends, and even before the funeral, Pa began to assert to anyone who would listen that his friend's death had not been natural, that somehow Farley Stuart was involved. At the time Colter and everyone else dismissed the accusations as the ravings of a man whose grief had affected his good sense. Now, he wondered if he had been too quick to judge his father. Wasn't it true that Stuart appeared bent on owning or controlling every scrap of land and every person in the Draft and probably beyond?

"I got news for you, Stuart. You ain't ever goin' to own me," he whispered, opening the Bible and removing the marriage contract. He unfolded it and looked at the signatures of his parents. Pa's was on the left side, its letters wavering and uneven; the writing of someone unused to wielding a pen. On the right, Ma's letters were smooth and rounded and exceedingly neat, evidence of hours of hornbook practice.

Eleanor Susan Marie Shields Colter. How she railed at the length of that name! *Pretentious and completely unnecessary,* she called it. *No one needs five names. Two are quite enough. After all, God has only one.* He remembered vividly the family gathering where she had stood up and announced that she would answer only to "Ellen Colter" from that day forth and that she would skin alive anyone who dared call her different to her face or behind her back.

Ma in a fury was not someone to disagree with so no one did. Not Pa. Not Colter. Not anyone in or out of the family.

Colter smiled ruefully and ran his thumb across the signature with its distinctive back-slanted "l"'s.

All at once his smile faded. Lorenzo had said it. Something was wrong. And now Colter knew what.

Farley Stuart's house stood backlit against a low sun, its outline crisp, its face murky and indistinct. A black maid opened the door to Colter's knock, but Elijah quickly supplanted her. "Massah's to dinner. You got to wait."

"Tell him John Colter's here, or I'll tell him myself," Colter demanded.

Uncertainty flickered briefly in the beefy slave's wary eyes. Colter seized advantage of the hesitation and pushed past into the entry hall.

Stuart stepped into the hallway from the right wing of the house. "Why, Colter. What are you doing here?"

The sight of this runt of a man preening toward him like the lone bull in a pasture of heifers set Colter's blood a-boil. "You know what I come for, Stuart. You goin' to get it for me, or do I have to take it?"

"We have guests for dinner, John. Your business will have to wait until tomorrow." Stuart spoke in the same tone one uses on a willful child.

"I ain't waitin'. Not for a th —"

The rest of Colter's sentence vanished into the dent Elijah's meaty fist pounded into his midsection.

"Take him out of here," Stuart commanded. "And never let him in again if you know what's good for you."

Colter did not have the strength to resist as Elijah forced him out the door and tossed him sprawling onto the porch. It took till he reached the main road for the pain of the slave's punch to subside enough to sit straight in the saddle. He made sure that his mother's Bible was still inside his saddlebag, then turned Blaze toward his uncle's.

A mile from his destination the road led through a dense stand of hardwoods growing on ground too rocky to be farmed, a reminder of what this country had looked like before men parceled it up and set plows to it. To Colter's mind, men with plows destroyed more than they created. Interfering with the Divine Order caused men to assume they were gods; to believe that they, not God, owned the land and that they could do whatever they wanted in the name of progress without suffering any consequences. Years in the wilderness of Kentucky Territory had taught him the opposite. God knew what He was doing, and men messed with His plan to the everlasting detriment of all living things.

Pszing! A shot rang out and something whistled past his ear. Then a second shot. He was scrambling off Blaze's back when the second ball grazed his skull. Ignoring the stinging pain on his scalp, he crouched in the road trying to figure out where the shots came from when a mounted figure burst out of the trees ahead and came straight for him.

He leaped aside, and the unidentified rider swiped up Blaze's dangling reins and started to ride away with her in tow.

Colter was not about to let anyone steal his horse. He let out a piercing whistle. The horse's ears twitched forward and she dug in her hooves, jerking the reins from the hands of the assailant. Once free, she trotted back to her owner.

Colter grabbed for his rifle, but before he could get it out of its scabbard, the shooter was out of sight.

While Aunt Dev cleaned the flesh wound and dabbed it with home-made salve, Colter related what had transpired. He pulled his parents' marriage contract out of the Bible. "It's this here convinced me you're right, Uncle. You know how Ma felt about her name. She wouldn't abide bein' called anythin' 'sides Ellen. But Stuart's bill o' sale shows this here name, writ exactly the same. Exactly."

Lorenzo's subdued nod was not the reaction he had expected. "I'll eat horse shit for a month if'n that paper ain't been forged. 'Tweren't no accident killed Ma neither." Colter stopped short of accusing Stuart of killing her. No matter what his gut told him, he had no proof. But he did have the marriage contract. Put it up next to the bill of sale and anyone with eyes, even weak ones, would know his mother had never signed it. No one writes her name exactly the same way twice. No one.

Still Lorenzo did not respond. He stared morosely at the piece of parchment.

"Say somethin', durn it!" Colter demanded, his voice cracking with built-up tension.

When his uncle finally lifted his eyes, he said, "You got to leave, Johnny."

"What?"

"This place is called *Stuart's* Draft for a reason, and that reason just about got you killed tonight. You're not safe here anymore."

"But I got this!" Colter jabbed a shaking finger at the yellowed document.

"That you do, but Farley Stuart owns every single person who could do anything about it. Next time whoever shot at you won't miss. Stuart doesn't put up with men who fail him." Lorenzo slid a glance sideways at his wife before going on. "Only way for you to stay alive now is to take off. Head west for a time. You can come back when things have cooled down a touch."

"No, sir. Stuart ain't gettin' away with what he done. Not this time."

His uncle clutched Colter's arm urgently. "Listen to me, Johnny. I know what I'm talking about. Stuart's run of luck is about to peter out. Elections are coming up — and this time those powerful friends of his down in Richmond are likely to lose. All you got to do is wait one year, two at the most. By then, there will be people in a position to do something about Stuart."

Colter's argument died in his mouth. His uncle spoke the truth. He could not fight Stuart. Not the way things stood now.

"I can set you to a stake, Johnny. It's not much, but it ought to help get you on your way over to Kaintuck."

Colter shook his head slowly. "Cain't take your money, Uncle. I'm the one lost what I had. Now it's for me to get 'er back." *There's always McBain's bet*, he thought to himself, then immediately dismissed the idea. Anyone else would jump at the chance to show the man up. Only, he was not someone else, and he was not going to bet. Not with McBain, no matter how much he might stand to gain from winning.

Aunt Dev leaned forward. "Quent told me he asked you to guide him and his friend over to Maysville and that you said no. Won't you reconsider, Johnny? For me? He's my only child." Her hands raised in supplication finished her sentence more eloquently than any words.

Lorenzo produced a small drawstring pouch and plunked it down on the table in front of Colter. "Maysville's a long ways. You'll need supplies."

Colter started to protest but his uncle's beseeching eyes stopped him. These two people had been as much his parents as Ma and Pa. He owed them more than he could ever hope to repay. If he had to leave the Draft, why not take Quent to Maysville? His cousin was bound and determined to go anyway. Who else could Aunt Dev trust with her son's well-being?

Colter looked from her to his uncle. He could not say no. Not to them. Somehow he would find a way to stomach McBain for the length of the journey. He had to. For their sakes. He picked up the pouch and forced a smile for his aunt. "All right. Quent's got his guide."

4. *Strange Goodbyes*

"You are going with your mother and me to church, Son. No more discussion." The set of his father's jaw told Shannon the conversation was over. He had no choice. He would have to face Sarah Cooper again.

"This is your last Sunday with us, after all," his father said, adding quickly, "for awhile, that is."

"Last Sunday?" Shannon asked.

"The term at the University starts October 20th, so you will need to leave by week's end. That will give you time to settle in. And," his father paused, "get lost a time or two on the way. You know how you get turned around."

The news stunned Shannon enough that he did not react to the criticism. He assumed he had a couple of weeks, not mere days, before he had to leave home.

His father coughed. "Your mother and I want only the best for you."

"He wants to say we love you, George." His mother bustled in from the kitchen. The smell of fried chicken clung to her clothing. She gave Shannon a hug and pecked his cheek. Before she released him, she whispered, "Your father finds it hard to say such things."

He managed a smile at his mother. "I'll go get ready."

Shannon left his parents off at the entrance to the church, then drove the family buggy to the open field beyond. He had just set the brake when he saw Parson Cooper hurrying toward him accompanied by Sarah Cooper. The parson grasped Shannon's hand. "I was so sorry to hear about what happened with your father over your West Point plans. Sarah told me as soon as I got back Wednesday. I wish I had been there to help you."

I wish you had been there, too, Shannon thought.

"You must not despair, George. Try again next year. Your father will change his mind," the parson urged.

"Parson, sir, if you think that, you don't know my father."

Sarah moved in front of her husband. "You must come to Sunday dinner, George. This afternoon."

Her stare was so bold that having less than a week until he left for Philadelphia suddenly seemed a blessing. "Thank you, ma'am, but I have to leave by week's end. I need to spend as much time at home as I can. For Mother's sake."

The church bell tolled. "Time for services, dear," the parson said, taking his wife's arm and guiding her away.

Shannon expelled the breath he had been holding before following. As she entered the sanctuary, however, Sarah shot a glance over her shoulder — a look that announced she was not about to give up so easily.

After services, Shannon fled to the buggy to wait for his parents, but his hopes of escaping Sarah's detection vanished in a word: "George."

She had managed to approach him yet remain hidden from the people socializing in front of the church. "Here's your hat. You left it the other day."

He took the hat, his stomach lurching precariously. "Thank you, ma'am."

"Sarah," she hissed, clamping hold of his wrist and digging in her nails. "Please, George. I need to apologize."

"No need," he said, prying at her fingers.

"Yes, I must. Listen to me, please."

Not wanting to attract attention, he ceased struggling. "All right. I'll listen. Just let go."

She released his arm and bent her head so he could not see her face. "The other day —" She hesitated. "All those times you came to the house to see my husband —" She stopped again, shaking her head. "No man has ever affected me like this before. I — I can't stand the thought of your leaving. Of not seeing you for months. Perhaps forever."

When she lifted her eyes to meet his, the longing in them made him want to take off running. He fought the urge.

"George, I have to see you before you go. Won't you give me that at least? We'll talk. That's all."

The tears welling in her eyes broke through his resistance. "All right."

"Oh, George, thank you. Come Tuesday."

With the memory of last Tuesday still fresh, he countered, "Wednesday's better."

"In the morning?"

A single tear traced a shining path down her right cheek. He could not refuse. "In the morning."

She rewarded him with a brilliant smile before heading back to the church. Her skirts billowed from her trim waist and swayed with the motion of her inviting hips.

As he watched, part of him remembered the scent of her and the pleasure of feeling her body pressed against his. The rest of him argued that this was the parson's wife and that keeping his promise would only lead to trouble. By the time she disappeared into the crowd, neither part of him had won the argument.

On Wednesday, Shannon awoke before dawn with an erection so profound that he had to shove his hands between his backside and the mattress to keep from relieving it. He knew a man could go blind or crazy if he gave in to such animal impulses. What he did not understand was why God would give men such urges in the first place.

By whispering the multiplication tables to the nines, he got the swelling to subside enough that he could flop onto his stomach. He was in that position when his mother knocked on the door to his room.

"Breakfast, George?"

"Maybe later, Mother."

"Are you ill?"

"No, ma'am. Just thinking."

She gave an understanding cluck. "Take all the time you need, dear."

After her footsteps receded, he rolled onto his back to study the ceiling and the thorny problem of keeping his appointment with Sarah Cooper. He had known her since his family moved west from Wheeling. She had been like a big sister to him. That is, until a few days ago. Usually he could will his morning erections away before he got to the fives. Since a week ago Tuesday, it had taken to at least the nines, plus he found himself getting hard at the most embarrassing moments during the day.

She had apologized for her behavior, hadn't she? Didn't she deserve his forgiveness? She said she only wanted to talk. Didn't he owe her that, after all the times she and the parson had listened to him? Besides, the parson was due back from his circuit today. He usually arrived around noon. If he dawdled enough, he could get there just before the parson. Then nothing untoward could possibly happen, and he would still keep his promise to Sarah to be there in the morning.

Yes, that was just what he would do.

*

Even walking the long way, he reached the parsonage gate before he felt completely ready to face Sarah. She opened the door before he had touched the gate latch. He glanced toward the stable set to one side of the property. The parson's horse was gone. A look up the road revealed no one moving. The village felt deserted in the noontime heat.

Sarah gave him an impatient wave. Reluctantly, he opened the gate and trudged down the gravel path lined with the low-trimmed honeysuckle alive with bees. Before stepping onto the porch, he slid another glance at the empty road. Still no one in sight.

"Don't let the flies in, George," she said, holding the door open for him.

The instant the door shut, Sarah was upon him, arms encircling his neck, her mouth possessing his.

*

Two days after deciding to guide his cousin to Maysville, Colter sat in his aunt's kitchen at daybreak, enjoying the farewell breakfast she had prepared for him and her son. Despite the delicious food and wonderful smells, sadness hung heavy in the room. Aunt Dev moved jerkily and kept her eyes downcast while Lorenzo's sunken eyes attested to several sleepless nights.

By contrast, Quent seemed oblivious to his parents' plight. He talked excitedly about the trip ahead and the expedition. If he had any doubts that he would be chosen or that the expedition would find the Passage when so many others had failed or that he would survive such a perilous journey, the stream of his chatter did not reveal them. In his view he and McBain were on their way to being rich and famous. Period.

Colter listened without hearing. His mind was on his mother's Bible and the evidence of Stuart's crime that it contained. How would he keep those two things safe on such a long journey? Or should he leave them here?

At the sounds of an approaching horse, Quent popped to his feet and rushed to the door. "It's Mac!"

"He'll be hungry," Aunt Dev said mechanically, getting down another plate and tin cup.

McBain entered with a courtly tip of his round-brimmed hat to Aunt Dev. In his other hand was another hat. A dusty black shovel hat, the kind favored by preachers. "Found this over by your place, Colter. In that dry ditch up where the lane meets the road. You lose it?"

Colter ignored the man's weak attempt at humor and examined the hat. It had not been in the ditch for long for it showed no evidence of the rain that had soaked the Draft four days back. And he knew immediately who it belonged to. Josiah Hartley had looked naked without it when he had seen the preacher at Stuart's.

He looked up to find his uncle watching him. Lorenzo's eyes reflected what he was thinking. Of course, it made sense. Stuart had found out about the marriage contract being in Ma's Bible from Hartley, his future son-in-law. The preacher had probably discovered the document during one of his visits out to the farm. No one would suspect a preacher who asked to use the family Bible of anything other than piety. It would not have taken much for him to arrange for Ma to "accidentally" leave the book behind after a Sunday service either. Ma was always forgetting things.

And it was Hartley who stood to gain the most from the forgery. No wonder he had tried so hard to convince Colter to bury the Bible with his mother. It contained the one piece of evidence that could topple Farley Stuart from his status as undeclared king of Stuart's Draft and cause the preacher to lose the life's work he had helped to steal from the Colters.

"You want me to return it, Johnny?" Lorenzo asked.

Two nights back Hartley's bullets had raised the stakes between them beyond the point where he would risk involving his relatives. "No, Uncle. If'n he wants it, he'll have to come to me get it."

"Then that preacher'll have some ridin' to do. Right, Johnny?" Quent added, his crooked grin making him look half his seventeen years of age.

Colter pushed back from the table. "Time to go."

While Quent crowed his delight, his mother blanched. Colter laid a hand on her arm and murmured, "He'll be all right. You got my word, Aunt Dev."

She managed a quivering smile of acceptance. Five minutes later Colter, Quent and McBain waved their final goodbyes and rode away. At the top of the lane Colter tied the shovel hat onto his saddle before he swung Blaze onto the trail leading west into Kentucky Territory.

"You have plenty of time, Son. There is no need to rush off today," Father said.

Shannon checked the knots on the cord that tied his rolled-up militia uniform onto the saddle. He was taking it to Philadelphia over his father's objections, a small but vital victory as far as he was concerned. He wanted to get these farewells over and get gone. The more distance between him and Sarah Cooper, the better. He had barely gotten away from her intact Wednesday. He never wanted to be put in such a position again.

His mother handed him a heavy parcel bound in burlap. "Meat pies and some cheese."

He started to protest, but the sadness on her face made him cup her cheek instead. "Thanks, Mother. I sure will miss your cooking."

Her lower lip quivered. Dreading her tears, he turned to tuck the food parcel into his already-bulging saddlebags. That done, he swung into the saddle.

"One last thing, Son." His father pressed a small but heavy leather sack into his hand.

"Money? But you already gave me some, Father."

"It is a long trip, not without its challenges. You must be sure to keep this separate from the other."

His father's sudden generosity confused Shannon until a glance at his mother told him who had insisted on the extra purse.

After he tucked the pouch into the top of his boot, his father gave him a packet of letters, each sealed with wax and pressed with his father's distinctive signet. "Letters of introduction to old friends of mine. Places for you to stay along the way."

His mother clutched Shannon's hand. "Promise me you will stop and ask for directions, George. I can't stand the thought of you lost and alone."

He bit back a retort. He was almost eighteen and the best rider and marksman in the militia unit, yet his parents treated him as if he were still a child. First they denied him West Point. Now they were treating him like an incompetent instead of a lieutenant in a top militia unit. Well, he would show them. Tonight he would stop in to see Fergus O'Toole, but after that, he would find his own way. "I promise, Mother."

His father put an arm around his mother's waist in a rare display of affection. "Study hard, Son. Some day you will see the wisdom of my decision. This country needs men educated in the law, not professional soldiers. The War was over before you were born, but if you had lived through it, you would know that I speak the truth."

Shannon was too restless to endure that old speech again and still too irked at having to swallow his father's plan for his life. "I'll write."

He spurred his horse, tossed off a final wave, then headed out of town at a lope without a backward look.

His hunger sated with roast beef and Yorkshire pudding, Shannon laid his fork across the empty plate and stifled a burp behind his palm. "Excellent meal, sir. Thank you."

Fergus O'Toole's merry eyes glistened in the candlelight of the chandelier. Those eyes were set off by rampant brows of black hair that seemed poised to invade other parts of the man's moon-shaped face. Above the brows, his head was smooth and hairless, and buffed to a shine worthy of a mirror. Such distinctive appearance had earned him the nickname of "Moonbeam."

A more serious man might have taken offense at that moniker. Not O'Toole. According to gossip, O'Toole had tried to change his first name legally to Moonbeam, but the local court in Wheeling denied the request on grounds of frivolity. Ever since, O'Toole had held all lawyers in contempt with the single exception of Shannon's father.

"So, George, tell me what happened," O'Toole said.

Shannon decided that nothing would be gained by blaming this man or rehashing the details of how he came to be heading for Philadelphia instead of the Hudson River valley. "Not much to tell. University session starts on the twentieth."

"Philadelphia?"

"I am to read the law."

O'Toole's fingers rippled a rhythm against the lace tablecloth. "The law. I see."

Shannon went on, anxious to fill the uncomfortable silence, "Father arranged my tuition and a place to live."

O'Toole's hand fell still except for the index finger that tapped a lace rose petal. "So he killed your appointment to West Point."

Shannon held back his nod, afraid O'Toole would see it as an accusation.

"I'm sorry I caused this trouble for you, George. Your plans to go to West Point just slipped out last time your father was here. Those ears of his never miss anything." His fingers curled into a fist. "Your father is brilliant but far too obstinate when it comes to his opinions."

The fist relaxed into a palm laid flat upon the lace. "Thank the Maker. His stubbornness saved my skin more than once during the War. Living with such a man though, that has to be a trial."

O'Toole patted Shannon's arm. "He raised a good one. I'll hand him that." He sat back and laced his fingers across his round stomach. "You want the law?"

Shannon dared not answer.

"Silence speaks louder than words, my boy. What do you know about the Northwest Passage?"

"It's a trade route from the Mississippi to the Western Sea."

O'Toole nodded. "Aye. One nobody's found. Not yet anyway. What do you know about Louisiana?"

"That's the land west of the Mississippi that Spain owns." Shannon shifted on his chair. Why was this man testing him?

"Not any more. These United States own it now." O'Toole leaned forward. "I know you're thinking 'What's that got to do with anything?' Right, my boy? Well, it happens that I don't agree with your father. This country needs more than volunteers to fight its battles. The Revolution proved that. Which is precisely why Congress created a military academy. To train officers like the ones who saved our rears. Because of attitudes like your father's, it took twenty years to charter West Point."

O'Toole's fist hit the table, startling Shannon. "This country needs its brightest men trained and ready to defend her. Not more mealy-mouthed lawyers twisting words into meanings no one intended.

"With Congress chock full of lawyers, it's a wonder anything gets done. Tom Jefferson, he knows their ways though. He's the one persuaded them to buy Louisiana and now he's managed to get them to finance an expedi-tion — a military expedition — to look for the Passage."

The man thrummed his fingers against the arm of his chair. "Old Tom has a vision. He has had it for as long as I have known the man. Wants this nation to stretch from the Atlantic to the Western Sea. 'Westering Vision' is what he calls the notion. You have to give things fancy names, you know. To keep all those lawyers in Congress happy. Gives them some-thing else to argue about so somebody else can get real work done. You ever consider how many terms they have come up with so they don't have to call themselves lawyers?"

As always, O'Toole took forever to get to his point. Shannon struggled to ignore his bladder which was uncomfortably full from the French wine he had consumed with dinner.

"Jefferson has never been wrong before. And he is not wrong this time either." O'Toole shoved away from the table, causing Shannon's fork to clatter off his plate. "The man in charge of the expedition is an Army Captain, name of Lewis. Meriwether Lewis. Meriwether. How's that for a handle? Worse than Fergus."

O'Toole's wagging head gleamed in the candlelight. "As we speak, Lewis is on his way down the Ohio in a custom-built keelboat. I met him when he passed through here a month ago. He is intelligent and cunning, charming when it suits his purpose, and single-minded."

"Like my father," Shannon ventured to say.

O'Toole honked a laugh, then fell serious again. "Lewis's plan is to re-cruit men for the expedition once he gets down into Kentucky. He asked me to be on the lookout for any I thought he could use." He scratched at his shiny top ridge. "He is due to be at Maysville, Kentucky around the fifteenth of this month. You just have time to make it if you get going."

"Me?" Surprise made Shannon's voice too loud.

"You carry yourself like a soldier, like an officer. How long have you drilled with the militia?"

"Eight years."

"Your father bragged about how you can shoot and ride. You are a little short on experience, and you will have to qualify no doubt. With Lewis's criteria, that won't be easy. But using my name should help your cause."

Shannon interrupted, "Mr. O'Toole, I can't do that. I have to go to Uni-versity. Father made all the arrangements."

O'Toole reared back in his chair with a chuckle. "Spoken like a true son of your father." He tapped Shannon's wrist, his face suddenly earnest. "But is that what *you* want, George?"

He held up a hand peremptorily, cutting off Shannon's reply. "Sleep on it, my boy. We will talk again in the morning."

"All right, sir, but don't expect me to change my mind."

At that, O'Toole shot Shannon a knowing glance, then turned to pour the brandy.

Outside his gate the next morning, Fergus O'Toole raised his disap-pointed face toward Shannon who sat in his saddle, anxious to be away. "You're sure?"

"Philadelphia," Shannon answered.

O'Toole sighed resignedly. "I will send word to your father then. Let him know you got here all right." He stepped back. "Have a safe ride, my boy. You are always welcome whenever you come back this way."

Shannon patted the pouch slung across his chest, then tapped the top of his boot to make sure the two bags of coins were still in place. "Thank you, sir. For everything."

He stopped when he reached Wheeling's main street, waved back at his host, then urged his mount into a trot until they rounded the bend. There he pulled up his horse Rosie, checked the road in both directions and scanned the flanking woods. Satisfied that no one was paying him heed, he rode off the road into the trees and made a wide circle around the town.

He paused in the cover of some maples before he rejoined the road. This close to home, someone might see him riding west instead of east. He talked to himself for courage. "Keep your ears open. You know the way to Zanesville. From there you go west to Columbus and south to the Ohio by way of Chillicothe. And you *will* ask for directions."

5. *Sarah's Ploy*

S hielded from the road by a stand of brush, Shannon crouched low over the saddle horn and waited for the riders to pass. This had been the closest call yet. *Durn you, George. Quit your daydreaming and pay attention*, he chided himself.

Once he figured the coast was clear, he prodded Rosie back onto the road, and in no time his mind was wandering again. The more he thought about the expedition, the more excited he got. This was his chance, the one he had dreamed about for so long. The opportunity to take charge of his life and prove that he could stand on his own two feet. Fergus O'Toole had ruined his dreams for West Point, but the man had given him something even better: the chance to become a legend. With O'Toole's recommendation, he was a shoo-in for the expedition. Imagine being the one who discovered the Passage. George Shannon. His name would go down in history like Alexander, Marco Polo, Columbus. Conquerors and explorers. They were the men whom history remembered. Not lawyers.

A tremble rippled along Rosie's back. Too late, Shannon heard the thud of galloping hooves rapidly approaching from the rear. Damn it all it! He'd done it again, wool-gathering instead of keeping his mind on his business.

There was no time to hide. He tugged his hat low over his brow, bowed his head and gave the fold of skin between his thumb and index finger a painful pinch to punish himself for not paying attention. Maybe the rider would gallop past without a second look. He prayed for a stranger.

"George!" Parson Cooper reined in his horse, a piebald animal with endurance and energy that made up for her spindly legs.

"Parson," was all he could get out at the sight of the one person on earth — besides Sarah Cooper — he did not want to see at that moment.

"Oh, I am delighted! Absolutely. The weather delayed me. I was in Wheeling on business, and I was afraid you would be gone before I got back."

The parson's effusiveness disconcerted Shannon. "I — I forgot something and had to turn back home."

"Marvelous! A stroke of luck for us both. Of course, you must stop at the parsonage. I know, supper. I insist. You can't head out again until morning anyway. Sarah and I simply must give you a proper send-off. After all, you are like a son to us."

The parson's enthusiasm made it impossible for Shannon to refuse.

"Well, come on. Let's not keep Sarah waiting. She will be so pleased." Cooper trotted off, leaving Shannon to follow with his stomach wrapping itself into a knot.

At the parsonage, Cooper dismounted. "You go on to the house and keep Sarah company. I'll be along after I tend both our horses and slop old Hambone and her shoats.

Shannon watched helplessly as the man made for the barn, taking Rosie with him. He did not want to face Sarah, but now he had no choice. He walked to the house like a man condemnned to death.

She was at the window, watching the barn when he reached the back door. He let himself in and stood waiting for her to say something.

Her voice was low. "Why? Am I so ugly?"

"Oh, no, ma'am. Not at all. It's just that, well, you're his —"

"Don't say it." She crossed the floor and fell to her knees at his feet.

Shannon tried to elude her grasp but she latched onto his pantleg. "No, this is wrong. Stop. Please." He backed to the wall, desperate for some way to extricate himself from her clutches without alerting the parson.

"God Himself gave me these feelings toward you, George," she pleaded, trying to pull him down beside her. "Nothing between us could ever be wrong."

"This is!" he exclaimed.

She let go of him as precipitiously as someone releases a hot coal. She got to her feet with a swish of her skirts and went to the oven. "I'm surprised you came back," she said coldly, opening the oven door. The fragrance of hot corn bread wafted into the room.

"How did you know I was gone?"

"Your mother. She came to see my husband right after you left. She cried most of the day, you know. But she wasn't the only one who cried."

He refused to take the opening she left him. "I forgot something. Had to come back. From Wheeling."

"Whatever you forgot must be awfully important for you to waste a couple of days. Especially since you could not even give me five minutes."

The edge in her voice kept him silent.

She turned toward him, a crafty look rearranging the planes of her face. "You know what I think? I think you didn't forget anything. I bet you're taking off. You're running away, aren't you?"

Before he knew it, she was beside him whispering into his ear. "Yes, that's just what you're doing," she purred. "Little George Shannon is finally showing some gumption. He's finally standing up to his daddy."

The tip of her tongue thrust suddenly into his ear. He heard himself moan.

"I should go straight to your father, George. But I won't. It will be our little secret." Her hands slid around his shoulders. "Provided —"

With her voice and tongue caressing his ear, gooseflesh exploded across his arms and legs. His words came out in a breathless tumble. "Oh, Sarah, what?"

"He has a meeting at the church later. After dinner, I'll ask you to help me clean up before you leave. Say yes, George."

Boots thudding on the back steps gave them enough warning to separate before the parson bounced into the kitchen. "I am hungry!" he declared, rubbing his hands together in anticipation. He reached for the pan of corn bread, but Sarah slapped his hand. "In a few minutes, dear. Why not pour cups of cider for you and George?"

The parson grabbed a jug and two cups off the shelf, giving Shannon enough time to edge quickly into a chair to hide the unmistakable bulge in the front of his trousers.

Dinner with the Coopers seemed to last for hours. Shannon choked down enough to be polite, then shoved the rest around with his fork, half-listening to the parson's prattle and offering an occasional nod.

Cooper finally pushed his empty plate away and reached for his frock coat. "Hate to rush off, George, but tonight is the deacons' meeting."

"George will help me tidy up, won't you, dear?" Sarah smiled sweetly in his direction.

With his thoughts and urges now under control, Shannon wanted to be gone, but the look in her eyes warned him of the consequences of going back on their agreement. "Of course, ma'am."

"Good." She turned to her husband. "I probably won't wait up for you, dear."

"Then I will remember to be quiet." The parson pecked her cheek and hurried out the door.

Sarah took her time closing the kitchen curtains. "He's gone. Thank God. I thought we would never be rid of him. Come." She took Shannon's hand and led him through the front room. At the doorway of the bedroom, he pulled back. "No, this isn't right."

Sarah left him there and went to light the oil lamp, then she sat on the bed and began to take the pins from her hair, one after another, with slow deliberate movements. With the last pin, the end of the braid she always wore in a bun at the back of her head came free. He could not take his eyes off her graceful white arms as she unwound the coils. She held out the bound end of the loosened braid to him. "Help me."

He was powerless to refuse. She drew him down next to her and guided his hands in separating the braid's three strands. The silken softness of the honey-colored tresses in his fingers mesmerized him. As her long hair leapt free of its bonds, he had the urge to bury his face in it. He knew he was on dangerous ground, but he lacked the will to move.

She swept the hair from his grasp and stretched her arms above her head. Arching her back, she studied him as the glorious tresses sifted down across the swell of her breasts. Still holding him prisoner with her eyes, she began to undo the row of buttons that stretched from the neck to the waist of her blue calico. The top of the dress came apart, revealing the milky skin of her shoulders.

"I, uh, have to go," he stammered.

"No, dearest," she whispered huskily. "We had an agreement."

The buttons across her bust sprang free of their holes, and she nudged the material aside. Her finger traced the top edge of her stays, drawing his gaze along with it. Smiling knowingly, she guided his hand to the next button and helped his clumsy fingers work the carved bone through the bound hole. "That's right," she coaxed.

Another button. Then two. Then the last.

"Now you," she whispered.

"W-what?"

"Your clothes, dearest."

When he was slow to respond, she helped him. Before he knew it, his shirt, belt and boots lay in a heap on the floor. Sarah stood up then and slowly drew the top of her dress down to her waist. She smiled and caressed his cheek. "You must look at me, dearest. After all, you have never seen a real woman before, have you? Do I please you?"

"Oh, yes." The words came in gulps. "Sarah, I —"

"Shhh. Don't talk. Sit. Watch."

He could not have done anything else.

Her hands moved mysteriously behind her until her stays fell away. She tossed them aside and smoothed her shift. The sheer cotton did little to hide the womanly swell of her hips or the erect nipples and shadowed aureoles of her breasts.

A moan escaped before he could bite it back.

"I see I have your full attention now," she teased, staring pointedly at his crotch. "Do you still want to leave?"

"No." His answer came too quickly.

She gave a throaty laugh and lay back on the bed. "I'm not taking any chances tonight. Why not slip out of those trousers?"

His fingers had never been so wooden. He struggled with the eight buttons at his fly, ripping off the last two in his rush.

"There now." She patted the bed next to her. "Come join me."

He peeled off his trousers and was about to heave them on top of his other clothes when a loud voice cut the darkness. "George Shannon!"

Parson Cooper stood framed in the bedroom doorway. Shouldering Shannon aside, he charged the bed. Shannon stumbled over a low stool and fell onto the pile of his clothes.

"Harlot!" Cooper's open palm connected with Sarah's cheek. The force of the blow slammed her head against the wall, and her scream rent the air. Her hands flew up but too late to ward off a second slap.

Shannon threw himself at the parson. The man fell against the bed but managed a kick backward, burying the heel of his boot in Shannon's gut. Shannon staggered into the wall and the parson pounced on him. "Adulterer!"

The man's fist glanced off Shannon's left ear and smashed into his nose with an explosion of pain that laid Shannon out on the floor.

Through a haze, he saw Cooper launch a kick aimed at his face. Instinctively his arms flew up to block it. The parson's heavy boot slammed into his wrist. The resulting jolt of pain ripped a scream from Shannon's innards and whetted his reflexes.

The parson's next kick was meant for his groin, but Shannon caught the man's foot and gave it a wrench that pitched Cooper off his stance. The parson's head connected with the overturned stool, knocking him out.

Escape was the only thought Shannon's mind could form. He scooped up his clothes and staggered out of the room, out of the house. He flung the saddle across Rosie, jerked the cinches tight, and swung onto her back naked. Clutching his clothes and digging bare heels into her sides, he rode away like the demons of hell were after him.

In the brooding darkness of the overgrown creek bottom that night, Shannon came to understand that he alone was responsible for all that had occurred at the Cooper's. Something shadowy and unsavory within him had driven Sarah to act the way she did. Worse, his failure to counter her actions had aggravated the situation. As a result, he had betrayed his friend, the parson.

He had always tried to be the son his father would be proud of. In his lessons, the militia and everyday life, he strove to conduct himself properly. More than once, that meant refusing to go along with the other boys his age, and such refusals had cost him popularity.

Then, a year ago he had awakened one morning to an idea so compelling that he could not deny it: he would apply to West Point, the brand-new military academy the Congress had just established. For the first time in his life, the rebel within him overcame his desire to please his father. He pursued applying to West Point behind his father's back, appealing to his father's many influential friends for references. Parson Cooper had helped at every turn, believing in him and encouraging him.

And now what had he done? Repaid that trust with betrayal.

There was way to right such a wrong. He needed to face the parson and beg his forgiveness, then leave. Forever.

That decided, Shannon fell asleep.

6. *Two Roads to Maysville*

Shannon woke the next morning to bright sun filtering through the trees of the peaceful glade. The sunlight lent everything around him a gilded glow. Chickadees flitted about in the oaks. Bracken fronds wafted on a gentle breeze perfumed with the clean morning scents of tree sap and warmed earth. While he savored one of his mother's meat pies, a pair of gray squirrels scurried about gathering acorns for the winter. The whole world seemed bursting with possibility.

He washed himself in the creek and dressed, then realized that he no longer felt guilty about what had happened at the parsonage. After all, wasn't it Sarah's doing that led to that awful scene with the parson? She was the one who had thrown herself at him. Not the other way around. In fact, he had been trying to get away from her when Fate led him to run into the parson on the Wheeling Road. No, there was no need to ask for forgiveness, so no need to go back there.

Yes, Sarah had guessed his intentions, but she did not know where he was going. If she went to his parents, they would assume he was bound for West Point, not Kentucky. Then again, his father was well-known in Ohio because of his efforts to win statehood for the territory, and Shannon looked enough like him that he was bound to be recognized unless he was careful not to be seen. *Of course I can do that*, he assured himself. He saddled Rosie and off they rode.

For the next five days, he skirted towns and settlements, keeping away from those places where he might be recognized while still stopping after every detour to confirm that he was on the right trail. There was a slim chance his father might be able to track him through those he talked to, but Shannon figured asking was better than getting lost and not reaching Maysville in time to join the expedition.

He ate the last of the food his mother had packed on the fourth day. On the fifth he reached the outskirts of the settlement of Columbus. He was hungry but decided it was too chancy to buy food there. Instead, he skirted the town, trusting that he could pick up the trail again on the other side. What he found was a confusing number of tracks leading south.

With his stomach protesting its emptiness, he picked what seemed like the right road to Chillicothe and the Ohio River. He rode along it for half a day before he came across someone to ask about his choice of roads. The itinerant peddler did not hesitate. "She's a-ways still, but you're goin' right."

I can do this. I can find my way, Shannon thought proudly as he rode away from the man. His confidence had been boosted enough to ignore his hunger until sundown when he came upon a rough clapboard structure with the sign "Livery and Rooms." He needed a hot meal and longed for a night's sleep on a real mattress so he decided to forego caution. "Sign says they have horse food, girl," he said to Rosie. "Hope they have people food, too."

He left the mare in the care of the stable boy and let himself into the public room. Blinking against the smoke curling from a badly-drafted fireplace, he found himself in a narrow room. Scraps of food littered the floor and greasy soot filmed the single window. He wrinkled his nose at the rancid odor.

A couple of shadowy characters hunched over their cups at opposite ends of the long shelf that served as a bar. Behind the shelf stood a paunchy, sallow-faced man who studied Shannon as if he were a bug to be squashed.

Shannon was too hungry and tired to leave. He drew himself up to full height and strode toward the bar. "I need a bed for the night."

"Do you now?" Sallow Face drawled. "And I suppose you'll want to pay me with that fetchin' smile of yours, instead of money?"

Shannon felt himself flush. He regretted not paying more attention to the details of dealing with innkeepers when he had traveled with his father. He fumbled for his purse and would have got it out of his shirt except that Sallow Face stayed his hand while darting warning glances at the other drinkers. "Welcome to Callahan's. You're speakin' to Callahan himself." He thrust out a grimy hand.

Shannon tucked the purse away and shook the hand. "I'm White, George White."

Callahan motioned Shannon to lean toward him. "Mr. White," he whispered, his breath reeking of rotten teeth and putrid food. "I'd be keepin' my purse out of sight if I was you." He stepped back and resumed his normal tone. "A room for the night it is. And you'll be wantin' a meal, I can see. 'Course that's extra."

Before Shannon could answer, the innkeeper ducked through a narrow doorway cut into the back wall. Minutes passed with the two strangers taking his measure. Shannon grew uneasy.

He was on the verge of leaving when Callahan reappeared with a steaming plate which he carried to a rickety table set into the corner next to the fireplace. "Take your seat, Mr. White."

Shannon did and Callahan produced a spoon from his ratty apron pocket, breathed on it, and wiped it with his shirt tail, then plunked it on the crumb-stewn tabletop. "Eat up."

While Shannon eyed the contents of the plate, the innkeeper took the chair opposite. "What are you starin' at, laddie? Eat."

"What is it?"

"My own special recipe. Best food you ever tasted. Try it."

He had never smelled such an odor. Not from anything edible. His hesitation seemed to vex Callahan. "You pay for it whether you eat it or not. Rule of the house."

In the dim light, Shannon could not tell what might be mixed up in the malodorous concoction, but he was much too hungry to turn down any food. He held his breath and downed a spoonful.

Callahan beamed. "Delicious, ain't it?"

Struggling not to gag, Shannon forced himself to smile.

"Where you be headed, Mr. White?"

"Chillicothe."

"Comin' from?"

"Zanesville."

Callahan's laughter bewildered Shannon. "How you expect to get there? By way of China? You're goin' north, laddie. Chillicothe's south. It's marked plain as this bulge above my belt." He grabbed his paunch for effect. "That sign at the crossroads in Columbus is painted bright green. How could you miss it?"

Shannon shrugged. He was not about to tell Callahan he had deliberately avoided Columbus and that his directions came from a peddler, not a signpost. *Confound it*, he thought. *Here I've been so careful to stop and check the way. And still I get lost. At this rate, how am I ever going to find the Passage?*

To stop the scolding in his head and cover up his dismay at his lack of direction, he set to work eating the disgusting meal. It was food. Who cared what was in it?

Callahan watched him until he cleaned his plate. "Possum and grits," he announced expansively. "An old family recipe. Knew you'd like it once you got started." He swooped up the empty plate. " Stairs're on the west end of the buildin'. Your room's on the right inside the door. In the mornin', I'll see you get pointed in the right direction."

He disappeared into the kitchen with a wink, and Shannon went off to find his bed — with a stomach full, but decidedly queasy.

Five days of McBain had shredded Colter's patience. The man questioned his every decision by trying to turn it into a bet. Colter had lost track of the number of times he had told McBain, "I don't bet." He had pressed the ride in order to put distance between them and the Draft and anyone Farley Stuart might possibly send after him. The ride would have been enough to wear him out without McBain. With McBain, he had about reached his limit.

By the end of the fifth day's ride from Stuart's Draft, with more than half the journey to Maysville still ahead of them, Colter craved some solitude and distance from McBain. He told Quent to care for the horses and McBain to set up camp, then took off afoot to hunt for some dinner.

Once he was alone, the forest began to work her magic on him, smoothing away his edginess. He passed up three larger deer before he shot a yearling buck that would supply more than enough meat for the rest of their journey. Though he would have preferred to stay out by himself, he swung the carcass across his shoulders and turned back to camp.

He returned to find the horses still saddled and standing in the same place he had left them three hours ago. Quent had not done a blessed thing. Drunken laughter rose beyond the windbreak of bushes that marked the edge of the clearing where he had located their camp. His anger flaring dangerously, Colter strode into the campsite to find McBain and Quent deep into a jug.

His cousin greeted him with an effusive "Johnny! Here, have a drink."

McBain had left the Draft well supplied with Hen's whiskey, a fact Colter had discovered at their first night's camp. He ignored the jug his cousin held out. "Why ain't them horses unloaded, Quent?"

Quent waved him off. "There's lots of time for that. Huh, Mac?" He gave the gambler an idolizing smile.

"Unless you want raw meat, one of you best get a fire goin'," Colter said.

"Flip you for it," McBain drawled, tossing a coin into the air.

Another bet. Colter's jaw tightened. "I got the meat. That's all I'm goin' to do."

"'Course you did," McBain said. "You're the famous dead-eye of the Blue Ridge, right?"

Colter had had a crawful of McBain's sarcasm. Ever since they left the Draft, the man had been on him about his refusal to participate in a shoot-off. "Damn right, I am." He turned his back on the drunken pair and set to dressing out the carcass.

"How about I get the fire started?" Quent offered.

Colter kept quiet. He was too angry to trust himself not to say something he would later regret. He listened to the sounds of his cousin thrashing around in the brush gathering fuel and to his slurred curses as he struggled to get a fire going. Finally, Colter relented and went to help. In no time he had a fire blazing. Quent hiccuped thanks and lurched back to McBain and the jug.

Colter turned to McBain. "Since he done your chores, you can do his. You best be for seein' to them horses if'n you figure on eatin'."

McBain yawned openly as if the challenge bored him. "I just got comfortable, Coal-Tar. Think I'll go hungry."

Coal-Tar. How he despised that nickname and the way Mac tossed it at him every chance he got. He was on the verge of smearing his impatience all over McBain's smirking face, breaking his life-long rule of never being the first one to throw a punch, when Quent swayed to his feet. "I'll do 'er, Johnny. You see to dinner. I'm starved."

Quent's youthful bravado and drunken state could not mask his stiff movements. Five days of hard riding had taken a toll on his body. Colter felt a twinge of empathy but did not interfere. The boy had to learn. Instead, he went back to carving up the meat as a way to cool his blood. He was disgusted with himself for letting McBain prod him into a temper. He knew better than to let someone like the gambler get under his skin. Knew better but did not seem to be able to stop it.

He threaded one of the deer's haunches on a pair of stout green sticks and positioned the meat over the fire to cook. That done, he carved up the rest of the meat for future meals.

He had just finished when Quent returned from caring for the horses, walking considerably straighter than when he left. When he made straight for the jug, Colter bit back the objection that rose to his lips. It was not his place to mother Quent. All he had promised was to get his cousin to Maysville safely.

His thirst quenched, Quent settled on the ground with his back against his saddle. "Tell me again about Kate's place, Mac."

Colter's jaw tightened. He rued the day he had ever heard about Kate's place. McBain started talking about that whorehouse soon as they left the Draft, and now it was all Quent could talk about.

McBain took a swig and tucked the jug under his arm. "Kate's is the kind of place a man won't soon forget. Her house in New Orleans was the grandest place you ever saw. I hear her new house in Charleston is even better. But it is what's inside that makes a man's blood heat up. Inside there is more pleasure than most men can handle. What kind of women do you dream about, my young friend?"

McBain did not wait for an answer from Quent. He rambled on. "Whatever you want, Kate has exactly the right woman to make your dreams real."

"Oh, God. I can't wait," Quent slurred. "How far to Charleston, Johnny?"

"Tarnation! Would you give it a rest?" Colter snapped.

The outburst confused Quent. "What'd I say?"

"Kate's place. Is that all you got in your head?" asked Colter.

"Prett' near," Quent answered slowly.

"You ever bedded a woman?" Colter asked.

"Lay off the lad, Coal-Tar," McBain said. "Why you getting so riled?"

"I'm as tired of your stories, McBain, as your bellyachin' and wagerin'. Tired of you feedin' Quent a passel of lies every night."

"Women are one thing I never lie about," McBain said, humor leaving his face. "Then again, with that blotch covering half your face, I can understand how you don't get many opportunities with the fairer sex."

"Listen to Mac, Johnny. He knows about these things," Quent said.

Knowing that his cousin had a bellyful of whiskey did not help soften the blow of his taking sides with a sharper like McBain nor did it prepare Colter for the impact of the memory that came careening into his head at that moment. A memory named Livy.

At the time, she was the most beautiful thing he had ever seen. She was one of three sporting women working out of a couple of gloomy rooms behind the tavern in a settlement where he and Zoob had stopped to sell their pelts at the end of their second season as trapping partners. They were both barely fifteen.

On one particular night, they decided to celebrate a lucrative season of partnering by blowing off some steam. After a few drinks in the tavern, they decided to cap their evening with a visit to the ladies out back.

At the door, one of the harlots, a woman with an overly ample body and pitted skin, confronted Zoob. "Your kind ain't welcome here. Git or I'll sic the dogs on you."

Usually Zoob's Shawnee looks did not pose a problem since they were out away from folks most of the time. But that night they did. Zoob managed to keep his face neutral, but Colter saw the hurt and anger in his partner's eyes as he turned away. In any other circumstance, he would have gone with Zoob to show solidarity with his partner, but that night he was too eager for his first taste of a woman to care about anything else.

Afterward he remembered everything about the experience: how Livy smiled, how smooth her white skin felt under his hands, how her body curved and swelled in all the right places. He remembered his body reacting, then acting as if it were separate from him. He remembered being swept along like a twig caught in a river current without the power or the will to stop himself as his need surged into unbearable pressure, then exploded with a torrent. Next came the peace, the lethargy in his limbs.

Too soon, he found himself standing in the road, aching to go back again. It was then he discovered his purse was gone.

At first he did not want to blame her, but after searching his clothing a third time, he crept back to the door. It took two tries for him to get the words out.

Livy flew into a rage. "God, you're ugly. Get out of my sight!" she screamed, and two enormous men who had not been there before heaved him out the door. He remembered the sound of her cruel laughter and the glint of lantern light on the men's skinning knives. He stumbled around in the dark, sick at heart but powerless to do anything in the face of such odds until Zoob appeared from somewhere in that ghostly way of his.

Zoob never asked what happened. He guided Colter away and rolled him into his blanket to let him sleep off the experience.

"Looks like the cat's got Coal-Tar's tongue," Mac said.

Colter let the taunt slide past. He pulled out his knife and began whittling on a piece of wood.

McBain smoothed down his longish brown hair. "You know, Coal-Tar, you ought to consider wearing a patch over that mark of yours. Something that ugly puts people off. Especially women."

The remark, coming on the heels of the memory of Livy, landed like a fist in the gut. Colter decided it was time to respond with a blow of his own. "Women? Why, I plum forgot to tell you. I changed my mind. We ain't goin' to Charleston."

Quent's lower jaw went slack. McBain peered at Colter as if he had never quite seen him before.

"If'n we're goin' to make Maysville by the fifteenth, we got some ground to make up so I'm takin' us by a different trail." He let that sink in while he tucked away his knife and drew out his blanket. "We best be turnin' in, too. You got first watch, Mac."

For once, there was a hard glint of anger in McBain's eyes. "If we aren't going to Charleston, then I'm not standing watches. You want watches, you can stand them yourself, seeing as how you're the reason someone's after us. If they are. Which I doubt."

Quent glared his disappointment at Colter. "I'm with Mac. No Charleston, no more watches."

Colter realized that McBain had matched his move. Even without the threat of someone following them, this trail west was dangerous. Without someone to keep watch at night, anything could happen. All of it bad.

He tossed aside his blanket and took up his rifle. For him, it would be long sleepless night.

"Get that Bible and be back here by November 15 to marry my daughter, Hartley, or rot in hell!" Farley Stuart's angry words had pushed Josiah Hartley relentlessly along the rough mountain track. Every bone, every muscle in his body ached from five days in the saddle.

Five days of jarring torment and five nights of sleeping on the unforgiving ground had dissolved all traces of neutrality he might have felt toward John Colter. Colter had become the spreading cloud that threatened to blot out the bright dream he had worked so long and hard to bring to reality. As long as the man possessed that Bible and the evidence it contained to tie Stuart with forgery, and the hat that tied himself to robbery and to Stuart, Hartley could not rest. He needed those two pieces of evidence, or his dream, his whole future stood in jeopardy.

He lashed his quirt across the rump of his lagging mount. "You worthless nag, don't give up on me now."

Instead of being prodded to greater speed, the horse's pace slackened even more, a warning that he better ease off unless he wanted to be stranded with only his two feet to carry him home again.

Though there was still just enough light to see by, he stopped beside a little brook and let the horse drink while he walked on stiff legs a few yards upstream to quench his own thirst. That was when he heard voices.

Leaving the horse to forage along the creek, he crept in the direction of the glow from a campfire showing through the thick tangle of thorny undergrowth off to his left. He concealed himself in some brush and studied the scene.

Next to the fire lounged the gambler McBain and young Quent Colter. They were sharing a jug and complaining drunkenly about missing something called Kate's. Just beyond the edge of the firelight, John Colter stood with his back to the other two, rifle in hand and saddlebags at his feet, obviously standing watch.

After five days of following whatever track seemed right, Hartley could scarcely believe his luck in coming upon the very one he had come seeking. All he had to do was wait for the chance to grab those saddlebags and he would be on his way home.

Once he got on the right trail, thanks to Callahan, Shannon's spirits revived. Rosie, too, seemed to have renewed energy in her step.

The day passed quickly. Near dusk, he turned off the narrow river trail and rode through the undergrowth along a creek to a clearing that promised a good camp for the night. He tended to his horse and, after much fumbling, got a fire going. Back against a tree, he stretched his saddle-weary legs toward the sputtering fire and untied his mother's food parcel. He divided the victuals into thirds, laid one third aside to eat and rewrapped the rest.

He forced himself to take small bites and chew slowly, but the amount of food barely scratched the surface of his hunger. Though he tried to ignore the demands of his stomach, the longer he sat, the more tempted he was to eat what was left. Finally he gave in to his appetite. Why not? He had plenty enough money to buy food along the way.

It wasn't until all the food was gone that he realized the flaw in his thinking. Now he would have to stop at Chillicothe, the one place he had to avoid since, as the new state capital, he was bound to run into one of his father's friends.

Miffed at his lack of foresight, he curled onto his side, drew his blanket around his shoulders and stared into the fire until his eyes drooped closed.

"Lost again, boy-o?"

Shannon snapped awake at the sound of a reedy voice. As he sat up, his head collided with something hard and the world went pitch-black.

All day a sullen Quent and an uncharacteristically quiet McBain trailed far behind. Colter reckoned it was just as well. He halfway regretted depriving Quent of his first chance to taste a sporting woman. Then again, sporting women had not been part of the bargain he had made for this journey until McBain started talking up the possibility.

By midafternoon Quent was clearly faltering, the result of too little sleep and too much whiskey. Colter found a campsite on a bare knob of land on the upper lip of a small valley. At the rear of the clearing was a sheer drop down a hundred-foot rock face. To Colter's mind, that and the sparse vegetation around the spot gave it clear defensive advantages, necessary since Quent and McBain were likely to refuse to stand night watches.

After a silent dinner of cold deer meat, Quent turned in, leaving Colter and McBain to sit up together until they, too, grew sleepy. Colter did not relish any more arguments so he pulled out his whittling and set to work.

McBain had his usual jug, but, for a change, he was not talking. The comforting sounds of the forest settling for the night and the familiar motions of liberating a shape from a chunk of wood soon absorbed all Colter's focus.

Then McBain's voice pulled him back to reality. "That was a dirty trick to play on Quent, Coal-Tar. Kate would've seen he got broken in right."

Colter let the words wash over him without comment.

McBain pulled out a corn husk, poured crushed tobacco leaves into it from a pouch he carried on his belt and rolled the husk into a tight cylinder that he called a *papelete*. Sticking one end of the rolled husk between his lips, he lit the other end with a stick from the fire and sucked in a mouthful of smoke. Exhaling, he went on. "You're a hard one, Coal-Tar. And that makes us alike. You and me, we don't fit in most places because we don't live like other people think we should." He grunted a short chuckle. "'Should.' Now there's a word for you. If folks spent less time doing what they should and more time doing what they want, this would be a lot better world."

He rolled the *papelete* between his fingers and studied its burning end before sucking in more smoke. "Yep, you and me. We're two of a kind."

Colter would not brook being put in the same category as the cheating conniver across the fire. "You got it dead wrong, McBain. Ain't two more different men than you and me. When I give my word, I keep it. Your word ain't even worth the air you use up in speakin' it."

McBain's expression lost some of its smugness. "Every man comes to a point where he has a choice to make. Either he can live out his days bound by his word or he can go after his dreams. Duty and desire. They drive everything we humans do. They're the real gods. No man was ever born who can serve both. Me, I'll choose my dreams. And I'm willing to bet my whole purse that I'll die happier than you."

"Happy or not, you'll still be dead. And livin' your way, there ain't gonna be many folks at your funeral."

McBain's lips tilted into a mocking smile. "Folks or not, it's still a funeral. Question is: which of us will have the better life? My money's on my way."

"From what I can see, that's how it always is with you and your kind. Fool's the man who ever believes you. Men like you die young."

McBain regarded Colter through the smoke from his *papelete*. "Better to die young and happy than old and angry, Coal-Tar." With that, he tossed the rest of the husk into the fire, wrapped his blanket around him, closed his eyes and promptly began to snore.

Dew dripped off the bracken onto Shannon's forehead. He opened his eyes to the glare of morning sun. When he tried to sit up, intense throbbing surged from the back of his skull. Investigating with stiff fingers, he discovered a bump just below the crown, encrusted with dry blood.

The bump brought the reedy voice back to him. His rifle was gone. His saddle and saddlebags, all gone. He had been robbed.

He swayed to his feet. "Rosie!"

He hoped desperately that she would come lumbering through the undergrowth, but, when he saw the hobble rope dangling from a limb, he had to accept that she too was gone.

"Dear God, the money!"

When his fingers felt the lump of the second purse inside his boot top, he had to gulp back the tears that rose to his eyes. "You didn't get everything, you useless piece of offal," he muttered. A wave of pounding blurred his vision as he struggled to his feet with the help of the nearby tree. *No horse, no food, no rifle. What am I going to do out here in the middle of who-knows-where? Whatever made me come this way? O'Toole and his big ideas..*

"No, you're the idiot, George," he muttered. "Blame yourself, not O'Toole."

He had no idea where he was. Alone, without a horse or gun, he was a target for every predator, thief and murderer around. A fresh stab of pain preempted his anxious thoughts. He clutched his throbbing temples and squeezed his eyes closed against the onslaught.

The torment subsided but left him too weak to continue standing. He sank to the ground, curled onto his side with his lanky legs against his chest and fell into a lethargic doze.

When he opened his eyes again, the sun was nearly overhead. He sat up slowly and glanced around the clearing. His initial anger had vanished along with his panic.

"I'm alive. I still have some money, a blanket and my militia uniform. So what'll it be, George: go forward or go back?"

He took comfort from the sound of his own voice and counted the money in his boot purse. Twenty dollars. Not enough for a horse or a gun. That meant turning back, but the thought of facing his father brought on another wave of nausea. He leaned against the tree until the feeling passed and he could stand. Callahan. Yes, Callahan was his best hope.

He took one last look at the place he had hobbled Rosie, hoping against reason that she would be there and that this had all been a bad dream. Still, no horse appeared so he set off down the creek toward the river on foot.

The effort of fighting through the undergrowth quickly wore him out. When he reached the river trail, he eased onto a fallen log to rest. A sense of failure overwhelmed him. Failure and desperation. He buried his face in his hands and wondered if he would live to see tomorrow. He was so lost in despair that he did not hear the noises approaching from the north until they grew loud enough to cut through his anguish.

Someone was coming, but who? Taking no chances, he hid himself behind some bramble bushes a moment before a team of horses, drawing a wagon loaded with freight, came into view. Behind it came a second team and wagon.

From his hiding place, Shannon could see just two people, each driving one of the wagons. The first was a short man, thin enough to make one wonder how he could control the massive draft horses. Two limp braids hung from under the man's sweat-blackened hat. The only generous thing about his body was a beard the color of dried mud. It bushed from his chin so luxuriously that the man had gathered it into a clump and tied it with a hank of string.

By contrast, the second driver's body was generous all over — arms, legs, head and a bosom generous enough to give her a swayed back. The sight of a woman sitting where he expected a man to be made his decision for him. He left his hiding place and yelled, "Hey!"

The lead team shied in startled unison. "Damnation!" the male driver yelled, fighting to control the spooked animals. "Bloody hell! You spooked my team. I oughtta shoot you for that!"

A gale of feminine laughter drowned out the man's threat. "If you're gonna use a bullet, shoot yourself, Hedges. Don't waste it on someone as flat-out pretty as this here feller."

The little man whirled toward the second wagon, but the pile of freight behind him blocked his view of the driver. Getting his horses under control, he halted them, set the brake and leaped to the ground. Flexing his hands into fists, he glared at the woman driver.

She waved him off and turned her full attention on Shannon. "Howdy. What is a handsome thing like you doing out here by himself?"

Her kindly tone dispelled Shannon's hesitation. He limped to her wagon. "I got robbed last night. They took my horse and gun." He waved in the direction of the clearing.

"Tarnation, Wilma. We ain't got all day to chat," the male driver complained.

She answered the man, never taking her eyes off Shannon. "Hedges, if you listened as much as you talked, you'd be a genius instead of the boringest man I know. Now, you were saying, Handsome?"

"Would you have room for a passenger, ma'am?" Shannon asked with a nervous smile.

"Depends."

"I can pay."

She examined him slowly from head to boots. "I need to see the color of your gold."

He hesitated. It had occurred to him that showing his purse at Callahan's was the reason he had been robbed.

"Well?"

He swallowed hard, "How much?"

"Depends."

By now, he had reached the limit of his tolerance for being viewed like a side of prime beef. He drew himself up. "On what now, ma'am?"

Interest replaced the boredom in her eyes. "Ah, you got some spirit, I see."

"Wilma!" Hedges said impatiently.

"Hedges!" The wrath in her tone was unmistakable.

With the captive end of his beard trembling with agitation, Hedges scuttled around his team out of view.

"We're headed down to the Ohio River. To Portsmouth," she said.

Shannon's pique vanished instantly. They were headed exactly where he wanted to go. He gave Wilma as winning a smile as he could muster. "That would be fine."

She glanced after Hedges. "I sure could stand some new conversation." She studied Shannon some more. "Smile at me again."

He put all his effort behind it.

"Nice," she muttered, running her eyes along his body again. "Five dollars."

Shannon bit back an objection to the outrageous price, stepped to the back of the wagon where she could not see what he was doing and pulled five dollars from his pouch. That left fifteen dollars, enough, he hoped, to get him to Maysville.

Walking back to the front of the wagon, he handed her the coins which she promptly stashed inside her well-filled shirt.

"Hand?" she asked.

The hand that he grasped felt more like a man's, Wilma's glorious female attributes notwithstanding. He settled himself onto the hard plank next to her, conscious that she observed his every move. She leaned toward him. "Ready?"

He nodded. "Ready."

"Hedges! Where are you, you lazy polecat?" she yelled.

Hedges reappeared, beard twitching, fists balled. He clambered onto the seat of his wagon without a glance in their direction and whipped his team into motion. When Wilma's wagon lurched forward, Shannon grabbed the edge of the seat for balance.

"Enjoy the ride." she said with a sideways grin. "I know I will." Then she pinched his thigh.

7. *Dirty Tricks*

C olter jerked awake, sure he had heard a sound that did not fit his su r-roundings. Once he remembered where he was, he lay under his bla n-ket, tensely listening for an intruder. Hearing no sound and sensing not h-ing out of the ordinary, he relaxed a bit and took his bearings.

That was when he heard it: a small sound as faint and indistinct as the cry of an unseen bird. Propping himself up on an elbow, he surveyed the camp through the graying darkness.

A few paces away McBain snored off last night's whiskey. Beside him, Quent's blanket lay in a heap. Colter did not immediately find that blanket disturbing. Quent's bladder never had been able to hold much.

Then the cry came again and he suddenly knew what it was.

He hurried to the lip of the drop-off that formed the back side of the campsite. Heights unnerved him, but he forced himself to peer over the edge.

The dim light of early dawn revealed the sprawled shape of Quent on a narrow ledge fifteen feet down. Straight down. And below Quent's perch, it was another good hundred-foot drop to a creek in a narrow rocky vale.

A weak "help" drifted up from his cousin. The cry got Colter moving. He needed to get Quent off that ledge, but he could not do it alone. "McBain!" he yelled.

The gambler's blanket twitched feebly.

"Mac, damn it! Wake up! Quent's hurt."

McBain groaned and flopped onto his back. His eyelids opened a slit. "Quent?"

"He fell. Come on. We got to go down and get him."

McBain stared stupidly back as if waiting for Colter to explain what his whiskey-soaked mind could not comprehend. Colter wanted to shake the man silly, but this was no time for fighting. Quent's life was in danger. There was no time to waste on rousing McBain or even putting on his own boots.

He yanked a coil of rope from his saddle and attached one end of the rope to the only tree handy. He wrapped the other end around his chest and under his arms twice and tied it securely. Then he backed to the edge and lowered himself into the nothingness of the drop-off, praying that the rope and the tree were strong enough to hold his weight.

The toes of his bare right foot found a crack in the rock face. Slowly, he shifted his weight until he was sure that step would hold. His left foot sought and found another crack. Again he tested as he shifted onto the step with his feet planted, his fingers found holds to trust before he shifted his stance.

Seeking, testing, shifting, left, then right, feet, then hands, he moved downward, keeping his disquiet over the height at bay with concentration. With each toe- and handhold, his mind chanted: *Small steps. Test 'em each. Slow and steady.*

"Colter!"

Pebbles showered onto his head from above and he started in surprise. The movement caused the perch beneath his left foot to crumble. The rope snapped taut as he slipped, catching him and cutting painfully into his ribs. He slammed against the rock face. The force of the collision scoured the skin off his bare toes.

He flailed for something to grip, knowing that, at any moment, the rope or the tree might give and send him tumbling to severe injury or death.

The rope held, however, and eventually his right toes found a solid tuft of grass upon which to rest. Then his left foot located a crack to wedge against, and his fingers found places to worm into. Stable again, he clung to the rock, unable to move, fear clenching his guts like a vice and the sour-sweet taste of bile in his throat.

Another shower of pebbles.

"Sit down and shut up, Mac!" His voice sounded like a stranger's, but hearing it helped get him going again.

One halting downward step. Then another. Each one strengthened his focus a little more and reduced his fear. After what seemed hours, he reached Quent's ledge.

His cousin smiled weakly. "Guess I fell."

It was beyond Colter to return the smile. "Can you move?"

Quent nodded.

"Careful now. This here ledge is a mite narrow for a barn dance. Move your arms one at a time," he instructed.

Quent did, though the effort clearly caused him considerable pain.

"Now your legs."

The right one seemed fine, but when he tried the left, Quent yowled. "My ankle!"

Colter felt a surge of relief despite his cousin's discomfort. An ankle he could deal with. A broken leg or worse . . . He did not want to think about that now. He yelled upwards, "McBain!"

An ashen face appeared at the top of the cliff.

"After I tie this rope around him, you haul him up. Hear?"

"One minute," McBain yelled, disappearing before Colter could object.

"So help me, if he went to get a jug, I'll . . ." A moan from Quent stopped him. Colter asked the question that had been in his head since he met McBain. "Why're you so set on trailin' after Mac anyway?"

"I'm back," McBain yelled before Quent could answer. "Rope him up,

Coal-Tar. I got this end tied to your horse."

It had not occurred to Colter to use Blaze. Give McBain credit for quick thinking. He unwrapped the rope from his body and tied it around Quent. By the time he got his cousin cinched up, hs knees were vibrating, the re-sult of the proximity of the steep drop-off.

Quent gave him a grateful smile. "It's sunrise and I'm up. Can you be-lieve it, Johnny?"

"Ready?" McBain yelled.

"Ready,"the two cousins replied simultaneously.

As the rope drew taut and tightened around his ribs, Quent's eyes bulged wide open. "Lean on back," Colter ordered. "Hang onto the rope and use your good foot to keep you away from the face. Blaze'll draw you up. You just got to keep yourself balanced. Got that?"

The younger man nodded uncertainly.

Colter watched Quent's ascent nervously. His cousin's life was in McBain's undependable hands and there was nothing he could do except hope they all lived to see this day through.

After agonizing minutes, Quent reached the top and McBain pulled him in. Colter sagged against the rock face as far back from the lip of the na r-row ledge as it was possible to get just then. His legs were trembling now from the effort to contain his fear of heights. He closed his eyes so they would not be tempted to stray toward the plunge that lay below. Then he waited, waited for the rope to be lowered down to him, to get him back up to an expanse of solid ground.

Long minutes passed. The rope did not appear.

He waited some more, then called out "McBain?".

No answer.

"Quent?"

Still no answer.

He craned to look to the top of the precipice, an effort that made him lean toward the drop-off and caused his gorge to rise again. There was no sign of the rope or Quent or McBain.

Then McBain appeared at the top of the drop-off. "You about ready to bargain, Coal-Tar? Quent and me agreed. We'll send down the rope when you agree to take us to Charleston."

Colter could not believe what he was hearing. His voice shook with an-ger. "Get that there rope down here now, damn it, or so help me."

"Now, now. You'll get 'er soon as you say the words."

"Damn your hide, McBain! Get that rope down here. Now!" The rock face picked up his shout and threw it outward in a long mocking echo.

The gambler's lips curved into a self-satisfied smirk. "She's right here." He dangled the end of it for Colter to see. "Say we're going to Charleston, and you'll get it quick as we can run her down to you."

McBain had him. Either he agreed with the pair's terms or he stayed here when here was the last place he wanted to be. "All right. Charleston."

"That mean we got your word on it, Coal-Tar?" McBain asked, flipping the rope nonchalantly.

"Yep," he grumped.

McBain cupped his ear. "Speak up. Quent 'n me can't hear you. What?"

"Yes!" Colter shouted.

The gambler pulled back from the edge and, the next moment, the rope began to snake downward. Minutes later, Colter cleared the top in a fury over how he had been manipulated. Quent was sitting on the ground nursing his injured foot. "Mac says all I got's a bruised ankle. That whiskey was good for somethin', huh, Mac? Made me too loose to get hurt bad."

McBain lounged against the rope-anchoring tree, rolling one of his obnoxious smoking sticks. "Thank your lucky stars for that, Quent. If you'd been hurt any worse, you would miss Kate's place, now that your cousin here has changed his mind. Hand me that jug."

Colter let the dig pass and addressed his cousin. "Time you quit drinkin', Quent, or next time you go stumblin' around in the dark drunk, you might break your back or worse."

"I didn't stumble and I weren't drunk, durn it. Someone pushed me," claimed Quent.

Colter snorted in disbelief.

"If you don't believe me, Johnny, then look around. Where're your saddlebags?"

They were not where he had left them, or anywhere else in campsite, but Colter was not about to take any more bait. Not after what McBain had just forced him into. "All right, Mac. Where'd you put 'em?"

The gambler stuck the smoke into the corner of his mouth. "Don't look at me, Coal-Tar. I know better than to touch anything of yours. Hell, you're liable to shoot me and then I'd miss out on Kate's *and* Maysville."

"It wasn't Mac, Johnny," Quent said. "I'm tellin' the truth. Someone was here. That's how I got pushed over that ledge. It's a wonder you didn't hear his horse takin' off. Sounded like an army to me."

Colter was not listening. He yanked his leather hunting pouch off the broken snag where he had hung it last night. Its weight told him what he needed to know: whoever took his saddlebags had not discovered Ma's Bible and the now-flattened shovel hat which he had moved to the pouch from the saddlebags last night before turning in.

"Quent's saddlebags and mine are still here," Mac said. "Guess they wanted something you had, Coal-Tar. At least we still got whiskey. Looks like you could use a drink, too."

Colter did not hear the offer. Now he knew for certain why he had been feeling so uneasy the last few days. Farley Stuart had indeed sent someone after him. The question was: who would he send? Elijah? Smoot? Someone he had hired for the job?

A more pressing question was how to throw that someone off his tracks. On his own, that would be easy, but he had Quent to worry about. The first order of business was getting his cousin to Maysville as fast as possible. Then he could fade into the wilderness, disappear where no one could find him until he was ready to be found.

There was a thorn in that plan however: his promise to take them to Charleston. *Damn you, McBain*, he thought.

Quent interrupted his thoughts. "If you want to leave, I can ride, Johnny."

His cousin's brave words did not match the grooves pain had traced on his young face, but they touched Colter. He tried to see the bright side. It would be hard for someone to ambush them in Charleston, and there they could buy supplies to replace the ones that had been stolen with his saddlebags. He nodded. "Let's go."

Hartley flung the useless saddlebag against a tree. It slammed against the trunk and flopped down atop the other one. He kicked impotently at the debris strewn around his feet.

From jerked meat and hardtack to a spare tin of lead shot and a supply of fishhooks, the bags had contained everything a man might need for a long journey into the wilds. Everything but what Stuart had sent him to get. Everything but Ellen Colter's Bible and his own lost hat. "Damn you to hell, John Colter!" he yelled at the surrounding trees.

"Preacher Hartley?"

Hartley whirled at the sound of his name to see riders staring at him. "Matt Elwes? Luke? What are you two doing here?"

Matt was the suspicious one of the pair. He answered. "We come after a varmint named McBain. He's got somethin' of ours we intend to get back. What're you doin' out here?"

Hartley sized up the situation in the space of a breath. For one, a week on the trail had worn him to a nub. He knew he could not keep going much farther alone. For another, he also knew that it would not do to reveal his real connections to Farley Stuart to these two brothers since their father was the senior deacon of the Draft's church. "I'm on my way to Charleston. On the Lord's business."

Luke, the more open of the pair, responded. "Maybe you didn't know it, Preacher, but it's not safe out here for a man alone. Whyn't we ride with you?" He nudged his brother. "I hear tell Charleston's got some doin's might interest us."

Hartley let the comment pass. Everyone knew Charleston's reputation for hospitality of the least respectable kind, but he hoped he would not have to go that far to get his own business done. Besides, he might be able to put these two to good use in his cause. He put as much enthusiasm into his reply as he could muster on short notice. "Why, I'd be much obliged for the company."

Despite Quent's badly sprained ankle, he and McBain were both jubilant to be heading to Charleston and Kate's. They were in such high spirits in fact that they neglected to complain when Colter pushed them harder than ever the next day. McBain chattered the whole day, the sound of his voice grating on Colter like a rasp on a fresh wound. He was so fed up with the gambler that he was prepared to have it out with the man if he, like always, refused to do his part in setting up that night's camp.

McBain, however, did not give him the opportunity. For once, he took care of their horses *and* built the fire, both without Colter's telling him to. He even volunteered to stand two watches, his own and Quent's. "Quent won't be needin' his rifle, so I'll take it with me for good measure," McBain grinned. Colter was glad for the gambler's turn-about because he could finally get a full night's sleep, but he knew better than to expect the change to last for long.

He was floating just below consciousness when a rifle boomed in the nearby woods, yanking him back to consciousness. The shot was followed by muffled cursing and the pounding of horses' hooves, galloping away from camp. Then came a second shot from the direction of the camp's perimeter. "Got him!" McBain shouted triumphantly.

Colter scrambled out of his blanket to find Mac standing over a downed man, staring into the darkness after the retreating horse.

"Think I winged the other one," Mac said. "But this one's done for." He used his foot to roll the man over. It was Luke Elwes from Stuart's Draft.

McBain swore under his breath. "Must be Matt got away then. Too bad. He's the real troublemaker. Wish these rifles had more than one shot. I'd have downed them both."

Looking down into the lifeless face, Colter crossed Luke Elwes and his brother off the list of men Stuart might have sent after him. Farley Stuart would have picked someone easier to manage. Still, that did not explain why they were all the way out here from the Draft. He turned to the one man who could answer that question. "We're not budgin' an inch unless you tell me what's goin' on, McBain."

Instead of his usual line of sarcasm and argument, McBain beckoned Colter to follow him back to the fire. Quent had just awakened, his face a confusion of sleep, his eyes barely open. "Somethin' wrong, Mac?" he asked.

Waving off the question, McBain extracted four sacks from Quent's saddlebags and lined them up in the dirt. "These are my winnings, thanks mostly to Luke and Matt."

"What's Quent doin' with them?" Colter demanded, his anger rising like a spring creek to realize the danger carrying such a sum of money posed to his cousin.

"I took them for Mac, Johnny," Quent said. "My bags were prett' near empty and Mac's were full."

Yeah. Full of whiskey, Colter thought.

"Every one of those card games was on the square," McBain asserted. "You can't blame me that those two never knew when to quit. I can't help it if I'm lucky."

"Lucky?" The word exploded out of Colter's mouth.

"Mac always plays fair, Johnny," Quent said flatly. "I know that for a fact, and I won't stand for you thinkin' any different."

Until that moment, Colter had assumed he was the object of the attack the previous night. Now he was not so sure. What if McBain and his money had been the target instead? What if the Elwes boys had mistakenly taken his saddlebags when they were really after Quent's?

McBain stifled a yawn and consulted his pocketwatch. "It's two o'clock, Coal-Tar. Time for you to take the watch." He stretched out next to Quent.

"Oh, no, you don't," Colter said. "There's a dead man to bury."

"Who cares?" Mac said through another yawn. "Burying that one is a waste of good muscle. Let the crows have him. He's no good to anyone anymore — if he ever was." He pulled up his blanket and immediately fell to snoring.

Colter looked at his cousin.

"Don't look at me, Johnny. I ain't helpin'. Mac's right. Let him lay right there. No one'll know or care otherwise."

"I will, Quent," Colter said, angrily hefting up the camp spade. "I will."

Waiting in the dark of the woods for the Elwes brothers to attack Colter and his companions gave Hartley his first chance all day to sort out what his next step should be. He was deep in thought when a shot rang out from the direction of the camp. The sound brought home to the preacher the prospect that Colter might die during the Elwes's raid. If that happened, he could be on his way back to the Draft by dawn, his mission accomplished without ever firing a shot or drawing his knife.

Another shot boomed, followed by a yell of "Got him!" Then came the sounds of a horse crashing through the undergrowth, coming straight toward his position.

He tensed. Something had gone wrong. He could feel it.

A horse and rider broke out of the woods a few yards ahead. It was Matt's buckskin, with Matt slumped over the horse's neck. A low moan carried to Hartley over the thundering of galloping hooves as the horse passed him and continued on into the surrounding forest.

Where was Luke? Hartley wondered.

On the heels of the question came the realization of how much danger he had put himself in. For Colter to discover him out here now would not only put his life in jeopardy but his future as well. Farley Stuart would see his discovery as failure and he would obliterate in a blink everything the preacher had worked so long and so hard to win.

Like a candle flaring into the midnight dark of a room, Hartley saw that following Colter in this way was the height of stupidity. He needed to get out in front of the man and lay a trap for him to fall into.

By now, it was clear: Colter and company were headed to Charleston. If he rode the rest of the night, he could be there first. He leaped onto his horse and wheeled away into the darkness.

8. *Kate's House of Pleasure*

C olter, McBain and Quent arrived in Charleston near noon the next day. Quent was determined to head straight to Kate's, but Colter insisted on stopping first to get supplies, knowing that harlots tended to induce amnesia in even the most conscientious man. McBain again surprised Colter by siding with him and directing them to a supplier where he assured Colter they would get first-rate treatment and the lowest prices.

The storefront wore a fresh coat of whitewash, an elegant lettered sign that read "Jarvis's General Merchandise," and real glass instead of oiled cloth in the windows. Not at all Colter's kind of place or the kind of place where anything close to the lowest prices was possible, but with Quent about to burst from frustration over the delay, he swallowed his prejudice and followed McBain inside.

McBain greeted the shopkeeper effusively. "Melvin Jarvis! Greetings! It's been too long since I was last in your fine establishment here."

With a sour look, Jarvis regarded McBain, then Colter. If McBain noticed the less-than-cordial reception, he gave no sign. "This is my friend John Colter. He has need of some supplies. Give him everything he wants."

"Yeah, and who's paying, McBain? You?"

Colter wanted a few supplies and a quick leave-taking, not trouble. "I am," he said.

"You a friend of his?" Jarvis asked, jerking his chin toward McBain.

"I'm travelin' with him," Colter answered, slapping a gold piece from Lorenzo's stake on the polished counter.

The sight of the money instantly transformed the shopkeeper from suspicious to fawning. "What do you need?"

While Colter ticked off his list, Jarvis fetched the items and tallied the charges. Colter was putting his purchases into a burlap sack when McBain laid a pair of beautifully-tooled new leather saddlebags across the counter. "You'll need these too, Coal-Tar."

Colter knew quality workmanship when he saw it. He also knew how much they had to cost. "This sack'll work fine, Mac."

"How did I know you'd say that?" McBain said. He turned to Jarvis. "How much?"

"More than you've got, McBain," Jarvis sneered.

Drawing a bulging leather purse from his vest, McBain's tone turned from playful to contemptuous. "Oh?"

This time the prospect of money did not alter the shopkeeper's attitude. "Twenty dollars."

The sum was outrageous, three times what the bags were worth. However, McBain did not argue or even try to bargain. He pulled two gold coins out of his purse and laid them out on his open palm.

When Jarvis reached for the money, Mac grabbed the man's hand, squeezing it hard enough to leave bruises. "It's a pleasure to do business with you again, Jarvis." He flung aside the man's hand and the coins like so much garbage. "Take the bags, Coal-Tar. They're yours. From me."

The deadly flatness in McBain's eyes brooked no discussion and no dissension. Colter scooped up the saddlebags and the burlap sack and left the shop.

Outside Quent rocked restlessly in his saddle. "Thought you two'd never get done. Come on. We got things to do, and women to sport."

Ten minutes later the three of them reined in their horses at the top of a lane. By now the flatness had gone from McBain's eyes and his usual expansiveness had returned. He swept an arm toward a house set at the end of a corridor of autumn-leafed maples fronting the river. "Gentlemen, we're here. We have come to Kate's."

The building was two stories of expertly-dressed limestone stretching on both sides of a central portico. Sounds of laughter and the smell of wood fires drifted through the crisp air from the slave quarters and work areas behind the structure. Colter might have taken the house as a rich man's mansion except for the bronze plaque set into a horse-high rock column at the top of the carriageway. On it, twin script "K's" twined together in the center, encircled by bronze ivy, with "K. Kilgallen Est. 1802" at the bottom.

Quent whistled tonelessly. "Looks way out of my league, Mac. And my price range."

"A man does not come to Kate's to quibble over the price. He comes to Kate's to make memories." A smile grew from a seed to full flower on McBain's face in the time it took him to glance down the tree-lined lane. "In fact, my bruised young comrade, I feel in such fine fettle right now that this treat is on me." McBain looked over Quent's head at Colter. "I want to give us something to remember about the last eleven days besides saddle sores, bad coffee and uninvited guests. Shall we?"

Quent let out a whoop as McBain led them down the drive. A boy with skin the color of blackstrap molasses and eyes that blinked too much scurried from the shadows of the porch to take charge of their horses. Though his hands were filled with reins, he managed to catch the penny McBain tossed.

When Quent raised his hand to knock on the door, McBain stopped him. "Kate can't abide loud noises. If you want to be allowed inside, you scratch."

Quent did as he was told. Sure that McBain was playing one of his jokes on the younger man, Colter was surprised when the door opened promptly. Quent fell back a step at the sight of the ebony giant who filled the doorway and regarded them through hooded eyes set under a jutting brow. "May I help you?" The question sounded like an ultimatum in the giant's clipped baritone.

McBain shouldered past Quent. "Jericho, good to see you."

The man studied McBain. Though his expression was neutral, the man's tone was frosty. "Mr. McBain."

"We're here to sample the merchandise, my man."

Jericho did not move immediately. He gave McBain a look that could have served for either a warning or a challenge before stepping to one side with a curt bow.

They entered a broad room with wood floors, gleaming under a massive central chandelier. By Colter's estimate, the chandelier held enough candles to supply a large family for a year. Two staircases, one on each side of the room, curved up to a landing on the second floor. Chairs and settees trimmed in crimson velvet and piled with tasseled pillows were placed at interesting angles around the floor, leaving the center of the room open. Crystal vases of fresh-cut flowers and small potted trees provided privacy between groupings of seats. Curtains from the same crimson velvet draped the windows, and paintings decorated the other walls. A woman with cinnamon skin, dressed in gray homespun and a starched white apron, moved about the room clearing china plates and pewter goblets from the low tables onto a silver tray.

"I will summon the mistress," Jericho said.

As the giant ascended to the top of the right-hand staircase, McBain muttered, "You do that, you uppity darky."

McBain's sudden mood shift and the nervous glance his words brought from the cinnamon-skinned woman set Colter on edge. Quent seemed oblivious of anything but the room however. Mustache twitching, eyes wide to every detail, he wandered around, touching things.

"What do you think?" McBain asked, his manner swerving back to cheerfulness.

Quent ran his hands along a velvet drape. "Even better than you said, Mac. But it looks expensive."

"Don't give it a second thought. We're celebrating."

"Celebrating what?" The throaty question came from a woman descending the steps with Jericho in her wake.

"Kate!" McBain rushed to the bottom of the stairs to meet her. "We're celebrating getting here from Virginia. Eleven days' ride and a few unfortunate adventures."

McBain's wink earned a faint smile from Kate. She let him take her hand and peck her cheek though she quickly reclaimed both. Wisps of hair straying from their pins and a button only halfway through its hole at her neck announced that their arrival had caught her unprepared. Under the scrutiny of her grayish eyes, Colter felt he had no secrets.

"The house is sure quiet," McBain said.

Kate swept them with a cool gaze. "My ladies are resting. We entertained until late and have not yet had the chance to clean up." She frowned toward the servant girl. "It's early. Perhaps if you gentlemen returned later."

"Later? We're busy men, Kate. We have a long ride ahead of us," McBain insisted.

"All the more reason for you to spend some time relaxing. Perhaps some whiskey? Or a hot bath?" Colter could have sworn her nose wrinkled when she said that though her tone stayed neutral. "You really should come back later. Between Army officers moving upriver and politicians getting ready to leave town for the winter, my ladies and I have had little relaxation for a week."

"You mean you won't make time for one of your old customers and his friends? Remember New Orleans?"

"I try not to."

"Let's come back," Quent said.

"No, we're here. And we'll get what we came for." McBain pulled out his purse. "Won't we, Kate?"

The woman's dismissive manner shifted only slightly at the sight of the bulging leather bag. "Three men, six dollars. Half an hour each. Liquor is extra."

Colter blanched at the cost which was triple what he had ever paid for a poke.

"Price has gone up," McBain said. "Why, New Orleans —"

"New Orleans was a long time ago, Mr. McBain. But the rules are the same. If you wish to bargain, you are welcome to find another establishment."

McBain looked ready to argue more but gave in and counted coins into Kate's well-kept palm. "Six dollars plus three more for drinks."

With money in hand, Kate smiled fully for the first time. The smile transformed her from businesswoman to hostess and hinted at the beauty of her youth. "Fetch Ruby, Tess and Flower," she said to a short thick slave who had entered from the back of the house.

As the slave's stocky legs carried him to the upper floor, Kate motioned for the men to take seats on a velvet settee. "It will be just a few moments, gentlemen. What can we bring you in the way of refreshment?"

McBain ordered without consulting the other two. "Something good. Not that swill you serve your other customers."

Despite McBain's insulting manner, her voice remained courteous. "Jericho." The black giant disappeared into the back of the house, returning quickly with three pewter goblets full of whiskey.

"No crystal, Kate?" McBain asked.

"Crystal does not travel well, and pewter seems more appropriate for Charleston. Please drink up."

Lifting his cup, Colter felt Kate's eyes studying the birthmark on the left side of his face. The smoothness of the whiskey did not dispel the sense of wariness her stare raised in him.

After they finished their drinks, McBain ran through the introductions. "This is John Colter."

Kate's eyes flicked across his left temple a second time. "John Colter."

"And this is his cousin Quent. It's his first visit to a fancy house," McBain said.

Quent blushed a shade of crimson barely lighter than the upholstery. Kate granted him an understanding smile. "In that case, I have just the woman for you. Ruby."

A woman sauntered toward them. Small in height, she wore a shade of satin that befit her name. Voluptuous flesh strained against the laces that held the top of her gown together. Below a nipped waist, satin skirts rustled with the slow rhythm of her walk.

Quent's gaze took on a feverish cast.

"Ruby prefers fresh ones," Kate said, nodding the woman toward Quent. "Don't you, my dear?"

Ruby stopped close enough to Quent to touch knees. "That I do." The tip of her tongue traced a slow path across her bottom lip, leaving Quent struggling to swallow.

"Is she what you want?" McBain asked Quent.

Ruby held Quent's eyes and dropped her voice to a murmur. "Say yes, Quent."

"Yes," he croaked.

"Then you come along with me," Ruby said, taking his hand, helping him to his feet and leading him up the stairs.

After they were out of sight, McBain asked, "That the same little Ruby?"

"I doubt that the Ruby you are referring to would be in the same room with you, Mr. McBain." Kate's pointed look at the man made Colter wonder what had gone on between them before.

"Her loss," McBain said. "Just hope you have someone who can keep up with me. Someone fresh, maybe?"

"Fresh costs considerably more than two dollars, Mr. McBain."

"Not fresh like Quent. Young. Eager. New, but not too new. Like that one gal last time in New Orleans."

A frown painted Kate's face, dispelling all traces of humor. Colter was growing less sure by the moment that he wanted to stay when two more women appeared on the stairs. "Gentlemen, Tess and Flower," announced Kate.

The shorter of the women wore a plain shirtwaist in a dusty green that robbed her pale skin of any hint of health and added to the bored expression on her narrow face. The color, though, was the perfect backdrop for the rich auburn hair that tumbled below her waist in thick waves. With hair like that, few men would care what the rest of her looked like.

The taller woman had better skin and a better sense of what looked best on her. Her creamy lace shift hinted at a ripe willing body that momentarily took Colter's mind off his doubts.

The two women approached the settee with identical walks of practiced languor and matching professional smiles. Tess, the taller one, curtsied in a way that gave them a clear view of her assets. McBain shocked Colter by grabbing one of her breasts as she was rising from the curtsy.

The woman squealed and McBain snorted a laugh.

"Mr. McBain!" warned Kate. "I will not tolerate that kind of behavior. You'll treat my ladies with respect. Or —"

"Or what?" McBain's laughter died as quickly as it began. "If this is the best you can do, Kate, no wonder you moved out of New Orleans."

"Perhaps you prefer a refund, Mr. McBain."

He backed down from the challenge with a dry chuckle. "We've been talking about this visit all the way from Virginia. I just want to be sure we see the best you have before we choose. Isn't that right, Colter?"

Before Colter could answer, the door at the back of the reception area flew open, and in skipped a girl. When she spotted them, she stopped short and turned at once to leave. McBain stood up, roughly brushing off the hand Tess was using to massage his neck. "Wait."

The girl froze.

"Come here," McBain ordered.

Eyes downcast, she did as he commanded.

"What's your name, my sweet?" The leer in McBain's tone matched that in his gaze.

"Lotty, sir."

"Lotty." The name rolled off McBain's tongue like something obscene as he ran his hand along the girl's thin arm. Colter guessed from the undefined roundness of Lotty's face that she was perhaps nine or ten years old.

"I choose Lotty, Kate," McBain said without taking his eyes off the girl.

"No, Mr. McBain. Not her." Kate reached for the girl, but McBain whisked Lotty onto his lap, encircling her with his burly arms. "How much?" he demanded in a low voice.

"No, Mr. McBain. Not after New Orleans."

"How much, damn it!"

Jericho moved as if to intervene, but Kate waved him back. "She is not for sale."

McBain's mouth curled into a cruel smile. "Kate, my dear, you, more than anyone, know that's a lie. For a price, any woman is for sale. How much?"

Colter had to speak. "Let her go, McBain. She's just a child."

"Mr. McBain loves children. Or didn't he bother to mention that to you, Mr. Colter?" Kate said.

The idea sickened Colter to muteness.

Lotty sat rigidly on McBain's lap, enduring his hands smoothing her brown hair. The raw hunger on his face made Colter's stomach knot with revulsion. Worse than that look, however, was Kate's reply. "Ten dollars."

McBain tossed his money pouch to Colter. "Pay her."

Colter made no move to catch it. "I ain't doin' nothin' of the sort."

McBain angrily scooped up the pouch, poured out some coins and tossed them on the table next to their empty goblets.

"Remember New Orleans, Mr. McBain. We certainly do." Kate nodded toward Jericho. "If such a thing happens again, I promise that you won't get off as easily this time."

McBain seemed not to hear. He stood up, cradling the girl in his arms. "I got my fun. Now you pick yours, Colter."

McBain's actions had doused any fire that might have been burning within Colter. "Another whiskey," he said.

McBain shrugged. "Have it your way."

"My way's a sight better'n yours, McBain."

Another shrug. "You're entitled to your opinion, Coal-Tar. Me to mine. Now if you'll excuse me." With that, McBain crossed the floor and started up the stairs, carrying Lotty.

Once the pair reached the landing, Kate motioned Jericho to follow. The giant moved with the stealth and deadly intent of a panther stalking prey. "Are you sure you don't want a woman, Mr. Colter?" Kate asked.

"Lotty ain't no woman, ma'am."

She gave a short laugh. "Lotty's no virgin either. I collected that thirty dollars a month ago. This is a business, Mr. Colter. Fantasies. Dreams. That is what I sell." She moved closer to him. Her voice fell to a hush. "What do you dream about, Mr. Colter?"

The scent of her rosewater which he had found so appealing before, all but gagged him now. "Got such a bad taste in my mouth, I cain't rightly remember."

Her mouth hardened. "Then, by all means, we must bring you something to soothe that." At her nod, Tess and Flower wandered out and Kate vanished through the rear door.

Colter had forgotten the cinnamon-skinned woman until her whisper startled him. "Gots a bad taste in my mouth, too." She shifted her gaze to the upper landing. "She be a chile no older than my Beatrice. That man, he be evil."

Though she spoke in anger, her accent was musical. Her plain dress could not disguise her proud posture. Shiny eyes danced among the chiseled planes of her face. The few lines that graced her skin gave no hint at her age. Her hair was thick and nappy as a lamb's winter coat, black at the scalp and red on the ends. "You be a good man. I tell you a thing to save your life."

The hair on Colter's neck rose. Was she one of those Creole women who could steal a man's soul with a charm?

She made sure Jericho was not looking before she stole closer to where Colter sat. She moved so gracefully that the contents of the loaded tray did not make a sound to draw the giant's attention. She knelt and pretended to clean off the low tripod table where the three just-emptied whiskey cups rested. "A crooked man, he looks for you. He searches at all the bawdy houses," she murmured, keeping her head bowed and tilting her shoulders so that there was no doubt in Colter's mind who she was trying to ape. Josiah Hartley.

"When?" he asked.

"Here, last night." She cast him a side-long look. "This crooked man, he offers much money to find the one with the shadow of a flying bird on his face."

Colter's hand went automatically to his birthmark. "How much money?"

A squeak of the wood flooring on the upper landing caused her to flinch and she nearly upset the little table.

"Jericho's not lookin'," Colter reassured her. "How much?"

"Enough to buy freedom for me and my two childs."

Foreboding roughened his voice. "How much?"

"A hundred dollars."

He could barely contain the fury that leaped up like a scorching flame. "Farley Stuart, you son of a snake!"

She put a finger to her lips, warning him to keep his voice down. Her eyes darted to the door Kate had gone through. Her words lost their music. "She sees you wear this mark. She will bring the crooked man here after you. She worship money like a god."

After what he had witnessed between Kate and McBain over Lotty, Colter had no doubt that, the instant she left the room, Kate had sent one of her slaves in search of Hartley.

"You a good man. You go now. Leave quick," the slave woman urged.

McBain's purse lay on the settee where he had tossed it after paying Kate. Colter picked it up and pressed it into the slave woman's hands. "You go, too," he said. "You and your children."

With eyes made brighter by welling tears, she reached out a tentative finger to brush his birthmark. "This be no bird. This be the shadow of the angel standing in the light of God's smile."

Her words surprised him. They were the same words his mother used to describe his mark. He had no time to reflect on the coincidence because a child's scream from the second floor rent the silence.

Instantly, Jericho bolted from the landing into the upper hallway. Kate burst through the rear door, followed by four armed men who raced up the stairs in her wake. A second, louder scream. Then the sounds of a door banging open, followed by a scuffle and McBain's angry "Take your hands off me!"

At that moment, Quent appeared on the landing. He seemed dazed and unaware of the commotion in the opposite wing. He had reached the bottom step when Lotty emerged onto the landing and stumbled barefoot and sobbing down the stairs. Her frock hung in tatters as if someone had shredded it from her shoulders. One side of her face showed signs of swelling under a red welt. Six steps from the bottom, she missed the riser.

Colter lunged forward in time to break her fall. She wrapped her arms around his neck and whimpered incoherently. There was fresh blood on her thin legs and arms.

The shouting upstairs increased in volume with the number of voices — Kate, McBain, Jericho, and at least three others Colter did not recognize.

"She was trying to cheat me," said McBain.

"I warned you, McBain!" Kate shrieked.

"Like New Orleans," boomed Jericho.

McBain. "I paid. I had the right."

Kate. "You'll pay now, and pay dearly!"

McBain. "Bitches always cheat. Her and you, both cheating bitches."

Kate. "Jericho, grab him."

The slave woman took Lotty gently from Colter's arms. "Go, good man. Run. Now."

Colter grabbed the bewildered Quent's arm and jerked him out the door to the horses. "We got to wait for Mac," Quent protested as Colter pushed him into the saddle.

"He gets to fend for himself from now on. We're leavin'." He swatted Quent's horse before his cousin had a chance to change his mind.

9. *A Gathering of Misfits*

On the afternoon of the third day after Shannon had joined up with Wilma and Hedges, the wagons pulled into Portsmouth. While Hedges parked his rig and went off to find where to deliver their freight, Shannon stared at the Ohio River. His stomach knotted at the thought of crossing all that deep flowing water. Yet, cross it he must in order to get to Kentucky. The question was how. There was not a boat in sight, not another person stirring.

An arm encircling his waist brought him out of his thoughts. He found himself the object of Wilma's leering gaze. "Why not stay with me, Georgie? You and me, we could have us one good time."

Her hot breath against his ear sent a shiver all the way to his toes. "Oh, Georgie likes that. Here, take your money." She pressed five dollars into his palm, then let her hand fall into his lap and begin exploring places he did not want her to be. "You don't want to go to Kentucky, do you? Change your mind and stay here with me," she whispered. "We'll get rid of Hedges and travel together. Just you and me." She blew directly into his ear, raising the hair on his neck.

First Sarah. Now Wilma. Women were fast becoming the bane of his existence. He pushed out of her hold with enough force that she tumbled backward into the cargo box. He yanked his uniform bundle from under the seat, leaped from the wagon and took off running.

"Hed-ges!" Wilma screamed. "Help!"

Shannon heard rather than saw Hedges run to Wilma's aid. "Get him!" she yelled. "Bring him back here."

The idea of having to go back to her lengthened Shannon's stride. Then, the riverfront ran out. He came to a halt and frantically looked around for a way out. To his right rose a mass of boulders too smooth and high to scale. To the left, a deep eddy. He could not swim and the thought of going into that pool petrified him.

A glance over his shoulder showed Hedges closing fast. As Shannon turned back to the river, something caught his eye. A john boat rested on a narrow lip of the sand in the shadow of a waist-high rock at the edge of the eddy, partially hidden from view.

Fighting down panic, he leaped across the finger of eddy onto the rock, shinnied over it, and dropped into the boat. Pushing off, he grabbed up the lone oar and maneuvered the craft into the current, narrowing his eyes to shut out as much of the river as possible. Soon as the nose turned toward the opposite shore, he set to paddling furiously, counting strokes aloud in hopes that the sound of his voice would keep his fear at bay long enough to get out of Hedges' reach.

Shouts sounded behind him. He craned back to see Hedges drawing aim on the boat with his musket and Wilma loading another musket while yelling "Thief! Blackguard!"

The musket discharged, sending a lead ball zinging past Shannon's shoulder into the water to starboard. He reacted to the closeness of the shot by jamming the paddle into the water. Mossy-smelling water splashed into his face and set him choking. He faltered but somehow kept paddling. His bowels churned, his lungs burned, his eyes watered but he kept at it, stroking and pulling, stroking and pulling.

More shouting. Another blast of musket fire. Another splash, this time mere inches from the boat's nose.

Gasping for breath, he redoubled his efforts, plunging the paddle into the river again and again. He was too intent on escaping to pay attention to the wind-whipped waves that were washing over the side.

He was well out on the river before his mind registered how heavy the boat had grown. That was when he noticed the inches of riverwater sloshing around his ankles. The sight of it froze his hands, stopped his rowing.

Another boom from the shore. *Thwack*! The ball burrowed through a plank below the waterline on the boat's left side, opening a thumb-sized hole. Instantly, riverwater began to spurt through.

"Oh, God!" Shannon's cry flung across the broad river as he jammed his boot over the gushing hole.

Horrified, he twisted round to see Wilma hand Hedges a reloaded musket and Hedges take fresh aim. "Shoot him, Hedges! Shoot the son of a bitch!"

Wilma's voice sliced through Shannon's hesitation and got him to paddling once again. By now, his arms, shoulders and back were aching, but he could not stop, could not give up. He had dreams to fulfill. No lecherous wagon driver was going to rob him of those.

Because he dared not look at the river while he rowed, he kept his head down and his eyes shut and concentrated on paddling and pulling, paddling and pulling until his muscles were screaming for relief.

Slacking off for a stroke, he opened his eyes and took stock. On the Ohio shore, Wilma and Hedges were standing nose to nose, arguing, their muskets discarded on the sand. He was safe from them for the moment, but the Kentucky shore still seemed an impossible distance away. "I can do it," he told himself. "I have to. Have to."

The foot he had pressed against the bullet hole had grown numb. He tried shifting feeling back into it. When he did, however, water geysered through with a force too great to re-stopper. By now the level of the water in the boat's bottom was well over his ankles. Soon the level would reach the top of the gunwales. Then . . .

Without the impetus of Hedges' bullets to keep him moving, Shannon became acutely aware of his precarious position — in the middle of the Ohio, in a sinking boat, unable to swim, terrified of drowning. He clutched the sides of the boat, paralyzed by the creeping water level, unable to put together a coherent thought. Then his eyes fell on the roll of his militia uniform.

The sight of it gave him a boost of courage. Militia lieutenants did not quit. *He* would not quit. *Eyes forward*, he thought to himself. He tore his gaze away from the river and looked toward the Kentucky shore. *You can make it. Now paddle.*

His hands resisted releasing their hold on the boat. "Let go or we die!" he commanded in a raspy voice.

It took some moments, but eventually his hands released the side of the boat and picked up the paddle. *Don't panic, keep rowing*, he thought rather than said, saving his breath for the task at hand.

Slowly, his arms plunged the paddle into the river and swept the stroke while he fought against thinking about how heavy the boat was or how weary his muscles.

Then his elbow grazed water, and he froze. He did not need to look down to understand that the boat was on the verge of sinking. His worst nightmare was about to come true. He was going to drown. Despite his best efforts, he had failed.

He picked up the soggy militia uniform. Hugging it to his chest, he rose unsteadily to his feet and stood at attention, ready to meet his maker.

Quent poked the small fire. "We should've stayed to help Mac."

Colter looked up from the square of rawhide he had been shaping. "That's ten."

"Ten?"

"Ten times you've said that since we stopped."

"Well, we should have."

"We didn't, Quent, and if'n we'd stayed, there's no tellin' what mighta happened to us."

Quent stared sullenly at the fire. He had not witnessed McBain's transaction with Kate over Lotty. He had not seen how young Lotty was or the results of the terrible things McBain had done to her. But Colter did not yet trust himself on the subject of the gambler. What could you say about a man who prefers girls to women, then beats and terrorizes them? He decided to change the subject. "You ain't said much about Ruby."

Quent shrugged. "Not much to tell."

"You mean I heard about nothin' but Kate's for a solid week 'fore we got to Charleston and that's all you got to say?" Colter teased. The younger man would not look at him so he tried another route. "His first woman is somethin' a man never forgets."

Quent stared at the fire. "Not if he doesn't want to remember." Colter kept quiet, waiting for more. Finally Quent went on, "I'll never do that again. Ever."

The vehemence behind his cousin's words surprised Colter though he knew better than to react. Quent bowed his head and stayed quiet for a long time. "She laughed at me." He pinched the bridge of his nose as if to stifle a stab of pain. "When she laid back on that feather bed and told me to crawl between her legs, I didn't want to take my eyes off those silky white thighs of hers, but I did what she said. Laid on top of her, like she told me, though I was afraid I'd crush her. Her skin felt so smooth and she smelled so good."

He paused. "Then she touched me. Down there."

He gave his head a violent shake as if to erase the memory. "I couldn't hold back, and she took to laughin' at me."

Colter let the silence settle between them before he spoke. "Don't know if'n it makes you feel any better, but my first time weren't much good neither. Since then, I come to understand that sellin' herself a poke at a time takes the gentle out of a woman. She starts to worship money. Starts to get hard and mean. I ain't sayin' you got to stay away from sportin' women. Just know what you're gettin' into when you do."

Quent managed a grimace that almost served as a smile. Colter went on. "Next time you won't be so quick. If'n you get on that there expedition, I expect you'll be busier than the only rooster in the barnyard what with all the women you're bound to meet up with. Sure would be a shame for you to pass 'em up on account of one bad experience."

At the mention of the expedition, Quent's shoulders drooped and he fell to poking at the fire again. Colter let him be alone with his thoughts and finished cutting out a piece from the hide square. Using the tip of his carving knife, he poked holes in the corners and strung some rawhide laces through them, then he positioned the creation over his left eye and tied it in place. He looked around the clearing, trying to get used to being one-eyed.

Quent glanced up. "What's that?"

"A patch."

"Why? What ain't you tellin' me, Johnny?" he demanded.

Colter hesitated. He did not want to go into everything that had happened at Kate's. They still had a long ride to Maysville. The less his cousin knew, the better.

"It's that preacher. He didn't go back home, did he?" Quent asked.

The guess forced Colter's hand. "He was in Charleston, at Kate's the night 'fore we got there, offerin' money to anyone'd seen me."

"How much money?"

"A lot."

"How much, dang it! Quit treatin' me like some kid."

"A hundred dollars."

A low whistle issued from Quent.

"Hartley's lookin' for a man with a birthmark so I figured I'd wear a patch over mine till I leave Maysville. Between the War, gougin' contests and drunken brawls, there're lots of men wearin' patches. Won't nobody notice another one."

Quent stared at him for a long time as if he were making up his mind about something important. "If you was alone and you knew Hartley was followin' you, what would you do, Johnny?"

"I ain't alone."

"If you were, would you stand and fight? Would you run? What?"

Colter untied the patch and bunched it up in his hand. "Depends on the time and the place. And the odds."

"Which way are we headed now?"

"Prett' much west to Huntington, then we follow the Ohio to Maysville. Trail's along the river, but we'll ride up-country, keep out of folks' way."

Quent shook his head slowly but determinedly. "No, I'll head on back. You take off."

"It's a long way home to the Draft, Quent. Too far for you to go it alone. I ain't about to let you do that."

"Not alone and probably not home. Not yet. Now that I got a taste of adventure, I want more. I figure to go back to Charleston and find Mac."

"Quent, there's a lot about Mac you ain't found out yet."

"Just because you and him don't see eye to eye —"

"Ain't that."

"Don't tell me I'm wrong or who I can have for my friends. You take care of you. I'll take care of me."

Colter let the heat of Quent's outburst fade before he spoke again. "Back at Kate's, after you went upstairs with Ruby, a young girl come walkin' into where we was sittin'. Pretty little thing, maybe ten years old. About the same size as them little girls always wind the May Pole back at the Draft every May Day. Remember?"

Quent gave a peremptory nod.

"This one's name was Lotty. Mighta been Kate's daughter for all I know."

"Why are you telling me this? What's it got to do with us goin' our separate ways?"

"That was Lotty who come runnin' down the stairs with her dress half torn off."

Quent's face showed no comprehension.

"That there was McBain's doin'. She ain't nothin' but a child, Quent. And she weren't the first little girl McBain's took." He stopped, hoping he would not have to tell Quent any more.

His cousin flung the poking stick into the fire and watched while the flames consumed it. "I shouldna left home."

"No, a man's got to go where he's got to go. Every man owes himself an adventure. Your pa'd be the first one to admit that."

"Not my pa."

"More'n once he said he wished he'd done some livin' first 'fore he settled down."

"He never said such a thing to me. All I ever heard was how no-account I am."

"Now you come this far, seems a mite foolish not to see it through. It ain't all that far to Maysville. You with me?"

Quent did not answer right away. Finally he nodded and said, "I'll take whichever watch you don't want."

Shannon stood rigidly in the bottom of the john boat while a thousand wet tongues of riverwater licked relentlessly up his body. Even if he had tried to scream for help, he couldn't. His jaw was locked in a rictus of terror.

As the water level crept above his chin, he sucked in one last breath and squeezed his eyes shut to block the sight of the blanket of water about to smother him. *Father. Mother. I love you. Forgive me,* he prayed in silence.

As the held breath ran out, his lungs began to burn. Soon his body's need for air overwhelmed his mind's ability to prevent breathing. *Goodbye, my life,* he thought and let himself breathe.

At the sensation of air, instead of water, filling his lungs, his eyes shot open. Air meant that . . . that he was still alive!

Peering down, he saw that a miracle had happened. The level of the water was no longer rising. From the mouth up, he was above the level of the river.

Counting heartbeats, he waited, not ready to accept the miracle as real.

The level of the water remained steady, and he began to believe his life had been spared. When he could get his neck to swivel, he saw that the john boat had come to rest on the riverbottom. That was small comfort, however, since the shore was still many yards of open water away. He could not stay where he was. He had to leave the boat. Had to commit himself to the river. *But I can't swim,* part of him screamed, all but drowning out the other tiny inner voice saying, *I don't have to swim. The river is shallow here. I can make it.*

Somehow the small voice prevailed and he began inching to the side of the boat. He lifted his right foot and stepped onto the river's bottom — and instantly sank into the silt.

There was no time to think, no time to be afraid. His body reacted to save itself. Kicking and clawing, fighting its way to the surface, beating at the water as if at an attacker. His efforts bobbed him to the surface, but then he sank again. His mouth was still open to gulp air as he submerged and river water flooded into it, gagging him.

Again his body responded, kicking off the bottom and shooting him upward. He broke the surface in an explosion of water, gulping air and thrashing to stay free of the river's grasp.

Panic was eating away at his strength, but he refused to give up. He squirmed and kicked, flailed and grasped. He did everything he could, yet it made no difference. The river was stronger and more persistent. It began to pull him down for the third time.

He felt his consciousness slipping away, not knowing that the neck of his leather shirt got caught in a drifting snag of broken-off trees, that the snag carried him to within five yards of the Kentucky shore before grounding it-self in the shallows.

He came to to find himself ensnared in a snag of branches and broken-off trees five yards from the Kentucky shore. Whatever had hit him had saved his life and his uniform which had also been caught on a broken limb on the other side of the snag. All he had to do was extricate himself and he could be on his way.

Pulling free of the snag was not easy. It cost him two bloodied palms and over an hour. Then he hauled himself and his militia uniform to shore and collapsed onto the sand. With solid earth underneath him again, his fear of water veered into shame. *You're acting like a boy instead of a man*, ac-cused the voice of his father that he carried around in his head. *Fear is for cowards. And no son of mine will ever be a coward.*

Sitting up, Shannon took stock of his situation. He had no rifle, no horse, no food. On the other hand, Hedges had not followed him. And he still had his uniform, his knife, and — he tapped at the top of his boot — some money. And a destination: Maysville.

According to Wilma, that settlement was two days by wagon from the landing on the Kentucky side of the Ohio. Counting the days since leaving home, he figured the date to be the tenth. That gave him five days to get to Maysville if Moonbeam O'Toole's information had been correct.

A broad track rutted by wagon wheels and horses' hooves lay a few yards beyond the bank where he had landed. The road to Maysville. It had to be.

He bent his head in a short prayer of thanks then, squaring his shoulders, off he walked with nary a backward glance.

⚓

Between riding all day off the trail to avoid people and standing night watches, Colter was bone-weary by the time they reached the vicinity of Maysville five days out of Charleston. He needed a few days rest here be-fore striking out on his own so he covered his birthmark with the patch he had made and followed Quent's lead into the settlement.

Besides being an Army post, Maysville was the main port of entry for goods and settlers coming into Kentucky Territory. People and wagons thronged the only road despite the early hour. A partially-built fort lay off to the right amidst a cluster of military tents. To the left, warehouses stretched into the distance. A keelboat was moored at the river's edge. The name painted on her bow: "Discovery". A queue of men snaked from the boat to disappear among the tents.

The dust and noise made Blaze skittish, and her mood transferred to Colter. "You go find out what you got to do, Quent. I'll be over yonder in them trees." He pointed to a copse of alders beyond the warehouses.

Quent hustled off, and Colter made for the shelter of the trees. After seeing to the horses, he stretched out against his saddlebags, tipped his hat over his face and dozed.

Quent's call awoke him sometime later. "Johnny, look who I found."

Colter lifted his hat to a sight he had hoped to never see again: McBain walking beside Quent, a proprietary arm slung across the younger man's shoulders. "Why, Coal-Tar, you old son of a she-wolf!" McBain exclaimed.

Colter sat up, wide awake. "You break out of jail?"

McBain waved off the question. "Nobody takes a harlot's word over a gentleman's. I got to tell you: riding a boat sure beats the back of a horse." His mouth tilted into a lazy smile. "Before I left, I heard that that preacher from the Draft was in town. Seems he was doling out money all over Charleston, paying for information about where you headed. He must want you pretty bad." The gambler's mouth crooked into a lazy smile.

"That's not something to smile about, Mac," Quent said indignantly. "We had to watch our backs all the way here on account of that preacher. 'Bout wore us both out."

The gambler held up a placating palm. "I wasn't smiling about that. Was Kate I was remembering. You should have seen the conniption she threw when that preacher refused to pay her. But why should he? You were already gone by the time he got there and she couldn't tell him where you two were off to. She was mad enough to scratch his eyes out. Took the sheriff and his deputy both to hold her back. That preacher, he made tracks, I'll tell you. Rode straight out of town, I heard. Couldn't get out of there fast enough. That woman's got a temper worse than a man's.

"By the way, Coal-Tar, I want you to know I don't blame you a bit for clearing out of there the way you did. I'd have done the same if I were you — only I'm not."

Under his breath, Colter muttered, "Praise the Lord."

McBain gave him an appraising look. "Where you headed next?"

Colter distrusted the motivation behind the question. It was more than possible that McBain and Hartley had made some kind of deal. Mac was the kind who would not let a fat purse get away unemptied. He shrugged vaguely. "West."

"Where?"

"Wherever the notion takes me."

McBain snorted and poked Colter's boot with the toe of his. "You're missing a sure bet if you don't latch onto this outfit, Coal-Tar. All you got to do is answer a few questions and prove you can shoot. Hell, there's nothing to it."

"Mac's made the first cut," Quent volunteered.

"Easy as can be," Mac went on. "The man in charge is an Army Captain name of Meriwether Lewis. He has his sergeant — name's Floyd — screen everyone first. It cost me half a jug to find out what questions he was asking and a minute or two to figure out the kind of answers he'd want to hear. Tomorrow the ones who made the first cut do some target-shooting. Then me and others who pass that get to talk to the captain."

McBain stretched as if the whole process bored him. "We leave for the

Passage day after tomorrow."

"We? Ain't you takin' a whole lot for granted, McBain?" Colter said.

"Oh, I'll make it all right. No problem."

The man's absolute confidence nettled Colter. "What'd this here sergeant ask you about? And what'd you tell him?"

"Oh, no. That information will cost you, Coal-Tar."

"I ain't interested in joinin' up. Figured you could help Quent here so's he won't tell the same lies as you."

The gambler barked a laugh. "Lies, huh? Well, call it whatever you want, but I sure as hell will do what it takes to get on that keelboat down there. Rich and famous. That's what I intend to be, and finding the Passage is the quickest, surest way to do that."

"What'd he ask you, Mac?" Quent prodded.

McBain stifled a yawn. "Oh, things like why do I want to join up and what kind of frontier experience have I had. Am I married or single? Do I have a trade?"

"Frontier experience? What'd you tell 'im?" Colter asked.

"The truth," McBain said, pulling out his tobacco pouch and preparing a smoke.

"Which is?"

"That I'm as good a frontiersman as anyone in line, and better than ninety-nine percent of them."

Colter's turn to snort. "All he had to do was look at those soft hands o' yours to see what a whopper of a lie that is."

McBain shrugged. "Too late for him to do that now. I made the cut. A little shooting tomorrow and in two days I'm headed for the Passage."

"You ain't a-goin' to make it, Mac," Colter said.

"Oh?"

"I been out in these woods most of my life. You won't last a week *if* they take you, which I doubt."

Quent interrupted. "That line to join up's a mile long, Johnny. We got to quit jawin' if we're goin' to make it up to the Sergeant before dark."

"I ain't interested."

"Why not, Coal-Tar? You can tell the sergeant about all that great wilderness experience you're so proud of. Hell, you might even get picked." Though McBain's mouth smiled, a dare glinted in his eyes.

Watching his cousin fall so quickly back under the gambler's sway vexed Colter. He struggled not to sound defensive. "Joinin' the Army don't interest me, Quent. You go on, get in line. Me, I'm restin' up a day or two, then I'm on my way."

Quent persisted. "But I remember you and Zoob all the time talkin' about findin' the Passage."

"That was Zoob's dream. Not mine. His dreams died with him." Colter got up and dusted off his behind. "Time to get away from these here crowds, look this country over. Meet you back here at sundown, Quent?"

"All right, Johnny, but I sure wish you'd try out."

"See you later."

"You run along, Quent. I'll come find you later on," McBain said. He let Quent get out of earshot before turning to Colter. "You don't like me much, I know, but, for what it's worth, the way Hartley's throwing money around, he acts like a man with a lot to lose if he doesn't find you. You know as well as I do that the money comes from Stuart."

Colter gathered up his saddlebags without comment.

"I'd think twice about this expedition, Colter. If that preacher's still on your trail, Stuart's money gives him an advantage, and you need to even up the odds. You can't hide behind that patch for long. If I were in those worn-down boots of yours, I'd find me a group with firepower to join up with. And firepower is exactly what this expedition has."

Joining a group that included McBain was not an option for Colter, Hartley or not. He hefted his saddle off the ground. "Like I said, Army life ain't for me."

"Stubborn to the end, huh? Then you better pray that preacher rode on back to the Draft."

McBain strolled away and Colter resaddled Blaze. "Let's get out where we can think, girl."

She tossed her head in agreement and trotted off as soon as he swung onto her back.

Once he hit the Maysville road, Shannon's luck deserted him. The first misfortune came after several hours of walking. He had stopped at the river's edge to drink when it hit him: he had been walking the wrong way, upstream, when Maysville lay downstream. Retracing his steps cost him most of the afternoon.

Then, at dusk, he accidentally stumbled into a camp of flatboaters. Before he could stammer out apologies and move on, six burly half-drunk men surrounded him.

"Lost yer gun, son?" The question came from a man with no front teeth and a continual wink caused by a tic under his left eye. He appeared to be the group's leader.

"I–I had an accident," Shannon managed to reply. "O–on the river."

"You be hungry then?" the man said, looking him up and down.

Shannon did not want to stay but he also did not want to give these men offense. "Y–yes."

Someone brought him a plate of beans and some kind of roasted meat, then the whole group proceeded to sit in a ring around him, passing jugs among them while watching him eat. Every few minutes one of the group would lean over to his neighbor and mutter something that caused both men to break out in raucous laughter. Laughter that grew more sinister the more the men drank.

Between the menacing laughter and six malevolent pairs of eyes upon him, Shannon could scarcely swallow. His imagination ran wild conjuring up what these ruffians were planning for him while he nursed his food and kept up a smile of fake enjoyment, all the while launching fervent prayers to the sky that the group's liquor supply would outlast the drinkers.

His plate was nearly empty when the flatboaters began to slide into unconsciousness. Their leader was the last to succumb. The instant the man's eyes closed, Shannon chucked the plate aside and bolted for the woods.

He kept moving all night despite the inky darkness, afraid to stop for fear the boaters would come after him. At dawn, he had to make a choice: stay on the river path and hope that he could avoid more flatboaters, or turn upcountry into the tangled undergrowth where walking would be difficult but also where he was not likely to meet anyone. He chose the latter.

The going was tortuous and slow. By mid-afternoon his legs were scratched, bleeding, and on the verge of giving out. Worse, he had made little headway toward Maysville. If he did not pick up the pace, he would miss Captain Lewis. And the only way to do that was to return to the road.

Reluctantly, he headed back. By the time he reached the rutted track, every muscle in his body ached. He was more hungry and tired than he had ever been. Too tired to go on and ready to give up, he slumped onto a fallen log beside the Ohio. In despair that he would never make it in time, he looked out down the river. "Where are you?"

He meant Maysville, but a nearby voice answered, "Here".

Colter studied the face of the young man whose head had snapped around in surprise at the sound of his voice. The man looked to be Quent's age, about seventeen. He also appeared to be alone, unarmed and on foot.

The younger man clambered to his feet. His voice was abnormally high-pitched. "Come out where I can see you."

Leading Blaze, Colter left the shelter of the stand of sycamores. "I talk to myself, too. I'm John Colter. You got a name?"

"Shannon, George Shannon," the stranger answered.

"You lost?"

Shannon blinked nervously and backed up a pace. "I was resting. I'm on my way to Maysville."

"You and everyone else," Colter said. "Where's your group?"

Shannon's eyes shifted left and right.

"Surely you ain't alone out here?"

"My friend is up ahead. We came to enlist in an expedition."

Colter knew it was a lie. He had just come from that way and had seen no one on the road. "Like I said, you and every other man hereabouts. You got a sight of competition."

"You a hunter?" Shannon asked, nodding at the fresh deer carcasses slung across Blaze's hindquarters.

"If'n I get the chance, I usually take it. I ain't much good at sittin' around, and there's a passel of men to feed back there."

"Then you're part of the expedition?" There was hope in the question.

Colter shook his head. "Nope. The Army ain't for me. Looks like you could use a ride."

Shannon drew himself up and looked pointedly at Colter's travel-stained clothing. "No one would mistake you for an Army man. That's for sure."

Colter swung into the saddle. "We best be on our way, Shannon. Your competition's already in line, and they all remembered their rifles and horses."

"I prefer to walk."

"Bull-headed, ain't ya?"

Shannon sniffed contempuously and took off hobbling down the road.

"Where'd you say you was goin'?" asked Colter.

"I just told you," Shannon answered without looking back. "Maysville."

"Then why ain't you headed there?"

Shannon spun around to face him. "Are you blind as well as vulgar, Colter? That's just what I'm doing."

"Nope. Maysville's that a-way." Colter did not try to keep the amusement out of his voice and expression as he crooked his head the opposite direction.

Shannon limped past him without so much as a thank-you or a sideways glance. Colter watched the younger man's progress with bemusement. He had now encountered three misfits looking to join the outfit Captain Lewis was putting together. Quent, Shannon and McBain. Two boys off on a lark and a con man looking to get rich quick. What a bunch. "I hope you realize what you're gettin' in for, Captain Lewis. Ain't one of them three I'd trust to cover my back, or my front."

Blaze whiffled, her way of agreeing with him.

The sun lay low in the west when Colter stopped on the edge of Maysville to adjust the patch and cock his hat down over his brow. He let Blaze pick her way toward the dock while he scanned the vicinity for anyone resembling Josiah Hartley.

A commotion near the keelboat caught his attention. A crowd of men were arguing with a harried soldier in a sergeant's uniform. "No more today," the sergeant said. "Come back in the morning."

"No way," one man shouted"I been waitin' all day for my turn. You cain't stop now!" "'Tain't fair!" came the stormy protests.

The exasperated sergeant managed to duck through the opening between two of the expedition hopefuls and slip past a pair of Regulars who used their rifles to block the crowd from following.

As the sergeant stalked past him, Colter spoke up. "Who's in charge of provisions?"

"You're looking at him. Provisions and just about every other blessed thing the captain needs done." Though his tone was gruff, the sergeant looked more worn out than angry.

"Got a couple of deer to lend to your cause then."

The sergeant glanced suspiciously at the carcasses draped across Blaze's rump. "You aren't one of the hunters we hired."

"Nope. Does that mean you don't want the meat?"

The sergeant's face and uniform showed the strain of his efforts to separate the curds from the whey for the upcoming expedition. He prodded one of the deer and his tired smile took five years off Colter's first estimate of his age. "Two deer? Where on earth? You realize that no one's been able to find fresh meat since we got here?"

"Too many folks hereabouts. Man-smell drives critters away."

"Of course I'll take them. How much do I owe you?"

"They're yours for the askin', if'n you promise not to waste any of 'em."

"You don't have to worry about that. Captain even saves the hides. You sure we can't pay you something? Powder? Rum? Something?"

"Got everythin' I need 'cept for some sleep."

The sergeant stuck out his hand. "Name's Floyd. Can I at least put in a word with Captain Lewis on your behalf?"

"I'm John Colter. Don't need no word. I ain't interested in your expedition. I only come along with my cousin."

"Colter? The one with the skimpy mustache?"

"If'n the one you mean keeps feelin' his lip to make sure the hair's still there, that's Quent."

"If he is anything like you, John Colter, he's what we need."

Colter hefted one of the deer across his shoulders. "Quent's his own man. Judge him on his own skill."

Floyd shouldered the second deer. "You must be the only man within three hundred miles who doesn't want to be on this expedition. Never dreamed there would be so many."

Colter followed the sergeant to a cook tent where they deposited the meat. Floyd gave some instructions to the cooks, then led Colter outside. "We'll be recruiting here two more days, at least. If you change your mind, you let me know."

"Thanks, but that ain't likely."

"Offer's open just the same. Thanks again for the meat." With that, the sergeant trudged back to the keelboat.

At the copse of alders, Colter unsaddled Blaze and hobbled her to graze, then went in search of Quent, keeping alert for signs of Hartley. He found his cousin among a group of boisterous men. He had to tap Quent on the shoulder to get his attention over the din of laughter and loud talk.

"I made the cut, Johnny! Here, help me celebrate." Quent thrust a crock into his hands.

Colter took the offering with little enthusiasm. From the droop of Quent's eyelids, the celebration had been going on awhile.

A groan followed by an outburst of cheering drew Colter's attention to the other side of the rowdy crowd. There McBain and a grizzled fellow with a strip of green cloth tied around his forehead faced each other across a wooden plank that was slung across two barrels at waist height. A dozen or so other noisy men crowded around the pair. While Colter watched, Green Cloth slammed a copper down on the plank with a curse and pushed away through the crowd.

McBain quickly stashed the coin in his pocket and swept an arm over three nut shells sitting cup-side down on the plank. "So who's next?" he said, tossing a pebble into the air, catching it and setting it on the board beside the shells. "Two bits to a dollar to the man who guesses where the stone ends up."

A ruddy-cheeked man shouldered his way forward. "By God, for them odds, you're on. My eye's quicker'n any man's hand."

McBain made a show of placing the pebble under one of the nut halves, then shuffled the shells' positions for a few seconds before lifting his hands theatrically. "Your guess, friend."

Without hesitation, the ruddy-cheeked man pointed to the left-most shell. "There."

"You're sure?" McBain asked in a wheedling tone. "It'll cost you two bits if you're wrong."

"Oh, it's there all right," the man declared.

McBain heaved a sigh. He thumbed over the man's choice. No pebble. "I tried to warn you."

McBain took the man's coin with a tap of his hat brim. "Why, thank you, friend. Now, who's next?"

From among the onlookers who were grumbling ominously about how much McBain had already won, another man stepped forward. Mac manipulated the shells again. "That one," the man said, pointing.

McBain's generous lips curled into a sympathetic smile. He tapped the designated shell. "This one?"

"That's what I said."

With another sigh not quite as deep or dramatic as the previous one, McBain flicked over the shell to reveal the stone. The man received McBain's pay-off with a triumphant whoop. "See. I told you."

Two more men jostled for position at the board, but McBain waved them off, and went around behind a wagon. "Thirsty work. Bring the jug, Quent." He grabbed the crock Quent brought to him and tossed back an enormous swallow before coming up for air. "So Coal-Tar, you got here just in time to see me lose."

"Hard to believe anyone'd fall for that old trick these days," Colter said.

"What trick?" Quent asked.

"Palmin' the pea it's called. Mac keeps the stone in his hand till he figures it's time to let some sucker win. He loses just enough to keep folks interested. You're smooth, McBain. I'll hand you that."

"Why, thank you, Coal-Tar," the gambler said, sweeping a bow.

"What're you sayin', Mac?" Quent said.

"It's all among friends, Quent. A bit of harmless fun."

Colter bit back a retort. Cheating was wrong. Quent knew that, but it was his choice whether to be associated with a man like McBain.

"Did Quent here tell you he made the cut?" McBain asked.

"Shoot-off's tomorrow afternoon," Quent added proudly, slurring his words.

Colter chose not to probe about his cousin's answers to the sergeant's questions. He had been coached by McBain, after all. "Then you oughtta put the cork in that there jug."

McBain passed the whiskey back to Quent. "Leave the lad alone. He's celebrating."

"Durn right." Quent took a pull from the crock and leveled drowsy eyes at Colter.

"You ought to try for a spot, Coal-Tar." McBain's mouth curled in a smile that his eyes did not share. "Instead of acting like Quent's mother."

"Durn right," Quent lisped.

"I ain't interested in no expedition or in motherin' nobody."

"I don't think 'interested' is the right word. 'Afraid' maybe. My guess is you're afraid you won't make the cut. Afraid someone like me can outdo you at your own game," McBain said.

Colter locked stares with the man. "You guess wrong then, Mac. Instead of mindin' my business, you ought to stick to the things you do best. Like gettin' drunk and schemin' how to separate other people from their money."

Someone at the back of the crowd yelled for McBain to return to his board. Mac tossed down another slug, came out from behind the wagon, and smilingly faced his audience.

"You got no call to talk to my friend like that, Johnny," Quent said, sloshing whiskey onto his shirt as he wrapped a protective arm around the crock.

"Mac ain't the kind of friend you need, Quent."

"You're wrong. He's just what I need." The belligerent angle of Quent's jaw announced that further argument was useless.

"Then you and Mac enjoy each other. I'm goin' for a walk now. I'll be leavin' first thing tomorrow."

He was at the edge of the crowd when Quent yelled after him, "Good riddance!"

⚓

Shannon reluctantly put the empty tin plate down on the ground beside him. After three helpings of stew, he was still hungry. However, the last time at the cooking pot, the cook had demanded to know why he was not in proper uniform. Up to that point, no one seemed to notice that his jacket was militia, not regulation Army. He had mumbled something and hurried away, banking that the man would not follow.

When he had first arrived in Maysville, seeing the long line of men stretching from the keelboat had all but crushed his confidence. It had taken a good rest and some hot food before he could think clearly. Then it became clear that, like the exercises in strategy his father used to give him as part of his militia training, this situation called for a plan of attack.

First, he settled on a strategy: forget standing in line to talk to some underling. He needed to get an audience with this Captain Lewis as soon as possible by whatever means. For that, he needed to make himself presentable. First a bath.

He had walked up one of the creeks flowing into the Ohio to a private spot. There he beat the dust out of his militia uniform against some rocks and took a long soak before putting it on.

The next step required that Captain Lewis be as relaxed as possible. Shannon figured he would wait until after the captain had eaten his dinner and had some time to rest from the day's activities. Waiting, however, required patience, and patience had never been his strong suit, especially when he was hungry.

He looked down at the empty plate. So what if the cook questioned him about his uniform? He would make up some story about delivering supplies for the new fort. Drop Father's name if he had to. Why not?

He scooped up the plate, rose to his feet, threw back his shoulders and marched back to the kettle for another helping.

Colter's pique had settled by the time he returned from his walk hours later. He would leave Maysville tomorrow with a clear conscience. He had fulfilled his promise to Aunt Dev. From now on, Quent's life and decisions were his own business.

During Colter's absence, the crowd of drinkers and gamblers had grown in size. As he worked his way through them, a powerfully built man with a jagged scar from his mouth to his right ear swaggered up to McBain's plank. McBain shuffled the shells and stepped back. "Make your choice, friend."

"'Fore I choose, you hold up both them hands, palms out," the scarred man said.

McBain's joking tone faded a bit along with his smile. "My good man, you already won five dollars."

Sensing impending trouble, Colter scanned the area for Quent but could not find him.

"Then you ain't goin' to mind, right?" Scar Face said.

"I mind any man implies I'm a cheat."

Scar Face turned to the men behind him. "Any of you hear me call this man a cheat?"

A dozen voices chorused "No."

Quent lurched up from the ground beside one of the barrels supporting McBain's counter. He still clutched the whiskey crock, but he was rapidly losing the battle to stay conscious. "Well, I heard you," he declared drunkenly.

Scar Face cast Quent a warning glance. "Seems liquor's affected your hearing, boy."

Colter pushed forward to take charge of Quent, and Scar Face turned again to the crowd. "I didn't call you a cheat, McBain, but that don't mean you ain't one."

"How do you know my name?" McBain demanded warily.

"Why, we go back a long way. I'm Joe Chase."

McBain looked confused.

"Could be you remember my sister better. Celie Chase."

A momentary shadow darkened McBain's face before he could recompose it into a bland gambler's mask.

"Ah, you do remember her," Chase said. "Then, of course, you remember how you got her with child. Ain't you goin' to ask me about her, McBain?"

A pulsing vein on the firelit side of McBain's neck was the only sign of a reaction.

"She's dead, from the beating you gave her before you high-tailed it out of town. We found her lyin' in a pool of her own blood, her face all bashed in."

A hush fell over the crowd. Chase stepped closer toward McBain. "I been lookin' for you ever since."

Suddenly there was a knife in McBain's hand. "No, Mac!" Quent yelled, staggering between the two adversaries. The gambler's knife thrust caught Quent in the shoulder. Quent shrieked and crumpled to the ground. Chase lunged for McBain, and the crowd erupted into a melee of fists and feet.

Colter dodged fists and jabs to get to his cousin. Quent lay in the dirt, staring stupidly at the knife handle protruding from his shoulder. Rather than stop to pull it out, Colter grabbed his cousin by the feet and dragged him out of the battling mob.

"Attention!" A voice boomed over the fray, throwing the fighters into confusion. A squad of blue-coated soldiers pulled McBain and Chase apart under the watchful eyes of a man in the immaculate uniform of an Army captain. His stern gaze caused the brawlers to quickly forget their reasons for fighting. They edged back from the captain who demanded, "Sergeant Floyd, do you recognize any of these men?"

Floyd pointed to McBain. "That one is scheduled for the shoot-off tomorrow."

"Correction," said the captain in a tone that brooked no disagreement. "He *was* scheduled. Instead, he will spend the next two days in detention. Same for his brawling partner. See to it, Sergeant."

Either McBain failed to hear the finality in the captain's tone or he did not care about the consequences of arguing with such a man. He struggled free of the grasp of one of the soldiers restraining him. "No, that's not right, Captain Lewis. Chase here started it. He's the one to punish. Not me. He isn't even here to try out for the expedition."

Captain Lewis's icy tone turned contemptuous. "Take them away, Sergeant."

McBain had just enough time to get out one last "But" before Sergeant Floyd and a Regular hauled him off, followed by two more Regulars bracketing Joe Chase. Then Captain Lewis fixed the remaining men with a scowl. "I order every one of you to leave Maysville by noon tomorrow. I will lock up for a week anyone who defies my order and the next man who makes a disturbance gets escorted east."

No one moved.

"Dismissed."

Colter held his ground in the dispersing crowd.

"You heard me. Leave," the captain said to him.

"No, sir," Colter shot back.

"What did you say?" The captain's voice was tight with control.

"Quent here tried to stop them two, and he took a knife in the shoulder for his trouble. You ain't sendin' him away with the rest of that lot. Not if I got anythin' to do with it."

Immediately, Lewis's attention went to Quent. He examined the wound. "He was lucky. No serious damage, but I'll need to remove the knife and dress the puncture. Help me get him to my quarters."

"What about makin' him leave?" Colter demanded.

"Neither of you have to leave. Only, he will not be joining the Corps. Not with that wound. You say you are his cousin? What is your name?"

"John Colter."

Quent's voice wobbled from shock. "But I got to go, Captain. I made the first cut."

"There, there, Quent, is it? Be thankful that knife landed where it did. You will be sore for awhile, but you will be able to use that arm soon enough. Unfortunately, not soon enough for the expedition."

"No, Johnny, no!" Quent wailed through the shivers of pain wracking his body.

Together Colter and the captain carried Quent to the captain's cabin on the keelboat. They stretched him out on one of the two berths that hung from opposite walls. Quent clutched weakly at Colter's hand, murmuring "But I made the cut" over and over.

Lewis pulled a heavy wooden box filled with vials and medical implements to the berth. "We have to remove the knife, Quent. Do you understand?"

Quent nodded weakly.

"It will hurt, so I want you to bite down on this." Lewis slipped a piece of thick rawhide between Quent's teeth. "Bite when you are ready."

Colter firmed his grip on his cousin's hand. As soon as Quent bit down, the captain yanked the knife out of his shoulder in one strong, sure motion and flung it aside. Quent had passed out before the knife hit the decking.

"Bring that water over here, Colter."

The water pitcher was adorned with pink cabbage roses. Its delicacy seemed incongruous next to the solid, unadorned furnishings of the excessively neat cabin. The captain carefully peeled Quent's grimy shirt away from the wound. "Good. The blood is flowing well. Pour all the water on the wound, Colter. Never mind about the blanket."

Colter tipped the pitcher, trickling its contents onto the oozing seam of blood.

"Good. Now for this." Lewis uncorked a bottle of powder from the wooden chest and tapped some into the wound. "Peruvian bark and gun powder."

"Waste of good powder," Colter said. "A poultice of river mud and moss's better. Mud 'n moss don't leave no scar."

"Where did you learn that?"

"From my partner. We trapped together."

With lips pursed as if he were weighing Colter's advice, Lewis pressed a folded piece of muslin against Quent's wound. "It is probably a blessing your cousin had so much to drink. He will sleep through the worst of the pain."

"If he hadn't been drinkin', he wouldn't be lyin' here," Colter grumbled under his breath.

The captain sat back on his heels. "A trapper, huh? How did you lose your eye?"

The unexpected change in the direction of the conversation caught Colter off-balance. "It ain't lost."

"Oh?" The captain's look challenged him to explain, but at that moment knuckles rapped on the partially-open door. "Captain, sir?"

"Sergeant, come in. We were just finishing our business."

Sergeant Floyd stepped across the threshold and did an immediate doubletake at the sight of Colter. "Captain, this is the man who brought in the deer."

Lewis's eyebrows arched with approval while his eyes focused on the left side of Colter's face. "May I?" Without waiting for permission, he lifted off the patch and studied the birthmark. "You say you had a partner?"

"Name was Zoob. He died awhile back."

"What are you doing for a partner now, Colter?"

"Still lookin'."

"Is this patch part of your search?" he asked, placing it in Colter's hand.

Colter chose not to answer. The captain got to his feet, snapped the medicine box closed, put the box back in its place and walked around the carefully-ordered writing table to the open rear window of the cabin to gaze out at the Ohio. "What do you know about this expedition, Colter?"

"I know you're out to find the Passage."

"Do you think the Passage exists?"

"Maybe. Maybe not."

"Outside earlier, when you defended your cousin, you did not hedge. Why do so now?"

"Maybe there's a Passage. Only findin' it ain't goin' to be as easy as stories tell."

"Go on."

"Lots of times a man'll think he wants a thing, and, when he gets it, it turns out to be exactly what he don't need."

Lewis moved to the berth opposite Colter. He held himself so steadfastly erect that Colter sat up a bit straighter, too. "Tell me more, Colter. What else do you know about the Passage?"

"Don't know much for sure. Only what I hear and what I suspicion."

"That is why I am asking you." Lewis waved at two large wooden crates stacked next to the writing table. "Those boxes contain every scrap of information the President and the most brilliant minds in America could gather about the Passage. Yet most of it is speculation. Dreams and myths based on no experience."

Lewis placed his hands on his thighs, palms down. The fingers of his left hand fanned out in an exact mirror of his right, the habit of a meticulous man. "There is danger in any exploration of the unknown. My job is to reduce the risk. I can do that only by talking to men like you. Men who understand the country, who have lived in it and on it. Please, I want to hear what you have to say."

The fervor flaring in Lewis's eyes encouraged Colter to respond with candor. "Way I figure, there's a lot more land west of the Mississippi than most folks think. There're more and bigger rivers, and more and higher mountains than anyone's ever dreamed. Because of them mountains, the courses of the rivers got to run all over the place. Not straight and orderly like folks'd expect. That means the Passage — if there be such a thing — ain't goin' to turn out to be what folks expect, neither."

Lewis stared at him for so long that Colter started to fidget with the leather patch. "You have just described the goals of this undertaking, Colter. As we speak, Congress is about to ratify a treaty transferring the entire territory of Louisiana to the United States from France. The purpose of this expedition is to explore that Territory: to map it, to study its flora and fauna, to learn about the peoples who inhabit it."

"Indians? You're goin' to study Indians?" Colter could not keep the scorn out of his voice.

"If you mean as opposed to shooting them on sight, yes, that is precisely what I mean. We go to explore a land mass that will more than double the size of our country, Colter. We shall follow the course of the Missouri River to her headwaters in the Shining Mountains. If luck is with us, we will cross those mountains and find the Columbia River on the other side to take us the rest of the way to the Western Sea. I intend to find the Passage, and, in so doing, lay claim to all that land for our country. Think what that would mean. Direct trade with the Orient and land for all the people on earth who see this country as their hope and their future."

When Lewis began to sound like a politician, Colter lost interest. He tied the patch back on. The captain's eyes never left him.

"I want you to consider joining us, Colter."

Colter rose from the berth, careful not to jostle Quent. "Not interested."

"May I ask why?"

"Got my reasons."

"Reasons that I suspect are connected to that patch you do not need." Lewis rose, too. "I have no right to pry."

"That's right. You don't."

"I need you, Colter."

"No, you don't, Captain. You got hundreds of men who want to be on your expedition. I ain't one of them."

When the captain touched his arm, he stopped moving toward the door. He pegged Lewis as someone who did not make human contact easily. "I need you, your practical experience, your knowledge of the land and how to survive off it, your straight-forwardness and definitely your forthrightness."

"Captain, may I add something else?" Floyd's interruption reminded Colter that another person was in the cabin.

"Please, Sergeant."

"We especially need a man who can find game when no one else can."

The tight line of Lewis's mouth relaxed slightly for the first time. "As you see, Sergeant Floyd takes his duties as my second-in-command most seriously." His mouth returned to a serious line. "The sergeant and I have heard enough — how can I say this delicately?"

"Fiction, sir?" Floyd offered.

"Exactly. We have heard little but fiction the last two days. It seems we have attracted every opportunist and adventurer on the planet. This expedition will succeed only on the strength of the character and will of its men." He heaved a sigh. "Besides the glory, each crewman will receive a generous grant of land, so that each will own a tangible piece of the territory he helped to explore. And rightfully so, for this is deadly serious business. There is no room on this expedition for dreamers and adventurers who treat this as a Sunday social or a quick way to fame and fortune."

Lewis rubbed a spot of Quent's dried blood off one of his knuckles. "To be frank, that little fracas this evening was a God-send. It will save hours tomorrow when we have to weed out the men who lied their way through the sergeant's interview and who might make it through the target shooting."

Colter was not aware he was smiling until Lewis said, "I see you understand what I mean."

"'Fraid that's Quent you're describin'. He can shoot and he's got spirit, just not much else."

"Where is his family?"

"Back in Virginia. Near Staunton."

"The President and I both hail from Virginia. Where near Staunton?"

"Stuart's Draft."

"Stuart? As in Farley Stuart?"

The way Lewis said the name, the captain, and possibly President Jefferson, knew more about Stuart and thought less of him than Stuart would like. Colter nodded.

Lewis glanced down at Quent. "No doubt you are concerned about getting your cousin home now. What if I offer to arrange transportation home for him on the next troop transport to Richmond, providing you join us?"

Colter looked at his sleeping cousin. There was no telling how long Quent would have to mend before he could head home. And winter was not that far off. Colter could not stay in Maysville. Not with Hartley so close and so determined to find him. But he also had Quent's welfare to think of.

There was another rap on the cabin door. A fresh-faced young man in a private's uniform snapped a crisp salute. "Captain, sir, someone to see you."

Lewis passed a hand wearily across his eyes. "Who is it, Private?"

"Says his name is Shannon."

"Is he Army?"

"He's in uniform, sir."

Colter recognized the name but could not immediately place it.

"Why not let it wait till morning, Captain?" Floyd asked. "I'll go tell him."

"Thank you, Sergeant."

After Floyd left, Lewis turned back to Colter. "We will stay moored here until morning after next. Will you please think over my offer for another day?"

"I'll think about it."

"May I ask that you tell me your answer in person, whether yes or no?"

Though Colter had no intention of wasting energy weighing the expedition among his options, he saw no reason to let the captain know that. He nodded, then excused himself.

Once outside, he paused to breathe out the tension from his conversation with Lewis. As he was doing so, Sergeant Floyd challenged a figure on the gangplank. "That's far enough. State your business."

"I'm here to see Captain Lewis," the newcomer responded. "Urgent business." The voice was familiar, but Colter could not put a face to it.

"He's resting. Come back in the morning," Floyd countered.

"You will address me as Lieutenant, Sergeant." The condescension in the newcomer's voice did not disguise his youth.

"A *militia* lieutenant? Ha! I'll address you as *gone*. Now!"

The door to the captain's quarters opened. Lewis stepped out, carrying a lantern. Colter moved over to give him room. "Something amiss, Sergeant?"

The lantern's light revealed the newcomer as George Shannon, the haughty young man Colter had met earlier in the woods; the one who had huffed off in the wrong direction.

Shannon beat the sergeant to a response. "Captain Lewis, sir. I bring news for you from Fergus O'Toole."

Lewis brightened at the mention of the man's name. "O'Toole, is it? Well, come inside where we can talk."

Shannon's eyes widened in recognition as he shouldered past Colter into the captain's cabin. Once the door was closed, Floyd motioned for Colter to follow him onto the riverbank.

"You *are* going to join us, right, Colter?" the sergeant asked.

"Told the captain I'd think on it," he replied noncommittally.

"Do more than think, man. You just saw what I'm up against." He scowled toward the keelboat. "Why, that one doesn't even shave yet and here he is trying to wangle his way onto this crew by dropping names. Bet his father's a politician. Did you see him? Strutting around like he's in charge. It's his kind that will sink this Expedition. And what we go to do is too important to this country's future for us to fail."

He kicked a stone in frustration, sending it splashing into the river. "This isn't some garden party. This Expedition is the most important thing that has happened to this country since Independence. Heading into uncharted territory is dangerous business. There's no telling what we will face. No telling if any of us will come back. Our success rests on the shoulders of the men we recruit. Men like you, Colter. Men with solid experience and native intelligence – and years of seasoning. That's who we need. That's who *I* need. Not some mama's boy out for a lark."

He shook his head. "So while you're thinking on it, I'll be praying that you make the right choice."

He left Colter looking out over the river. Quent's injury presented a quandary: Did he wait for Quent to get back on his feet, then take him back to the Drift? Or did he leave his cousin to his own devices and head west as planned? Or was there another option he had not thought of? What was he supposed to do now?

🪶

"Captain." Shannon snapped a salute, grateful for all the hours his father had made him practice. Though he held his gaze rigidly forward, he saw enough to know that the cabin and the captain were Army exact, as he must be if he were to succeed in his quest.

Lewis returned the salute. "At ease, Mister . . .?"

"Shannon, sir. George Shannon. Lieutenant, First Ohio Militia." Despite the captain's command to stand at ease, he had no intention of relaxing his posture. He had one chance to make an impression and he was determined to make the best of that chance.

"So what news does Moonbean send?"

"It's not exactly news, Captain. It is me. Mr. O'Toole recommends me to you as a recruit for your company." The phrase came out exactly the way he practiced it.

"He does, does he?" Lewis leaned back on the bench. "Your father's war record and that fine militia organization of his are well known in Washington. I had the opportunity to make his acquaintance when he was in the capital lobbying for Ohio's statehood. You bear a remarkable resemblance to him, Mr. Shannon."

Shannon had to swallow before he could speak. "So I am told, sir."

The captain rose and paced to a window that stood open to the river. When his back was turned, Shannon hazarded a glance around the cabin which was orderly, despite being crammed with barrels and boxes. He was surprised to see a man about his own age asleep on one of the berths. There was a fresh bandage on the man's shoulder. A bloodied knife lay in the corner apparently forgotten, the only hint of disorder in the cramped quarters. He had heard a commotion earlier but was too involved in his own strategizing to investigate. No doubt it had been another drunken brawl, this man had been knifed, and the captain had been left to repair the damange.

A rap sounded at the door. The sergeant who had tried to turn him away earlier let himself into the cabin. What Shannon had taken to be a shadow beneath the writing table turned out to be a huge dog that raised its head and cast a suspicious eye toward the sergeant before sighing and resuming its nap.

"How old are you, Shannon?" Lewis asked, breaking the silence.

"Eighteen, sir." His answer sounded incomplete so he added, "But I have drilled with the militia for eight years and was recently promoted to lieutenant, based upon my proficiency in military strategy and marksmanship."

Sergeant Floyd coughed, a small skeptical sound in the quiet cabin, but the captain did not seem to notice. "And why would you consider our enterprise instead of, say, studying law to prepare to follow in your father's footsteps?"

Shannon would not let himself scratch the itch that suddenly cropped up where his uniform collar rubbed across his sunburned neck. Memories of what he had gone through to get this far added force to his voice. "I intend to become a professional Army officer."

"I see," Lewis mused. "An unpopular choice, if what I have heard about your father is true."

Shannon allowed himself a small nod, hoping the captain would probe no further.

Lewis picked up a goose quill from the writing table and twirled it absentmindedly. The itch at Shannon's neck grew more persistent, threatening his concentration and discipline.

The captain laid the quill precisely parallel to an open journal, then lifted his gaze to Shannon. "If Fergus O'Toole recommended you and if you are the kind of man your father is, I have every reason to believe you will succeed as a member of our venture. Welcome to the Corps of Discovery, Mr. Shannon."

The suddenness of the decision caught Shannon by surprise. His "Oh, thank you, sir," did not cancel out Sergeant Floyd's gasp.

"Do you have something to add, Sergeant?" Lewis asked.

"No, sir," the sergeant answered, though his expression said different.

"Then see to issuing our new recruit here a gun and a uniform and the rest of the supplies." Lewis looked back at Shannon. "You will be sworn in morning after next. Congratulations."

"Thank you, Captain Lewis. You won't be sorry. I promise."

As Shannon followed the sergeant off the keelboat, he struggled to choke back the whoop of triumph that threatened to undermine his decorum.

Once they were out of earshot of the keelboat, Floyd lit into him. "Captain might be impressed by all those names you just dropped in there, but I'm not. Don't think you can fool me like you fooled the captain. I judge a man by what he can do, not who he knows. My job's to weed out the ones who don't measure up. You won't last a week. Do us both a favor. Don't show up for the swearing-in."

In the face of the sergeant's diatribe, Shannon drew himself up to full height. "I have every intention of being there day after tomorrow, Sergeant. So I suggest that you do as the captain asked and get me what I am supposed to have in the way of supplies." Such insolence would have earned him a day of boot-polishing from his father, but his success with Captain Lewis made Shannon cocky. Nothing was going to stop him now, especially this sergeant who was trying to discredit him and his victory. Let Floyd try to throw his weight around all he wanted. He, Shannon, had the captain's ear — and, just as soon as he could, he would see to it that the sergeant got the comeuppance he deserved.

"You'll get your things when I'm ready to give them to you. Not before," Floyd said.

"When, may I ask, is that, Sergeant?"

"When, may I ask, is that, Sergeant?" Floyd aped in a falsetto voice. "Oh, but you do have a high opinion of yourself, don't you, *loo-ten-ant*?"

Shannon refused to be baited. He had dealt with recalcitrant underlings in the militia. This was no different. There would be time enough to work out their differences when they were underway. "When, Sergeant?"

"Take my advice. Head back home to your mother. You don't belong here. *I* don't want you here."

"Your advice is noted. I will be here an hour before the swearing-in to collect my things." He executed an about-face and marched away from the sergeant, feeling more pleased with himself than at any other time in his life.

10. *Making the Cut*

C olter checked on Quent the next morning, then left Blaze to rest some more and went off on foot to explore the sparsely-settled land southwest of Maysville. The solitude and the beauty of the autumn foliage colors helped to collect in his scattered thoughts. Quent's injury, McBain's reappearance, the threat that Josiah Hartley might still be on his trail – those aggravations faded into the background, allowing him to enjoy the day and the exercise.

He was on his way back to Maysville in the late afternoon when he chanced upon two bucks, surprising one drinking from a forest pool. Later, he spooked the other from a thicket of thornbushes. He downed both with single, clean shots and hoisted the carcasses into trees to keep them out of casual reach of predators until he could return with Blaze to retrieve them.

He was tired but content when he arrived back in Maysville with the two deer slung across Blaze's rump around nine that night. Retying the patch over his face, he went in search of Sergeant Floyd to give him the meat.

With the shooting and selection interviews over, the settlement had the feeling of a mountain meadow lying in wait for the onslaught of winter. Most of the unsuccessful expedition hopefuls had left the settlement, but a few men unwilling to accept their rejection still hung about the keelboat's mooring place.

The sergeant was on the quarterdeck jotting entries in a ledger. Seeing Colter, he slammed the notebook shut, swung down to the rowing deck and bounded onto the bank. "More meat? Colter, you're amazing." Floyd slapped him on the shoulder. "You're saving my tail and my belly. I don't care what you say, I have to pay you. Something, anyway."

"It's me who owes you and the captain for tendin' to Quent. How's he doin'?" Colter asked.

"He was in pain most of the day, but the last hour or so, he settled down. Captain went off for a walk to stretch his legs. Lord knows he needs it after a day like this."

"Problems?"

"Wasted most of the day when there's no time to spare. And I only have myself to blame. I did the first cut. Used to think I was a pretty fair judge of men, but this afternoon's shooting showed me how much I still have to learn."

"Pretty bad, huh?"

Floyd grimaced. "Worse. Good thing the spotter was standing at the line and not down with the targets during the shooting or his wife'd be a widow now. Maybe one in ten balls ever hit the target. And only one in ten of those hit the mark. Worst shooting I ever saw, bar none."

"How many men'd you get?"

"Six."

"That's six more'n you had yesterday. Seems to me you did your job."

"Sure wish you'd join us, Colter. If you don't, you'll pass up the chance of a lifetime. We're going places no white man's ever been."

White men and Indians. The two did not mix. Colter had seen evidence of that too often. Floyd did not need to hear about that, however. "I better check on Quent."

His cousin lay huddled under blankets in the captain's cabin which felt stifling despite the night's chill. Colter ruffled Quent's hair.

"Johnny," Quent murmured with a wan smile. "You're not waitin' around here for me to get better, are you? You ain't thinkin' about takin' me back home?"

"That did cross my mind."

Quent struggled up on an elbow. "No way. You're not goin' back where Farley Stuart can get you. Not on my account."

"Don't get all riled up or you'll start bleedin' again."

Quent sank back on the pillow but would not give up his argument. "I know how you are once you make a promise. Your word's your law. My ma had no right to burden you with me."

"Don't blame her for worryin' about you. That's what mas do."

"You can't stay here. Not when Preacher Hartley might show up any-time. You got to leave."

"When you're better."

The younger man's eyes blazed with conviction. "Hellfire, Johnny, stop that! Get out of Maysville. Now. Today. Don't give that preacher a chance to find you. Get yourself off somewhere to hunker down till it's time to go back to the Draft and hand Farley Stuart what he deserves. Promise me you'll do that."

"Nope."

Tears of frustration welled in Quent's eyes. "Why is it that you'll make promises to everyone else but me?"

Colter could not leave his cousin to fend for himself. He kept quiet rather than risk saying something to upset the younger man more.

"I could be here for a month. Maybe more. What if Hartley finds you? Then your blood'd be on my hands. I couldn't live with that," Quent pleaded. "I could — A surge of pain contorted his face, curtailing his speech.

Colter stayed at his cousin's side, sponging his feverish face with a cool rag until his eyes closed and his breathing grew regular. When he was sure Quent slept, he moved aside the blanket to check the wound. A poultice of mud and moss covered the area. That Captain Lewis had heeded his advice gave him little satisfaction. What was he going to do about Quent?

He replaced the blanket to find Quent awake and watching him. "Johnny, would you go see Mac for me? I got to see him before he leaves Mays-ville."

"Doubt the captain's goin' to allow him visitors."

"Then you have to get the captain to let me see Mac. I got to know where he's headed so's I can find him when I can ride again."

Colter bit back an admonition for Quent to forget the gambler. "If'n you'll promise to get some rest, I'll see about talkin' to him."

Quent gave Colter's hand a weak squeeze of gratitude. "Sergeant Floyd said they got him over to the fort."

"Shouldn't be too hard to find him then." The comment was wasted on Quent who had fallen asleep before Colter got to his feet.

Although it was full dark outside, he still slid the patch over his eye be-fore heading toward the fort. No sense taking chances in case Hartley had found his way here.

Canvas Army tents stood in rows on both sides of the thoroughfare that led up to what would be the fort's main gates when the palisade wall was completed. Inside the unfinished walls, log buildings ringed an open pa-rade ground on three sides. Several of the windows showed lights, but only one of those appeared guarded. Colter headed for it, figuring that was where he would find McBain.

At his approach, the sentry pushed away from the door where he had ob-viously been eavesdropping and blocked Colter's path. "I'm next. If you want a turn, you got to wait," he announced testily.

Female laughter sounded from inside which explained the guard's puzzling comment. "I come for McBain, not his company," Colter said.

"Better knock then. They ought to be about done. Only it's my turn next. You better not try to horn in." The guard spit a stream of tobacco juice at Colter's feet before moving aside.

At Colter's rap, McBain drawled, "You're early. Come back later."

"It's Colter, McBain."

"Coal-Tar! You just hold your horses. I'll be right with you."

Inside, McBain's female guest complained about being interrupted. The gambler placated her with murmured promises of later resumption of activities if she would get dressed and leave while he took care of some business. After another minute or so of rustling clothing and creaking bed boards, the door scraped open and out stepped a curvaceous woman. She smoothed down her skirts and met Colter's stare with a toss of her head and a look that promised her undivided attention, for the right price. The neckline of her brown dress was cut low enough to advertise her possibilities while retaining a small semblance of propriety. The cummerbund that cinched her midsection thrust her bosom forward in an invitation most men would find hard to ignore.

The sentry snapped to and, in the process, swallowed his tobacco plug. He doubled over, gagging, and she brushed past him headed toward a formation of soldiers on the parade ground. The closer she got to them, the slower she walked and the more her hips swayed, a motion she emphasized by propping one hand on her waist.

McBain's voice boomed through the open doorway. "Don't stand there gawking, Coal-Tar. Come on in."

Mac waved him to the lone stool and offered him a jug. Refusing the offer, Colter took in the man and his surroundings. The room consisted of four log walls enclosing a square of dirt six feet on a side. The furnishings consisted of the stool where Colter sat and the narrow bed where McBain sprawled, legs outstretched, back propped against the logs.

The gambler's shirt appeared freshly laundered; his coat, brushed; his knee-boots, polished to an impressive shine. His hair and beard showed signs of a recent trim. And the fingernails of the hands resting languidly against the bed's dark blue blanket showed no traces of the grime that had been caked underneath them the previous day.

"Welcome to my humble quarters." McBain belched into the back of his well-maintained hand.

"That there was your sister, right?" Colter asked.

McBain grinned. "Definitely not my sister. Definitely the key to my future, however." He propped the jug between his legs. "That fight last night might have knocked me off the expedition but it landed me in tall cotton. Cotton by the name of Lil, the one who just left. With her, there's no reason to risk my life on some dangerous journey when I can get rich faster staying right here."

He tossed back a slug of whiskey and smacked his lips. "Been living by my wits as long as I can remember. It's time to put my brains to work and let others make my money for me."

Others had done McBain's work for most of the trip to Maysville, but Colter chose not to point that out. "What you got in mind?"

"As we speak, every one of those recruits out there has a full ear of corn stiffening between his legs from watching Lil sashay past them. Another fifteen minutes they'll be lining up outside that very door, fighting for the chance to let her help them shuck those ears clean. Her and me, we got us a captive audience here. Men with ready money who'll pay for entertainment. Lil's just a start. Women, gambling, liquor. Those are the things I know best."

The idea of McBain being in a position to exploit the Lils and Lottys of the world turned Colter's stomach. He stood up. "Quent wanted me to ask you not to leave without saying goodbye. Message delivered."

"Whoa, Coal-Tar. Where are you going so fast? What about Quent?"

Remaining on his feet, Colter filled McBain in on his cousin's condition as briefly as he could.

"You tell Quent that I plan to stay around here long enough to get myself established before I move on," McBain said. "Tell him I have a present for him soon as he comes round to collect it."

Colter grunted. He had no intention of relaying such a message to his cousin. He did not want Quent mixed up in any scheme of McBain's. When it came time to tell his cousin about this visit, he would make something up. Something safe.

"How about you? You up for a poke? It's on me," McBain said.

"Keep your poke, McBain. Any woman has anythin' to do with you I ain't interested in.

"Ah, Coal-Tar. If it's Quent you're worried about . . ."

"It's Quent and everybody else you use, McBain."

Instead of rising to the provocation, McBain laughed. "I'm going to miss you, Coal-Tar, even if you won't miss me. You're about the only one anymore can make me laugh. You still planning on setting off by yourself?"

"I ain't got much choice."

"But you do. You belong on the expedition, Colter." It did not escape Colter's notice that McBain had used his real name for once instead of that irksome nickname. McBain went on. "With that preacher close by."

"Here? You saw him?"

"If he isn't yet, he will be. The way he was acting, Farley Stuart has the power to take away something that preacher really wants. That's Stuart money Hartley was flashing around. Enough of it to buy all the cooperation he needs while all you got is your wits. The only safe place for you now is a group like this expedition. I doubt the preacher is desperate or stupid enough to try to attack the U. S. Army."

McBain ran his fingers through his hair twice. "The only way to counter

Stuart is with power. Money's one kind of power. Reputation's another. The reputation you'd get by being a member of the group that finds the Passage would equal things out between you and Stuart. You'd be on his level then. Even odds, that's what you need, Colter."

What McBain said made too much sense to deny. Had he been too hasty in discounting the expedition? Captain lewis wanted him. Floyd, too. Certainly he had the skills and experience. The question was — and it was a big one — could he put up with the kind of obedience and discipline the military required? What if he got an order he disagreed with? Then there were the men he would be thrown together with. How did you trust people you had never met before, trust them with your life?

Out on the parade ground, someone barked an angry order. McBain sidled to the door and peered into the darkness. "What's going on, Murphy?" he asked the guard.

"The sergeant of those recruits don't like it much that Miss Lil's out there stirring up his men. She be back soon?"

"Is your pump primed, friend?" McBain asked.

"Damn right, I'm primed. Thought you said I was next." The frustration in the man's tone announced that his condition was reaching critical.

"Next is exactly what you are, Murphy." McBain winked in Colter's direction. "Why not step inside to wait for her?"

Private Murphy's hesitation about leaving his post was hardly long enough to notice. McBain shoved the jug at him. "Might as well take some comfort while you're waiting."

"Oh, no, Mac. Can't drink while I'm on duty."

McBain patted the private on the shoulder. "Anyone ever tell you you're a fine man, Murphy? I'm proud to have you guard me. What say I go get Lil and let her know you're waiting here? A good soldier like you shouldn't be gone from his post long."

Murphy's eyes took on a feverish glint. "Would you, Mac?"

"Of course. You make yourself at home. She'll be here directly."

Murphy abandoned his rifle against the wall and tested the bed while McBain led Colter outside. At the edge of the parade ground, Colter could not hold back any longer. "You mean, you just walked away?"

"Private Murphy and me worked out a deal last night. Seems each of us had something the other wanted. I'm not leaving. I'm just taking a stroll, giving him some time to do his business in privacy. Wouldn't do to get him in trouble now, would it?"

McBain stopped and turned to Colter. "You think over what I said about the expedition. Nothing would give me more pleasure than knowing you called Stuart's bluff. I'd sure love to see you knock him off his high horse. You do and all the women you can handle will be on me. That's a promise."

"Keep your women, McBain."

The gambler smiled his irritating, all-knowing smile. "Oh, by the time the expedition gets back, you'll change your tune. A woman'll be the first thing you'll want. Old Mac has no doubts about that. By then, I reckon to be in St. Louis. That's where the expedition starts and ends. I'll be waiting for you. Ah, St Louis. Now there's a place to appeal to our kind of man."

Colter would not be lumped into the same category with a whoremaster who lusted after children, but he was not about to waste breath saying so and giving McBain a chance to rile him more. He was heading away when the gambler caught his arm. "You know, that patch is a definite improve-ment in your looks. You ought to think about wearing it all the time."

Colter scraped off the man's hand and made for the gates. Heading down the main aisle of tents, he pondered the audacity and supreme self-assurance of a grifter like McBain. Puddles of mule piss and mounds of manure littered the path, forcing him to pick his way carefully. Soldiers lounged around small fires set in cleared spaces between the tents. Snatches of conversations, singing, laughter and arguments blended on the night breeze with the smells of boiled coffee, roasting meat, and burned beans.

He liked the feel of this male place, devoid of the softening influence of women or children, but he also recognized the restlessness inside him. Hartley or not, it was time to be gone, to lose himself in the mountains, to fall silent for the winter so he could once again listen to his heart.

" — got him a red splotch across his left eye looks like a flyin' bird." The words came from one of two soldiers who walked past him into a tent. Colter ducked into the shadows to eavesdrop through the canvas walls.

"I heard you tell some whoppers before, Tink, but this takes the prize. No way am I fallin' for some cockamamie story. First of all, that feller don't look to me like he's got one nickel let alone a hundred dollars. Second of all, a mark like that you'd notice right off on someone's face, but I sure ain't seen nothin' like it around here."

"If there is a man with that there mark around Maysville, I'm a-goin' to find him," the one called Tink said. "And when I do, that reward's all mine. Don't say I didn't give you no crack at it."

"I'm tellin' you there ain't no money."

"Oh, he's got it all right. He showed me."

"When?

"When you and Marsh went off to piss. He only showed the color of his gold to those he trusted. That's what he said anyhow."

"Still don't mean you'll ever get no gold to hand, Tink. Just where do you plan on findin' the one he's lookin' for?"

Colter's hand strayed to his eye-patch. Hartley was here — way too close for comfort.

"Maybe I don't have to," Tink said in a lowered voice. "Maybe I got a better idea. One that'll get us a lot more'n a hundred dollars. That gent's got him a purse the size of a possibles pouch. Got to be mighty heavy to tote around. What say we do him a favor and lighten his load for him?"

"You see where he settled for the night?" the second one asked in a hushed tone.

"I got a general idea."

"Well, what are we waitin' for?" the unnamed man said.

The two men burst out of the tent so suddenly that Colter barely managed to duck out of their way. Learning that Stuart's money made Josiah Hartley into a target for thieves gave him no comfort. If anything happened to the preacher, Stuart could easily buy a dozen other men desperate or greedy enough to take his place. If Hartley had been able to follow him here, others could, too. If he was ever to bring Farley Stuart down, he had to stay alive. And there was only one way to do that.

The gangway of the keelboat groaned under Colter's step. In the darkness a hunched-over figure moved on one of the rowing benches. "Sergeant Floyd?" The voice was Captain Lewis's.

"No, Captain. John Colter."

"Ah, Colter. Come." There was a strange tightness in the captain's voice, as if he had to force out the words. He rose, steadying himself momentarily against the swivel cannon. "So, you have come to tell me your decision. We have to talk out here. Your cousin is finally asleep. I do not want to disturb him."

"What I got to say is short enough," Colter replied.

"I hope you brought good news." Lewis passed one hand across his brow.

"If you still want me to join up, I do." He thought he saw Lewis wince. "You okay, Captain?"

"Just a little headache. Would you mind if we sat down?"

After they sat, the captain did not speak for a few moments, causing Colter to wonder if he had made up his mind too late.

The captain threw his shoulders back as if changing positions eased the pain in his head. "I count this as my lucky day, Colter. I hoped you would say yes. You are our seventh recruit. Seven has always been my lucky number. I promised to see that your cousin got back to his home. Like you, I keep my word."

Colter's doubts eased. "Then I got another favor to ask, Captain. Since I'm goin' off with you, I got to leave my horse with Quent."

"My offer extends to your animal as well." The captain's hand lifted again to his brow. "This expedition will test each man in trials none of us can foresee. The only way for us all to survive is as a group. A group needs rules. I will expect you to follow those rules. I will expect you to use your experience and skill to set an example for the rest of the Corps. And I will expect you to do nothing that will in any way bring harm to the others. For a man used to being solitary, that is a lot to expect. Can you abide those expectations?"

Colter hesitated. He had always hated rules. The ones he could not break, he always found a way around. However, that was before Farley Stuart and Josiah Hartley. Before Quent got hurt. "Yes, Captain, I can."

"Indians and how we treat them is one subject you and I have not discussed and it is one area I will not — cannot — budge on. We will pass through lands occupied by many native populations. No one knows their numbers or extent. Our job is to establish peaceful relations with them all. We go to open trade routes. Not to fight. There is no room in the Corps for any man whose trigger finger twitches whenever he sees copper skin. How do you feel about that?"

Colter gave himself time to think through what he had to say. This was no time to be misunderstood. "I got my reasons for not likin' Indians, but I try to avoid fights, not start 'em. And I don't kill nothin' unless I figure to eat it. You got your orders. If that means treatin' with Indians, then, by signin' up, I got to help you do that."

A man hurried down the riverbank toward the keelboat. Sergeant Floyd. His churning arms signalled that he was on a mission of importance. He took the gangplank in two steps. Seeing Colter with the captain seemed to throw him off. "Captain, I . . ."

"Speak up, Sergeant. What is it?" Lewis said.

Floyd cast a sideways glance at Colter. "Some man's been asking around about a man with a birthmark over his left eye, sir. And not just asking. He's offering money — a lot of money — for the information."

Lewis's expression was impossible to read across the darkness. "Is there anything I ought to know about this, Colter?"

In the space of a heartbeat, Colter decided to tell the truth. "Yesterday you said you knew Farley Stuart."

"I know of Stuart, yes."

Colter sucked in a deep breath. "He stole my ma's land. I can prove it, but right now Stuart controls everybody who could help me do anythin' about it."

"So Stuart has come here after you?" The captain's gaze seemed to penetrate the blackness between them.

"No, he sent Josiah Hartley, a preacher from the Draft. That's Stuart's money Hartley's offerin' for a reward. He's been on my tail since we left Virginia."

"Why?" the captain asked.

"I got somethin' proves Stuart's a forger and a thief."

The captain tilted his face toward the night sky. In the long ensuing silence, Colter grew suddenly desperate to be part of this expedition, to get as far away from Farley Stuart and Josiah Hartley and the Draft as he could, to go West and never look back. Yet, with every passing moment, he sensed his chances eroding. Stuart had powerful friends in Washington. The kind of friends an ambitious man like the captain would cross at his own peril.

At last, the captain spoke. "The induction ceremony is scheduled for an hour after sunrise tomorrow. We will get underway immediately afterward. Sergeant, I hold you personally responsible for keeping this Hartley person away from this boat and from Colter. Understood?"

"Yes, sir," answered Floyd.

"Colter, I want you to wear that patch until we are underway. Just as a precaution. And I want you to sleep aboard tonight."

"Cain't, Captain. I got me some goodbyes to say."

"Very well, but perhaps you ought to bring to me for safekeeping that proof you said you had."

Colter readily agreed. At least the Bible and the flattened hat would be safe in the captain's possession. For himself, he needed solitude, and he knew the perfect place.

He had discovered the spot during his wanderings outside Maysville — a wide grassy shelf, rising above the surrounding area, protected at the rear by tree-high boulders and shielded from view in the front by rocks and tangled vines.

Through her usual uncanny intuition, Blaze seemed to know that they would part in the morning. She did not stray more than a few feet from him all night while he wrestled with the confusion of thoughts that clogged his mind, pre-empting sleep. Had he been too hasty in joining the Expedi-tion? Could he keep the promises he had made to Captain Lewis? Was he right to run away from Hartley? Or should he take a stand? Would Hartley or Stuart try to hurt Quent, or Lorenzo, when they failed to lay hands on Colter's proof? Why was Captain Lewis willing to side with him? What about the other men chosen for the Corps? Was his being among them putting innocent lives in danger?

At dawn, with eyes scratchy from lack of sleep and no clear answers to those questions, he mounted Blaze for the last time and rode into Mays-ville.

Fog lay thick over the river and its banks. His first thought was that their departure would be delayed. His second, that the fog was an ideal place for Hartley to hide.

He repositioned the patch and hat before urging Blaze forward. The few figures that materialized out of the swirling mist proved to be strangers who gave him only cursory glances. Then the shape of the keelboat loomed ahead.

Floyd was sorting piles of clothing. "Mornin', Colter." He held out a wool jacket. "See if this fits."

The jacket was dark blue with a white lining and scarlet facings. Far too fussy for Colter, but he shucked off his roomy buckskin hunting shirt and shrugged on the jacket. It was tight in all the wrong places, especially at the neck where the scratchy wool felt like a noose rather than a collar.

Floyd's hands went up in a gesture of futility. "It's the best I can offer without a tailor. We're stuck with what the captain managed to requisition from Army stores. Dadblamed things never do fit right."

"Why bother? Buckskins're what we need," Colter said.

The sergeant nodded sympathetically. "But soldiers wear uniforms, though you won't have to wear it much. Just for official ceremonies." He waved toward the rifles arranged across two rowing benches onboard the keel-boat. "Pick the one you want."

As he walked onto the boat, Colter unbuttoned the jacket but left it on while he handled and sighted each rifle until settling on one that felt best in his hands. The stock was half the length of any rifle he had seen before. Its barrel just reached his shoulder when the gun was standing on its butt-end. A patchbox, covered in brass etched to match the guards and stockthimble, was fitted into the stock. The barrel had been rounded for half its length to reduce its weight and balance the short stock. A rib soldered to the barrel held the ramrod. In short, a rifle made to stand up under hard use. Though he had always found his own rifle reliable and accurate, he knew that where they were going, it would not hold up. He would give his personal rifle to Quent, to keep for him until his return.

"Like it?" Floyd asked, coming to stand beside him. "Captain Lewis designed them special."

Colter nodded. "He done a good job. It's a far sight better than anythin' I expected."

Floyd looked at the piles of clothing draped across the tops of boxes. "You'll get more kit once we get to Clarksville. Captain doesn't want to unpack anything we don't absolutely need right now."

"I can wait." Colter thought a minute. "Clarksville? Ain't that where the falls are?"

Floyd ran his eyes down the length of the keelboat. "'Fraid so. Means unloading everything and moving *Discovery* and several tons of supplies to the bottom of the rapids. We get our other captain there, too." He shook his head skeptically. "Two captains. I don't know how that's going to work. Never heard of such a thing in any man's army before. Captain Lewis, though, is convinced that's what this expedition needs. Captain Clark —"

"Clark? As in George Rogers Clark?"

"I'd give up a year's pay to serve with the General," Floyd said. "But, no, not him. His younger brother William. He and Captain Lewis served together a few years back."

The Clarks were legends. The thought of serving with a Clark, be it George Rogers or William, made more palatable to Colter the idea of all the military hoo-ha he was letting himself in for.

"That you, Johnny?" Quent lay on a pallet in the far corner of the deck, Colter had not noticed him before and he hurried over to his cousin. Quent fingered a button on the uniform jacket. "You joined! By God, Johnny, you'll do us Colters proud."

Colter squeezed Quent's hand. "Captain Lewis said he'd see about gettin' you home."

The younger man returned the squeeze weakly. "Captain told me Hartley's here in Maysville."

"He's here all right, offerin' money to anyone's seen me. That's why I joined up. I told the captain what's happened and gave him Ma's Bible and the preacher's hat for safe-keepin'." Colter hoped his expression and tone did not give away the uncertainty he still felt over his decision. He changed the subject. "Got a big favor to ask, Cousin."

The ends of Quent's scrawny mustache twitched with curiosity. "Shoot."

"Need you to see to Blaze and my rifle till I get back home. Captain promised to see you got home to the Draft."

"Oh, Johnny," Quent gasped, reverting momentarily to the youngster Colter had once rough-housed with. "I promise I'll treat Blaze like my own."

"That's why I asked you. Just don't get too attached. I plan on bein' back 'fore too long."

Floyd broke the spell. "We ought to move your cousin ashore soon, Colter. We're shoving off right after the swearing-in."

11. *Peckerwood*

M ore of the expedition's recruits had arrived. They were trying on their new uniforms. It concerned Colter that he had paid no heed to their arrival. Not good, when he needed to be on guard with Josiah Hartley somewhere out there in the fog.

He helped Quent up and supported him to some boxes piled up on the bank. From there, his cousin could see the departure and Colter could better watch the crowd gathering to watch the swearing in now that the fog was thinning. As he got Quent settled, a squad of Regulars appeared, the crew that had brought the boat down the Ohio to Maysville. At the Mississippi confluence they would head for other assignments, leaving Colter and the other recruits to wrestle the keelboat the rest of the way to the Passage — or whatever else they might find.

Watching the Regulars, he wondered why the captain had never asked him a single question about his experience with boats. Come to think of it, Quent and McBain had never mentioned any such questions either.

He turned his attention to the gathering crowd and, as he searched faces for Hartley's, George Shannon appeared, walking at the measured pace of a military drill. Back straight, shoulders square, chin high, he marched past the other recruits who waited awkwardly at the bottom of the gangway, then continued up the gangplank, executed a square corner at the top and came to a halt in front of Sergeant Floyd. Floyd did not look pleased to see him.

Sitting at a distance, Colter could not hear what transpired between the two men. He could read their expressions however, and those made it clear that neither liked the other. They broke off their exchange when Lewis emerged from his cabin, resplendent in an immaculate red uniform jacket whose brass buttons shone like mirrors. Floyd thrust a jacket into Shannon's hands, gave a peremptory wave toward the dwindling pile of rifles and followed the captain to the bow.

As soon as the sergeant turned his back, Shannon flung aside the jacket he had been given and began to rummage through the pile for another more to his liking. By the time he found one, jackets were scattered everywhere. Then Shannon moved to the rifles. Of these, he grabbed the nearest one without so much as a second look and carried it off the boat. Colter watched, flabbergasted that anyone would pay more attention to his choice of coats than to his weapon.

"Recruits, line up!" Floyd's boomed order cut through his astonishment. Quent patted him on the arm. "Go get 'em, Johnny."

Colter tousled his cousin's hair and went to join the line. He found himself standing next to Shannon who was fussing with the sleeves of his uniform. "Sergeant said they never fit," he offered.

"It's the sergeant's duty to set an example of proper appearance for his men," Shannon responded curtly. "This is appalling."

As Colter rebuttoned his own scratchy coat, Shannon turned to the man on his other side and plucked some loose lint off his jacket. The man grabbed Shannon's wrist. "Just what do you think you're doin'?"

"Removing lint from your uniform," answered Shannon through clenched teeth.

"I like lint. What I don't like is some peckerwood touching me." The man torqued Shannon's wrist, eliciting a grunt before releasing it.

Shannon's actions had not gone unnoticed. The glares that the other men aimed his direction did not bode well for him, and they had not even shoved off yet.

While Floyd administered the oath of enlistment to the recruits, Shannon's mind was on his future. He had had a day to think about his set-to with the sergeant, and he had come to the conclusion that this outfit desperately needed someone who understood the value of discipline, of rules, of paying attention to details. That someone was himself, George Shannon. *Lieutenant* George Shannon.

The rude shock of being set back to the rank of private had passed, replaced by a determination to regain his lieutenancy. The key to that promotion lay with Captain Lewis. That meant finding a way to work around the sergeant. He had to do that carefully, for, if Floyd found out what he was up to, there was no telling what he might do to wreck Shannon's chances, especially if the sergeant himself had designs on a commission.

Floyd finished the oath of enlistment and stepped back to allow the captain to address the men. Shannon glanced down the line at the other recruits. What a slovenly lot! Not one of them knew how to stand at attention properly. Their uniforms were dirty and unkempt already. From their collective stench, none of them had bathed recently. When he was in charge, he would order them to shave every day and keep their hair trimmed. And, by God, they had better bathe daily if they knew what was good for them!

The man to his right, Colter was his name, shifted from one foot to the other. He looked so awkward in his uniform that he might have been comical if he had not looked so pathetic. Then there was the matter of his eyepatch. Why on earth would the captain choose a man with only one eye?

Lewis ended his remarks with "Say your farewells, men, then come aboard. We will be underway shortly."

Colter hurried over to a young man with a bandaged shoulder, sitting on a crate at the edge of the crowd. Shannon recognized the youth as the one who had been asleep in the captain's cabin during his interview. The obvious affection between the two men and the realization that most of the other recruits had someone to say goodbye to made him feel suddenly lonely.

Half-turning toward the keelboat to mask the emotions on his face from anyone who might be watching, he noticed a woman on the edge of the crowd looking directly at him. A beautiful woman in a dress that challenged the rules of polite society. She was smiling at him so brazenly that his face went immediately hot under a blush.

The next thing he knew she was standing next to him, an invitation in her striking gray eyes. She leaned toward him, drawing his gaze to her cleavage despite his best efforts to hold back. Her voice was low and caressing. "My, my, but I do love a man looks as good in a uniform as you. I can't believe I haven't seen you before now. Where have you been hiding, you beautiful man?"

She pressed into him. Her voice was so soft that he had to lean toward her mouth to hear. "I'd like to take a bite out of you right now. A big juicy bite."

He was too flustered to speak even if he could have thought of something to say.

Rube Field, the taller of a pair of brother recruits, spoke up. "Don't waste your time on him, Miss Lil. He won't taste near as good as me."

Lil paid no heed to Rube. "Well, I just have to do this." She rose on tiptoes and locked Shannon's mouth in an energetic kiss.

Shannon could not see the crowd — her head blocked his view — but he could hear their laughter. He tried to push himself free from her, but she countered his efforts and, to his embarrassment, he found himself returning her embrace. It took a long time for her to break off the kiss. "That is a sample of what you'll get when you come back, Handsome,"

Chagrined to realize that he was holding onto her, he tried to cover his embarrassment. "No, thank you, ma'am. I'm not that kind of man."

Rube Field guffawed. "Somethin' must be wrong with your equipment then, or you ain't much of a man." He dragged a grimy finger across Shannon's cheek. "I thought so, Little Brother. This here peckerwood don't even shave. I say we call him Fuzz."

"Yep, Fuzz fits," Joe Field agreed. "I give odds fuzz's all he's got between his legs, too."

Captain Lewis's stern voice sliced into the exchange. "That'll be quite enough, you three. I suggest you get aboard immediately. All except Privates Shannon and Colter."

With muttered "Yes, sirs" and downcast eyes, the Field brothers and other recruits began to board, leaving Shannon and Colter with the captain.

"Captain, I — Shannon stuttered out of humiliation.

Lewis waved him to silence and addressed Colter. "Private Colter, I have two assignments for you, starting now. I want you to take Private Shannon here under that competent, experienced wing of yours and help him adjust to the hard work we are about to face."

"Captain, I protest," Shannon said.

The disapproving wrinkle in the captain's forehead evaporated Shannon's objection. He could not afford to alienate the expedition leader. Not if he wanted that promotion, and at that moment he wanted a promotion worse than anything in his life.

"And, Private Colter, once you get aboard, remove that patch," the captain said.

"Yes, sir," responded Colter.

"Good. Come aboard," the captain ordered.

Shannon waited until the captain was up the gangway before whispering to Colter, "I don't need your help and I don't want it. You stay out of my way and I'll stay out of yours."

Colter's expression mixed amusement with annoyance. "I don't like you much neither, but if'n the captain asks me to do somethin', I'll do it." He paused, his eyes gleaming with spite. "Peckerwood and Fuzz. Both'a them names fit you so good that it's goin' to be a hard choice which one to use from now on."

Shannon replied to the sarcasm by giving Colter a view of his back. Obviously, the captain had bigger plans for him. Let the others call him whatever they wanted. Names meant nothing. He had found that out early in his life. Let them say what they wanted. Soon enough they would all be answering to George Shannon. Soon enough.

Colter spit a wad of disgust into the wet sand of the riverbank before stepping onto the gangway. Not only did the enlistment oath bind him to Army rules, but now he was also responsible for a puffed-up greenhorn without a single lick of sense. But for the promise he had made to the captain, he would fade through the crowd now and take off into the western wilderness.

"Captain wants you next to Shannon." Floyd directed, then added in a lowered voice, "He'll be gone before you know it, and I plan to help him. You can count on that."

There were eleven benches in all, each one wide enough for two rowers to sit side by side facing the stern. Still, counting the Regulars that had boarded earlier, barely half the seats were occupied.

Shannon was seated on the bench closest to the captain's cabin. With a sigh of aggravation, Colter slid into the space next to him and undid the strings holding the leather patch in place. The air felt good on the skin where his face had been covered.

"Why, you have two eyes," Shannon said in a surprised voice.

Colter rolled the patch into a ball. "Same as you."

One of the Regulars on the bench behind him gasped and whispered urgently to his seatmate. "It's him, Rut."

Seeing the man cross himself against the evil eye compounded Colter's aggravation. He twisted around. "Him who?"

The other Regular, the one called Rut, answered. "There's a man lookin' for you."

Colter forced himself not to react. "Must be somebody else. Ain't nobody lookin' for me."

"Oh, it's you all right," Rut said. "That there's the mark he was talkin' about. He's willin' to pay a purseful of money to the one who finds you for him."

Colter kept his tone and expression as neutral as his roiling emotions allowed. "He must not be lookin' very hard then. I been around here all week."

The first Regular tugged at Rut's sleeve. "Rut, be careful. That mark!"

Rut silenced his partner with a sideways glance. "Yeah, but you been hidin' 'hind that patch."

A commotion on the dock interrupted them. The aide to the new fort's commanding officer shoved through the crowd and hailed Lewis. "Captain Conners asks you to come up to the fort, Captain. He needs to speak to you. It's urgent."

"We are about to leave, Lieutenant. What could be that pressing?" Lewis asked curtly.

The aide's pursed lips showed that he did not want to discuss the matter openly, but it was equally obvious that Lewis did not intend to budge without an answer. "A man was attacked and robbed last night. A civilian. He claims his assailants came from your company."

Colter thought of the conversation he had overheard last night and guessed that Hartley was using the attack on him as an excuse to keep the expedition — and Colter — from leaving. No doubt Hartley meant to blame him for the robbery. If that happened . . .

Lewis signalled for Floyd to remove the gangplank. "Express my apologies to Captain Conners, Lieutenant."

"You mean you're not coming?" the aide demanded incredulously.

"That is precisely what I mean," Lewis said, motioning for the six Regulars to take up positions along the *passe avant*, the narrow raised walkway along both sides of the rowers used by the polers. The captain nodded and Floyd bellowed, "Shove off!" The Regulars set their poles in the shallows and pushed in unison. The keelboat began to move slowly away from the riverbank.

The aide's face flushed. "Captain Lewis, I must protest. Captain Conners insists on your immediate presence. One of your men is a thief. Why, he nearly cut off the civilian's ear in the attack."

"Whoever did that is not among my crewmen, Lieutenant. Now we have delayed long enough. I have faith that Captain Conners will resolve the matter without me. Wish him my fondest regards." The captain turned his back on the aide and disappeared inside his cabin, leaving the man to return to the fort alone.

Colter looked at the wadded up piece of leather in his hand. That had been close. Too close.

"Man those oars! Get ready to sweat!" Floyd bellowed.

Dropping the patch to the deck, Colter moved the sweep oar out of its lock. Beside him, Shannon looked down at his oar as if he did not know what to do next.

"Take it out of the lock, Fuzz." His voice was quivering from the strain of what he had just witnessed.

"There's been a mistake. I-I — Shannon stammered.

"You what, Private?" Floyd appeared on the *passe avant* next to Shannon. "You better not let me catch you slacking off, Shannon. You talked your way into this thing. Now you're going to get a chance to show us you aren't just another pretty face. Now grab that oar, or get off the boat!"

Shannon managed to fumble the oar out of the lock. Floyd gave him one long, lingering sneer before he straightened up and shouted, "All right, ladies. Stroke."

As he leaned forward, Colter took a last look toward the dock. He was relieved to see neither Hartley nor Captain Conners, but he had little time to enjoy the feeling because the moment the head of his oar struck the water, the current tried to wrest it out of his hands.

He prevailed and heaved his body backward with the sweep movement. The muscles in his shoulders and back strained with the effort to finish the stroke. Then it was time to lean forward, sink the head of the oar and pull again. And again. And again. It would be like this all the way down the Ohio. And this would be the easy part. Once they hit the Mississippi, the current would be against them, and they would have to tow the boat up to St. Louis, then up the Missouri. Suddenly, joining the expedition seemed like a very bad idea.

Beside him, Shannon let go his oar. "I won't —"

Floyd was there in an instant. "Won't what, Private?"

With the sergeant glaring at him, the younger man regrasped the oar. "I suggest you row, Shannon. And keep on rowing until I tell you to stop." The sergeant's tone left no doubt who was in charge on this boat.

Colter leaned forward again. As his oar hit the water, he wondered, *Dear God, what did I get myself into?*

PART 2

RECRUITS

Fall, 1803 — Spring, 1804

The Commanding officer feels himself mortifyed and disappointed at the disorderly conduct.
— Meriwether Lewis, 1804

1. *Blisters and Sweat*

Above the Falls of the Ohio River

S hannon winced as another blister on his palm popped with a gush of sticky fluid. He dropped the oar to examine this latest insult to his body. Damned oar! Between it and the daily assault of water and sun, his hands looked like a ditch-digger's. He was not cut out for this kind of brutal labor. He was educated, for heaven's sake. Educated men made the plans and gave the orders. They directed those who did the grunt work; they most certainly did not do the work themselves. Physical labor was for the ignorant, the less-capable, the undisciplined. None of those adjectives applied to him.

"You goin' to study them hands all day so's the rest of us have to haul your sorry behind all the way to the Passage?" Colter's familiar complaint came with an elbow in the ribs.

"Can't you see I'm hurt? I'll row when I'm good and ready," Shannon shot back.

Colter bent forward in the rhythm with the cadence count. "Hurt? A goldurn blister don't hurt. Not a man anyway."

Shannon pretended not to hear the gibe and glanced toward the riverbank with its endless stands of trees. How he longed for a town, for people and houses and civilization — any diversion from the daily drudgery of rowing and putting up with Colter and the rest of his kind! "Butt out, Colter. No one asked for your opinion."

"I'll butt out when I ain't got to sit here and sweat while you loaf. Pick up that oar, damn it!"

Shannon reluctantly took up his oar. Not because of Colter's implied threat, but because he did not want to attract more of Sergeant Floyd's wrath. It was clear the sergeant disliked him. Yet, the man was his immediate superior and the captain's next-in-command so he needed to toe Floyd's line until he had time to work his way solidly into the captain's favor.

By now, there was not a muscle in his shoulders, back, arms or legs that did not ache from the strain of rowing. Lift and pull, lift and pull. Again and again, an endless cycle of daily agony on this endless river.

Supplies and equipment packed every inch of *Discovery*'s fifty-five-foot length. Between the weight of the load and the low level of the Ohio, even a full complement of twenty-two rowers would have had a struggle propelling the boat, but to expect eleven men to do so was asking the impossible. Yet that was exactly what he was up against.

Colter abruptly stopped rowing. "If you can take a break, Fuzz, so can I. Maybe I can raise the level of the river some."

As Colter stood up, on the next bench back, Elliott, the Regular, made a warding sign. The ignorant oaf believed Colter's birthmark could hex him. Worse, he also believed that some flumadiddle hand motion could cancel the curse! Unbelievable.

Sharing the bench with Elliott was Rutledge, another Regular with the attitude of an approaching rainstorm and a face to match, who muttered something under his breath.

"What say, Rutledge?" Colter demanded.

"Weren't talkin' to you," Rutledge said.

"Then why're you starin' at me?"

"Move it, Colter," Sergeant Pryor yelled down from the quarterdeck. "We're not running a pleasure cruise here." Pryor had joined the Corps as a second sergeant not long after leaving Maysville. He had dark eyes that seemed to follow you everywhere without moving. He and Floyd were cousins and as close as brothers.

With a parting glare at Rutledge, Colter threaded his way through the sweating bottom-polers on the *passe avant*. Shannon had the bench to himself then. He gritted his teeth against the groans that forced their way up from his straining, complaining muscles as he attempted to keep rhythm with the other rowers.

"My Lord, is that Peckerwood making all that racket, Little Brother?" The sarcastic comment came from Reuben Field. Rube shared the bench behind Rutledge and Elliott with his brother Joe. "I must be dreamin' 'cause my eyes tell me he's rowin'. Didn't think he knew how, did you?"

Shannon considered a smart retort but stifled it. Arguing with Rube served no purpose. Besides, the door to the captain's cabin was ajar and Captain Lewis might hear. It wouldn't do his cause a bit of good to give the captain reason to think he could not keep cool in the face of a little razzing.

Shannon surreptitiously checked through the partially open door to see if the captain was paying attention to the exchange. Seeing Lewis was bent over an array of maps and journals spread out on his worktable caused an idea to swirl into form. Shannon glanced toward the bow. Sergeant Floyd was studying the riverbank through a telescope, his back was to the rowing benches. Good!

He threw aside the oar, popped to his feet and rapped on the cabin door. "Captain?"

"Come," came the reply.

Shannon stepped quickly over the threshold and quickly closed the door. Captain Lewis looked up from his work. "Private Shannon. What is it?"

"It's my hands, sir." He held out his damaged palms for the captain's inspection. In the corner, Seaman, Lewis's dog, gave a low disapproving growl before yawning and propping his head back on his front paws.

Lewis flung down his writing quill. "Curse that boat-builder! He cost me months of delays and still did not do his job. None of those oars was smoothed right. Not one."

The captain's angry outburst momentarily rattled Shannon. "Maybe I should come back later."

Lewis waved him to silence. "There will be boatwrights in Clarksville to do what ought to have been done properly to begin with. Until then, we will have to make do. Lord, I wish we had room on the crew for a doctor."

While the captain treated his hands, Shannon went over in his head the speech he had prepared. It had to come out exactly right. His future hung on its success.

The captain turned to snap the wooden medicine box closed. Shannon took a deep breath and began, "Captain, it seems to me that —" The boom of the keelboat's cannon obliterated the rest of his sentence.

"Captain, the falls are ahead," yelled Sergeant Floyd from the bow. "Clarksville landing coming up to starboard."

"Excellent, Sergeant!" Lewis scooped his uniform jacket off the bunk. A broad smile so transformed his face that Shannon realized how seldom he had seen the captain happy. "You do not want to miss this, Shannon."

Coat half-buttoned, his formal shako forgotten on the bunk, the captain rushed from the cabin and up to the quarterdeck, leaving Shannon smarting from a golden opportunity lost. Chances to get the captain alone had been few and far between so far. Now he would have to bide his time until the next chance came along.

Stepping out of the cabin, he blinked against the brilliant fall sunshine. Floyd's voice at his shoulder startled him. "Having a cozy little chat with the captain, Private?"

Shannon slid stiffly onto the rowing bench without answering. The sergeant bent to look him directly in the eye. "You disobeyed an order, Private." Shannon stared over the sergeant's right shoulder, but Floyd moved his head to that side and locked gazes. "A *direct* order not to leave your bench without my permission. Correct, Private?"

"Yes, Sergeant."

"Did you have my permission to leave?" Floyd persisted.

Reaching for the oar forced Shannon to lean forward until his face was only an inch from Floyd's. "No, Sergeant."

The sergeant picked up one of Shannon's bandaged hands and announced in a voice loud enough for just the rowing crew to hear, "Private Shannon here has done you ladies all a favor. He will stand a double watch tonight so you can all go enjoy yourselves. Wasn't that thoughtful of him?"

At the chorus of catcalls, Shannon ducked his head to hide the flush of resentment. He had to get out from under Floyd's control. Had to. And soon, before the man completely undermined him in the eyes of the crew and the captain.

The sergeant murmured in his ear, "Midnight to dawn, it's all yours, Mister Shannon. Hope you enjoy it. I know I will."

Colter listened to Floyd's announcement with a mixture of satisfaction and futility. He had tried to be patient with Shannon, tried to reason with him and teach him in keeping with his promise to the captain, but Shannon ignored or rejected all his efforts. Shannon behaved as if he considered hard work beneath him, as if he were better than the rest of the crew. He was the weakest rower on the crew, and he showed no inclination to improve.

The best that could happen was for Captain Lewis to release Shannon from his enlistment before his superior attitude created any more problems. Lord knew no one would miss him, especially Colter.

The keelboat angled into the settlement of Clarksville on the north bank of the river. The place had been named for George Rogers Clark, hero of the Revolution. It consisted of a ragged line of newer cabins and buildings strung out along a shallow bluff. As the keelboat approached, people began to gather at the landing stage at the base of the bluff to meet it. Those people were mostly men — burly, broad-shouldered, half-wild from their looks. Colter saw no children and only one woman — a thin, pale wraith in a faded calico dress who quickly disappeared, leaving him to wonder if she had been a figment of his imagination.

Elliott and Rutledge exchanged murmured comments on the bench behind him. Elliott's habitual curse-warding motions annoyed him, but Rutledge's silent stares provoked him as few men other than McBain ever had. The man talked little, but whenever he did speak, a chord of recognition vibrated in Colter. Somewhere he had heard the man's voice before, but where?

On the quarterdeck, Lieutenant Lavendar, the stiff-backed leader of the squad of Regulars, went to stand next to the relaxed-looking Lewis during the landing. Pieces of their conversation drifted down to the benches and Colter.

"I hope Captain Clark has recruits for you, sir," Lavendar said. "With water this low, you'll need every hand and back you can get, especially to rope the boat down the rapids."

"With Will's luck, he'll have a boatload of men by now," the captain said.

"You'll need all we can get. Winter can't be far off and St. Louis is a long way yet."

"We will manage, Lieutenant."

Behind Colter, Reuben Field grumbled, "Roping the boat? Who said anything about roping any boat?"

"Captain did, you ninny," Shannon snapped back.

"That ought to be a sight, Peckerwood: you hauling on a rope," said Rube. "If those dainty hands o' yours hurt now, just wait."

"Up oars! Polers to port. Prepare to beach," Floyd yelled.

Colter shoved the oar into its lock, then ducked his head and pulled in his elbows to keep from being kicked, as the men assigned to the bottom-poles clambered up to their positions on the *passe avant*. While the rest of the rowing crew stretched their sore backs and arms, Shannon left the bench and scrambled up to the quarterdeck. The only time he moved fast was when Captain Lewis was his destination.

Seaman greeted Shannon's appearance with a ominous growl. One of the crewmen called out, "I second that motion!" The whole crew laughed. The dog did not fancy Shannon, either.

Three horses — one riderless — galloped into view at the top of the bluff. One rider spurred ahead, racing down the bank and straight on into the river where he recklessly flung himself out of the saddle into the knee-deep water. A mass of unruly red hair framed his freckled face. "Meri, you old teaser! Thought you'd never get here!"

Seaman forgot Shannon and plunged into the river with a splash that showered half the crew. The 150-pound Newfoundlander made straight for the red-headed newcomer. Amidst barking, splashing and baritone laughter, dog and man met and tumbled out of the river onto the sand in a playful wrestling match.

Lewis surprised the crew by swinging down to the rowing deck and splashing over the side and up onto the bank to embrace the stranger. "Will Clark, you old son-of-a-she-bear!"

As Colter studied William Clark, the man who would share command of the expedition with Lewis, the second rider, an ebony giant, taller and wider than Clark, drew up and dismounted.

Flinging riverwater and sand in his wake, Seaman left off playing with Clark and raced toward this man who easily caught the dog mid-leap. Momentum carried man and animal into a joyous spin. "Looks like you've made a friend, York!" Clark called.

The black man laughed, a rich delighted rumble. "A big friend, Master Will."

"So that's your best-boy, York. About time we met," Lewis said to Clark.

Clark laughed. "Best is the right word for him, too. The extra horse is for you, Meri. We'll ride to the house and get caught up over dinner."

"Hold on, Will. Aren't we forgetting a few details? Like the boat and the falls?"

Floyd let himself over *Discovery*'s side and splashed to the pair. Lewis introduced him and Clark shook the sergeant's hand. "Floyd? Didn't your father serve under my brother George?"

"That he did," Floyd said proudly.

Lewis interrupted. "Sergeant, you organize the men into an unloading brigade. Start in the bow."

Clark's hand on his arm stopped Lewis. "Let it wait, Meri. Till tomorrow."

Another horse and rider trotted onto the sand. "Greetings, Meri. I brought a little something for a celebration." The rider brandished a crock jug that he nearly dropped in his enthusiasm. The crock explained his unsteadiness in the saddle.

York released the dog and hustled to take charge of the newcomer's horse. Some of the pleasure slid off of William Clark's face as he addressed the rider. "George, I said we'd come down to the house shortly."

Colter looked at the rider in consternation. "George" could only mean this drunken man was General George Rogers Clark, the man responsible for wresting Ohio Territory away from the British-Indian alliance during the Revolution.

"That's right, you did, Billy," the general slurred. "But that doesn't mean I can't come down here. Hell, this is my town. I can do what I want."

"York, see to it my brother gets back in one piece and let Rose know we'll be along directly," Clark insisted.

"Don't dismiss me, Billy," demanded the general. "It's not every day I get to greet the man who's in charge of the expedition I ought to be leading."

"Take him home, York. Now," ordered Clark, all hint of joy leaching from his face.

"Oh, no, you don't," responded the general, attempting to dismount but getting his boots tangled up in the stirrups.

York pushed the general back into the saddle, took hold of the reins and quickly led the horse and the protesting man away.

"Sorry about that, Meri," Clark said.

"No need for apologies." Lewis looked up at the sky. "We've got five good hours of daylight. Let's get started."

"Tomorrow, Meri. Please. Right now, you and I need to talk, and your crew deserves a rest."

Lewis seemed inclined to argue further but didn't. "Sergeant, release the men until dawn with the usual restrictions."

While the captain and Clark headed up the road, Floyd addressed the crew. "Bratton has first watch. Except for him and Shannon, the rest of you have the run of Clarksville until dawn tomorrow. Don't leave the area of the settlement. No fighting. No trouble."

The crew responded with an eager "Yes, Sergeant,"and, as they filed off the boat, every one had some cutting remark for Shannon. For a time, Shannon held his peace like a sensible man. Then Reuben Field called him a peckerwood again. "It's woodpecker, you ignoramus. A bird," Shannon shot back. "Do I look like a bird?"

Rube's face settled into gloating lines. "You look like someone who makes the rest of us do his work so's he can stick his nose up a certain captain's crack whenever he feels like it. It's about time you got brought down a peg."

Mindful of his promise to Lewis, Colter stepped between the two men before words could turn into flying fists. "Oh, no, you don't. Ain't goin' to be no fights."

"Peckerwood? Hell, he won't fight, Colter. He don't know how. And he might get his little self hurt," Rube jeered.

Joe Field pulled his brother away. "Come on, Rube, let's go. Peckerwood's not worth missin' a good drunk."

Rube gave Shannon one last smirk before leaving. Colter kept a grip on Shannon until the men had cleared the boat.

"I'll thank you to mind your own business," Shannon said, shrugging Colter's hand off as Sergeant Floyd sidled over.

"Too bad you can't join the celebration, Shannon," Floyd said. "I'm sure Captain'll miss you. You do know the penalty for sleeping on post, don't you?"

"Yes, Sergeant."

"Why don't you tell me what it is, Private?" Floyd goaded.

Shannon's Adam's apple moved up and down with a swallow. "A firing squad, Sergeant."

"You wouldn't want that to happen, now would you?" Floyd said, giving his head an exaggerated shake.

"No, Sergeant," Shannon said defiantly.

"Then you better get some sleep before you go on watch."

Colter followed the sergeant onto the beach. Let the other men have the liquor. He wanted to get off by himself for a time, to stretch his legs and enjoy some solitude. Yes, Floyd had said to stay in the settlement, but who would know if he left? He knew his way around the woods. Nothing could happen to him except for restoring his equilibrium and restocking his supply of tranquility.

"That Shannon's a piece of work," said Floyd. "I got to hand it to him though. He's stuck it out longer than I thought he would." He chuckled. "Then again, if it were up to me, he'd get double watches every night. The sooner he quits, the better. Why, the captain . . ."

He pulled back from whatever he was going to say and clapped Colter on the back. "Don't you let him get under your skin, Colter. He'll quit. Won't be long now. Leave it to me." And off he went, toward the sound of men getting into their cups.

Colter waited until Floyd was not likely to look back, then he struck out for the woods, and some peace and quiet.

🦅

"Break! Thirty minutes!" Captain Clark shouted.

A grateful Colter slung down the load he had been hauling, plodded to the nearest spot of shade, and stretched out on the ground. Getting out of the sun felt good; resting, even better. All along the line, crewmen sprawled wherever they could shelter out of the beating sun. Low water had exposed the limestone ledges that formed the Falls of the Ohio. It had taken the crew five long, hard days to unload *Discovery* and maneuver it by ropes down the deepest remaining channel. Now they were in the process of reloading the cargo so they could continue their journey.

Shirtless and sweating, Floyd came to share Colter's shade. He swiped a grimy kerchief across his brow. "We ought to finish in a couple of hours." He spit a stream of tobacco juice into the dry autumn weeds. "Captain says we leave tomorrow right after services."

Colter shifted restlessly. If in fact they were leaving Clarksville tomorrow, attendance at the church services would be mandatory. Churches gave him the willies. All that going-on about hell and sin. For peace and contentment, nothing beat a few hours alone in the woods.

Floyd nudged him. "Town's going all out for the celebration tonight. You ought to see the spread of food and whiskey."

"Join you?" Pryor did not wait for an answer. He flopped next to his cousin. As he did, Colter noticed Rutledge watching him again. "Damn his eyes!" He started to get up, but Floyd grabbed his shoulder. "Rein it in, Colter."

"His starin's drivin' me daft."

"A stare never hurt anyone. Now, cool off before you do something that'll make me keep you away from tonight's doin's."

Colter did as Floyd asked, although he could not relax with Rutledge's galling gaze still on him.

Too soon, Captain Clark clapped his hands. "Up and at it, men. Another hour or two and we're done."

Rising, Floyd glared down the line of men. "Tarnation! Where's that Shannon got to now?"

"Last I saw, he was headed into the bushes," someone offered.

Floyd scowled. "Then he better still be there, or else."

"Something wrong, Sergeant?" Clark said, walking over.

"It's Shannon. sir. He's gone again."

"When you find him, I want to talk with him." The glint in Clark's eyes was the first sign of a redhead's temper. *Peckerwood better watch out,* Colter thought.

Shannon stopped on the porch to catch his breath after the long sprint. The hill up to the Clark cabin was steeper than it appeared from the river.

As his heart rate slowed, he wiped the worst of the mud from the toes of his boots with his kerchief, slapped more mud out of his trousers, tucked in his shirt tail, dusted his hat against the porch railing and smoothed his hair. Then he threw back his shoulders and stepped to the entrance.

The door cracked open in answer to his knock. A pair of brown eyes appraised him through the opening. Their yellowed whites softened the edges of the pupils and gave them a dreamy quality. "Yes, suh?"

"Captain Lewis, please."

The door opened fully to admit him. A black woman of ample proportions led him down a narrow hall, barely wide enough to accommodate her width, to a cramped room at the rear of the house. "Cap'n Lewis? A gent'man here to see you, suh." The woman's voice was as husky as a man's.

"No visitors, Rose. Tell him I . . . Oh, Private Shannon." The captain sat at a narrow table with his quill poised above a piece of parchment. A growl from the captain's feet signalled Seaman's presence.

The pinched expression on the captain's face made Shannon regret his timing. "I-I —"

"Come, come, what is it?" Lewis demanded.

The captain's brusqueness threw him into a panic and the speech he had prepared so carefully dissolved.

"Why aren't you working with the rest of the crew?"

"Work break," Shannon managed to get out.

"Then you had best return." Lewis dipped his quill in the inkpot beside the parchment.

"Captain, I . . . you need an aide." The captain's pen paused in mid-air. Shannon forged ahead. "You have so much to do, so many details to worry about. The President has asked too much of you and Captain Clark. You both need help. Help I can give. I want to be your aide, sir."

Lewis set the quill in the inkpot and squeezed the bridge of his nose. "Captain Clark and I do indeed need an aide. That and much more." He toyed with a corner of the table. "But I am afraid you are too late."

Shannon's heart seemed to stop momentarily. "Sir?"

"We made the decision last night. York will serve as our aide."

"But, but, he's just a nigger."

The captain's palm slammed down on the tabletop. "That he definitely is not, Private. You will never, never say that word again. He is your fellow crewman, and you will treat him as an equal. Do you hear me?"

Shannon swallowed against the lump of disappointment in his throat. His path had been blocked, because of a slave.

"You are an educated young man from an excellent family, Private Shannon, " the captain said. "This expedition needs your enthusiasm, your fresh ideas. I need them."

The words and the hint of softness on the captain's face plunged Shannon immediately into confusion. Was this a test where the captain's "no" really meant "try again"? Or was the captains' choice of York a sign that Lewis doubted his abilities?

With those questions reeling through Shannon's head, Floyd burst into the room. His face was purple with anger. "Shannon! I thought so, you little — Oh, sorry, Captain."

"Is there a problem, Sergeant?" Lewis asked.

"Yes, sir. We were missing the private here. Break was over half an hour ago."

"Then, by all means, both of you need to get back to work. As I must, if the President is to hear about our progress. Oh, and thank you, Private Shannon." The captain returned his attention to drafting the letter.

Shannon trailed the sergeant out of the house. Outside, Floyd clamped onto his arm with a force that made him grimace. "Just what, pray tell, would the captain be thanking you for, Shannon?"

"A suggestion I had, Sergeant."

"Such as?"

Under the sergeant's glare, Shannon decided that telling the truth was the best policy. "That he needed an aide."

"Let me guess: The captain needs an aide, and you're it, right?" The sergeant clasped the front of Shannon's shirt and yanked his face forward until their noses were touching. "You'll be lucky to be in one piece by the time we leave here. You know who sent me to find you?"

The smell of breakfast bacon on the sergeant's breath assaulted Shannon's nose.

"Captain Clark wanted to know where you were. It wasn't hard to guess where you'd gone. I came straight here."

The reek of the sergeant's unwashed body, added to the stench of his breath, made Shannon tilt his head back.

"As of this minute, you're on report."

"Sergeant, I —"

"Oh, so you want to argue, do you?" Floyd tightened his grip on Shannon's collar. "An extra watch ought to take that out of you."

Shannon stifled the arguments that he wanted to hurl at Floyd. He had done nothing wrong. Nothing. He had carried boxes and barrels until his legs were ready to give out from fatigue. He had stood a watch every single night they had been here, plus two on the night they arrived. That he would miss the big farewell celebration was completely unfair.

Floyd shoved him away. "You don't think that's fair, do you, Private? I've got news for you. No one cares what you think. Not Captain Clark. Not me. Certainly not a single one of the crew."

When the sergeant released him, Shannon resisted the urge to straighten his shirt. *Captain Lewis cares*, he thought. *I know he does, and that's all that matters. The rest of you can go hang.*

"Want to quit yet, Private?" Floyd goaded. "Just say the word. Make me a happy man."

Shannon forced all emotion out of his expression and focused his gaze on a blemish on the sergeant's ear lobe. He was not going to quit, no matter what the sergeant did to him. "What word, Sergeant?"

2. *Sendoff*

T hreatening weather forced the citizens of Clarksville to move the expedition's farewell send-off into their church. By the time Colter arrived, the room was already crammed with crewmen eager for some entertainment and townsfolk eager for a break in their normal routine. As with most frontier settlements, women were in short supply and the crewmen had to trade off dancing and flirting with the few available females. Colter did not join in. Instead, he found a place near the back wall to watch.

Even that grew too close for comfort after awhile and he refilled his cup from the barrel of hard cider, grabbed some johnny-cake from the refreshment table and went outside. The night air was heavy with humidity from the afternoon's thundershowers, but it was a welcome change after the din inside the church. He had just downed the cider when someone barrelled into him from behind, sending him sprawling into a mud puddle. Then that someone pounced on top of him.

Hartley was Colter's first and only thought as he fought back savagely, punching and scratching and biting whatever flesh came within range.

"OOOWWW! Damn it all, Colter! You about bit my hand off. Cain't you take a little funnin'?"

The voice was not reedy and it did not belong to Josiah Hartley. "Scratch Wilkes, that you?"

"Durn tootin' it is,"said Wilkes rolling off Colter's back and sucking on the bite. "By Jesus, Colter, them fangs of yours drew blood. That's some fine howdy-do for an old friend."

"Same to you, Wilkes," Colter said, sitting up.

Wilkes looked at him through the darkness, then they both burst out laughing. "Where'd you come from, you mangy old varmint?" Colter asked.

"Was over to Louisville and heard about this here expedition," Wilkes answered. "Thought I'd come check 'er out. Got here around noon and was about to head back when I seen you come outta that church house yonder. What are you doin' here? When I didn't see your ugly face in Louisville by the fifteenth, I figured you got waylaid somewheres."

"I did get waylaid. Someone stole the stake I'd been savin' to join your outfit. That and a couple of other things kept me from leavin' the Draft to get over here in time. Instead, I ended up joinin' this here expedition you came to check out."

Wilkes's huge right hand pounded Colter's shoulder with bruising force. "By God, Colter, that's the smartest damn thing you coulda done. Hell, if I'd'a heard sooner, I'd'a joined! Where you're goin', there's streams ain't never seen a white man, let alone a trap. Hell, with your eyes and your memory, ever' one of my competitors are goin' to be jumpin' outta their worthless skins to sign you on once you get back."

Wilkes's beefy fingers squeezed Colter's upper arm. "Only, them other galoots are goin' to be too late 'cause the minute you get back, you're goin' to be my partner. My full partner. The first one I ever had. And it ain't goin' to cost you so much as a plugged nickel. All you got to do is lead me and our men — how'd you like the sound of that: 'our men'? — lead our men back out to them Shinin' Mountains, show us where them beavers are. What do you say?"

The possibility that being on the Expedition could lead him to fulfilling the dream of a lifetime had never occurred to Colter. Such a proposition coming from Wilkes went beyond extraordinary. The man's tight-fistedness was legendary. So was his reputation for honest dealings.

When he did not answer right away, Wilkes's grip on his arm tightened. "Don't let me down, Colter. I ain't never made such an offer to any man, and I ain't likely to do so again neither. What do you say?"

"I say . . . yes."

Delighted, Wilkes impressed more finger welts on Colter's shoulder. "Well, ain't this my lucky day! This here calls for a drink. Come on down to my boat. I got some fancy French brandy that'll cure what ails ye."

Colter fell in beside Wilkes, scarcely able to believe his good luck after so many months of everything but.

The smell of hard cider and stale sweat from the previous evening's festivities permeated the air of the little church for services the following morning. The crew and the squad of Regulars stood shoulder to shoulder in the center of the room, ringed by those local residents who managed to push their way inside. The rest of the settlement had to stand out in the drizzling chill of the late October day.

Lewis and Clark occupied the front row along with York and the sergeants. Two rows behind them Shannon had an unavoidable view of the back of the slave's head. The sight kept him from concentrating on the service. He had spent the night watch mulling over what he might have done differently in his meeting with Captain Lewis. He had reached the conclusion that his mistake had been too much caution. If he had gone to the captain just one day earlier, he would have been on the front row right now instead of that–that darky.

The longer he looked at York's nappy black hair, the worse he felt. When he could stand it no more, he shifted his gaze and discovered another pair of eyes studying him. They belonged to a comely young woman who, instead of lowering her gaze as proper decorum dictated, gave him a flirtatious smile. He looked away but not before a sharp elbow jabbed his ribs. He grunted and turned red.

The offending elbow belonged to Rube Field whose glower conveyed a proprietary interest in the young woman. Shannon had been the target of Rube's constant harassment since Maysville and he was tired of it. He waited for the man's attention to drift back to the service, then returned the favor of an elbow in the side, catching Rube off balance so that he lurched against his brother Joe who immediately launched a fist at Shannon. Colter stepped in front of the punch, blocking it so it glanced harmlessly off his forearm.

"Outta the way, Colter," Rube whispered.

The disturbance drew Captain Lewis's attention. His glare caused the four to break off.

Outside after the service, Rube grabbed Colter's sleeve. "I ought to deck you, Colter."

"Why? So you can have the midnight watch instead of Peckerwood?"

"That name's demeaning and I won't stand to be called it," Shannon said indignantly.

Colter regarded him with a smirk. "Okay, I'll call you Fuzz, then."

"Why'd you butt in anyway, Colter? This is between me and him," Rube demanded.

"It'll be between you and Sergeant Floyd if'n you don't get away from here now," Colter warned in a dropped voice as the sergeant looked their way.

Floyd's scrutiny changed Rube's mind, and he grudgingly headed down to the keelboat.

"I'll have you know I don't need your help or anyone else's, Old Man," Shannon said. "You don't mind if I call you that, do you? After all, if you call me Fuzz, then I ought to have a name for you, right?"

"What you need is to quit, Shannon," Colter said. "Now, before Rube or somebody else beats you to a pulp. You are 'bout the orneriest son-of-a-hamhock I ever come across. Ornery and ignorant. You don't belong here."

"Ignorant! Why I have more education than this entire crew put together."

"Book-learnin' don't mean squat where we're headin'. It don't help you row or pole or shoot or shiver your way through no blizzard."

"Why, you . . . you . . ." Shannon raised a clenched fist.

"Sure. Go on and hit me. Sarge is just waitin' to bust you outta here."

The threat cooled Shannon off like a bucket of spring water. He dropped his hand at the exact moment the young woman who had started the whole affair came out of the church. One look at her and he took off for the boat before anything else could happen.

Elliott and Rutledge were already on their bench when Colter boarded *Discovery*. Immediately, Elliott ducked his head and traced a warding sign. Tetchy after dealing with Shannon, Colter thrust his face toward Elliott's. "Good to see you, too, Elliott. Here, have yourself a good long look at me."

The man recoiled and fell back against Rube. Rube shoved him away. "Cut it out, Colter. He smells worse'n a dead skunk."

Just then, the captains started down the path to the boat surrounded by an admiring entourage. Captain Lewis cut a dashing figure in spotless white trousers, gleaming kneeboots and an impeccable dark blue jacket with polished brass buttons and loops of gold braid. A woman dressed in a shade of rose that accentuated her porcelain skin clung to his arm. From the woman's adoring glances, the captain had not spent all his time in Clarksville working.

Clark's group of followers was considerably bigger, noisier and less tidy. As usual, the captain's uniform looked rumpled, his hair ribbon did not keep the hair out of his face and his boots were spotted with mud. At his side, General George looked completely sober for once. The effects of years of hard drinking and leading men into battle were evidenced by his stooped back and weather-worn face. Smiling uncertainly at his younger brother, he moved cautiously like a man unused to steady legs, and he blinked frequently as if trying to wake up from a long sleep.

After saying their private goodbyes, Lewis and Clark walked up the gangplank and turned to address the gathering. First Lewis; then Clark.

The remarks dragged on interminably. Colter had had enough of sitting and waiting. He was anxious to get on with things, not sit and listen to a bunch of useless speeches. "Sit still, Colter," came Shannon's irritated whisper. "I can't concentrate with you twitching."

"Then tell 'em to git it over with," he whispered back.

At long last, Clark shouted "Cast off!" The mooring lines were loosened and the gangway removed, then the bottom-polers set their poles and, in unison, shoved the boat away from the landing stage. The gathered throng erupted into wild cheering, punctuated by rifle shots.

The gun shots made Colter flash back to Maysville and Hartley. What had become of the preacher? Had he gone back to the Draft? If so, would Stuart send someone else after him and the evidence?

Floyd's yell of "On the oars, ladies" brought him out of his thoughts. Beside him, Shannon unlocked his oar reluctantly. *If McBain was here, he'd be takin' bets on how much longer Fuzz lasts*, Colter thought.

Thinking of McBain led him to wonder about Quent and Blaze. He hoped that they had not fallen in with the gambler. And that thought led him to consider that he ought to write to Lorenzo and Aunt Dev, tell them about Quent.

With his mind preoccupied, the keelboat swung into the Ohio's main current and soon rounded a jut of woods. Movement among the trees drew Colter's attention. In the shadows a man sat on a horse, watching them.

A chill shot up Colter's spine. The man was Josiah Hartley.

3. *Water Demons*

"**S**hip oars!" Floyd yelled.

Shannon jammed his oar into the lock and slumped forward with an exhausted moan. Colter glanced at the younger man with grudging respect. In the three weeks since leaving Clarksville, Sergeant Floyd had ridden Shannon unmercifully, yet he hung on, showing more tenacity and fortitude than Colter ever imagined he possessed.

"Captain's coming, Peckerwood. Sit up now and beg like a good little dog," Reuben Field whispered just loud enough to benefit the crewmen nearby.

Captain Lewis emerged from the cabin, cutting short the snickers Rube's remark had caused. With obvious effort, Shannon straightened and managed an expectant smile toward the captain. Lewis, however, went on up to the quarterdeck without taking notice, and Shannon fell back into his slouch.

The captain had left the cabin door ajar, allowing Colter a view of Captain Clark's prone shape stretched under blankets on the second berth. York knelt beside the berth, attentive to his master even as he slept. Clark had been ill most of the way down the Ohio. His condition had many of the crew doubting that the expedition would make it as far as St. Louis.

While Colter rubbed at the soreness in his shoulder, the poling detail struggled to move *Discovery* into the eddy above a willow-cloaked point of land. After a pair of crewmen scrambled overboard to tie off the mooring lines, Captain Lewis called the crew to attention. "We have reached the confluence of the Ohio with the Mississippi. Since the current runs against us from this point, we will stop to rest here for a few days."

Lewis waited for the crew's cheering to subside before continuing sternly, "Captain Clark and I are well aware of the reputation of this place. Let me warn you that your conduct here will determine your treatment for the rest of our journey. There is to be no trouble. None. Do I make myself clear?"

The crew's muttered "yeses" were markedly less enthusiastic than the preceding cheers.

"Your sergeants will direct you in unloading the necessary supplies. Once that is accomplished to their satisfaction, you will be granted liberty. Are there any volunteers for sentry duty?"

Only one arm shot up: Shannon's.

Lewis nodded approvingly. "Anyone else?"

No response.

The captain pursed his lips. "In that case, Sergeant Floyd will assign watches."

The captain turned to confer with the sergeant, and Reuben Field whispered, "What is it with you, Peckerwood? You and the captain got somethin' goin'? What goes on behind that there door when you two're together?"

"Yeah, Shannon, what?" Rutledge echoed.

"You can malign me, Rube, but never, never impugn the character of the captain. He is beyond reproach," Shannon hissed.

"Oh, my, would you hear Peckerwood toss around them high-falutin' words!" Rube taunted.

"What's a 'may line'?" Joe asked, feigning ignorance.

Colter frowned over his shoulder at the two brothers whose voices were approaching a level that would carry to the captain. The moment he turned, Elliott recoiled, his stubby fingers tracing the air.

"Elliott, you idiot! Stop that!" Shannon demanded, grabbing the man's hands and forcing them down onto the bench. "That's a birthmark on Colter's face. A birthmark, a blemish. The devil had nothing to do with it. Nothing! Now get that through your thick skull before I beat it in with my oar."

"Leave him be, Peckerwood," said Rutledge. "He's got the right to protect himself from a freak however he sees fit." He spat onto the deck. "'Cause that's what Colter is — a freak. Where I come from, we kill his kind at birth."

Colter was out of sorts after three weeks of putting up with such nonsense. He shot back, "How'd they miss you then, Rutledge?"

"Bet your mama cried the first time she saw you," Rut said. "Bet she wondered what she did to deserve you. Bet other folks thought the same, too."

There was something obscene about the way the word "mama" rolled off the man's tongue. "We ain't talkin' about my ma. We're talkin' about the freaks that didn't get killed back where you come from," Colter said.

"Hit a sore spot, did I?" Rut said.

Elliott flinched. "Rut, watch out! He's liable to put a spell on you."

"Colter won't do anything to me," Rut said. "He don't want to get his buddy Sergeant Floyd in trouble."

Shannon's dropped, studying something intently, as he asked, "One of you drop something?" He pointed. "There, under the bench."

When both Rutledge and Elliott bent over to investigate, Shannon gave a slight nod to Colter who saw his opportunity and took it, slipping the oar out of its lock and drawing the handle back. The oar caught Rutledge on the bridge of the nose with a satisfying *thwack* when he raised up.

Rut's howl brought the two sergeants running. Floyd ordered all the men except Rutledge and Colter off the boat. Then, while Pryor tended to Rutledge, Floyd demanded of Colter. "All right, what was that about?"

"A difference of opinion," Colter said.

"Had to be more than that to get you worked up enough to react."

Now that he had cooled off, the whole incident seemed senseless. What could he say that was not obvious? He had lost control, and that rankled him. Then again, Shannon had stood up for him and seized the initiative to retaliate. That realization combined with the exceptional perseverence the younger man had shown since Maysville caused Colter to revisit his opinion of his benchmate. There might be hope for Shannon yet.

"I can't play favorites so I got to restrict you to camp tonight," Floyd said. "You'll have to stand guard duty along with Shannon. Stay out of trouble, or there'll really be hell to pay with the mood the captain's in. Understand?"

Colter nodded glumly. His act of venegeance had cost him a night's liberty when he was overripe for some carousing after three weeks of rowing. It was also time for another small personal celebration — after three weeks with no sign of Josiah Hartley, he was finally ready to believe that the man had given up and gone back to the Draft.

Floyd went to help Pryor, and Colter watched them tend Rutledge. Since the day Colter had first met Rut, there had been bad blood between them. But it was more than simple disharmony. Colter was convinced that he had run up against Rutledge before. He knew he'd heard his voice before — somewhere significant. But where? That was the question.

◄

The few crewmen who were awake and able to stomach breakfast the next morning reeked of whiskey and women, odors that added to Colter's regrets over missing liberty. The pleasures available at this confluence were the stuff of legend. He had spent his entire watch last night tormented by the sounds drifting down from the sin camps. *Tonight,* he promised himself. *Tonight, I'm makin' up for lost time.*

Captain Lewis left his tent and came to the fire, exuding a purposeful air. "We have a unique opportunity today, men. The chance to launch the diplomatic efforts of our Expedition by visiting a large Shawnee camp across the river." He swung an arm toward the Mississippi. "Who wants to join me?"

Colter kept his eyes focused on the cup of gruel in his hand. Captain could go traipsing off to all the Indian camps he wanted. He was staying put.

"Yes, Private Shannon," Lewis acknowledged Shannon's hand. "Who else?"

Silence.

"You all know that one of the missions of this expedition is to establish trading relationships with the native populations along our route."

Still no hands went up, and Colter felt as well as heard the captain's growing irritation. He held his body still despite the nagging itch in his crotch. He was not about to call attention to himself. He had lost out on women and liquor last night. He was not going to do so tonight.

"Then you leave me no choice," Lewis snapped in frustration. "Colter, Bratton, Newman."

"Hellfire!" Colter muttered under his breath, giving in to the itch, scratching it harder than necessary.

Figuring they had escaped, the crew not picked for the detail relaxed into a buzz. It did not last long. "Since the rest of you are so interested in staying here rather than pursuing the prime goals of this expedition," Lewis said, "all liberties are cancelled. And from now on, each of you will work for your privileges. Sergeants, organize work details. For those in my party, assemble at the boats in full uniforms in fifteen minutes," said the captain, his voice still tight with annoyance.

While the sergeants dealt with the indignant crew, Colter poured the rest of his gruel onto the sand. The idea of Indians always made him lose his appetite. On the way to the keelboat, Shannon fell in beside him. "I can't wait to see how real Indians live. I can't believe our luck! This is the opportunity of a lifetime, Old Man."

Lucky was the last thing Colter felt. "Far as I'm concerned, we oughtta let all them Indians be and get on upriver 'fore winter hits."

"We can't, don't you see? Indians are the key. Just like Captain Lewis said. Imagine the things we can learn from them," Shannon said.

"You mean like scalpin' a man whilst he's still alive? Or carryin' off white women as slaves?"

"You don't believe that claptrap, do you?"

"Call it whatever you want to. Far as I'm concerned, the only good Indian's the one I ain't got to see or smell."

Shannon followed him onto *Discovery*. "But those are lies, Old Man. Deliberate fabrications by men who profit from exploiting the ignorance of men like you."

Colter was in no mood for such a discussion. He turned his back on

Shannon and opened his locker.

"I'm surprised Captain Lewis would pick a man with opinions like yours for his crew," Shannon said.

Colter jammed an arm into his uniform jacket. "Look who's talkin'. You ain't pulled your weight since Maysville. Only thing you're good at's chasin' after the captain like some starvin' dog. That and actin' like you're better'n the rest of us. Don't talk to me about who should be on this crew. If it was a choice between me and you, there ain't no contest. You ain't goin' to last a day once we start up the Mississippi."

"Oh, I'll last all right. And once Captain Lewis promotes me —"

"Promotes you? For what? Makin' every blessed one of us hate you?"

"It's obvious the captains need a junior officer. They are overwhelmed by details and logistics. They need someone who understands proper military procedure. And I'm that man."

Colter banged the locker shut. "You? Hell, you don't even shave yet."

"Scoff all you want, but you'll be reporting to me someday. Someday soon." Shannon turned on his heel and strutted off.

Colter wanted to laugh, but he was too disgruntled over the unpleasant duty ahead of him. He finished dressing, regretting for the hundredth time his promise to the captain to watch out for Shannon. No one could protect someone like him. The sooner the captain realized Shannon was a mistake, the better off they would all be. Maybe this trip across the Mississippi would prove the younger man's undoing. He could always hope.

Shannon walked tall. He was enormously pleased with himself. Although the idea of promotion had been forming in his head since Clarksville, he had not voiced it until his exchange with Colter. Now that the words were out, he intended to make the idea a reality.

Let the other crewmen squeak by with minimal effort. Let them run off to drink and carouse. The captains could always count on George Shannon to volunteer for extra duty and to improve himself at every opportunity — reading the captain's books, seeking his advice, acting as the captains' ears and eyes at Indian councils, recording his observations, learning the finer points of command.

Backward attitudes like those Colter held about Indians had made each day since Clarksville a trial for him. Then again, there was always blessing hidden in tribulation. His enlightened ideas set him above the others and made him the obvious choice for promotion. No one else came close to him in enthusiasm and education.

He understood now the reasoning behind the captains' choice of York as their aide. In the slave, they had someone who could act as a crewman as well as perform the functions of a lackey, seeing to their physical comfort. Such a lowly position did not suit an educated man like himself, a fact the captain had recognized.

The Regulars would be leaving in a few days. With four new recruits added to the expedition since Clarksville and more expected to be waiting at their stops along the Mississippi, the captains would need to modify the structure of the company. A solid junior officer with the education, training and discipline to help them control the crew and get things done would be an indispensable addition to the command structure of the Corps.

In all fairness, he had come onto the crew soft and ill-prepared for the rigors of the journey, and Colter had been correct to point that out. However, he had toughened over the last three weeks. He had the calluses on his hands and new muscles in his arms to prove that.

Even proximity to deep water did not bother him like it used to. Not that his indisposition had ever been anything more than a nuisance. Indeed, he had begun to wonder if it had ever been more than some inconvenient aberration that his newly-earned maturity had overcome.

He retrieved some charred sticks of wood from the fire, tucked them into his pocket, and felt the other pocket to be sure his journal was there, ready for the sketches he planned to make at the Shawnee camp. As far as he knew, no one else on the crew had any artistic ability. He did, and he intended to exploit it as another way to further his cause with the captains.

Spotting a squall line advancing across the river toward the camp, he draped a length of oiled canvas around his shoulders as a way to keep his uniform presentable. Appearances mattered to Captain Lewis.

When he got to the pirogue, Colter was already there along with the other privates, Bratton and Newman. Bratton was nondescript except when he opened his mouth to reveal teeth so worn and spaced that they looked like odd pieces of corn set into his gums. Newman always seemed to be listening to something no one else could hear. In addition, there was the civilian Clement, the beefy Creole river pilot who would guide them across the river.

Captain Lewis arrived with the spring in his step of a man looking forward to his task. He settled into the bow and Clement took the stern. Bratton had the seat behind the captain with Newman behind him, leaving Colter to take the seat in front of Clement and Shannon the next place forward.

As soon as the pirogue moved out of the shelter of the willows, a stiff chill wind bore down on them, driving before it a wall of black clouds. A sudden gust caught the corner of Shannon's hat and peeled it off his head.

He just managed to grab it, but, in doing so, he came face to face with the undeniable fact of the Mississippi River. Its gray-blue surface boiled with foam peaks that rose and fell and rose again like so many hands reaching out to drag him into the water. Wind-driven spray blasted his bare face with the force of hail stones, yet he could not turn his gaze away from the terrifying spectacle of all that moving water, waiting, waiting for its chance at him.

A wave sloshed over the side into his lap. The icy fingers of the water creature clawed at Shannon's uniform. He tried to scream, but the sound lodged like a rusty nail in his throat.

Colter had no love for any Indians, especially Shawnees. Zoob's Shawnee mother had returned to her people after Zoob was born, abandoning her husband and newborne. Zoob had never forgiven her for giving him her looks while robbing him of her love and care. That he looked Indian made Zoob's life hell and turned him into an Indian-hater. Hatred that had rubbed off on Colter.

Colter's mind was occupied with memories of his old partner when Shannon suddenly broke off paddling and sat up, holding his paddle with rigid hands while he stared at the river as one would watch a crouching mountain lion preparing to spring. Colter poked at him with the end of his oar.

Shannon did not respond, so he prodded again.

This time Shannon dropped his paddle and bent forward, resting his head on his knees. Colter gave off in disgust. Pretending to be sick. That was just like Shannon who had used every excuse in the book not to row on the way down the Ohio. Well, his act wouldn't work here. Not in a boat as small as this pirogue. It was high time the captain saw what Shannon was really like instead of how he pretended to be.

The headwind that buffeted them on the crossing was brutal. Colter's shoulders and back were screaming for relief by the time they came within twenty yards of the high tree-lined bluff and steep bank of the western shore.

When the water was just waist-deep, Shannon straightened, took up his paddle and set to rowing as if he had been doing so the entire distance. The pirogue scraped bottom and he bounded into the shallows to help draw it up on the sand with a hearty "Good crossing!"

Colter had other things on his mind than Shannon's miraculous recovery. He had a plan, a way to get out of going up to the Shawnee camp. Shannon wasn't the only one who could volunteer. Soon as the pirogue was tied off, he spoke up. "I'll stay with the boat, Captain."

Lewis was preoccupied with the meeting ahead and agreed quickly. The captain led the rest of the party off to the Shawnee village and left Colter to enjoy the demise of the storm in solitude.

It was late afternoon before the captain and others reappeared. The storm had long since cleared out and Colter had had time to mull over Shannon's strange behavior on the crossing. That pondering had led to a theory, one that the return to camp would either confirm or deny.

He did not have long to wait. The boat was only yards out from the bank when the same thing happened to Shannon. He stopped paddling abruptly and spent the crossing doubled over as if in pain. That is until just before the landing when he resumed rowing. Astonishingly, for the second time, no one but Colter seemed to notice. As soon as the others were out of hearing range, he confronted Shannon. "Are you goin' to tell the captain, or do I have to?"

"Tell him what?"

"How'd you ever think to last it out? You think no one'd notice?"

"I don't know what you're talking about. You're standing in my way when I have important things to discuss with the captain about our meeting with the Shawnees."

"Forget the Indians. You best be tellin' him about your problem instead 'cause if'n you don't, I will."

"The only problem I have is you, Old man. You and your warped imagination."

"My old partner couldn't cross deep water neither. It ain't nothin' to be ashamed of, but you sure don't belong on an expedition that's set to follow the Missouri and who knows what other rivers as far as they go. You freeze up. I seen you. And that could get somebody killed. Either you tell the captain or I'll do 'er for you."

"Why, you spiteful old man!"

"All right then. It's up to me to set things straight."

Inside the captain's tent, Captain Clark lay sprawled on a cot, snoring, one arm thrown across his forehead. Captain Lewis motioned for Colter to keep his voice down. "Yes, Private?"

"It's Shannon, sir. He's got a problem. He's afraid of water."

The captain's eyes narrowed. "What gives you that idea?"

"Soon as we got out on the river, he froze up and didn't move again 'til we was comin' into shore. Happened goin' and comin'."

Lewis watched him but did not speak. Colter went on. "It's somethin' I seen before. My old trappin' partner wouldn't go near water deeper'n his waist."

There was an edge to the captain's voice when he finally spoke. "Private Shannon has been with this expedition for over a month now. He has been on the river every day of that time, sharing a bench with you, Colter. If your theory is true, how do you explain that he has never exhibited before the behavior you describe?"

Colter had no explanation. He just knew what he knew.

"Private Shannon is not the kind of man to withhold such vital information from his superiors." The captain stood up, a sign that the conversation was over.

Colter refused to give up. "Shannon's got him book-smarts, but he ain't got a lick of sense. Sergeant Floyd has to ride him every durned minute 'bout somethin'."

The captain looked down his nose at Colter. "In Maysville I asked you to take Shannon under your wing, to shore up his lack of practical experience. You gave me your word you would take on that responsibility. Is this how you keep your promise? With far-fetched tales?"

"Shannon don't belong, Captain," Colter said, his voice rising.

"He's a member of this crew, and he will remain so. Answer my question," Lewis demanded.

"If he stays, then I go."

"You are a member of this crew, Private. The only way you will leave is with a court-martial."

Colter knew better than to voice the retort that rose to his lips. A heavy silence settled between them. When the captain spoke, his tone had lost some of its hardness. "What do you want, Colter? Why are you here?"

Colter gave his anger a moment to cool before he answered. "I want to make Farley Stuart pay for stealin' my land. That's why I joined. That's why I'm here."

"Are you sure there's no other reason behind your decision to enlist?"

Since Scratch Wilkes's offer had come to him after he joined the expedition, he did not have to lie. "No, sir."

"Back in Maysville, you entrusted me with something important to you — the things that prove Farley Stuart's crime. I returned the favor by entrusting to you something important to me — Shannon. I ask you again: Can I count on you to watch out for him?"

Colter stared at the captain, this man who had believed him about Stuart and Hartley and who had countered the preacher's attempts to capture him at Maysville. Joining Lewis and the expedition had begun as a way to escape Farley Stuart's long reach and, thanks to Scratch Wilkes, it was now the road to fulfilling the dream he had thought was lost. That dream came with a cost: to continue shepherding Shannon. It wasn't the arrangement he would have chosen, but it was what he had to work with. He swallowed hard. "Yes, sir."

"Very well then." Lewis nodded him out of the tent.

Sergeant Floyd broke away from the group at the fire and came to Colter as soon as he stepped outside. "With Captain Clark still sick, we'll be here a few more days. I need someone to go out hunting tomorrow. Know anyone might like the job?"

"Would I have to drag Fuzz along?" Colter answered bitterly.

Floyd shot a glance at the captains' tent. "Something happen in there I ought to know about?"

Colter related what had happened on the river crossing and his conclusions about Shannon.

"I take it you told Captain Lewis," said Floyd.

"Yeah, for all the good it did."

Floyd shook his head. "Smart as the captain is, he has a big blind spot when it comes to Shannon."

"That don't help me none, Sarge. Fuzz's an anchor 'round my ankles. One that's gettin' heavier ever' damn day."

"Would getting off by yourself help any? A day of hunting, say?"

"That's better'n nothin', I guess. Okay, I'll do 'er."

After Floyd returned to the fire, Colter decided to work on his carving, hoping that would soothe away his edginess. He opened his pack and knew from the disorder that someone had been at his things. He dragged out every item and took inventory. That nothing was missing gave him small comfort. Who had been rifling his things and why? Two questions and no answers.

⬩

Shannon furtively observed the exchange between Colter and Captain Lewis through the open flap of the captains' tent while pretending to be engrossed in polishing his boots. *Discovery* was a substantial boat, big enough that he had been able to ignore the fact of the deep water he was floating on. A month aboard had convinced him that he was no longer af-flicted by a fear of deep water. Then today the wall of that denial came crashing down. He had been so shaken by crossing the Mississippi to the Shawnee encampment that half the meeting with the Indians was over be-fore he could lift up out of his fear enough to pay attention. Then it took every ounce of strength to step back into the pirogue for the return trip to camp.

Of course Colter noticed his problem. How could he not when Shannon had been sitting right in front of him? Now Colter was in telling Captain Lewis and all he could do was wait in silent agony for the nullification of all his hard work and sacrifice, for the termination of his tenure with the expedition. His spirit wilted at the prospect of the public humiliation he was about to face.

He needed to think about tomorrow, to plan what he would do and where he would go after he was discharged in disgrace. He needed to, but his mind would not go beyond the mortifying moment when he had to own up to his failure and hear the captain dismiss him from the Corps.

Abruptly the pair broke off their conversation and Colter left the tent, his mouth drawn into a tight angry line. Sergeant Floyd hurried over to Colter and those two conversed before breaking apart, Floyd going back to the fire and Colter to his pack.

Shannon looked anxiously toward the captains' tent, expecting at any moment to see Captain Lewis coming his way.

A minute passed. Then two. No captain.

He did not know what to think. Should he continue to wait for the ax to fall or should he go straight to Captain Lewis and launch a defense of him-self?

While he weighed the two options, one question nagged at him: What was taking the captain so long?

As time passed, his anxiety subsided, replaced by a faint but growing hope that either the captain did not believe Colter or that he viewed any af-fliction of Shannon's to be outweighed by his persistence and potential. By the time full darkness had set in, hope had grown into conviction that he was too valuable to the captain to be let go.

Assured, he pulled on his boots and got to his feet, drawing a sour stare from Colter who had moved to the fire. Shannon met the man's frown with his head held high. He had nothing to be ashamed of and nothing to fear. George Shannon was soon to be *Lieutenant* George Shannon, a force to be reckoned with.

4. *Longings*

Whatever enjoyment hunting might have brought Colter the next day was marred by lingering bitterness over the captain's reaction to his reporting of Shannon's problem. Sergeant Floyd was right. The captain had a blind spot when it came to Shannon. A blind spot that could lead to tragedy.

He made it back to camp after dusk with a brace of possums and an assortment of turkeys and quail. He arrived late, too weary to do more than wolf down some stew and roll into his blanket.

The next morning he crawled out primed for visiting one of the nearby pleasure camps now that the captain's pique had passed and the restrictions on the crew had been lifted. Yawning and stretching as he wandered to the fire, he did not immediately notice the black eyes, bruises and split lips on the few crewmen already gathered there.

One of them, Newman, sported a muslin bandage around his head and his eye was swollen shut. "'T'ain't fair, by gum! They started the fight, but we have to pay for it. We been workin' hard. Ain't right to spoil our fun."

Colter nudged Rube Field. "What happened?"

"Big fight last night. Crew's restricted to camp again," Rube answered.

"Don't joke like that, Rube," Colter said, now fully awake. "Tonight's my first chance at some fun."

"Ain't no joke, Colter," Newman said in a brogue that thickened whenever he got angry. "Captain said blame's ours because we're soldiers. Like that's supposed to stop me from defendin' what's mine when some galoot tries to horn in? He could've waited his turn. I'd have been done with her soon enough." He ripped a string of meat from a deer rib with his yellowed teeth.

Colter's stomach went hollow. Last night's dream had left his loins aching. He could go months without bedding a woman, but when the need came on him, it hounded him until he satisfied it. Here he was at the confluence of the Ohio, a place famous for the amount and variety of sinning a man could indulge in, and suddenly that meal had been whisked away before he could even pick up a fork.

"Weren't much of a fight," Newman muttered on. "The Fields and me, we made short work of them buzzards. Once it was over, that gal dragged me back to her cot. Ripe as a blackberry in the sun, she was. Me, too. But I didn't even get my pants unhitched before Sarge come bustin' in there. Now we cain't go back tonight, and that's wrong."

"That fight was over too quick," Rube said. "Sarge got there way too fast. Somebody snitched on us."

Newman flung the gnawed rib into the dirt. "York. That's who. He spies for the captains. I know it."

After three weeks of rowing on the bench directly outside the captains' cabin, Colter found the accusation ludicrous. Either York was rowing, or he was with Captain Clark. And Clark had been so sick the last week that the black man rarely left his side. How could York have known about the brawl? "No way. Ain't York," Colter said flatly.

Newman's brow beetled. "Oh, it's him all right."

"York's been nursin' Captain Clark. He ain't been out of that cabin to do more'n piss since we got here," Colter said.

Newman's face hardened into fighting lines. "I say it was York."

"Then you say wrong, Newman."

The man's vacuous blue eyes snapped into rare focus. "Then who else could'a told the sergeant?"

"You're forgettin' we was drunk, New. Drunk and rowdy," Joe Field said. "A deaf man could've found us as much noise as we was makin'."

Colter nodded, agreeing with the younger Field's explanation, but Newman's expression said the subject of York's guilt was not about to be dropped.

Colter did not have long to nurse his frustration. After breakfast, Sergeant Floyd assigned him to lead a hunting detail composed of Newman and the Field brothers. Although he did not cotton to leading others, he welcomed the chance to get away from the sullen anger that hung over the camp, the result of the crew's second restriction. Floyd's parting words to him were, "Whatever you do, stay out of trouble. I got enough to handle already."

Colter struck out north at a fast pace, feeling better for the exercise and fresh air. He led the way north until he began to see tracks of game, then he turned toward the river. By the time he came in sight of the Mississippi, the other three crewmen had fallen far behind. He stopped to gnaw on some deer jerky and wait for them to catch up.

A scowling Newman arrived last. "Where's the durned fire, Colter?" He broke off in a wolf howl. "By God, would you lookie there? We done struck gold, boys."

South of where they were standing, mud and debris had dammed off a secondary river channel, creating a bridge of land to a narrow island. On the island stood a pair of grimy tents. A line strung between two trees was draped with frilly, though dingy, female undergarments. Colter had led them straight to a sin camp.

Rube slapped him on the back. "Why, Colter, you old snake! No wonder you were so het up to get here."

Colter was torn between his loyalty to the sergeant and his unresolved physical needs. On the one hand, he did not want to cause Floyd any more grief than the man already had. On the other, he had twice been denied the experience of the sin camps. Wasn't he due some fun, too?

"What're you waitin' for, Colter? Lead on," Newman urged.

"This ain't what we come to do," he responded halfheartedly.

"Sure it is," Joe said. "It's just a different kind of huntin'."

"Durn right, Little Brother," Rube agreed. "Huntin' — that's just what it is."

"We can say we didn't find no game. The other kind, I mean," Newman said with a sly chuckle.

"Yeah, all we got to do is stick together and won't nobody find out what we did," Rube chorused.

The more the others talked up the idea, the less Colter liked it. Sinning was one thing. Lying about it, another, especially lying to someone who trusted him. "I'll know."

"Then you go off by yourself," Rube said. "We've found what we were after. Ain't that right, you two?"

"I cain't do that, Rube. I cain't lie to Sarge," Colter said.

Ever the peacemaker, Joe Field chimed in. "Won't be no lie. All you got to do is say you and us got separated. Which is the truth, as far as it goes."

The other two agreed and, without waiting for Colter's response, the trio took off for the tents.

"I ain't no good at lyin'," Colter said to their retreating backs.

Newman craned over his shoulder. "You better be, 'cause if we get caught, we'll know it's you and not that darkie tellin' tales out of school."

Colter bit back a snappish response. He was annoyed that he had been put in this position. Equally put out that his conscience and sense of loyalty would not allow him to go along with the others and take care of his needs. "Damn it all!" he said, heading off northward alone.

Over the next several hours, he followed half a dozen game trails only to have them peter out without leading to quarry. The farther he went from the area of the confluence, the heavier the brush and the more difficult it was to make headway.

Midafternoon, fast-moving clouds obliterated the sun and the temperature plummeted. Soon a cold rain began to fall. Still he pressed onward, unwilling to return to camp empty-handed.

Within an hour, the rain turned to sleet. He tramped another mile without shouldering his rifle, then gave up and turned back south. He was not far from the island and its tents when he stopped to drink out of a stream. He was raising a cupped hand to his mouth when he spotted something moving in the trees up the creek. Certain it was game, he forgot his thirst and crept into cover behind the exposed root ball of a fallen tree. He primed his rifle with fresh powder before chancing a peek out.

Beyond his place of cover, the ground sloped to a marshy depression. In the center of the hollow knelt York. Surprised, Colter drew back. What was the slave doing out here so far from camp? Was Newman right? Were the captains using York to spy on the crew? If so, his instincts about the black man were wrong, and he had long ago learned that his intuition was rarely, rarely in error.

Unwilling to concede that he might be wrong, Colter decided to stay where he was and find out what York was up to. The slave was crawling along on hands and knees as if searching for something he had dropped. The fabric of his shirt had split open along one shoulder from the strain of his muscular build. The cold breeze carried his low muttering to Colter's hiding place.

Abruptly the man stopped moving, plunged his huge hands into the wet soil, and yanked something up. Sitting back on his heels, he smiled triumphantly at the darkish man-shaped root he held up before his face. "There you are, you little rascal! I knew I'd find you."

Mandrake. Colter recognized it from the times he had hunted medicinal plants with his mother. So that was what York had been after: a plant to make medicine to help Captain Clark recover from the affliction that had kept him abed most of the last month.

Colter considered revealing himself to the black man, then decided that would serve no purpose. He knew the truth now. His gut had led him right. And he would set Newman straight about York when that time came.

Shannon huddled deeper into his blanket, trying without much success to concentrate on Captain Lewis's botany book. The problem was the other crewmen and the stories they were telling — stories about the harlots they had visited before the captains put the pleasure camps off-limits. The men's lurid descriptions painted images in his mind that made him both uncomfortable and curious. How much of the scandulous tales were true? Would women really stoop to the debauchery attributed to them? What would it be like to experience such licentiousness, to indulge one's basest physical whims?

He pulled his thoughts back from this last question as too dangerous to contemplate and shifted his position in an effort to shut out the voices and the stories. That was when he saw Newman and the two Field brothers stroll into camp. They had been sent out to hunt, but here they came with no game, sporting the smirks of men who had been up to no good. He was close enough to hear the three tell the two sergeants that they had become separated from Colter and had wandered around lost most of the day before finding their way back to the camp. It was clear as daylight to Shannon that the trio had been doing a lot more than wandering around, but Floyd did not question their story. He waved them off and went back to working on his log book.

As the three went to join the other crewmen around the fire, they passed Shannon. The odor coming off of them confirmed his surmise. They all three reeked of cheap whiskey and women. Either Sergeant Floyd did not care or he was too lazy to punish them for disobeying captain's order. Whatever the reason, the sergeant was undermining the captains' authority which was precisely why the captains needed a junior officer. When George Shannon was lieutenant, no one — private or sergeant — would get away with flaunting orders. No one.

Shannon was preoccupied with how to present what he had just witnessed to Captain Lewis when Colter plodded into camp. He, too, showed up with no game. He, too, told the sergeant he had gotten separated from the others. *How convenient*, Shannon thought cynically, taking note of the looks that passed among Rube and Joe and Newman.

As Colter walked by Shannon on the way to the fire, their gazes locked. "No luck?" Shannon asked, pouring as much sarcasm into the question as he could muster.

"Not a blamed critter anywhere," Colter answered.

"Shannon!" Floyd's yell prevented Shannon from further conversation. He laid the botany book aside and went to find out what the sergeant wanted. The sergeant's smile did not reach beyond his mouth. "Newman's sick. You get midnight watch. Enjoy it."

Floyd's mocking tone prompted a bitter retort to rise to Shannon's lips. He bit it back but barely. Newman was drunk, *not* sick. If anyone was sick, it was him. Sick of standing midnight watches because some lazy, incompetent sergeant had it in for him. He added another mark next to the long string of negative marks next to Floyd's name on his mental check list, and saluted, "Yes, Sergeant. Thank you, Sergeant."

The energy behind his response caused Floyd's mocking smile to slip. Shannon turned away so he would not be tempted to laugh with satisfaction over scoring a small victory in his war with the man. Sergeant Floyd might think he had power, but just wait. A new day was coming. A day of reckoning for everyone who had tormented George Shannon.

5. *A Face for a Snake*

T he camp was dark, the crew slumbering when Colter awoke with a full bladder. The earlier sleet had subsided, but clouds masked the sky, promising a reprise, perhaps even snow, come dawn. Reluctantly he unwound from his blanket and pulled on his boots. Shivering in the cold, he headed toward the bushes at the rear of the camp, picking his way around the blanket-shrouded forms of the sleeping crewmen.

After five days at the Ohio-Mississippi confluence, they would break camp in the morning and the Expedition would start the long pull up the Mississippi to St. Louis while the Regulars would head south to their new assignments. For the first time since Maysville, Colter would be free of the irritation of Rutledge and Elliott. That thought made him yawn luxuriously.

His approach startled the perimeter sentry. "It's me, Newman. Colter," he whispered.

"In that case I might shoot you anyway. I ought to shoot you and Newman both for what you pulled today."

The voice belonged to Shannon, reminding Colter that Newman had claimed illness to get out of midnight watch. "You best let me pass 'fore I piss on them nice boots of yours."

"Piss on your own boots," Shannon said, turning back to continue pacing the camp perimeter.

Colter waded into the brush, unbuttoned his trousers and did his business while musing about the rude awakening Shannon was in for when they got on the Mississippi. Rowing with the current was one thing. Pulling against it, bent under a *cordelle* with the considerable weight of *Discovery* and all the expedition's supplies attached to the other end, was quite another. Shannon had made it this far by pluck. He would need a lot more than gumption to tackle the Mississippi's current head-on. Floyd had said again and again, "He won't last," and now that might just happen.

Yawning again, Colter tucked himself back into his trousers and did up the buttons. He was turning toward camp when something heavy and hard crashed down on his head. He heard himself grunt, felt his legs buckle, felt his body topple into the dirt, then . . . nothing.

Something cold and wet flooded onto Colter's face and a voice hissed, "Damn you, Colter! Open your eyes. I want you to see what you've cost me."

Colter's closed lids would not lift, and his sluggish memory would not supply a name to go with the angry, demanding voice.

"By now I should be a rich man. But you, you kept me from getting back in time for the wedding. I didn't work this long and this hard to lose. Time for you to pay what you owe me."

A slap stung Colter's cheek and he struggled to open one eye a slit. He lay on his belly on the damp ground. All he could see of the person speaking was a pair of worn boots. When he tilted his head to see the man's face, he discovered that his neck was encircled by a rope that ran down his back to his ankles, binding them in such a way that moving his legs at all tightened the rope round his neck.

A worn boot pushed him onto his side, and Colter found himself looking up at Josiah Hartley.

"Even if you handed that Bible over now, Colter, it wouldn't be enough. Not after what I've been through chasing you down." Hartley got a piece of stropping leather out of his saddlebags, and, tying one end of the strap to his horse's stirrup ring, proceeded to sharpen his knife. "What, no questions? Don't you want to know what I'm going to do to you?"

Colter was not aware that another person was in the clearing until one spoke up. "Come on, Hartley. I got to get on my way. I done my job. Now where's my money?" It was Rutledge.

"After I lift his face," Hartley answered, working the blade of his knife against the leather. "That's right, Colter. Stuart's going to get your face as a souvenir of this goosechase you led me on."

Hearing what the preacher intended, knowing that that snake Farley wanted the skin from his face as proof of his demise, jarred Colter's memory—now he remembered where he had heard Rut's voice before. And he knew he'd better put that memory to good use now. "Heard you got robbed back in Maysville, Preacher."

"Attacked. Not just robbed. If I hadn't fought back, they would have cleaned me out and probably killed me. As it was, they took half my money and half my ear." His hand went to what remained of his left ear. "If I ever catch those two, I'll teach 'em a lesson."

"You don't have to chase 'em, Preacher. One of 'em's right over there," Colter said, cocking his chin at Rutledge.

Hartley's stropping hand stopped, and he darted a glance toward Rutledge.

"Nice try, Colter, but you're wastin' your breath. Come on, Hartley. We had a deal. Now pay up," Rutledge demanded.

Colter pressed on. "The last night we was in Maysville, I overheard two soldiers talkin' about how some man was willin' to pay big money to the ones what found me. Only, they reckoned lookin' for me was too hard. Instead of earnin' the money, they decided to just take it."

Hartley dropped the strop and tested the edge of the knife against his thumb, drawing blood.

Colter decided to put some heat on Rutledge. "So you wasn't satisfied with half the preacher's money, huh, Rut? Came back for the rest, did you? How about his ear? You plannin' on takin' the right one this time?"

"The money, Hartley," Rutledge growled.

"When I'm done," Hartley warned.

"Now!" Rutledge said, taking a menacing step toward the preacher.

Hartley pointed the knife at Rut. "That's far enough."

Rut lunged for the preacher and the two began to grapple.

With the two men engaged elsewhere, Colter realized he'd better try to escape while he could. He squirmed into a roll, heaving onto his side, his back, his other side, then his front, slowly and painfully maneuvering himself toward the cover of the deep brush. Fighting for air over the choking ropes, he registered the sounds of the struggle going on behind him.

There was a loud grunt just as he rolled onto the side where he could see the clearing. In that moment he saw Rutledge wrestle the knife out of the preacher's hand. A shaft of moonlight through the ragged clouds glinted off the sharpened blade as it plunged into Hartley's chest. The preacher shrieked with pain, the sound setting off a paroxysm of replies from the waterbirds.

The sound propelled Colter onto his feet. He tried to mince along but the rope binding his ankles proved too tight and he tumbled into a patch of nettles.

*

"Halt! Who goes there?" Shannon's jittery hands tightened on his rifle while his ears strained for the sound that had jolted him out of his daydream. *A sentry who failed to remain vigilant deserved the ultimate punishment.* How many times had he heard Father say that? Yet here he was, guilty as a raw recruit of woolgathering on watch.

There. There it was again. A low moan. Was it an animal? Or was it Indians?

Indecision gripped him. Should he leave his post to identify the source of the sound, or give the warning, or wait to be sure he was not imagining things?

He decided to investigate. As he tiptoed into the undergrowth, his mind was so alive with the stories he had heard about Indian attacks that he stumbled over a body on the ground. "Colter?"

The name drew a groan and Shannon squatted down to see what was wrong. There was a rope around Colter's neck. It had rubbed the skin raw. Closer examination revealed the reason: the other end of the rope bound his ankles, trussing him like a turkey ready for the spit.

The discovery thrust Shannon into dilemma. He remembered letting Colter pass, but he did not recall seeing him return to camp. Since Colter was not one to sit quietly while someone tied him up, there had to have been a struggle, and a struggle meant noise. Noise that he, the sentry, should have heard — if he had been alert. Only, he had heard nothing which could only mean he had been lost in his imaginings instead of paying attention.

Colter's weak "Help" broke through his ambivalence. "Sergeant!"

Floyd was out of his blankets and running to Shannon in the space of a breath.

"It's Colter, Sergeant. He's been hurt."

Floyd cut Colter free of the rope. "What happened, John?"

Colter answered in a strained voice. "Hartley's here. Rut's in with him. I come out to pee, and Rut jumped me." A shudder coursed through his body. "Hartley was goin' to skin my face. Only him and Rut got into it 'fore he could do it."

While Colter talked, Shannon's nose picked up the strong smell of liquor coming off the man and all his indecision vanished. Colter was faking! Just like Newman and the Fields brothers had done earlier. Worse, the sergeant was buying his phony story.

Colter struggled on. "Rut stabbed him. That was the last thing I saw."

"Sergeant, I —"

Lieutenant Lavendar, leader of the Regulars, arrived on the scene, interrupting Shannon. "Did I hear you say 'Rut,' Colter? Do you mean my man Rutledge?"

Colter coughed a "yes."

"That can't be. My entire unit is sleeping down on the beach so we can be ready to leave at dawn as planned. I'd know if anyone left. No one has." He turned to Floyd. "This man smells of rum, Sergeant. He's obviously lying to cover up a trip to the off-limits camps. I trust you will punish him accordingly."

Floyd ignored the allegations and the challenge. "Where's Rutledge? I want to see him."

It was less a question than an order, and while Lavendar went to get his charge, Shannon made another mental note to reprimand Floyd for showing such a lack of respect to a commissioned officer.

Meanwhile Floyd peppered Colter with questions. Was he sure it was Rutledge who attacked him? Sure that it was Hartley? Where did the attack happen? When? How did he manage to get away with his body trussed up the way it was?

Shannon noted that he never once questioned Colter about drinking. Before he could point out that failing, Floyd turned the questioning on him. "All right, Shannon, you were sentry. What did you see and hear?"

Shannon was ready. "I saw and heard nothing, Sergeant, for the simple reason that there was no attack. There is, however, an off-limits camp about three miles that way and probably a dozen more beyond that. Why, you can smell the rum on Colter from ten paces." He lowered his voice. "Frankly, Sergeant, your favoritism toward this man is getting in the way of your judgment."

The reappearance of Lavendar leading Rutledge and Elliott squelched Floyd's response. "As you can see, Sergeant," Lavendar said. "Private Rutledge was where I said he was. Which means your man here is lying to cover up his disobedience."

Colter raised up on one elbow with difficulty. "What you're smellin' is the rum Hartley threw in my face to bring me around after Rut there knocked me out."

Elliott stepped forward. "No way, Lieutenant. Rut's been asleep next to me all night. I'd know if he moved."

A jagged streak of lightning split the gathering clouds, followed by a loud crack of thunder. Floyd had to shout to make himself heard. "This is one for the captains. We'll get to the bottom of it in the morning when there's some light to see what we're doing. Meantime I'm taking Colter and Rutledge into custody."

The lieutenant stepped in front of Rutledge, turning aside the sergeant. "You'll do no such thing. I am completely satisfied that Rutledge is not involved in this matter except as part of your private's vivid imagination. We leave at dawn. What you do with Colter is your business. Yours and the captains'."

"I ain't no liar!" Colter insisted. "There's a dead body out there'll prove me right."

"That I doubt. Good night, Sergeant," Lavendar said, pivoting on his boot heel and leading Elliott and Rutledge back to the beach.

"Why, you pompous donkey's rear," Floyd said in an undertone in the direction of the lieutenant. "I'm going to fetch that body back here and see you eat your words."

"Sergeant!" Shannon exclaimed. "You have no call to say such a thing about Lieutenant Lavendar. Don't make any more mistakes than you already have."

Floyd whirled on Shannon. "And *you'd* better be ready to explain to the captains why you didn't see or hear the ones that attacked Colter. I can't wait to hear that little tale, Private. Ought to be worth enough laughs to make worthwhile all the grief I've had to put up with since Captain Lewis took you on as his pet project. Only, no one can pull you out this time, Shannon. Not even the captain can overlook something as serious as dereliction of duty. I can't wait to see your court-martial."

Shannon stood his ground in the face of the sergeant's threats. "Then you'll wait a long, long time, Sergeant."

"Not long, Shannon. A couple of hours. Now get back to your post."

With his guts roiling under a load of doubt and dread about facing the captain when he knew he had been in the wrong, Shannon executed a proper about-face and marched away from the sergeant and Colter. He managed to maintain a ramrod posture until Floyd had pulled Colter up on his feet and supported him back to the center of camp. Then panic seized him and would not let go. Colter's ropes and bruises were real. He could not deny that fact, could not deny that he had heard nothing, that he had been fantasizing instead of keeping watch. But he also could not admit to daydreaming while on duty. Such an admission would bring an immediate end to all his dreams and everything he had struggled for.

But how did he explain? He needed a story, and he needed on fast.

"You're sure this was the place?" Floyd's expression begged Colter to say it wasn't.

"This is it, all right." Colter knelt as if to examine the ground for blood when he knew there was nothing to see — no blood or drag marks or foot-prints. The two of them had been searching since dawn without finding Hartley's body or any sign of him. Then there was the question of Rutledge. Why would he return to camp? Why not just take off? With the kind of money the preacher was rumored to have, compliments of Farley Stuart, Rut could live high for a long time. Sticking with the Regulars made no sense.

Colter got back to his feet and thrust his hands into his pockets in frustration. "I weren't dreamin'. Rutledge knifed the preacher. I heard the screams. This here's where it happened. So why ain't we seein' some sign?"

Floyd scanned the clearing, hands on his hips, his lips pursed in uncertainty. "Whatever happened, all we have is your story, another story from Rutledge and Elliott, a length of rope, that welt on your neck and a sentry who claims he never heard or saw anything." He heaved a stone into the river. "There's nothing here. We might as well give up."

"What'll you tell Captain Lewis?" asked Colter.

"I'll tell him what I found, which is nothing. No harm done. He's got more important things to worry about." He shifted his weight and gave Colter a sidelong glance. "I doubt you'll have to worry about that preacher again."

"You believe me then?"

"Of course I do. A man like you doesn't make up stories, especially ones about a man I know for a fact is following us. I know, too, you aren't a killer. Can't say the same about Rutledge."

He toed the dirt. "What I don't understand is Shannon's part in all this. Either he was mixed up with Rutledge and Hartley, or he was asleep at his post. The kind of scuffle you're talking about would make plenty of racket."

"Weren't much Fuzz coulda done against Rut," Colter said.

"Are you defending him?" Floyd demanded.

"Shannon ain't the problem here, Sarge. I am. It's my story against Rut's, and mine ain't worth a tinker's dam without the preacher."

"You're right. Shannon is one subject always makes me forget what's important. We better get back before they take off on us."

"Leavin' me behind might be the best thing," Colter said.

"Oh, no. You're one man we can't do without."

"That's what you think."

"That's what I know. Now come on. We got us an expedition to do."

Colter looked around the clearing one last time, hoping to see something he had missed before. He had seen Rutledge bury the knife into Hartley's chest. Either the preacher was dead or badly wounded which meant he had to be here somehere. But where?

6. *Fort Kaskaskia*

T o Shannon's immense relief, Colter and Floyd returned from their search empty-handed. Less than an hour later the expedition struck out from the confluence without another word from the captains about the purported attack.

Shannon's relief did not last long. The next nine days turned out to be the worst he had ever lived through. Instead of rowing, he and the other crewmen spent their days bent under the chafing *cordelle* rope, slogging through the ankle-deep mud of the river shallows pulling *Discovery* and her heavy load up the Mississippi. Sergeant Floyd aggravated his misery with a constant barrage of criticism and murmured insinuations that Shannon had abetted Colter's attackers.

The charge was preposterous, yet he had to live with the knowledge that someone had set upon Colter, had tied him up in a way that could have strangled him and he, the sentry, had heard nothing, had seen nothing when *that was his duty*. That awareness weighed like a two-ton boulder on his shoulders.

The ninth day after leaving the Ohio confluence, the expedition reached Fort Kaskaskia. Few of the crew had the energy to cheer the sight of the fort's imposing palisade wall sprawled across a promontory above the river. The men, Shannon included, sagged onto the half-frozen ground while Captain Clark and Sergeaant Pryor hurried up the trail to the fort to search out Captain Lewis. Lewis had gone ahead of the expedition a few days earlier to qualify additional recruits, a move necessitated by the number of potential candidates who had failed to pass muster at their previous stops.

Reuben Field sniffed the air. "I can smell 'em, Little Brother. Women. They be close, and I be ready."

Whores were all the other men talked about, and Shannon was sick to death of listening. It was time for them to quit acting like rakehells and start acting like soldiers. "No doubt they can smell you, too, Rube," Shannon jabbed. "A week-dead goat smells better."

"Least my pecker's hard which is more than I can say for yours. Where women are concerned, that is," Rube shot back.

Shannon refused a retort. Arguing with Rube was a losing proposition, especially when it came to slinging filthy innuendos.

"What's wrong, Peckerwood? Did I hit a nerve?" Rube needled.

Floyd's "Attention!" intruded on the exchange. Shannon got wearily to his feet.

"Listen up," Floyd bellowed. "We stop here for three days. Captain Clark ordered an extra ration of rum as a reward for your hard work. Collect it at the fort in one hour." He waited for the buzz to ripple through the tired crew, then continued in a sterner tone. "You are all restricted to the fort and the boat. Every place else is off-limits. *Every* place."

Shannon listened to the crew's grumbling with detachment. Extra liquor and restriction. Neither mattered a speck to him. The physical hardship expected of the enlisted crew was wreaking havoc on his body and spirit. He could not wait any longer. He had to press his case for promotion. Soon.

Floyd dismissed the men and Shannon went to get his journal to take up to the fort. He had just propped open the cover of the locker when angry voices drew his attention to the beach where Newman and Colter were arguing.

"It's that black son-of-a-bitch's fault we cain't have no fun while we're here," Newman groused. "And we mean to make him pay for spyin' on us for the captains."

"You and Rube and them others picked the fight with them flatboaters down at the confluence," Colter shot back. "Was your doin' that forced the captain to do what he done. Weren't York's."

Newman thrust his flushed face toward Colter. "What makes you so damned sure of that darky, Colter?"

"I'm sure 'cause I'm sure. Now get outta my way."

Newman gave Colter a shove. "I'll move when you talk."

"It ain't York. Now move!"

Newman's second shove caused Colter to trip over a coil of rope and sprawl into the mud at the edge of the river. He came up swinging, but Floyd and Pryor appeared from nowhere to pull the two men apart. Floyd slapped Colter with a three-day restriction to the boat and Newman with three days in the fort's holding cell.

After Pryor hauled Newman away, Floyd turned on Colter. "Jesus H. Christ, Colter. What's going on with you? We haven't been here ten minutes, and already you and Newman get into it. You've been at each other's throats for a week now. And it's got to stop."

Colter looked genuinely sheepish. "Sorry, Sarge. I know better than to let him get to me like that."

The apology took some of the edge off the sergeant's anger. He threw his hands into the air. "For God's sake, I rely on you to keep a level head. Shannon gives me enough trouble. Until he quits, I don't need any more trouble from you." With that, he stomped off toward the fort.

Shannon rose from behind his locker. Colter saw him and said, "So now you're snoopin' too, huh, Fuzz?"

"I was getting things out of my locker. I can't help it if I overheard your little set-to." He let the lid of the locker bang shut to emphasize his disapproval. "It surprises me that you would defend a slave. York's a piece of property. Not a man."

"He's as much a man as you are. Maybe more. And I'll stand by any man, black or white or green even, who ain't done what someone else claims. He no more spied on the crew than I did, and you know it."

The words caused a muddle of random thoughts to snap into a fully-formed idea in Shannon's head. In fact, the perfect idea to support his suit for a promotion and get his life back on track.

"What're you smilin' at?" Colter demanded.

"Nothing," Shannon replied.

Colter stretched out his legs and leaned back against the low wooden lockers that lined the sides of the keelboat's quarterdeck. After three days of restriction to the boat with too much time to wonder about what had become of Josiah Hartley, he was ready to burst from the frustration of confinement.

Floyd settled onto a nearby locker. "Aren't you leaving? Thought you'd be off this tug as soon as you could."

"Waitin' for the crowd to clear," Colter replied. At the bottom of the gangplank, Newman tossed one last hateful glance in Colter's direction before trailing the Field brothers up the path to Fort Kaskaskia.

"You ever going to tell me what's between you two?" the sergeant asked.

"Can't tell what ain't there," Colter replied, as weary of the question as he was of the boat. "Any chance the cooks could use some fresh meat?"

Floyd sighed and looked toward the fort. "I'm not supposed to authorize anyone to leave the immediate area of the fort."

Colter shifted against the wooden locker. He needed an hour or two of trotting to unknot his muscles, or he would be in sorry shape.

"If you'd open up, I'd tell you something I found out. It's about your old friend Hartley," Floyd said.

Colter's head whipped toward the sergeant. "What'd you hear?"

Amusement brightened Floyd's eyes. "Absolutely nothing. I talked to a fellow who makes it his business to know everyone who travels this river, and nobody around here's seen that preacher."

Colter's relief was tempered by doubt that Farley Stuart would forget the matter, whether or not Hartley had survived Rutledge's knifing.

"Now what's wrong?" Floyd asked. "I thought my news'd make you happy. Makes hunting a whole lot less complicated when you don't have to keep looking over your shoulder to see who might have his rifle sights trained on your back."

"If you ain't supposed to let us go nowhere, I got no reason to care, do

I?"

"I'm supposed to feed all of you, too. This morning Captain Clark said we have to wait here until Captain Lewis gets back from up north. Could be a week. Maybe longer. The news didn't exactly thrill the fort's commanding officer."

Floyd scratched his thigh. "There's not enough to eat and certainly not enough to do to keep everyone busy. You can bet some of the crew have already found ways around the restrictions. The more creative ones always do. At least they've kept out of trouble." He faded into thought momentarily. "With all these extra mouths to feed, the least we can do is help out with some fresh meat."

Colter played along with the sergeant's game. "Any way I can help, Sarge?"

"You might get your rifle, make sure your horn's full and get out of my sight before I change my mind."

Colter was on his feet in a flash, rifle and horn in hand.

"Now you'll pay heed to the restrictions, right, Private?"

Colter waved in answer and hustled off the boat. The skies were heavy with impending snow, but he didn't care. Even a blizzard could not slow him down today.

7. *Betrayal*

S hannon signed his name at the bottom of the page with less of a flourish than usual. He blew the ink dry, then folded the letter into a neat rectangle. He wrote his mother's name and address across the front, then sealed the back with wax which he imprinted with his signet ring, the one she had given him for his sixteenth birthday.

When the wax hardened, he placed the finished letter inside a tin box with the others. He had written one to his mother each week since joining the expedition, but he had never sent any of them. Not yet. Not till the expedition started up the Missouri, and he was out of reach of his father's wrath. Besides those to his mother, there were letters to Fergus O'Toole, expressing thanks for guiding him to this expedition, and to Parson Cooper — after half a dozen false starts — to apologize and try to explain what had happened that last awful night with Sarah. There were none to his father because he could never get past the salutation before the image of the man's unforgiving visage dried up whatever he planned to say.

Once the letter was done, Shannon wondered what to do next. The lowering clouds promised snow at any moment. Sulky crewmen jammed the fort's small mess hall, bellyaching about how bored they all were and going on endlessly about the whores they had bedded and the fights they had been in. He had no experience with such things nor did he wish to accumulate any. In one way, the fact that the others treated him as an outsider made things easier. With no friends in the ranks, his transition to command would be that much easier.

On the other hand, not having friends made for some lonely moments. In the past he had filled those times by seeking out Captain Lewis for serious discussion. However, the captain was now on expedition business in Cahokia, a settlement to the north across the Mississippi from St. Louis. True, Captain Clark was still with the crew, but he had never responded to Shannon's conversational overtures, and Shannon got the impression that Clark did not exactly approve of his relationship with Lewis.

The door to the mess hall banged open. In came Newman and Rube and Joe Field. "Close the door, please," Shannon requested.

"Close it yourself, Peckerwood," Newman growled.

Shannon rose to shut the door. When he was in charge, Private Newman would learn better manners or find himself off the expedition permanently.

Closing his ears to the derisive comments the three directed at him, Shannon took his seat again and opened Lewis's navigation book to the diagram that described the method of using stars to shoot a ship's course across the Atlantic. The Atlantic. In his mind's eye the diagram dissolved and another image formed: an endless expanse of black water. Deep, cold, black, smothering water. Water that took control of his imagination and made it hard to breathe. He slammed the book shut and sucked air into his grateful lungs.

How ridiculous! He had made it this far up the Mississippi, and he would make it the rest of the way to the Western Sea. And he would get through this book. He would overcome this–this difficulty. All he needed was time and effort.

Across the crowded room, reeking with the sour odor of bodies long unbathed, Newman and his cronies huddled around a table. Noting the conspiracy evident in their postures, Shannon raised the book and surreptitiously observed them.

After a time one of the men rose from the table and left the room. A short time later, another man followed.

Neither of the two returned before a third departed, confirming Shannon's suspicions that the group was up to something and stoking the fires of indignation within him. These men had been given a direct order to stay away from the whores and grog shops that infested this frontier outpost, yet they chose to disobey, chose to flaunt the very authority they had pledged to follow.

Newman left the table last. He strolled to the door, leaned over Shannon's shoulder, and blew a fetid kiss against his ear, then went out, deliberately leaving the door open behind him. Shannon no longer cared about the door. This was the chance he needed to alter Captain Clark's opinion of him for the better.

He tucked the navigation book inside the tin box, slid the box into a safe spot beneath the lowest log of the wall in the corner and hurried outside.

Newman was sauntering across the fort's central plaza, whistling a tune like a man in no hurry. Reaching the latrine wall, he paused, glanced around him, then took two quick steps to the right and disappeared down the narrow passage between the latrine and the rooms along the fort's west wall.

By the time Shannon got to the latrine, Newman was crawling through a knee-high door that had been cut into the pickets of the fort's back wall at ground level. Shannon counted to twenty-five to give the man enough time to get a headstart before following. Once outside the walls, he had to sprint to keep the loping figure of Newman in sight.

At the top of a rise, Newman stopped unexpectedly to look behind him and Shannon dove for cover. Newman laughed at something with a triumphant note in his voice, then continued down the other side. Shannon left his hiding place and crept cautiously up the slope to see what the man was about.

A flatboat some thirty feet long sat on supports above the level of the Mississippi on the banks of a protected cove. A single cabin occupied most of the boat's span. Smoke curled into the low gray clouds from the tin chimney in the center of the cabin's roof. Whiskey barrels in tiers marked the stern, and a narrow walkway leading to a garishly-painted door defined the prow.

Voices raised in greeting and female laughter carried up the rise to Shannon as Newman went inside. His suspicions had been confirmed, and he raced back to the fort just as snow began to fall fast and thick.

He stopped outside the captains' quarters to brush snow from his knees, tuck in the tail of his shirt and swipe his fingers through his hair. York opened to his knock. "I need to see Captain Clark. It's urgent."

The black man motioned him inside where the captain was sitting across the work table from Sergeant Floyd and a second man whose uniform epaulette identified him also as a sergeant. Clark's face was pale and drawn. "Yes, Private?" he said hoarsely as if his throat hurt.

"Some of the crew have left the fort against your orders, sir," Shannon answered firmly.

Floyd bounded to his feet, hot anger burning in the glare he leveled at Shannon. Shannon swallowed hard. Oh, Lord. He had been so intent on his own priorities that he had forgotten to use the chain of command.

The stranger rose from his seat. "I'll handle it, Captain. I know every place within a ten-mile radius where a soldier would think to go against orders."

"I can show you where they went. I followed them," Shannon volunteered.

"You what?" Floyd growled.

Realizing he too had technically disobeyed orders, Shannon tried to explain himself. "It all happened so fast. I had to make sure before pointing a finger at anyone."

A flicker of pain crossed Clark's face. "I don't care how it's done. Just get those men back here. I leave it to you sergeants to handle it as quickly and quietly as possible."

Outside, the snowfall had picked up force. The new sergeant turned to

Shannon. "I'm Sergeant Ordway. Private Shannon, is it?"

"Shannon. Yes, Sergeant." He answered crisply, conscious of Floyd's furious glower.

"Where did they go?" Ordway said.

Shannon described the flatboat.

"The man who runs that place has been trouble for two months," Ordway explained. "He's been moving his boat every few weeks. The troops always seem to know where he sets down, though I haven't been so lucky. Till now, that is. How do you get there?"

Shannon had hardly begun to tell the way when Ordway interrupted, "If we followed those directions, Private, we'd be heading east. The river lays to the west, in case you hadn't noticed."

The new sergeant's criticism threw Shannon into confusion. He was sure those directions were correct. "Why don't I just lead you there?" he offered curtly.

Ordway waved him ahead, and Shannon lit out.

It wasn't long before Ordway stopped him again. "No, Private. It can't be this way."

"But it's just over that rise," Shannon said, growing exasperated at the man's refusal to trust him.

The two sergeants exchanged a knowing look before Floyd spoke. "If they went this way, Shannon, they went in a circle. The fort's over there."

Ordway pointed in the opposite direction. "River's yonder. Why don't you just describe the place where the boat is?"

Shannon barely managed to keep the irritation out of his voice as he described the cove.

"I know it," Ordway said. "Now, Private, do you think you can manage to get back to the fort without getting lost?"

Shannon refused to legitimize the new sergeant's patronizing question with an answer.

"On second thought, it's better you take him back, Floyd," Ordway said. "I'll go round up *your* men."

After Ordway headed off, Floyd whirled on Shannon. "You're playing with fire this time, Shannon, and you're going to get burned."

Shannon drew himself up tall. "I don't know what you're talking about, Sergeant."

"The crew'll find out right quick who informed on them. And when they do, believe me, you'll be sorry."

"Those men are your responsibility, Sergeant. Are you condoning their actions?"

"You're always so sure you're right. Well, this time you've shot yourself in the foot. From now on, you better watch your backside and watch it close because those crewmen are going to get even with you."

"Don't count on it, Sergeant," Shannon said, standing his ground.

Floyd's index finger dug into Shannon's breastbone. "Mark my words. This crew's too small to keep a secret for long, yours or anyone else's."

By the time Colter's route led him back to the river, the snow was still falling. Except for a renewed attitude, a head clear of thoughts of Hartley, and a set of well-exercised legs, he had nothing to show for the seven-hour arc he had swept north and west of the fort. If there was any game hereabouts, it was keeping well hidden. He had not come across a single track.

Reaching the high bank above the towpath, he paused to look across the Mississippi. Clumps of collected snow glided on the surface of the grayish water, forming islands that would soon freeze and jam together until the river was covered in ice from bank to bank. If Captain Lewis did not get back soon, the crew would be stuck at Fort Kaskaskia until spring. Not an unpleasant prospect, provided he and the rest of the crew could find a way to visit the local liquor purveyors and sporting women.

He drew in a deep breath of the snow-freshened air and caught the familiar scent of wood smoke in a place where there should not be any. Hanging clouds swallowed any visible smoke trails, so he followed the smell. He rounded a curve in the bank and came upon a beached flatboat. The smoke came from a rusted chimney protruding from the roof of its cabin. Faded letters over the door spelled RUM.

He gave the area around him a quick once-over. He was two miles from the fort. The crew were all restricted, and any patrols were not likely to venture out until the snow stopped. Three days of restriction had meant missing his daily liquor ration, and he had a big thirst to quench. What could be the harm? One drink, two at the most, then he would go on his way with no one the wiser.

Close up, the boat amounted to a cabin on a raft, crudely constructed and carelessly maintained. The wooden sides and decks of the craft cried out for paint, in contrast to the bright crimson color of the door. He shouldered the door open and paused to allow his eyes to adjust to the interior's gloom. Smoke belched into the room around the ill-fitting door of a battered stove. Next to it, in the back corner, a narrow doorway connected with a second room. Along the left side stood a bar, two slabs split from a tree trunk laid side by side across whiskey barrels.

"Well, well, if it ain't the nigger-lover hisself."

Colter squinted into the dimness for the speaker of the slur. A few rough tables dotted the room, with only one of them occupied.

"I said it. Over here." Bratton, who was sitting with Newman, Rube and Joe, pushed back from the table and made a show of sniffing the air. "Place smells real bad all of a sudden. Must be you, Colter."

Colter ignored him and walked to the bar. "Cup of rum."

"You serve him, we're leavin'," Newman warned the barkeeper.

"Cup of rum," Colter repeated.

The bartender had a dark complexion, a pair of thick braids and a permanent scowl. He looked from Colter to the other four men and back again. "I don't want no trouble."

"You heard me," Newman said. "If he stays, we go. Your choice."

Two Braids moved to the keg to draw Colter's drink. Newman slammed down his cup and stomped out the door, taking Bratton and the Field brothers with him, leaving behind a breathless quiet. Colter broke the spell by tossing his coin on the plank bar.

The bartender set a dented cup in front of him and scooped up the coin. "Ain't enough," he said, laying his empty hand, palm open across the top of the cup. "Since you run off four good customers, that'll be a dollar."

Colter fished out the extra coins and placed them on the bar top. Two Braids pocketed the coins and moved off. Only then did Colter pick up the cup.

The liquor had a burned taste, evidence of the rum-maker's carelessness. Instead of soothing him, it made Colter grimace. This detour had been a mistake. He put the empty cup down on the bar and turned to leave.

Just then, the door swung back and in strode a sergeant he did not recognize. The man's piercing gaze swept the room and came to light on him. "Your name?"

"Colter."

"State your business."

"I'm through, and I'm leavin'."

The sergeant stepped over to him and peered closely at his face. "You with the expedition?"

Colter nodded, figuring it was better to be honest than to lie since he was no good at lying.

"Then you're coming with me." The sergeant grabbed his arm and yanked him out the door where he slammed him against the cabin wall and jammed a forearm across his throat. "I want to thank you, Colter. A sergeant needs to make his mark on a new outfit right away. You're mine. You and me are going to show the rest of your crew what happens to those who go against captains' orders. By the way, I'm Sergeant Ordway. Starting now, you can think of me as the bad dream you can't ever shake. Now move!"

⌁

Shannon stared blindly at the open book in his lap. What he thought would be a scheme to gain favor with Captain Clark had fizzled. Floyd would never let him live down having to be led back to the fort. Never. Then there was the new sergeant's — Ordway's — condescending treatment. His mind churned with arguments in his defense, but what good would arguments do him once the captain learned that he had not been able to locate that blind pig again and that he had to have help to get back to the fort?

The door opened and Newman, Bratton, Rube and Joe trooped in, all stinking of liquor and smiling smugly. Shannon's senses went on immediate alert. How did they escape Sergeant Ordway's clutches?

The four shoved their way into places at the table next to Shannon's and began a desultory poker game. Straining to overhear their muttered conversation, Shannon learned that the four had left the whiskey mill, rather than drink in the same place with Colter who had come in later. The issue seemed to be the men's belief that York was spying on them for the captains versus Colter's contention that York was innocent of such doings. Shannon's first thought was *Good, that'll teach Sergeant Ordway not to wave me off.* His second thought was *Oh, Lord, it's me who'll be blamed because Ordway didn't catch the others.*

All at once he could not stand being inside. He stashed the book and let himself out into the deepening dusk. He paused at the corner of the building, trying to figure out where to go, when Ordway strode through the fort's front gates with Colter firmly in his grip.

Floyd banged out of the room the sergeants had been assigned at the fort and hurried forward to intercept the pair. Shannon ducked back into the shadows to listen in.

"Colter? What's the meaning of this, Ordway?" Floyd demanded.

"Means I found him where Private Shannon said he'd be," Ordway answered.

Shannon could not see Floyd's reaction in the dim light, but there was no mistaking the testiness in his voice. "I'll take him to the captain."

"No need to bother the captain," Ordway said. "He told the two of us to take care of things, and that's what I'm doing. You just go on about your business."

Floyd's wariness was obvious in the set of his shoulders as he turned away and left Ordway to manhandle Colter toward the back of the fort. The pair came within three feet of where Shannon was hiding. As they passed, Colter spotted Shannon and for an instant their eyes locked. In that instant Shannon got the message. Colter knew that Shannon was responsible for whatever this new sergeant was going to do to him. If Colter knew that, then the whole crew would know. Sergeant Floyd's warning came back on Shannon with the force of a kick in the gut. He slumped against the wall. *Oh, God, what have I done?*

⚓

Passing the forge, Ordway hailed the blacksmith and his brawny apprentice. "You two, I need your help."

The pair took charge of Colter and hauled him to the rear corner of the fort. There, refuse and discarded equipment — cracked whipple trees, parts of traces, partial wagon beds, barrels with missing staves, legless chairs, rusted traps, moth-eaten hides, broken pottery, and the like — had been heaped into a pile taller than a man.

"I have to take a piss," Colter said.

Ordway ignored the demand. "You know what to do," he told the smiths.

The pair shoved Colter into a small shed. While the apprentice forced him against the wall, the blacksmith tied his hands at his sides, then strung a stout chain across his throat, attaching the ends into rings that had been bolted into the wall. The arrangement forced Colter to stand tall or choke himself.

"I said I have to take a piss!" Colter insisted.

Ordway waved his two accomplices back to their forge, then dusted some imaginary dirt off his sleeve. "Unfortunately, our guest accommodations don't include a privy, Private."

"I ain't goin' to piss myself," Colter said through clenched teeth.

"Then you have a real problem, don't you? Good night." Ordway scraped shut the ill-hung door and walked away.

In the pitch-blackness of the tiny airless room, Colter began to sweat. He had gotten lost exploring a cave when he was seven years old and, ever since, he had steered clear of cramped spaces. Now the memory of that terrifying experience came flooding back on him, awakening sensations long hidden. His imagination began to play tricks on him. The roof was sinking down. The walls were drawing in. His body was being squeezed from all directions. The little shed was running out of air to breathe

Stinging sweat poured into his eyes, but his hands were tied to his sides and he could not wipe it away. He struggled against his bonds, raking the chain against the skin of his neck and gagging against its pressure. But he could not get free.

He gulped at the air but could not seem to get enough to fill his laboring lungs. Rasping breaths compounded the noise of his heart's thudding, making him deaf to all other sounds.

He had to get out. Had to get into the open air before the walls closed in on him. Had to. Had to.

"Help," he cried but his throat was too dry, his panic too great to lend any strength to his voice. *Help. Help.* He continued to cry out, tortured whispers of sound that barely penetrated the enclosing walls.

The strain proved too much for his extended bladder which unleashed its burden. Hot urine gushed forth, running down his legs, soaking his trousers, puddling at his feet.

Shannon could not sleep that night for worrying about the consequences of his actions. Every time he tried to close his eyes, Colter's furious face appeared on the backs of his eyelids. At the first hint of daylight, he gave up trying to sleep and walked to the fort. The gate guard admitted him, snarling a curse in response to his "Good morning."

Without knowing how he got there, he found himself in the rear of the fort where the garrison disposed of its refuse. The reek of rotting garbage wrinkled his nose. If he had not been so distracted, he would have gone straight to the fort's commanding officer. Garbage belonged away from the fort, not inside the walls where the inhabitants had to put up with it and its noxious odors and the vermin it attracted.

A small sound intruded on his preoccupation. The sound of metal upon metal, coming from what looked to be an abandoned lean-to.

"Someone there?" he whispered uncertainly.

The sound repeated. Definitely a *clink*.

Shannon tugged tentatively on the flap of leather that served as a handle for the warped door. The top of the door budged slightly but the bottom remained stuck.

It took another harder yank to pull the door open.

"Old Man!"

Colter was trussed against the wall with his arms bound to his sides and a length of chain stretched tightly across his throat. The smell of urine was strong enough to make Shannon's breath catch.

"I pissed myself," Colter hissed. "Like a baby."

Even in the gloom, the dark stain running down the insides of Colter's pantlegs was obvious. Shannon backed up a step. He had never intended for something like this to happen. This was torture. This was wrong.

"This is your fault," Colter rasped. "You little weasel!" In his fury, he moved and the chain dug into his throat, choking off his voice.

Shannon backed up another step. He had no business being here.

"For God's sake, Fuzz! Help me 'fore this here thing strangles me," Colter rasped.

Shannon's mind raced back over the last two days and all the missteps he had made. If Sergeant Ordway had put Colter in shackles, it was definitely not a private's place to release him. Then again, he could not allow Colter to continue to suffer.

He spun round and hurried off to find help.

He met Sergeants Floyd and Pryor coming up from the keelboat. "It's Colter. He needs help."

He explained Colter's situation as quickly as he could, then Floyd exploded, "You mean you left him like that?"

"It wasn't my place to interfere," Shannon answered.

"Interfere? Hell, you got him into this fix."

"I only did my duty," Shannon said.

"Duty," Floyd sneered. "Try that one on the crew, when they find out what your duty did to Colter."

"I didn't do anything to anybody," Shannon said in exasperation.

"Tell that to Colter next time you see him." The sergeant shouldered Shannon aside and rushed into the fort.

It felt to Colter that hours passed between the time Shannon ran off and Captain Clark showed up, trailing Floyd and Ordway. "Sergeant Ordway, release this man immediately," Clark ordered, each low-pitched word distinct and forceful.

A tight-lipped Ordway cut the rope binding Colter's arms and unhooked the chain. Colter crumpled to his knees with a groan. The chain had chafed away the scab from the wound caused by Hartley's rope and his neck was on fire with pain.

The captain turned to Ordway. "You owe this man an apology, Sergeant."

"But, Captain —"

"Now, Sergeant!"

Ordway's jaw tightened and he seemed to be deciding whether to continue to protest.

"Now!"

"I apologize, Private." Ordway's reluctance painted each word.

"His name is Colter. Use it," ordered the captain.

"I apologize, Colter."

"And so do I, Colter," the captain said, the harshness of his voice softening into compassion. "This should never have happened and you have my promise that it will never happen again. Isn't that right, Sergeant Ordway?"

"Yes, sir." There was no meekness, certainly no remorse in the response.

"Sergeant Floyd, help Private Colter to my quarters so York can see to that wound on his neck. We depart in two hours." With that, the captain stomped off.

Floyd waited until Clark was out of earshot before speaking. "Well, Ordway. Congratulations. Took you less than a day to rile the captain. That's a record. Maybe next time you won't be so quick to throw your weight around."

Malice glittered in Ordway's eyes. "There might be three sergeants on this crew, Floyd, but only one on top. The sooner you accept that, the sooner we can get on with our real business, which is shaping rabble like this man into soldiers."

"I was here first, Ordway. And first is where I intend to stay," Floyd bristled.

Ordway's mouth twisted into a mirthless grin. "I would wish you luck, but I'd be lying." He turned to Colter. "As for you, Private, this is only the beginning. From now on, I intend to make your life hell."

Colter lifted his head with effort. He made no attempt to disguise the venom in his voice. "Then you can count on the same from me."

"Oh, really? Guess we'll see about that, won't we?" Ordway turned and strode away.

Floyd looked after him. "Why, that cocky son-of-a-bitch. I'd like to throttle him."

"I got a chain you can use," Colter said, hooking a thumb toward the shed.

"And I'd use it if I thought I could get away with it. Damn that Ordway! Now I got him and Shannon to contend with. This is going to be a long, long trip."

Colter could not have agreed more.

8. *Camp du Bois*

S hannon's hands were so cold that he had to look at them to make sure he no longer had hold of the ice-stiffened cordelle rope. His back was so stiff from bending under the rope to haul the keelboat up the Mississippi that he had to prop those icy hands against his lower back before he could straighten up and look at the place that would be the expedition's home for the next five months. What he saw did not make him happy.

A small river, the Riviére du Bois or Wood River, coursed through a densely-tangled bottom, emptying into the Mississippi a few yards beyond *Discovery*'s nose. Though it was already December 12 and freezing cold, it would take days, even weeks before the crew could clear the bottom area and build a camp. They would be lucky to have roofs over their heads by New Year's.

"Check out Peckerwood, Little Brother," said Rube.

"He don't look too good, does he?" Joe said. "What you think's wrong with him anyhow?"

"Why he's missin' Captain Lewis, don't you know?" Rube made some exaggerated kissing sounds that brought sniggers from the crewmen within earshot.

Shannon turned his back on the stale innuendo and the sniggers. Yes, he did miss Captain Lewis but not for the reasons these oafs insinuated. Let them think what they would. They had no ambition. He did, and he counted on Captain Lewis to help him realize his dreams. But the captain had been in St. Louis lately, seeing to expedition business. The few times he had rejoined the crew, there had been no chance to speak with him. No time to press his case for promotion. To make matters worse, ice would soon close the river which would force Shannon to bide his time until spring. If that happened, he would lose all hope.

"How many times do I have to tell you to police that rope, Private?"

Shannon jumped, unaware that Floyd had come up behind him. Back muscles protesting, he bent to wind the rope into a proper coil and deliver it to Colter who was charged with securing the boat. Colter snatched the rope out of his hands with a scornful "Thanks, Fuzz."

Shannon refused to be bullied by the man's continuing anger. He had nothing to apologize for. Indeed, Colter ought to be grateful to him. After all, he was the one who got Colter out of that torture chamber back at Kaskaskia. If it had not been for him, Sergeant Ordway would have gotten away with what he had done, and, if he had, there was no telling the torments the crew might have had to endure at the sergeant's hands.

He lifted his chin, threw back his shoulders and walked away, leaving Colter with the rope and his anger.

◢

For the next three weeks, every able man, including Captain Clark and the three sergeants, worked from dawn to dusk in all weathers to prepare their winter quarters at Camp du Bois, or Camp Wood, as they began to call it. They cleared the river bottom, erected the cabins and walls, hauled *Discovery* up onto blocks for the winter and cut a wagon road up to the nearby prairie for bringing in supplies from Cahokia.

The camp consisted of five cabins. The large one in the center was divided into two rooms, one for the captains; the other for the sergeants. Around that building, spaced at compass points, stood four smaller crew cabins. Since there were no hostiles in the area, rather than erecting the higher walls that normally enclosed a fort, the captains opted to build a seven-foot wall between the outer cabins with half of each building protruding beyond the wall.

The crew moved into their quarters on Christmas Day, and most of the rest of the major work for the camp was completed by January 1. The following day formal military drilling began, conducted by Sergeant Ordway. For Colter, this meant going from three weeks of little contact with the sergeant while the camp was under construction to a minimum of four hours a day under the man's direct scrutiny on the parade ground. He was not looking forward to the shift when he took his place in ranks next to Shannon.

No sooner had the men begun to march single-file than Ordway yelled for them to stop. He strolled down the line, looking each man over as one examines a sway-backed horse. He paused next to Newman, leaned toward his ear and yelled, "Didn't your mother teach you right from left, Private? Or were you too busy sucking on her tit that day?"

The man behind Newman shifted nervously.

"Who gave you permission to move, Gass?"

Pat Gass braced and Ordway's attention swung back to Newman. "Not only are you clumsy, Newman, you're stupid. You're going to wish those were discharge offenses, because, starting today, you get to be the first member of a very special unit. I call it 'Stupid Drill.' First muster is this afternoon. I promise you my undivided attention. Won't that be fun?"

The sergeant sauntered on to Rube Field. "And, since we don't want Newman to feel lonely, you get to join him." And on to Rube's brother, Joe. "What about you, Private Little Brother? You don't want Big Brother to be the only one keeping Newman company, now do you?"

Joe blinked.

"That's the spirit. See you this afternoon," Ordway sneered.

Colter held his breath while the sergeant walked past him, then stopped and came back. "Why, I must be slipping. Here I almost forgot my favorite recruit, Private Colter." Ordway walked a slow circle around him. "You know, you wouldn't be half bad-looking if it weren't for that mark on your face. Looks like a puddle of purple bird shit. I'm tired of looking at it."

He rocked back on his heels. "Any of you others tired of looking at Private Colter's butt-ugly face?"

A loud "Yes" came from a recent recruit named Leakins.

"Hear that, Colter? Private Leakins agrees with me. So starting tomorrow, I order you to wear a patch anytime I have to see you. That means every drill. Got that?"

Colter held himself rigid against his growing hatred of Ordway while the sergeant returned to the head of the column of crewmen and called out, "Private Shannon, front and center."

Shannon marched to the sergeant, executing two perfect square corners despite the frozen mud ruts underfoot. Ordway addressed the line of men. "Did you see that, ladies? Shannon here can tell his right foot from his left.

He can also walk a straight line, turn a square corner and salute properly. He can but not one of the rest of you seem to be able to do those things. Why is that?"

Shannon's gloating expression brought back to Colter memories of the night he had spent locked in that stinking hole at Kaskaskia. The night he would never forget, compliments of Private George Shannon.

"Stumped, are we?" Ordway needled. "Well, then Shannon here will be your drill leader from now on. Assume your duties, Private."

Smiling exultantly, Shannon faced the ragged column of recruits. "Company! Forward! *March!*"

As Colter moved past Shannon, he was sorely tempted to hawk his plug of tobacco into the center of that smug visage, to wipe that smile away once and for all. High and mighty Shannon, the one who would do anything to get ahead. Anything including informing on his fellow crew members. So far, only Colter knew what he had done back at Kaskaskia. Much as he would like to have told the others, he was not about to become an informer himself. It was up to the others to find out the truth about Shannon. And when they did, Shannon had best watch his butt.

*

"Left . . . left . . . left, right, left." Shannon marched, calling the cadence through lips numbed by the bitterly cold air. He refused to acknowledge the icy footing, the blisters his frozen boots had rubbed on his heels, the lack of feeling in his fingers and toes. His own discomfort had to take second seat to the larger responsibility Sergeant Ordway had given him.

Squad leader. Of course, it made perfect sense. Of all the crew, he was the only logical choice. It was a perfect fit for his experience and training, plus he was fulfilling a genuine need — shaping this ragtag group of ruffians into a team of dependable, obedient soldiers.

The more he thought about his new duties, the more he saw the hand of Captain Lewis behind Ordway's decision. This was an ideal way for the captain to groom him to take on larger responsibilities when the expedition left to begin their explorations in the spring. The idea that the captain had selected him for such an honor thrilled Shannon to the marrow of his bones.

"Left, Newman! Left!" bellowed Ordway from his position next to the flagpole.

Shannon smiled inwardly. When it came to drilling recruits, the sergeant reminded him of his father. Ordway had correctly identified Newman and Rube as the leaders of the rowdies. *Break the leaders, tame the herd.* That was how Father had put it.

"Right turn . . . march!" Shannon yelled, turning the words into guttural military approximations. "Left . . . left . . ." He understood now why Ordway had come down on Newman and Rube, but ordering Colter to cover his birthmark — that was uncalled for. That smacked of superstition and ignorance. He would have a talk with the sergeant about the subject once their relationship was more firmly established. Meantime, Colter would have to comply with the sergeant's order.

Shannon stepped away from the head of the column, letting Private Whitehouse take the lead. Continuing to call cadence, he sized up his task. Shaping these recruits into a respectable unit by May was going to be a monumental task. However, he was determined to show results.

For an hour, he drilled the full squad under Ordway's watchful eye, then dismissed all the men to see to their other duties except for the four assigned to the sergeant's special detail. He gave those men a five-minute latrine break, warning them not to be late returning for their remedial session. The four went off and Shannon turned to Ordway. "Thank you, Sergeant."

"No need to thank me, Shannon. You're the obvious choice. You have the appearance, discipline and behavior of a true military man."

The praise rendered Shannon temporarily speechless. The sergeant had said the very things he had longed to hear from his father for years.

"I've been keeping my eye on you since we first met back in Kaskaskia," Ordway said.

"I apologize for getting turned around that day, Sergeant," Shannon stammered.

Ordway brushed the apology aside. "It's your sense of right and wrong that impressed me, Shannon. Not your sense of direction. You saw something wrong, and you took it upon yourself to correct it. Choosing to do the right thing — that can make for a lonely life."

The flash of sympathy in the sergeant's gaze said he understood how isolated Shannon had felt as part of this crew.

"Unfortunately, it is the responsibility of a few to make this expedition work. You are one of those few, Shannon." Ordway's eyes widened slightly. "I need to be able to rely on you. In all things. I need you to be my eyes and ears. Can I count on you?"

Shannon did not hesitate. "Eyes and ears. Yes, Sergeant."

9. *Grog*

F loyd was furious when he found out that Ordway had ordered Colter to cover his birthmark. There was nothing he could do however, since the captains had handed Ordway total responsibility for the crew's military instruction. The best he could do was commiserate and see to it that Colter got a regular turn in the hunting rotation.

So Colter fashioned himself a patch, and, for the next thirteen days, he wore it whenever he was around Ordway, his loathing for it growing to match the feeling he harbored for the man who forced him to wear it. On the fourteenth day, his turn in the hunting rotation finally came up. Floyd arranged for him to have the detail alone. Still, it took most of the day to work off his accumulated resentment and it was with reluctance that he turned back to camp with his take of six turkeys and two large geese.

A mile above the camp, he stopped to eat some pemmican and put off his return another few minutes. As he chewed, he thought about how his life since the Draft had come to be defined by enemies. First Stuart and Josiah Hartley. Now Ordway. And not just enemies, either. McBain and Shannon were not as much foes as major irritants. Especially Shannon, now that Ordway had put him, the least capable of all the crew, in a position to lord that inexperience over them every day for the next four months.

About the only good thing to happen since they got to Camp Wood was that Newman had backed off his contention that York was the captain's spy. That, in turn, had allowed Colter to relax his guard against blurting out the truth about Shannon.

Deep in thought, he did not pick up on the sound of an ax for several minutes. Since he was too far from camp to come across the firewood detail, he went to investigate the source.

A half-raised cabin stood in a clearing dotted with fresh stumps. Two men were busy felling a sugar maple while a third man was guiding a draft horse dragging another log toward the new structure.

As Colter approached, a fourth man emerged from the trees beyond the cabin. He was broad of torso and thin of leg. Sweeping off his broad-brimmed hat, he swiped a rag across his sweating bald pate. The absence of the hat revealed a ruddy face, its bottom half engulfed by a beard of bushy hair the color of ripe persimmons. "She's cookin' up just fine, mates. She's a-cookin' fine," he announced.

An unmistakable odor carried to Colter's nose on the wind and caused him to sneeze.

The sound stopped the work of the men in the clearing. Colter sneezed a second time, then stepped forward. The ruddy man bustled to him. "A customer, a customer. Welcome, welcome. Ramey, Gideon Ramey."

Colter shook Ramey's meaty hand. "John Colter."

"Colter. Colter. I knew a Colter once. Once." Ramey's eyes strayed to Colter's left temple and stayed there for a long moment.

"It's a birthmark," Colter explained.

"Never seen the like of it," Ramey said. "Never have, but come, come. You must sample my wares. My wares."

Ramey led him to a lean-to built against the trunk of an oak. "Here. Here." He slid aside the lid of an upended cask, dipped two tin cups of tawny liquid, handed one to Colter and raised his own cup. "To John Colter, John Colter."

Colter drank, expecting the harsh jolt of too-young whiskey. Instead of burning however, Ramey's concoction caressed a pleasantly warm path to his stomach.

"More? More?" Ramey asked.

"Do you always repeat yourself?"

"Repeat myself? Repeat? Why, no, no."

At the perplexity on the man's face, Colter chuckled and accepted another cupful of Ramey's creation. "Best whiskey I've had since I left home."

"Today is on the house since we aren't officially open, open. You'll tell the others where I am? That I'm here?"

"The smells from your still'll do that."

Before he completed his sentence, Colter realized that if he could smell the still, so could everyone including Shannon, Ordway and the captains. Ramey made excellent whiskey, just the kind of thing that would help a restless man pass the time till spring. Colter was not willing to lose this treasure he had found before he had the chance to enjoy it. "And that ain't good. Listen, you got to cover your mash so's it won't smell."

"But what about —"

"Don't you worry none. Keep your mind on the whiskey-makin' and I'll make sure you got all the business you can handle."

"Cookin' up a new batch now. A batch."

Bolstered by the warmth of the whiskey and what that meant for the rest of the winter, Colter hefted his take of game and took off for camp at a fast clip. He would have to find a way to spread the word about Ramey's to the crew while keeping it from Shannon. And do so without letting on to Newman what he was doing and why. But that was a small problem. For now, the future looked brighter than it had in a month.

Shannon stooped to shove his stiff, mittened fingers under a length of log and lifted it out of the snow. The muscles in his lower back cramped as he straightened and he had to fight to hold on to the heavy awkward load as he staggered over to the crude wood-hauling sled. When he became squad leader, he had assumed he would be excused from all afternoon details. How wrong he had been! This week he had had firewood detail every af-ternoon *after* putting in a full day of drilling Ordway's two squads. He used to dislike wood detail. Now he despised it. The only time he had feeling in his feet anymore was at night in his bunk when they warmed up enough to throb.

"Break!"

Shannon checked to be sure it was Sergeant Pryor yelling and not one of the crewmen pulling another puerile stunt in the name of fun. He sank down on a stump and pulled his blanket up over his head, paying no atten-tion to the derisive comments of the others who teased him for doing so. They could sit in the snow or let the sweat freeze in their hair. He had a better way.

Blowing on his fingers to warm them, he pulled out his journal and a piece of charcoal. He preferred not to use charcoal — it smeared if he was not careful — but ink froze in this cold.

More waiting.

The same scrawled entry as yesterday's. He had never been good at waiting. Now it seemed that was all he did. Waiting for food. Waiting for warmth. Waiting for Captain Lewis to return from St. Louis.

It has been seven days since. . .

He broke off writing. He had promised himself a week ago that if the captain did not return by today, he would seek out Captain Clark to plead for promotion. But is that what he wanted — to take a chance that Captain Clark might turn him down flat because they did not yet have a working relationship? Wouldn't it be better to wait for his mentor?

A blast of icy wind drove him deeper into the inadequate shelter of the wool blanket.

"Best grog I ever tasted."

His ear snatched that phrase out of the whispered conversation going on behind his back. Ordway had been pressing him all week for information about how men were sneaking out of camp and where they were going. Resisting the temptation to glance around at the speakers, he strained to hear more.

"Better we go separate," one murmured.

"How'll I find it in the dark by myself?" the other asked.

"Goin's easy. You move off a-ways now. I'll draw a map in the snow. When I leave, you mosey back over here and study it."

The snow crunched behind Shannon as one of the pair moved off. He imagined the other finger-tracing a crude map in the snow. He heard that one leave and the other return. This second man's joints cracked when he knelt to study the drawing, then cracked again when he rose and walked off.

Shannon faked a stretch, then slid off the side of the stump onto one knee and pretended to adjust his boot while he scanned the upside-down drawing.

It was no use. The map made no sense from this angle. He had long been able to read words and formulae upside-down, but not diagrams or maps. And it was too risky to move around to view the map in the right orientation. What to do?

He sat back up on the stump, opened his notebook, and began recording the map as just a pattern of lines rather than trying to make any sense out of it. He kept his head bent and used the edge of the blanket to cover the page from prying eyes. He was only half-finished when Pryor yelled, "Back to work!"

He kept working, frantic to get the whole drawing done before someone trampled it.

Pryor clapped his hands and bellowed, "Work!"

Shannon sketched in the last three lines and slammed the journal closed a moment before the sergeant reached him. "Mr. Squad Leader, are you deaf?"

Shannon shot to his feet. The journal slipped down inside his trousers, lodging in the space where his pantleg tucked into the top of his boots. "No, Sergeant. Coming."

"Since you're the last one to rejoin our little work party, Shannon, you win the honor of pulling the sled to camp. Mind your back now. We couldn't have our squad leader hurt his precious self, now could we?"

Shannon draped himself in the sled's harness, amid a chorus of catcalls from the rest of the detail.

"Newman, Gass, get on the back end to push," Pryor ordered.

Newman took a spot at the rear runner. Gass took the other side. "Mush, your highness," Newman muttered.

Shannon let the remark pass. No doubt Newman would be among the men sneaking out tonight. When he did, he would be sorry. George Shannon would see to it.

Colter's discovery of Ramey's prompted the men housed in Barracks 4 to dig a tunnel beneath the cleared ground outside the picket walls into the woods beyond. The tunnel allowed the men easy access to the escape valve of Ramey's hospitality and drink, but they were careful about using it so as not to attract the attention of the officers. They made a rule that no more than five of their number were absent at any one time, spreading out their departures and returns to minimize the risk of discovery. Although the precautions kept Colter from going as much as he would have liked, just knowing that he had Ramey's to look forward to restored his equilibrium whenever it started to sag.

This was his night to go but he was third in line. Newman was first. Ten minutes after he left, Rube rolled off his bunk. "Got the damn watch," he groused, winking at Colter.

Although he could not see Rube's wink from his angle, Shannon looked up from the book he was reading to watch Rube go out the door. Taking note of the younger man's interest, Colter chose to put off heading out the tunnel for another half hour. Shannon must never get wind of Ramey's. The place and the man were too important to the crew to be careless.

With eight men, their belongings, four pairs of bunks, and a fireplace, the little room was too crowded to accommodate much movement. Never fond of tight spaces, Colter spent as little time there as possible. Tonight, as he waited to make his escape, the room felt even smaller.

He was just putting away his whittling when sergeants' voices sounded in the compound. He muttered a curse under his breath. The coast had to be completely clear before he could head for the tunnel.

Eventually the voices faded away, but Colter scratched away at his carving for a few more minutes just to be sure. Then he set it aside, mumbled something about needing some fresh air, shrugged on his coat and let himself out as if he intended to visit another barracks.

He was two paces from the door to Barracks 4 when the three sergeants slammed out of the captains' quarters. In the flickering light of Floyd's lantern, Colter could see that Ordway had something in his hand. A page torn from a journal. He knew immediately whose journal it had come from and, reading the victorious look on Ordway's face, he guessed what was on that page. Shannon had found out about Ramey's.

He watched impotently as the three sergeants marched out the gate. There was no time to warn the other crewmen, nothing he could do to stop Ordway from finding them at Ramey's. He banged his fist against the log wall of the barracks. "Damn your traitor's heart, Shannon, you worthless peckerwood! You done it now, and this time it's your hide."

Seeing Colter come back into the cabin just moments after leaving threw Shannon into turmoil. This was Colter's night to sneak off. His observations had made him certain of that. Yet here he was, joining into the crew's never-ending poker game. If concentrating on the book had been difficult before the man left, it was impossible now as doubts rained down on Shannon. He had taken the traced map directly to Sergeant Ordway upon returning from wood detail and explained how he came to have it.

"Good work, Shannon," Ordway had said, clapping him on the back. "Excellent work, in fact. Deserving of reward."

Deserving of reward. Shannon had clung to that phrase throughout the long hours of waiting for this night's drama to play out. There was only one reward he wanted and, after tonight, that reward would be his.

Or would it? If something had gone wrong —

Bang! Joe Field shot to his feet, overturning the box he had been sitting on. "Cheater! You dealt that card off the bottom, you son-of-a-slut!"

Joe Whitehouse jumped up. "Did not!"

"You prove you didn't, you dirty slacker!"

Shannon's tension snapped. "Sit down and shut up! You have the same tired argument every blessed night and I'm sick of it!"

Whitehouse pooched out his lips and waggled a limp wrist. "Dear me, Peckerwood's sick of it. Whatever shall we do?"

"No one cares what you are, Shannon," Bratton declared. "You ain't no squad leader when you're in this here room."

At shouts from the compound, the men forgot their argument and piled outside. Shannon was the last out. A blustery wind was blowing and thick clouds raced across the night sky. Outside the captains' cabin, Newman, Pat Gass and Rube Field stood in a ragged line flanked by Sergeants Floyd and Pryor.

As Shannon watched, the door to the captains' cabin opened and Captain Clark hobbled out on arthritic knees. Behind him came Sergeant Ordway who was saying, "It was a grog shop, sir. I took the worm from the proprietor's still to be sure he's out of business." He held up a length of coiled copper tubing.

Clark barely glanced at the sergeant's trophy. His full attention was on the three crewmen. For a long time he said nothing while he studied each man in turn. Then his hand slashed the air. "Ten days' restriction to barracks, starting now. No drilling. No details. See to it, Sergeant."

Shannon was stunned. What kind of deterrent was that? Restriction was a slap on the wrist for miscreants like Newman and Rube. This was no way to rein in disobedience. No fit punishment for the infraction. He followed his barracks-mates back inside.

"It was that darky, I tell you," Newman said, his voice rising above the angry talk. "He followed us, like he's been doin' since we started out."

The accusation brought a chorus of agreement.

"Someone ratted on you, but it weren't York," Colter countered.

"Only way you're so all-fired sure it ain't York, Colter, is if'n you know who is," challenged Newman.

"There's a rat among us, but I ain't sayin' who except that it ain't York," Colter answered. "I lived by my word my whole life, except one time. That were back at Kaskaskia when I lied to protect you and Rube and Joe. That lie cost me good, too."

There was muttered agreement before Bratton demanded, "Then you owe us the truth. Who's the spy, Colter?"

"It ain't me or Newman or Rube or Pat Gass. Or Joe. Or York. But that's all I'm tellin' you. It's up to you to figure out who your enemy is. Not me," Colter said. With that, he took up his carving and refused to say anymore.

Shannon took this all in and did not know what to think. After Kaskaskia, he had spent several anxious days waiting for the boom to fall, waiting for Colter to spread the word about the part he had played in his getting caught and for the boom to fall. When nothing happened after several days, Shannon figured he was in the clear and relaxed. Now though, he saw that he had escaped because of Colter's moral code and not a conscious decision on the part of the crew. What would happen if Colter broke his silence? Was there a way to deflect the blame away from himself and onto York who was already under suspicion?

There was too much noise in the little room for him to think clearly. As he stepped out of the cabin, he saw the one person he could safely talk to enter the storeroom, carrying a lantern.

Deer and rabbit carcasses strung up on the rafters threw ghostly shadows against the rough log walls in the lantern's light. Ordway was on his knees, rooting among the piles of boxes and bundles of expedition supplies. Shannon waited for the sergeant to regain his feet before revealing his presence.

"Ah, Shannon, just the man I wanted to see," Ordway said.

"I wanted to congratulate you on a job well done, Sergeant."

Ordway dusted himself off. "Then you need to congratulate yourself, too. Getting that map did the trick."

The sergeant's words felt like a soothing balm on Shannon's tension. "We are an unbeatable team, Sergeant. Diligent and disciplined. When I am promoted, we'll really be able to turn this unit around."

"When you're what?" Ordway asked.

"Promoted. To lieutenant."

"Lieutenant? Where did you get that idea?"

"Lieutenant is my militia rank. It is obvious, isn't it, that my talents and education are completely misused as a private? The expedition has enough brawn. What it lacks is brains. That's what I have to offer, a fact I intend to bring up with Captain Lewis as soon as he returns."

Ordway shook his head. "In my opinion, you'd be wise to wait for that talk."

That was not what Shannon wanted to hear. "I happen to disagree. I have proven myself time and again. I am simply too capable to be wasted as a private."

Ordway ran his fingers along the flank of a deer carcass. "It's your best interests I'm thinking about. That's why I advise you to wait. You need to have the strongest case possible when you do go to the captain. You'll get only one chance."

The sergeant's avuncular tone took some of the heat out of Shannon's argument. Though more waiting was the last thing he wanted, he said, "I see. Thank you, Sergeant."

He turned to go but the touch of the sergeant's hand on his arm stopped him. "From now on, we shouldn't be seen alone together. I'll leave first and you wait fifteen minutes. All right?"

Shannon agreed and remained in the stinking, cramped room while the sergeant left. He spent the time getting used to the idea of waiting even longer to realize his ambition.

Waiting. He had never been good at waiting.

From the deep shadows outside Barracks 4, Colter watched Ordway leave the storeroom. Shannon followed some minutes later. That Shannon had brought punishment down on Newman, Gass, and Rube was one thing. Shutting down the business of a hard-working man like Gideon Ramey was quite another. Ramey had taken considerable risks to come all the way out here to provide the crew with a service vital to helping them endure the long idle hours of winter. Besides, Ramey had a big family to support downriver, but, thanks to Shannon, he could no longer make whiskey.

Colter watched Shannon strut across the compound like a stallion on the scent of a dozen mares. The sight burst the seam on his determination to let the crew discover for themselves the Judas among them. After what he had done to Ramey, Shannon deserved whatever punishment the crew dished out.

First, however, Colter had to help Ramey get back on his feet. He would find and return the worm, then he would see that Shannon got his comeuppance.

Through a curtain of falling snow, Shannon watched the men of the remedial squad go through their desultory paces. Six weeks of endless repetitive drills with precious little success. They resisted everything he tried to do. They openly disdained him and his authority and made his life difficult at every turn. As a result, his enthusiasm for the task he had been given was fast ebbing away. Between that and awaiting Captain Lewis's often-delayed return, he was at his wits' end.

The expedition had been at the Camp Wood site for over two months, and Captain Lewis had yet to make an appearance. The heavy snowfall of the last four days precluded the possibility he would show up anytime soon. Shannon heaved a sigh. What was the use?

Although it was early, he dismissed the members of the squad. Displaying more zeal in two minutes than they had in four hours, the four made for the barracks, leaving Shannon alone in the compound with enormous snowflakes filtering down from an unbroken ceiling of gray clouds.

He looked around at the rough cabins that made up the camp. Even the snow could not hide the ugliness of the place. If he felt this low now, how would he ever last until departure, the first of May?

The bundled figure of Sergeant Floyd came out of the sergeants' quarters and kicked through the accumulated snow to Shannon. Only his eyes and the tip of his nose were exposed. "You're on wood patrol, Private."

As much as he despised wood detail, Shannon refused to give Floyd the pleasure of a negative reaction. "Yes, Sergeant."

Floyd chuckled humorlessly. "Yeah, I'll bet you can't wait to get out there. Have fun."

Shannon watched the man disappear into the sergeants' cabin. This expedition had turned from a grand adventure into pure torture. How he longed to leave this detestable, God-forsaken place! He had no friends, no sense of belonging, nothing to show for all his effort except some pages in a journal, layers of calluses covering the palms of both hands and a few unrealized dreams. Nothing was keeping him here. He no longer cared about the expedition. No longer believed in its goals. Why not just take off?

To where? came the next question. St. Louis lay across the Mississippi River, but to get there meant crossing a mile of ice-laden water in a small boat, a journey he knew he could not face. Home was hundreds of snow-covered miles to the east. To stay here meant two and a half months more of the same idleness. Seventy-five days, each one of which would seem a year long. How would he ever endure the boredom?

The front gates opened, hinges squealing in the cold, to admit a rider. The sound exacerbated the pain behind his eyes. He started to turn away, then stopped. The rider was Captain Lewis!

He forced himself to hold back against the urge to run to the man, to pour out at the captain's feet the dream he had been holding onto for so long. That would be the wrong way to act. The two captains needed time to talk, to catch up. Better to wait and make sure of his timing and his argument.

◂

Rube burst excitedly into the barracks room. "It's time. Captain Lewis just rode in. You got that map ready, Little Brother?"

Joe held up the piece of deer hide. "Just got 'er done."

"Lemme see that." Colter snatched the hide from Joe's hand.

"Don't smudge it," Joe said. "The ink's not near dry."

"Hang the ink. I got to make sure you keep 'em away from Ramey's," Colter said.

Bratton paused from dealing the cards to the poker players. "Hell with Ramey's, Colter. It's McBain's we don't want the sergeants stumbling onto."

"McBain's?" Colter asked, sure he had not heard right.

Bratton nodded. "Whiskey and women. Tasty women."

"McBain's, you sure that's the name?" Colter probed.

"McBain, yep. That's how the man introduced himself when I paid for my first poke," Bratton said.

"Droopin' eyelid? Looks half-awake?" Colter pressed

"Rolls tobacco leaves in paper to smoke. Durnedest thing I ever saw," Bratton answered.

McBain's *papeletes*. There could be no mistake. Mac had found his way here, and he had brought whores with him. The thought made Colter frown.

"McBain's is the biggest thing that's happened to us since liberty back in Cahokia," Rube said. "How'd you miss hearin' about him, Colter?"

"Looks like your buddy Ramey's got hisself competition," Joe Field said. "No reason to go to Ramey's for just whiskey when McBain's got *every-thing* we want."

The men's ribald laughter told Colter that Ramey was already losing out. The man was a whiskey-maker — the best there was. He was not a whore-master.

The sound of footsteps approaching outside silenced the room. Rube grabbed the map away from Colter and stashed it inside his shirt. The card players returned to their game. As Colter took a seat on an upturned barrel, Shannon entered. The trap was set to spring.

Shannon could tell that something was up the instant he walked into the room. Although the other men acted casual, the air crackled with tension. The kind of tension that signalled a plot. A plot to sneak out again tonight, no doubt.

But he could not go to Captain Lewis with just his suspicions. He needed proof. He could always follow the scofflaws; however, Kaskaskia had taught him the downside of that option.

He was wrestling with the problem, pretending to write in his journal as his barracks-mates began to filter away. Newman first, then Rube, then Colter, until Shannon was alone in the room with Joe Field. He knew he had to come up with something fast or lose this opportunity.

Joe stretched and yawned. "Guess I'll mosey on out, see if I can find somethin' to do besides sit. Wanna come along, Shannon?"

The unexpected offer took him totally by surprise. "No, thanks. You go on."

"All right, but you're missin' out on somethin' good."

After Joe left, Shannon tossed down the journal and lunged for the door, stopping when he realized the foolishness of following too closely. In his hesitation, something on the dirt floor beside one of the boxes the card players used as seats caught his eye.

It was a scrap of deerhide with lines and symbols drawn on it. One glance told him he had found his proof.

He was tempted to go straight to Captain Lewis but remembered the problems that had caused him at Kaskaskia and turned aside to the sergeants' quarters. Ordway answered his knock. Floyd and Pryor were not around. Shannon handed him the map. "This is more than a whiskey mill, Sergeant. I've heard whisperings. About women."

"You sit tight, Shannon. I'll take care of this."

Shannon did not move. "You'll tell Captain Lewis where you got the information, right?"

"Of course. Of course. Now get back to your barracks and let me get on with this."

Colter spent the midnight watch anticipating the return of the sergeants from the goosechase the crew had sent them on. By the time pink nudges of dawn began to light up the eastern sky, they still were not back and he began to fret. Had something gone wrong?

No sooner had he asked himself that question than he heard voices outside the gates. Among them, Ordway's unmistakable boom. He slid back the heavy bar and shouldered open one side of the double gate to admit four men: the three sergeants and a thin man sporting a mustache whose ends trailed far below his chin and the stern expression of a man who had come about an overdue debt.

The man and Ordway continued on to the captains' quarters. Floyd hung back. "What do you know about this, Colter?"

Colter had to work to keep his face and voice neutral. "Know about what, Sarge?"

"Last night Shannon came to Ordway with a map, claiming it showed the way to a new whorehouse hereabouts and that a bunch of you had sneaked off there. Only, the map led us to a settler's cabin, not a whorehouse. We didn't know that till we busted down the door. We scared the bejesus out of those womenfolk and chased off their rooster. Our mistake is going to cost Captain Lewis a lot more than a new door and new rooster, mad as that settler is."

Colter ducked his head to hide his smile from Floyd.

"Now, why would anybody here have a map to some settler's cabin?" Floyd asked.

"Maybe they found it?" Colter suggested.

"Right. They found it, then left it for Shannon to find."

"Could be you'll get your wish," Colter ventured. "Maybe Captain'll decide to get rid of Fuzz now."

Floyd shook his head. "Won't happen. Ordway never told the Captain where the map came from. He made it sound like he found it. If he tried to foist it off on Shannon now, it'd make him look worse than he already does. Ordway's too smart for that."

Floyd trudged to his quarters and Colter paced out his watch, swallowing his disappointment. The trap had been sprung, but unfortunately the intended prey had escaped.

10. *A Trap is Laid*

C urled under his blanket, Shannon teetered on the cusp of sleep while his head danced with sweet images of himself as a lieutenant, leading the crew and carrying out the captains' directives. Those visions shattered when the cabin's door banged open and John Shields, a crewman from Barracks 2, crowed, "You done it. You got Ordeal!" He used the crew's nickname for Ordway.

"How'd you know?" Newman asked through a yawn.

"I just saw him come through the gates with a settler. Seems our three fine sergeants raided the feller's cabin, and he's madder'n a wet cat. He's in seein' Captain Lewis and Ordeal right now. Says he won't leave till he gets fifty dollars to pay the damages."

The news shredded every trace of Shannon's contentment. Amid the chaos Shields's news caused, he slunk out the door and headed to the privacy of the latrine until he could get a handle on his churning emotions.

Someone was already there. A recent recruit named McNeal, a repulsive man who would talk your ear off about nothing if you gave him the chance. Shannon turned toward the storeroom just as the door to the captains' quarters opened and a thin man came out, clutching a fat purse. Shields had been telling the truth.

Ordway trailed behind the stranger. He spotted Shannon and cocked his head toward the gates. Shannon nodded and headed off to their private meeting place where *Discovery* rested on supports at the edge of the river.

Ordway showed up a few moments later. His voice was unnaturally quiet. "Where did you get that map, Shannon?"

"I told you, Sergeant. It was lying on the floor next to the box the others use for a cardtable."

"You are a fool, Shannon. An idiot."

Fool? Idiot? He was neither of those things and he would not allow himself to be so disparaged. "I did what you asked. I was your eyes and ears among the crew. I won't take the blame for your mistake."

"My mistake? Mine? You're the one had to be led back to Kaskaskia, Private. Why, it's a wonder you can find your way to the latrine."

To have that embarrassment thrown back in his face was too much. "I advise you to be careful what you say to me, Sergeant. When I'm lieutenant —"

Ordway grabbed hold of Shannon's shirt and yanked him forward. "Lieutenant is one thing you'll *never* be, Shannon. Not if I have anything to do with it."

Nose to nose with Ordway, Shannon ran out of words to fling back at the man. The sergeant released him with a violence that caused him to stumble backwards. "What a mistake I made not telling Captain Lewis where I got that map! You'd be off this crew by noon."

Shannon stared at the sergeant while the implications of what he had said sank in. The captain did not know he was involved. Ordway had planned to take all the credit. Instead he was getting all the blame. "Like I said, Sergeant, your mistake."

Ordway's face contorted like that of a man about to strike, but just as suddenly, the mood passed, as he turned and stalked away.

Shannon walked the trampled path back to the camp with a lighter heart. The sergeant had just done him an enormous favor, one he needed to move swiftly to take advantage of. First he needed an opening. For that, he went back to the barracks for the captain's navigation book. Returning it would be his excuse to speak to Lewis.

Inside the room the captains shared, Captain Lewis was seated at the small table before a heap of account ledgers and receipts. "What is it?"

It had been over two months since they had been able to talk, and Shannon was not prepared for the captain's brusqueness. "Have I interrupted you, sir?"

Lewis tossed a confirming wave. New lines around his mouth and eyes gave him a pinched look.

"It's a pleasure to have you back with us, sir," Shannon began.

"Yes, yes. Get on with it."

Shannon had to swallow before he could forge on. "Sir, it has been my observation the last two months here at the camp that, given the short time left until we leave, Captain Clark needs additional help."

"The whole Corps needs a lot of things — more time, more money, a break from this interminable cold, less political maneuvering," Lewis said.

"I was referring to discipline, Captain. A junior officer would take some of the burden off the captains' shoulders. And I would be honored to be considered for such a position."

Lewis leaned against the chair back and rubbed his eyes. "I see." He ran a thumb along the side of the open ledger. "You are an astute young man, Private."

Shannon's heart raced with renewed anticipation. The captain leaned forward and steepled his fingers in front of his chin. "You are right. Discipline is an issue. The Corps will succeed only if we work together. Every man must do his part."

He dropped his hands onto the open ledger. "However, another officer is not the answer. We have too much overhead as it is. Thank you for your suggestion. Be sure the door latches when you leave." He picked up his quill and went back to work.

Incredulous and dazed, Shannon let himself out and stumbled through sleet he did not see or feel to the barracks. He curled onto his bunk and stared at the wall without seeing it. Since joining the expedition, he had done his very best to be an exemplary soldier. For what? To be slapped down not once, but twice. To feel completely alone and isolated in the midst of a crowd of men he could barely stomach. To face a future trapped in a position he was utterly unsuited for. A position that wore him down physically and emotionally and starved his intellect.

In his bewilderment, he paid no attention to the comings and goings of the other men throughout the day. It took a full bladder to finally bring him back to reality. The room was empty and he realized he was shivering. He slogged to the latrine and back on leaden legs, then stoked up the fire, stripped the blankets from three bunks and wrapped himself in them.

He was huddled by the fire when Rube bumped in, back from hunting. "Oowee! Got me two elk and two deer with four shots! Four shots! Can you believe that?"

Shannon listened dejectedly to the elated chatter. Who cared about food? Or hunting? He wanted to be warm.

Rube took the box next to Shannon. "That my blanket you got there?"

Shannon started to unwind it, but Rube waved him off. "Use it. Looks like you need it. You sick or something? Maybe I ought to go get Captain?"

"No. That's okay. I'm just cold."

"York could make you up some of his special tea. It'll put you right back on your feet," Rube offered.

Shannon again demurred, but the man's concern touched him. This was the first real conversation they had ever shared, and it revealed a whole other side to Rube. A kind and gentle side that Shannon needed so badly at that moment.

"You sure there's nothin' I can do for you, Shannon?"

That Rube had called him by his name rather than "Peckerwood" was not lost on him. "No, nothing. Thanks."

Rube stared into the fire. His voice was soft, almost sad. "Place like this sure can get lonely, can't it? A time or two this past month I've felt, well, downright lost. You ever feel like that?"

Shannon was astonished to hear Rube describe exactly what he was feeling at that moment. He nodded.

Rube reared back on his seat and slapped his palms on his thighs. "You do, huh? Then you're in luck, Shannon. I happen to know just the thing'll fix you up. Only — He slid a sideways look at Shannon.

Shannon did not want anything to spoil the camaraderie blossoming between them. "I'm part of this crew, Rube, and that's just what I want to be, although that hasn't always been obvious by my actions."

Rube studied him as if weighing a decision. "You up for a drink?"

Shannon understood the implication and Rube's hesitation. "I'd love one. No. Make that several."

Rube tapped him on the knee. "Then you best come along with me right now. I got the cure for what's ailin' you." He leaned toward Shannon conspiratorially. "Bunch of us got a celebration planned tonight. In honor of bamboozlin' Ordeal."

Sneaking off to a grog shop meant going against everything he'd been taught. Yet, Shannon did not think twice. He needed a release. Badly. "Lead the way."

From his hiding place behind the screening wall of the latrine, Colter watched Shannon leave the barracks with Rube. The crew's plan was working. Tonight they would get their revenge on Fuzz. From the looks of him, Shannon suspected nothing. As much as he would love to be there to witness the reckoning, Colter had no intention of making McBain's acquaintance again. Not after Maysville. Whatever McBain dished out tonight, Shannon deserved.

*

"Am I seeing a ghost or is that really Peckerwood?"

Shannon could not pick the speaker out from among the crewmen packed into the cabin's front room. That he had chosen to defy orders to sneak off to a place where men drank whiskey and committed who knew what other sins both excited and intimidated him. He followed Rube into the room with his heart in his throat.

Newman pushed forward to meet them. "So you finally decided to join us, Shannon? Here, first one's on me." He pressed a cup into Shannon's hand.

Rube tapped the cup he had just acquired against Shannon's. "To Peckerwood."

The group pressing around them echoed the toast. Their encouragement overcame Shannon's hesitation. He followed Rube's example and drained the drink in a single swallow. His mouth, throat, and stomach all caught fire at once. He doubled over, coughing and gasping for breath.

Rube thumped him between the shoulders. "Second one's easier."

Rube's jollity and his own pride would not let Shannon refuse the refill someone shoved at him. Rube raised his cup again. "To good friends, and to hell with certain sergeants."

"I'll drink to that," Newman declared, clunking his cup on Rube's, then Shannon's.

Rube was right. The second drink was easier. After the third, he felt pleasantly warm all over. He relaxed against the bar, basking in the buzz of conversation and the press of the crowd.

Rube pushed another refill toward him. "So, how do you like it?"

His affection for the man grew stronger by the minute. "Better than I ever imagined. Thanks, Rube." His tongue felt sluggish and thick, but he had so many things he wanted to say to Rube. "I know I haven't been much of a friend before."

"Don't go mushy on me now. Drink up," Rube said.

Shannon tossed down the drink. He lowered the cup to find a stranger wedged next to him. "I don't believe I've had the pleasure. McBain's the name — for me and this place."

The hand Shannon shook was soft to touch and firm to grip. Before he could get his mouth to work, Rube said, "This here's Shannon."

"Welcome to McBain's, Mr. Shannon. Please accept this drink from me as a token of my thanks for your business this evening."

The man's generosity drove Shannon's sense of well-being even higher. He could not remember when he had felt this good, this accepted. At last he was coming to understand what attracted men to places like this. He had been so wrong to condemn what he did not understand, to look down on the other crewmen, to chase promotion at all costs. These were good men despite their lack of education. *From now on, things'll change*, he thought. *I'm one of this crew and I'll act like it.*

He gulped down the free whiskey. "Thanks, Mr. McBain," he said through numbed lips.

"No need to be formal, Shannon. We're all friends here." McBain leaned toward him. "Whiskey's only one of the pleasures I offer. Perhaps you'd be interested in others. Say, something like this?"

Shannon blinked in the direction of McBain's outstretched hand. The room grew suddenly hushed, and the crowd parted to reveal a woman in a figure-hugging gown of jade green. Though she stood no taller than a girl, she had a prominent bosom and womanly hips. She glided forward until she stood directly in front of him. She had full red lips and enormous eyes made wider by an outline of black.

"This is Lisette, Mr. Shannon," McBain said.

Shannon could not get his mouth around her name. She rescued him from his temporary muteness, speaking in a low, caressing voice. "Lisette, she is *enchanté*, Monsieur Shannon."

Her fingers on his cheek felt electric as she murmured against his ear. "Lisette, she likes what she sees. Does Shannon?"

The scent of rose petals clung to her, filling up his senses. He managed a breathy "yes."

"Then with me you will come." Lisette took his hand and led him toward the back rooms. Shannon did not resist.

◆

Shannon came awake to a wave of throbbing pain dashing against the insides of his skull. "Oww!" He grabbed for his head as if to squeeze out the agony.

Carefully swiveling his eyes but not his head, he saw nothing recognizable about the room he found himself in. Women's clothes hung from pegs along one wall. A patchwork quilt lay in a jumble at the end of the bed. He was lying on a feather mattress, not his usual hard pallet. *Where am I?* He thought.

The door banged open, causing a fresh surge of throbbing inside his head. Sergeants Ordway and Floyd entered the room. "Private Shannon!" Ordway bellowed.

Shannon tried to sit up, but pain exploded behind his eyes. Without warning, his stomach erupted and vomit spewed everywhere.

"Good God!" Ordway boomed in disgust. "Drunk, AWOL and still in the whore's bed."

Whore? Shannon stared dumbly at the putridness splattering his half-covered body. A name washed up onto the sterile beaches of his brain. "Lisette," he gasped.

His stomach convulsed again, but he managed to lean out over the floor in the nick of time.

"Jesus!" Floyd muttered. "What a mess!"

Shannon pushed himself into a sitting position, clamping his eyes shut against the pain knifing through his skull.

A woman pushed her way into the room then. Lisette, he remembered. When she saw the mess he had made of her bed, she gave a strangled cry and flew at him, her nails raking his face. "Clean it up! All of it! Now, damn you! Now!"

"Whoa, there, ma'am." Floyd captured her hands before she could inflict serious damage. "Get up, Shannon, or I'll turn her loose."

Even through his haze, Shannon could see Floyd's effort to suppress a grin and hated him for it.

She struggled against the sergeant's hold, screaming at Shannon, "Damn you, you shiftless drunk! Damn all of you!"

Shannon got to his feet but nearly toppled over from dizziness. He was sure that the Lisette he remembered spoke with a French accent unlike this women. It was not until the next wave of nausea passed that he realized he was naked, and erect. He spread his hands in front of his groin and looked numbly around the room for his clothes.

Ordway lifted a pair of vomit-splattered trousers from the floor with the toe of his boot. "Shannon, you are pathetic."

He was too embarrassed to disagree. He pulled on the pants with difficulty, then found his boots. Buttoning his trousers, he stumbled from the room and out into the blinding sunlight. There he collapsed into a snow bank and retched up the rest of the contents of his stomach.

"It's a pity the captain can't see you now," Floyd said. "Maybe then he'd see what a mistake you are, and I'd be rid of you. You sure got what you deserved. Now you get to march back to camp and face 'em."

"Them?" Shannon croaked, too ashamed to meet the sergeant's eyes.

"Oh, the crew got you good. Paid you back for snitching on them."

Then it sank in. He had walked right into the trap, eyes open. He had swallowed Rube's overtures without question and violated every principle he had been taught. He had betrayed his parents and his superiors. He wanted to die. Only, he knew God would not be that kind.

11. *Risen From the Dead*

F ingers of bitter cold thrust like daggers through the thin pallet of filthy straw into the marrow of Josiah Hartley's bones. He lay on his side, pretending to sleep while he waited for the other residents of the tumbledown shanty to clear out. On this of all mornings, the wait to be alone seemed interminable.

The boy Jethro left first, off to spend the day fishing through cracks in the river ice. Despite having only a shaved stick and length of twine to work with, Jethro had managed to keep them all fed. Or at least he had until four days ago when his usual luck failed him. Four days with nothing to eat except a few swallows of lukewarm water flavored with moldy potato skins had made up Hartley's mind. It was time to leave.

A sour odor announced the family's mangy yellow cur a moment before the pathetic creature's inquiring nose brushed against the exposed skin on the back of Hartley's neck. He managed to stifle an involuntary jerk. There was too much at stake to give himself away now.

"Come away, Tater," the widow woman wheezed from the direction of the fireplace. The mongrel broke off exploring Hartley's prone form, but then Hoopy, Jethro's little sister, started to cough, a croupy hacking sound that set the preacher's teeth on edge. Her coughing made the wound in his ribs itch, and it took all his control not to dig at it.

He remembered so little of the last three months. His only memories consisted of a few disjointed scenes separated by long tunnels of blackness. His clearest remembrance was of the moment he rose out of a pool of pain in the clearing where Rutledge had left him for dead to see Jethro passing by on his way to fish. Somehow he had summoned the strength to push his bleeding body off the ground and flag the boy down. Knowing he would die without help, he had thrust his purse into the youngster's hands, then fainted.

After that, he remembered nothing until he came to days later to find a gaunt, graying woman changing the bandages that bound his torso from armpit to waist. She was a taciturn soul, and it had taken extraordinary persistence to prod her into talking. Even then, he gleaned precious few details.

She was a destitute widow, struggling to keep herself and her two children alive through the winter. She had only agreed to care for him in return for the contents of his purse. Yet, she proved a gentle and attentive nurse.

The woman and her sickly daughter went out at last. Hartley listened to the sound of Hoopy's coughing recede until he could hear it no more. Only then did he throw off the thin blanket, plant his feet on the cold earthen floor and pull himself into a standing position, using the leaky cabin wall for support. Moving cautiously against the twinges of his mending wound, he peered out a knothole toward the slowly collapsing lean-to that served as a stable for the family's horse.

Good. They had not taken the animal.

He slowly dragged himself the six paces to the tiny room's darkest corner where he figured the widow would have buried his purse. The family cur growled menacingly at his approach.

Hartley had grown to hate the miserable creature, but he tried to keep that feeling from sounding in his voice. "Good dog. Good Tater, move away and let me see what you're guarding."

The volume of the dog's growls rose as the hair on its back lifted.

There was too much to do and too little time to get it all done to mess with this now. "Stop that now," Hartley demanded.

The dog's growls gave way to full-fledged barking. Barks that could draw the widow back to the cabin. If that happened . . . He picked up the family's one pan, a rusting iron skillet, from the lip above the fireplace. "Move, you leprous bag of worms!"

Tater's lips pulled back over its yellow teeth and it sprang for Hartley's throat. The preacher swung the skillet at the creature's skull. The pan connected with a wet *thwack*. Tater's barking ceased abruptly, and it fell into a heap with blood oozing from the flattened side of its skull. The blow had killed it.

Hartley viewed the carcass with satisfaction. "Damn you!" he snarled, giving the animal a vicious kick in payment for the pain that swinging the skillet had caused his unhealed rib wound.

The dog's hind leg twitched as if mocking him, and the preacher lost all control. He forgot his wound, picked up the animal's limp body and flung it onto the banked coals of the fire. Immediately the tip of one thin ear began to smolder.

"Burn in hell!"

With the curse still ringing in the room, the smoking ear caught fire, flames spreading to engulf the whole of Tater's head, filling the little room with the stench of burned hair.

While the dead dog burned, Hartley fell to his knees and ripped at the soft dirt with his bare hands. In no time he found the purse. Feeling the hard lumps under his fingers brought a grim smile to his cracked lips. The widow had spent little, if any of his money.

His smile faded, however, as he considered the full purse from another perspective. The woman had chosen to let him go hungry for four days rather than spend money — *his* money — for food. Stupid woman! She should be horse-whipped for such parsimony. Since he did not have a whip and did not intend to be there when the widow returned, he decided taking all the blankets would serve as just punishment for her avarice. The family should have taken better advantage of him when he was down. Now it was their problem how they would keep themselves warm the rest of the winter.

At the door, he paused for one last look around the miserable hovel. A bit of fat from Tater's skinny body sizzled in the fire. The sound prompted an idea to take shape: If the dog could burn, why not Colter?

The idea proved so pleasing that Hartley stepped into the cold, crisp winter air, feeling better than he had in months.

12. *Writing in the Snow*

From his usual leaning spot against the wall of Barracks 3, sheltered from the swirling end-of-February wind, Newman yelled out, "Left . . . left!"

Shannon held his eyes fixed straight ahead and continued with his punishment drill, closing his ears to the hazing. The rest of the crew had grown tired of their sport. But not Newman, who continued to harrass him as he marched endless circuits around the compound every afternoon. He wished he could hate Newman and Rube and the others for conspiring to make him fall from grace, but admitting his transgressions to Captain Lewis had left him too humiliated to work up loathing for anyone but himself.

"Come on, Peckerwood," Newman called. "Put some li —"

Shannon craned around to see what had cut Newman short. Captain Lewis emerged from his quarters, trailed by the three sergeants. York took the captain's saddlebags and secured them to the saddle, then held the horse while Lewis mounted. The captain was headed to St. Louis to join Captain Clark for the ceremony formally transferring the Territory of Louisiana from France to the United States.

"In my absence, I leave Sergeant Ordway in charge," Shannon heard Lewis say. He could see the gloating on Ordway's face from across the compound, and it unleashed a new emotion within him. The urge for revenge.

The moment the gates closed behind the captain, Floyd and Pryor turned away from Ordway with an abruptness that conveyed their opposition to the captain's decision. Seeing that gave impetus to Shannon's impulse, and he knew just where to start to set things in motion.

"So why are you tellin' me this?" Colter demanded moments later.

"Ordway had no call to make you wear that patch. No call," Shannon answered.

The candidness of the answer disarmed Colter who had been on his way back from wood detail when Shannon accosted him and prodded at the guilt he had been carrying around over his role in exposing the younger man to the crew's revenge. "It ain't a-goin' to work."

"Of course it will! There are only three of them versus all of us," Shannon insisted.

"But the captains?"

"They're both in St. Louis. Captain Lewis rode out awhile back. I'm on the gates tonight so you don't even have to sneak over the walls."

Colter was still not convinced. He distrusted the sudden change in Shannon.

"Look, Old Man, it's a good plan and one sure way to show Ordeal up. I've done my part. Now it's up to you what you and the others do with my idea." With that, Shannon stalked off.

Colter watched him, weighing suspicions of the younger man's motivation against the idea Shannon had suggested. He decided in favor of Shannon and entered the barracks.

After he had laid out the plan to the others, Newman slapped down his poker hand. "Count me in, Colter." The rest of the crewmen quickly echoed agreement.

"Hope Ramey's ready for us," Colter commented.

"Ramey, hell," Newman said. "I'm heading for McBain's. And a woman."

Newman's comment drew another chorus of agreement. Colter was caught off-guard. He had put McBain and his establishment completely out of mind.

Amidst the welter of conversations spawned by the prospect of visiting McBain's, Rube sidled over. "I'm with you, Colter. They can have McBain's. Me, I got a hankering for a whole lot of Ramey's good rum."

Although he guessed that Rube was going with him out of some misguided sense of loyalty, Colter accepted the offer with gratitude. At least there would be two of them at Ramey's tonight. Two was better than none.

With no one else in the barracks, normally inconsequential night sounds bothered Shannon: the hiss and crackle of the fire, wind whistling through cracks in the chinking, the popping of the building's logs as the night temperatures plummeted below zero. Tension had him too wound up to sleep. What was taking the sergeant so long?

The door banged open. "On your feet!" Ordway ordered.

Shannon took his time getting off the bunk. He intended to enjoy every moment of this spectacle.

The sergeant stomped to the nearest bed and ripped away its blanket. "Empty! By God, I'll have heads this time. Where did they go, Shannon?"

"Who, Sergeant?" Shannon said. A smile tugged at the corners of his mouth despite his attempts to control it.

"Unless you want another month of extra drill, Private, you'll tell me where they went."

Since Shannon did not know, he could not lie. "I don't know, Sergeant."

"By God, Private, you're in for it this time!" Ordway threatened.

There was not one thing Ordway could do to him that had not already happened. Even being denied membership in the permanent party that would head up the Missouri when the ice cleared — even that would be a blessing after what he had endured the last two weeks.

"I'm warning you, Shannon. I can see to it that this is the end of the line for you."

Shannon gave up all attempts to control his incipient smile. "Yes, Sergeant."

Rube stood next to Colter, slouching pathetically. His woeful expression contrasted sharply with the crooked grin he had sported last night when he traced his name in a snow bank with a stream of piss, crowing with delight when he succeeded in dotting the "i" in his last name. It was Rube's crowing that got him, Wiser, Shields, and Colter caught.

Colter stared at the outside wall of the captains' quarters and considered the irony of what had happened. When Shannon had come to him yesterday with the idea for the whole crew to break out, no one had taken into account that dangerous ice conditions would keep Captain Lewis from crossing the Mississippi as intended. The captain was still in Cahokia when Pryor showed up with news of the crew's escapade. The captain immediately postponed his trip and returned to Camp Wood to mete out punishment to those crewmen unfortunate enough to get caught. As much as Colter disliked Ordway, he respected Lewis and he did not relish having to stand before the man who had steadfastly supported him, to answer for a stunt that seemed so pointless in the thin light of a gray morning.

"You're gone now, Colter," Ordway had told him on the way back to the camp last night. His dismissal from the Corps would be the answer to the sergeant's prayers. At one time it would have been the answer to his own prayers, too. Now, though, he saw things in a different light. For one, he had Scratch Wilkes's offer of a full partnership once he returned from the expedition. For another, he had endured five months of hardship since Maysville — six since Stuart's Draft. All that time and effort ought to count for something besides a memory or two. The only way to make it count was to stick it out with the expedition. Now, that seemed like a remote chance, at best.

Lewis emerged from his quarters. His face was clouded and drawn. He climbed up on a stump and the crew fell immediately silent. Colter focused on a knot in the horizontal log behind the captain's left knee. He felt Lewis's eyes raking him, but he could not bring himself to meet the captain's gaze. Beside him, Rube shifted nervously. Colter held his body still against the urge to follow suit.

Lewis began to speak. "As your commanding officer, I am appalled by your misbehavior. You have each been entrusted with a mission of critical importance to this nation. The money to train, supply and support you derives from the sweat and toil of your countrymen. Do you think they would approve of the way you chose to dishonor their trust last night? I know they would not, and so do you."

He paused to let his words sink in.

"This mission requires the full effort of each of us. You, the sergeants, Captain Clark, me. Everyone. If any one of you is not willing to promise that, speak now."

Silence.

"Very well. Sergeant Ordway will act as commanding officer in my absence. That means his orders carry the same weight as Captain Clark's or mine." He fixed his scowl on each of the recruits in turn to emphasize his point, then addressed Colter and his three companions.

"The four of you will be confined to Barracks 3 under guard for ten days. Sergeants Floyd and Pryor will adjust living arrangements accordingly. Dismissed."

Colter stared at the door for a long time after it closed on the captain, trying to absorb the fact that Ordway had been wrong. He was still a member of the crew.

Ordway took hold of his arm, lifting him out of his thoughts. "Let's go, Colter."

Since the dispersing men were paying no attention, Colter gave into the impulse to prod the sergeant over what had come to pass. "Seems you and Captain don't never quite see eye to eye, Sarge. Thought you said he was goin' to send us all packin'.'"

A slight shift in the sergeant's expression told Colter he had scored a hit. "It's only March first, Private. At least a month until the captains name the permanent party. Only reason Captain's hanging onto you and the others is that there's so much work left to do."

"Goin' to be real hard for us to help out much seein' as how we'll be in-side for ten days," Colter shot back.

The sergeant held out his hand. "Give me your patch, Private."

Colter pretended not to find it in his pockets. He wanted to know why Ordway was asking for it.

"I know you've got it. Now hand it over," Ordway demanded, his voice rising.

"Does this mean we ain't got no more drills, Sarge?"

"It means I want it," the sergeant said.

"You'll git it when you tell me why you're askin' for it," Colter said.

Ordway appeared to struggle with what to say before he spoke. "Captain Lewis wants it."

Pulling it out, Colter wadded the leather into a ball and tossed it high into the air, forcing the sergeant to catch it. "There, you got it. Guess you're goin' to have to put up with my butt-ugly face from now on. Huh, Sarge?"

"Don't push it, Colter."

"Don't have to. You're doin' enough for both of us." With that, he strolled whistling to his barracks to begin his sentence. No matter what else happened on this expedition, he would never forget the look on Ord-way's face when he admitted that the captain wanted the patch. That was worth ten day's confinement, easy.

13. *Pox*

O*ne more day. Just one more.* Colter lay on his bunk, repeating the phrase to himself again and again. Nine days of his punishment were over. Nine long, boring days with nothing to do but stare at these four walls and try to shut out the presence of the other three men. Even whit-tling had lost its magic ability to take him out of his surroundings.

Today, Day Ten, would be the longest and most tedious.

Since trips to the latrine were the only times they were allowed out, he welcomed the pressure growing in his bladder. He pulled on his boots, shrugged on his coat and told their guard where he was going. He walked across the compound slowly in order to prolong the experience.

Inside the latrine, he found Shannon standing at the lip of the trench with his trousers open, examining his penis. "Howdy, Fuzz."

Shannon started at his greeting and fumbled to tuck himself away.

Colter studied Shannon's face briefly. "Looks like you got yourself some trouble. How long you had it?"

Shannon tried to leave without answering, but Colter grabbed his wrist. "How long?"

"It's this cold weather. Always makes me tighten up," Shannon said, prying without success at Colter's gripping fingers.

"It ain't the weather and it ain't goin' away by itself, Fuzz. Only one thing gives a man sores like that there. And that's the pox. You been with any other woman besides McBain's whore?"

Shannon blushed bright red at the question. "Her name is Lisette. And I tell you it's the cold."

"If'n it's her, then some others're likely to have it, too. Captain Lewis is due back tomorrow. You go see him. He'll fix you right up."

"I'll do no such thing," Shannon shot back. "And don't you go running to him either. I don't have the pox and that's final."

The guard Leakins yelled from across the compound, "Hurry it up in there, Colter. I can't wait on you all durned day."

Reluctant to have his brief freedom end, Colter finished his business and rebuttoned his trousers. "Pox ain't nothin' to fool with, Fuzz. It can blind you or drive you outta your mind. Best go see the captain soon as he's back."

"For the last time, Colter. I don't need to see the captain because I don't have a problem! End of story."

"And I'm tellin' you for the last time: Go see the captain."

"Either you come out, or I'm going for the sergeant," Leakins yelled.

"I'm comin'," Colter shouted back, and with one last look at Shannon's stubborn face, he returned to the barracks and his last day of confinement.

Shannon lay wide awake on his bunk surrounded by the snores and mutterings of his sleeping barracks-mates. In the hopelessness of deep night, his earlier exchange with Colter in the latrine haunted him.

The pox . . . the pox . . . oh, God, why is this happening to me? Haven't I paid for my misdeeds? I can't even remember what happened to me that night. Can't even put a face with the name Lisette.

"Captain Lewis'll fix you right up," Colter had said. But how could he go to the captain? How could he bring himself to admit such a grievous moral blunder?

One of the men chuckled in his sleep, a sound so incongruous with Shannon's mood that he was driven from the room. Outside, the inky blackness of the slumbering camp closed in around him, and he was struck by a wave of loneliness that made him long for the familiar, for home, for his mother and father. Beginning with his impulsive decision at Moonbeam O'Toole's, he had made a royal mess of his life. As far as his parents knew, he had dropped off the face of the Earth. He was their only child, the one into whom they had poured their faith, their hope, their love, and how had he repaid them? By vanishing without a trace. He deserved a lifetime of loneliness as punishment for the pain he had inflicted on those who loved him most.

The hunched figure of the gate guard stepped to the front of the little watch shelter. Recognizing Shannon, he waved, then returned to the shadows.

In the short space of that exchange, Shannon made a decision. He no longer belonged on this expedition, if he ever had. He needed to go home, to throw himself on his parents' mercy, to re-establish a bond of trust with them, and to rebuild a life for himself, modelled on their vision for him, from whatever scraps of his old life he could salvage.

The image of the angry red sore on his manhood popped to mind, and he knew he had to go now before his courage failed.

He walked to the latrine, skirted the shield wall, stepped gingerly over the trench and boosted himself to the top of the picket wall. With one last glance at the slumbering fort, he bid farewell to what had turned out to be an impossible dream, then dropped to the ground outside the walls.

He paused to take his bearings, knowing that he could ill afford to get turned around since his absence would be discovered at morning roll call. Then he struck out for Cahokia where he could get across the Mississippi to St. Louis. From there . . . well, winter or not, there had to be a way to get back to Ohio. A way he intended to find.

*

"Colter," Ordway called out.

"Sergeant!" Colter responded with a gusto that brought glances from several of the other men lined up for morning roll call. *Let 'em stare*, he thought. *They ain't the ones been locked up for ten days.*

"Shannon," the sergeant called.

No response.

Ordway's voice rose, "Private Shannon!"

For the first time since lining up, Colter noticed that the place next to him was empty. Where was Fuzz?

"Shannon!" Ordway boomed.

Someone behind Colter grumbled, "Try the latrine. He's there an awful lot lately." The comment brought snickers from other men who had obviously noticed Shannon's problem, too.

Ordway motioned for Floyd to check the latrine, then went on with the roll call. Floyd returned, shaking his head. "At ease," Ordway ordered, stepping down off the stump and going to report the situation to Captain Lewis, who had just returned from St. Louis.

Rube caught Colter's eye. To his questioning look, Colter could only shrug. He should have known better than to trust Shannon not to do something stupid over a simple case of pox. Where Shannon was concerned, nothing was ever simple or easy.

*

Shannon sagged against a sapling, grateful for any kind of support. The walk from the fort to Cahokia had been long and difficult because of the icy ruts formed by the hooves of the horses traveling the route.

His stomach clenched around a pang of hunger. He hugged himself and waited for the ache to pass. When he could stand it, he sat up and took stock of his situation.

Even in the dead of winter, Cahokia had a comforting air about it. Its thirty-odd neat houses, row of business establishments and two substantial timbered buildings, the church and the territorial courthouse, were all laid out above the high-water mark at the mouth of its namesake stream. Beyond it lay the Mississippi, its swift current bearing ice in huge sheets, small chunks and every size in between.

He shivered at the sight of all that water. If he was to get to St. Louis, he had to find a way to cross, but how could he possibly submit to such a journey?

The smell of frying bacon from a cabin nearby curtailed his thoughts. Emboldened by hunger, he plodded straight to the door and knocked.

The door opened to reveal a girl of perhaps fourteen whose face brightened into a welcoming smile at the sight of him. "Hello," Shannon said. "I . . . I need to get across the river. Can you help me?"

A man with permanently narrowed eyes and a mustache that drooped below the level of his thin pointed chin pushed the girl aside and probed Shannon with a suspicious gaze. "You from that there fort up on the Wood River?"

The tenor of the question told Shannon that telling the truth would not be a wise decision. "No, sir, I came from the south." He waved in a direction that he hoped was south.

The man did not accept the answer immediately. He continued studying Shannon, then finally said, "From the looks of you, you could stand some grub. Come on in."

Shannon tried with limited success to keep the gush of relief out of his "Yes, sir." He followed the man to a rickety table and took one of the two chairs. The girl and an older woman whom Shannon took to be her mother moved about the cramped room getting plates served up. He watched them out of the corner of his eye while half-listening to the man go on about the weather.

"Be glad you ain't from that there fort," the man said. "This here family ain't got no use for them kind."

"What kind is that, sir?" Shannon asked warily.

"The kind what busts in on law-abidin' folk for no reason. Why, they tore our place up so bad and scairt Molly there enough that we had to move way down here to shelter out the rest of the winter in this here rat's nest of a town. Remains to be seen if we can repair our place, let alone live in it agin." He spit a wad of tobacco juice into the corner of the room.

"I never seen such high-handed goin's on. Never thought I'd be on the wrong end of folks what's paid to protect us. All that fort's done is brung us problems and misery." The man pushed back from the table and went to fetch his jug.

In the ensuing silence, Shannon inwardly cursed the bad luck that had delivered him to the very group of settlers whom Ordway had raided a month ago. He groped for a way to extricate himself from these people.

The girl slid a plate of food onto the table in front of him with a wink.

Shannon managed a distracted nod and picked up the spoon although his appetite had deserted him. At that moment the cold metal of a rifle muzzle jammed against the flesh of his neck.

"Don't you make no fast moves now, and I won't have to hurt you," the man said. "Woman, tie his wrists and ankles. Him and me are goin' for a ride."

*

"Never knew Peckerwood could look so good on a horse," Rube said, grinning broadly.

Colter grunted noncommittally. Shannon lay belly-down across the swayed back of a winter-thin nag. Colter had immediately recognized the man leading the horse as the settler whose cabin the sergeants had erroneously raided last month.

The settler did not acknowledge Captain Lewis's greeting. "I brung back this here deserter of your'n. Now where's my reward?"

Without hesitation or argument, Lewis drew a purse out of his jacket and dropped it into the settler's outstretched hand.

"This ain't near enough. Not for all the trouble I gone to," the settler complained.

"It's what I have, sir," the captain answered.

The settler appeared to want to argue further but finally pocketed the money. "Get him off'n my horse so's I can be on my way."

Ordway waved Colter forward to help Shannon down. "Jesus, Fuzz!" Colter whispered. "What the hell are you thinkin', takin' off like that?"

Shannon leaned against him but would not meet his eyes until Colter forced his chin up. What he saw pricked his conscience. The light of ambition no longer shown in Shannon's eyes. Instead there was a dull sheen, a glassiness, as if the spirit behind them had fled.

He released Shannon's chin, aware that the blame for everything bad that had happened to the younger man in the last month rested squarely on his own shoulders. Now he wished he had never opened his mouth, never revealed who had informed on the crew. He mentally kicked himself for not sticking to his principles.

"Come with me, Private Shannon," Lewis said.

Shannon pushed away from Colter's supporting hold and shuffled after the captain. The door closed behind them, and Colter turned away. There was no use agonizing over what had happened. At least now Shannon would have to admit his pox to the captain, would have to submit to treatment. That took care of one problem. Now for the other.

*

Shannon was too mortified to meet the captain's eyes. He waited for Lewis to speak, waited for the final indictment, the bitter end to what had once been a wonderful dream.

"So, George?" Lewis said.

The captain's familiarity that he had once treasured now cut Shannon like a rapier. His head drooped even lower.

Impatience crept into the captain's tone. "Explain yourself."

Nothing about the choice he had made lent itself to explanation because no part of it made sense anymore. If he could not understand his own actions, how could he possibly explain them to anyone else?

He felt the captain's growing disapproval. Lewis had stood behind him from the start. He owed the man an explanation. Something. Anything. "I deserted and I'm ready to face the consequences of my actions, sir." His mouth was dry and his voice quavered, yet he got out what he wanted to say.

"But why, George? Why did you desert?" the captain demanded.

With his throat aching from bottled-up pain, Shannon could not bring himself to reveal his grievous sin to this upright and moral man whom he so admired.

The captain circled behind him. "A month ago, Sergeant Ordway discovered you absent without leave at an illicit establishment called McBain's. I can understand such indiscretions. They are a rite of passage for every soldier. But leaving camp with the intention to desert is quite another matter. One entirely out of character for a bright, eager young man from an excellent family."

Shannon needed to swallow but his jaw was too tight to allow it.

The captain stopped directly in front of him. "When did you first notice the lesions?"

Shannon's head jerked up in surprise.

"Just as I thought," Lewis said. "Unbutton your trousers."

"I have sinned, sir, and I am being punished. I accept that."

"Nonsense. You have contracted a serious disease. The buttons, Shannon."

He fumbled his trousers open while the captain sorted through the vials in his box of medicines. Lewis removed the stopper from a small bottle. "From what I have observed, this affliction and its treatment will be worse than any punishment I could give you. This will hurt."

Shannon kept his eyes on the far wall, feeling more than naked under the captain's gaze. "Yes, sir."

The captain applied the solution. Shannon gasped at its piercing sting. Captain Lewis was right again.

14. *Rousted*

McBain's was easy to find. All Colter had to do was follow one of the many tracks leading to it from the camp. The place mirrored the braggart's high opinion of himself, and his impracticality. Built of expensive sawn planks, rather than whole logs, it was fancier and larger than any other structure around. It featured generous windows, a pair of fireplaces on opposite walls, and a raised boardwalk along three sides overhung by extensions of the roof.

Colter approached quietly from the side and peeked in a partially open window to size up the situation. There were two people in evidence: Mac and Lil, the whore from Maysville. They were standing at the bar with their backs to him. Since he did not see the other woman, the one named Lisette, he figured she must be sleeping behind one of the three closed doors that led off the main room.

He was about to move toward the front door when a snatch of the conversation stopped him. "That third sergeant, Ordway. He's our problem," said McBain. "We need to find a way to buy him off."

Lil snorted in a most unladylike way. "You're dreaming, Mac. No one can buy that one. Hell —"

McBain slapped her viciously across the mouth. "How many times do I have to remind you? Ladies don't swear." The violence in his tone reminded Colter of Charleston and Lotty's bruised and bleeding body, the result of another fit of McBain's rage.

Whimpering, Lil cringed away from him, but McBain caught her and drew her toward him, cupping her chin and coaxing, "Please, my precious, I need your help on this. For us."

He smoothed back a lock of her hair, then bent to kiss her ear, letting his lips stray onto the soft skin between the base of her neck and her shoulders. She sucked in an audible breath. "I need you, Lil," he crooned. "Say you'll help me."

She turned to him with shining eyes and leaned into his embrace, tucking her head against his chest so she could not see the revulsion that flickered across his face. "Just give the word, Mac darling, and I'll have him eating out of my hand."

Colter watched the gambler stroke Lil's hair, his touch a contradiction to his grimace. "I want you to coach Lisette," McBain said.

Lil pushed out of his embrace. "So that's how it is, huh? Well, if I'm out, there's no reason for me to stick around. Lisette can have you, for all I care." She started for the front door but McBain grabbed her and threw her to the floor.

Colter burst in to find him straddling the prone woman, choking her. He leaped on the gambler, pried his hands free from their stranglehold, and dragged him off Lil. Then he wrenched McBain's arms behind his back and torqued them upward, forcing the man down until his forehead touched the wooden floor.

Despite his position, McBain turned on the charm. "So you finally showed up, Coal-Tar. How about a drink?"

Colter answered by binding the man's wrists to his ankles with a length of rawhide.

McBain persisted. "Is this any way to greet an old friend?"

Colter finished tying up the gambler and turned to Lil. "Get the other gal up, and both of you pack your things. Be quick about it. I ain't got all day."

Clutching her bruised throat, Lil staggered out of the main room to do as he said.

"What's this all about?" McBain asked with concern finally coloring his tone.

"I'm puttin' you out of business, Mac," Colter said.

McBain laughed. "Okay. So you're playing a joke. But enough's enough, all right?"

"Pox ain't no joke."

All the humor left McBain's face. "Pox? Not here. Not my women."

"They ain't your slaves and you don't own 'em, but at least one of 'em's poxed. And it'd be like you not to give a hoot who gets hurt. So I'm helpin' out."

"I don't believe you. Prove it," McBain demanded, struggling against his bindings.

"Ain't time for that. Got to get goin'." Colter started for the other room to hurry the women up.

"Get back here, Colter!" McBain yelled.

He paused in the doorway. "About damn time you got my name right, McBain."

"Damn you, Colter! No one gets the better of me. No one!"

He looked at the man on the floor. "Well, it looks like somebody did."

"You're going to pay for this," McBain hissed.

He shrugged. "With what? Preacher robbed me, remember?" And he went to get the ladies moving.

He led the overburdened horse away from the cabin toward the supply road. He had tried to limit the two women to one bag each, but he had to relent in the face of their angry outbursts. The women needed to get on their way if they were to get to Cahokia before nightfall.

Lil's throat was swollen and purpling where McBain had choked her. Riding behind her, Lisette seemed unconcerned with the other whore's condition. She kept looking behind them.

When they reached the supply road, Colter stopped and handed the reins to Lil. He pointed south. "That's the way. Cahokia's ten, twelve miles so you ain't got time to dawdle."

"We don't want to leave," Lil said and Lisette agreed with a nod.

"He beat you, woman," Colter reminded her.

"It doesn't happen much. Mac loves me," Lil declared.

He could not believe what he was hearing. "A man don't hit a woman he loves."

Lisette spoke up for the first time since Colter set her on the horse. "No, it is me he loves."

He refused to get caught up in that argument. "One of you has the pox. Maybe both. It ain't right you spreadin' it."

"If we can't work, how do you expect us to eat?" Lil argued.

"I didn't get you out of McBain's clutches for sport. You ain't passin' the pox if I can help it. Take this here road and you oughtta reach Cahokia by sundown."

"And then what, Bird Man?" Lil groused.

"They got a big church there where you can ask for help."

"Oh, right. Of course they're going to help women like us. The sight of you makes me want to puke." Lil jammed her heels angrily into the sides of the horse.

Colter watched till they disappeared over the rise. When they did not come back, he dusted his hands and turned toward Camp Wood. He would get back late, but, whatever the consequences to himself, at least he had taken care of the problem of McBain. Knowing that, he could put up with just about anything.

15. *Decisions*

T wo days later Colter learned from two of the crew who had risked going over the wall at night that McBain had disappeared, abandoning his place, leaving the doors wide open and six barrels of whiskey untouched. The satisfaction he felt at knowing he was rid of McBain once and for all was curtailed by his growing concern over what was going on with Shannon.

In the space of a few days, Shannon had turned into a sad, silent shell of a man. He resisted all attempts to draw him into conversation and dragged through the days as if under a spell. Off-duty, he lay on his bunk with his face to the wall. He no longer read or drew or wrote in his journal. He had little appetite and his youthful face became gaunt.

Colter blamed himself for Shannon's state, and he wanted to put things right again. The long winters of unremitting boredom stuck out on his traplines had created in him a keen appreciation for any man who could make life interesting, and one thing about Shannon was that life around him was never boring.

Five days after his first and last trip to McBain's, Colter's name came again to the top of the hunting rotation. He left camp feeling unlucky, and, in the space of four hours, he missed what should have been three sure shots. After the third, he stared after the escaping stag in disgust. "Where's your mind today, Johnny boy?"

"What in hell am I doin' in the Army?" The second question popped out of his mouth before he could stop it. It hung in the winter air like an indictment. The next thing he knew, he was at Ramey's.

Ramey greeted him like a long-lost son and drew him a cup of rum. Colter tossed it down, glad for something to take his mind off his problems.

As he reached into his pocket for a coin to pay, Ramey waved him off. "No charge today. I'm celebrating. McBain is gone! Hooray!" For once, Ramey did not repeat himself.

His elation rubbed off on Colter. He accepted a refill and drank it a bit more slowly than the first. He put down the cup to find the rum-maker watching him closely.

"What's got you down this fine day, John Colter?"

"Cain't hit the side of a barn this mornin'," Colter said.

Ramey cocked an eyebrow. "Is that right? Well, these old eyes of mine tell me there's more. My guess is that you are finally wondering why you're with that there expedition. What's the name of that young buck you're always complaining about? Tanner or some such?"

"You mean Shannon?"

"That's it. Shannon. Hear tell it was you brought him down a peg or two. Never figured you for doing such a thing. From the looks of you, you never figured yourself that way, either. Army life must be getting to you pretty bad."

Colter checked a nod.

"It's awful to feel trapped. Been there a time or two myself." Ramey's gaze shifted to the small window where the ragged hide that covered it lifted on the breeze. "You don't have to stay with that crew, you know. I got a friend over in St. Lou who's looking for a man just like you. Name's Lisa. Manuel Lisa. He's getting up a team of trappers to go out to the Shining Mountains. His idea's to have his men do the trapping and not rely on Indians to bring in the furs like the other fur outfits do. He figures to make more that way and pay better'n any of the others. A word from me and you're on his crew. You won't need no stake, neither."

Colter stared into the clear amber liquid at the bottom of the tin cup. The temptation to say "yes" to Ramey's suggestion was strong, stronger than he wanted to admit. If what he said was true — and Ramey had always been completely trustworthy — Colter would not have to wait for God knew how long to get back to the trapping life he loved and missed. Yet, taking Ramey up on the offer, much as he wanted to, would mean going against the oath of enlistment he had made at Maysville.

"Much obliged, Ramey, but I got to say no," Colter said. "I made a promise and I got to stick by it. Only way out now is if'n the captains don't choose me for the permanent party."

Ramey heaved a regretful sigh. "Always the man of your word. A promise made . . ." His words tailed off and a cunning gleam began to glow in his eyes. "Still, we all change our minds from time to time, no? So I leave the offer open to you, my good friend. You say the word, I'll tell Lisa about you. Here. Let me fill that up again."

This time Colter said "yes."

The day had finally come, the one Shannon had been dreading since his ill-fated desertion attempt three weeks back. Today the captains would announce the names of those men who would comprise the permanent party and continue west to find the Passage. He took his usual place in formation, consumed by a mixture of dread and resignation.

He understood now why Captain Lewis had not had him executed as a deserter. The punishment he had meted out was worse. Much worse. Condemning him to a kind of living death whose coup de grâce would be delivered today.

"Get your butt in line, Shannon!" Ordway bellowed.

Shannon's leg muscles felt weighted with lead. He kept his eyes on the ground in case anyone was looking at him with pity. His self-control was too shaky at that moment to handle pity. He was liable to break down and embarrass himself beyond redemption.

Captain Clark came out of quarters and stepped up onto the speaking stump. Shannon braced himself for what was coming — the moment when he would be proclaimed a failure to the world.

"Gentlemen, I have great news," Clark said. "Captain Lewis and I have set a date for departure. April 18th."

The crew erupted in boisterous cheering, but Shannon was rooted in place by a terrible sadness, unable to join in the celebration, unable to feel anything besides a kind of numb resignation.

Clark called for attention. "To meet that date, we have lots of work to do in order to get the boats and supplies ready. Captain Lewis will leave this morning for St. Louis to help speed up the process. Before he goes, he wants to speak to you. Meri."

Lewis replaced Clark on the stump. In his right hand, the orderly book. His eyes swept the assembled crew. "Following is a list of those men who have been chosen to continue forward with this expedition."

Around Shannon, men shifted nervously. Only Colter and he remained still.

"Private Bratton. Private Collins."

With the reading of each name and each excited response, the ground under Shannon's feet seemed to ripple, making it hard to maintain a stance.

"Private Colter."

Shannon's thoughts raced. *Colter? After all the trouble he had gotten into? Then again, no one could match him for sharp-shooting and success at hunting.*

Colter's "Aye, sir" caused a keen sense of loss to sweep over Shannon. Though he and Colter had their differences, he had grown to rely on the man as a steadying influence, and now that was being taken away.

"Privates Field and Field," Lewis called out.

Out of the corner of his eye, Shannon saw the two brothers grin and elbow each other with a boyishness that compounded his sense of abandonment.

"Private Shannon."

He was too enmeshed in his own turmoil to hear Captain Lewis speak his name. Colter nudged him. "What say, Fuzz?"

Shannon stared at the man, trying to figure out what he meant by "What say."

"Private Shannon," Lewis repeated.

He shifted his uncomprehending eyes to the captain. "Say 'Aye, sir,'" Colter prompted in a whisper.

His "Aye, sir" came out in a gasp, as the import sank through his despondency and took root in understanding.

Shields, Thompson, Werner, Whitehouse, Willard, Windsor, Wiser. He barely heard the other names or the hearty responses for the buzzing between his ears. Then the captain was done and the crew was dismissed.

Rube grabbed Shannon's hand and began pumping it. "How about that, Peckerwood? We made it. We're about to be famous."

Shannon blinked at Rube, still trying to absorb his unexpected change of fortune. Then Rube turned away and Colter put out his hand. "Looks like you and me're stuck with each other awhile longer, Fuzz."

As he grasped Colter's hand, Shannon understood. He wasn't a failure after all. He had passed muster. He was going onward with the expedition. On to the Shining Mountains, the Western Sea. On to discover the Passage, to go down in history as one of the world's great explorers. And to think that he had almost thrown his chance away by deserting.

He shook Colter's hand. "You and me, Old Man. Together all the way to the Passage."

"And back," Colter said. "I ain't a-stayin'. Got some things back this way to see to."

Floyd's approach broke up the conversation. "You look happy, Shannon," the sergeant said.

"I am, sir. About as happy as a man can be," he answered.

"Then you won't mind mucking out the latrine pit," Floyd said.

At that moment Shannon would have mucked out three latrines for the privilege he had been granted. He fairly shouted in his relief, "No, Sergeant. Glad to, Sergeant."

Bafflement glazed Floyd's stare. "Then get to it, Shannon."

Shannon could not suppress the bubble of laughter that popped into his throat. "Yes, Sergeant!"

16. *The Devil Must Die*

Mounds of equipment and supplies for the Corps' journey up the Missouri littered the ground outside the walls of Camp Wood. Organizing and packing it all aboard *Discovery* and the two expedition pirogues was a daunting task, and, for that purpose, Captain Lewis had arranged for John Hay, U.S. Postmaster from Cahokia and an experienced upriver trader, to come to the camp to help.

From his seat on an upturned barrel, Colter watched Sergeant Ordway follow Hay and Captain Clark through the piles. Now that he had been named to the permanent party, he was wrestling with a weakening commitment to the expedition. The problem was Sergeant Ordway.

Four months under the sergeant's thumb had convinced him that the friction between them was bound to get worse once they started up the Missouri. Ordway had nursed a grudge against him since they first laid eyes on each other back at Kaskaskia. Over the months at Camp Wood, that grudge had festered into open hostility. Hostility that showed no sign of abating.

Why go on? The question niggled at him day and night.

Captain Clark's beckoning wave curtailed his thoughts, and he went to see what the captain wanted. He arrived while Hay was delivering a long-winded lecture about packing small quantities of various supplies together to minimize the risk that all of some critical item would be lost in case of the accidents. "Accidents will happen," the man repeated again and again in a supercilious tone that grated on Colter's nerves.

When Hay showed no sign of winding down, Clark cut in, "So what do we need from St. Louis?"

"Oil cloth. Lots of it," Hay said in a tone that proclaimed his annoyance at being interrupted.

Before the man could take up his lecture again, the captain turned to Colter. "The small pirogue's ready, so take it. Once you get to St. Louis, ask someone to direct you to Chouteau's. You get your pack and rifle. I'll draft a purchase order for you to take along."

Ordway spoke up. "Current's still too tricky for just one man to negotiate, Captain. It'd be better to send two. Private Leakins is free."

Clark nodded impatiently, "Good idea, Sergeant," and off he went to draft the necessary document.

On the way to his barracks, Colter wondered at Ordway's choice of Leakins. Leakins was a strange-acting man that no one seemed to know very well. Someone always on the fringes, looking on but never participating. Then again, another pair of hands would come in handy to row the loaded pirogue back up to camp later on.

"Hard left!" Colter yelled, plunging the head of the paddle deep into the frigid water and throwing his back into the sweep. In the prow Leakins responded but ineffectually. The stern turned but not enough to keep the pirogue from scraping the jagged chunk of ice that the current had flung at them."Damn it, Leakins! What're you doing up there? This ain't no time for a nap."

Leakins said something too low for him to hear above the rush of the wind and the creaking ice. Colter let it pass. Maneuvering across the Mississippi was too dangerous to let himself be distracted.

Leakins was inadequate as a rower in the best of conditions. Today he was not even that good. He seemed upset about something and he was talking to himself. "Some help, Ordeal," Colter muttered.

The first glimpse of the houses and buildings of St. Louis, spreading across three yellow limestone bluffs, checked his frustration. Having to put up with Leakins on the way across the river had decided him. He would follow up on Ramey's recommendation and go talk to Manuel Lisa. He would see what the man had to offer. Not that he planned to join Lisa. That would go against his grain. No, this was just to talk, a way to satisfy his curiosity. He thought to learn something that would be useful when he returned to Scratch Wilkes's outfit.

Enough sand had collected at the base of the city's bluffs to form a landing stage. The river was still too ice-choked for navigation by bigger boats, but there were several canoes and pirogues resting on the beach. With minimal help from Leakins, Colter guided their craft into the shallows and hopped out. Between them, they wrestled the pirogue out of the water and tied it off, then climbed to the top of the bluff.

Colter handed Leakins the leather letter pouch Captain Clark had given him. "You take this to Captain Lewis. I'll go after the supplies."

"W–where is he?" Leakins looked up the road as if he expected to see the captain standing there.

Colter curbed a sarcastic remark. "At Government House. Ask somebody to show you where it is."

When Leakins did not seem inclined to do as he was told, Colter left him to figure things out on his own. He had more important things to do. The man could stand in the road all day if he wanted. It was not his job to make sure Leakins did his task. That was Ordway's problem and he could deal with the result.

The loaded wagons all seemed to be going in the same direction so that was where he headed, figuring to come across Chouteau's — and Lisa's — along the way. He found Lisa's place first. The building was so new that it smelled of sap and the paint on the sign above the door was still wet. A line of men stretched across the street in front of it, partially blocking traffic.

"What're you all waitin' for?" he asked the nearest man.

The man's eyes narrowed suspiciously. "You're pullin' my leg. Everyone knows Lisa's gettin' up a party to go furrin' out yonder. But if'n you're thinkin' of tryin', end of the line's down that a-way."

Colter nodded his thanks and found a place to stand on the edge of the crowd. From there, he listened in on the surrounding conversations. That he had happened to come this way on the very day that Lisa was choosing his party was an eerie coincidence. Maybe this was not such a good time to try to talk with Lisa. Then again maybe it was the best time.

As he waffled over what to do, he got the feeling that someone was watching him. Checking around, however, he recognized no familiar faces and spotted no one paying particular attention to him.

"Ah, what the hell," he decided at last and joined the end of the line. He had been in line only a couple of minutes when a man brushed past him, nodding as if he and Colter were acquainted. It took a moment to place the man. He was George Drouillard, the civilian the captains had hired to be the expedition's guide and interpreter. After his hiring last fall at Fort Massac on their way down the Ohio, Drouillard had seemingly vanished and Colter had completely forgotten about him.

To run into the man now in this particular place abruptly changed Colter's mind. A rumor had circulated around camp that Captain Lewis had argued with Manuel Lisa and now considered him an enemy. Since rumors tended to be based on truth, he decided it was best to forget Manuel Lisa and go on to Chouteau's. If Drouillard told the captains that about seeing

Colter in line at Lisa's, they were bound to take the information the wrong way. Better to see to his business and get back.

He stepped out of line and headed up the road.

*

Colter dropped the armload of oil cloth onto the sand and motioned for the helper from Chouteau's to deposit the rest of the bolts in the same place. The helper put down his burden, waved off Colter's thanks and hurried back to the store.

Where was Leakins? Colter scanned the landing stage for the man's ragged black hat. No Leakins. No sign of him either on the road leading up to the top of the bluff. That Leakins was not back annoyed him. They had a long trip to camp and it was getting late.

He waited a few minutes more, then decided to load the rolls of cloth into the pirogue to be ready when the man finally got there.

He had just tied the last knot in the last binding cord when Leakins showed up, dressed in a set of clothes he had not been wearing earlier. It was obvious from their well-worn creases that the clothes were not new, but Colter had more important things on his mind than Leakins' clothing. "'Bout time you got here. Come on. We got us a tough pull to home and durned little daylight left."

Once they were on the river, the glare of lowering winter sunlight on the water's surface forced Colter to focus all his concentration on holding a course. He ignored Leakins's muttering in the prow until the man started to row erratically. He could have let that go if Leakins had not stopped paddling entirely and cocked his head to one side as if he were listening to something.

"Leakins, damn it!" Colter slapped the head of his paddle against the river's surface, splashing a wave of icy water against the man's back.

When that drew no response, Colter gave up. They did not have that much further to go. He could make it paddling alone. Soon as he had some supper, he would report Leakins' strangeness to Ordway and let him deal with the problem.

Ten minutes below camp as Colter manueuvered the pirogue northward along the shore, Leakins's muttering grew into audible ranting, Biblical references jumbled with exhortations that made no sense.

Suddenly Leakins pounded the head of his paddle against the gunwale and shouted, "I shall smite him down!"

Colter had had a crawful of the man's weirdness. "That's it! I ain't takin' no more off'n you, Leakins. Either you shut up and row, or I'm puttin' in and you kin find your own way back. Which'll it be?"

"The Devil must die!" Leakins whirled toward Colter, swinging his paddle like a sword and catching him squarely on the side of the head. The blow lifted Colter off the seat and threw him over the side.

A string of bubbles floating upward past his eyes was the last thing Colter saw before he lost consciousness.

*

With the bulk of the expedition's supplies out in the open, Captain Clark ordered an additional sentry to guard them around the clock. Thanks to Floyd, Shannon drew the four to eight watch which meant he would miss supper. And that meant he would go to bed hungry since the cooks rarely set any food aside.

With everyone else inside the camp eating, solitude hung heavy on Shannon's shoulders. Now that the euphoria of being chosen for the permanent party had passed and departure loomed just eight days away, he had begun to have doubts. Doubts that he was cut out for such a dangerous journey. Doubts that he could survive. Doubts that he wanted to go on. These doubts made it impossible to concentrate on any one idea long enough to create a coherent thought. The only thing he knew for sure was that nothing in his life anymore was certain.

Splashing sounds from the river drew his attention toward the white pirogue approaching the landing beach. He was slow to take in the fact that the boat held only one man: Leakins.

"Where's Colter?" he asked, going to help pull the pirogue onto the sand.

Leakins's frame jerked as if wracked by a spasm. "The Lord hath spoken. 'Rid my people of this scourge.'" He turned feverish eyes on Shannon and whispered, "The evil has infected us all. It is upon you! Seek atonement now before it's too late."

With a lunge too quick to parry, Leakins snared Shannon in a hammerlock that he could not break despite having nearly a foot of height and thirty pounds' advantage over his assailant., "Let me go!" Shannon rasped, struggling against the hold.

The man's hold intensified. "Pray! Pray to be cleansed of evil, Shannon!"

Realizing that Leakins was beyond reason, Shannon did the only thing he could think of to summon help. He fired off his rifle.

The shot was still echoing off the trees when crewmen and officers poured out the gates, armed and ready. It took three men to pull Leakins off Shannon.

"What's the meaning of this?" demanded Captain Clark.

Now it was Leakins who struggled, trying to break free of the men who restrained him. "Shannon is cursed! The devil has touched him!" he shouted. "He must be cleansed."

"He's been ranting like that since I asked where Colter was, sir," Shannon explained in gulped phrases.

"Colter wasn't with him?" Clark said.

"No, sir," Shannon said.

"All right, Leakins. Where is he?" Clark thundered.

Faced with the captain's anger, Leakins's voice lost some of its fervor. "The Lord spoke and I obeyed. The devil is no more." Then he fell to muttering, his face raised to the darkening sky, his eyes darting left and right.

"Floyd, Pryor, get this man to my quarters. Don't let him out of your sight," Clark ordered. "Sergeant Ordway, Shannon, stay here. The rest of you back inside." Clark turned to Ordway. "Explain this."

"Sir, I don't know what to say," Ordway stammered.

"A man does not completely lose his senses overnight. Surely you noticed something wrong with him before now?"

"No, Captain. Nothing."

Shannon burst in. "For God's sake, Captain, forget Leakins and think about Colter. What did Leakins do to him?"

Ordway recovered from his discomfiture. "The only thing that's happened to Colter is desertion. He's been looking for a chance for weeks. If I know him, he's hiding out somewhere in St. Louis, waiting for the expedition to leave so he can go on about his business."

"That's a lie, Captain," Shannon retorted. "Leakins couldn't row his way out of an eddy by himself, let alone get back up here from St. Louis. He's done something to Colter. He could be hurt or dying. We need to find him before it's too late."

"Face it, Shannon. Your friend's a deserter," Ordway said.

"He is not!" Shannon fairly shouted. "Colter's one of the best men on this crew and everybody but you knows it. Captain, permission to go looking for him."

Clark had kept silent during the exchange between the two men, but now he spoke. "Thank you, Private. But I can't grant that. It's nearly dark."

"But, Captain —"

Clark held up a hand for silence. "Best we wait until morning. Sergeant, organize a search party and head out at dawn."

The look in Ordway's eye told Shannon not to bother to ask to be part of that search detail.

A force that he did not have the strength to counter had hold of Colter's lower body, pulling him down, down under the water. He knew he ought to claw upward, to heave himself toward the air, but his muscles would not obey. Down, down he was dragged. Air, precious air, draining from his lungs. Water closing over him pressing down, crushing, choking. "Oh, God, no!"

Suddenly, he came to, the sound of his own screams reviving him. Shannon was kneeling beside him, peering worriedly into his face. "I'm here, Old Man. You're safe now."

From the bed, Colter glanced around the room. He was in the barracks on his own bunk with no recollection of how he got there.

"You caught on a snag," Shannon said. "Thank God for snags, huh?"

Colter grunted. He remembered being in the pirogue coming back from St. Louis, but, beyond that, everything was blank.

"Leakins is gone," Shannon said.

Hearing the name drew back the curtain from a hidden place in Colter's memory and flooded his mind with images: Leakins's contorted face, the paddle's arc through the air, the thud as it connected with his skull, his body tumbling out of the pirogue, a stream of air bubbles. "That whoreson tried to drown me." His voice was a hoarse, halting rumble.

He tried to struggle up from the bed, but Shannon caught him by the shoulders and gently forced him back down just as Captain Clark came into the room "Ah, Colter. You're awake. Excellent. I want you to take it easy the next few days."

"There ain't time, Captain," he protested weakly. "Not if we're leavin'."

"Yes, there is. We had to slip the date for our departure to May 1st. You've had quite a shock. Now you need to rest."

After the captain left, Colter looked up at Shannon. "Where'd that son-of-a-bitch Leakins go?"

"Who knows? He was crazy, Old Man. Forget about him, and concentrate on getting your strength back."

Colter tried once more to sit up but found he no longer had the strength to do so. Much as he hated to admit it, Shannon was right. He needed to forget about Leakins and rest up. May 1st was not that far away.

17. *First Blood*

T he night of May 1st was dark and brooding; the air heavy with moisture. Thick ominous clouds blanketed the sky. As Shannon walked his post along the front gates, lightning flashed, illuminating Colter walking his post at the rear of the camp. This was the older man's first watch since the search party found him thrown up on the bank of the Mississippi after Leakins had tried to drown him.

Today was to have been the expedition's new departure date, but something still delayed Captain Lewis in St. Louis so that date had been pushed out yet another week. Another delay had pushed Shannon's doubts about his suitability for the expedition to a critical level and filed his nerves to a thin edge. The lightning, thunder and brooding quality of the night only made things worse.

He was pacing past the front gates when a streak of lightning rent the sky and caused him to freeze mid-stride. The bar had been moved back and the main gate was open.

As much as he hated midnight watches, Colter was enjoying this one. He had had enough lying around thinking about Leakins and Hartley, wondering if there was a connection between them. Time to get back on his feet and do something useful

Two delays in departure had everyone champing at the bit to be gone. He was no exception. Only, his agitation had another side to it — the nagging sensation that Hartley was close by. The feeling did not make sense, but he could not shake it.

A sudden slash of lightning startled him. *Get a-hold of yerself, Johnny Boy*, he thought. *You're jumpier than a fart on a skillet. You cain't . . .*

He did not get the chance to finish out the thought because someone jumped him from behind and dragged him to the ground, pinning him on his stomach, his right arm under him and his left immobilized.

Hartley. The name and face slammed into Colter's mind as the attacker's fist slammed into his jaw. He took the blow, bucking and heaving against the man's weight.

The attacker rode out his efforts, then yanked Colter's head back by the hair and jammed the blade of a knife against his exposed throat. Only then did Colter realize he was wrong about his assailant.

Hatred glittered in McBain's eyes as his knife blade dug into the skin of Colter's throat. "So we meet again, Coal-Tar. Too bad I don't have time to do this up slow. You deserve all the pain I can give you. But as long as you're dead, I —"

The boom of a rifle shot cut the gambler short. He grunted and jerked upright, a look of surprise painting his face. Then the knife slipped from his fingers and he flopped across Colter's back.

Colter shoved the gambler's body off his and bent to listen to his chest. There was no heartbeat.

He put his cheek to McBain's mouth. There was no breath.

His fingers felt for the bullet hole and found it in the man's back directly over the heart.

Across the compound, Shannon stood with his rifle still raised and smoking. "Is he dead?" he whispered hoarsely.

"Yep."

"I killed him?" Shannon's voice wavered.

Touching the stinging cut on his neck where McBain's knife had sliced the skin, Colter's fingers came away sticky with blood. "If you hadn't, he'd'a killed me."

Shannon flung his rifle down and sank to his knees, his hands covering his face. "I killed him. He's dead. Dear God, no."

When Colter tried to stand, his knees refused to support him. It took two tries before he could push himself to his feet. Meanwhile, the men awakened by the shot came out of their cabins to investigate.

"What's the problem here?" Captain Clark rushed to where Colter steadied himself against the wall.

"That one's dead, instead of me, thanks to Shannon," Colter said.

York held the lantern up to allow the captain to examine McBain's body and Colter's neck. "You were lucky, Colter. If that knife had cut any deeper, we would have two corpses. Sergeant Floyd, double the guard and pick men to relieve these two. The rest of you, back to bed. Colter, Shannon, come with me."

The crew shuffled back inside their cabins, and the captain headed toward his quarters. Colter limped over to pick up Shannon's rifle and to help Shannon stand. "Come on, Fuzz. Captain wants to see us."

Shannon would not move. He was trembling, his teeth were chattering and his head was shaking "no."

Colter put a comforting hand on his arm. "You saved me, Fuzz. Thank God, you did."

A flash of lightning revealed Shannon's shock-glazed eyes and quivering mouth. He was in no shape to listen to reason. Colter took him by the hand and led him to the captains' quarters.

"It's time, Fuzz," Colter said, touching Shannon's shoulder.

Shannon shrank away from the hand. He felt dirty — the kind of dirty no amount of water could wash off. He had taken the life of another human being. The smudge that that sinful act had left on his soul would never go away, no matter what Colter or anyone else claimed. The smudge made it impossible for him to go on with the expedition. He had one last duty to perform, then he would ask the captains to release him from his enlistment.

He swung off his bunk and dragged himself outside where the blanket-shrouded body draped across the back of a horse brought a fresh lump to his throat. He had done this, this horrible thing. He could devote the rest of his life to making amends, but this man, this being he had hardly known would never come back to life.

Colter gestured impatiently. "Come on, Fuzz. We ain't got all day."

He followed Colter and the horse out the gates and east along the course of the Wood River. After a mile of picking their way through the tangle of new spring growth, Colter stopped on a small knoll. "Here's a good spot. Ground's thawed."

Overcome by a sense of unreality, Shannon watched his hands take a shovel and begin digging. He watched, his mind detached, as his body dug and dug into the earth.

"Good enough, Fuzz. We better both carry him. He's heavier than he looks." Colter untied the ropes securing the body to the horse. "How 'bout you grab his legs?"

Shannon watched himself climb out of the grave and walk to the horse but that was as far as his body would go. "I can't touch him."

"Sure you can. He ain't a-goin' to hurt you. He's dead."

That last word destroyed Shannon's control. Tears flooded into his eyes and he had to turn away to hide his disintegration.

"Judas H. Priest, Fuzz! It'd be me instead of McBain you'd be buryin' here today if'n you hadn't'a shot him. Get a-hold of yourself!"

A weak sob escaped Shannon's trembling lips. Colter came up behind him. "You're the one wanted to be an Army officer. What do you think bein' in the Army's all about anyways? Dancin'?"

It took a long time for Shannon to collect himself enough to answer. "I don't think I can go on — upriver."

"Then you best not. No tellin' what we'll get into from here on out. We got them Sioux to get past."

The mention of the Sioux brought back to Shannon his visit to the Shawnee camp down at the Mississippi-Ohio confluence. So far that had been the highlight of his life. That memory nudged aside his guilt over killing McBain and gave him strength. "The Sioux," he whispered.

"Yep, Sioux and who knows how many other blood-thirsty heathens we'll have to plow through 'fore we get where we're goin'."

Shannon tilted his chin. "Didn't you listen to Captain Lewis?"

"About what?"

"Besides finding the Passage, the primary purpose of this expedition is to treat with those "blood-thirsty heathens" as you call them. To make peace with them, to ensure safe passage for those who will follow in our wake. Peace is our mission. Not war."

Exasperation replaced sympathy in Colter's expression. "For pity's sake, Fuzz. Ain't you heard a word I said? Them Sioux'll lift your hair in a wink if'n you don't kill 'em first. I don't give half a hoot about no mission. This here's my hair and I plan to keep it anyway I can."

"Then it's you who ought to quit the Corps. With your attitude, you could destroy everything Captain Lewis has worked so hard for."

Colter's face darkened. "You're the one wants to quit, Shannon. Not me. I don't quit."

Shannon was not about to let Colter's challenge go unanswered. "Neither do I." He marched to the body and waited for Colter to help lift it over the saddle. Without speaking, they carried McBain to the grave and laid him out. Colter was about to heave a shovelful of dirt onto the corpse when Shannon thought to ask, "Why did he come after you?"

With a glance at the body, Colter related a story stretching from his first meeting with McBain to an incident at a whorehouse named Kate's to bundling Lil and Lisette off to Cahokia. The story held Shannon spellbound. When it was over, his annoyance at Colter had dissipated, replaced by a melancholy that made him speak of something he had kept to himself. "Her was Lisette. I remember that and how she smelled like roses. But I can't remember her face or anything else."

Colter's heat had cooled too. "There'll be plenty more like her, Fuzz. Seems you got somethin' attracts women. While the rest of us fools is chasin' 'em, you have to fight 'em off."

"Don't get me wrong, Old Man. What I did that night at McBain's was a sin. And I got punished for it. I learned my lesson. I don't intend to be that weak again." He fell to shoveling dirt into the grave.

"We ain't goin' to have much in the way of temptation once we leave here," Colter said. "If'n I was you, I wouldn't turn down no chances came my way. All you'll get upriver is squaws. I'd as soon plant my carrot in a polecat as bed one of them."

Shannon drew back. "If I were you — and I'm glad I'm not — I'd keep such advice to myself. First of all, I didn't ask for it. Second, I would never consider it since it's based on prejudice and ignorance. And third, I have no intention of repeating my mistakes, with any woman, white, red or yellow."

"Well, la-di-da. Ain't you the uppity one all of a sudden. Whatever happened to all them regrets about killin' McBain?"

"The sooner we finish here, the better," Shannon snapped.

"Amen." Colter was none too careful where he aimed the last few shovelfuls of dirt. Neither was Shannon.

Without another word or look, they finished their work and went back to camp, by different routes.

18. *Under Way — At Last!*

A steady rain was falling when the crewmen lined up for roll call on the morning of May 14, 1804. After waiting ten minutes for the officers to make an appearance, Newman spoke up. "Three-to-one odds it's another delay. Who's wagerin'?"

A few diehards jumped at the chance to wager. Not Colter. Betting — any betting — reminded him of McBain, and any thought of McBain made him wonder if the gambler had been linked to Hartley, if not back at Stuart's Draft, then later on. After all, McBain's prime motivator was money and Hartley had Stuart's fortune backing him.

The sense that the preacher was somewhere close by had not left him. In fact, it had grown into a near-conviction and he wanted to be gone. Now.

Yesterday Clark ordered the crew aboard *Discovery* for a brief trial run up the Mississippi. The experiment proved sobering for Colter. Moving the keelboat was a slow laborious proposition. Someone as determined as Hartley would have no trouble following him. He did not relish having to watch his back for the entire journey up the Missouri. Still, moving at any pace would be better than standing still.

The creak of the captains' door brought an end to the betting. Clark emerged, looking drawn and hungover. He was followed by the three sergeants.

After everyone was accounted for, the captain mounted the speaking stump. Colter endeavored to look attentive, but he already knew from Clark's expression that they were in for another delay. It seemed to be not a question of *when* they would leave but *if* they would.

Clark's eyes rolled down the ranks of crewmen. "We are leaving — *today*. As soon as we can get our belongings on the boat. We'll stop in St. Charles to wait for Captain Lewis."

The crew reacted with whoops of joy. Everyone had heard about St. Charles and the pleaseures it offered to upriver travelers. Pleasures that had the crew hoping that Lewis would take his time in joining them.

Colter gave a half-hearted cheer and turned to find Shannon watching him. "What are you lookin' at, Fuzz?"

"Someone who doesn't seem all that happy to be leaving," Shannon shot back.

"What's that supposed to mean?"

"Just what I said."

"You know somethin', Shannon? You talk way too much for someone who don't know diddle."

"I never met Diddle so I don't know him, but it's a good thing for you I know how to shoot."

"Shannon! Colter! Get a move on!" Ordway's bellow broke off their conversation. Turning to their cabin, Colter could not resist getting in one last lick. "You might can shoot, but can you swim?"

As the smugness drained out of Shannon's face, Colter smiled.

PART 3

INTO THE WEST

Spring, 1804 — Winter, 1804

I can foresee no material or probable obstruction to our progress, and entertain therefore the most sanguine hopes of complete success. I have never enjoyed a more perfect state of good health. Capt. Clark and every individual of the party are in good health, and excellent sperits; zealously attached to the enterprise, and anxious to proceed; not a whisper of discontent or murmur is to be heard among them; but all in unison, act with the most perfect harmoney. With such men I have everything to hope, and but little to fear."

— Meriwether Lewis in his report to President
Jefferson, April, 1804

1. *Lessons Unlearned*

May 16, 1804 — On the Missouri

Colter dropped the setting pole and slumped wearily down on the *passe avant*. Around him, the rest of the poling squad did the same. Just two days of fighting the humbling force of nature that was the Missouri had wrung all the fight out of the entire crew.

Sergeant Floyd dropped the anchor, and Captain Clark transferred into the red pirogue to be rowed across the river to the settlement of St. Charles on the south bank. Colter watched the *engagés* struggle to move the little boat across the runoff- and obstacle-choked main current, glad he wasn't one of them.

"Captain'll give us a couple days here," Rube Field said from his place next to Colter.

"Bet he don't," Joe Field countered. "With our luck, Captain Lewis'll be over there when Captain Clark lands and we'll be on our way west quicker'n you can spit."

Rube shook his head stubbornly. "No way. Captain Clark'll make sure we get us one last fling. He knows better'n anybody some of us might not come back."

"Now, Rube, why you got to get all gloomy? You know how I hate that kind of talk," Joe complained.

Not one to deliberately upset his brother, Rube backed off. "I say we pool our money, Little Brother, and spend it all on having a real good time soon as we put in over yonder. What do you say to that?"

Joe brightened. "Now you're talkin'. Them St. Charles women better be ready 'cause they got a lot to handle in the two of us. Ain't that right, Big

Brother?" The pair exchanged playful punches, then broke out a well-worn deck of cards and got a game going.

Colter pulled out his carving, and, while the rest of the crew speculated on the entertainments St. Charles had to offer, his mind churned over a disturbing idea. Once they started up the Missouri from this point, there would be no turning back. He would be stuck with Sergeant Ordway for the duration.

As he had promised the first time they met, the sergeant had become a bad dream that Colter could not shake, and the prospect of continuing to live with such a nightmare put a strain on his resolve to remain with the Corps. The way things were going, the sergeant would push him too far one day and too far to avoid a lethal confrontation.

Colter pushed away the memory of what he had done to the last man to goad him into a rage. That memory was so loathsome that he relegated it to the deepest recesses of his mind and held it there behind the wall of a pledge that he would never again get that mad, never again be at the mercy of emotions that robbed him of all reason and restraint. Ordway, however, was hacking away at that barrier of resolve, and, unless he found a way to separate himself from the sergeant, there would be hell to pay before long.

He was still brooding on this problem when he heard Rube scramble to his feet. "Oh, oh," Rube announced. "Captain Clark's comin' back."

"Is Captain Lewis with him?" Joe asked.

"Don't see him."

The pirogue drew alongside *Discovery* and Clark climbed aboard to tell the crew what he had found ashore. "Captain Lewis has been detained in St. Louis, and he sent word for us to wait here in St. Charles. You'll all be happy to know that the townspeople are holding a dance in our honor to-night."

Clark waited with a brittle smile for the crew's cheering to subside. "Any trouble — any — and we'll move upriver, out of the reach of temptation. Understood?"

After a murmured chorus of yessirs, the two squads of crewmen changed places. The second squad, Shannon's, climbed onto the *passe avant* while the first, Colter's, took over the rowing benches. The strain of pushing the heavily-laden keelboat across the power of the main current to St. Charles's landing stage set Colter's back and shoulder muscles quivering. The crossing seemed to go on for hours, and he could barely lift his arms by the time they reached their destination.

While the rest of the crew piled off the boat, anxious to taste the pleasures of St. Charles, Colter chose to stay aboard and catch his second wind. He was slumped against the gunwale when Floyd began yelling at Shannon, "Your pole, Private! Park it, or I'll park you."

While Shannon scrambled to get the setting pole properly lashed down, Floyd stood over him, hands on hips. "Face it, Shannon, you aren't cut out for this. Why not make both our lives easier? Quit now before we get into real work, and I'll see your discharge is quick and honorable."

With obvious effort, Shannon threw back his shoulders. "I have no intention of quitting, Sergeant."

"You are as useless as tits on a boar to the rest of us," Floyd said, shaking his head in disgust. Either you're too stupid or too stubborn to know that. Just remember: Captain Lewis can't protect you forever."

"You got more gall than sense, Fuzz," Colter said to Shannon after the sergeant had left the boat.

"I won't let Floyd brow-beat me, Old Man. No way." Shannon stretched out on the *passe avant* and flung an arm over his eyes with a conversation-ending grunt.

Colter got stiffly to his feet. Ordeal and Fuzz, between the two of them he had a bad taste in his mouth, the kind only whiskey and a ripe willing woman could clear up.

Shannon lingered aboard *Discovery* the rest of the day. He had had his one bout of indulging in whiskey and women back at Camp Wood. He did not need that kind of trouble ever again. What he did need was rest and lots of it so he took advantage of the quiet and solitude of the keelboat to nap.

When he awoke, it was evening. The breeze was alive with the sounds of fiddle music and laughter coming from the townfolks' celebration. Along with the music wafted the aromas of fresh-baked bread and rabbit stew, reminding him that he had not eaten since that morning.

The ground was spongy underfoot from an early morning downpour. His steps squished to the tempo of the reel that was playing as he approached the church-turned-dancehall. Spotting Sergeant Floyd through the open front door, he immediately altered his course for the rear entrance. He was rounding the corner of the building when his nose picked up a new smell. A familiar smell: rose petals.

A soft palm cupped his cheek. "Yes, it is you, my handsome one." The voice with its faint trace of huskiness was also familiar, but he could not put a name to the woman's face.

In stature, she was the size of a schoolgirl. In development, she was definitely a woman, dressed to emphasize her endowments. "Tsk-tsk. You do not remember. Such a pity." She sighed. "I remember you, mon cher. You are a man not to forget." She tossed her head. "So much pleasure we shared, you and Lisette."

Lisette?

She brushed his cheek with her lips, and memories from that night at McBain's came flooding back. On the heels of those memories and sweeping all other thoughts aside came a tidal wave of guilt and embarrassment over the humiliating malady she had given him.

He turned away, but her hand on his shoulder drew him around to face her. "So, you do remember," she cooed. "A man never forgets his first woman. Lisette, she was your first, no? Perhaps we will make another memory together. Tonight?" Her voice turned to a low purr. "For you, there is no charge. Lisette does this for pleasure."

He pried off her hand. "I wouldn't touch you if you were the last woman on earth. You gave me the pox."

She thrust away from him indignantly. "Not from Lisette, you did not get such a thing. Filthy lies!"

Her outburst was bound to attract the wrong kind of attention. He put a hand on her wrist in an attempt to calm her, but she raked it aside with her nails. "How dare you touch Lisette!"

"Lisette, hush."

"Lisette will do no such thing! She gave you pleasure. Not pox. Lisette is a lady. You will tell her you are sorry for your lies."

One of the crewmen glanced out the open window, drawn by the commotion. Shannon had to do something quick or draw even more attention. "I apologize. I didn't mean it. Just please, please, lower your voice."

She regarded him with hauteur but deigned to speak more softly. "Lisette accepts your apology."

Shannon glanced around. With no ruckus to watch, the curious crewman lost interest and turned back to the dancing.

"She accepts your apology if — " she paused for effect "—you accept her offer."

"I can't do that."

Her voice shot to a shriek. "Then you are no gentleman!"

Another person poked his head out the back door of the church. Shannon knew he had to get her physically away from the building before they attracted an entire crowd.

"Okay, I'll go with you. Just keep your voice down."

Abruptly her manner changed again. She stepped closer to him, pressing her jutting breasts into his midriff. She tilted her chin up and draped one dainty wrist up over his shoulder. "You are a lucky man, my handsome one. Lisette grants her favors only to special men."

Several crewmen emerged at that moment from the party. Spotting Shannon with Lisette, one of them pointed and called out to him. He had taken enough ribbing from the crew over that night at McBain's to want no more. He grabbed her hand. "I'm honored. Let's go."

She refused to be hurried. He tried to steer her away from the church, but she insisted upon walking past the gawking crewmen. Accompanied by calls of "Go Peckerwood!", Shannon followed her up a muddy path to the two-story clapboard building that housed the tavern. She led him up the creaking outside stairway into a room lit by a kerosene lamp with a soot-smudged chimney.

"You like?" Lisette asked, settling on the bed, kicking off her shoes, and pulling up the hem of her flounced skirt to reveal a bare thigh.

When she began to roll down her stocking, he knew he had to leave. "No, I can't do this. Goodbye."

A hairbrush flew past his ear and crashed against the doorjamb. "No, you will stay!"

"But you don't understand. The pox . . . the treatments . . . I can't."

She was on her feet and ripping at the buttons of his britches before he realized what she was doing. "Lisette, stop." He grabbed her hands but she eluded him.

The last button came free and his baggy pants slid down to his ankles. She stood back and surveyed the effect she had had on him. A sly smile blossomed on her face. "My handsome one cannot leave. Not now." She took hold of him in a most intimate way. "You will stay, yes?"

At the mercy of her fondling, he could barely rasp out a "Yes" over the surge of lust constricting his throat.

"Then you must watch." She glided back to the bed and resumed taking off her clothing. She moved with a languidness that built his need to the critical level. Once she was naked, she stretched out on the bed and wagged a finger at him.

Close to bursting, he rushed to her. Her outstretched palm stopped him. "No, first you must look at Lisette," she ordered, dragging her fingertips along her leg from ankle to hip, then from hip to shoulder, pausing to linger beside one erect nipple. "Now, how can you accuse Lisette of bad things? She is beautiful, no?"

His erection had reached such throbbing proportions that it was difficult to think, let alone speak.

Her fingertips traced a return journey along her torso, pulling his eyes with them. "You will not speak ugly words about Lisette again, yes?"

"No. No. Never, never again."

She held her hand out to him. "Then come to Lisette. To lie here by herself is lonely."

He did not need a second invitation.

Colter was enjoying a cup of hard cider generously fortified with a shot from Newman's flask when he noticed a woman at the threshold of the church where the townfolks' party was in full-swing. She was dressed in brilliant green satin with her hair twisted and crimped into an elaborate style. Her face was carefully powdered and her eyes lined with kohl. He recognized her immediately. Lil, McBain's whore.

Fire smoldered behind the eyes with which she searched the room, and he decided to make an exit through an open window rather than cross paths with her again. He had one leg hitched over the window frame when he heard, "Caught you, you son-of-a-bitch!"

"Good to see you, ma'am," he said lamely.

Her slap stung his cheek. "Don't you 'ma'am' me. You ruined my life!"

"How could I do that, ma'am? I ain't been here till today."

"This is a worthless one-horse town. I've never been so miserable in all my life."

"Looks like a right fine little place to me."

"Don't argue with me, Bird Man. You don't know. You can't know. This town's the end of the world. I have to get back to Mac, and you're going to help me."

"Cain't do that, ma'am. Even if I wanted to, I cain't."

"Of course you can. You can tell Mac how you made me leave. He'll take me back then."

"No, ma'am, he won't. Mac's dead."

It took several moments for the news to sink in. Then her anger crumbled into disbelief. "He can't be dead. I loved him. I need him. No!" A sob swallowed anything else she was going to say.

Colter looked at her, unsure what to say or do in the face of her anguish. He tried to touch her arm, but she jerked away from him. "All I wanted was to get back to him. Mac loved me. No one ever loved me before. What'll I do now? Where'll I go?" Lil cried. "My life's ruined. It's over, and it's all your fault!" She stumbled off sobbing.

He let her go. He believed he had done the right thing in getting her away from McBain's beatings, only she did not see it that way. He also thought he was doing the right thing to remove the other whore, Lisette, the one with the pox, from the crew's temptation before every man in the crew had it, but the reaction of most of the men when they learned she was gone had been: better a poxed whore than no whore at all.

He assumed he was doing the right thing by keeping his word to see this expedition through. Was he wrong about that, too?

Shannon trudged back to the keelboat from Lisette's room just after daybreak the next day. Though he was physically tired, he was also jubilant. Memories of his night with Lisette buoyed him through all his assigned tasks, and, by sundown when the crew was turned loose on the settlement, he was primed for another night of exploring the wonders of her body. He took the steps up to her room two at a time and burst through the door to find her sitting at her dressing table, looking more beautiful than he remembered. He spread his arms wide. "I'm here!"

She gave him a cursory glance, then turned aside to regard her reflection in a cracked mirror. Her cool reception, so in contrast to the emotions boiling within, baffled him. "Lisette?"

She patted a strand of hair into place. "So, you return for more. Of course you bring money, yes?"

"Money?"

"Lisette, she has a hard life. She must earn her own way. Surely my handsome one he understands this."

"But you said —"

She turned toward him, her chin cocked at a stern angle. "Last night was Lisette's gift. But that was last night. Tonight she has no more gifts to give."

Shannon's mind could not square what she was saying with how he was feeling.

"Ah, so you do not speak. Then you will stand aside. Lisette has work to do." She moved past him and he followed her down the steps and into the tavern, struggling to comprehend what was happening.

St. Charles's lone pub was crowded. Besides the crew, there were upriver traders, enjoying one last drunk before they headed west for the season. In addition to them, there were *engagés* and a scattering of taciturn locals who grudgingly shared the local entertainment with these outsiders.

The moment Lisette entered the room, every head in the place turned her way. Conversations ground to a halt as she strolled toward the bar.

"My, my, ain't she somethin'." The murmured words came from Moses Reed, one of the crewmen, sitting with some of the *engagés* closest to the door. "Ain't I glad I got me a fat purse."

The sight of Reed's bulging money bag and the thought of Lisette sharing herself with anyone else spurred Shannon into action. He shoved his way through the crowd gathered around her, scooped her into his arms and carried her back outside. Angry shouts followed them with Moses Reed's protest rising above the rest.

Lisette was furious. "You have no money. You will put Lisette down!"

"You'll get your money. All you want."

Her anger cooled into interest. "All?"

Shannon had to set her down in order to extricate his money sack from his pocket. She took one look at it and flung it to the ground. "You insult Lisette. Now, out of her way."

She tried to go around him. Desperate, Shannon grabbed her arm. "There's more. Lots more. I just don't have it on me."

"Then you must get it," she commanded.

"I will, but you have to promise to wait, up in your room, until I get back."

"Lisette will wait one hour. No more. And my handsome one will pay for the time she waits."

By now he was prepared to spend every cent he had to keep her out of the clutches of any and all of his crewmates while they were in St. Charles. "One hour and, yes, I'll pay."

"Good. Be quick. Lisette does not like to wait."

2. A Tempting Offer

A misting rain settled over St. Charles and the river at dusk. The rain and three nights of carousing had mellowed the crew gathered in the tavern. Colter sat at a table with the Field brothers and Newman, trying with mixed success to dodge the pointed looks of a plump tart named Annabelle whose favors he had enjoyed two nights back. Right now he had more important things to mull over than what she had in mind.

Last night he chanced to strike up a conversation with an upriver trader named LeBlanc. According to LeBlanc, there were riches beyond measure waiting for those trappers courageous enough to push west into the Shining Mountains. Prominent in his talk and praise was one name: Manuel Lisa. In LeBlanc's opinion, Lisa had no equal for foresight when it came to recognizing the West's potential and audacity for going after it. The conversation served to intensify Colter's ambivalence about the expedition. He was sunk deep into that uncertainty when Rube asked, "I ain't seen Peckerwood for three whole days. Where the hell's he got to anyway?"

Joe had drunk so much of the over-priced, watered-down whiskey that he slurred his reply. "Where he's been for the last three nights? Why, with that pretty little whore used to be at McBain's, thass where."

The comment seized Colter's attention. He knew Lil was here. However, no one would call her pretty and she definitely wasn't little. Now the other one, Lisette — she was both. He waited for one of the brothers to mention the obvious — that Shannon should have known better after his last experience with the woman. Instead, Joe said, "That ain't hardly fair. Least he can do is share with us."

A spirited group of men sporting identical blue caps tumbled through the door just then. Their entrance boosted the noise level in the room.

The increased racket was too much for Colter. He needed a place to think. As he let himself out into the misty darkness, a figure stepped out of the shadows. "*Buenos noches, compadre.*"

Unable to place the voice or the thick accent, Colter replied, "Howdy."

"Señor Ramey. He is a friend of yours, no?"

"That he is," Colter said suspiciously.

"Señor Ramey, he tells me many things about you. He say he tells you about me, too. *Bueno,* now we speak face to face. You come."

"Maybe I'll come. Maybe I won't. Depends on who you are."

"Aye, *caramba.* I forget we just meet. My name is Manuel Lisa."

Colter sucked in a surprised breath at hearing the name of the man who had been so much on his mind of late.

"I see that you know my name," Lisa said. "Come." He led the way down to the river to a boat moored fifty yards upstream from *Discovery.* Following the Spaniard to the small cabin, Colter had the chance to look the craft over. She was a compact compromise between being light enough for a small crew to cordelle upstream and large enough to carry sufficient trade goods to make the trip worthwhile.

Inside the cabin, Lisa motioned Colter to take a seat on a box, uncorked a dusty bottle and poured out two generous cups before launching into a summary of his plan to go upriver with a hand-picked crew. While Lisa talked, Colter studied his face in the dim light of the lone candle. He liked what he saw: passion, intelligence, honesty.

"Each man of my company, he spend one year, two years with the western peoples. He traps, he enjoys their women, and when he returns, one-half the profits from his peltries are his. One-half. This way of mine, it is the best way. Join me, *amigo,* and you will be more rich than even your President Jefferson."

"Wait. Back up. What do you mean by 'with the western peoples'? You talkin' 'bout livin' with Indians?"

"Such an ugly word, Indians. And incorrect. This is not the Indies. I prefer to say 'western peoples.' You live with them and they show you where to trap the beavers. You do the work, you keep the profits. My way, no man takes a *peso* who does not work for the money."

For years, Colter had railed about the difference between the price he received for his furs and what people paid for the finished products. He saw the wisdom, and justice, in Lisa's plan and agreed with everything. Everything except living with the Indians. Ramey had never mentioned that part.

"I stake on this plan all my fortune," Lisa said. "It must work. It *will* work. The trapping you know. Ramey, he say you hunt and shoot better than any other man. Such a man I need. You, *amigo*, I need." He jabbed a finger into the flesh of Colter's forearm. "To you I offer a double share to join me. All the profit for you only. No one else."

All the profit and no middlemen — Lisa's offer was worth three times Scratch Wilkes's. Three times. But the part about living with Indians — that was a price he could not pay, no matter what the reward.

Lisa eyed him. "Colter does not say 'yes'. But," he held up a thick forefinger. "he does not say 'no,' either. And that is good. I like a man who thinks before he speaks."

He picked up the bottle and looked at the candle through it. "While you are thinking, I tell you something. Your captains plan to pass through the land of the Teton Sioux. That is foolish thinking. The Teton Sioux, they are pirates. And worse. They will try to stop you, *amigo*. They will fight you." He paused. "My crew, we will turn west at the Niobrara River. We do not go into the land of the Tetons, for that is the quick way to die."

He put the bottle down. "Tomorrow, we leave at dawn. I give you until then to think. Yes?"

Colter nodded.

"*Bueno*. You will find me here. *Vaya con dios, mi amigo*."

A noise awakened Shannon from the slumber he had fallen into after another session of sporting with Lisette. He opened his eyes to see her buttoning the top of her dress. "Come on back to bed, Beautiful. I miss you."

In reply she tossed an empty leather bag onto the quilt. "She is empty."

It was his purse. His empty purse.

"Lisette must earn her way. You will leave now."

"Leave?"

"Yes, leave. Go before Lisette returns. And take that," she motioned dismissively at the limp bag in Shannon's hand, "with you."

Shannon was sure that she was pulling one of her little jokes on him. He watched her finish dressing, anticipating what her inventive mind planned for him next. That anticipation vanished the moment she sat on the stool and began pinning up her hair. She really was going.

He rolled off the bed onto his feet. "Please don't go." He did not care that he sounded desperate. He was. He could not live with the thought of her with another man.

She threw him a look of pure disgust. "Lisette is a lady. You must cover yourself."

He grabbed the pillow and held it before his nakedness.

Another dark look from her. "Dress and go. Now."

His mind was a blur of thoughts, all of them centering on the disaster that was about to shatter his world. Lisette must not go down to the tavern. He must find a way to keep her out of the clutches of the men down there. "Don't go. Please."

She heaved a sigh and spoke to him in a tone women reserved for recalcitrant children. "Go, Shannon."

It was the first time she had addressed him by name, and it cut him to the quick. He picked up his empty purse. "I have more," he said in desperation. "Lots more. I'll go get it."

She paused in the act of pushing a pin into her hair and regarded him in the mirror through eyes narrowed in suspicion. He knew he had to act fast or lose her. He flung on his clothes and dashed to the door. "I'll be right back. Say you'll wait for me?"

She did not answer right away, and he feared she did not believe him. Then she laid the pin on the table and rested her hands primly in her lap. "Lisette waits thirty minutes. No more."

Shannon burst out the door, flew down the outside stairs, then pulled up short. He had spent all the money he had on her. There was no more. What on earth was he going to do?

"Comin' up for air, Peckerwood? Or is it my turn with her, finally?" The words stretched out and wandered around Rube's liquor-soaked tongue. He stood under the staircase, holding up his semiconscious brother Joe.

There was only one man with enough money to save him from pending disaster. "Have you seen Colter?"

"He was headed down to the boat last I saw. So when do I get my turn?" Rube demanded.

Shannon loped away, hoping that Rube was too drunk to climb the stairs and that Lisette would keep her promise to give him a half-hour.

A crewman named McNeal, whose one redeeming quality was that he could cook something edible, was standing watch on *Discovery*. When Shannon inquired after Colter, the cook asked, "What's it worth?"

Shannon had no time for games. "Captain's looking for him. Is he here?"

The lie worked. McNeal gave a straight answer. "Not here. Try up at the pub. That's where I'll be soon as my relief shows up."

Before the man could finish his sentence, Shannon shot back up the path. Minutes later, he puffed his way toward the pub door.

"Where you off to in such a hurry, Fuzz?" The question came from Colter who was sheltering under the overhanging roof of the tavern.

Shannon motioned for him to come away from the building. "So what's got your tail in such a knot?" Colter asked.

Shannon did not have time for small talk. He went straight to the subject. "I need a loan."

Colter looked up toward the rooms on the second story, then at Shannon.

"She take all your loot already?"

"Look, Old Man, I can't stop to talk. This is an emergency."

"Ain't they all. What about the pox, Fuzz?"

Shannon braced himself for a lecture. He prayed it would be a short one. Lisette — and his own need — would not wait.

After a moment's thought, Colter sighed. "Guess it's the only way you're liable to learn. Here." He pulled out a bulging sack and began to count coins into Shannon's outstretched palm, then changed his mind and shoved the entire bag at him except for one coin which he slipped into his own pocket. "How much is she chargin' you, anyways?"

It was a question that Shannon had not thought to ask of Lisette, and he was too anxious to return to her to make up an answer. "I'll pay you back."

"I might not be around," Colter replied.

Shannon thought to ask Colter what he meant by that remark, but the weight of the money in his hand banished the idea. With a firm grip on the bag and renewed hope in his heart, he bounded up the steps into Lisette's room.

She had made up the bed where she now sat curling a lock of hair around a finger. At the sight of the heavy sack, her peevish expression relaxed, and she rose to greet him. "Ah, my handsome one returns." She took the bag from his hand and weighed it, then looked back up at him through her long eyelashes. "You bring all of this for Lisette, yes?"

"Just like I promised."

"Lisette likes a man who keeps his promises. Come."

I might not be around. Colter was surprised to hear those words come out of his mouth. Even more surprised to find out he meant them. Before Shannon showed up, he had been chewing on Lisa's offer. The more he weighed that opportunity against the specter of months of rubbing up against Sergeant Ordway, the more his commitment to the expedition eroded. But leaving meant betraying the principle upon which he had based his entire life — keeping his word. It also meant losing out on Scratch Wilkes's offer and erasing whatever advantage he might have gained against Farley Stuart if the expedition succeeded in locating the Northwest Passage.

Ordway. The growing bad blood between them was leading them toward a show-down. A show-down from which only one of them was likely to walk away. There was only one way to side-step such a confrontation and that was to leave the expedition here in St. Charles before they started up-river.

Yet leaving posed its own dilmma. What was he going to do instead? The terms of Lisa's offer — having to live with Indians — he could not live with, and not seeing the expedition through nullified Scratch Wilkes' offer. He no longer had a home to go back to — Farley Stuart had seen to that — and he had no other prospects.

At a loss for an alternative, he headed for the tavern.

He had just crossed the threshold when his jaw collided with a doubled fist. The force of the blow sent him reeling into one man who immediately shoved him off into two others. Before he knew it, he was in the middle of a melee. He had never been one for fighting, so he dropped to the floor and crawled outside.

He was halfway out the door when his progress was stopped by a group of men, the mayor of St. Charles and Sergeant Ordway backed by two burly men with lavish beards.

"Well, Colter. At it again, I see," Ordway said with a satisfied smirk.

"Zis ees zee man?" the mayor asked in heavily-accented French.

"Oh, it's him all right," the sergeant replied.

"*Bon*," said the mayor, motioning for the other two men to pull Colter to his feet.

"Seeing as how you like tight places so much, Private," Ordway said. "I fixed it with the mayor here for you to spend the night in the best St. Charles has to offer." He nodded to the mayor, then turned and walked off while the mayor's muscular helpers yanked Colter to his feet and wrestled him to what served as the settlement's jail, a narrow block building set in the space between the tavern and the church. As one of the helpers scraped open the door, Colter knew he had little time to save himself from another harrowing night of confinement. He reached into his pocket for money for a bribe, but all he had was one solitary coin. He had foolishly given Shannon everything else.

At the sight of that single coin, the mayor became incensed. "You insult me. In!"

"Look, I — *ooff*!" A fist jammed into Colter's gut and hands grabbed him from behind, picked him up and heaved him into the cell. The door slammed behind him. Colter doubled over, coughing, and could not protest. The padlock slid into place and snapped shut with the click of finality.

The walls of the tiny cell were made of brick. There was no window and the only way air could get in was through the crack around the door. He felt along the walls, hoping to find a loose brick. All were firmly mortared into place.

He banged on the door until his knuckles bled and yelled himself hoarse, determined not to give into the panic that had taken hold of him at Kaskaskia.

When no one came to investigate, he became aware of a strange tingling in his feet and hands. Within minutes, his hands began to quiver, then shake, then cramp and spasm. The convulsions jumped to his legs and drove him to his knees, then onto his side. He curled into a defensive ball while convulsions racked his body.

The one and only coherent thought he was able to put together was a reproach: *Lisa'll be gone 'fore I get outta here. Why didn't I say 'yes' when I had the chance?"*

When at last someone came to free him, he was still on the ground, unable to move. He did not see who opened the cell door. He did not care.

All that mattered was that the door was no longer shut or locked.

It was a long time before he could sit up or stand. As his mind cleared of the formless dread that had gripped it, he became aware that the morning was well-advanced and that the sun was out. Laughter and drunken arguments sounded from the tavern next door.

When he could trust his legs to support him, he hobbled to the edge of the low bluff and looked down to where Lisa's boat had been moored. It was gone and so was the chance he should have taken.

A large group of horses and riders approaching from the south intruded on his regret. At their head was Captain Lewis which meant that the expedition's stop in St. Charles was over.

The door to the tavern opened and out came the owner, a greedy blob of a man named Strauss. He hurried to where Colter was standing. "You are Colter, ja?"

Colter nodded.

"I have a message for you." Strauss stuck out a grimy palm and Colter handed over his one remaining coin. Strauss fingered it as if dissatisfied. "That there's all I got," Colter growled. He had been through too much to put up with more. "Take it or hand 'er back."

Strauss quickly stashed the coin in his vest pocket. "Herr Lisa, he tonight for you waits." He paused as if expecting Colter to produce more money to prompt him to go on.

"I told you. I ain't got more coins. Now either you tell me all he said or I want my money back ."

Strauss started to walk away, but Colter grabbed him. "Are you going to tell me, or do I have to make you?"

"He upriver this night camps. Ten miles," the man said, wresting his arm from Colter's grip and scuttling back to the safety of his saloon.

Ten miles. He could make that on foot before dark. But so could a certain vengeful sergeant who would revel in the chance to bring him in as a deserter. That was unless he could figure out a way to delay the sergeant from discovering his absence.

There was one way, one that required lying to Sergeant Floyd. Colter detested the idea of duping his friend, but, after last night, he had to get away from the expedition. He *had* to.

Colter trotted along as quickly as the faint path and the tangle of spring growth allowed. To his right, the Missouri ran high and furious, alive with floating logs, massive jams of uprooted trees and tons of earth from the upstream banks she had undermined. The crew would have its hands full from now on. The raging river would fight them for every foot of progress.

Stepping around a snag of trees, he shifted the rifle to his other hand. He had turned down Floyd's offer of a horse to help in hunting, but he could not leave without his rifle. To do so would have aroused suspicion. Now he had to figure out how to return it to the expedition once he reached Manuel Lisa. Betraying the sergeant's trust was one thing; taking something that did not belong to him was another. He knew Lisa would have an extra rifle that he could pay for out of his own take.

The going was harder than he anticipated. Moving as quickly as he could through the dense foliage, he had covered a mere seven miles by sunset. He had just stopped to readjust his pouch and catch his breath when the sound of snapping twigs brought him instantly alert. He squinted into the dimness and saw the brush moving a few yards ahead.

From the movement, he guessed that whatever was there was big. Fresh meat was something every camp needed. Bringing in game would be an excellent way to begin partnership with Lisa. He shouldered his rifle, aimed just ahead of the direction of movement and squeezed off the shot.

The creature grunted and fell with a thud.

Colter hurried forward to see what he had bagged. He parted the bushes and gasped, "My God!"

He had not shot a deer or a bear. He had shot York.

He dropped to his knees and frantically scanned for the wound his ball had inflicted. The light was so bad he had to use his fingers to help his eyes. It was his fingers that found the oozing crease above the slave's right ear.

Colter sat back on his heels in relief. The bullet had knocked York out, but the wound was superficial, not life-threatening. Relief quickly turned to anger at himself. He knew better than to shoot before he had identified his target.

York's eyes blinked open. "C-Colter?"

He positioned himself in the slave's line of sight. "That's me."

"W-Where am I?"

"West of St. Charles, seven miles or thereabouts."

York's expression went from puzzled to horrified. "Oh, no," he groaned, his face crumpling in pain.

"Were an accident, York. I thought —"

The black man rolled away from Colter, concealing his face.

"Want to tell me what you're doin' out here?"

York flinched away from his touch.

All at once, Colter knew the answer to that question. "You're runnin', ain't ya?"

That York did not speak or look at him confirmed his suspicion. "Look, I don't blame you a bit. If'n I was you, I'd run, too. Ball grazed your head's all. I'll wrap a rag 'round it to stop the blood. You'll have a headache, but that ain't goin' to slow you down much. Let me help you up and you head on. Far as I'm concerned, I never saw you and this here never happened."

The black man faced him then. "I got a woman at home. Tallie. She's carryin' our baby, and I forgot her birthing time." His voice turned husky with anguish. "I met up with an old friend of mine in St. Charles. Used to be a slave. Worked for Tallie's master, but he bought his papers. Name's Caesar."

Colter nodded, hoping to keep the normally-reticent York talking until he could figure out what to do next.

"Caesar's out here now, working for a man named Lisa. Manuel Lisa."

The hair on Colter's neck stood straight up at the coincidence.

"They headed upriver this morning. Wanted me to go with them, but I couldn't. Not just then, anyway." York paused to swallow. "Then Captain Meri showed up and, and all of a sudden, the idea of going out west . . . I . . . I . . ."

"All the more reason for you to get on your way."

York's gaze sank. "I can't."

"What do you mean, you cain't? Good Lord, go whilst you got the chance!"

"You being here. This." He touched the wound gingerly. "It's a message."

"Message? It was an accident. Here, I'll tie on this here kerchief and you get outta here."

York would not be deterred. He gripped Colter's wrist fiercely. "It was no accident. I was making a mistake. Your bullet was a message from God."

"What kind of fool notion is that, man? Get goin'."

"This was no accident, Colter. God sent you. You were here to stop me. This was God's way of telling me I'm supposed to go back, not run."

Colter could not bring himself to argue further. York was talking about instincts and a man's hunches were nothing to dismiss. Trusting a hunch had saved his life more times than he wanted to count. He started to tie his kerchief over the wound, but York objected. "I can't wear this back. Someone'll want to know why I got it on."

"Then I'll wrap it over your head like them Frenchies wear. It'll look like you're takin' after the *engagés*. Ain't nobody goin' to notice, what with everyone in a tizzy gettin' ready to leave."

York agreed to this. Colter wrapped the make-shift bandage in the style of the French rivermen, then helped the slave to stand. "Path's a mite overgrown, but she's right along the river. It'll take you straight back to St. Charles."

York took only two steps before his legs gave way. He fell, hitting the wounded side of his head against the limb of a fallen tree. The fall knocked him out. Now Colter was left with two choices: to leave York where he lay and go on to Lisa's camp, or to help the slave back to St. Charles. Two choices, but his conscience would let him live with only one.

After Captain Lewis had finished treating York's wound, he turned to regard Colter. "It's late. Better get some sleep."

Colter was glad to get out of the captain's presence. Lewis had accepted that York's wounding had been a hunting mishap. He had not pressed further, for which Colter was glad.

Outside the keelboat's cabin, clouds obscured the night sky hanging over *Discovery* as the fluctuations of the Missouri's current rocked her. The boat was deserted except for a sentry on the quarterdeck and another lounging at the gangway. The rest of the crew were making the most of their last night in St. Charles.

The brooding stillness of the night matched Colter's mood. He had no one else to blame for missing the chance to catch Manuel Lisa. He always, always made sure of his target. That is, until today.

He made his way across the gangway to the beach and up the low bluff to the settlement. The tavern was in full swing, but he was not in the mood for alcohol or a lot of talk or much of anything else. With every passing minute, he was feeling more and more like a condemned prisoner.

He was walking away from the tavern when a female voice hailed him. He turned to see Annabelle hurrying toward him. She was the whore he had bedded their first night in St. Charles, a plump willing woman with a serious overbite and the habit of talking nonstop. He figure she was looking for more business and held up his hand. "You're outta luck, missy. My purse is empty."

Despite his efforts, she came ahead. "He figured you'd have trouble and he was right. How'd you like our jail?"

He wanted to forget that experience, not talk about it. "Who's 'he,' missy? Who're you talkin' about?"

"El Señor. Manuel Lisa. He's a regular of mine. That is, when he's not off gallivanting. He gave me a message for you. Said he'd stay at the Niobrara till September 4. That mean anything to you?"

Colter nodded noncommitally. Of course he knew what it meant, but he did not know what he could do with the information.

"You going to join him?" she asked.

"I don't know," he said, when what he meant was *Soon as I can get there.*

3. *The Adventure Begins*

T he waiting was getting to everyone — the crowd that had come to see the expedition off, the twenty-five crewmen, the *engagés* hired to paddle the two pirogues supporting *Discovery* were all there. What was keeping the captains?

Manuel Lisa's message had Colter wound up tighter than a watch spring. He had to get to the Niobrara River by September 4 and every passing minute moved that date ever closer. He was too keyed up to be much good at carving, but he tried anyway just to give his hands something to do.

A piercing wolf-whistle startled him and he dropped the chunk of wood he was working on. He looked round to see the whore, Lisette, sashaying through the crowd to the accompaniment of catcalls and lewd comments from the crew.

Uncombed, unshaven, unwashed, Shannon had been standing apart, looking like someone who had lost his way and his will. The sight of Lisette transformed him instantaneously. His jaw lost its slackness; his expression, its forlornness; and his posture, its slouch.

She glided up to Shannon, wrapped her arms around his neck and gave him a passionate kiss that drew cheers from the spectators. "You come back to Lisette with a full purse, yes?"

"Oh, yes," Shannon gushed.

"Then Lisette, she waits for you. *Adieu, mon amour.*" She tossed her abundant curls and waltzed back through the crowd, leaving Shannon gaping after her.

"That was some goodbye, Peckerwood. Now you best forget her," Rube said.

"I'll never forget —"

An unearthly shriek cut into Shannon's declaration. Lil flew out of the crowd and barreled into Colter, pummeling his chest with her fists. "Coward! Murderer!"

Colter managed to catch her clawing hands before they could do much damage to him. She screamed even louder, each expelled breath putrid with cheap liquor. "Mac's dead and you're to blame. I hate you, you bastard!"

"Weren't me killed him," he countered.

"I didn't want to leave, but you made me. And now he's gone, and I can't go back. My life is over."

He tried to reason with her, but she would have none of it. She flung out of his grasp. "You won't get away with it. I'll make you pay for his life!" She spit in his face and lurched away. He heard her wailing long after she was out of sight.

"Whew! That woman was mad enough to scratch your eyes out. Here." Newman handed Colter a clean kerchief.

Colter was wiping the spittle off his face when the captains finally began to make their way to the boats. Behind the two men trailed Drouillard, York with Colter's kerchief tied around his head and a cluster of dignitaries.

"Bloody half-breed," Newman muttered in Drouillard's direction. The gossip among the crew was that Drouillard was to receive twenty-five dollars a month pay for his services. That was five times what Colter or any of the other crew earned. And, because he was a civilian, he would not be subject to standing watches or performing other camp duties. Colter had not put much store in the gossip, but now, watching the man's arrogant swagger and self-possessed manner, he decided that he did not like the man one whit.

"Hear his ma was Shawnee," Newman said.

Yes, there's Shawnee in his face, Colter thought. *Shawnee, like Zoob's ma.* That realization doubled his dislike of the man.

The crew filed aboard *Discovery* and took up their assigned positions while the captains said their final farewells. Sliding onto the bench next to Shannon, Colter was too preoccupied to care about his bench-mate's mournful look.

At last the captains came aboard, the gangplank was drawn in, and Floyd gave the order to cast off. As the first mooring lines were undone, cheers and rifle fire erupted from the crowd on the bank. Colter viewed the celebrating throng through the cynical eyes of someone who did not want to be there.

Thwack. Something slammed into the gunwale next to the oar lock, splintering the wood. A rifle ball, he guessed, then immediately thought, *Lil*.

However, scanning the crowd revealed no sign of the woman or any rifle aimed his direction. He relaxed. The ball had been a stray, not meant for him.

Shannon let out a low groan. "Oh, God. Look."

Colter followed Shannon's pointing finger to see Lisette leading a man up the stairs to her room above the tavern. "What'd you expect, Fuzz? She's a whore after all."

The pain in Shannon's face flared into anger. "Don't you dare call her that! Her name is Lisette."

Shannon's outburst drew Floyd. "What's the problem, Private? Why aren't you rowing?"

Shannon mastered his faculties enough to fall to his oar. *Sotto voce* Floyd said, "You had your chance to quit, Shannon. You should've taken it."

Colter waited for the sergeant to leave. "She's a whore, Fuzz. Don't expect her to be nothin' else."

"She said she'd wait for me."

Colter wanted to say *wait for your purse, you mean,* but he held his tongue. Let Shannon keep his illusions. Where they were headed, he would need them.

⚓

Josiah Hartley threw down his rifle in exasperation. He had had Colter in his sights, had the perfect shot, only to see the rifle ball swerve and bury itself in the keelboat's side, rather than in the man's skull. He kicked the weapon and stomped on the stock.

"You're goin' to break it, mister." The comment came from a freckle-faced boy of about six, peering at Hartley from the other side of the leaning elm the preacher had used for cover.

The youngster's innocent expression was too much for the preacher to stomach at that moment. He grabbed up the rifle and swung it against the tree, smashing the wooden stock. One of the splinters struck the boy in the cheek, eliciting a yowl of pain. The boy ran away crying.

"Serves you right, you little meddler," Hartley yelled after him.

⚓

The next two days were the most difficult of Shannon's eighteen years. The Missouri was running at full spate, hurling one obstacle after another at the crew — massive uprooted trees, floating islands of deadly splintered branches, rolling sandbars, sawyers, the bloated bodies of drowned animals. After months of relative inactivity at Camp Wood, fighting the river wore everyone to a nub.

But, hard as the physical exertion was for Shannon, it was nothing compared with the aching in his heart and loins for the woman he had left behind. To compound his misery, every time he turned around, Sergent Floyd was at him. *What am I doing here? What's to be gained by going on? Fame? Glory? That's not what I want. I want Lisette and she's back in St. Charles. Why not quit? I could be back to St. Charles in two days.*

"What'd you say?" Colter grunted, heaving back on his oar.

"I didn't," Shannon said.

"Sure did. I heard ya. Somethin' about two days."

Shannon did not answer. He was nonplussed to have spoken his most intimate thoughts aloud.

"You best get over her," Colter said.

"And you best butt out," Shannon shot back.

"If you're thinkin' she'd settle down with you, think again. She sells herself a poke at a time. Money's all she cares about. The only way to keep her attention's with a full purse. Which mine was 'fore you borrowed it off'n me."

"You don't know her and you don't know what I'm thinking so stick your nose in someone else's business."

"This is my business, Fuzz. Has been ever since you took all my money. And it'll stay my business till you pay me back. By the by, when's that goin' to be?"

The question took Shannon unawares. Once he handed Colter's purse over to Lisette, he had put the debt out of his mind.

"That there was fifty dollars, Fuzz."

Fifty dollars? That much? In his rush to get back to Lisette, he had not bothered to count the money or question how much she was charging him for her company.

Colter spit a wad of tobacco juice onto the decking. "Fifty dollars pays for a lotta pokes. A month's worth I reckon, but you didn't even get a week, did ya? You got took, Fuzz. That whore played you like a fiddle and you never even knew it. When do I get my money?"

Shannon had no way to repay Colter at the moment and no answer to the question, but he was saved from saying so by the order to head into shore. While Colter's squad was called up to the *passe avant* to pole the boat in, Shannon added another to the growing list of reasons to question continuing with the expedition.

Their stop was a large cave, dubbed the "Tavern", carved out of the base of a soaring cliff by the grinding current of the Missouri. The walls of the grotto were inscribed with the names of previous passersby. As soon as the keelboat was tied off in the wide eddy at the cave mouth, the crew crowded off to eat lunch and add their names to the walls.

Colter was already on the beach and Shannon was disembarking when

Captain Lewis called out, "Colter, Shannon, come with me." Lewis strode to the far end of the beach with them in his wake. "Ah, just as I thought," he muttered and began pulling himself up a steep, pebble-strewn break in the cliff face.

Colter stared up at the route the captain had chosen. "He's outta his mind."

"If you can't take it, Old Man, stay here," Shannon said, scrambling after Lewis.

For Colter, the climb proved an obstacle course of crumbling handholds and sliding steps while dodging debris kicked loose by the captain and Shannon above him. His legs were shaking by the time he reached the top. Heights. He would never get used to them.

The captain stood with his hands on his hips, taking in the view. "Magnificent! I wish the President could see this."

The top of the cliff angled sharply downward to a vertical precipice that plunged into the river. Wind and water had scored deep grooves into the cliff top, making the footing treacherous. The captain prowled about examining pieces of sediment and gathering rock samples, seemingly oblivious of the peril.

"How's your geology, Shannon? Can you identify this?" the captain asked, bending to pick up a chunk of rock. Without warning, his feet slid out from under him and he went down on his knees. He grabbed for something to arrest his skid, but the friable rock crumbled under the pressure of his grasping fingers and he pitched onto his belly and began sliding feet-first toward the edge of the precipice.

Shannon was closest to the captain, but stunned surprise rooted him to the spot. Colter realized that, even running, he could not reach the man in time so he yelled the one thing that came to mind. "Knife!"

The captain got the message. He managed to fumble his knife out of its scabbard and jam it into a fissure in the decomposing rock. The blade buried deep enough to stop the captain's slide. Lewis lay sprawled on the cliftop, the fingers of his left hand clawed into the rock, his right arm stretched long, his right hand clutching the handle of his knife and his feet dangling out over the drop-off.

Shannon sank down to his knees as though he had lost the power to stand in the face of the captain's danger.

"Fuzz, get up. We gotta help the Captain," Colter urged.

Shannon's mouth moved, but the rest of him did not.

"Please hurry," the captain pleaded in a ragged voice.

Colter realized it was up to him alone to pull the captain back from the edge of certain death. His legs were already shaky, the result of his dilike of heights. He could not trust them to hold him upright so close to the yawning drop-off, so he got down on all fours and crawled toward the captain.

He crawled maybe five feet before the proximity of the cliff edge halted his progress. He simply could not get closer if he had to look at that drop-off.

"Don't stop," the captain implored through gritted teeth.

Colter rolled onto his stomach with his head pointed away from the precipice and began inching feet-first down toward the captain, occasionally glancing over his shoulder to check his position, but never allowing his eyes to fixate on the cliff edge or the river below.

When he was close enough, he felt about for depressions and cracks to use for bracing his knees and fingers. He set himself as best he could, then said, "Here's far as I can go, Captain. It's up to you now to grab a-hold of my ankles. Then I'll see to pullin' us both back up."

There were three sharp intakes of breath from the captain, followed by the sickening sound of falling rocks. A heartbeat later, a hand clamped around Colter's left ankle. A second heart-stopping rock shower, more wrenching of Colter's leg, and a grunt before the captain let go of his knife and flailed to secure a grip for his right hand on Colter's other leg. The attempt missed the ankle and the hand latched onto his boot instead.

Absorbing the captain's full weight destabilized Colter, unseating one knee and uprooting his handholds. His heart pounded in his chest, but he managed to keep the other knee braced and that held him long enough to reset himself. "Ready?"

"Yes," came the captain's labored reply.

Swallowing against the parched desert of his throat, Colter crept upward using his fingers, elbows, hips and knees, dragging the bulk of the captain away from the cliff rim one fraction of an inch after another until he was forced to stop for a breather.

"I–ah–I'm slipping," the captain said.

Colter sucked in a deep breath and forced himself onward, clawing, pushing, heaving, dragging until the captain said, "I believe you can stop now."

Drained from the rescue, Colter remained on his stomach while the captain let go his foot and ankle and pushed himself into a kneeling position. Getting to his feet, Lewis slapped dust from his pants and coat, and adjusted his jacket. His movements were so normal and controlled that no one would guess that he had come so close to plunging to his death. "Quick thinking, Colter. You, too, Shannon. My thanks to you both."

Shannon nodded at the captain, the only movement he had made since Lewis's fall, a fact that apparently escaped the captain's notice.

The captain smoothed his hair before replacing his hat. "I think it best that we make no mention of this incident to the others. No need for unnecessary alarm." He spoke matter-of-factly, but his tone left no doubt this was an order, not a suggestion.

Lewis turned and looked at the spot where his knife was still jammed into the cliff's fissure. "That is a perfectly good knife. Shame to leave it."

Colter found a piece of his voice. "No, Captain. Leave it be."

"I suppose you're right. Shall we descend?" He did not wait for an answer before starting the climb down to the beach.

When Shannon moved to follow, Colter said tiredly, "Time to quit play-actin', Fuzz. This ain't no Sunday picnic. You freezin' every time there's danger means someone's goin' to get hurt."

"Don't be ridiculous. I'll admit I was surprised, but that's not a crime."

Colter snorted. "Like hell it ain't. If'n it'd been up to you, Captain'd be dead now."

"I'm not about to stand here and listen to this nonsense. I'm leaving."

Colter watched him go. No sense arguing with someone who refused to admit the truth about himself. Time and circumstance had a way of catching up with folks like Shannon. *Just don't be takin' anyone else down with you*, he prayed.

Shannon was halfway down the precarious descent to the beach when the question he had been mulling for three days solidified into a decision. He arrived at the beach to find Sergeant Floyd lounging against a house-sized boulder. "Had enough yet, Private?" Floyd asked.

"In fact, I have," Shannon replied. "I quit."

"Oh, you do, huh?" Floyd said with surprising casualness, given how hard he had worked to hear such an answer.

"Yes, I quit. I am not going another foot with you or anyone else on this crew."

"Think again, Shannon. You waited too long. The only way any of us leaves now is to stop breathing for good."

"But, but, you said —"

"No 'but,' Shannon. You blew your chance to quit when we left St. Charles. Too bad, because you and me are stuck with each other now. Believe me, I don't like that any more than you do."

Shannon looked at the river in disbelief. *Lisette, Lisette, Lisette*, the name beat against the walls of his yearning, imprisoned now for as long as the expedition took.

Hartley mopped sweat from his face and neck. The noon sun beat mercilessly down on the canoe. The boat belonged to two surly rivermen, the shifty-eyed Bonhomme and his tongueless partner with the ironic name of Parler, French for "to speak." He had hired them in St. Charles to take him up the Missouri in pursuit of the expedition.

After his shot missed Colter during the expedition's departure, he spent two days searching St. Charles for the woman who had attacked Colter at the expedition's farewell. After he found her, it took a surprising amount of persuasion in the form of expensive brandy to get the woman to tell her story. Yet, once he got her talking, she told him everything he needed to know. Playing on her anger at Colter over the death of McBain, he found it easy to manipulate her into finding rivermen willing to do what he wanted.

Those men did not come cheap. It had cost the rest of his purse and the three barrels of whiskey now secured in the canoe to persuade them. In return, they agreed to supply him with food and gear for the trip as well as doing all the rowing. Their one condition was that they would not go beyond the Platte River.

In the bow, Bonhomme suddenly barked an order in French to his partner, and the canoe angled sharply for the bank where a cluster of crude cabins stood beside a foaming creek.

"Wait! What are you doing?" Hartley demanded, pounding his fists on the whiskey barrel lashed down in front of his drawn-up knees. "I paid you to paddle. Not to stop. Turn us upriver! Now!"

When Bonhomme did not react to the demand, Hartley leaned across the barrel and poked him in the ribs. "Did you hear me? No stop!"

The head of Bonhomme's paddle punched the preacher in the midsection. "Here we stop. Comprenez?" the riverman growled.

Chastened by the blow and the menace in the man's tone, Hartley settled back on the splintery seat. For the first time, it hit him squarely between the eyes just how tenuous his position really was: he was at the mercy of the boatmen. Yet, he quickly realized that their slow progress didn't necessarily mean defeat. Moving the keelboat was slow work for the expedition. A lot slower than paddling a canoe. Stopping for an hour would not make that much difference.

Bonhomme guided the boat to a narrow spit of sand upstream from the mouth of the creek. He and Parler slid the craft expertly onto the bank. No sooner had the canoe beached than six women, skirts lifted to display a shocking amount of leg, came running from the cabins to greet them. The women welcomed the two rivermen with enthusiasm that bordered on the salacious. Parler managed to break away from their attention long enough to wrest one of the liquor barrels out of the canoe. Then he and Bonhomme went off to the cabins, enveloped by a hovering cloud of randy women.

Alone and ignored, Hartley turned his back on the scene. He wanted no part of the debauchery that was about to go on inside those cabins. Those women were French, after all. He would wait here and try to figure out some way to regain control of things.

4. *Cordelle into Hell*

D evil's Race Ground. The name fit. The Missouri roared her displeasure and threw up huge rolling waves to protest being squeezed between an island and the cluster of projecting rocks that crowded the south bank.

The water's drag on the boat made every step under the cordelle an exercise in agony. Colter bent forward, focusing on the ground with vision blurred by sweat, judging his progress by the inches of ground he managed to shuffle over. At times, the river held *Discovery* so tightly in her grip that he had the sensation of standing still or even of losing ground.

With his muscles screaming in protest and blood pounding in his ears, he did not hear the low rumbling sound until the ground under his feet began to vibrate. He flung aside the rope and scrambled toward the trees, away from the river. He was almost there when Shannon plowed into him from behind and they both fell flat.

Raising up, Colter saw the stretch of riverbank upon which he had been trudging collapse into the river. "Whew! That was a close one, Fuzz," he said, regaining his feet and offering Shannon a hand up.

The earth began to shake again. And a crack opened, separating the two of them from the safety of solid ground. Without thought, he shoved Shannon across the gap, then belly-flopped after him.

From down the way came shouts, "The rope! She's loose!"

The cordelle rope had been abandoned in the crew's efforts to escape the collapsing riverbank. Without a force to oppose her will, the river had pulled *Discovery*'s nose around until the boat lay broadside to the current. The few crewmen still aboard fought to bring her around, but the Missouri swept the boat into a sandbar before their efforts had any effect.

The river's surging power pushed *Discovery* against the mass of sand, causing her to heel at a dangerous angle. With Colter and the other pullers watching helplessly from the bank, the remaining boat crew scuttled to the high side to counterbalance the current. Their efforts stabilized the angle of cant, but the boat did not come level. One by one, men slung themselves over the side, hanging by their hands from the gunwales using the weight of their bodies as ballast to help settle the boat.

Slowly, their combined efforts worked, but, just as the boat leveled, the sandbar broke up under the scouring action of the water, sending *Discovery* floating free.

The on-board crew scrambled back to their oars, but before they could sweep one stroke, the Missouri grabbed the boat a second time and wheeled it end for end onto another, larger sandbar. A few of the boat crew managed to clamber to the high side, but, before the rest could get into position, the boat broke loose with a shuddering jolt that sent those on-board sprawling across the rowing benches.

That was when Colter noticed something black bobbing on the surface of the roiling water. It was a man's head. York's head. Despite the danger, the slave was swimming out to the keelboat!

On *Discovery*, Clark hustled to the bow and hauled in the loose cordelle line. As York drew near to the boat, Clark threw him the coiled-up rope. The slave snatched the line cleanly out of the air, then disappeared beneath the churning surface of the river.

Colter sucked in a breath, fearing that York had been pulled under by a submerged snag, or worse.

"The fool!" Shannon exclaimed.

Agonizing moments later, York's head and shoulders popped to the surface halfway between *Discovery* and the chewed-up bank. Colter dashed to the water's edge and intercepted the black man, grabbing the cordelle from him and passing it into the hands of the other crewmen. When he tried to help the exhausted swimmer out of the water, York waved him off. "Save the boat," he gasped breathlessly.

It took an hour of harrowing struggle to secure *Discovery*. Once that was done, Colter flopped down, too weary to do more than stretch out and fling one arm over his eyes.

"Old Man?"

He squinted around his arm to see Shannon standing over him. "You saved my life."

Colter grunted.

"Next time, don't bother," Shannon murmured in a faraway tone.

Colter watched Shannon plod away, then shook his head and closed his eyes. Before he could form a thought about what Shannon had said, he fell asleep.

The excitement of the Devil's Race Ground left Colter feeling restless. The following night, he stuck up his hand when Captain Clark asked for a volunteer to help take readings of their geographic position.

Colter's part was to carry the bulky instruments and set them up. Then he hauled them back to the boat and stowed the equipment in the captains' cabin. He was turning to leave when Clark said, "You might find this interesting, Colter."

The captain smoothed out the master map he was in the process of creating and pointed out two positions. "Here's the Mississippi, and here's our current position."

He went on explaining more details of map-making, but Colter quit listening when his eyes landed on a squiggly line marked "Niobrara River" in the captain's distinctive script. He mentally measured the distance from where they currently were to where the Niobrara emptied into the Missouri, then compared that with the distance they had traveled so far. His jaw tightened at how far they had yet to travel by September 4.

He went ashore to find the crew back to normal, complaining about the food and grumbling about how hard they were working. He found a place on the fringes of the group and set about tending his sore feet as a way to calm the anxiety the captain's map had raised within him. The day after leaving St. Charles, he had given Newman his boots and taken to wearing moccasins like the *engagés* wore. The moccasins consisted of folded pads of supple deer hide secured to the foot by thongs. Unlike boots, they provided firm footing on slippery rocks; they dried overnight; and, since the hunters brought in new hides daily, they were easy to replace.

While he wrapped his feet, Newman and three others played a fitful game of poker, Joe Field picked out a mournful song on his mouth organ, and Rube cleaned his rifle. On the edge of the group, Shannon sat staring at the fire, shoulders slumped, a doleful expression on his face. *He's got the pox again*, Colter guessed, shaking his head. *Well, maybe this time he'll get the message.*

He was tying on his second moccasin when Captain Lewis joined the men at the fire, called for attention, and began reading an order outlining duties that would rotate among the three sergeants. Colter listened for a time, then closed his ears. What the sergeants did was no concern of his.

"Shit!" Rube muttered, reclaiming Colter's attention.

"What happened?" he asked.

"Where you been?" Joe replied. "You, me, Rube, Newman, and Fuzz all got us a new squad."

From Joe's pained expression, it was no stretch to guess who their sergeant was. Ordway sidled over to their group. "Well, ladies, looks like you're in luck." He turned to a square-jawed private named Collins. "Draw some extra powder, Collins. You'll be hunting with Drouillard tomorrow."

"Hold up there, Sergeant. I'm up to hunt tomorrow," Colter said.

One corner of Ordway's mouth hitched upward. "Seems Private Colter wasn't listening to the captain's order. For anyone else who missed it, let me repeat. I'm in charge of rations for this expedition. Not Sergeant Floyd. Not Sergeant Pryor. Me. I'm also in charge of placing the men of my squad at those positions they are most suited for. For you, Colter, that means at the oar and on the cordelle. Every day."

Inwardly, Colter's guts churned at the idea that, with Ordway in such a position, he would be denied the opportunity to periodically escape into the solitude and quiet of the hunt. Solitude and quiet kept him sane. Outwardly, however, he forced his expression to remain neutral.

Ordway's parting look promised that, from now on, every day with the expedition would be a long one for Colter. *Until the Niobrara*, he vowed.

Shannon stood outside the door to the captains' cabin, unable to bring himself to knock. He could no longer ignore the festering canker on his penis. The sore made it impossible to deny that Lisette had lied to him. Worse was the knowledge that he had believed her — because he wanted to.

All of a sudden the door swung open, and there stood Captain Clark. "Yes, Private?"

"Is Captain Lewis — available?"

Clark went back into the cabin, motioning Shannon to enter. "Yes," Lewis said, looking up from his work.

"Sir — I —" Shannon stammered, unable to think under the captain's gaze.

Lewis's face settled into sternness. "*Again?*"

Shannon could barely manage a nod.

Lewis sighed heavily. "Let me see."

Shannon fumbled open his pants. The captain glanced at the lesion from across the table. "So, that's what that little scene at our departure from St. Charles was all about. Don't think you're protecting her honor, Private. Women like her make a choice to forfeit their honor. I hope she was worth it to you."

Shannon could not bring himself to indict Lisette to the captain. As he submitted to treatment, the question echoed in his mind: *Had she been worth it?*

Half an hour later, he left the cabin. Without an answer.

"Up and out!" yelled Ordway.

Colter jammed his oar into its lock, grabbed the shovel from under the bench, and crawled over the side into the river without enthusiasm. For the last ten days, the Missouri had added even more tricks to the arsenal she threw into the fight against the expedition. A fickle wind teased the crew, remaining steady long enough for them to raise the sail, then either dying away or shifting directions and rendering the sail useless. Overhanging branches snapped the mast, forcing a day's delay while the crew felled, dressed and stepped a new one. More insidious were the dense clouds of mosquitos that drove the crew to distraction. And now this. Another sand-bar, another dig, another damn delay.

He glanced back at Shannon who was always the last one into the river when it came to digging the keelboat off a sandbar. "Comin', Fuzz?" he asked sarcastically.

Shannon grunted something and made a show of bending to retrieve his spade from under the rowing bench. Colter looked toward the prow to see if Sergeant Ordway was paying attention to Shannon's procrastination. For once, he was watching and coming Shannon's way.

Colter splashed into the waist-deep water, waded to an empty spot beyond Rube and Joe and set to work digging away at the leading edge of the sand-bar. The theory was that, once they removed enough of the sand, the river's current would clear away the rest. Sometimes the theory even proved out.

Out of the corner of his eye, he saw Ordway push the dawdling Shannon over the side with a push. Shannon landed in the river with a satisfying splash some six feet away. It was about time someone rode herd him. About time he admitted that deep water spooked him. It was his fault he refused to quit when he had the opportunity. He had had more chances than anyone, had enjoyed more leniency from the captains and sergeants than anyone. And now it was time he paid for all that coddling. *Past time*, Colter thought.

Hearing the creaking sound of a loose oar, Colter craned around to make sure he was not in its path. He wasn't, but Shannon was, and the oar hit him smack in the back of the head, knocking him face-first into the murky water.

Colter glanced around, but could see no one else who had witnessed the accident. He watched to see if Shannon resurfaced.

A minute passed, then two.

No Shannon.

The diggers were making too much noise for him to get anyone's atten-tion so he tossed his shovel up into the keelboat and took off swimming toward the place where Shannon had disappeared.

The water was choppy and muddy from the digging. Too choppy for making headway so he dove beneath the surface. The water was a-churn with sand from the crew's shoveling, rendering his eyes useless. Robbed of sight, he had to rely on his hands to feel for Shannon's body.

He stabbed around him, but his hands did not connect with anything.

He forced himself down to the bottom of the river, using his arms as antennae, surveying left and right, above and below.

Still nothing.

Lungs burning, he bobbed up to the surface, saw no sign of Shannon, gulped air and immediately sank again. He jabbed and poked, circled and probed. Left, right, forward, backward, stretching arms and fingers, lunging this way and that.

His lungs were close to bursting when at last his hand brushed something. He could not tell if it was hair or moss, but he grabbed for it anyway and kicked back to the surface. He broke into the air and breathed too soon, sucking water as well as air into his lungs. Coughing, he lost his grip on whatever he had caught. Still choking, he went down after it.

He caught hold again, then launched himself and his burden upward. He broke the surface and, with the last of his strength, pulled up his catch. It was Shannon.

Others had, by now, become aware of his plight. Rube and Joe took charge of the unconscious Shannon and handed him up to Floyd and Ordway on the keelboat, then they helped Colter aboard. Ordway intercepted him before he could take two steps. "That was your oar, Colter."

A quick glance showed that the sergeant was telling the truth. It was his oar that hit Shannon.

"So you were getting even with your bench-mate before you take off. Is that it?" Ordway needled.

Colter was too tired to spar with Ordway. "Whatever you say, Sarge."

Ordway lowered his voice so that the captains who were working to revive Shannon could not hear what he said. "We've been on the river for eleven days now. In my experience, now's when someone like you gets it into his head to take off because you think I'm not watching. Well, I am. You know what happened to the last four men who tried to desert my outfit? Firing squads for two; hanging for the others. I prefer hanging myself. It takes longer. In fact, I brought along a rope with your name on it, Colter."

"Then you'll be takin' it back home with you, won't you, Sarge?"

At that moment *Discovery* lurched free of the sandbar, throwing Ordway off his stance. Colter used the opportunity to slide past him to the rowing bench where the now-conscious Shannon sat slumped and bedraggled. He looked up at Colter, "You should have left me be."

You should'a stayed back in St. Charles, thought Colter, but he said, "That wouldn'a got you back to that whore."

A fire blazed up in Shannon's eyes and he sat up a little straighter. "Hellfire, Old Man! I've told you before not to call her that!"

Colter shrugged and turned away satisfied. Shannon would live to see another day at the oar whether he liked it or not.

During the three-day orgy of drunkenness and womanizing at the Femme Osage settlement, Bonhomme and Parler ignored Hartley. He stayed near the canoe, preferring the heat and mosquitos to the depravity going on within the filthy cabins.

Once they finally got back on the river, Bonhomme and Parler bent to their paddles and made a respectable distance for two days. Then around noon on the third day, the canoe again swung into shore. This time there were no cabins or women at the landing site which did not make sense until the pair took up their guns. "We hunt. You stay," Bonhomme had said on his way out of camp.

Hartley stayed by the boat and the pair returned at sundown with a string of rabbits and quail. "You cook. We drink," Bonhomme said, jerking the bung from a new whiskey cask.

Hartley was ravenous. He set to work cleaning the kill, building a fire and cooking the meat while the rivermen applied themselves to drinking. When the meat was done, they waved it off so Hartley ate as much as he could down, then turned in.

The next morning he could rouse neither man from his drunken stupor. When Parler finally came to in mid-afternoon, Hartley had had enough. "Now see here. We had a bargain, and you're not keeping up your end."

Parler lifted him off the ground in a strangling embrace and held him that way until he was on the verge of blacking out. At that point, Parler dropped and kicked him. The kick connected at the point where Rutledge's knife had pierced Hartley's ribs and he cried out in pain.

After that, the preacher learned not to complain. He had made a major mistake in entrusting his life and mission to two brutes whose main aim in life was to stay drunk. The problem was how to get out of the situation alive.

This dilemma was on his mind the next day when two rafts glided into view upstream. Bonhomme motioned the craft to the bank and turned in to join them. From the amount of cheek-kissing, hugging and rapid-fire French, it was obvious that these newcomers were old friends of the two rivermen. Seething with frustration over what looked to be another prolonged another stop, Hartley waited in the canoe.

After a time Bonhomme broke away from the group and came to the boat. "No more stops. We go now," Hartley demanded.

Bonhomme grunted and bent to untie the ropes holding down the whiskey cask. Hartley grabbed the man's thick forearm. "Now! Vite! I've put up with your drunkenness and debauchery for more than two weeks. I demand that it stop this minute!"

Bonhomme spread his hands in supplication. "These men, zey are my brothers. Zey live with zee Sioux all weenter. Come, we talk weeth them."

"No, absolutely not. Get back in this boat now, or I'll —"

Another hand lifted Hartley out of the boat by the collar of his shirt. Parler carried him thus to the top of the bank and deposited him there with a look that warned him to shut up. Bonhomme followed with a cup of whiskey which he held out to the preacher.

"No, I don't want any filthy drink. I want you to do what I hired you for," Hartley said.

Parler cocked his head, snorted like a pig and, grasping Hartley's hand, nearly broke his fingers bending them around the cup. With his other hand, the riverman pried open Hartley's mouth and jerked back his head. Whether he wanted to or not, Hartley drank.

5. *Battle Lines*

I *brought along a rope with your name on it.* Before Ordway's taunt, Colter had been chafing under the sergeant's constant scrutiny. After it, he knew that the only way he would make it to the Niobrara and Manuel Lisa without having a major confrontation with Ordway was to get out from under the sergeant's thumb regularly. And the only way he saw to do so was to get back in the hunting rotation. How to do so was the problem.

A month passed without a solution presenting itself. Every day, pairs of crewmen went off to hunt while he remained behind, his tolerance for the sergeant deteriorating. To aggravate the situation, July began hot and grew steadily hotter. The stifling heat that ground Colter down made Shannon talkative. The more Colter sweat, the more the younger man's incessant yammering grated.

On the afternoon of July 7, in the middle of one of Shannon's deadly dull discourses on geology, Colter reached his limit. "Shut up, Fuzz."

Shannon went right on lecturing as if he had not heard. Colter raised his voice. "I said shut up, Fu —"

A rifle boomed, drowning the end of his sentence. Colter looked up to the quarterdeck where the smoke of exploded powder hung around the breech of Captain Lewis's rifle. Then he glanced toward the nearby river-bank to see what the captain had been shooting at.

A huge wolf rose out of the reeds, yipping in pain and snapping at the seam of red the captain's ball had opened along its hindquarters. Less than ten feet separated the animal from the rowing deck, an easy leap for such a powerful body.

"What's that?" Shannon asked.

"Trouble," Colter answered, shoving away his oar, grabbing up his rifle and rushing to load it.

Shannon started to stand to get a better look. "'Less you want to die, you best sit down," Colter warned.

"Die? Don't be ridiculous," Shannon said. "A wolf wouldn't dare attack a boatful of men."

Jamming a ball and patch down the barrel, Colter flung down the ramrod and stood up.

On the bank, the wounded wolf dropped into a snarling crouch. Ears flattened, the animal sprang at the boat. At the instant of that spring, Colter dropped the hammer.

His ball slammed into the wolf's skull as the animal flew through the air. The wolf fell, its forepaws raking the gunwale next to Shannon before flopping into the shallows next to the boat.

Newman and Rube leaped over the side to look at it. "Great shot, Colter!" exclaimed Newman. "Right through the brain."

Colter lowered his rifle and sat down on the bench. Good shot or not, that had been close. Too close. A wounded wolf was the most dangerous critter alive.

Lewis swung down from the quarterdeck to view the carcass. He turned to Colter with a satisfied smile. "Beautiful specimen, Colter. One to send back to the President." He pointed to Ordway at the bow. "Extra rum for Colter tonight, Sergeant."

Colter was ready. He spoke up. "I'd rather hunt, sir."

Lewis looked at him curiously. "Hunt? I thought you were in the rotation."

"No, sir," Colter said, deciding the less he said, the better.

The captain glanced at the wolf, then beckoned Ordway to him. "Sergeant, besides the extra rum, see to it that Colter is put in the hunting rotation, starting tomorrow."

Colter could not see the sergeant's face from where he sat, but he heard the anger in his "Yes, sir" before the sergeant spun on his heel and returned to the prow.

"What was that all about?" asked Shannon.

Colter looked at his rifle. "There's a war goin' on, Fuzz. And I just won a battle. Only, it ain't over yet. Not by a long shot."

Once Colter was back in the hunting rotation, Shannon found himself sharing the rowing bench with the mess cook, Moses Reed. Reed had been in Pryor's squad at Camp Wood so Shannon knew little about him other than that he mostly hung around with the *engagés* and that the man had would have bought Lisette's favors their first night in St. Charles if he had not intervened.

The memory of that incident still stung. He did not want to believe that she was less than the goddess his heart and memory wanted her to be. Just as he refused to think of her entertaining other men, he would not allow himself to blame her for the pox he had contracted not once, but twice. As a consequence, he rarely spoke to Reed.

Lisette. Her face formed the backdrop of all his thoughts and nettled his conscience. *Why did I ever leave her? Why? Why?* The question haunted him. And so did the answer. It was painful to admit that he allowed his determination not to let Sergeant Floyd force him off the expedition to take precedence over his love for her. Yet, beneath all this was the beginning of a nagging doubt about Lisette that he barely managed to suppress. He knew so little about women, but he could not, would not believe what Colter said about Lisette.

By now they had moved far enough up the Missouri that they ought to be encountering Indians. Shannon knew from the few conversations he managed to have with Lewis that the captain was especially anxious to make contact with tribes along the river and begin carrying out the diplomatic assignments President Jefferson had given him. Half a dozen times a day the captain scanned the surrounding countryside with his telescope for Indian sign. Each time, he came away disappointed.

Late in the afternoon of July 14th, a storm blew in from the north with winds so strong that they forced the expedition off the river. The storm continued unabated into evening, making for a soggy supper and an early turn-in. Shannon was so exhausted that he fell asleep the moment he wrapped himself up in his damp blanket.

He slept soundly until awakened by an odd creaking. He looked out the flap of the little tent he shared with Rube, Joe and Colter. The storm was far from over but it had lessened in intensity. Puddles dotted the camp. Over the rain pattering a tattoo on the canvas walls of the tents, he strained to hear a repetition of the strange noise.

Yes, there it was again, down by the boats.

Using his blanket for cover, he splashed to the riverbank. *Discovery* and the two pirogues appeared like spectral shapes out of the rain. He stopped and listened again.

Hearing nothing, he shrugged and turned toward the tent when something moved, catching his eye. He looked back at the boats and realized that something was wrong. The white pirogue was not where it had been a moment ago. In fact, it was moving away from the other two craft.

The crew of the red pirogue had secured their craft, but the crew of the white boat either forgot or tied off carelessly for now the rain-swollen Missouri had hold of it and was about to carry it off.

Shannon skidded down the bank and dashed into the river, but as the water rose above his knees, he came up short. Fear would not allow him to go futher. "Help!"

The storm swallowed his weak cry.

The white pirogue drifted past the stern of the red boat and swung toward *Discovery*. The current then flung it at the keelboat and the two boats collided. The force of the impact flung the white pirogue further out into the current. It was only a matter of moments before the boat would be lost unless he could summon help.

"Help!" This time his yell rang out and roused several of the crew. One man, then a second, then a third, then three more dashed past him in pursuit of the loose boat. One caught the painter which allowed others to grab the gunwales and wrestle it back to shore. Captain Clark came up behind Shannon and slapped him on the back. "Quick thinking, Private."

The captain splashed into the river to help drag the pirogue onto the sand. Shannon backed out of the water and slowly climbed the bank. There he met Colter. "You're a might peaked, Fuzz. You should'a owned up a long time back. We're way past the point of turnin' back. We got a lot more river ahead of us 'fore she gets any smaller or gentler."

Shannon heard the truth of Colter's words, but still, he ached to lay the blame for his predicament on someone, on anyone else. He longed to leave this god-awful place, the mosquitos, the heat, the daily drudgery, and the fear that always hung on the edges of his days ready to immobilize him. He longed to be back in Lisette's bed, free to taste her lush body, free of harassment, free of cares. "How long before we get there — where we're going?" He tipped his chin in the direction of the keelboat.

"Depends on the river and the weather. And the Indians. Could be three months, maybe four."

Shannon groaned. Three or four months was a lifetime to go through when facing deep water every day.

"Well, you had your chance," Colter said, heading back to the tent.

Shannon gave him a few minutes to get settled before returning to the tent himself. He wrapped up in his soggy blanket and turned his face to the wall. "Why me?" he whispered at the canvas.

In reply a drop of rain dripped onto his neck just below his ear. The tent had sprung a leak.

Colter had spoken the truth when he said he and Ordway were engaged in a war. Although he was back in the hunting rotation, Ordway arranged to always partner him with Drouillard. From the start, the half-breed rubbed Colter all wrong. The man's luck at finding and bringing down game was out and out unnatural. To make matters worse, he was a civilian, not subject to military discipline or duties, and he was Indian-arrogant. Drouillard as a hunting partner made it hard to relish the time away from Ordway. The sergeant had played him to a draw. Again.

Colter and Drouillard were off hunting the day the captains sent out one of the *engagés*, a taciturn Oto-speaking man named Liberté, to search out bands of Oto Indians in the area and convince them with gifts of tobacco to travel to the expedition's camp for a council. When Colter got back to camp that night, he had to pitch in to the preparations for the proposed council. Then, they waited to see if Liberté had been successful.

To Colter, talking with Indians was a waste of time. They said one thing and did whatever they wanted. Take Zoob's ma. Up and walking away from her husband and baby, leaving them to pick up the pieces and patch their lives back together, all because she decided to go back with her people instead of staying to see to her responsibilities.

Irked by what he saw as an unnecessary delay in his quest to get to the Niobrara by September 4, Colter quickly tired of carving. He then wandered down to the river to skip stones. He managed one three-hopper and was trying for a four-hopper when Joe Field crashed out of the nearby brush, looking frantic.

"That you, Colter?" Joe asked breathlessly.

"Nope. Tom Jefferson," he cracked.

"Any chance you see the horses come back this way? They wandered off on us. Rube and me been lookin' for 'em since last night," Joe said.

The news could not have come at a worse time for the expedition. "They ain't come back. Better let the captains know," Colter said.

He followed Joe up to the camp and listened to him tell the captains what happened. When Joe finished, Colter spoke up, "Send me after 'em, Captain."

Lewis's gaze swung to him. "All right, Colter."

"Better send Drouillard along, too, sir," Ordway chimed in. "He can hand-sign if they meet up with Indians."

"Good thought, Sergeant. George, you go with Colter." The captain's familiarity with Drouillard added one more to Colter's list of reasons for despising the half-breed.

Half an hour out of camp, Colter and Drouillard came upon Rube, plodding along, leading the mulish roan packhorse named Brimstone. "Where's the others?" Colter asked.

Rube shook his head and kept on trudging.

Half an hour after that, Colter and Drouillard located the place where the two Field brothers had bivouacked the previous night. Colter immediately paced the site, looking for tracks to indicate which direction the horses had gone. He had scarcely begun the search when Drouillard announced, "This way" and took off without waiting for him.

Even Drouillard could not find a trail that fast. *Goodbye and good riddance*, thought Colter, continuing his own search. After a lot of looking, he found a hoofprint with the tell-tale notch that identified Lump, a dun-colored mare with the soulful eyes and even temperament that made the animal his favorite among the three expedition horses.

Once found, the tracks were easy to follow in the rain-softened ground. He found Lump and the other horse, Burr, in a small clearing two miles away. Both animals broke off grazing to watch his approach. Burr returned to the grass, but Lump snuffled and came to him. She nuzzled his hand, allowing him to easily gather in her lead.

Walking her over to the other horse, he reached for Burr's dangling rope only to have the animal prance away. It was typical of Burr to want to play when he was in no mood for such shenanigans. With day waning, he wanted to get back to camp and some supper, not chase some fool horse around the countryside. "Stand still, durn you."

Burr's ears twitched forward, the usual signal that it was ready to cooperate, but when Colter went for the lead, the horse waltzed away with its tail held high.

That tail prodded Colter like a red flag prods a bull. He picked up a stone and hurled it at Burr's front flank. His aim was off, and the stone smacked the horse on the nose. Burr neighed in protest.

Colter felt instantly remorseful over mistreating a harmless animal. He calmed the horse with mumbled assurances, then allowed Burr to come to him. "There, there," he murmured, stroking the horse's muzzle, looking around for some special treat he might offer in apology.

That's when it hit him: here was the perfect chance to take off for Manuel Lisa's camp. He had the two best horses and a good half-day's lead on Sergeant Ordway. He had seen enough of Clark's master map to find his way to the Niobrara. All he had to do was take off.

He had a grip on Lump's mane when another thought stopped him. The loss of two horses was likely to cripple the expedition. The crew had to live off the land as they went. It took the equivalent of two large deer or an average-sized elk to keep them all fed every day. Even on the best days, hunters had to range miles in search of game. He knew from experience that without these two animals, the hunters could not get to the game, let alone bring in their kills. Taking even one of the horses would work a hardship on the other men, a hardship that his conscience would not bear. *Confound it! Why's everything always so gol-durned complicated? Why can't I be selfish like McBain who never give a second thought to anybody or anything?*

Thinking of McBain curtailed his stream of thought. Mac was dead and buried. Now that he had the missing horses, it was time to get back to camp.

After six weeks on the river, Hartley was no closer to catching Colter. Though his ribs hardly bothered him any more, he had new problems: mosquitos, chiggers, fleas, boils, sunburn, dysentery, and all the treachery Bonhomme and Parler had up their grimy sleeves.

Last night the whispers of the two rivermen had awakened him. He did not need to understand their patois to know they were plotting something. He possessed nothing of value save his rifle, but he had no doubt these two would strand a man for less. Whatever they had in mind, he was determined to give them a battle.

From the prow now, Bonhomme grunted an order at Parler, and the nose of the canoe swung to an island in the middle of the channel. *Here it comes*, Hartley thought, his nerves tingling with tension.

Stepping out of the canoe, Bonhomme fixed him in a squinty gaze. "We go back to St. Louie *maintenant*."

"You made a bargain to take me as far as the Platte, and, by God, you'll keep that bargain." Hartley lifted his rifle to show that he meant business.

Bonhomme swept a hand toward the west. "*Voilà, La Platte.* We turn back."

Hartley was not about to fall for that old trick. "The Platte's a big river. And it's a long way from here. You showed me on that map of yours."

Bonhomme pulled the river map out of his pack. He stabbed at the line labelled "La Platte." "*Nous sommes ici. Maintenant*, we rest, then we go back."

"You're lying. Get back in the boat this minute, and row me to the real Platte before I lose what little is left of my temper."

"No lies. You no catch those men. We go home."

Hartley aimed the butt of his rifle at Bonhomme's face, but the Frenchman caught it and brought a knee up into Hartley's groin. The preacher screamed and grabbed at his testicles.

For good measure, Bonhomme jammed a meaty fist into Hartley's Adam's apple. Choking, the preacher collapsed on the sand.

"We go back, yes?" Bonhomme declared.

Hartley cradled his throbbing private parts and searched for his lost voice. When at last he found it, he croaked, "Yes."

6. *Deserter*

A ugust 7th. Four days since the Oto council. Not only had that meeting and all the time the crew had spent waiting and preparing for it been an utter waste, but absolutely nothing had been resolved or decided that Colter could see. The only thing to come out of the whole useless exercise was that the *engagé* Liberté had been declared a deserter after he failed to return. Even that did not mean much since the man was a hired boatman, not a crewmember, and the captains would not waste the time or manpower to drag him back.

Liberté's desertion hit Colter hard. Although he had chosen not to head for the Niobrara and Manuel Lisa when he had the chance, the notion would not leave him alone.

Now it appeared that Moses Reed had also deserted. Four days ago, the man had been let off the boat a couple of miles upriver from the Oto council site to go back after a knife he claimed to have left behind. No one had seen him since.

Colter's mind was mulling over Reed's actions when the call came for their midday break on a willow-cloaked island. He was good and ready to get out from under the merciless August sun and made a beeline for a clump of willow and sumac bushes where he discovered a natural bower of intertwined branches. He crawled into the welcome shade, stretched out on his back, and drifted into sleep.

Sometime later a commotion at the boat ripped him out of a dream of Zoob. "Drouillard!" The anger in Captain Lewis's shout was unmistakable. Sergeant Ordway stood rigidly beside the captain, his fists clenched tight, making the knuckles stand out like pale knobs against the weathered skin of his hands. Shannon stood immediately behind the sergeant, waiting with obvious impatience for the captain to finish conferring with the half-breed. What was Fuzz up to now? Since the incident of the loose pirogue, Shannon had changed. He had lost his hang-dog bearing and regained the superior attitude that had so annoyed Colter and the crew from Maysville through most of the stay at Camp Wood.

As soon as Drouillard turned away, Shannon said something to the captain. Whatever he asked for, the captain shook his head, and Shannon turned away as if he had been slapped. With nothing else to hold his attention, Colter laid back down to resume his nap.

The next thing he knew, Shannon had crawled in next to him. "Always Drooler. Never me," Shannon griped, using the crew's nickname for the half-breed. "Captain's shouldn't play favorites." He poked angrily at the sand. "The crew ought to hunt Reed down. After all, he's one of us. Instead, Drooler gets to do it. Drooler! The man's a civilian. Who knows where his loyalties lie?"

Colter kept quiet, hoping Shannon would go away and let him sleep.

"I volunteered to go along, but Captain chose Rube and Labiche instead. Why those two? They don't give a hoot about Reed or what he's done. Me, I want to see the man brought to justice. Deserters are the lowest form of life." Colter knew better than to be drawn into the conversation given his own thoughts on the subject.

"What on earth was Reed thinking?" Shannon continued. "Why would he stoop so low? Answer me that, Old Man."

Shannon's shrillness made it clear that he would keep pestering until he got an answer. "Maybe this life ain't for him."

"So what? The man swore an oath to see the expedition through. When he did that, he forfeited the right to change his mind. That's what promises are all about. Commitment, loyalty, perseverance — all the things you're always talking about. 'This life ain't for him'. I can't believe you said that."

"Then forget I opened my mouth."

But Shannon would not let up. "What's with you anyway? Sounds like you're having second thoughts yourself."

The younger man's challenging expression forced Colter to nip the accusation in the bud straight away. "Only place to run off to's some vermin-ridden Indian camp. I'd as soon starve."

Shannon's posture stiffened. "From what I observed at the Oto council, life among the Indians would be a big step up for most of this crew. You included."

Colter snorted a laugh. "What you observed? A step up? Holy thunder, Fuzz, what was you drinkin'? How many Indians do you know, anyways? None, right? Well, by the time you get to know a few, your tune'll change right quick. Either that or somebody'll be dead. You maybe."

"The trouble with you, Old Man, is that you've swallowed too many scare stories. Your mind is too clouded to see reality."

Shannon's condescending tone pushed Colter past his limit. He grabbed the younger man's wrist and wrenched it hard. "I'm goin' to tell you about reality, Fuzz, so listen good. Them Indians that you claim are so peaceable — they killed my partner Zoob. Shot six arrows into him whilst he was eatin' his breakfast. He ended up dyin' in my arms."

Shannon struggled against the hold, but Colter tightened his grip and went on. "Them Indians didn't care that Zoob was the spittin' image of his Shawnee ma. They was out for blood. Didn't matter that they kilt one of their own kind. Bloody damn savages! They kilt my best friend for no good reason, and you call that a step up? You ever again dare talk to me like that agin, you best be prepared for the fight of your life 'cause that's what you're in for. That there's a promise."

He flung away Shannon's wrist, got up and stalked away. It had taken him a long time to lock away those old memories, yet, now they were out again — the memories and the hurt — and all mixed up with the other vexing notions that had been bothering him lately. Then again, the conversation had served one positive function. He had thrown Shannon off any scent of his deserting.

Had the trade-off been worth it?

Only time would tell.

The argument with Colter in the willow bower solidified in Shannon a conviction that had been growing since the Oto council: since he had to stay with the expedition, he would make the very best of it. That meant using his education, power of observations and skills at sketching to futher the course of the history they were making.

Since the party searching for Moses Reed had not yet arrived when the expedition reached the rendezvous point, the crew established a camp and set about preparing for a second Indian council in case the search party located more Oto bands and Drouillard succeeded in enticing their chiefs to come in for talks with the captains.

With the site prepared and Colter too surly to countenance, Shannon turned to Joe Field for companionship. He soon regretted his choice. Joe was too nervous about his brother Rube to be good company. "They've been out too long," he moaned, referring to the search party. "Somethin's happened. Indians got 'em. I just know it."

No amount of reassurance altered the man's refrain, and Shannon gave up trying. He steadfastly refused to consider that the peaceable Indians that he had witnessed at the last council might have harmed Rube or anyone else.

On the morning of the third day of waiting, Ordway paired him with Colter to hunt since they needed to lay in extra meat in case the Indians showed up. They were about to leave camp on foot — the searchers had taken the horses — when Colter stopped. "If we're goin' to get along today, I don't want to hear one word about that whore or Rube and them or how wonderful you think Indians is. Got that?"

"And what if I won't?" Shannon countered.

"Then you kin stay here. I don't want you taggin' along and ruinin' my good day."

Shannon snapped a mocking salute. "Why yes, sir, General Colter. Lead the way, sir. Oh, yes, sir."

Shooting him a murderous look, Colter loped off. Although Shannon tried to follow, the man's pace proved too much. Finally, Colter stopped to let him catch up. "Pace you're goin', we ain't goin' to get much game. Maybe you oughtta wait here and rest up whilst I go do what we got sent out for."

Shannon flared at the sarcasm. "Why wait? Let's split up." He pointed to the right. "I'll go that way."

Colter eyed him skeptically. "Don't waste no powder and get back here by two. No later." Shannon nodded, but Colter was not done. "Means keepin' an eye on the sun, Fuzz, *and* rememberin' where 'here' is."

"Just who do you think you're talking to, Old Man? Some greenhorn?"

he snapped. "I can take care of myself without your advice." And with that, he strode off, head held high, arms swinging, satisfied that he had set the record straight.

Within a mile, Colter flushed several flocks of wild turkeys out of the high grass. He shot all he could carry and still manage his rifle, then plucked the longest tail feathers and stuck them in his cap the way Zoob used to do. With plenty of time before two o'clock, he walked a long slow arc back to their meeting point, reveling in the solitude, the far-off horizon, the caress of the August wind, the summer-yellowed grass around him.

He arrived at the meeting spot a little early by the sun's angle, his confidence and good mood restored. Shannon was nowhere to be seen, but he refused to let that bother him. He addressed the turkeys. "Looks like we wait a spell. He coulda got lucky. If'n he did, he gets to lug his take back. My hands is full up."

He sat down next to the pile of birds, tucked a plug of tobacco into his right cheek and closed his eyes, imagining the taste of the roast turkey he would be eating tonight. The chaw and the vision lasted for half an hour.

Still no sign of Shannon.

He looked in the direction the younger man had gone. "You got half an hour more, Fuzz. Then I'm a-leavin'." He settled back down and tried with mixed success to conjure up the turkey vision. Thirty minutes later, with his good mood melting away, he stood up.

Shannon was still not back.

"One shot, then I'm headin' to camp with you or without," he muttered through clenched teeth as he loaded his rifle. He aimed at a passing cloud and released the hammer. The rifle's boom flushed five quail out of the surrounding brush. The whir of wings, combined with the echoing crack of the shot, made his ears ring.

Still Shannon did not appear.

"That's it. I'm gone!" He picked up the turkeys and started off toward camp. At the top of the next little hill, he paused to adjust his load. A dark dot on the horizon drew his attention. Something moving, coming his way.

"Durn you, Fuzz, how'd you get clean over there? I swear you ain't got the sense God gave an acorn." He put the turkeys down again, tucked another plug into his cheek and waited.

The figure kept coming. At one point Colter waved his hat. In return he got a wave and a letdown. The approaching man was not Shannon. The choppy gait identified the stranger as the co-pilot Labiche who had gone with the search party. He hoped the man brought good news that would get the expedition underway again.

Hefting the turkeys, Colter trotted out to meet Labiche. The Frenchman was exhausted to the point of stumbling. He grabbed onto Colter's already burdened arm for support and rasped, "How far?"

"Two miles that-a-way." Colter used his free elbow to point in the right direction.

Labiche crossed himself and muttered something in slurred French.

"Where're the others?" Colter asked.

"With Reed zey come. Liberté, we find but away he run."

"You see Shannon out there anywheres?" Colter asked.

Labiche shook his head tiredly. "Non, ami. Now I go."

Once Colter was sure Labiche was headed right, he struck off in search of his hunting companion. The trail was easy to find. Shannon's footprints veered one direction, then another with no discernible pattern and for no discernible reason. At one point he had stopped, turned this way and that as if looking for something, then resumed walking in an entirely new direction. Colter scratched his head in frustration. There was no way Shannon could be following game. Animals did not waste energy zigzagging. "What are you doin', Fuzz?"

No sooner were the words out of his mouth than he spotted a lone figure a quarter mile off. The man walked one way for a few steps, looked around, then turned and walked another way for a few more steps to stop again.

Colter watched for as long as he could stand it, then, shifting the turkeys into his rifle arm, he cupped his mouth and yelled, "Fuzz!"

Shannon whirled toward him.

"Lord help us. He's got hisself lost," Colter muttered, waving the younger man to come on.

Shannon took his time getting there. Colter laid into him the moment he arrived. "Where in thunderation you been?"

"Ask the question nicely and maybe I'll answer it," Shannon said defensively.

"This ain't no time for nice and you know it. You been wanderin' all over creation 'cause you was lost. Pure and simple. Lost! By God, Fuzz, what are you thinkin'? This here's Indian country."

"What's that got to do with anything? You were at the council. Those Indians wouldn't hurt anyone. If I can do only one thing on this expedition, I intend to make sure the truth, the *real* truth about these noble people, gets told."

"Them's big words comin' from one who'd be out here all night 'cept for me."

"I was not lost! I was hunting."

The claim was too ridiculous to waste any breath on. Colter turned on his heel and trotted away. Shannon could keep up or he could get lost again. He did not care which.

The rest of the search party arrived at the expedition's camp around noon the next day, August 18. Drouillard rode at the head of the column, leading the horse that carried the deserter Moses Reed. Reed was dressed in a leather breechcloth and moccasins. Except for his white skin, he looked and smelled like an Indian.

The captains welcomed the Oto chiefs and a French trader named Fairfong who was staying with the Otos, and settled them aside to eat while they turned their attention to the deserter. Colter did not listen to Captain Lewis explain the court-martial procedure. His attention was on the Indian horses. Spirited and muscular, the animals fretted at their picket ropes with the energy of creatures born to carry a man to freedom.

His observations were curtailed when the captains assigned him to the court of crewmen sitting in judgment on Reed. The evidence against Reed was presented. The search party had found him in one of the Otos' hide lodges, living with two squaws. The accused made a rambling contradictory statement in his defense. Then it was time to cast votes: guilty or innocent.

Given his own intentions, Colter held back. How could he indict someone for doing what he himself planned to do?

"We're waiting, Colter," Collins said impatiently.

"Guilty," he said with reluctance.

The two captains conferred momentarily, then Lewis beckoned for the sergeants to bring Reed forward. "Moses Reed, this court finds you guilty of desertion and stealing public property. Henceforth, you are discharged without honor. Your name will be removed from the rolls of this expedition."

Reed stared defiantly ahead. Shannon watched him without pity. Deserters were the worst kind of cowards. They deserved to die.

The captain continued. "You are hereby sentenced to four rounds of the gauntlet, and you are assigned without pay to Patron Deschamps to serve in place of his missing *engagé*. It is with him that you will return to St. Louis."

Shannon could not believe his ears. The gauntlet? What could the captain be thinking? This man was a deserter, not a sneak thief. Army tradition called for hanging or a firing squad, not a mere beating.

"Sergeant Pryor, direct the men into formation," Lewis ordered. "Sergeant Ordway, Sergeant Floyd, see to the switches. Nine per man. The sentence will begin immediately. Court is adjourned."

Shannon's chin dropped. Switches, instead of clubs? He glanced around. No one else seemed surprised at the sentence. However, something had to be done and quickly. He broke ranks and hurried over to the captain before Ordway could stop him. "Permission to speak, sir."

Lewis nodded distractedly.

"Sir, aren't you forgetting something? I mean, the punishment for desertion is death."

The captain's gaze sharpened and his low voice turned icy. "Return to your place, Private."

Stunned by the captain's lack of receptivity to his suggestion, Shannon executed a quick turn and marched stiffly back to his position. Colter greeted him with a murmured, "Good job, Fuzz."

By the time the two sergeants returned with armsloads of cut willow, the crew had formed two facing lines. After each crewman received nine switches, Captain Lewis stepped to the head of the columns. He spoke sternly. "Each of you will lay on with gusto or run the gauntlet yourself. Sergeant Ordway, bring the prisoner."

As Reed stepped into place, the Otos became agitated. Lewis held up the punishment to see what was causing the Indians' unrest. Trader Fairfong provided the translation.

Curious to grasp an understanding of the Indian mind, Shannon paid close attention. When the Otos heard that Reed was to receive a group whipping, they were horrified. To them, inflicting bodily harm on one of their own kind was unthinkable since they regarded each Oto as sacred.

Such reasoning hit Shannon as a revelation. Suddenly everything he had read in the Bible and everything Parson Cooper had ever tried to tell him about loving his neighbor snapped into such clear focus that he was lifted to a higher level of understanding. Looking at Reed, he no longer saw a deserter, but rather a precious life deserving of compassion, not punishment. Suddenly ashamed that he had urged Lewis to condemn the man to death, he threw down his bundle of switches and turned to step out of line, only to bump into Sergeant Floyd.

"Just where do you think you're going, Shannon?"

"I won't participate."

Floyd thrust his face close to Shannon's. "Pick up those switches and resume your position."

Shannon wanted to stand firm, but he also knew Army rules. He did as he was told. The Otos and Captain Lewis arrived at an impasse and the captain gave the signal to proceed with the punishment.

As Ordway cut the thongs binding Reed's wrists, the man's confident expression slid into uncertainty, then into fear.

"What are we waiting for, ex-Private?" Ordway asked scornfully.

Reed took a tentative step into the corridor between the two files of men. The first two bundles of switches whizzed and popped against his bare back, driving him into a lurching shuffle down the length of the gauntlet. The air came alive with the sounds of the beating: willow tips snapped, branches *thwacked* flesh, men grunted force into their blows, Reed moaned. By the time he reached Shannon, his back was laced with welts. His frantic eyes held Shannon's a moment, then, he stumbled and pitched onto his knees.

Someone laughed and the men around Shannon increased the intensity and frequency of their blows. Their frenzy sickened him. He could not, he would not strike a man on his knees.

Beside him, Colter's voice was low with warning. "Better swing, Fuzz. Floyd's watchin'."

No, I won't, Shannon thought with disgust.

Sobbing now and trying to shield himself from the blows with his arms, Reed crawled to the end of the human tunnel where Pryor set him back on his feet. The noise level of the crew subsided. Floyd came up beside Shannon. "You swing or you're next, Private."

Pryor pushed Reed back into the gauntlet and the air again filled with the sound of whips lacerating flesh. With Floyd right there watching, Shannon drew back his switches unwillingly. Every fiber of his being rebelled at the idea of adding to the stripes of oozing blood crisscrossing the deserter's neck, shoulders and back.

Reed staggered within range.

"Swing, Private," Floyd said quietly. "Swing or run it next."

Shannon directed his bundle of whips to graze Reed's side but his aim was off and they struck the man's upper shoulder, deeply slicing his left ear. Out of his peripheral vision Shannon could see the horror on the faces of the Indians chiefs, and his shame deepened.

7. *Opportunity Lost*

A s the council with the Otos dragged on under the hot August sun, Colter studied the Indian horses. One in particular drew his eye: a paint gelding that belonged to Chief Little Thief. The horse stamped and snorted with displeasure at being tied up. It acted out the edginess that Colter had been holding in for weeks. Like the horse, he longed to break free of the rules that bound him under the will of others, to run where he would, to be his own master once again.

At long last the council ended. Colter was on his way to the river to wash the sweat from his face when Ordway intercepted him. "You have dawn watch, Colter. On that perimeter." He pointed to the side of the camp closest to the lodges of the visiting Otos and the picket line of Indian ponies.

Ordeal did not know it but he had just handed Colter the break he had been looking for. "Thank you, Sarge," he said as he bent to dash his face with river water.

Colter walked slowly along the imaginary line dividing the expedition's camp from that of the Otos. With his senses at hyper-alertness, he remarked the positions of the other two other sentries and the layout of the Indian camp. Good, the Otos had posted no watch. This would be easier than he expected.

One more pass, he judged, *Just to make sure this isn't a trap.*

His assigned post stretched along a little creek that tumbled into the Missouri. He reached the mouth of the stream and cast one last look over the three expedition boats. Never again would he have to strain at *Discovery's* cordelle or curse the river's current as she fought his oar. Next time he came this way, that current would carry him down to St. Louis to the fortune he had long dreamed of.

He did an about-face, took two paces and stopped. Something or someone was moaning.

That was when he saw Sergeant Floyd, kneeling in the wet sand at the river's edge. The sergeant was shirtless and sweating heavily despite the pre-dawn chill. "Sorry . . . sick," he mumbled. He then doubled over and vomited.

Colter figured it was a case of the sergeant's excesses catching up with him. At the earlier celebration Floyd had spent more time in the dance circle than even York.

The sergeant's retching did not subside, however, and Colter's first impression gave way to concern. There had not been all that much to drink. Just two cups of rum per man. Not enough for the sergeant to overdo. "You need some help, Sarge?" he asked.

Floyd tried to smile, but it turned into a grimace. "Don't know what — Another round of puking sliced off the rest of his sentence. Colter did not need to lay hands on the sergeant to feel the heat coming off his skin.

"I need Captain Clark." Floyd's voice was a shadow of itself.

Colter hesitated. The eastern sky was beginning to lighten into indigo. Soon it would be too late for him to act.

A tortured groan issued from the ailing man. "Please, Colter."

The plea overcame his equivocation. He whistled for the inner camp guard. McNeal came over, stifling a yawn behind one grimy hand. He looked down at Floyd. "What's his problem?"

"Fetch Captain Clark," Colter answered.

"Why? He's just puking."

Colter knew that every second counted if his plan was to succeed. "You stay here then. I'll get him."

Floyd moaned, "No, stay, Colter."

"Get him, McNeal. And make it snappy," Colter said.

"I don't think —"

From somewhere, Floyd found some strength to fill out his voice. "McNeal, go!"

The cook had never been able to bamboozle Floyd like he had Ordway. He curtailed his backtalk and took off at a run. Colter squatted beside the sergeant, with one hand on the sick man's shuddering shoulder and one eye peeled on the string of Indians' ponies. Time was slipping away fast.

After what seemed an hour, Clark appeared and took Colter's place crouching beside the sergeant. "Where's it hurt, Charley?"

"All over, Captain. And I'm burning up."

"Colter, help me carry him up to my tent. McNeal, you take over Colter's watch here."

Colter swallowed the urge to ask to stay at his position. He lifted Floyd by the shoulders and the sergeant looked up at him. "I don't mean to cause such a fuss."

"Ain't no fuss. You just hang on. Captain's goin' to fix you right up."

Floyd nodded weakly.

At the tent Colter helped lay the sergeant out on the captain's recently-vacated blankets, then ducked back outside. There were streaks of dull orange on the eastern horizon. If he was going to go, he had to move fast. He made for the line of thorn bushes that provided a windbreak for the cooking fire. The bushes would give him cover up to the little bench where the Indian horses were staked. After that, his last obstacle was McNeal.

He was three steps from the cooking fire when Ordway stood up. With his mind screaming *Not Ordway! Not now!,* Colter forced himself to say "Sarge?"

"What was all the racket?" Ordway asked.

"Floyd's took sick." Colter could not believe how normal his voice sounded.

"Why are you away from your post?"

"Captain Clark relieved me."

"He did, did he?" From the tone of the question, Colter realized that the sergeant had guessed his intentions and had been waiting for him to make his move. If he had tried to make a getaway, he could not have made it ten feet. Sergeant Floyd had saved him from Ordway again.

While he endured a long morning standing under more hot sun in his scratchy uniform, tolerating the interminable speeches of the Oto chiefs, Colter had an excellent view of Chief Little Thief's paint gelding. The sight underscored how narrowly he had escaped falling into Ordway's trap. It also made him question the bad turn of fortune that had thrice blocked his efforts to join Manuel Lisa.

At last the council wound up and he helped carry Floyd's stretcher onto *Discovery.* One glimpse at the sergeant's pain-contorted face and dull eyes wrenched him out of his own concerns.

"Captains ought to know better than to coddle drunks, even if they are sergeants," Shannon said as Colter slid onto the rowing bench.

"Drunk ain't his problem," Colter said grimly, watching the Otos riding off on their handsome ponies.

"How would you know? You were sound asleep while he made a complete fool of himself, prancing around like some crazed prairie chicken. The way he was acting he had a lot more than just two cups of rum to drink. Why, if this were my father's outfit, he'd be demoted." Shannon seemed to find pleasure in the idea. "He would be reduced in rank and I'd be promoted. Father always considered me a natural leader."

"Natural pain in the rear, you mean. Sarge ought to get a month's extra pay for puttin' up with you all this time."

"A man does not deserve extra pay for merely doing his job."

"Look who's mouthin' off about doin' his job — the great riverman hisself."

Shannon's wild punch glanced off Colter's chin. Colter managed to capture the balled fist before any of their superiors spotted the incident. The last thing he needed right now was Ordway breathing down his neck. In fact, Ordway was the last thing he needed. Period.

The next day, Colter's relief at escaping Ordway's snare had changed into discouragement. He watched dejectedly as Drouillard gathered the expedition's horses for hunting. The sight of Burr, Lump, and Brimstone heading away from camp drove his spirits even lower. Three failed attempts to leave Ordway and the expedition behind. Would he get a fourth?

He was chewing on the question at his oar when the captains ordered a stop near noon. He had just shipped his oar when York called him into the captain's cabin.

"Sergeant Floyd asked for you," York said, one of the first times they had talked since both of them tried to desert back at St. Charles. That was all the slave said before he left the cabin.

The little space was dark and the smell of sickness hung thickly in the air. Floyd's eyelids flickered open. One hand lifted off the blanket, but fell weakly back. Colter came to kneel beside the berth and took up that hand. "You're lookin' better today, Sarge." he said without sincerity.

The sergeant's head wobbled in denial. His speech came in halting two-word wheezes. "I'm worse — but I — have something — to say."

Under the sergeant's dull gaze, a protest died in Colter's mouth. He felt as if Floyd had hold of his soul instead of his hand.

"That night . . . in Maysville . . . when you . . . brought in meat." Floyd hunched around a rattling cough, then gasped for the breath to continue. "The Almighty . . . sent you . . . to us . . . That's what . . . I told . . . Captain Lewis."

"Weren't the Almighty, Sarge. You know that."

Floyd's gentle squeeze cut off the protest. "We got . . . this far . . . because of . . . the few . . . like you, John. Don't fail . . . us . . . now."

"I ain't goin' to."

He honored another, weaker squeeze from Floyd. "You're a . . . good man . . . You're a . . . spark . . . for the others." His eyes fluttered shut and he appeared to struggle at swallowing.

When he looked back at Colter, there was serenity in his gaze as if he had accepted something long resisted. "Without . . . the likes . . . of you . . . we won't . . . make it . . . especially Shannon." Another difficult swallow. "He's stubborn . . . someone needs . . . to show him . . . the way . . . You, Colter . . . you."

The light behind Floyd's eyes began to dim like a guttering candle. "I rode him . . . pretty hard . . . Please . . . tell him . . . I . . . " His voice splintered.

Colter pressed the sergeant's hand. "I'll tell him."

Floyd's gaze drifted to the shuttered window. Colter raised up to open it. "There. Some fresh air for ya."

The sergeant dragged in one shallow breath, turned his gaze back to Colter and spoke in a calm, quiet voice. "I'm going away now." The strength seemed to flow out of his hand, and it fell from Colter's grip. At the same time, all traces of pain faded from his face, leaving behind the gentle mask of a man deep asleep.

Colter stared at the transformation, not yet able to accept the fact of the man's passing.

Clark burst through the door. "Charley?"

"He's gone," Colter said quietly, folding Floyd's hands over his chest and aching with the emptiness that comes when a cherished friend departs.

Outside, the sun was too bright. Where were the clouds that ought to darken such a moment?

Crewmen littered the bank. Some lay stretched out asleep. Others engaged in idle chatter. A few played cards. Colter wanted to shout the news at them, to yell out his sorrow for the confidant and friend he had lost, but the pain was still too private, too fresh to put into words.

He slumped down on the rowing bench and looked out at the river. Floyd's words kept cycling through his mind: *Without the likes of you, we won't make it, especially Shannon. Don't fail us now.* He did not want to believe the words, did not want to take the responsibility attached to them. Yet, he knew a man on his deathbed always spoke the truth. Whether prophesy or recollection, did he dare ignore it?

Colter stared at the earth mounded at the edge of the grave while Captain Lewis read the service. The captain finished his eulogy. "Is there anyone else who wishes to speak?"

Beside him, Shannon shifted but did not step forward. Across the grave, Pryor, Floyd's cousin, appeared too stricken to do more than stare at the blanket-shrouded body. Silence stretched. The wind pelted dust from the grave at the crewmen gathered at the top of the bluff.

"Anyone?" Lewis asked.

Colter could not allow Floyd to be buried without trying to express what the man had meant to him. He stepped to the side of the grave and addressed the remains. "You said I was a good man, Sarge, but I'm sayin' it back to you: You're a good man. A fair man. Privates ain't supposed to like sergeants, but I couldn't help myself. I suspicion there're others here'd say the same thing if'n they could find the words. You believed so much in what we're doin' that you got us believin' too. This here crew ain't a-goin' to be the same without you."

He stepped back before his voice could crack, then York moved to the foot of the grave, raised his face to the flawless blue canopy of sky and began to sing:

Swing low, sweet chariot,
Comin' for to carry me home.
Swing low, sweet chariot,
Comin' for to carry me home.

The song ended with much sniffing and throat clearing. A squad shoveled dirt over the body, and the crew straggled down the hill to the boats. Colter stayed behind. He needed time alone with his sadness, time to gather his wits. He looked out over the surrounding country. So much emptiness, waiting to swallow anyone who entered it.

Ordway's voice broke into his reverie. "Nice little speech, Private. Real touching. Makes sense you'd whine about the expedition not being the same. After all, Floyd won't be around anymore to side with you."

Colter made himself turn slowly in order to rein in the hatred that demanded to be unleashed on this spiteful man. "I can see you're real broke up, Sarge. Too bad it ain't you in that hole."

"I got you figured out, Colter. Desertion is written all over your face. I'm just waiting for you to try. You won't get off easy like Reed. Oh, no."

You're the key, a spark to the others. Floyd's words rattled around Colter's mind like rocks in a tin box, urging him to reclaim his commitment to the expedition. "You're right sure of yourself, ain't you, Sarge?"

"I know men. I know *you*, Colter."

"You don't know a durn thing about me, Sarge. Sarge Floyd might be gone, but you ain't won. Not by a long shot. I'll see to that. That's my promise."

Shannon was halfway down the bluff when he changed his mind and returned to the top. Colter was the only one still at the grave. Shannon stared at the mound. He could not get used to the idea that Sergeant Floyd was no more. He had never experienced the death of someone close to him. Until now.

A hand squeezed his shoulder. "Sarge give me a message for you," Colter said.

"Go away."

"He said he didn't mean to ride you so hard."

Shannon shrugged off the intrusive hand. "I don't want to hear."

"Then close your dad-blamed ears," said Colter hotly.

Shannon held his silence until long after Colter had walked off. When he began to speak, his voice was muffled with sadness. "I never got the chance to know you, Sergeant Floyd. Now —" The incessant wind moaned into the pause. "Colter's right. You are . . . were . . . the best there is. I wish things had been different." Another pause. "You were right to ride me. I need riding."

He touched the rough cedar post that marked the head of the grave. The raw wood felt almost smooth under his callused fingers. "We're going to find a way through the Shining Mountains, Sergeant. And when we reach the Western Sea, I'll wade in it — for you."

He stepped back and saluted the grave. As he turned away, the image of Floyd that he carried in his head smiled.

"There's no way Pat Gass got that many votes," Shannon fumed. "No way. The count was rigged."

After four days of the same litany, Colter was sick of listening. "Pat Gass won. You got one vote — your own. Now shut up!"

"I did not vote for myself."

"That don't matter. Gass won 'cause he listens two, three times more'n he talks. Lord, all you do is talk, and a body cain't learn nothin' when his lip's flappin'."

Shannon was quiet for two miles. When he spoke again, he sounded chastened. "Thanks, Old Man. I deserved that. And I promise to do better from now on."

The change so surprised Colter that he had to look over to see if someone else had taken Shannon's place next to him. About that time, Ordway appeared on the *passe avant*. "Shannon, you go out with Drouillard tomorrow." He spoke to Shannon but looked at Colter.

"I'm not in the rotation," Shannon said.

"Everyone is now, thanks to *Sergeant* Gass."

After Ordway left, Shannon looked at Colter. "What's that mean?"

"Means you're huntin'."

"But you're the hunter."

Colter shut his ears. Knowing that he could count on getting away from the close confines of the crew every few days kept the walls from closing in and dissipated his aggravation toward Ordway. This change to the hunting rotation would mean that his turns would be spaced out weeks apart. Weeks, when even five days around Ordeal pushed him to the limit of his tolerance.

Something Shannon said brought his attention back to the moment. "What say?"

"I said, maybe Drouillard and I can make contact with the Sioux. We ought to be getting close to the Niobrara River by now. There are supposed to be several villages around that confluence."

Colter sat up. "What day is this?"

Shannon figured for a moment before answering, "August 27. Why do you care?"

Eight more days to get to Manuel Lisa. The lethargy that had settled over Colter since Floyd's death began to lift. "Just askin'."

Shannon crouched behind a fallen tree, studying Drouillard who was stalking a trio of elk cows. What did the half-breed see: regal creatures, or just food on the hoof? Shannon closed his eyes. Now that he was away from the river he realized how profoundly tired he was. The constant mind-numbing manual labor and the strain of holding his fear of water in check for so long had taken more out of him than he wanted to accept.

He opened his eyes to watch Drouillard prepare his rifle. He envied the man's economy of motion and wanted to learn all his secrets. Drouillard signalled for him to cover the shot. It was an unnecessary precaution since the half-breed never missed, but Shannon went through the motions anyway.

The shot felled one cow and scattered the rest of the animals. To make himself useful, he headed off to fetch the horses. Drouillard's whistle stopped him.

The half-breed pointed curtly in the opposite direction. "That way."

Shannon averted his face to hide the flush of embarrassment and changed course. This country was so blamed deceiving. A body could get turned around in a heartbeat.

His mood improved a bit when he spotted the split-trunk tree that marked the stand of ash where they had left the horses. As he stepped around the tree, he muttered, "See, I'm learn — Oh, no!"

The horses were gone.

Since Brimstone broke its leg and had to be destroyed, hunting for forty hungry people had become an onerous chore with only two horses to help out. Without Lump and Burr . . . he did not want to contemplate the bleak prospect. He simply had to find them.

It took three passes over the hard ground to locate the distinctive notched tracks left by Lump's hooves. He followed them north and west, and, half an hour later, he came upon the two horses grazing contentedly in a patch of sweet grass. Lump, the mare and everyone's favorite, raised her head and twitched her ears in recognition.

"Oh, Lump, you're a trial. If some Sioux brave had found you out wandering around, you'd be stew by now."

He gathered in both horses' reins, and Lump nuzzled his hand. "Come along. We'll see if we can't find you a prairie turnip or two on the way back."

He set off, following the notched prints backward. Even Burr, who was not known for his willing disposition, followed docilely. The three were crossing a rocky area when the tracks gave out. The spot did not seem familiar but that was the usual case for Shannon. Shrugging in exasperation, he tied the horses to a bush and paced around the area, looking for tracks. Would he ever learn to remember landmarks?

When he could find nothing, he went round again, expanding the radius of his search.

Still nothing.

He turned one way, then the other; forward and back; left and right. The only tracks he found were his own. "Not again," he cried, sinking down on a boulder. "I can't be lost. Not again."

When Rube asked him a question, Colter grunted and pretended complete absorption in his carving, hoping the man would take the hint and leave him alone. Tonight he had a big decision to make. He wanted to think, not talk.

"Here comes Drooler now, Little Brother," Rube said, standing up and looking into the distance. "Oh, oh. No Peckerwood and no horses. Looks like trouble."

Drouillard's normally expressionless face was clouded. He marched straight to the captains' tent. Rube sidled over to eavesdrop and returned frowning. "Looks like Peckerwood took him a wrong turn. Captain's goin' to wait till mornin' to send out after him. How about it, Little Brother? Want to go lookin'?"

"Not really," Joe said. "If you want to, you go."

"What if Captain asks for two men. You'll go, right?" Rube wheedled.

Joe seemed ready to disagree, then nodded. Rube slapped his brother's back and went off to volunteer. Joe turned to Colter. "He might be my brother, but sometimes I'd like to —" He ground a fist into his palm. "We argue a lot, but not as much as you and Fuzz," Joe said. "The way you two carry on, a body'd think you were married."

"At least married folks has got a choice," Colter grumped. "I got stuck with him."

"Thought you two was friends."

"My last friend died two years back."

"That isn't what the man in the canoe said."

"What man?"

"The one Rube and the others run into back when they were out looking for Reed. You mean he didn't tell you?"

"I ain't got a clue what you're talkin' 'bout."

"Rube said they come upon him this side of those bluffs where that first Oto meetin' was. Man was in a canoe all by hisself. Asked after you. Said he was your best friend. Now what did Rube say his name was? Seems like it was Carter or Harper. Hartson maybe. Nope, that's not it. Barley or —"

The hair on Colter's arms prickled. The name gushed out. "Hartley?"

"That's it! Where'd you know him from?"

Colter did not answer. He had assumed that Hartley died back at the Ohio confluence.

"Man's darn lucky to get so far alone," Joe said. "Lucky and foolish for ever tryin' such a thing, I say. Must be some God-awful powerful message he's bringin' you. Wouldn't tell no one. Said he had to tell you personal. Got any idea what that could be?"

He ain't comin' all this way about my health. That's for sure. Colter thought. *And he ain't comin' 'cause of no reward money neither. No man'd be this far upriver for just money. He's out for my hide.* "Who knows?" he said, trying to sound casual.

"Strange Rube never told you."

Colter ceased to listen to Joe. He did not believe in coincidence. That Joe had told him about Hartley now, at this particular moment, was a sign that it was time to head for the Niobrara as soon as Rube and Joe brought in the horses. And Shannon.

Once his initial panic faded, Shannon swept another search of the ground around him. This time he found the tracks. His victory whoop spooked Burr. The animal reared in alarm, and Shannon had to spend precious time calming the horse before it would let him lead it.

By the time they got to the place where Drouillard killed the elk, it was deep dusk. The half-breed had dressed out the carcass and hung the slabs of meat from tree limbs to keep them out of the reach of predators.

It was too late for Shannon to try to find the boats. The weather was clear and not too cold. He had his blanket. Might as well bivouac for the night.

By the time he got a fire going, he was too tired to bother cooking any-thing. He broke out the jerked meat the captains insisted the hunters carry for emergencies and ate lying on his back. Once he got used to the night sounds and the solitude, he fell into a deep sleep.

He woke the next morning full of energy and full of pride for handling the situation so well. He wrapped Drouillard's elk meat in burlap and loaded the bundles on Lump, then gathered his bedroll and climbed aboard Burr. "Adventure's over, you two. Time to find the boats. We have till noon before they take off. That's the drill."

Burr tossed its head and away they went.

⚓

Every time Colter shut his eyes that night, Josiah Hartley's familiar face appeared on the insides of his eyelids. As a consequence, he spent a wake-ful night and took his place on the cordelle the next day, dreading the hard pull to come. *Damn it! Where was them horses and Fuzz?*

Late afternoon Rube and Joe caught up with the boats. They had found the tracks, but it appeared that Shannon and the horses were out in front of the expedition, headed upstream.

"Good work, you two," Lewis said. "We're bound to catch up with him soon."

Seeing the chance he had been waiting for, Colter jumped in immedi-ately. "Beg pardon, sir, but I ain't so sure. He's got them horses. No tellin' how fast he's movin' especially if'n he thinks we're ahead of him. This bein' Sioux country, somebody oughtta go after him."

Lewis shook his head. "Shannon knows the rules. Every man is respon-sible for himself."

Clark spoke up. "Colter's got a point, Meri. We need those horses."

Colter pressed on. "Let me go, Captain. It's my place after all. Shannon's my charge, and I'm used to movin' quick afoot."

Clark and Lewis exchanged a glance, then Clark nodded agreement. "Draw plenty of extra powder."

Lewis's upraised hand kept Colter from hurrying away. "If you don't find him, you must turn back after eight days. Agreed?"

Eight days meant September 6. He would be long gone before then, with enough of a head start that neither Hartley nor Ordway would ever find him. "Agreed."

8. *Hungry Pursuit*

T wenty-five days. That was how long Hartley had handled Bon-homme's canoe solo, a fact that made him bitterly regret all the time and money he had wasted in hiring the intractable rivermen. It made him furious to think that he could have caught the expedition days, maybe weeks ago and been on his way back to the Draft. Instead he was still on this infernal river, chasing after Colter. And now he was out of food, which meant another maddening delay.

He spotted a creek running into the river on the near bank and turned in. His skill at fishing had kept him from starving after he was orphaned. Back then, respectable people did not eat fish. To them, fish was pauper's fare, but he had been too hungry to care what other people thought.

The day he took up preaching, he had sworn off fish forever. Yet here he was, back to eating it in order to save his dwindling supply of powder and shot.

He had tracked the expedition up the river, campsite by campsite, since May. He had even talked to some of the crew when they happened upon his camp one morning. He had been too surprised to concoct much of a lie, so he told them he was an old friend of Colter's with important news meant for his ears alone. It tickled him to imagine how stunned Colter must have been to hear about that encounter, and he chuckled now as he nosed the canoe into the overhanging bank. He pulled the canoe tight under the ledge where it could not be seen by passersby, then tucked the spy-glass and rolled leather river map into the pack that had been Bonhomme's and set off along the creek's course, keeping parallel to the stream, but avoiding its banks for fear of leaving tracks in the soft dirt. Bonhomme's map was labelled in French. Most of the words made no sense. However, the label on this area did: "Sioux." *Those* he wanted to avoid at all costs.

He rejoined the creek a mile above the Missouri and followed it until he found a good-sized hole. As he sat on the ground to make a drag line, his thoughts turned back to how he had escaped from the rivermen.

After Parler grabbed him, the man had frog-marched him to a stout sycamore where Bonhomme bound him to the trunk and gagged his mouth with a strip of filthy cloth. Instead of leaving him to rot as he feared they would, the pair settled down to polish off the last of his whiskey.

While they drank, Hartley grappled with the knots that bound him. His fingers were awkward and the knots were tight and he had prayed that the liquor would hold the attention of his captors so they would not notice what he was doing.

As the day waned, he had abandoned the knots and tried working his wrists through the loops. He was still trying when Bonhomme's head slumped onto his chest. Moments later Parler fell into a stupor as well. No longer afraid that he would be discovered, Hartley managed to rip one hand free and, to the snores of his captors, undid the rest of his bonds.

He thought to leave them the worst rifle and a small supply of ammunition, then changed his mind. Why give them a break when they had done nothing but cheat him from the start? He loaded anything of use, including their boots, into the canoe and left.

Later in Bonhomme's pack, he found a pipe, some tobacco, fish hooks and a supply of dried meal. The meal lasted him a week. After that, he fell back on the hooks. So far, he had not gone hungry.

He tied the last knot in the drag line, kicked over rocks for grubs to bait the hooks, and dropped the line into the pool. In no time, he felt the tell-tale tugs of fish hitting the bait and the drag of hooks biting the fish back.

The good catch gave him scant satisfaction. He resented having to stop at all. Resented the constant demands of his body: hunger pangs, the need for sleep, the aches and the too-frequent signals from his bowels like the urgent one coming on him right now.

He floated the string of caught fish in the creek, grabbed up his few possessions, and sought the privacy of the bushes to relieve himself.

The bout of diarrhea left him temporarily dizzy. He remained squatting while it passed, then waited longer for the strange babbling sounds to clear from his ears.

The dizziness left, but the sounds persisted.

A chill washed over him. These were not imagined sounds. These were voices, speaking in some unknown tongue.

He peeked through the foliage. Two half-naked bronzed men squatted on their haunches beside the creek. One of them held up his string of fish.

His heart lodged in his throat. They were Sioux. He was caught.

Colter swiped the back of his hand across his sweat-beaded forehead. He had been on Shannon's tracks for most of two days and still had not caught up. Why on God's own earth was Fuzz pushing himself and those horses so hard? Surely he had figured out by now that the boats were behind him.

The search was turning out to be a lot harder than he had reckoned when he volunteered. Shannon's pace was one problem. The lush vegetation along the river was another. Unseen roots tripped him up two or three times every day, plus he had to keep picking his way which slowed him down. The only way to speed up the pace was to get out on the river which meant stopping to build a raft or . . .

There was another possibility. The river occupied a trench between low-lying grass-covered bluffs. A man could move along a lot faster in grass than in tangled brush. Even accounting for dropping down to the river periodically to check for Shannon's tracks, he would be time and distance ahead.

He headed up the nearest bluff. At the top, he adjusted his pack and shifted his rifle to the other hand, then bent his head against the ever-present wind and set off at a trot. The sound of voices brought him up short. Dozens of voices. That could mean only one thing: Indians.

He dived into the cover of a rock outcropping. Chancing a look, he saw a column of people and horses strung out across the plain. Behind a group of mounted braves walked women and children, leading dogs and horses, pulling drag-frames piled high with household goods, foodstuffs and personal belongings. More men fanned out along the sides of the column as defenders and scouts. At the back, older boys on foot formed a ring around the extra horses. Most likely a village on the move.

Colter looked longingly at the horse herd. What he would not give for a horse!

The procession moved at a snail's pace. By the time he felt safe enough to leave his hiding place, the sun had dipped to a low angle in the west. He would not find Shannon today.

＊

Shannon fumbled at the strings of his food pouch. He ripped the last knot apart and thrust in his hand. Instead of jerky, his fingers found air.

He turned the bag upside down in disbelief. Surely he would have remembered eating the last of his food.

He flung the bag to the ground, but anger did nothing to take away the gnawing pain in his guts. The sounds of the two horses cropping grass teased him. Two hard days of moving against a strong wind and sputtering rain, and still no sign of the expedition. How could they be so far ahead? What was he doing wrong that he had not caught them?

In his anguish, he suddenly remembered something else he had forgotten: Drouillard's elk meat.

Five feet from Lump, the odor of rotting meat made him gag. He could hardly bring himself to touch the burlap wrapping of the elk meat for the stench. How could he have not noticed that smell? All that meat, spoiled, worthless.

Breathing through his mouth to keep from throwing up, he cut the cords that bound the reeking cargo to Lump's back and watched the bundles fall to the ground. Such a waste. *It is a sin to waste food when others are hungry* was his father's constant litany. Angry with himself, he turned away from the spoiled meat and the scavengers it would inevitably attract.

He continued upstream until hunger forced him to stop. Unsaddling Burr and Lump, he spoke aloud to try to lift his sagging spirits. "Tomorrow's the day, my friends. The day we catch them. So you rest up tonight."

The animals did not seem to care what he said. They went on searching for food. Shannon wrapped himself in his blanket, curled up under a tangle of overhanging vines, and fell asleep counting the growls from his empty stomach.

＊

Shannon peeked around the tree trunk. At the sight of the four does browsing in the glade, his heart thumped wildly against his rib cage. Hungry as he was, he shouldered his rifle nervously. If he missed, the deer would scatter and he would be out the first meal he had had since getting separated from the expedition. His bowels muttered and gurgled, the aftermath of a spell of diarrhea brought on by the unripe berries he had eaten two days back. He prayed the noise would not alert the animals to his presence.

Mindful of the elk meat he had let spoil, he sighted on the smallest doe and was set to shoot when a profound dizziness struck, forcing him to grab for the tree to keep the earth from tilting out from beneath his feet.

In the time it took for him to feel steady again, his target had edged closer, making for an easier shot. He sucked in a ragged breath, bit his lower lip, and released the hammer. The rifle exploded with a bruising recoil.

The smoke cleared, to disappointment. The glade was empty of deer, standing or fallen. His shot had missed.

He leaned against the tree, too frustrated to hold back the tears that puddled in his eyes. *Why? Why? Why?* The question wore grooves through his mind while he struggled to regain control.

Finally he shook his head clear of all self-pitying thoughts and forced himself to consider that something good might have come out of the miss. Where there were four deer, there were bound to be more. By the law of averages, a miss was a good thing. The important thing was to keep heart and not give up; to keep on until he succeeded.

He stood the butt of his rifle on the ground and reached into the shot pouch for a new ball. His fingers pulled out a spare patch. "What're you doing in there? You belong here," he said, putting the patch in its box. "A ball's what I need now."

When his fingers did not find one, he turned the pouch over and shook it. The only thing to fall out was dirt.

He checked his pockets.

Still no ball.

He tried the shot pouch again.

Nothing. He had patches and plenty of powder but without shot, they were worthless.

He lifted his face to the sky. "Dear God, now what am I supposed to do?"

No one answered.

All day Colter kept to the high ground above the river trench, driving his tired body hard. He was determined that this would be the day he caught Shannon and could finally take off for the Niobrara and his future.

The sun was low in the sky before he dropped down to the river trench for the first time that day. He could not believe his eyes when he came across the familiar tracks. Shannon was still ahead of him, still heading upriver.

In frustration, he yelled, "Turn around, Fuzz!" The surrounding trees bounced the words back in a mocking echo. Only then did he realize what a risky thing he had done in shouting. Someone could be nearby. Someone bad for his health. He decided he had better move on and fast.

He had climbed halfway out of the trench before it registered that he was leaving tracks of his own. In pursuing Shannon so singlemindedly he had grown careless, and, in Sioux country, careless men lived short lives. First he would cover his tracks better; then, tonight, because he had not been thinking clearly, he had better stop for a full night's sleep instead of the quick cat-naps he had been grabbing.

He veered off to a nearby creek and waded up its rocky bed to the high ground. He stopped at the top to get his bearings before continuing and spotted a hawk gliding down the sky toward an odd structure that stood silhouetted against the backdrop of the sinking sun. The structure appeared to be the frame of a flat-roofed house. Curiosity drew him to investigate.

He was several paces away when he realized that it was a burial scaffold. A recent one, from the condition of the robes wrapping the body laid out on the platform.

Beyond the raised platform, a pattern of circles and ash heaps marked the site of a recently-abandoned Indian camp. That explained the group he had seen earlier. Before he could turn to leave, an eerie keening drew him to notice a waist-high bower of grasses and vines placed to one side. A small fire blazed in front of the dome-shaped structure with what looked to be a large discarded sack next to it.

He crept forward, rifle to hand, an found not a sack, but a person; an ancient Indian man, wrapped in a worn buffalo robe, rocking slowly from side to side and chanting in a low quavering voice. At Colter's approach, the singing stopped, and the head raised to reveal a brown face wrinkled so heavily that it seemed to be caving in on itself like the last apple in the barrel come spring. Blindness had turned the old man's eyes milky blue.

The man raised a crooked finger to his lined temple and slowly traced a pattern against his leathery skin. The hair on Colter's arms lifted when he recognized that the sightless man was drawing the outline of his own birthmark. "But you're blind," Colter said.

The Indian responded with a cackle and a stream of gibberish, then pointed to the opposite side of the fire, inviting Colter to sit. Every muscle in Colter's body wanted to get out of there, but he took the seat anyway.

The old one's hair had been recently combed and braided. Though his clothing was worn, the moccasins on his feet looked new. Three bowls of food and a full waterskin sat within easy reach. The bower had been swept clean, and there was enough wood in a stack to keep the fire going for several days.

It struck Colter then that the migrating Indians had left this old man behind to die. *Trust Indians to be so cruel,* he thought. *Fuzz ought to see this, see how Indians really were. This'd set him straight.*

The Indian held out one of the bowls of food and insisted that Colter take it. "In the morning, I'll see you get more food, Grandfather." The honorific popped out before he was aware of it.

The old one grinned as if accepting the title and began to talk. Colter's instinct told him that the Indian was relating the story of his life. The unknown language flowed around him, lulling him. He felt as if he were floating. He lost track of his limbs. His cares melted away.

He was not aware of nodding off until he woke to find the night sky hanging like an indigo backdrop beyond the fire's light. The old one greeted his awakening with a toothless smile before lifting his face to the heavens and beginning another song.

Colter knew in his bones that the Indian was singing a prayer to his gods.

When he finished, the old one continued to stare sightlessly upwards, his head cocked as if he were listening to something in the carpet of stars above them. He grunted approvingly and removed the draw-string bag from around his wattled neck. He held the bag up to the heavens, spoke a few words and nodded, then held it out to Colter.

Colter hesitated before taking it. The pouch was still warm from contact with the Indian's flesh and he could feel three or four objects through the supple leather.

The old man motioned for Colter to put it around his neck. Again, he did so with reluctance. The old one nodded, his etched face lighting with a satisfied smile. Then he pulled the buffalo robe closer around his thin shoulders, curled onto his side, closed his eyes and, with a sigh, went to sleep.

Colter fed the fire and watched the sleeping man. He could not shake the feeling that the Indian had been waiting for him. Again and again, he reached for the pouch, intending to remove it and return it to its owner. Each time, something stopped him.

After a while, he decided that his tired mind was playing tricks on him. There was a logical explanation for everything that had happened here tonight. He would figure that out in the morning, after a good night's sleep. He pulled his blanket out of his pack and, like the old Indian, fell fast asleep.

The next thing Colter knew, the sun was shining into his eyes. He sat up, wondering where he was. Once he figured that out, he reached over to rouse the old Indian.

The old one would not be roused. His song last night had indeed been a prayer. A death prayer.

First Sergeant Floyd, now this old man. Before that, Pa, Zoob, Ma, and McBain. Death had once again reached out a bony hand to take away someone near him. The next moment he remembered why he was out here. "Oh, Lord, Fuzz."

He could not allow himself to leave the old one to scavenging animals, so he carried the body to the burial scaffold. He laid the man out next to the other body and tucked the edges of the buffalo robe carefully around him.

Though he was anxious to be off, he took note of the personal possessions of the other corpse decorating the platform — a painted shield, a quiver of arrows, a bow — and knew that his task was not quite done.

He collected the old man's few belongings from the bower and carried them to the scaffold where he arranged the food bowls and waterskin near the old man's head and laid the carved walking stick at his side. For a moment, he considered leaving the pouch, too, but the image of that kindly wrinkled face made him reconsider. Instead, he pulled out a nearly-completed carving of an elk and placed it in the cupped palm of the man's right hand. "A gift for a gift," he said, taking up his rifle and hurrying off to resume the search for Shannon.

Back in the river trench, he came across Shannon's tracks straight away. Only today something was different. Lump, the horse he had planned on taking when he caught up with Shannon, was limping badly.

Squatting, Shannon clung to the bark of a downed log to keep from falling backward into the puddle of watery burning excrement. In his weakened state, he marveled at how his body could keep spewing forth matter
when there had been nothing for his stomach to digest.

He was haunted by thoughts of how failing to refill his shot pouch before
going hunting with Drouillard had put him in this situation. He had been
desperate enough to use pebbles in place of rifle balls. He had even carved
a bullet out of wood. But all his attempts to shoot animals had come to
nought. Either the substitute ball had failed or he had missed the shot.

Then he tried setting snares, and failed again. The worst part of all these
failures was that every minute he spent searching for food put him that
much farther behind the expedition.

He pulled himself hand over hand into a standing position. "You got to
get hold of yourself, George." The weaker he got, the more he sounded
like his father.

Burr raised its head and blew impatiently through its nose. Shannon drew
himself up as best he could and set off upstream one wobbly step at a time.
He no longer bothered to lead the horses. They followed of their own ac-
cord.

He marked off one hundred steps before he allowed himself to rest. That
was when he realized only Burr was with him. "Lump, get up here," he
croaked weakly.

A faint snuffling came from the direction of his last stopping place. "You
have to stay up or we'll leave you," he pleaded.

Silence.

"Stay here," he said, pointing a warning finger at Burr before retracing
his steps.

Two hundred yards back, he found Lump lying down, her sides heaving.
"Oh, no. Not you. Not now." He fell to his knees beside the horse, took the
animal's head in his lap and stroked her muzzle. "Please don't die on me."

He glared up at the lamb's-fleece clouds scudding overhead. "I'm the
one to blame for this mess. I'm the one that made the mistakes. Punish me.
Not this poor creature."

The benign silence of the sky filled him with despair. What was the use?
He had bungled everything. He didn't even have a bullet to put the ailing
horse out of her misery.

Lump sneezed. To Shannon, it sounded like a demand for him to leave.
"You're right. It's all my fault. I'm sor —" His voice failed. He laid the
mare's head gently on the ground and struggled upright. Lump's eyes
closed.

Ignoring the dizziness that threatened to knock him off his feet, Shannon
stumbled away, feeling like a murderer.

September 3rd. The knowledge that he had one day to find Shannon and
still make it to Manuel Lisa's camp kept Colter on the move all day. He refused to think about the decision that would face him if he failed to find

Fuzz. It pained him to think how certain he had once been of success.

All day he kept to the high ground, moving strongly after a night of rest. He pushed onward until dusk, then descended into the river's trench, determined to finally find Shannon and turn him around, then strike off for the nearby Niobrara and a whole new future. Even if he had to travel all night, he resolved to get to Lisa's camp before day-break tomorrow.

With his mind focused inwardly, he nearly passed the dun-colored mound before he recognized it. Lump, his favorite horse, lay on the ground, scarcely breathing. She barely had the strength to open her eyes at the touch of his hand. "Oh, girl. What's happened to you?"

He scanned her legs for signs of a break and her coat for wounds. Nothing. Nothing except exhaustion and starvation. Suddenly he was furious. Shannon had pushed the horse into this state, yet he did not even have the decency to put the mare out of her misery.

Colter turned away to load his rifle. Steeling himself, he turned back and shot the horse.

Afterward he knelt at the river and scooped water into his mouth to purge the bad taste. On the second swallow a new possibility occurred to him, sweeping aside his anger. Shannon might be a lot of things, but he was not deliberately cruel. He would never leave a horse to suffer. Not if he had a choice.

Colter's cupped hand paused at the level of his chest. He knew without knowing how that something had happened to Shannon's rifle. That meant he was defenseless against the Sioux — and liable to starve. In that moment he realized that he might never find Shannon alive. Shannon, who had been such a trial, who was always ready to show off his book-learning, who argued about anything and everything, who thought Indians were exotic creatures to be studied — in that moment Colter understood how much a part of his life Shannon had become. An aggravating, yet interesting part.

He glanced at the position of the sun. Dusk already. What was he going to do: take off for the Niobrara and leave Shannon to deal with his own problems, or keep up the search, hoping to catch him before the Sioux or hunger did him in?

He sat back heavily on the damp sand. Why did his life always seem to come down to decisions like this? Why was he always having to choose between his dreams and his duty? Ma called it Fate. Others called it Destiny. No matter what you called it, it seemed to complicate his life at every turn.

After a long time, he pushed himself up to his feet. Dream or not, he could not let a friend die without making every attempt to save his life. Manuel Lisa would have to go West without him.

Battling the vertigo that kept his world tilting and swaying, Shannon stooped awkwardly to drink from the brook. He was long past caring that Burr was lapping water a short distance upstream.

Thirst quenched, he leaned back and squinted across the Missouri. Just downstream, the river curved to the south. The water's surface rippled in the sunlight like a thousand tiny dancing mirrors. Foliage along the river sported the dusky green of waning summer. His breath caught momentarily at the beauty of the place.

He no longer knew where he was or why. All he knew was that he had made a tragic mistake and now he was paying for it. A mist filmed his eyes. He blinked against it.

Wait. What is that? Downstream, at the bend. Something moving.

He squinted into the glare, scanning for movement.

There. Men! On horses.

There were five of them, bare-chested, deeply tanned, with long black hair and no beards, riding bareback. Two riderless horses carried deer carcasses roped across their backs. It was a hunting party, probably Sioux, and they were moving away from him.

In a split second, his dilemma overcame caution. He pushed himself to his feet. "Hey! Here! I'm here!"

He was staggering forward, off-balance and woozy, waving his arms over his head when a root caught his foot and sent him sprawling. By the time he struggled onto his knees, the Indians had disappeared, and so had his chances.

9. *Too Stubborn to Die*

"**N**o!" The cry ripped out of Colter's bowels at the sight of the unmistakable tracks pressed into the earth damp from the overnight rain. He had given up praying after Zoob died, but last night, still behind Shannon and knowing today he had to turn back to the expedition in keeping with his promise to Captain Lewis, he had turned to prayer out of desperation. Now this — proof that God had ignored him. A wavering line of Shannon's footprints continued to head upstream.

He shook his head in wonder, and sadness, at the young man's resilience and stubbornness. One last time, he cupped his hands around his mouth and yelled, "Turn around, Fuzz!"

Though he listened hard for a reply, none came.

He aimed a wobbly kick at a rock. "Damnation!" he swore, turning downstream.

The morning's storm matched Colter's mood perfectly. Lump was dead, and, from the tracks, Burr was close to it. Lisa had gone on without him. And Shannon was out alone in this vast dangerous country without a working rifle. He had no one to blame but himself for underestimating the task of tracking down Shannon and for not pressing the search until it was too late.

He was walking along, head down, absorbed in his own thoughts when a fat buck stepped out of the brush ahead. He did not bother to raise his rifle.

He had been the cause of enough loss.

Before trudging on, he glanced over his shoulder on the remote chance that Shannon might have materialized since the last time he looked. Nothing there but trees and bushes.

Around noon, he came to a shelf of sand where yesterday he had left a pair of crossed branches to signal the expedition that he was ahead of them. He uprooted the sticks and flung them into the undergrowth. He had wasted eight day's worth of time and energy because his mind had been on Manuel Lisa, not on finding Shannon.

In a fit of frustration, he grasped the pouch given to him by the old Sioux, but before he could rip it from his neck, a shape outlined in faded black on the leather stopped him. Although he had worn the pouch for three days, he had never really looked at it. Now he recognized the figure as a bird with its wings spread in flight.

A chill rippled along his spine. The figure was the same as the one he wore on his face. What kind of witchery was going on here?

The sound of splashing drew his attention downriver as the white pirogue hove into view. For an instant, he had the overwhelming urge to take cover; to let the expedition pass by, then take off after Manuel Lisa. But the feeling vanished like smoke before a gale, leaving him feeling a complete failure. He let the pouch fall back against his chest and settled down on the bank to wait for the flotilla to reach him.

A dozen pairs of arms helped pull him aboard *Discovery*, and both captains came to greet him. "Shannon?" Lewis asked.

"Never caught him." Colter admitted.

"That Shannon's got wet dough for brains," Collins said.

"What's he thinking?" Joe said.

"The Sioux're going to cook his liver for sure," said Rube.

Clark's hand slashed the air. "Back to work, men!" He nodded at Lewis, who motioned for Colter to follow him into the cabin. Once inside, Lewis's voice was soft and full of concern. "What happened, John?"

Colter had to look down at his hands in order to compose his faltering emotions. "Yesterday I come across one of the horses down, but not dead. Had to shoot it. Shannon never would've let a critter suffer. Not if he could help it. I figure his rifle's broke or lost or somethin's happened to his powder or ammunition."

The captain paced slowly to the window. He stood with his back to Colter for a long time. The silence stretched. At last, Lewis spoke. "Thank you for all your effort. Take a couple of days to recover your strength. I will have Sergeant Ordway bring you some food."

"But what about Shannon, sir?"

"He is on his own. Our mission is too important to risk any more lives searching for him. Shannon knew the risk he was taking when he signed on."

Colter could not abide the idea that the captain was giving up on Shannon. "You're wrong, Captain. Fuzz has book-learnin' but he don't know dirt about what's really out there. Tarnation! He thinks Indians're crosses between pet dogs and deacons."

A dark look from Lewis dried up his protest. He threw up his hands, left the cabin and climbed to the quarterdeck where he sank down on one of the lockers and gazed at the river.

His eyes caught movement on the bank, and, immediately he thought of Shannon.

The object proved to be nothing more than the sun playing tricks, but it took awhile before the hope it raised in him died away.

Ordway appeared and tossed a chunk of roasted meat onto the top of the next locker. "Food for our returning hero."

Colter ignored the comment and the food, hoping the sergeant would go away. He didn't. Instead Ordway caught hold of Colter's pouch. "This is something new."

Colter pushed away the sergeant's hand and stuffed the pouch inside his shirt. "It's private."

"You really disappointed me, Colter. Here I was all set for some fun. There's nothing I like more than a good chase. What made you change your mind about deserting us?"

Colter could not resist the urge to taunt the man. "Why, I couldn't never leave you, Sarge. You cain't do without me."

Ordway coughed a laugh. "You flatter yourself, Colter."

"It ain't flattery. It's a fact. Ain't no one in this here crew's a better burr in your britches than me."

A snort from nearby revealed Rube Field, listening in and obviously enjoying what he heard. Colter raised his voice a bit for Rube's benefit. "Seein' as how you need me, Sarge, I weren't about to let you down by not comin' back when I said I would. Gave my word, remember?"

"Only thing I need from you is the pleasure of giving the order and watching a rope choke the sass out of you."

Colter curled up the corners of his mouth, mocking Ordway. "Ain't you forgot somethin'? Captain Lewis and Captain Clark, they don't go in for them old-fashioned Army ways."

There was the slightest tensing around the sergeant's eyes. "When it's your turn, Colter, we'll see. Meantime, I'll wait. Sooner or later, you'll trip up. Your kind always does." He swung down to the rowing deck.

In the absence of his enemy, the heat of anger drained out of Colter, leaving him bone-weary. He leaned his chin on the railing and closed his eyes. From St. Charles on, he had made a royal botch of everything. He should have found Shannon. He should be with Lisa. "Damn it all, Fuzz. Turn around," he muttered.

"What say?" Rube asked.

"Said I had enough restin'. Time to do somethin' worthwhile." He pushed past Rube, climbed down to the rowing deck, and slid into his usual place. Since he was bound to go West, he would row or pull or whatever was needed. Just because he had come a cropper did not give him the right to make someone else pick up his slack.

⚜

Two hours later the expedition reached the confluence of the Niobrara. Colter had to turn away from the sight of Lisa's abandoned campsite on the western bank. He did not go ashore with the rest of the crew. He could not delight in picking through the litter the previous occupants had left behind. To know that he had come within minutes of reaching Manuel Lisa — *minutes* — before he turned back, made him ill.

Rube returned from the camp and tossed something into Colter's lap. "A present for you."

It was a broken chain link. Colter was about to toss it overboard when his hand stopped. The broken ring was a perfect symbol for his life: always gaping open, never quite joining into one strong whole, never fully connecting with others. He slipped it inside his hunting shirt until he could stash it in his locker.

Two miles above the Niobrara a sudden storm blew up with a torrent of cold rain driven before a strong wind. As the crew struggled to draw in the sail, the mast snapped in two with a sickening crack.

"Bring out the cordelle!" Ordway's bellow was all but swallowed by the wind. Colter straggled off the boat along with the other crewmen.

Not wanting to lose the chain link, he decided to put it into the old Indian's pouch. As he pulled the pouch out of his shirt, Drouillard materialized beside him. The half-breed grasped the little sack and examined its design, then looked pointedly at Colter's birthmark.

"I found it," Colter volunteered.

Drouillard shook his head emphatically. "Such medicine cannot be lost. Only given."

"I found it," Colter repeated, snatching the pouch out of the half-breed's hand and tucking it away.

Drouillard continued to watch him. "The Hawk Spirit flies closest to Him Who Sees All." He pointed to the lump of the pouch under Colter's shirt. "Him Who Sees All sends this medicine to guide you on your way to that place He chooses for you."

Then, as suddenly as he appeared, the half-breed was gone, and Colter was left to acknowledge the notion that had been nibbling at the edges of his thoughts the last few days. A notion that he was being pulled onward by some force he did not understand. A force capable of undermining his attempts to deviate from the course it had set. A force beyond his ability to counter, pulling him toward . . . what? And why?

⚜

A tangled loop of berry canes caught Shannon's ankle and pulled him down. Stinging thorns dug into his skin, infuriating him. Cursing words he had never uttered before, he kicked and slashed weakly at the bushes until he ripped free of the thicket. "I will not be stopped!" he muttered hoarsely as he crawled away.

When a sharp spine stabbed deep into the soft flesh beneath his kneecap, he did not have the strength to cry out. He rolled onto his side, groaning weakly and clutching his knee.

Burr regarded him with a blank expression while its tail swished listlessly at flies.

"Don't stand there. Help me," Shannon croaked.

Burr bent to sniff a tussock of sun-burned grass.

Shannon's anger bled into dejection. The drifting clouds overhead mocked him. He had fought a losing battle. He was never going to catch the expedition. His only hope was to flag down a trading boat headed back and convince them to take him to St. Louis. *If* there was a trading boat.

As if it read Shannon's mind, Burr turned and plodded away downstream, leaving Shannon to struggle up and follow however he could.

Three days later Shannon lay on his back on a shelf of flat rock that jutted into the river. He took no comfort from the heat radiating from the surface of the stone. In the whispers of the passing water, a thousand voices scolded him for his defeat.

It had been three days since he turned downstream. In that time there had been no sign of any other human life. The moment had come to accept that he would never meet a trading boat this late in the season.

He closed his eyes. No traders. No expedition. No food. No hope of walking all the way back to St. Charles. No chance of surviving out here. His life was forfeit.

He clung to the consolation that Captain Lewis would inform his parents of his death. He could picture them in the parlor, his father holding his mother while she wept inconsolably over the death of her only child. At least he would not die unmourned.

"If I should die before I wake, I pray the Lord my soul to take." His voice sounded strange after so long without speaking. Heaving a final sigh for all the thoughts he would never think, experiences he would never savor, books he would hever read, and pleasures he would never enjoy, he folded his hands across his chest and waited for the end.

Sometime later a noise intruded.

He lay still, eyes closed, hands folded, ears cocked to the wind which carried a hint of murmuring.

In the course of a few minutes, the murmuring grew into voices. Definitely voices. *Angels*, came the thought. *I'm dead and angels are coming to lift me to heaven.*

He opened his eyes and cocked his head toward the sound. He did not want to miss his first glimpse of the heavenly messengers. But, instead of winged creatures and heavenly scenery, he saw nothing but the place he had laid down by the Missouri to die.

Not dead yet, he decided, putting his head back down and reclosing his eyes.

The silence was broken by a familiar snorting laugh. *Newman?* he thought. *Maybe he's dead too. And God has sent him to welcome me to*

Heaven.

"Shannon!" came a shout.

He struggled up onto an elbow, blinking against the glare off the river to see who might have called his name.

What he saw down the river brought him up to one wobbly knee. "Dear God," he whispered and pitched forward in a faint.

The crew spent the next morning slogging through knee-deep river mud and man-high willows. Colter was primed for a rest break when the call came. All he wanted was to be left alone to nurse his misery, but Joe Field flopped down next to him and proceeded to chew his ear. "It's time you quit moping about Peckerwood, Colter. It's his fault he got lost. Not yours. And he's paid for it. Those are the breaks. So come on. Buck up."

He kept still, hoping Joe would take the hint. He didn't. "Say, did you ever figure out who that man is who's followin' you? Whatever he's got to tell you's got to be mighty important for him to come all this way."

Colter had been too immersed in self-recrimination and sorrow over Shannon and his own lost opportunity with Lisa to think about the danger that was following him. Danger by the name of Hartley. As casually as he could, he said, "Why're you askin'? You seen him?"

"No, but I figure he ought to be up with us by now. If'n it'd been me, I'd have slipped on by whilst we was stopped with them Yanktons and waited for us somewheres upriver. But I sure wouldn'a gone far enough to risk gettin' stopped by the Teton Sioux. Jesus H. Christ Almighty, not them!"

The idea that Hartley might be close held Colter's full attention so that he jumped when a whistle pierced the air.

"Who on earth is that?" Joe said as three tattered figures emerged out of the brush upstream, one of the *engagés* from the white pirogue, a horse and a hunched shadow of a man in filthy ragged clothes.

"By God, it's Peckerwood!" Joe exclaimed, popping to his feet and loping toward the trio.

Colter rose slowly, trying to find the Shannon he remembered in the scratched and shrunken apparition with the mangy beard and weed-matted hair. He hobbled toward the mob that hoisted him up onto their shoulders and carried him to the boat.

The relief and happiness Colter felt over Shannon's miraculous reappearance got immediately nudged aside by a sudden upwelling of anger. Anger at the younger man for continuing upriver long after common-sense should have turned him around. Anger at himself for not taking into account Shannon's stubborn naïveté. Anger at Ordway. Anger at the tricks life kept throwing at him.

With so much anger churning inside him, Colter decided to put off greeting Shannon until he calmed down some. He turned away from the welcoming crowd and walked into the brush to cool off. He was almost away when Ordway stepped into his path. "What, no welcome home for your buddy?"

"Gotta piss first, Sarge," he answered without conviction, side-stepping the man and continuing his walk.

At the time of Shannon's miraculous reappearance, the expedition had already traveled over a thousand miles up the Missouri, according to Captain Clark's calculations. A thousand more could lie ahead of them. Maybe two thousand. No one knew for sure. What everyone did know with certainty was that any day now they would encounter the formidable Teton Sioux.

For Colter, the issue of the Tetons took a second seat to the issue of what to say to Shannon. The younger man had been confined to the captains' cabin while he recuperated, and every time the cabin door opened, Colter got a glimpse of his sleeping figure, lying on Clark's berth, swathed in blankets despite the late summer's heat. Every glimpse served to reinforce, rather than diminish, his bitterness. Consequently, a full day passed and he still had not talked to his benchmate.

York sought Colter out that night. "Shannon's been asking for you."

The plea in the black man's eyes was clear, but Colter was still not ready to face Shannon when he climbed aboard *Discovery* that night after supper to see him.

"Is that you, Old Man?" came a weak voice.

"Sure is." Colter forced a smile and stepped into the cabin. In the gloom, Shannon's eyes looked huge against the thin pale oval of his face. Upon seeing Colter, those eyes softened and the mouth, still framed by a straggle of beard, parted in a tremulous smile. "Come sit where I can see you, Old Man."

Colter complied, but he was unable to find a comfortable position under Shannon's gaze.

"Rube said you came looking for me on foot. Said you volunteered." A fit of coughing stopped the stream of Shannon's conversation momentarily. "How can I ever thank you?"

"Don't have to. Didn't find you, did I?"

"The point is that you tried. Thanks."

Colter pushed himself to his feet. "Damn it all. Don't do that! I don't want your thanks."

"Colter, I — What?"

Colter stopped at the threshold and faced Shannon, too angry to keep it in any longer. "You were traipsin' up this here river for more'n two weeks, Fuzz. Two weeks! Why in the hell didn't you turn around?"

Shannon's face crumpled into confusion and his lips moved without producing any sound.

"Why, damn it?" Colter demanded.

"I — I — It never occurred to me. Till the end," Shannon rasped.

Colter fell silent, suddenly ashamed of himself. "Lord Almighty, if that don't take all." He turned to leave, but a question from Shannon stopped him. "Why did you come after me?"

"Because, because — ah, hell, Fuzz."

"Why? I have to know."

He tried to frame a response. "'Cause who else am I goin' to argue with?"

Shannon's Adam's-apple worked. He kept his eyes averted for a long time before he found his voice. "Couple more day's rest and I'll be back in regular form. Think we can pick up where we left off? How's that?" A wan smile revealed the familiar gap between his teeth.

"Hell, I don't know. I'm a mite outta practice right now."

"Me, too," Shannon said. "I'm . . . " His words trailed off into a soft snore.

"Goodnight, Fuzz," Colter murmured and tiptoed out, relieved and a little guilty for getting so worked up.

Shannon had to wait ten days before the captains allowed him to resume his regular duties. He was on the verge of laughing for sheer joy when he took his place on the bench next to Colter. For the first time since joining the expedition, he was grateful for the scrape of the oar handle against his palm, for the tug of the current, for the sweat and the strain of rowing. He treasured every sensation, every smell, every sound as confirmation of the life that still coursed through his veins. He could not help grinning, and meaning it, when Ordway assigned him a watch that night.

Before his ordeal, he hated the midnight watch most of all, but this night he rolled out of his blanket and hurried cheerfully to his post, drinking in the sweet air, enjoying the gurgle and swish of the ever-flowing river, admiring the canopy of stars overhead. Had there ever been a more gorgeous night?

Since the expedition had moved into Teton Sioux country, the captains had them camping on sandbars with double guards posted for all watches. This night's sand island was an oval with a five-foot drop-off at the downstream end. The keelboat and two pirogues had been tied off in the protection of that bank while Shannon's post was at the opposite, upstream end of the bar.

Half the crew were sleeping on the island. The rest were bedded down on the keelboat. He smiled toward the blanket-covered form that was Colter. He had never considered bickering as the basis of a relationship. Yet, as he reviewed the near-year he had spent with the expedition, he realized that disagreements formed the foundation of his friendship with his benchmate as much as the experiences they had shared.

A low rumbling sound slowed his pacing. He searched the sky for signs of a storm. That was strange. The sky was clear, a brilliant splash of stars across black velvet. How could there be thunder?

The rumbling came again. He inspected the sky a second time. No lightning that he could find. At that moment the ground began to shiver, a gentle movement that rapidly grew in intensity until his legs were vibrating.

He turned toward the river in time to see a line of willows disappear as if the earth had swallowed them.

More rumbling, more shaking and another width of the sandbank vanished in a swirling cloud of dust.

The rumbling grew louder, the vibrations intensified until they rattled his whole body. More of the island's upstream edge vanished. If this went on, the whole island would disappear. "Attack!" he yelled for lack of a better way to alert the sleeping crew to the disaster that was about to overtake them.

Heads popped up around the camp.

"To the boats!" he yelled, running in that direction.

He glanced side to side to make sure that the crewmen all got the message. In doing so, he tripped over one of the sleeping men.

"What the . . .?" came Colter's sleep-thickened question.

Shannon sprang up and yanked Colter off the ground. "Run! River's eating the island!"

As the two of them reached the lip of the downstream bank, the crew of the white pirogue shoved it off with the red crew right behind it. The two craft had just cleared the overhang when it collapsed, unleashing a cascade of sand that would have destroyed both canoes and buried their crews had they not escaped.

The scene on-board *Discovery* was chaos. Those men awakened by the noise and shaking were at their oars trying to move her away from the island while the rest groggily tried to comprehend what was happening. The three sergeants had been on the island and they had not yet made it onto the boat. Without them, none of the crew seemed to know what to do. Shannon did.

He leaped aboard, followed by Colter. "To the poles!" he yelled.

A few men followed him onto the *passe avant*, but by then a five-foot high bank of collapsing earth was advancing toward the boat like a juggernaut. "Set!" he thundered, putting as much authority into his voice as he could muster and jamming his own pole into the river. Four of the bewildered men on the walkway followed his lead.

"Push!" he yelled, putting all his strength behind his effort.

A small margin of water opened between the keelboat and the collapsing island. "For God's sake, set!"

There were a dozen men on the walkway now. They had to make it out into the current this time or be crushed. "Dig!"

With this push, the ribbon of dark water on the island side of the boat widened by five yards.

"Out of the way, Shannon," Ordway ordered, pushing him roughly aside. "You're not in charge. I —"

Just then the rest of the island disintegratd with a roar worthy of the Biblical Beast. The collapsing banks narrowly missed *Discovery*, which rocked wildly, but remained unscathed.

Shannon closed his eyes. For the second time in ten days, his life had been spared. There could be no mistaking the Divine message in those occurrences. God expected him to make something of himself and this second chance at life he had been given. "I'll try," he mumbled toward the sky. "I'll really try."

"Shannon!" Ordway bellowed.

Shannon plunged his pole in the river and leaned into it, happy to be alive.

10. *Teton Sioux*

E xcept for losing a night's sleep, no one was hurt in the sandbar's collapse and no vital supplies were lost. Next day the expedition passed Cedar Island with its forlorn abandoned trading post. The crew had all heard stories about how the Teton Sioux followers of Chief Partisan harassed the St. Louis-based traders who built the post, stealing their goods and threatening them until the traders gave up in frustration and retreated downriver. The sight of the gutted structure sobered everyone, and that night the captains tripled the guard. As usual Ordway assigned Colter the dawn watch on the outermost exposed perimeter.

The next day, September 23, three Teton boys swam out to *Discovery* with news of a village just upriver. The captains sent the boys back to their people with gifts of tobacco and invitations for the chiefs to come in for council. Figuring Ordway would assign him another dangerous watch when he was already edgy from lack of sleep, Colter was surprised when Captain Clark approached him instead. "Are you up to some hunting, Colter?"

"Yes, sir!" he answered with enthusiasm. After being on his own searching for Shannon, he had had a rough time, adjusting to being back under Ordway's control. He was willing to take any risk to be away from the sergeant, including the chance that he might run into Tetons.

"We need meat and lots of it for the council, but, for safety's sake, keep to the islands," Clark said.

Burr, the only horse remaining to the expedition, was still too run down from his trek with Shannon to be ridden. Colter led the animal two miles upriver, then across a shallow channel to a sizeable island that, to his practiced eye, looked like a good one for game. Right off, he found elk tracks. He tied Burr's reins to a stout willow in a shady thicket and took off in pursuit of the quarry.

The trail led him to the opposite side of the island where two summer-sleek elk cows browsed. He dropped one, slit its throat and strung it up to bleed before going back for Burr.

The horse, however, was not where he had left it. What he found instead was Burr's hoofprints leading toward the other end of the island, and, next to those, the unmistakable imprints of a pair of moccasined human feet.

Josiah Hartley or Sioux? The tracks did not tell him who to expect.

He moved cautiously along the tracks until he came to the point where a third set of tracks joined the other two. The tracks of another horse. An unshod horse.

Colter felt only momentary relief at discovering the footprints were not Hartley's. The Teton Sioux had Burr, the expedition's last horse.

"Burr." Shannon's voice cracked when he spoke the name. Colter could not fault him. Losing the animal you had gone through so much with was almost as bad as losing your best friend. After a long moment, Shannon said wistfully, "Captains'll get him back."

"Ain't likely to happen, Fuzz. Best you get used to the idea that Burr's gone for good."

Shannon shook his head adamantly. "They will get him back. You'll see."

Colter held back on his arguments. Let Fuzz believe whatever he wanted. He would have to admit the truth soon enough.

"Captain! Indians!" came a cry from the quarterdeck.

Both captains came out of the cabin while the pilot maneuvered *Discovery* toward a campsite on the bank. Colter counted five Indians. Burr was not among their horses.

Once the boat was in position to carry on a conversation, Captain Lewis did the talking. Using the pilot Cruzatte to translate from English into halting Sioux, he went through the greetings and formalities all these Indians expected, then told them that the expedition's missing horse was to be a gift for the head chief of their nation.

This came as a complete surprise to Colter who, knowing how valuable the horse was to the expedition, expected the captains to demand that the Sioux own up to their thievery.

There was much muttering and head wagging among the five Sioux before they denied all knowledge of Burr.

"Like hell," Colter muttered. "They got him stashed somewhere."

Shannon elbowed him. "Wasn't that brilliant, Old Man! By saying that Burr was meant for a gift, whoever took him won't be able to keep him. Brilliant!"

"Hold on there. Burr ain't nowhere that I can see. And if'n he was here, Captain just give him away. In my book, that's plumb crazy."

"In my book, he took the only option open," Shannon shot back.

"Then we all better hope it works."

"Amen," Shannon replied.

Amen. The word prompted Colter's thoughts to bounce back to Hartley. The preacher was somewhere close — his gut told him so. The man was persistent, but he was also alone. Alone in Teton Sioux country. Given the stories about how Partisan and his band of dog soldiers treated every white man unlucky enough to cross their path, the preacher was likely to end up very sorry he got this far upriver. *Serves him right*, Colter thought, smiling.

Josiah Hartley dipped his paddle methodically: three strokes left; three, right, the way he had learned from observing Bonhomme. The last two mornings, he had awakened to frost and realized he'd best figure out the exact date.

It took him a long while to come up with September 25th, a month, give or take a few days, since he peeked through the bushes to see the two Indians with his string of fish. God had been on his side that day for sure. Not only had his seeping bowels sent him into the brush at just the right moment, but the rocky ground had hidden his tracks, so the heathens had not discovered him. His miraculous escape from them had pumped him full of enough fear to drive him upriver as fast as his strength allowed.

God had continued to be on his side for the last month, too, despite coming across Indian signs every day.

Spotting a cove overhung with trees, he guided the canoe in and tied the painter to a bush before pulling out his food pouch. Munching on wild grapes he had gathered the day before, he unrolled Bonhomme's hide map and studied it. He located his approximate position and saw that he had entered Sioux country. Time to be extra alert.

Once he had dulled the edge of his hunger, he tucked away the rest of the grapes and resumed his journey. Ahead, the river curved sharply to the west. With instincts born of daily experience, he nosed the craft into the line of least resistance and dug hard against the water's swirling counterforce. His muscles began to burn from exertion, but he lowered his head and kept paddling.

Rounding the bend, he poured the last of his strength into a final pull that propelled the canoe out of the current into an eddy. There in the quiet water, he dropped the paddle into the bottom of the canoe and slumped forward, resting his chest on his thighs and dangling his arms until they quit hurting.

The pounding of his own heart covered the other sounds for a long time. When he became aware of them, he looked up and nearly fell off his seat. The banks ahead were swarming with Indians. He had nearly paddled into a whole village full of Teton Sioux!

With his heart racing, he swung onto the opposite thwart and cautiously maneuvered the canoe back around the bend into the first available cover. Trembling from the close call, he checked the nearby bank for signs of Indians.

Seeing nothing, he slid into the river and pushed the canoe into the cover of a partially-submerged log. Then he grabbed his belongings and waded through the muck to the bank where he scuttled through the undergrowth until he found a protected vantage point to observe the Indian situation through Bonhomme's telescope.

Two pirogues filled with Indians were on the river headed for a large island that split the Missouri's current into two equal strands. He did not need the telescope to see their destination: there, at the upper end of the island, sat a familiar keelboat. At last, he had found John Colter.

"Look lively, men. We have guests," Ordway announced.

"Guests," Colter grumped. He was fuming over the sergeant's latest spiteful move: assigning him to guard the cooks preparing food for the up-coming Teton council. The captains had decided to hold the meeting on a sparsely-grown mid-river island just below the mouth of the Bad River. While the rest of the crew remained aboard *Discovery*, Colter had to stand guard on the open sand, completely exposed.

Worse, he had to endure the whining skittishness of McNeal, the head cook, who managed to dump more food on the sand then he cooked.

Then, aggravating the situation, Colter and the cooks had to spend the night on the island in full view of the Sioux encampment on the western riverbank. By the time the red pirogue brought a relief contingent to the island the next morning, there were enough Sioux swarming the banks to make him long for Virginia *and* Farley Stuart.

Back at *Discovery*, Shannon gave him a hand over the gunwale. "We're making history today, Old Man. Imagine a meeting with real Sioux. Captain asked me to make sketches. Hope I have enough charcoal to last out the day."

Shannon followed Colter to his locker, yammering on and on about the council to come. "Today, at last, you and the rest of the crew will see that all those terrible stories about the Sioux are just so much hot air."

Colter stopped in the process of shrugging on his uniform. "I cain't believe you, Fuzz. You ain't for real."

"What do you mean? Of course, I'm real. As real as you are."

Colter grabbed Shannon's chin and physically turned his head so he was facing the riverbank. "What d'you see?"

"Indians. Teton Sioux."

"How many?"

"I'd say sixty, maybe seventy."

"How many on this here crew?"

A surprised frown furrowed Shannon's brow. "I don't know exactly. I never counted."

Colter held his grip on Shannon. "Guess."

"Thirty, maybe thirty-five, not counting engagés. Come on, let go. You're hurting me."

"Seventy agin' thirty-five. I ain't good at ciphers, but near as I recollect, that's two a them for every one of us. That makes us outnumbered, in case you cain't figure it out."

"Don't be ridiculous. Why would they bring women and children if they planned on trouble?"

Colter arched an irritated eyebrow in reply.

"You're incorrigible, Old Man. To you, all Indians are killers."

"And thieves and liars."

"Well, you're wrong, Colter. Wrong."

"No, you're wrong, Shannon, and you might just be dead wrong — and bald — 'fore this day's out."

Shannon started to say something but stopped and turned to look out at the council site. Several minutes of silence passed before he spoke again in a low subdued voice. "You came after me when I was lost. I will never forget that." He turned his gaze on Colter. "You are my friend. I don't want to argue."

The words took the teeth out of Colter's argument. He was the only one who knew that his true purpose in going after Shannon had been driven by his desire to join Lisa, not by charity or friendship.

Captain Lewis came out of his cabin, followed by Clark. Both were dressed in identical full uniforms, but, while Lewis looked brushed and crisp, Clark appeared rumpled and not quite put together. Lewis nodded to Shannon. "Ready, Shannon?"

Shannon, journal in hand, straightened. "Yes, sir."

"Then let's away."

Shannon followed the captains into the red pirogue and took the seat be-hind them before the canoe headed for the island. Colter looked after it. "But you're wrong, Fuzz."

Two trips later, the red pirogue carried Colter from the keelboat to the council island. Most of the crew were already in their assigned defensive positions around the encampment except for the few who were to remain aboard *Discovery,* manning the cannons and acting as backup should that be necessary. Colter's irritation flared at seeing McNeal standing where he himself was supposed to be. Only a coward and not a very bright one would try to duck out of his assigned position under the noses of his supe-riors. He marched up to the cook. "Outta here, McNeal. This here's my spot. Yours is over there." He thumbed toward the beach where the white pirogue was disgorging its latest load of Teton passengers.

The cook shook his head. "Not no more. Sarge Ordway shuffled us around. You're over there now."

Colter did not bother to look at the sergeant for confirmation. He could feel Ordway's eyes on his back, and he refused to give the man the satis-faction of seeing the disgruntlement that he could not keep off his face.

McNeal grinned slyly. "Maybe you ought to work harder to get Sarge on your side, Colter. Make your life easier."

"And maybe you oughtta shut up, McNeal, while you still got teeth in that there mouth."

"Don't threaten me, Colter. Sarge likes me a whole lot."

"He would," he muttered, moving away to take up his new position be-fore he gave in to the temptation to take the grin off the cook's face.

Ten minutes later the white pirogue returned, carrying three Teton men whose bearing identified them as principal chiefs. Two wore full bonnets of eagle feathers and elaborately painted buffalo robes. The third man wore only one feather sticking up from the back of his head, an unadorned breechcloth and plain leggings. Despite his simple dress, he walked with the swagger of the neighborhood bully.

Colter was close enough to hear Cruzatte's halting translation of the captains' welcome. He learned that the first two chiefs were Black Buffalo and Buffalo Medicine. "Lone Feather" was Partisan, the man Manuel Lisa had turned west at the Niobrara to avoid, the Sioux leader whose followers had chased traders out of their post on Cedar Island.

The keelboat's mainsail had again been stretched to create an awning. Captain Lewis motioned for the chiefs to take their places under its shade where a group of lesser Teton dignitaries had already gathered. While Black Buffalo and Buffalo Medicine walked to their places, Partisan remained stationary until four men separated from the gathered Indian throng and arranged themselves around him. The four wore identical headdresses: a split raven skin tied so the beak projected over the forehead. Similar raven skins adorned their girdles; the bare flesh of their chests, arms and legs had been blackened.

Watching them escort Partisan to the sail-awning, Colter guessed that these were dog soldiers, the bravest and most daring of Sioux warriors. Taking in their appearance and surly behavior, he decided he did not like what he saw. Not at all. With men like this, the expedition's odds were worse than two-to-one. Much worse.

Even in the tensest situation on the river, Colter had never seen Cruzatte sweat, but, as the pilot struggled to translate the captain's words into Teton Sioux, and the Indians' replies into English, perspiration sheened his face. The Sioux listened poker-faced, leaving Colter to wonder how much Cruzatte's nervousness affected his ability to get across the captains' message.

Recognizing the pilot's struggle, Captain Lewis cut short his usual speech and waved Clark forward to pass out gifts. Black Buffalo and Buffalo Medicine accepted medals and red uniform jackets with blank faces, few words and scarcely a glance at what they had received.

"Next we wish to honor Chief Partisan," Clark said.

Partisan did not move so the captain repeated, "Chief Partisan."

The man rose slowly but remained where he was, forcing the captain to bring the gifts to him. He waved aside Clark's offerings with a gush of guttural words accompanied by slashing hand signs. "Le Partisan, he ask why we who are so rich dishonor his people with gifts so poor," Cruzatte translated in a voice high with strain. "He say, that without better gifts, we cannot proceed. That we must stay here and trade only with his people."

A vein throbbing in Lewis's neck was the only indication of tension. He spoke calmly. "The Great Father in Washington sends many wonderful things to show to his children, the Teton Sioux. Observe." He signaled a crewman to plant a stick in the sand. "Please keep your attention on that target." He dropped his hand and Sergeant Pryor fired the airgun, an experimental device Lewis had decided to take on the expedition. The target stick exploded without a sound from the gun.

The demonstration had amazed the Otos, but the Tetons appeared completely unimpressed. The silence that followed seemed an eternity until Clark announced that he and Lewis would escort the three chiefs, along with one follower each, to tour *Discovery*.

Black Buffalo and Buffalo Medicine selected their attendants and followed Clark down to the white pirogue. Partisan trailed behind, surrounded by his four dog soldiers. Colter stepped aside to let the group pass and found himself and his birthmark the object of Partisan's scrutiny. He felt the touch of the man's glittering reptilian eyes long after Partisan and one of his bodyguards took their places in the canoe.

The other three dog soldiers lined up to watch the pirogue make its way to the keelboat, giving him a chance to study them. They exuded the strength and confidence of men pledged to stake themselves to the ground in battle and fight to victory or death without retreat.

Out at *Discovery,* the captains led the Teton chiefs on a tour of the craft. At one point, Partisan appeared to stagger into Captain Clark. York stepped in instantly, wedging himself between the two men and using his intimidating size to usher Partisan, then the other two chiefs back into the shuttle canoe. The *engagés* pushed off without delay and paddled for the island.

The pirogue landed with a crunch of gravel, and the trio of dog soldiers moved forward to meet it. Clark disembarked first. His face was flushed a red deeper than his usual sunburn. York came next. Eyes narrowed, he hovered protectively close to his master. Behind them came Black Buffalo and Buffalo Medicine, walking deliberately as if aware that their every move was being watched by men suspicious of their motives.

Colter had only a moment to wonder where Captain Lewis was before Partisan emerged from the canoe. Again he lurched into Clark. Colter was about to whip up his rifle when York moved to push Partisan away from his master.

The chief's hands slashed the air indignantly. Cruzatte stammered the translation. "This one, he want the paleskins' bitter water for his braves."

Clark drew himself up. "For the last time, Pilot, tell the chief that we are not traders, and there will be no liquor. Period."

Cruzatte started translating. For the words he did not know, his hands stuttered through the signs with a lack of assurance he never showed when he manned *Discovery*'s rudder. He had just finished when one of the dog soldiers sprang at the *engagé* holding the shuttle pirogue's painter, knocking the man aside and grabbing the rope.

Immediately, Partisan's remaining three followers went into action. Two of them wrapped their arms around the canoe's mast, and the third held the prow.

"What's the meaning of this?" Clark thundered.

Partisan swaggered forward. He swept a hand at the pirogue, then hissed a series of syllables while swatting the air with a few indolent signs. The unnatural pink flush on Cruzatte's face deepened to red as he struggled to interpret for the captain. "He say his braves take this boat and its cargo in return for us to go on upriver."

Clark's hand went to the hilt of his sword. "Well, Pilot, I guess we'll see about that." The blade came out of its scabbard with a swoosh and swept up into the sunlight. "I give your men a count of ten to release my boat." Clark glared at the Teton chief to the end of the pilot's translation, then began counting, "1 . . . 2 . . . 3 . . ."

Adrenalin flooded through Colter's body. He picked out his target: the dog soldier holding the pirogue's painter. When the time came, he would have just one shot. He intended to make it count.

From *Discovery* came the squeals of the cannon swiveling toward the sandbar and the thumps and clangs as the emergency squad scrambled into the second pirogue to reinforce the crew on the island.

"4 . . . 5 . . . 6 . . ." Clark counted.

Aware of how vulnerable his position was and how sparse the cover, Colter's hearing grew keener, gathering in other sounds: the twang of bow strings sliding into place, the sigh of arrows coming out of their quivers, the rattle of pebbles displaced by the Sioux women and children scurrying behind the wall of men.

"7 . . . 8 . . ." the captain continued.

Colter's mouth tasted like gunmetal. He could not blink away all the sweat oozing into his eyes from his forehead.

"9 . . ."

Cruzatte had not translated the word before Black Buffalo spoke up. The man's tone left no doubt that he meant to be obeyed. Reluctantly, the two dog soldiers released the mast and stepped out of the boat. The third also moved away. The fourth, however, Colter's target, continued to hold the canoe's tie line.

For a long moment, no one moved, neither Sioux nor crew. Colter's ears roared from the tension of knowing that the lives of the entire crew could end right here.

Black Buffalo barked one sharp word. The last dog soldier dropped the line but sullenly held his ground.

Black Buffalo strode to the painter and scooped it up. The chief spoke, gesturing with the rope, heedless of the spots of mud that spattered his new uniform jacket. "This chief, he say the river, she is closed to us," Cruzatte said.

Clark lowered his sword. "Like hell it is. York!"

York crossed the sand in two strides and yanked the rope out of the chief's surprised hands, flung it into the pirogue, and shoved the heavy craft back into the water. Immediately the *engagés* leaped aboard, grabbed up their paddles and took off rowing at full speed toward *Discovery*. While this was happening, Colter found himself less than an arm's length from the slave and smack in the center of the action.

"Good work, York," Clark said in a low voice, then loudly, "Pilot, tell Chief Partisan that we are not squaws to be ordered around."

Black Buffalo replied through the pilot, "If you try to go ahead, our warriors will follow you and pick you off one by one."

Where were those reinforcements?

Clark swept his sword toward the keelboat. "We have enough medicine on board to wipe out twenty nations like yours."

What medicine? This here's no time for bluffs. Even the cannon cain't overcome these here odds.

The sounds of men splashing into the shallows and the clank of swords and rifles announced the arrival of the emergency squad and broke the tension. Faced with a dozen more rifles, the Sioux began to unnock their arrows and fade back. The three chiefs withdrew into a huddle up the beach.

The breath Colter had been holding in for so long whooshed out with relief, and he realized how dry his mouth was.

Clark resheathed his sword, straightened his jacket and readjusted his cocked hat. "Time to see what we can salvage," he said half to himself, then nodded toward the white pirogue. "York, be ready to put her out quick." Then he marched to the chiefs' huddle and offered his hand to Buffalo Medicine.

The chief rebuffed the hand, so the captain turned to Black Buffalo. Same result. Likewise for Partisan.

"Have it your way then." Clark wheeled toward the pirogue and signalled the keelboat crew to send back the red canoe. "Sergeant Gass, load half your men. I'll go with the first load. Sergeant Ordway, evacuate your men next."

With that order, Colter knew he would be one of the last to leave — if he lived that long.

No sooner had Clark and the first load of crewmen left the shore than Black Buffalo and Buffalo Medicine broke out of their huddle and waded into the river, gesturing that they had more to say. York slipped over the side into the river to act as an anchor while Cruzatte translated for Black Buffalo. "Black Buffalo, he ask that we stop upriver at his village so that his people can see our big war canoe."

With a quick glance toward *Discovery*, Clark consented. The white pirogue returned to the beach to disgorge four crewmen who were replaced by the two chiefs and their attendants. Colter watched with disbelieving eyes. Who in his right mind would agree to another stop when they were not yet out of this fix? And what kind of nasty surprises were these wily Sioux planning?

The red pirogue landed, loaded and took off again, this time with Shannon and McNeal among the evacuees. Then the white pirogue returned to repeat the process. It left for *Discovery*, leaving only five crewmen, including Colter and Ordway, on the island. Under the glare of all those Tetons, seconds turned into hours. Colter's nerves stretched thin, his thirst more urgent.

At last the white pirogue returned. Colter was moving to it before its nose scraped on the sand and pebbles of the landing, but Partisan blocked his way. The next moment, a hawk screamed in the distance. Partisan galnced up at the sky and a hint of approving smile flitted across his lips. He allowed Colter to pass.

Colter helped shove off, then scrambled into the canoe to find Ordway on the bench next to him. "What was that all about, Private?"

"Guess he likes the way I look, Sarge."

That reply caused one of the *engagés* to burst out laughing, followed by another, and another. Soon everyone but the sergeant was laughing. Even Colter.

"Shut up and row!" bellowed the sergeant.

The laughter died away, but not the smiles. An *engagé* nicknamed Noir for the stumps of rotten teeth that dotted his gums leaned back to Colter. "*Bon, ami. Très bon.*"

"That Peckerwood's got guts, don't he?" Rube asked.

"It ain't guts. He ain't got a lick of sense," Colter said, watching the pirogue carrying Captain Lewis, the four Tetons, Shannon and a small group of other crewmen, moving toward the riverbank. The tepees of Black Buffalo's village were set back from the bank and partially obscured from view by the thick vegetation lining the river. Shannon's had been the only hand to go up when Captain Lewis asked for volunteers to visit the encampment. The other men in the canoe had to be pressed into duty.

"Hope the pirogue comes back with some nice-lookin' squaws. These eyes of mine sure could stand to see somethin' female for a change," Rube said.

Colter could not even work up a grunt at that comment. If it were up to him, they would be pulling upriver as fast and hard as they could, putting distance between themselves and the Tetons. Instead, here they were, only a few miles above the island where yesterday's face-off had happened, surrounded by even more savages. He had had enough Sioux yesterday to last him a lifetime, yet the pirogue would soon return full of Teton women and children, and he and the other crewmen were supposed to play host. Captain Lewis's parting order had been, "The Tetons will be our guests. You will treat them with respect and courtesy."

As the load of Indians tucked against *Discovery*'s side, Rube clapped his hands. "Well, don't that beat all. Captain must've heard me. Would you get a load of all them skirts?"

The Teton women and children swarmed aboard *Discovery* like a summer storm pouring through a gap in the hills, and began poking into every nook and cranny. Colter stood with his back against the wall of the cabin, feeling naked without his rifle. He was so tense that it took awhile to register that someone was staring at him: a small girl with enormous black eyes. At his glance, she smiled shyly, revealing two missing front teeth. That smile drew him down to her height. "How do, little miss."

The little girl reached out and, with one stubby finger, traced the outline of his birthmark.

"Hawk," he said.

"Hawk," she repeated.

He chuckled. "Good girl."

A fringed skirt swished up behind the girl and a woman's hand snatched the child's finger away from Colter's face. The hand belonged to a pretty Sioux woman with big black eyes, identical to the little girl's. She rewarded Colter with a frown before leading Little Big Eyes away.

Ordway was seated on one of the benches, dandling a Sioux toddler on his knee. Colter did a double take at the incongruous sight of the sergeant cooing at a baby. Ordway's eyes met Colter's and, swift as a cloud blocking the sun, Ordway's face fell into a scowl. "Off!" he commanded.

Not understanding the sudden change in his new-found playmate, the baby whimpered.

"Get away from me, you little savage," Ordway hissed.

Whimpering louder, the child recoiled. Whether that movement caused him to lose his balance or Ordway deliberately pushed him, the child fell, by some miracle barely missing hitting the next bench with his little head. He landed on his rump and burst into tears.

Colter scrambled over the intervening benches and retrieved the fallen little one. Relinquishing the baby to its mother, Colter flashed a look of rebuke at the sergeant.

"If you know what's good for you, you'll wipe that look off your face and get back to your post, Private," Ordway warned.

Colter let his glare stand as his reply.

11. *Celebration?*

T he canoes continued shuttling between the Teton village and *Discovery* all day. The last group of Sioux women and children returned to the shore in the late afternoon. Playing host had worn out the crew. Colter was not alone when he stretched out on the rowing bench for a nap after the order to stand down.

Ordway's rough shake ripped him out of a sound sleep. "Go see the captain."

Groggily, he joined the two Field brothers huddled with Captain Clark and Sergeant Gass. The captain's voice was too quiet. "Captain Lewis isn't back yet. I want you four to find out why. After yesterday, I'm sure I don't have to remind you that the last thing we want is a fight."

Ordway untied the pirogue's line and tossed it to Colter with a contemptuous "Good luck." Colter caught the rope but held his tongue.

On the way to the bank, Gass began his briefing in his usual positive way. "Chances are Captain Lewis just forgot the time. You all know how he is."

"Place is big, Sarge. How're we going to find the captain? We're way outnumbered," Joe said aloud the thoughts that were bashing against the walls of Colter's mind.

"By my count, there are only fifty warriors here," Gass replied. "About one for each tepee. Fifty warriors. But no guns. If you remember anything, latch onto that and the fact that you will not shoot *anything* without a direct order from me. Understand?"

Colter grunted noncommittally. By his count, the sergeant's estimate of fifty warriors was at least twenty too low. Besides, he knew from experience what damage arrows could do. He knew that, in the time it took a man to reload his rifle, even a fast reloader, a middling bowman could get off three arrows. That gave the Tetons a significant advantage. Add to that the problem of maneuvering their long rifles in close quarters, and the crew had a deadly challenge on their hands.

The pirogue nosed into the landing area, and two of the *engagées* got out to hold the boat while the search party disembarked. By the time Colter fell in behind Gass, curious Sioux lined the path up to the village. He walked into the human corridor with his heart in his throat.

Halfway up the path, Little Big Eyes appeared. She grabbed his hand and led him and the others the rest of the way into the heart of the Teton town, parting the crowd with imperious waves of one small brown hand.

Colter's heightened senses absorbed all the scenes he passed: the brilliant designs painted on the exteriors of the Teton lodges, each different from the others; the huddles of women and girls chattering in the alien babble of the Teton language while they fleshed out hides, stripped meat for drying, tended babies, and prepared food; the boisterous children and barking dogs racing among the tepees. Over everything hung the smoke of a dozen fires and the charnel smells of meat drying on racks.

The girl led them directly to a large tepee set in the center of the others. Its sides had been rolled up to allow the large audience of seated men gathered outside to see what was going on. Inside, Captain Lewis and the members of the expedition's party sat opposite Black Buffalo, Buffalo Medicine and Partisan. Shannon sat behind and to the left of the captain, absorbed in sketching.

Little Big Eyes interrupted Cruzatte's translation in a piping little-girl voice. Jerking his head around, Partisan glared fiercely at the child. In less than a heartbeat, the same pretty squaw as before appeared to whisk the little girl away. Colter realized then that Little Big Eyes was Partisan's child; the woman, his wife.

"Is there a problem, Sergeant?" Lewis asked Gass at the rescue party's approach. The captain sat cross-legged on a buffalo hide, his journal opened and balanced on his knees. Nothing in his manner suggested tension or fear.

"Not with us, sir," Gass said. "Captain Clark thought there might be one with you, though. He expected you back by now. It's been five hours."

"Five hours? Why, it seems that we just began," Lewis said, smiling expansively. Behind him, Shannon's pleased expression mirrored the captain's.

"Captain Clark's worried. What should I tell him?" Gass asked.

"Tell him that everything is under control. In fact, our hosts here have invited us to a celebration tonight."

"Apologies, sir, but is that wise, considering yesterday?" Gass asked.

"It is not a question of wise, Sergeant. It is the job the President gave us. We have to take every opportunity to salvage our relationship with these people. Now, you go relay my message to Captain Clark. The rest of you," he swung an arm at Colter and the Fields, "will stay here."

Shannon shot Colter a self-assured glance as Colter squeezed in between the Fields and the row of Sioux. He was much too close to Partisan for comfort and all too well aware that he was completely surrounded by Tetons to return Shannon's confident look.

Hartley crept through the undergrowth, choosing every step as if his life depended on it. Yesterday, he had witnessed two Sioux chiefs regaled in feather headdresses going aboard the keelboat. When the big boat weighed anchor to move upstream, the realization that he might lose his prey had made him reckless. And it was only by chance that he had spotted the Indian canoe and swung into the protection of a screen of willows before its Teton occupants saw him.

After lying low for what seemed like hours, worrying that he would lose his chance at Colter, he decided that using the canoe was too risky. With the help of stones, he sank the boat among a thick stand of reeds, then took off up the east bank on foot, relying on the remaining darkness to cover his passage.

Sometime after dawn he crept to the river to check his position from the cover of a tangle of driftwood. He was half a mile above the Teton village and perhaps a mile from the place where he had hidden his canoe. To his relief, he counted only three Indians on the opposite bank. The presence of so few Sioux gave him hope. The rest had probably followed the expedition upriver. If so, that would slow the expedition's journey considerably.

Hope eased his anxiety. He walked faster, his mind marking time with a silent chant: *Colter's mine. Colter's mine.*

Some time later — an hour or two by the length of the shadows — he again took his bearings and witnessed the expedition's white pirogue push away from the anchored keelboat, heading for the shore, and the red one returning, filled with Indians. He crept forward until he found a hidden vantage place abreast the keelboat and trained Bonhomme's telescope on the scene.

With his first sweep of the rowing deck, he located Colter. At the sight of his prey so close, a wave of euphoria washed over him. "You're mine, John Colter," he whispered. "All mine."

He entertained the idea of shooting Colter until he realized the folly in giving away his presence and position. Besides, he had come too far and endured too much to not stretch out Colter's demise.

Moments later, Colter and two other crewmen clambered into the white pirogue behind a fourth man in a sergeant's uniform. Through the glass, Hartley followed the canoe to the beach below the Indian village.

His elation collapsed when he saw the size of the Sioux encampment. Yes, the Indians had stopped the expedition, but they had also stopped him.

Under the star-studded sky, the Tetons arranged themselves in a ring around a large open space. In the middle of this, a group of squaws set about building a bonfire, while other women cleared away the remains of the meal. Shannon stifled a burp with a greasy hand. Delicious food. He never would have believed that dog meat tasted so good until he tried it. And, to his taste, the bread made from prairie turnips rivaled his mother's best efforts.

Although his back was stiff from sitting all day hunched over his journal and his fingers ached from jotting notes and sketching scenes from the Sioux town, he felt exhilarated. Today's talks had completely restored his good opinion of the Tetons and convinced him that yesterday's problems resulted from miscommunication.

The only sour note of the day was a wretched group of Omaha women and children, prisoners taken by the Tetons in a recent raid. They huddled together now off to one side of the main ring, eyes dull, downcast faces blotched and pinched with grief. During the talks earlier, Captain Lewis tried unsuccessfully to convince the Tetons to release the captives. Shannon hoped the captain would continue to press for their release tomorrow. After all his efforts, the captain deserved to score a diplomatic success.

A little girl with bewitching black eyes circulated among the crew, carrying a waterskin. Most of the men refused the water, instead wiping their greasy hands on their pants if they even bothered with that. Being in the wilderness was no excuse to ignore common cleanliness. Shannon held out his hands for the girl to pour water over them and returned her smile while he dried his hands on his kerchief. Only when his hands were clean did he pick up his journal, opening it to his last sketch, one showing Partisan sitting surrounded by his dog-soldier followers.

The little girl squealed with delight at the picture. She pointed at Partisan, then at herself.

"I don't understand," he said.

"She's sayin' Partisan's her pa." The comment came from Colter, who had come up on Shannon's right side.

"Hawk," the little girl said, beaming a smile at Colter who patted her head and smiled back.

"Thought you didn't like Indians," Shannon said.

"I don't," Colter said, sitting down when the little girl scampered off. "That's why I come to give you some protection. No tellin' how things are liable to go tonight."

A sudden throb of drums kept Shannon from replying. Two Teton men leaped into the ring and launched into a frenetic, yet mesmerizing dance. Shannon turned to a fresh page and began to sketch.

After a time, the rhythm of the drums changed slightly and more braves entered the dance. Another page, another sketch.

The tempo changed again. This time the men took seats and a line of women swayed into the ring. Shannon reached for a fresh stick of charcoal. Colter's hand stopped him. "You don't want to draw this, Fuzz."

"Why not?"

"Scalp dance. Omaha scalps. From their husbands and fathers." He hooked a thumb toward the prisoners.

Shannon's jaw dropped. In horrified fascination he watched human hair swing from poles to the accompaniment of eerie female keening. He was unaware he had not drawn anything until the women left the center of the ring and another men's dance began.

This time crewmen joined the dancing, led by York who leaped and whirled as if under the spell of the rhythm. Shannon set about capturing the black man's movements on paper. About that time, he noticed the smallish Teton brave following York around the fire, aping his moves with the perfection of a shadow. The incongruous sight dragged a laugh out of Shannon, relieving the tension built up during the scalp dance. In appreciation, he tossed a tail of tobacco at the feet of the short brave.

The Teton scooped up the gift, but, instead of tucking it into his waistband like the other dancers, he stalked to the captains and, brandishing the tobacco, spat out a string of demanding syllables. Cruzatte cleared his throat nervously. "This man, he say we are rich. Why do we give such poor gifts to our new friends?"

With the man's face in better light, Shannon's observant eyes recognized him as one of Partisan's followers, minus his usual paint and attire.

Captain Lewis's smile slipped. "Tell him this is a gift from the Great Father in Washington. There can be no better or higher honor than to receive such a gift."

The sneering brave let the tobacco drop into the dirt. He snatched a drum out of the hands of one of the musicians and flung it into the fire, then stomped off into the darkness among the tepees.

Even in the flickering firelight, the approval on Partisan's face was plain to see. Colter took up his rifle and whispered, "We're in for it now, Fuzz."

Shannon was skeptical. Still, he reached for his own rifle and powder horn. He found the rifle but realized that, in his rush to leave *Discovery* earlier, he had left his horn behind. How could he have done such a stupid thing? Hadn't he learned anything from his ordeal along the river about making sure he always had enough ammunition? All he could do now was hold his breath and wait for whatever was going to unfold.

The owner of the drum saved the moment. He dashed to the fire and pulled his damaged instrument from the flames. He tested it and found it still usable. Soon drum beats again filled the night air and the dancers resumed their gyrations.

"Let us put this incident behind us, men," Lewis counseled. "Keep dancing. We have nothing to be afraid of."

"And I'm the King of England," Colter muttered under his breath.

Shannon looked down at the unfinished drawing in his journal. Suddenly he had lost his appetite for being here. He wanted to be back on *Discovery* and he wanted to be far away from this place and these people. He closed the book.

"That last one ain't done," Colter said.

"I am," Shannon replied.

Colter watched with disbelieving eyes as Captain Lewis headed for the riverbank in the white pirogue. For no good reason that Colter could figure out, the captains had decided to stay with the Tetons another day.

Swinging down to the rowing deck, he was surprised to see Shannon still aboard. He had not gone with the captain as usual. Shannon held up a warning hand. "Don't say anything, Old Man."

"Who said I was goin' to?" Colter said.

"I didn't go back to the village today because I'm tired. And that's all."

"I wouldn't count on restin' up much then. Havin' Sioux crawlin' all over the boat ain't exactly restful."

"What are we supposed to do?" Shannon asked.

"Watch and make sure they don't take nothin'."

"Now you hold on! These people have done nothing, *nothing* to deserve being called thieves."

"Guess you forgot about Burr, huh?"

Shannon's combative expression turned strickened. "Burr. Oh, Lord."

"Burr what?" Colter asked.

Shannon struggled to get out the words. "The captain — didn't — He swallowed hard. "Yesterday Captain Lewis never once brought Burr up. Not once."

Colter kicked the gunwale in disgust. "I could've gone all day without knowin' that."

"What's worse, I forgot all about him myself," Shannon moaned.

"If'n the captain ain't tryin' to get our dad-blamed horse back, what in tarnation's he doin' stayin' here?"

"He's trying to open the river to American trade."

"Ain't that just dandy. We ain't got no horse, winter's comin', and Captain's jawin' about everythin' but gettin' us outta here."

"Listen up!" yelled Ordway, bringing an end to their conversation. "We'll use the red pirogue as a shuttle today with the following crew." He read off a list of names, ending with, "Colter, you take the rudder."

Colter swore under his breath. Shannon shushed him. "You want to get sent back like Reed?"

"Right now I'd go anywhere that Ordeal and them Sioux ain't."

"That's just what he wants, you know," Shannon said. "He wants you off the crew. And you're playing right into his hands."

Colter eyed Shannon who, for once, made sense. It was true. Ordway had been trying to get rid of him from the day they met back on the Mississippi.

Shannon touched his arm. "Don't let him get to you, Old Man."

Colter studied the earnest young face. "I'll think on it."

After Colter left in the shuttle pirogue, Shannon spent a restless day, alternating between feeling he had done the right thing by staying aboard the keelboat and suffering pangs of guilt for not going with Captain Lewis to record the day's happenings for posterity. At dusk, Sergeant Gass returned. He carried word from the captain that the Sioux had invited the expedition to another celebration that night.

By the time Captain Clark asked for volunteers to attend that night's celebration, Shannon's emotional pendulum had swung back to guilt and, after a slight hesitation, he stuck up his hand.

As he stepped into the pirogue, Colter said, "All rested up, are ye?"

Shannon gave him a disdainful smile. "Yes, thank you."

Colter saluted. "Then how 'bout rememberin' to make sure we get our horse back?"

Shrugging off the sarcasm, Shannon crawled to a vacant thwart and sat with his back to Colter, keeping his mind on the task to come and off the deadly river underneath him.

Upon landing, Gass took charge of the men headed to the Teton celebration, and Ordway assumed command of the shuttle crew. "We're to wait here for the captains," he announced. "Colter, you like excitement. You take the lookout up there." He pointed to the crest of the bank where a pair of Partisan's dog soldiers squatted on their haunches.

Colter spat into the dirt to show how he felt about once again being shoved into a dangerous position by a man he hated. "Problem, Colter?" Ordway asked.

Colter refused to honor the question with an answer. With his skin crawling under the Sioux pair's hostile gazes, he walked up the path.

While he stood waiting for whatever was to come, currents of cold night air lapped at the exposed skin of his arms and neck, while the throbbing of the Sioux drums stretched his nerves taut. What trouble did Partisan and his men plan to spring on the expedition tonight?

A figure appeared out of the darkness on the path near the tepees. Colter whistled down to the shuttle crew to be on the alert.

The figure drew closer. It was Labiche. Although the co-pilot walked slowly, Colter sensed the man's tension from ten paces. As Labiche reached Colter, Ordway joined them.

The co-pilot's tone was conversational; his message was not. "The Omaha prisoners say the Sioux mean to attack us tonight. Capitaine Meri, he say be ready for trouble."

After Labiche headed back to the village, Ordway turned to Colter. "That was one puny whistle, Colter. You wouldn't be nervous now, would you?" Ordway asked.

Colter's hatred for the man flared into an open flame. "If'n you're judgin' whistles, Sarge, here." He stuck his fingers in his mouth and let go a loud piercing whistle that brought a shout of "What's goin' on up there?"

from the crew down on the beach. "That better?"

"Some day, Colter, I'll —"

The drumming stopped abruptly, curtailing the sergeant's threat and turning the night suddenly colder. Torches appeared among the tepees, illuminating a crowd moving toward the river. Ordway and Colter returned to the canoe, and Colter took up a position near the stern to be ready for a fast getaway.

Gusting wind angled over the flames of the approaching torches. In that strange light, Colter picked out the captains behind Buffalo Medicine and Black Buffalo, and the protective shadow of York behind Clark. They were followed closely by Partisan and his usual entourage of dog soldiers.

Ordway saluted Captain Lewis's arrival. "Labiche brought your message, sir."

"The rumor was false, Sergeant. There is no need for alarm."

From where he stood, Colter had an unobstructed view of Partisan's face, lit by the flickering light of two torches. That face conveyed the wariness of a hunting wolf. The faces of the dog soldiers surrounding him echoed the same alertness. What was going on?

Partisan quirked his head slightly, and a woman came to stand at his side. Little Big Eyes's mother. Partisan's hand signs slashed the air. Cruzatte stammered through an unintelligible translation that forced Lewis to turn to Drouillard who was fluent in hand-talk. Speaking in a manner well-matched to Partisan's imperiousness, Drouillard said, "Le Partisan, he offers his woman to you for this night."

The offer rendered Lewis momentarily speechless. Recovering, he said, "I decline the offer."

"Capitaine, that you cannot do," Drouillard said in a flat voice that, nevertheless, warned of dangerous consequences.

The captain's tone turned shrill. "I can do so and I will. Now relay my answer to the chief."

Clark intervened. "Be sure Partisan understands that we mean no disrespect. Explain that it is not our way to accept such . . . gifts."

After Drouillard signed the captains' reply, Partisan's voice dropped into a string of rasped syllables. "Le Partisan, he say he has never heard of such ways."

Clark's eyes stopped smiling. "He has now."

Partisan moved three paces away from the captains before he spoke more. "Le Partisan, he wish to sleep this night on our war canoe — if such is our way."

"Why the — Clark growled under his breath. This time Lewis intervened. "Tell him we would be honored by his presence."

No sooner had Drouillard finished the translation than seven of Partisan's dog soldiers surged around their leader, ready to join him on *Discovery* for the night. Clark held up a restraining hand. "Tell the chief we have room for one of his followers. No more."

After a brief conference, all but one of the dog soldiers merged back into the crowd of Tetons, then Partisan and his chosen companion climbed into the pirogue. Clark and York followed.

The shuttle crew shoved off. Colter scrambled in last and took charge of the rudder. Between the day's rowing and the evening's tension, his arms and shoulders had stiffened up. Out on the river, the wind shifted quarters with every gust, and the current seemed equally fickle. To add to those challenges, Colter had to contend with the night's darkness and the lightest load of the day. With the rudder fighting his every move, he lined the canoe up with the middle of the keelboat, using the lanterns hung on *Discovery*'s stern and bow as guides.

Keeping the craft on course took every ounce of Colter's concentration plus both hands firmly on the rudder. His temples began to throb from the strain. As they drew close, he motioned for Ordway in the bow to take up the mooring line and prepare to toss it to the on-board landing crew.

At what he judged was the right moment, Colter swung the rudder to bring the pirogue's leeward side parallel to *Discovery*'s side. The canoe was almost in position when the current yanked the rudder out of his grip and the pirogue's nose came back round, slamming into the keelboat.

The blow threw Ordway into Partisan's lap in the pirogue and set *Discovery* rocking violently, in danger of capsizing. Then came the sounds of something tearing, followed by a snap. Clark braced himself against the sides of the teetering pirogue, shouting, "Anchor line's snapped! Boat's loose! All hands to oars!"

Colter scrambled to reclaim the rudder and held it for all he was worth. Up front, York, Rube, Joe, and even Ordway fell to paddling the pirogue away from the keelboat. Onboard *Discovery*, the remaining crew clambered onto the benches and jammed their oars into the water in desperation. Without synchronization, they worked against each other instead of helping. Meantime, the keelboat wheeled downstream, held firmly in the grip of the river.

"Make for shore! " Clark bellowed.

By now the bank had come alive with firebrands and movement. Along with whooping and shouts, the boom of a rifle carried across the water. Clark's voice was tense. "There's no telling what we'll find on landing, men, but we can't afford a battle. Not now. Have your rifles ready, but absolutely no shooting unless and until I give the order."

Armed Sioux thronged the banks. As the pirogue's nose scraped sand, Ordway and York leaped out to pull her in, Colter threw aside the tiller and grabbed up his rifle. Drouillard and a ruffled Lewis hurried over to the canoe. Although his hat was missing, the captain appeared unharmed. By contrast, to look at Drouillard, no one would guess anything out of the ordinary was going on. Shannon trailed the pair, hovering as close as a shadow.

"Good God, Will, what happened out there?" Lewis asked.

"Current caught us and rammed the canoe into the boat. Anchor line snapped," Clark said. "We heard shots. What's happened here?"

Partisan chose that moment to make his exit from the canoe. He signed disdainfully. "Le Partisan, he says his people come to defend their new paleskin brothers from the Omahas," Drouillard translated.

"Omahas?" Clark demanded. "What Omahas?"

Partisan went on signing. "The Omahas are our enemies. They lie and steal. They are not worthy of trust. Not like my people. The Teton Sioux will risk our lives to defend the paleskins from the Omahas."

Lewis looked down his nose at Partisan. "There are no Omahas. There is no attack. Call your men off." Drouillard performed the translation with nerveless skill that Colter had to admire.

The stalemate went on for more minutes before Partisan broke it. At a twitch of his hand his dog-soldier companion let out a chilling yelp that caused the armed Tetons to stop their advance and lower their weapons.

A shout from downstream alerted Colter and the others on the beach that the crew had managed to get the keelboat under control. "Without an anchor, we will have to tie up to shore tonight, Will," Lewis said.

Clark scanned the Sioux crowding the bank. "Looks like that's our only choice. Sergeant Ordway, move the pirogue down to *Discovery*."

While Clark walked down the bank with Lewis and York, Ordway turned to Colter. "If anyone got hurt because of that little stunt you pulled, you're going to pay and pay big."

Colter kept quiet. This was no time to point out that Ordway had put him on the rudder in the first place or that, without an anchor, they were sitting ducks for a Teton attack. This was going to be a long, long night.

He helped push the pirogue into the river, splashed into the stern and again took charge of the rudder. Shannon sat immediately in front of him. He was so pale Colter wondered if the younger man had been wounded. "You hurt, Fuzz?"

"N–no," came the shaky reply.

Before Colter could probe more, the pirogue hit the current, forcing him to apply his full attention to piloting. This time the river cooperated. He maneuvered the boat skillfully up beside the keelboat which was now moored under a low bluff.

Ordway was waiting for him when he stepped aboard. "Remember what I said, Private: your stunt will cost you. I'll see to it."

"You're out of line, Sergeant," Shannon said.

Thunder gathered on Ordway's face. "Oh?"

"Fuzz," Colter murmured, hoping to pull Shannon back before the sergeant savaged him, too.

"This is no time to ride anyone. We need to pull together," Shannon said. "All of us. In my father's unit, teamwork was the watchword."

Ordway's voice shifted into a squeaky falsetto. "Oh, yes. Daddy again." The voice slid back to a menacing register. "One more word out of you, Shannon, and you're in the log. Two more words, and you will be speaking to the captain personally. Three more words and you'll be headed downriver come spring."

Colter managed to push Shannon bodily away from the confrontation. "Get outta here, Fuzz. I'll handle this."

Glowering, Shannon reluctantly moved away.

Back to his falsetto, Ordway said, "I'll handle it." Then in his regular voice, "Why don't you, Colter? I'd like nothing better."

Colter yanked back hard on the reins of his rising anger. "I meant what I said. I will handle it, but not how you mean, Sarge. I ain't about to give you no such satisfaction. That'd be too easy."

"With you, Colter, nothing's too easy."

"Good. Wouldn't want you gettin' soft, Sarge."

"Captains'll want to talk to you tomorrow. You better get lots of sleep," Ordway said.

"Thanks. I plan to."

12. *Running Siege*

W ith the keelboat tethered to a shore teeming with armed Tetons, that night seemed endless. Everyone was exhausted, but no one slept. The captains ordered the lids of the on-board lockers raised to form a defensive bulwark and the crew to hunker behind that wall. Colter spent the night crammed shoulder to shoulder with Rube, Joe and Shannon.

At daybreak, Captain Lewis sent both pirogues out to search for the lost anchor. Colter and Shannon drew assignment to the red pirogue. No one had to say anything for Colter to feel that many of the crewmen blamed him for the mistake that had thrust them into such danger. He kept his head down and applied himself to his oar, praying that they could quickly locate the lost anchor and be on their way.

On the third pass he glanced at the shore to check their position and noticed that all the color had drained out of Shannon's face. "You OK, Fuzz?"

Shannon nodded, but his color did not improve.

"Colter and Shannon. Now there's a pair to draw to. A real cozy pair!" McNeal declared, making an obscene gesture for the benefit of anyone who missed the implication.

Colter let the remark pass without reaction and kept his attention focused on what the probing setting pole was finding on the riverbottom. The long pole was clumsy enough for a standing man to handle. It was even worse for a man kneeling. Still he did his best but to no avail.

Labiche turned the boat around and, once again, the men had to paddle hard to get back up to the right place to begin more testing of the riverbottom. The effort wrung the talk out of all the crew, except for McNeal. "This is your doin', Colter. You oughtta be out here searchin' the bottom by yourself."

"And you ought to shut up for once, McNeal." Although Shannon's voice was shaky, the glower he aimed at the cook was not.

Getting a rise out of Shannon goaded McNeal on. "Well, fancy that. Colter even lets Peckerwood fight his battles for him."

"I said shut up," Shannon warned.

"Fuzz —" Colter muttered.

"My, my, ain't you two the perfect couple," McNeal said.

Someone laughed, encouraging McNeal to go on. "Come to think on it, I always thought there was somethin' a might peculiar about how you and Colter stick together. Downright unnatural, I call it."

Shannon slammed down his paddle. "That's enough, McNeal."

"Truth hurts, huh, Shannon?" the cook said.

Shannon drew back his oar to take a swing at the cook. Colter caught it and wrested it out of Shannon's hand. "No, Fuzz."

This brought more derisive laughter from the other men, egging McNeal on. He leaned toward Shannon. "Come on, Peckerwood. Hit me."

Shannon reached out to retrieve the oar from Colter, but before he could grab it, his face contorted and he lost his breakfast all over McNeal.

Colter could not resist the opening. He said in a loud voice, "Couldn't have said it any better myself, Fuzz."

The pirogue crew exploded with laughter. Shannon groaned in humiliation. And the furious McNeal dashed himself in riverwater in an attempt to wash off the vomit. The laughter was just dying away when Labiche announced, "Capitaine Lewis, he signal us to come in."

At the bank, Lewis met them, with Ordway right on his heels. "Any luck?"

"*Rien*," Labiche answered.

With eyes driving into Colter like two steel spikes, Ordway said, "Captain, we need to talk."

Lewis waved him aside. "Later, Sergeant. Once we are away. We have wasted enough time here. Somewhere upriver we will improvise a new anchor. Get the men aboard. We are leaving."

Colter was too done in to feel any relief at the news of their departure. The best he could manage was a grim smile.

Shannon was rinsing out his mouth when Colter slid onto their rowing bench. "I know it don't taste good, but that there was a great shot. Just what McNeal deserved," Colter said.

Shannon smiled slyly. "It was, wasn't it?"

"The cook ain't likely to forget it neither."

Ordway's yell cut off whatever Shannon was about to say. "Shannon, untie us!"

"That son of a boil! What's he tryin' to prove, makin' you go in amongst them murderin' savages?" Colter snarled. "You stay. I'll go."

"Oh, no, you won't. That's my order. I'll carry it out." Shannon pushed himself off the bench and marched determinedly off the boat, down the plank, and up the bank, straight into the thickest part of the Teton throng. As this was occurring, Captain Clark ushered Black Buffalo into the keelboat's cabin and Captain Lewis had York shadow Buffalo Medicine, Partisan and the few followers back down the gangplank.

"Bring in the line!" Ordway called.

Shannon untied the rope and was coiling it as he walked back to the keelboat when a group of dog soldiers burst out of the crowd. One knocked him down and yanked the line out of his hands, and the others immediately stepped up to form a protective shield around their companion.

Colter was reaching for his rifle when Lewis yelled "Will!"

Clark came out of the cabin, trailing Black Buffalo. He quickly sized up the situation and called Cruzatte over. "Pilot, tell the chief here that those men are to return the line to Private Shannon. With an apology."

Cruzatte performed the translation and interpreted Black Buffalo's answer. "He say these men he does not control. These men follow Le Partisan."

At that moment, seeing the pleasure on Partisan's face, Colter understood that the expedition was caught in a power struggle between two rivals, Partisan and Black Buffalo. He saw too that the captains had already figured this out and deliberately separated the two chiefs. Whether this was a wise move or a deadly one, they would soon know.

A silent signal passed between Clark near the cabin and Lewis in the bow before Lewis whipped out his sword and positioned it over the mooring rope as if he intended to chop through it. "Private Shannon, come aboard," he ordered in a level voice.

Shannon appeared stunned as he started toward the boat. Clark took up the swivel cannon's firing taper and held it above the gun's touch point. "For the last time," he said to Black Buffalo.

Shannon still had half the distance to the boat to negotiate. If he did not pick up the pace, he would be the first one cut down when the shooting started.

Black Buffalo looked out over the throng of Sioux, then signed to Clark. "Give these men some tobacco in honor of our friendship," Cruzatte interpreted in a strained voice.

"No bribes. Release our boat," Clark demanded.

"A gift of tobacco." A note of pleading crept into the chief's manner.

Glaring at Black Buffalo, Clark plucked a twist of tobacco from his waistband and flung it into the wet sand at the edge of the river, then turned to the Teton chief. "You speak of your influence among your people. Show us that influence now."

A long unblinking look passed between Black Buffalo and Partisan before the latter gave an almost imperceptible nod and one of his dog soldiers hurried forward to pick up the tobacco. The man raised the twist into the air above his head and ululated as if he had just won a prize.

The fact of his own exposed position seemed to dawn on Shannon all of a sudden. He looked around frantically as if unsure where to go. "Just keep on comin', Fuzz," Colter said under his breath.

Shannon drew abreast of the demonstrating dog soldier, then hesitated. The sneering Sioux took a menacing step toward him, blocking his path.

"Oh, oh, Fuzz," Colter whispered.

Black Buffalo stepped to the gunwale and spoke to the Teton holding the mooring line. The man did not respond and a murmur passed through the crowd of Sioux gathered on the bank. Colter shifted his grip on his rifle, sure the fight of their lives was but a moment off.

Black Buffalo uttered one more curt syllable. The warrior let drop the mooring line as if it were an afterthought and stalked away, taking along the wall of his companions, including the Sioux menacing Shannon. *Come on, Fuzz. Hurry it up*, Colter urged silently.

Shannon bent to pick up the fallen line and looped it into a neat coil as he coolly paced back to the boat. Clark met him at the top of the gangplank and took the rope out of his hands. "Very good, Shannon," he said, with the hint of a grin playing at the corners of his mouth. "Let's away!"

The ribbon of water between the boat and the bank was the width of two pirogues when Shannon resumed his seat. There was a definite gray tinge to the skin of his face. "You're crazy, Fuzz," Colter said, clapping him on the back.

"But I'm alive, and it's finally over."

Colter did not have the heart to point out to him that Black Buffalo remained on board or that groups of Sioux were following them along the bank on horseback.

Horses. Damn it all! The Sioux still had Burr.

Every time Colter glanced at the bank during the next two days, Partisan and his followers were there, dogging the expedition's progress, trying any number of ploys to get the captains to stop again. The captains did pause twice, hoping for some positive result to show for their four-day delay. When nothing came of these halts however, they decided not to waste any more time. That decision was popular with all the crew, especially Colter.

Black Buffalo stayed aboard *Discovery*. Why he did so remained a mystery. He surveyed the passing scenery from the quarterdeck while smoking pipe after pipe of the expedition's tobacco. No one begrudged him the tobacco. As long as he was with them, the Tetons appeared unwilling to attack.

With their upriver progress little more than a running siege, there was no possibility to procure fresh meat or to escape the cramped quarters of the boats. A temporary anchor made from a net filled with stones allowed them to stay away from the banks at night, but the crew's conversations were as short as their tempers. The strain and lack of sleep were written on every man's face.

Since the incident with the mooring line, Shannon had been particularly withdrawn. Except for an occasional "yes" or "no," he did not talk for two days. Colter did not press him for conversation, figuring he needed time to sort out his thoughts now that he had finally learned some religion about Indians.

The second night, a wind sprang up. By the following morning it was strong enough to allow the crew to raise the sail. Throughout the morning, the wind continued to increase in intensity until, around noon, Black Buf-falo traded the quarterdeck for the cabin and the captains ordered the sail reefed.

The canvas had been secured only a few minutes when there came an ominous boom and a suspicious vibration coursed the length of the boat. Shannon tossed Colter a questioning look. Before he could say "hit a log," *Discovery* slid into a deep trough and landed with a jarring shudder that sluiced waves of river water over the gunwales. An unmoored box slid across the rowing deck and took a gash out of the wooden side while causing Colter's rifle to crash onto the deck. The combined cacophony of wind and water swallowed his curse and all but drowned out the order to let out some sail. Securing his rifle, Colter jumped up to help.

It took less than a foot of loosened sail to right the keelboat. He slid back onto the rowing bench. "Damn that wind! It'n the river are in cahoots. Won't neither of 'em give us an inch.

Shannon responded with a jerky nod. His eyes were clamped so tightly shut that his face looked warped. Colter had to lean in close to hear the words coming out of his barely moving mouth. "Are we sinking?"

The door to the cabin banged open and out wobbled a grimacing Black Buffalo. He looked around warily, then retreated back into the cabin.

"No, we're not sinkin', Fuzz," Colter said. "In fact, feels like the wind's a-droppin'."

Shannon nodded again but did not open his eyes. Colter let him be. If anyone had earned the right to be respected for his grit the last few days, Shannon had.

The cabin door opened again, and out came the chief and the two cap-tains. The trio climbed onto the *passe avant* where the chief made signs with nervous hands.

"He wants to be put off." Shannon's voice was brittle as a dried leaf as he watched the movement of the chief's hands through slitted eyes.

Clark waved the white pirogue alongside and helped hand the chief into it. The canoe headed to the bank carrying Black Buffalo.

"How'd you know what he was sayin'?" Colter asked Shannon.

With the keelboat out of danger, Shannon relaxed a trifle and opened his eyes. "Watching, mostly. At the councils. After awhile the signs started to make sense."

Colter looked at his seatmate in wonder. Whenever he thought he knew everything there was to know about Shannon, Fuzz surprised him.

They watched the chief step out on the bank, clutching the blanket and tail of tobacco the captains had given to him in parting. "Don't one bit like the thought of goin' on without a hostage," Colter said.

Shannon looked surprised, as if it had never occurred to him to think of the chief as such. Something about the look on Shannon's face brought thoughts of Hartley into Colter's mind. He realized he had not thought about the preacher for days now. Not since they reached the Tetons.

On the bank, Partisan swung off his horse and walked to meet Black Buffalo. Partisan. As much trouble as that surly Indian had caused the expedition, Hartley, out here by himself, was in for much, much worse. Colter found that thought most comforting.

In the two days since the keelboat headed upstream, the Sioux had been so active that Hartley could not risk following. Yet every minute he stayed put, Colter got farther away.

By noon of the second day, frustration overtook his caution. He decided to set out after dusk in pursuit. An hour later, a storm raced down the river, clearing the banks of Indians for the first time in a week. Hartley saw his opportunity and took it.

By the time he had refloated the canoe, rain had begun to pelt down. He kissed the paddle's handle. "God is with us. We both survived. Colter is ours now. Yours and mine."

As he dipped the paddle into the river, she seemed to echo, "Yours and mine."

13. *Arikara*

Whether the Tetons lost interest or decided they had enough of the freezing wind and soaking rain that continued for days after Black Buffalo's departure, they finally stopped trailing the expedition. After a layover day to hunt and make repairs, the crew continued upriver. Three long, hard-pulling days later, they arrived at the first of a cluster of three Arikara, or Ree, villages.

After setting up camp on an island, the captains engaged Tableau, a Ree-speaking French trader who was wintering there, to be translator and held another formal council. As a gesture of goodwill following the talks, the captains announced that parties of crewmen would visit all three Arikara villages: one party under Ordway; another under Gass; the third under the captains. The rest of the crew, led by Pryor, would remain behind to guard the camp and boats.

Primed by tales of the pliability of Ree squaws, for once the crew members clamored to be chosen for the visiting parties. And, for once, Shannon did not volunteer. He kept his head and hand down. The incident over the mooring rope at the Tetons had rocked his confidence. He no longer trusted his former views of Indians. He needed time to come to new conclusions. Time he did not get, thanks to Sergeant Ordway.

"Captain wants you with me, Shannon," Ordway said. "Bring what you need to do your drawing. The white pirogue in five minutes."

The trader Tableau was the third member of their party. He went along as interpreter for the visit. With the help of two *engagés,* they rowed up the river to the Ree village of Rhtarahe. It consisted of a cluster of large earth-and-grass-covered mounds, surrounded by a defensive wall, and stood on a bluff well above the high-water line. There was a landing stage at the base of the bluff and all the ground around the village had been divided into fields, delineated by brush fences. Shannon and the sergeant disembarked and followed Tabeau and the village headman, Chief Hay, up the path to the settlement. Curious Rees lined the route, their crush making Shannon uneasy.

The Indians' lodges resembled earth-covered beehives, built so close together that people had to walk single-file between them. At Chief Hay's lodge, Shannon ducked through the low entrance tunnel to discover an immaculate, well-organized, circular interior with a radius of thirty feet or so. Four central posts, placed in a square, supported large crosspieces to form the structure's basic framework. The rounded walls were shaped by a series of thinner posts positioned to run from the the ground to these crosspieces. Over this shell went a latticework of woven branches which was then mounded over with a thick layer of dirt and turf to form the exterior of the lodge. There was a central fireplace and a hole in the fifteen-foot-high domed roof for venting smoke.

Chief Hay waved the sergeant and Shannon to backed sitting platforms of stretched hides overlaid with buffalo robes. While they settled into their seats, Indians packed the lodge. Those who could not squeeze inside climbed up on the roof and peeked down through the smoke hole. So many people crowded onto the roof that dislodged chunks of turf began to fall into the fire. A short squaw screamed at the ones on the roof, shooing away all but a courageous few.

That accomplished, the squaw and two young girls served up a stew full of the vegetables grown in the surrounding gardens. Shannon was too nervous to have an appetite. He ate a few bites out of courtesy, then put aside his bowl and took out his journal.

As he opened the book, a group of young Ree women flocked around him. He attempted to wave them away so he could work, but they pressed in closer, jostling him and laughing. One of them snatched the stick of charcoal out of his hand. As he grabbed for it, his backrest collapsed and he fell into the lap of one of the women.

She spoke a few sharp syllables and the group backed away from him. He righted himself and smiled gratefully at her.

She smiled back, revealing a gap between her two front teeth. She pointed to the gap, then to his, then to the blank page of his open journal.

"Oh, you want me to draw a picture of you. Of course. Here." He dashed off a sketch and turned the book to allow her a better look. She clapped her hands in delight and began speaking. "Tabeau, what's she saying?" he asked.

"Your peecture. She weeshes to trade you for eet."

Tabeau's leering grin left little doubt what the woman offered to trade. Shannon had no intention of going along with it. After Lisette, he wanted nothing to do with women. "Tell her she can have the picture, for free."

"What's your problem, Shannon? You paid money for it in St. Charles. Only difference here is that the price is a sketch," Ordway said in a level voice that belied the calculation in his gaze.

"'It' is my business, Sergeant."

"No, Shannon. 'It' is the business of us all. Tell him, Tabeau."

The trader leaned forward. "Thees ees the wife of Chief Hay. To refuse her ees to deeshonor heem."

Nothing in Shannon's experience had prepared him for such a situation. He had seen enough councils now to understand the high value Indians placed on honor. But what about his honor, his vow?

The woman turned from Shannon and spoke to Chief Hay.

"Shannon," Ordway hissed.

Shannon realized that he was on the verge of creating a complication for the expedition. He had to act quickly to salvage the situation. He ripped the picture out of the journal and laid it in the chief's hands. Hay examined it and grunted to his wife who stood up and waited for him to do the same.

"Eet would be better eef you smile at her," Tabeau whispered as Shannon got to his feet.

"I can't," he murmured.

"Oh, yes, you can," Ordway said flatly. "There are only two of us, remember."

It took enormous effort to draw up a corner of his too-dry mouth. Whether the effort produced a grimace or a smile, the woman did not seem to care as she led him through the crowd to the back of the lodge. Shannon's mind swirled with thoughts he could not grasp. His body moved after her as if responding to the commands of an entity unseen and unknown. Ree chatter flowed out of the crowd, over and around him like water flowing around a rock.

Along the back wall of the lodge, several platforms had been built. These sat a foot off the dirt floor under the curve of the roof and were draped with hide curtains for privacy. The woman swept aside one of the curtains and waited for him to sit on the pile of buffalo robes. When she let the curtain drop and crawled in next to him, he experienced the sensation that had happened to him that last night with Sarah Cooper: it was as if his eyes had separated from his head and floated to the roof where they gazed down upon his body, sitting stiffly next to the Ree woman.

She stretched out on the robes. The curtains had not closed completely. Through the crack, the power of sight that remained in Shannon's head glimpsed the Indians standing inches away.

She touched his back. He flinched involuntarily and would have fled if his body had been able to cooperate. Strong hands pulled him down onto the bed. He had no strength to resist. From above, he watched himself. *This is your duty. You must do it.* The words rang hollowly in his unresponsive mind.

She muttered in Arikara and tugged at his clothing.

She is the chief's wife.

His body felt numb, unyielding. Her muttering grew louder; her tugs, more insistent. He had to move or face the consequences. He shut his eyes and tried to bring Lisette's image to mind. The face with its alluring pout wavered into his mind's eye, and, just as quickly, it vanished.

The squaw raised up on an elbow to frown at him. Petulance was gathering behind her eyes. He was only seconds away from total failure.

Another scene flitted across his mind then. One he would never forget: the sight of *Discovery* rounding the bend to save him from starvation and sure death. The moment that would forevermore define the sweet, sweet life that still coursed through his veins.

The squaw swatted his chest and started to slide off the bed. Shannon caught her hand. He loved his life, and he meant to keep it for as long as the Almighty allowed. "Don't go, please. I'm . . . a little off today is all."

The woman hesitated but moved back next to him. "That's better," Shannon said, brushing her cheek and winning a tentative smile from her. The gap between her teeth lent her a girlish quality that he found suddenly endearing.

Her hand brushed his cheek, and, in the matter of a moment, he cast away his former vow of chastity in favor of a brand-new experience.

The keelboat sat at anchor upstream from a big island containing a busy Indian village and expansive fields. Seeing this, Hartley knelt in the bottom of the canoe to thank God for answering his prayers.

He was almost too weak to get back up on the seat. He had spent eight nights creeping upstream in his canoe, and eight days hiding from Indians, catnapping for sleep, existing on the few fish he managed to snag when he could risk leaving cover, eating them raw because he dared not chance a fire.

Then terrible high winds on the ninth day forced him to stay off the river. The inactivity, combined with fatigue and his deteriorating physical condition, threw him into a depression. For the first time he allowed himself to consider that he might not catch John Colter. The idea of failure had forced him onto his knees to pray, a habit he had practiced before only in public when there was something tangible to be gained — tangible like the attention of some moneyed widow. This time, however, he had begged for God to help him in his quest.

Now, here in front of him, after ten long days of doubt, was proof that God heard and answered.

He backed downstream to an eddy on the northeast bank. He took pains to hide the canoe and struck off searching for a likely spot for fish. He quickly found a pool, and the instant he dangled the hook in the water, he felt it jerk. He smiled. God was definitely on his side.

When the pirogue bearing Shannon hove into sight, the last party to return from visiting the Ree villages, Colter heaved a sigh of relief. He had had a bad feeling most of the day. A feeling that Shannon was in trouble.

He helped draw the canoe onto the sand, then helped Shannon out. Seeing the younger man's dazed look, he waited for Ordway to leave before asking, "What happened, Fuzz?"

"Nothing," Shannon replied quietly. Too quietly.

"That ain't what your face is sayin'," Colter said.

Shannon shrugged and began to walk away.

"Ordeal give you any trouble?" Colter asked.

Shannon stopped. "For pity's sake, Old Man, can't you give a body a break? I sketched all day, and I'm tired."

There was little force or conviction behind the complaints, and Colter swept a stagy bow. Shannon could not keep quiet for long. He would be blabbing about the day soon enough. He was about to head to the camp when he spotted the younger man's journal lying on the pirogue bench. He thought to yell at him, but Shannon had already crawled into the tent.

Colter's curiosity overcame his opposition to snooping. He opened the book. He recognized the last sketch as one Shannon had made during the Ree council yesterday. Next to it, in the crease, were the raw edges of a torn-out page. If Fuzz had drawn all day as he claimed, where were the pictures? And what had been on the torn-out page?

He closed the book and glanced toward the tent. Whatever had happened today, if it was important enough for Shannon to hide, it was important enough for him to uncover — and soon.

Hartley's eyes shot open. He sniffed the air and listened hard for sounds of any other presence in the cave. Sensing nothing, he kicked off the dirty blanket, got to his feet and stretched the kinks out of his back. Today, his long quest would end. Today, John Colter would die.

Last night, using the cover of darkness, he had paddled past the expedition's camp, then backtracked through the undergrowth along the riverbank. His reconnaissance decided him to act now while the tired crew was not playing host to any Indians.

On his way back to his canoe, he had come across a cave where he could have a fire to cook some fish and dry others and warm himself. The cave had made possible his first real relaxation since St. Charles.

He knelt now to repack his belongings. The fish he had caught and dried filled his pouch. *Good for you, Preacher*, he thought. *Enough food to last you all the way back to St. Louis.*

Pleased with himself, he checked the cave to make sure he did not forget anything, then kicked apart what was left of the fire before heading for the river. With a full belly and a good night's sleep, he felt wonderful. He moved through the autumn-stained undergrowth that was thinning with winter's approach, charting his route up to the expedition's camp by the trees and boulders he had used as landmarks yesterday. For the hundredth time, his mind turned over his vision of Colter's death and the satisfaction he would get when the man breathed his last.

Rounding a point, he saw that the expedition's flotilla was already on the move. The three boats were working their way up the current on his side of the river. The keelboat was behind the two pirogues. As he had hoped, the keelboat's crew were strung along the bank, hauling on the cordelle. His spirits soared when he recognized the man on point: Colter. Bonhomme's telescope brought the man's face with its cursed birthmark into sharp focus.

Hartley scuttled on hands and knees into the undergrowth until he had enough cover to rise into a crouching run. He knew just the spot to set up an ambush. By now the crewmen he had run into downriver would have forgotten him, and no one would suspect that a white man was this far upriver. While they were looking for Indians to blame for killing Colter, he would be on his way downriver, ready to receive the rewards he had earned and content in the knowledge that Colter would never again pose a threat to him or Farley Stuart.

He arrived out of breath at the place where a substantial creek entered the Missouri. Tricky footing here would force the towing crew to spread out, making Colter on point especially vulnerable and giving Hartley enough time to make his get-away. He played the scene through in his head, then picked his position and hunkered down to wait.

A branch snapped. A pair of bronzed hands grabbed his left arm; another pair, his right; and he found himself dragged to his feet.

PART 4

MANDAN WINTER

Winter 1804 – 1805

The Mandans are the most friendly and well disposed
savages that we have yet met."
— Meriwether Lewis in a letter to his mother,
Winter 1804-1805

1. *Fragrant Grass*

End of October, 1805 — Confluence of Missouri and Knife Rivers

F ragrant Grass sawed at a clump of her hair with a stone lance blade,
biting her lower lip to keep from crying out at the painful tugging on
her scalp. The knot of hair came free an instant before a twig snapped on
the path leading to the clearing in which she hid. She flung the blade to the
ground and covered it with her foot.

She shoved the hand clutching the shorn hair up her sleeve an instant before a figure entered the clearing. Her fluttering heart calmed a little when
the figure turned out to be her sister Mint, rather than Sly Wolf, the man
the two women now shared.

"There you are, my sister. I have been looking everywhere for you,"
Mint said. Her eyes were merrier than usual, and there was an excited
pinkish cast to the tawny skin of her oval face.

"I was out walking," replied Fragrant Grass.

Mint sighed sympathetically. "It is not good for you to spend so much
time alone. You need to share your mourning with us who love you."

Fragrant Grass dropped her gaze. She could never admit her secret. Her
sister stood in too much awe of Sly Wolf for that.

"With winter coming, our husband will be in the lodge more," Mint said
in the indirect way she always used when approaching some scheme that
involved her husband.

Fragrant Grass kept her eyes down. *Sly Wolf is your husband*, she thought.
He will never be mine. No man can ever be such to me again.

Mint's tone became conspiratorial. "Next summer I want to give him a
son."

For the first time Fragrant Grass smiled. Perhaps her sister could keep
Sly Wolf busy enough for the winter that he would not think about coming
to her sleeping robes.

"There is so much weighing on our husband's heart. Sometimes I wonder
how he can rest. I wish I could help him more," Mint said.

For as long as Fragrant Grass could remember, Sly Wolf had aspired to
the highest status among their Mandan people. His marriage to her sister
had been one in a long series of steps calculated to reach that end. Although her own husband Strikes Two had been ambitious like all men, no
one matched Sly Wolf for conniving to better himself. Mint worshipped
her husband and refused to acknowledge his scheming for what it was.

"You keep his lodge presentable for his guests. You prepare his favorite foods and decorate his clothing with clever designs that are the envy of all. He is a fortunate man, indeed," Fragrant Grass said gently.

Mint flushed with pleasure at the flattery. "I try to be a good wife." Her fingers brushed the ragged ends of the just-cut clump of Fragrant Grass's hair. "I wish I knew why your hair will not grow back."

Fragrant Grass tensed under her sister's touch. No one must know that she had been cutting her hair instead of letting it grow back. No one, especially Sly Wolf. If he knew, he would surely demand his rights as husband. The thought sickened her.

Mint leaned forward, a hint of mischief in her eyes. "The first time our husband comes to your bed, you will forget your sorrow."

Fragrant Grass had to work to keep her thoughts separate from her expression. *Sly Wolf will never share my robes. Never!* She squeezed Mint's hand. "Speaking of our husband, it is late, and he will —"

The sight of three boats on the river made her stop talking. Two of the craft resembled the masted canoes used by the paleskins who came from the north every summer to trade for furs and buffalo robes. Behind them came the biggest boat she had ever seen. It resembled a monstrous insect with a dozen legs lumbering across the surface of the water. The sight of it sent a shiver coursing through her body.

"Indian town to port!" called Cruzatte from the quarterdeck. The two captains hurried to the bow. The town stood atop a fifty-foot bluff with the Missouri curling around its base. It looked to Colter like the Ree towns farther south: a cluster of forty or so large earth mounds set close together behind a defensive picket wall.

"Mandans," Rube whispered from the bench behind Colter.

"Mandan squaws," Joe corrected, playfully nudging Shannon in the back.

Shannon did not react to the prod. He had been entirely too quiet since he went to that Ree village with Ordway eleven days back. Colter had tried without success any number of times since to get him to open up, but Shannon refused to talk about what had happened there.

By the time the anchor dropped, Mandans filled the path from the beach to the blufftop and stood two deep along the picket wall with more gathered on the roofs of the mound lodges on the river side of the town. The captains and Tabeau rode the small pirogue into the town's landing stage. More delay. October would be gone in seven days. For the last two weeks, V's of geese, swans, cormorants and ducks had graced the skies. Soon they would disappear and winter would grip the land, the river, and the expedition who had yet to catch a single glimpse of the Shining Mountains.

Wondering how much more time would be wasted at this stop, Colter took out the knot of wood he was carving into the figure of a buffalo, inspired by the first one he had seen. Unsheathing his knife, he noticed Shannon staring at two women standing in the high grass downstream from the village.

The pair might have been twins except for differences in their height and hair. The shorter one had a full mane of long blue-black hair held away from her face by a leather band. By anyone's standards she was stunningly beautiful, yet it was the other woman who held Colter's attention.

She stood a head taller than the other. Her inky hair had been hacked into ragged clumps. Over her right temple there was an unusual streak of stark white hair, lending her an expression of perennial surprise. That she seemed so familiar troubled him and he countered the feeling by saying, "See somethin' you like, Fuzz?"

Shannon reacted as if he had been insulted. "Why do you always have to be at me, Old Man? Butt out."

"What's got you actin' like some sore head, jumpin' down my neck 'cause I'm tryin' to make conversation?"

"You know what's bothering me, Old Man? You. You and your annoying questions. All you do is talk. Why don't you shut up for a change?"

"Why, yes sir, General Shannon, sir," Colter said, shooting Shannon the mocking salute he had used on Colter more than once. He then turned to the Fields who looked equally baffled by Shannon's outburst. "The general here don't want no talk. Got him a hair up his behind."

The call came to bring the keelboat to the landing stage. "We gotta go now, Fuzz," he whispered.

Shannon shot him a frown and went back to gawking at the Mandan woman.

The village of Matootonha buzzed with speculation about the paleskins and their enormous war canoe. Fragrant Grass shut out the talk for fear she would say or do something that would give away the turmoil she had experienced since spotting the sign of Hawk Spirit on the face of one of the newcomers yesterday. Since Strikes Two's death, she had spent hours beside his grave, seeking guidance from Him Who Sees All for a way out of her grief and out of Sly Wolf's clutches. Now this newcomer had come wearing a powerful sign. Only she did not understand what she was being guided to do.

Mint dashed into the lodge, out of breath with excitement. "Our husband brings the paleskins here to our lodge. Quick, we must prepare food for them."

Fragrant Grass stashed her sewing under her bed platform, then went to help her sister uncover one of the lodge's sunken food caches. As they worked, she asked as casually as her nervousness would allow, "Which of the paleskins come?"

"They have two chiefs, both taller than any men you have ever seen," Mint said. "One has hair the color of red clay. The other one has pale hair the color of buffalo grass at the end of summer."

Playfully, she flipped several squashes from the cache to Fragrant Grass who caught them cleanly and piled them into a basket. "The chiefs are big but not as big as the black giant with them. That one is tall enough to see over any lodge, and his head is as big as one of our mother's prize pumpkins."

Fragrant Grass let pass the reference to their dead mother. Speaking of the dead inside the lodge was apt to bring bad luck. She suppressed a frown and waited for her sister to get around to telling her what she most wanted to know.

Mint jabbered on. "The giant's skin is the color of ripe acorns and the hair on his head looks like a mat of damp moss. One of his huge hands could reach around my waist."

Fragrant Grass had to smile at such an exaggeration. Mint went on. "Like the traders from the north, these paleskins are as hairy as bears, especially on their faces. Do you think, sister, that they are sent from the Great Bear Spirit?"

"Perhaps," Fragrant Grass said, then gave Mint a teasing wink. "Which one is your favorite?" When her sister did not answer or look at her, she made a guess. "Ah, so it is the one with the gap between his teeth. The one we saw yesterday. And your excitement tells me that he too comes to our lodge."

Mint hid her grin behind a hand. Fragrant Grass turned to prepare the vegetables for the stew. She wanted to ask about the other one, the one marked by the Hawk Spirit, but she dared not. Her sister must not know of her interest in the man. No one must know until she understood why Him Who Sees All had sent him.

Shannon made sure he was the last of the group to reach the pirogue that would shuttle Lewis and a contingent of guards back upriver to the Mandan town from the expedition's camp. Ever since Ordway picked him to be part of the squad, his emotions had been swinging unpredictably between the two extremes of guilt and anticipation. Guilt, because bedding the Ree squaw had caused him to stop denying his lustful nature. Anticipation, because the only thing he had thought about since yesterday was the beautiful Mandan woman and how very much he wanted to slake the carnal thirst she raised in him.

He took the last empty seat in the pirogue, feeling the familiar panic that came whenever he was about to set out on the river in a small boat. Colter and Rube sat in front of him. They were talking and did not acknowledge him which suited him fine, given the state of his emotions.

Lewis sat on one of the benches in the bow with a French trader named Jesseaume, whom the captains had discovered yesterday at the Mandan town and subsequently hired as translator. To Shannon's eyes, the only thing to recommend the man was his ability to speak Mandan. Otherwise, from an overabundance of filthy hair to his lumbering gait and bestial manners, he resembled a mangy, bad-tempered bear.

Behind Shannon, two of the *engagés* carried on a muttered conversation. He did not need to understand their words to hear their anger. Three days ago Captain Lewis had announced his decision to keep the entire crew together over the winter rather than allow the *engagés* to return to St. Louis as originally planned. The rivermen were paid only as long as the expedition was underway. Over the winter, they would be on their own for food and shelter. Shannon empathized but shut out their grousing. Complaining did not help them or him.

At Matootonha, Mandans crowded around the crew as they made their way up the path from the river. At the top of the bluff, the artist in Shannon quickly picked out the differences between this Mandan town and the Ree villages downriver: the set and spacing of the pickets in the defensive wall, the dimensions of the mound lodges, the designs on the pouches, shields and clothing of the people.

Once inside the defensive wall, Jesseaume pulled a squaw out of the gathered crowd and presented her to Lewis as his wife. Shannon was stunned. The woman was the beauty he had spotted yesterday. The one responsible for his fitful slumber last night. The one who had ripped down the walls he had constructed around his memories of bedding the Ree woman. This gorgeous creature, married to a half-human lout like Jesseaume — What a tragedy!

Shaken, Shannon followed the captain and the rest of the group to an open plaza in the heart of the village. In the center of it stood an odd circular fence, as tall as a man and as big around as the hogshead it resembled. Next to that structure stood Big White, the First Chief of Matootonha, and another man with the posture and bearing of a rising politician. The pair came forward to greet the expedition members and lead them into a nearby lodge.

As soon as Shannon ducked inside, he was jolted again. The same beautiful Mandan woman was bent over the cooking fire. It took a moment of looking before he realized that this Beauty was not Jesseaume's woman. That one had worn different clothing and had stayed out by the picket wall.

Colter whispered over his shoulder, "Twins, Fuzz."

Of course. His Beauty was a twin sister to Jesseaume's woman. He grunted at Colter when what he really wanted to do was cheer.

With every jouncing step, the bones of the horse's bare back jarred Hartley. There was not a muscle or bone or ligament in his body that did not ache. He bit back his groans. He refused to show his Indian captors weakness.

As near as he could figure, it had been fourteen days since they seized him, lashed him onto this horse, and forced him to ride along with them. Between fear of his captors and the difficulty of staying atop the spirited horse with his hands bound behind his back, his memory of the ride contained huge gaps. He had no idea where he was or how far they had come.

Over time he had gradually adapted to his mount's gaits and moods, and he had grown used to the Indians' rough handling. He found their language almost pleasant on the ear but, early on, he gave up trying to understand it even when he sensed them discussing him.

His captors belonged to a hunting party. He guessed that they were part of some Sioux band. The extra horses dragged travois filled with the meat and skins of elk, deer, buffalo, rabbits and fowl.

He did not let such evidence of the Indians' hunting skill keep him from considering escape. Overpowering one of the night guards would be easy, especially if it were one of the younger braves who guarded the horse herd. But there were two problems: he had no idea how to get back to the Missouri River and he had no weapon. Still, the longer he remained a captive, the farther away Colter moved, and he had come too far and endured too much to give up now, Sioux or not.

The leader of the hunting party yelled something that spurred the Indians into a gallop. Hartley's mount lunged after them, and the preacher had to hang on with all his might to keep from falling off.

Ahead, wisps of smoke tailed into the wintry sky. Drawing closer, he made out a cluster of mound lodges enclosed by a picket wall and, beyond them, a patchwork of fields, lying fallow for winter. Beyond the fields lay a river.

He blinked. Could it be?

He blinked again.

It was! He had found the Missouri.

"Thank you, Lord Jesus!" he croaked.

Riding up on Hartley's right, one of the Indians shouted something in reply.

"Damn right, you bloody savage. I have been delivered!"

2. Drooler

O nce the expedition arrived among the Mandans, winter clamped down on the land with a vengeance, and the captains decided to stop. They chose a site for their winter fort six miles below the confluence of the Knife River with the Missouri and three miles below, but on the opposite bank from, Matootonha. The hills bordering the broad river valley sloped upward from the bottomland to a height of five hundred feet. The fort was to be situated at the base of one of those rimming bluffs.

Although Colter immediately saw the strategic advantages of the site, he would have preferred something farther from the Mandan town — and the squaw with the white streak. Her image haunted him waking and sleeping. In Ordway, he already had enough to deal with over the winter. He did not need anything else, especially a woman and most especially a squaw.

The sergeant's sudden appearance curtailed his thoughts. "Colter, Rube, Joe, get your gear and meet me at the boat in five minutes."

"Want to tell us what's up, Sarge?" Joe asked. Of the entire squad, Joe and McNeal were the only ones who could get away with asking questions of Ordway.

"Captain Clark wants a squad to lay in some meat before the snow gets too deep. Drouillard will lead you." Ordway pronounced this last with a speculative glint in the gaze he aimed at Colter.

Colter smiled back. Going off on a hunt meant getting out from under the sergeant's thumb for a few days and escaping the drudgery of building another fort. For both of those gifts, he was willing to pay any price, even putting up with the know-it-all half-breed.

The first day out, the party found game in quantities none of them had ever experienced. Around the fire that night, they shared the congeniality that comes from seeing an early end to a shared task. Colter rolled into his blanket completely satisfied for the first time in weeks.

Overnight, temperatures plunged. The next morning he and the others awoke to find the world around them gripped in deep snow and a cold so intense that no matter how big the fire they built, no one could get warm. Moving at all became an effort.

Morale plunged along with the temperature, but Drouillard appeared unfazed by either the weather or the men's deteriorating attitudes. He insisted the squad lay in even more meat.

From glaring silences to loud complaints, nothing the men tried got the half-breed to relent. The freezing days dragged by one after another; the pile of meat grew; and, still, Drouillard showed no sign of heading back to the fort site. Instead he seemed to thrive on the biting wind and the sleet-choked days.

Listening to Rube and Joe's angry muttering one morning, Colter suddenly had enough. Time for someone to call the half-breed's bluff. He flung a full cup of lukewarm broth into the fire and stood up. "I count thirteen days today," he said to Drouillard.

The half-breed continued to coax more flames from the sputtering fire.

"Captain Lewis said two weeks," Colter said.

Still, Drouillard failed to acknowledge what he had said.

Colter jammed his hands deeper into his pockets. "We got us a heap of meat."

The half-breed shifted back onto his heels and looked at him for the first time. Colter went on. "River ice'll be solid before you know it."

No one had dared to challenge Drouillard's leadership before. Colter felt the other men holding their breaths and waiting to see what would happen. "It'll be hell to pay gettin' back upriver with all that meat, what with the Missouri as icy as she's gettin'."

Drouillard got slowly to his feet. He stared at the flames for a long moment before he looked back at Colter. He continued to remain silent.

"We're for headin' back right now," Colter said. "You hear me, Drooler?"

With the slur hanging in the air, Drouillard said, "You stay."

Colter shot a help-me glance at the Field brothers. Rube jabbed the air with a clenched fist of support. "We're leavin', and we're goin' now."

Colter turned to the other men. "Who else is for goin' back?"

Joe Field, Potts, Wiser, Bratton — each one said, "Me."

"Six against one, Drooler," he said. "In this here country, majority rules. You comin' with us, or stayin' here?"

The half-breed's face remained an unreadable blank. "Eat now."

"No, by God, we're —"

Drouillard's sharp look lopped off Colter's sentence. "Eat now, then go."

As the Arikara shaman's chant dragged on, Hartley struggled to keep from fidgeting. Every minute's delay put John Colter that much further out of his reach, yet he dared show no disrespect. These Rees were worse than the bloody Papists when it came to rituals.

It had cost him two weeks of effort to overcome the Indians' skepticism to get to this point. Two weeks that began when he walked into Chief Hay's lodge to find a display of the gifts the expedition had left behind: medals, pieces of Army uniforms, ribbons, strings of beads, mirrors. He had barely digested that stroke of good luck when he met Tabeau, the French trader who had acted as interpreter between the two captains and the Rees.

It was Tabeau who told him that the expedition had stopped for the winter with the Mandans to the north. Using that bit of information, Hartley cooked up a story to explain to the Indians why he had been traveling upriver alone: he carried secret information from the Great White Father to the leaders of the paleskins.

The Rees swallowed the story but balked at helping him catch the expedition. He spent several days talking in circles until he realized that some of the men on the village council believed his story too much. They saw him as a way to get ransom from the expedition leaders and argued to hold him at their village until a delegation of council members could ride to the Mandans to arrange for the right price for his release. Hartley had no intention of staying with the Rees now that he knew where Colter was. Realizing that winter would soon make travel impossible, he kept talking.

His life with the Indians was not all frustration. It had its rewards, too. Rewards in the form of the chief's wife who took him to her sleeping robes every night. His few previous experiences with women had not prepared him for such a willing partner. She had a responsive body and an adventurous streak.

His efforts to get the Rees to help him had seemed dead until yesterday when the two hold-outs on the council suddenly changed their minds. The Rees agreed to let him leave. Delighted, he bargained for a horse with the only thing he had left to trade: Bonhomme's telescope.

Once he was free, he wanted to strike off immediately. The Rees, however, offered to let him accompany a hunting party headed upriver the next day. In a weak moment he allowed the inviting smile of the chief's wife to convince him that he needed one more night in the village. As he sat now listening to the shaman's droning, he regretted his choice. He had not counted on having to endure an interminable ceremony before the hunters took off. All this chanting was giving him a headache.

Finally, the shaman gave his rattle one final shake and stepped aside allowing the hunters to ride out through the breach in the defensive wall.

When they had gone a hundred yards or so, Hartley glanced back at the town. He picked out the chief's wife among the women waving at the departing men. Fiona Stuart had wealth, but she would never stir his ardor like this Ree woman. Perhaps he ought to come back here after killing Colter. After all, there was no reason to hurry back to St. Louis. Winter would last for months. Wasn't it better by far to spend the cold nights wrapped in a warm buffalo robe with an enthusiastic woman rather than shivering alone on a musty straw mattress in some dark, smelly room, waiting to book passage on a boat up the Ohio?

He raised an arm to return the squaw's wave. Yes, he would come back — after he saw Colter die.

Colter had to look at his hands to see if he still had hold of the oar. He had not been able to feel his fingers for hours. While his hands were numb from cold, the rest of him sweated from the exertion of paddling. Though the mound of frozen meat, tied in the center of the pirogue between him and Drouillard at the prow, left scarcely enough room to kneel, he felt lucky to be in the boat. The rest of his five crewmates staggered along the snowy bank, bent under the pirogue's towing line, engaged in a tug-of-war with the Missouri's fickle currents.

The steely sky was just bright enough to tempt him to shut his eyes, but there were too many ice chunks in the river to risk such a thing.

In the bow, Drouillard rose on his knees and craned to look ahead. "*À droit*," he ordered.

Colter shifted his paddle to the port side and used it as a rudder. The nose swung, allowing a wedge of ice to slide past. Another of Drouillard's mysterious talents was the ability to read the river with uncanny accuracy.

"*Gauche!*" Drouillard called out.

Again Colter swung the boat out of the way of danger, then he lifted his paddle slightly in order to adjust his grip.

"*Gauche vite!*"

The half-breed's sudden urgency quickened Colter's pulse. He plunged the oar into the river and endured the icy water that splashed up his arm. This time, however, his ruddering had no effect. The canoe's nose did not come around.

"*Encore, vite!*" Drouillard yelled.

Colter dug again, but the pirogue seemed held fast. He chopped a third stroke.

Before he could set the oar for another, there came a thud and the sickening sounds of splintering wood. Icy riverwater flooded through a hole in the bottom of the canoe. "We're sinkin'! Pull us in!" he shouted to the men on the bank.

While he paddled furiously toward the bank, water rose steadily inside the boat and the canoe grew heavier and clumsier. It took the Fields wading into the river up to their chests and pulling the boat into the shallows to save the pirogue and its load from sinking completely.

Colter helped wrestle the canoe onto the bank, then collapsed on the nearly-frozen ground. By the time he caught his breath, Drouillard had a fire going. If the accident affected the half-breed, he did not show it.

"Now what?" Bratton asked, casting a side-long look at Drouillard.

Joe Field frowned at the half-breed's back. "We should've left yesterday."

"Looks like we're walkin'," Rube added, "The wolves'll have them a feast off'n all this meat."

The hunter in Colter hated the idea of abandoning his kill to other predators. The realist in him saw no other choice.

Drouillard looked up from the fire. "*Non.*"

"What do you mean, no?" Colter challenged, anger sparking new energy in him.

"We walk, take meat."

"I ain't no bloody pack horse, Drooler. I ain't carryin' no meat nowhere," Colter declared.

Drouillard tilted up his chin and regarded Colter down the length of his generous nose. "You lose the only horse. Now we must carry the meat."

Colter started for the fire, ready to have it out with the stubborn half-breed. Rube stepped in his path. "There's too much for seven to carry," Rube said. "'Sides, we got to get the pirogue back, too." The other crewmen murmured agreement.

"We walk, take meat," Drouillard repeated.

"You ain't our leader, Drooler," Colter challenged. "We don't got to follow your orders. You're just a durned civilian."

Drouillard cradled his rifle against his shoulder and stared placidly into the distance.

"I say one man goes to the fort and brings help back. The rest of us stay and guard the meat," said Colter.

Rube added, "In this cold, I'll wait three days. No more. After that, I head on back no matter what."

While the six crewmen were agreeing, Drouillard strode off.

"Where the devil do you think you're goin'?" Colter demanded.

Drouillard kept walking, speaking over his shoulder, "Help to get."

"Why, you ignorant, filthy —"

Rube's hand on his arm cut Colter off. "Let him go, Colter. Ain't worth bustin' no gut over. Simmer down." With the back of his other hand, Rube turned aside the barrel of Colter's rifle which was aimed at the retreating figure.

Colter looked with horror at the rifle in his hands. Aiming a weapon at a man? What had he been thinking? Thinking. That was exactly the problem. Exactly *his* problem. He had been running on emotion, and that always led to trouble. A man who resorted to violence to solve his problems was not much of a man. He had a lot of things to do before he died. Nothing was worth destroying another human life or his respect for himself. "Thanks, Rube."

Rube nodded. "That Drooler's a piece of work, ain't he? So what do we do now?"

The other men looked at Colter as if awaiting orders. "How should I know?" he said.

"Someone's got to lead. Might as well be you." Rube said. The other four agreed.

Colter kicked at a tussock of frozen grass. Telling others what to do was someone else's job, not his. He was a private, same as them. Yet they were all watching him like cows waiting to be milked. And like cows, they would stand there staring all day if he didn't say something. "All right then. Unload the meat and move the boat up outta the water. We'll camp here and wait for help."

Rube started to protest. Colter cut him off with a curt, "Get a move on."

Two days of fires consumed most of the dry wood the stranded hunting party had found and gathered. By the afternoon of the second day, there was only enough left for a small blaze that gave off little warmth. Colter sat alone on one side of the fire while the rest of the party huddled together on the other, glowering at him through the gray smoke.

Earlier, he had refused to go along with the Field brothers who wanted to abandon the meat and the crippled pirogue and make for the fort. "We said we'd give Drooler three days, and, by God, we'll keep our word," he told them.

As the angry silence dragged on, he thought about the unfairness of the situation. He had not asked to be leader of this group. The others had forced it on him. Now they were trying to force him to go back on *their* promise. Well, it was not going to work. "We said we'd wait. Ain't right to leave," Colter said.

"Right?" Rube exclaimed. "Since when was it right for Drooler to take off on us? The man's a cursed 'breed. I wouldn't trust him to wipe my behind, let alone come back with help."

"This ain't about him. It's about us holdin' up our end of the bargain," said Colter.

"You do what you want, Colter. Joe and me are headin' for the fort," Rube said, standing.

"Fine-a-ree," Colter said, angrily tossing the last two branches onto the fire.

The rest of the squad looked at each other in silence. Then Rube slammed his hat down into the snow. "Damn your stubborn hide, John Colter!"

Colter continued to stare into the flames, ignoring the other men's anger. They could do what they wanted, and he would to the same.

"We'll stay through tonight, but we're headin' back first thing tomorrow," Rube said.

"Noon," Colter said.

"Damn you, Col —"

"Noon makes three days," Colter said, cutting Rube off.

Joe pulled his angry brother back. "Okay, Colter. Noon. But not a minute more."

That night the temperature sank even lower. Between the cold and the howling of a nearby wolfpack, no one slept much. The next morning Colter put up with the glowers and glares of the other men for as long as he could stand it. "All right, it's noon. Let's go."

Joe groaned and pointed upriver. "Wouldn't you know it? He's back."

Drouillard lumbered into camp, throwing up snow and hopping strangely from side to side as if his feet were wedged apart. He grunted a greeting, then bent to untie a pair of strange contraptions from his feet. Each device consisted of an evenly-spaced mesh of interwoven rawhide thongs attached to an oval frame of bent wood two feet wide and three feet long. Tossing these aside, he unloaded a length of tin from his back and removed the coil of rope draped across his chest, dropping both into the snow.

"Where're are the others?" Rube asked.

"No others. This." Drouillard pointed to the pile at his feet. "The hole we fix with tin, then we pull with the rope the pirogue to the fort."

The man's complete self-assurance irked Colter. "For any of you what ain't paid attention, whenever Drooler here says 'we', he don't include hisself."

Instead of backing him up, Rube said, "If this is the help we got, I suppose we better get to patchin'. Come on, Little Brother."

Colter stared at Rube and the others. They talked real big when Drouillard was not around, but soon as he showed up, they acted like whipped dogs. He had a snootful of their shilly-shallying. Some other fool could play at leader next time.

It took an hour to patch the hole and reinforce the nose against further collisions. Bratton found some pitch to use around the patch, and the pirogue floated without leaking, although no one trusted it to hold more than the meat.

Colter had just attached the new rope to its ring on the canoe's bow when Rube asked, "What's he doin', Colter?"

Drouillard had donned the strange snow-walking contraptions. "Why're you askin' me?" Colter shot back.

"What're you doin', Drooler?" Rube called.

"I guard," Drouillard said.

"Guard? We don't need no damn guard. Get on over here and help pull," Colter said angrily.

"Let him be, Colter. After all, he went for help," Rube said.

"Pick a side and stay on it or run for office, Rube." Colter held up a length of the tow rope. "Here you go, Drooler. A spot just for you."

"I am civilian, Colter. Like you say. I do not pull." Drouillard struck out along the river bank without a backward look.

Colter looked hard at Rube. "You mean, you're just goin' to let him go? What happened to all that big talk?"

"Lay off, Colter," Joe said. "Let's get to pullin'. Time's a-wastin'."

Hearing the phrase he always used on himself coming out of Joe's mouth shut Colter up. There would be time enough to give Rube and the others a piece of his mind — after he got warm again.

3. *Fort Mandan*

Because of their late start, the hunting party had to camp along the river. Another night in the snow and cold plus the pull back upriver sucked all the anger out of Colter. With the river shallows frozen, the men had to let out more rope in order to get the canoe out into some free-flowing water. The longer rope and the stronger current slowed their progress. He was trying to get used to the idea of spending another night in the bitter cold when Rube said, "Smoke."

Half a mile ahead in a clearing hacked out of the riverbottom stood the raw walls of the new fort. From within those walls, smoke curled into the gray skies of early dusk.

"Drooler's been warmin' himself by a fire, while we been freezin'. Damn his red hide!" Rube groused.

Colter shut out the other men's grumbling. It would take a week's worth of sitting by a fire to get himself warm, cold as he was. First, though, he had to see to his feet. Their continued numbness had him worried. Cold like this killed flesh as well as men.

"I seen forts in squares and rectangles before, but I don't recollect nothin' like yonder," Joe said.

Colter examined the structure which was laid out in a 'V'-shape with the point toward the backing bluff and the opening facing the river. The legs of the 'V' were about sixty feet in length. Set along each leg inside were two rows of rooms whose roofs sloped downward into the compound. Although the front of the structure remained open, logs eighteen to twenty feet long lay on the trampled snow ready to be made into gates.

A shout went up inside the fort and crewmen poured out to meet them. Shannon was among the first to reach the hunters. He nearly bowled Colter over with his enthusiastic welcome. Whatever had been bothering him before Colter left was obviously forgotten.

"I was getting worried. You were gone a long time," Shannon said.

Colter glanced toward Drouillard who was shadowing the captains. That blamed half-breed got his dander up quicker than McBain used to. With a long winter's confinement ahead, it was going to be hard to keep out of the man's way, but that was exactly what he knew he had to do to keep his pent-up anger from getting the best of him. "Sure could use a fire, Fuzz."

"Well, come on then," Shannon said. While York and three other men took charge of the pirogue, Shannon and Colter both took loads of meat. Shannon led the way to the fort, talking non-stop about everything that had happened while Colter was gone. A heavily-pregnant Indian woman trudged past, headed toward a crude lean-to erected at the edge of the clearing. Colter was struck by how young she was to take on the mantle of motherhood.

As if he had tapped into Colter's thinking, Shannon explained, "She's one of the new interpreter's wives. Her name's Sacajawea." He lowered his voice. "She's the real reason the captains hired her husband, Charbonneau. She's a Shoshone and hails from the Shining Mountains. Captain Lewis is banking that she will help us get horses from her people when the time comes to make the mountain crossing."

"But she's pregnant," Colter said.

"Captains don't seem to mind. Why should we?" Shannon answered blithely.

They dumped the meat in the new storeroom. As they emerged into the compound, Joe Whitehouse waved from the roof of the storage area wedged into the apex of the triangle at the back of the fort. "You aren't going to like that one bit," Shannon said, cocking his chin at the rooftop. "That's a watch station. Worst duty you can imagine. Nothing stops the wind up there." To illustrate his point, he held up his left hand. The dead frostbitten skin on the last two fingers contrasted with the healthy skin of the others.

"Looks like somethin' Ordeal thought up just for me," Colter grumped toward the roof watch post.

"You're safe tonight," Shannon said. "Watches are already set. Here's our barracks." He held the door for Colter.

Except for a fireplace set against the rear wall, bunks, barrels and boxes crammed the small space, leaving precious little room to move around, even less than the crew cabin at Camp Wood. The smell of wet wool and damp wood overpowered the odor of wood smoke.

Shannon pointed to an empty bunk near the fireplace. "That's yours. I made 'em save it for you."

Colter was touched. Saving a bunk by the fire could not have been easy.

"Friend Shannon, is this Friend Colter?" asked the young Indian boy who hopped off an upturned box.

"Yes, Echo, this is Colter. Old Man, this is Echo. He's from Matootonha. He has the most amazing ability to mimic sounds. That's the reason for the name. Why, he's picked up English faster than you can believe."

Echo came forward with his hand to Colter. "I am honored to meet you, Friend Colter."

Colter ignored the hand. "Mind tellin' me what he's doin' here?"

"He's teaching me to speak Mandan and talk with hand-signs. I'm teaching him English. With Captain Lewis's approval, of course," Shannon answered.

"Have you gone daft, Fuzz? Mandan?"

"We're going to be here five months, Old Man. Why not use that time to improve myself?"

Colter narrowed his eyes. Improving himself, maybe; but a more likely explanation for Shannon's sudden interest in the Mandan tongue was a certain comely squaw. He wondered how far things had gone between Shannon and her by now.

"What's that look for?" Shannon asked.

"It's your business what you do, Fuzz. Only I don't never want to catch that there little brat on my bunk. Hear?"

"Friend Colter is angry?" Echo said.

"No it ain't —" An unmistakably female giggle stopped him mid-sentence. "What in the name of spit?"

A pair of legs in leather bindings appeared in the opening cut in the ceiling to the right of the fireplace. A moccasined foot found the top rung of the ladder which had been nailed to the rear wall, and a young Mandan woman climbed down to the floor level.

"That's the loft," Shannon explained. "Four men sleep up there."

"That ain't no man, Fuzz," Colter countered.

Shannon colored. "I figured you'd rather be down here since we agreed the loft's the only place women would be allowed."

"We?" Colter shot back.

"It's the same in all the barracks. Seems to be working out just fine so far."

Colter turned his back to hide his disgust. It was the captains' fault for putting a fort full of opportunistic rakehells so close to that Mandan town. If things had gotten to this point in less than three weeks, what would the rest of the winter be like?

The woman scuttled out the door. "Good riddance," he muttered.

"Friend Colter is not happy." Echo's open scrutiny disconcerted him. Colter looked at Shannon. "Ain't he supposed to be learnin' you somethin', 'stead of botherin' me?"

Echo answered instead of Shannon. "Friend Colter wears the sign of the Hawk Spirit. Such is special medicine granted by Him Who Sees All. Medicine given only to those who go where others fear to go, to do what others cannot, to make choices others will not make. The one who wears this sign walks a lonely trail."

A sensation washed over Colter. The same sensation he had felt upon seeing the outline on the old Sioux's leather pouch. "You're spoutin' nonsense, boy. Get along with you."

Echo did not move. "Only the Hawk flies high enough to reach the lodge of Him Who Sees All. Many seek to know the Hawk. Few succeed. You are one of few."

"I said git."

Shannon pulled the boy away.

"You best keep him away from me, Fuzz. For his sake."

"When did you get so touchy? Echo's harmless and he's a genius. He's going to be a big help. You'll see."

Between his barracks-mates fornicating with squaws in the loft and

Shannon's new pet, Colter had reached his limit for nasty surprises. He would tend to his feet some other time. For now he needed some fresh air and a place to be alone. He slammed back outside and ran smack into Ordway.

"Why, Private Colter, welcome back. You have the midnight watch. Up there." The sergeant thumbed toward the roof. "Enjoy it." He walked off, smiling.

The encounter happened too fast for Colter to react. Shannon had been wrong about watches being set, and he had been right: Ordeal would have him up on the roof, up in the biting wind, all blasted winter. He stomped out through the fort's unfinished front opening and plopped himself down on one of the raw stumps to stare at the river.

Except for a narrow channel in the very center, ice now spread from bank to bank. Soon, even that channel would be gone and the ice would grow to more than a foot thick. It would remain so until spring. He was stuck with squaws in the loft, an Indian urchin in the barracks, Drouillard, and Ordway. The next five months were shaping up to be the longest of his life.

Once the Rees set out from their town, Hartley had trouble keeping pace. His solitary trip up the Missouri had taken a toll on him physically. He did not realize how weak he was until he began to fall behind the Indians. To add to his misery, Tabeau had stayed behind at the Ree town so he had no way to communicate his difficulty.

Toward the end of the third day, scouts spotted tracks in the snow and the Rees turned wary. They camped that night without a fire and slept with the leads of their horses bound to their wrists. Older men took the late watches in place of the younger ones. Hartley lay on the ground, shivering despite two buffalo robes.

A cry pierced the night.

He sat bolt upright. The ground under him shook, and the frigid night air reverberated with the thunder of galloping hooves before his eyes managed to pick out a mob of mounted shapes bearing down on them.

One of the Ree horses reared, neighing wildly. Around him, Ree warriors sprang up, nocking arrows. The only thing he understood of their anxious conversations was the Arikara word for "Sioux."

One of the oncoming riders separated from the rest and headed straight at him. Realizing he was moments from death, Hartley scuttled on all fours toward a cluster of Ree warriors. The attacker launched a spear in his direction. A scream froze on his lips.

The closest Ree crumpled and Hartley realized he was in the middle of a battle with no place to hide.

Another attacker wheeled toward him and took aim with an arrow. *I'm going to die*, he thought, emptying his bowels into his trousers.

Shannon might have been wrong about night watches being set, but he was right about roof watch being the worst duty of the winter. Thanks to

Ordway, Colter drew that post eight nights out of his first ten back from hunting. Over those ten days, the weather grew steadily worse. Colter's thoughts kept turning to the cold as he slumped next to the fire in the barracks the last few minutes before he had to take the watch yet again, this time during the day.

He had decided that the best way to fight the sergeant was to take whatever the man handed out with nonchalance. He reasoned that, unless Ordway got a reaction from him, he would eventually tire of the game and turn to tormenting someone else. The problem was that that reasoning was not proving out.

With less than ten minutes until his watch, he did not have time to whittle, but he pulled out the block of wood and his knife anyway. He needed something to help him ignore the Mandan gibberish Echo was teaching to Shannon.

An unexpected outburst of laughter from that pair startled him. His knife slipped, decapitating the buffalo carving he had nearly completed. He flung the ruined lump of wood against the wall. "I'm sick of this hell hole. A body cain't think for all the racket."

"We did not mean to anger you," Echo stammered.

"Well, you did."

"You got roof duty again, right?" Shannon asked. "Ordeal's sure working you over."

"Ordeal," Echo repeated. "Working you over."

Colter glared at the boy. "I hate everythin' about this place. That blasted roof. Squaws fornicatin' over my head. You wastin' your time tryin' to learn how to talk to a bunch of savages.

"Savages." Echo perfectly imitated Colter's inflection, then grinned with pleasure at his ability at mimickry.

The boy's lopsided smile was more than Colter could take. He sheathed his knife, grabbed his rifle and headed out the door. As it slammed behind him, he heard Echo ask Shannon the meaning of the word "savages."

The day was cold and still. The frozen flag looked fragile enough to crack in a breeze if there had been one. His first breath shocked his lungs. *Damn this infernal cold! And damn them Mandans for bein' able to stand it like they do!*

Stiffly, he climbed the ladder up to the roof and relieved the previous sentry, then began trudging from one side of the roof to the other. Through the trees he could see the keelboat where she lay locked in river ice. The crew had been too busy yet to haul her onto supports. If they did not get to it soon, ice was liable to crush her hull.

Within minutes, cold wormed its way through his two blankets and settled deep inside his bones. Shivering, he silently cursed a system that put so much power in Ordway's vindictive hands. He would have preferred to use his time on the roof to plot ways to strike back at the sergeant but a large Sioux war party had been spotted in the area and he needed to keep his mind on his guard responsibilities. It would be just like the Sioux to use the cold to their advantage.

To keep his mind off Ordway, he silently counted steps: twenty-five up, twenty-five back. The fort's gates had just been completed and another unlucky soul, too bundled up to recognize, had drawn that post. Seeing him made Colter feel less alone in his misery.

Morning passed with agonizing slowness. He was wondering how much longer he had yet to go when he spotted an Indian across the river, gesturing frantically toward the fort. Colter's yell to the gate guard came out muffled because his lips were too cold to form words properly.

The gate sentry hammered on the captains' door and Captain Clark came out bundled in a buffalo hide.

"'Cross the river, Captain," Colter managed to say. "Looks like trouble."

"Fire a shot, Colter," the captain called up to him. "Let's roust everyone out."

While he did as ordered and welcomed his relief, Clark, York and the interpreter Jesseaume hurried down the rutted path to the river to meet the Indian there, who turned out to be a Mandan.

Colter had just climbed down from the roof to join the milling crowd of crewmen when the captain rushed back through the gates. His face was flushed from the cold and his eyes were alive with excitement. "A party of Tetons and Rees attacked some hunters from Matootonha. If they're looking for a fight, I think we ought to give it to them. Right, Meri?"

All eyes turned to Captain Lewis. "Of course! Sergeants, issue powder and shot and get your men to the boats on the double."

The crew had been confined to the fort by the weather so long that they were spoiling for any activity, especially a fight with the Tetons who had given them such a hard time only a few months back. They cheered the decision. Colter added his voice to the chorus. Enduring another roof watch had him spoiling for a fight. He would get warm — later.

Floating islands of ice made crossing the river tricky. Between his hydrophobia and the fact that he had never been in a real skirmish before, Shannon was wound tight as a windlass by the time the pirogues reached the other bank.

He had no chance to collect himself before Ordway ordered the squad forward. He found himself positioned next to Colter on the end of a skirmish line, creeping through knee-deep powder snow. His mouth filled with the bitter taste of tension at the sparse cover. His hope — one he had never shared with anyone — was that he would somehow be able to capture some Sioux horses as a way to avenge Burr's loss.

It did not take long before the deep snow and the tension wore him down. There was no sign of the rumored raiders. The line's advance came to a halt at the edge of the open field the Mandans used as a graveyard. Beyond it, the picket wall and domed hives of Matootonha. He studied the snow-heaped funeral scaffolds that dotted the field and wished he had brought along his sketch book.

Clark, Drouillard and Jesseaume walked forward to meet with the leaders of the Mandan town who came out to greet them. Charbonneau slipped and slid in a clumsy attempt to follow. Shannon stared after the man in disgust. Charbonneau had shown himself a coward since crossing the river, skulking along behind the skirmish line instead of taking his place in the advance with the rest of the crew.

After a brief conference, Clark beckoned the crewmen to follow him across the graveyard and into the Mandan town. That he might see Beauty again made Shannon forget his fatigue and his dislike for Charbonneau. Upon reaching the central plaza of the town, the captain split the group into two parts, one under his direction, the other under Ordway.

For once, Shannon and Colter both got assigned to the captain's contingent. They exchanged playful nudges over that fact as they ducked through the low entrance to one of the lodges. Inside, Shannon came out of his crouch to find Beauty, standing just behind their two hosts, Chief Big White and the grim-faced Mandan who seemed to be Big White's constant shadow.

It had been a month since he had last seen her, a month in which he doted on the image of her that he had stored in his memory. The woman in the flesh made that image pale in comparison. He gawked at her, drinking in the planes of her face, the contours of her bones, the way the light played on her golden skin, the luster of her hair.

Colter leaned over. "Ain't polite to stare, Fuzz."

Shannon shrugged off the remark, keeping his full attention riveted on Beau7ty as the crew took seats on the packed earth floor. When he began learning Mandan from Echo, he told himself that he was doing so to enrich his experience. Now he threw off that excuse and embraced the truth: she was his reason to learn the language. The other men bedded whatever squaw was handy like dogs in heat. Not him. When the time came, he would be ready to express to this gorgeous creature the depth of his feelings, to pay her proper court. The gracefulness of her movements made him yearn that that time would come soon.

Echo had followed the crew to the town. He now burst into the lodge, full of excited questions. "Did you find the Sioux? Was the fighting fierce? How did Friend Shannon show his bravery?"

Shannon dragged his attention away from Beauty to the boy with reluctance. He was answering one of Echo's questions when it occurred to him that he did not yet know Beauty's name or anything about her.

Because Colter was sitting beside him, he decided to ask Echo about her using the little Mandan he had managed to learn thus far. The boy listened patiently, twice correcting his pronunciation and responded, "She is called ___."

Shannon quickly put a silencing finger across the boy's mouth. "In your tongue," he murmured.

Echo switched to Mandan. "She is called Shakoka." He added in English, "It means Mint."

Shakoka. Mint. A beautiful name for a beautiful woman.

"Do you wish to know the names of the others, Friend Shannon?" Echo asked hopefully.

Colter roused himself. "Sure he does. Don't you, Fuzz?"

Echo went on without Shannon's nod, obviously proud to show off his newly-acquired English. He pointed at the woman with the white streak in her cropped hair. "She is Shakoka's sister, Pshanshaw."

"What's that mean, boy?" Colter asked.

Coming from Colter, the question grabbed Shannon's attention. Since when did the Old Man give two hoots about an Indian, particularly a woman?

"That means Fragrant Grass," Echo said.

Colter nodded curtly and Shannon detected a subtle change in his friend's expression: the alertness that comes with interest. What was going on here?

Echo continued, pointing to the various Indians in the lodge and giving their names. When he got to the grim-faced man next to the plump light-skinned Chief Big White, Shannon paid particular attention. Echo spoke a Mandan name he could not begin to pronounce. "In your tongue," Echo said, "his name is Sly Wolf."

Whoever had named the man chose well. Sly Wolf had the hooded eyes of one who allowed no detail to escape his seeing, no rumor to escape his hearing, no slight to go unavenged.

"He is husband to Fragrant Grass," added Echo.

The merest shadow of an emotion flitted across Colter's face. Pain? Resignation? Shannon could not decide which.

"He is also husband to Mint."

The comment caught Shannon completely off-guard. It had not occurred to him that Beauty, that Mint might be married. And that knowledge dampened his ardor like a pail of cold water snuffs out a fire. To harbor love for a woman who belonged to another man went against God's law.

"Two wives?" Colter said.

"When the husband of Fragrant Grass died, Sly Wolf took her, the sister of Shakoka, as his second wife. That is our way," Echo explained.

"Some way," Colter muttered.

"Are you unwell, Friend Shannon?" asked Echo. "You are so pale."

Shannon managed to shake his head. "I need to take a piss."

Echo bounced up immediately and accompanied Shannon to the village latrine. A woman was already there, squatting, her skirt pulled up to her waist. She smiled at Shannon and beckoned him to join her. "She welcomes you and your paleskin brothers," said Echo.

Put off by the woman's presence and her exposed situation, Shannon turned to leave. "Where do you go, Friend Shannon? Is this not what you desired?"

"I'll wait until she's done," he replied.

"I do not understand."

He had to rack his brain to explain his reaction in a way that Echo could understand and that would not offend him or the woman. "It . . . it is not our way to have men and women do this," he waved an arm at the area of the latrine, "together."

Echo cocked his head to one side in an attempt to comprehend this, then he spoke to the woman. She gave Shannon a puzzled look, but, with a re-signed shake of her head, she raised up from her squat, casually dropped her skirt and walked off.

Shannon needed to be alone with his churning emotions more than he needed the latrine. He asked the bewildered Echo to leave also. Alone at last, he heaved a shuddering sigh. Fate had played yet another cruel trick on him in the form of a woman. From Sarah Cooper to Lisette and now to Mint, something about him attracted the wrong kind of woman. If he did not correct that flaw, he was bound to suffer more pain, more heartbreak.

Hearing Echo coming back, he pretended to be finishing his business. On the way back to the lodge, the pair passed the woman from the latrine. She was with two other women. The trio stopped their conversation to stare at him. Feeling himself blushing, Shannon forced himself to walk even taller. Never had he felt so naked with all his clothes on.

4. *Dreams of Matootonha*

F ragrant Grass hugged the bundle of warm bread to her chest and waited at the edge of the empty plaza for her sister who had gone to fetch a pot of stew from a neighboring lodge. Was this winter colder than the last, or was it the presence in their lodge of the man sent by the Hawk Spirit that made her tremble so?

Mint's face was alive with excitement when she arrived, lugging the pot. "I have thought of a way to please our husband."

Fragrant Grass stifled her opinion that Sly Wolf did not deserve to be pleased and instead spoke her customary protest, "Your beauty alone would please the coldest of men. Surely, it is not necessary to do more than you already do for him."

Mint brushed aside the compliment. "I know a way to help improve his position among our people."

Fragrant Grass tilted her face so her sister would not see her disgust at the man's constant efforts to bring more importance to himself. For wis-dom and integrity, no man compared to the dead Strikes Two. Sly Wolf would always live in Strikes Two's shadow on both counts, but she could not hurt her sister by saying so. Mint prattled on. "Our husband says that the paleskins possess great powers so I decided that I will mate with one of them. This way I will absorb the medicine of the paleskins and pass it to our husband."

Fragrant Grass lowered her voice. "Have you told him about this plan of yours?"

"Oh, no. I want this to be a surprise. You know how much our husband likes surprises." She lowered her eyes in the coy way she had. "I have one of the paleskins already picked out."

Mint's twin, Kebeka, popped into Fragrant Grass's thoughts. Sly Wolf had arranged Kebeka's marriage to the paleskin trader Jesseaume because he coveted the goods the trader brought to Matootonha and the prestige that came with possessing such things. It did not trouble him that Kebeka now lived in a dark damp lodge in the paleskins' wooden fort across the river. He did not care that Jesseaume treated his dogs better than Kebeka or that her sister ached to be reunited with her clan and her people, living in the only way she had ever known instead of among the barbaric paleskin warriors who never bathed. To cover her thoughts, Fragrant Grass changed the subject. "This food will be cold unless we hurry."

Mint took the cue and followed her through the crowd of people gathered around the entrance and into their lodge. Fragrant Grass went directly to the fire, wrapped the bread in woven reeds and placed it next to the coals to keep it warm. Then she helped Mint rearrange the two pots of stew atop the fire-stones. They moved back into the women's section of the lodge to wait for a signal from Sly Wolf to serve the food.

Fragrant Grass deliberately stood behind her sister to prevent conversation. She tucked her hands into the sleeves of her deerskin tunic and studied the scene around the fire. With the paleskin Chief Red Hair and the giant Black White Man both in the lodge, Sly Wolf sat puffed with self-importance which he somehow managed to contain enough to let Big White lead the conversation.

Ever since boyhood, Sly Wolf had angled and schemed to improve his social standing among their people. His marriage to Mint meant a big step up the social ladder. Not only did it attach him to the ancient clan of Mint, Kebeka and Fragrant Grass but also to Big White, Matootonha's civil chief who was married to the women's oldest sister. That Mint's husband had set his sights on succeeding Big White was obvious. That Fragrant Grass seemed to be the only one who saw the manipulating, grasping, selfish being beneath the man's calculated image filled her with despair.

She turned her attention to the man wearing the mark of the Hawk Spirit. Why had Him Who Sees All sent a paleskin, instead of a Mandan, in answer to her entreaties? Pondering that question, she almost missed Sly Wolf's signal to begin serving the food.

Mint filled the first two bowls with stew and carried them to Sly Wolf and Chief Red Hair. The bowl meant for her husband slipped out of her hands, splattering stew across Chief Red Hair's leather leggings.

Fragrant Grass knew better than to go to her sister's aid with Sly Wolf right there. She had to watch from a distance while Mint wiped the stew from the paleskin chief's pant leg with the hem of her dress. Her sister's tawny cheeks were flaming with embarrassment when she returned to the cooking fire for another bowl of stew.

Fragrant Grass brushed Mint's trembling hand as a way to give comfort. The touch brought a trembling smile before Mint returned to serve Sly Wolf his food.

The two women worked together, delivering two bowls of food with each trip until only two paleskins remained to be served — the young one with the gap-toothed grin and the one marked by the Hawk Spirit. This time Mint filled only one bowl and carried it to the gap-toothed one, placing it into his hands with a beguiling smile. She left it to Fragrant Grass to serve the last guest.

Fragrant Grass hoped no one, especially Sly Wolf, would notice her trembling hands as she moved to the Hawk man, keeping her eyes down to avoid his gaze. The prospect of perhaps touching his pale skin intimidated her so she placed the stew on the earth in front of his crossed legs and hurried away as fast as her quivering knees would allow.

From the shadows at the rear of the lodge, she watched the Hawk man take up the bowl and eat the stew. *Why that one? Why not one of my people? What would you have me do, Great One?* The thoughts roamed through her mind like buffalo across the plain.

The conversation between Clark and the Mandan chief dragged on. Colter fought off the drowsiness brought on by the tasty stew and the warmth of the lodge. In his torpor his thoughts turned to the white-streaked squaw. Fragrant Grass. The name fit her. That his eyes kept swinging toward where she was standing in the rear of the lodge perturbed him. She was a squaw and there was no way he wanted anything to do with squaws.

At last the captain rose to leave. "We aren't sure that the Sioux have left the area, so we had best get back to the fort."

Rube stuck up his hand. "Captain, any chance some of us could stay? In case those Tetons try something, we'd be here. To help, I mean."

Rather than reprimand Rube for his gall, Clark flashed a knowing wink. "All right. Those who want to stay, can."

Bedlam ensued while the crewmen set to bargaining for their choices among the Mandan women. Colter moved to the edge of the group and took note of Drouillard edging away from the captain's side. He seemed to be searching for someone.

A trio of women converged on York, blocking Colter's view of the half-breed. "One at a time, ladies," York said with a laugh. "I'll get to you all, if you'll wait your turn."

The black man's obvious pleasure in the situation bothered Colter, but another, more pressing issue captured his attention. Drouillard had moved to Fragrant Grass. His hands made some signs, then he held three strings of beads out to her.

Instead of taking them, she slashed a signed reply, then brushed past the half-breed and out of the lodge. Colter was not aware he had been holding his breath until the exhale whooshed out.

He turned to see Shannon smiling like a moonstruck fool at the woman called Mint. She returned the smile with an invitation in her eyes. Colter walked over to his bench-mate. "Come on, Fuzz. Time we was goin' back."

"You go on. I . . ." Shannon's voice trailed off as if his mind had lost interest in words.

Mint held out an open palm and pointed to his pockets with the other hand. "What's she want, Old Man?" Shannon murmured.

"Like Lisette, Fuzz. You got to pay for it," Colter said, making no effort to keep the scorn out of his tone.

Shannon made a frantic search of his pockets but came up empty. When he produced no goods to seal the bargain, Mint's smile faded. She turned to leave.

"Don't. Please. I'll bring something next time," Shannon pleaded.

"Doubt she speaks English, Fuzz. Best try some of that Mandan you been learnin'," Colter said.

"Where's Echo?" Shannon asked, looking around for the boy who, for once, was nowhere to be found. "Old Man, have you got anything I can give her?"

"Nope. And I wouldn't give it to you if'n I did," Colter said.

"Some friend you are," Shannon said.

Colter noticed Mint's husband walking toward them. "Come on, Fuzz. Her husband's comin' and the boat's leavin'."

This time Shannon followed. Outside, Colter paused to draw his coat tighter against the cold that had more of a bite after the over-heated atmosphere inside the lodge. "Be glad your pockets're empty."

"They might be empty now, but they won't be empty next time," Shannon said.

"What are you plannin' to do: rob the expedition's stores? For a squaw?"

Shannon looked forlorn. "What I do is none of your business, Old Man." With that, he stomped off to the boats.

So many men had opted to stay at Matootonha that the fort seemed empty. After a stop at the latrine, Colter entered the barracks room to find Shannon rifling through Rube's pack. The younger man glanced up at his entrance, but went right on with his search until he came up with several colored hair ribbons which he stuffed into his pockets.

"What're you doin', Fuzz?" Colter asked.

"Rube owes me," Shannon said, cramming things back into Rube's pack. "I'll tell him what I took when he gets back."

"Ain't right, takin' things without him knowin' about it first."

"Is too right. He owes me," Shannon said.

"So what about that money you owe me? Same go for me? I take what I want of yourn any old time?"

Shannon's self-assurance wavered momentarily and he replaced the ribbons back into the top of the pack. Colter was not about to let him off the hook yet. "While we're talkin' about money, just when am I goin' to get mine?"

"Don't know," Shannon answered sullenly.

"That there was one hell of a lot of money," Colter said hotly. "A whole lot. For what? For a damn whore!"

For the first time since St. Charles, Shannon did not jump immediately to Lisette's defense. He flung Rube's pack down and flopped onto his bunk. Repelled that his outburst had exceeded the bounds of necessity as much as by Shannon's attitude, Colter banged out the door to cool off.

He was passing the captains' quarters when Captain Lewis stepped over the threshold. He gave Colter an appraising look. "Well, Colter, I am glad to see there are a few men in the crew I can count on to exercise good judgment."

Colter responded with an automatic "Yes, sir."

The captain started to walk away, then stopped and came back. He reached out a hand to cup Colter's shoulder. "Thank God for you, Colter." With that, he turned and resumed his walk.

Colter stood rooted to the ground, too surprised to respond. By the time he could move again, he realized he had received the answer to a question he had been asking since the Niobrara River. The question: Why was he here? The answer: Because Meriwether Lewis believed in him.

The travois lurched over a rut, jarring Hartley's wounded shoulder. He clenched his teeth against crying out. He was tired of hurting, tired of trying to hide that pain from his captors, tired of being afraid, tired of the blizzard raging around them. Just plain tired.

He had lost all track of time since his capture. After the attack on the Rees, he had come to to find an arrow sticking out of his shoulder and a group of Sioux braves standing over him. Their expressions made him wish he had remained unconscious.

When one of the Indians stopped and pushed against the arrow's shaft, Hartley did not have time to scream out before sliding into a black hole of pain.

He revived later to discover himself strapped to a travois covered with a ratty buffalo robe. The arrow was gone. In its place a sticky substance coated the bare skin of his shoulder.

For days thereafter, he slipped in and out of consciousness. Waking and dreaming blended into an undifferentiated tangle of confused images. Then, one day, he revived to find himself still lashed to the travois – with one difference: the conveyance had stopped and he was alone with the horses. In the distance, he heard the neighs of more horses. He craned around to see his Sioux captors breaching the defensive picket wall of an Arikara village.

The next minute the air filled with shrieking and the sounds of battle. That noise gradually diminished, then ceased entirely. In the eerie stillness, the Sioux returned with their arms laden with foodstuffs and other objects looted from the Rees. They also brought a collection of fresh scalps, each with a patch of bloody skin attached. One of the Indians brandished a scalp in Hartley's face. When he recognized the comb belonging to the Ree chief's wife, the one he had bedded, he gagged up all the food that was in his belly.

His heart was still heavy from that awful revelation as the horse dragging his litter drew up with an abruptness that set his shoulder throbbing. One of the front riders chattered excitedly. Hartley stared through the swirling snow at the tracks the travois had made. *Please, Lord, not another bloody raid*, he prayed to himself.

His horse lurched forward and the poles of the litter bounced across the frozen ground, jostling his wound until he moaned in spite of his efforts not to. From somewhere up ahead came shouts and the drumming beat of approaching horses. Moments later mounted Sioux surrounded Hartley and the raiding party.

One of the newcomers slid off his horse and came to the travois. The Indian wore a split raven skin as a head ornament, tied so that its beak hung over his forehead. The man's black eyes echoed the glittering gaze of the dead bird. He studied Hartley for a long time as if deciding what use the preacher could be to him, then he got back on his horse and led the expanded party forward. The preacher closed his eyes and fell into a welcome sleep.

For the next week, the temperatures remained too low to send crewmen out for anything except the most crucial tasks. Confined to the fort, the men had little to do except swap stories about their recent experiences at Matootonha. Every story aggravated Shannon's pain over missing his chance with Mint. On the morning of December 7, feeling low and bundled into all the blankets he owned or could borrow, he left the barracks to take his assigned watch on the roof. "About time you got here," grumbled Collins. "I'm froze."

"Glad to see you too," Shannon muttered at the top of the man's head as Collins descended the ladder and disappeared into his barracks room. Shannon braced himself before turning into the icy wind. He would not allow himself to think about how cold he would be by the time his relief came. If it was this way in early December, what kind of ice-bound hell would the rest of the winter be?

The fort's gates creaked open to allow a pair of mounted Mandans to enter the compound. Shannon recognized the lead horse with the unusual dark brown blotches splashed across its white coat as the one belonging to Chief Big White. Rumor had it that such horses were specially bred by a tribe called the Nez Percé, the pierced-nose people, far to the west across the Shining Mountains. Behind that horse came the smallish paint of Sly Wolf.

The sight of Mint's husband revived Shannon's Matootonha disappointment. To think that the lack of a simple hair ribbon or two had caused him to lose out on the opportunity to enjoy the pleasures of the beautiful Mandan woman. Such a thing would never happen again. *Never*, he vowed.

His understanding of hand signs had progressed to the point where he could read most of the conversation between the captains and the Mandans from his position on the roof. What he could not read, he interpolated. The cold had brought a herd of buffalo to the river and the Mandans came to invite the crew to join their hunt.

Clark clapped his hands and the sound resounded off the log walls of the little fort. "Just what the doctor ordered! A buffalo hunt's the elixir that will cure what ails us. Pass the word, Sergeant Ordway. Anyone who wants to go, can."

Shannon decided to be bold. "Anyone, sir?" he called down into the compound.

"You want to go, Shannon?" Clark asked.

"Yes, sir."

"Then you will." Clark turned to Ordway. "Find a replacement for Private Shannon." He started to turn back to his quarters but paused. "And that does not mean Colter, Sergeant. He has been on duty too much lately. Today I want him hunting."

The barracks room was alive with excitement when Shannon entered. He crowded his way to his bunk to gather his hunting gear.

"Way to get outta watch, Fuzz," Colter drawled.

Shannon let the comment slide by. He and Colter had been at odds all week. Maybe a hunt would set things to rights again.

A comment directed from Rube to Joe caught his ear. "Don't forget squaw do-dads, Little Brother. Could be we get us the chance for a little sportin' later."

Squaw do-dads. Shannon needed some and knew where to get them. He tried on his most winning smile and pointed at the hair ribbons Rube was about to stuff into his pockets. "You got any extra of those? For a friend?"

"Thought you swore off women," Rube said.

Shannon could feel Colter's eyes on him. He decided not to say anything and simply held out his hand. Rube surrendered two ribbons. "Thanks," Shannon said.

An hour later, a buffalo hunt seemed like a very bad idea. Barely halfway across the now-frozen river, Shannon's lungs and joints were aching from the biting cold. The scarf across his nose and mouth had frozen into uselessness. The small expanse of bare skin around his eyes prickled as if pierced by a dozen needles. His feet, hands and fingers all felt like ghost limbs.

By the time he reached the other side of the river, Shannon had decided to turn back for the fort. He plodded after Colter to let him know.

Colter shushed him and pointed into the trees where a group of buffalo were grazing. The great beasts' exhaled breath formed a cloud of fog around their snouts reminiscent of steam from a tea kettle. Shouts and whistles drifted into the silence from the north where the Mandans had begun their hunt. The sight of the buffalo changed Shannon's mind about going back.

Captain Clark quickly sorted the crew into pairs and directed Shannon and Colter to move south. The trek across the river had tired Shannon so much that walking in the thigh-deep snow took all his concentration. When he glanced up to get his bearings, he found himself less than ten yards away from a magnificent bull. The buffalo was so intent on digging at the snow with his front hooves to uncover the grass that lay beneath that he was oblivious of Shannon's presence.

Colter saw the bull as well and motioned for Shannon to cover his shot. Then the wind shifted and the bull's head swiveled toward them. The animal's nostrils quivered, testing the air for the scent of intruders.

Both men froze where they stood. Shannon did not even let himself breathe until the wind shifted back to their favor and the weak-eyed creature went back to foraging. Only now, Shannon wanted the shot. He signalled his intention to Colter who nodded doubtfully and moved out of his way.

Shannon took careful aim and released the hammer. With an explosion of powder, the ball went wide, dislodging a divot of bark from the trunk of a nearby tree instead of striking its intended target which snorted and lumbered out of sight. There was no covering shot from Colter.

"Tarnation, Old Man. You let him get away!" Shannon barked.

"Me? You did the missin'."

"You're supposed to cover me."

"You're supposed to hit what you shoot at."

Two more buffalo moved out of the trees just then, putting an abrupt end to the argument. Shannon hurried to reload, but Colter put a restraining hand on his rifle barrel. "Too small. Wait," he whispered.

"You wait." Shannon wiped off Colter's hand, brought up the rifle and fired. Another miss.

"That's two," Colter said.

"I suppose you could do better," Shannon flung back.

"A blind man could do better'n you, Fuzz." Colter took off, leaving him to make the choice whether to trail along or not. Two misses. Back home he always won the militia shooting competitions. But that was back home. Here was here, and once again, he had not measured up. Colter did not need to win competitions. Next to Drouillard, he was the best shot in the whole outfit. A voice sounded in Shannon's head — his father's voice: "Better pay attention, George. Between your mouth and your pride, you are missing the chance to learn something."

"Oh, shut up, Father," Shannon muttered.

"George!" the voice warned.

Shannon backed down. "Yes, Father. I'm sorry."

"That's better," the voice said. "Now do as I say or —"

Shannon shut down the voice by heading after Colter.

Colter slogged along, hoping Shannon would not follow. He didn't care if he downed a buffalo. He didn't care if his toes broke off from the cold. He was alone, away from Ordway, away from the confines of the fort. Out here for the time being, no one owned him, no one could tell him what to do.

"Old Man, wait up!"

"Damn!" Colter cursed. He leaned against a tree to wait for Shannon to catch up. Pulling even, Shannon pointed urgently toward a snow-covered deadfall. Behind it grazed a group of buffalo, all bulls, virtually obscured from view.

"Will you line up my shot?" Shannon whispered, adding, "Please?"

"Only if'n I get to pick the critter."

Shannon nodded cooperatively. "Never take the biggest or strongest. Always get the weakest. Got that?" Colter mumured, sighting Shannon's rifle on a smallish male.

Shannon nodded again a little less quickly.

"Line up the shot, then take a breath and hold her whilst you drop the hammer."

For once, Shannon did everything Colter told him. This time his shot brought the beast down.

"Hallelujah!" Shannon's triumphant shout was still echoing off the tree trunks when a horse and rider hurtled out of the trees beyond the deadfall. Sly Wolf on his distinctive paint horse.

The Mandan reined up beside the dead buffalo and shot an arrow into its neck. His ululating cry brought two more muffled figures out of the trees. Both were on foot. One led a horse dragging a travois. Each wore snow-walking shoes similar to the ones Drouillard used, and they kicked up clouds of snow with each lumbering step. They immediately fell to butchering the animal.

"Stop!" Shannon yelled, lurching toward them, waving his arms. "That's my buffalo. Mine. You can't have it."

Sly Wolf glared imperiously at Shannon as he slashed signs claiming hunter's rights.

Shannon was undeterred. "No, by thunder! I downed it. It's mine."

"He cain't understand you, Fuzz," Colter called.

Shannon switched to halting Mandan. Sly Wolf answered in a voice so calm it sounded bored.

"What's he say?" Colter asked.

"The buffalo's his because his arrow's in its neck. He asks where my arrow is."

At that moment, the hood covering the head of one of the butchers fell back. Through the steam rising from the warm carcass, Colter recognized Fragrant Grass. The animal's blood covered her bare arms to the elbows, glistening as it congealed in the frigid air. She gave a quick warning shake before bending back to her work.

"Better back off, Fuzz."

"The kill's mine. It's —" Shannon stopped mid-sentence as the other butcher's hood slid aside to reveal Mint. Abruptly he whirled around. "You're right. No sense fighting. There's plenty to go around." He brushed past Colter and disappeared into the trees.

Colter gave Sly Wolf and the women one last look, then followed. He felt Sly Wolf's eyes on his back long after they were out of sight.

5. *1805*

1804 passed and 1805 began. Once the fort was finished, there were only enough chores to keep the crew occupied a couple of hours out of every long dull day. The rest of the time, the men had to find ways to oc-cupy themselves.

Shannon spent his free time working with Echo to improve his skills at Mandan and hand-talk. Still, as the days dragged on, even the allure of those activities faded. The captains had allowed no crew visits to the Man-dan town since their unsuccessful search for the Sioux raiding party. Still, enough Indian women continued to come to the fort that the barracks loft seemed to be perpetually in use. Shannon was glad that Mint was not among them. He did not want to be tempted to sully her or their relation-ship by resorting to the vulgar coupling the other men indulged in. And he certainly did not want any of the other men to get their hands on her.

Echo finished the story he had been relating in Mandan and fell into an alert silence as he waited for Shannon to repeat the tale in English. Shan-non had been paying more attention to his drifting thoughts than the story, but he tried to cover up his inattention. "A bear awoke from his winter's sleep."

"No, no, Friend Shannon. Not a bear. A badger. Were you not listening?"

All at once Shannon had enough of the fort, the winter, the boredom, and, most especially, Echo's constant correcting of his Mandan. "Bear, badger. What bloody difference does it make?" He stood up with an abruptness that made the boy recoil.

His angry outburst stopped the other conversations in the room and Echo fled outside, leaving the door ajar. Colter rolled off his bunk to close it, tossing Shannon a knowing glance. "Mind your own business, Old Man. No lectures," Shannon said.

"Wouldn't waste my breath," Colter said, returning to his bunk and picking up his carving.

Out in the compound, a rifle boomed and the barracks door swung open on Captain Clark and York. The captain's rifle still smoked from the shot. "Roust out of there, men," Clark yelled. "New Year's Day.It's the first day of the year we find the Passage. Time for a celebration! Let's go visiting!"

The only place to visit was Matootonha. The atmosphere in the room in-stantly snapped to life. Only Colter appeared unmoved. He shifted from his bunk onto one of the vacated boxes next to the fire and resumed whit-tling. "Aren't you going?" Shannon asked.

"Nope," Colter said.

"Oh, yes, you are. This isn't optional, Colter." Ordway stood in the doorway, hands on hips, his mouth hooked into a tight, treacherous smile. "Captain wants everyone going who is not on duty."

"Then give me a watch, Sarge," Colter challenged.

"I already did. Get your things. Now." Ordway slammed the door behind him.

"Be glad he didn't take you up on that, Old Man. You could be on the roof again," Shannon said.

"Oh, I got that tonight," Colter groused. "Like always."

"Change of pace will be good for you and me both," Shannon said, trying to cajole the man into a brighter mood.

"Rather sit here by myself than watch you make a fool outta yourself over some squaw."

"What makes you think that?" Shannon demanded.

"Them there ribbons in your pocket."

"Doesn't mean I'm going to use them," Shannon said.

"Sure, Fuzz," Colter said.

"Colter! Shannon! Get a move on!" Ordway yelled from the compound.

Shannon bounded outside, delighted to be on his way to Matootonha and glad to escape Colter who always saw through his rationalizations. As he dipped into his pocket to assure himself the ribbons were still there, Rube punched his arm. "Ready, Peckerwood?"

"Ready!" he replied. The stirring in his loins was proof of that.

Fragrant Grass knelt on the buffalo robe spread beside the burial scaffold and arranged the bowls of food into the familiar ritual pattern. "For you, my husband," she murmured to the snow-shrouded mound on the platform. She settled down on the robe facing west and recalled the vision of Strikes Two, atop his favorite horse, riding at the head of that fateful raiding party. He had stopped, as he always did, at the top of the distant rise to look back at her. He did not wave — he never did — but she sensed his love even at that distance. It was her last image of him, the last time she saw him alive.

She held the vision in her mind, willing him to reappear in the flesh, to wipe away her pain with the light from his gentle smile. But the image eventually slithered away. As it faded, her ears caught faint sounds coming from the south. She tensed. Teton Sioux and Arikaras, the perennial enemies of her people, favored winter attacks.

At the sight of figures moving among the trees near the river, she whistled to the guards at the picket wall and took off toward the safety of the village. Fear weighted her legs, deep snow caught at her feet. She had been in too much of a hurry to get out of the lodge before Sly Wolf returned and she had not put on her snow-walking shoes, a choice she now regetted.

She floundered along, laboring to get enough air into her lungs. Terror chased all thoughts from her mind but one: if she did not reach the wall, if the intruders captured her, she would be enslaved. Or worse.

She reached the wall and staggered through the narrow opening to find not grim-faced warriors ready to defend the town, but rather a throng of children who raced out across the burial field toward the advancing figures. A woman caught her arm. "The paleskins come. And they make music. Strange music. Do you hear it?"

The group of newcomers were crossing the burial ground. For once, they were not carrying their long thunder-sticks. Two of them sawed branches across shaped boards, producing the most unearthly music she had ever heard. The rest were singing, laughing and jostling each other.

Fragrant Grass quickly picked out the Hawk man. Him Who Sees All still had not told her what she was to do with regard to this paleskin, and not knowing unsettled her.

Another source of distress for her was also in the approaching column. The dark-eyed one who tried to buy his way into her sleeping robes did not look like the other paleskins. Indeed, he looked like a Sioux, yet even the most brutish Sioux warrior would have heeded her shorn hair of mourning, instead of dishonoring her status as widow in such a manner.

Sly Wolf pushed his way to the front of the crowd of Mandans. "Explain this," he demanded of the boy Echo.

"This is a day of celebration for the paleskins. They come to share it with us," the boy said, beaming with pride over his knowledge of the strangers' ways.

Sly Wolf riveted his gaze on Fragrant Grass. "Do not stand there, Wife. Go to prepare food for our guests. We must honor them."

Inside their lodge, Mint was already at work preparing food. Poor Mint. She had been so sure she would win Sly Wolf's approval by taking the gap-toothed paleskin to her robes only to have that man refuse to offer the appropriate gifts to seal the bargain. In the weeks since, Sly Wolf had treated her so harshly that twice she had run out of the lodge in tears.

Now Mint was convinced that the only way to regain her husband's favor was to pick another paleskin to bed. Fragrant Grass did not know which of the strangers her sister would choose. She only knew which one she did not want it to be.

Colter had straggled near the end of the line of men crossing the frozen Missouri, deliberately putting off his arrival at the Mandan village for as long as he could. He did not know how he felt about seeing the one called Fragrant Grass again. Did not know if he wanted to know.

He and Shannon ended up in a group with Clark and Ordway in a different lodge than before. From the moment they sat down inside, Shannon began to squirm like a man preparing to bolt for somewhere else. Colter knew where the 'somewhere else' was and guessed that it would not be long before the younger man found an excuse to disappear in that direction.

Sure enough, within five minutes Shannon popped up and headed outside, drawing the attention of both Clark and Ordway. *Bad move, Fuzz*, Colter thought.

"She'd be a looker without all that clumpy hair and that white patch. Why, that patch looks like a big bird done shit on her head." The observations came from Joe Field who had offered a running commentary about every female they had seen since arriving in the town.

Colter had ignored Joe's chatter until his ears picked up the words "white patch." He spotted the woman Fragrant Grass among the group of Mandan spectators who had crowded into the lodge. During the eating and the dancing that followed, he tried to ignore her presence. He failed.

It was late afternnon when the captain signalled the fiddlers to stop playing. "Those who have no duties can remain here the rest of the afternoon," he announced. "The rest of you, it's time to go back with me."

Before Colter could get to his feet, someone grabbed his arm from behind. McNeal. "You got to help me out, Colter."

Colter pried off the clinging hand. "I don't 'got' to do nothin'. Especially for you."

"I'm about to bust from bein' around all these squaws. Got me so much juice built up, it's like to poison me if I cain't get rid of it. Only, I got the watch come dusk." While he talked, he caressed the bulge in his trousers and leered at a nearby cluster of women.

Colter rose. "I got me one watch already. Ain't interested in more."

The cook snatched at Colter's pantleg. "What if I got Ordway to ease off on you?"

As tempting as that offer sounded after weeks of pre-dawn watches in the freezing cold, he was not about to put himself in the cook's debt. "Nope."

McNeal tugged on Colter's trousers. "You got to. Cain't you see I need relief?" He pulled the top of his pants down, releasing his engorged penis to thrust obscenely toward the dome roof.

Being touched by the cook was one thing. Having to look at his ripe carrot was another. Colter pried loose the cook's grip and forced the man's hand into position to cover his exposed member.

The cook's yelp drew Ordway over. "Good God, McNeal! Cover yourself," the sergeant ordered.

"He attacked me, Sarge. For no reason," McNeal whined, fumbling to pull his pants back up. "I was only tryin' to get him to trade watches with me so's I could stay here awhile. He was goin' back anyways."

Colter snorted.

"You shut up, Colter. Let him speak his piece or I'll slap you with his watch, too," Ordway said.

"I already got a watch, Sarge," Colter said. "The same one you been givin' me all month. The ones I been enjoyin' so much."

"You goin' to let him talk back to you like that, Sarge?" McNeal said. "I'd say he deserves two watches for sassin' you."

"Good idea, Private." Ordway turned to Colter. "Two watches tonight it is, Colter, seeing as how you enjoy them so much."

While the cook scuttled away with his pants agape, Colter ducked through the tunnel before his hatred of the sergeant exploded. Eight hours on the roof! Eight hours. If Ordway was trying to break him, tonight might just do it.

He raised up from his stoop outside to find Echo. Beside the boy stood Fragrant Grass. Her gaze locked onto his. She glided toward him until only inches separated them, then she raised a hand to his face and lightly touched his birthmark. Reverence filled her gaze. She spoke to him in a soft, awed voice.

He had picked up a good knowledge of sign language from watching Echo and Shannon the last few weeks, but his knowledge of Mandan was too sparse to catch more than a word or two. "What's she sayin', Echo?"

"Of all my people," Echo said, "the Hawk Spirit chooses to guide only Pshanshaw. She say that you are the one she has seen in her dreams."

"Dreams," Colter scoffed. "I ain't no durned dream."

The woman's hand dropped to the pouch around his neck. She gasped at the outline of the hawk drawn on it. More incomprehensible words.

"Now what's she sayin'?"

"An old Sioux gave this to you. This she saw in a dream. The Hawk Spirit sends you to her."

A chill raced along Colter's spine. None of this made sense, yet he had the same sensation — that he had meant to come here. To come to her.

She turned away all of a sudden and hurried off. "What's she want?" he asked the boy in confusion.

"Do you know why you are here?" Echo asked.

"What kind of question is that?"

"When you know why you are here, you will know the answer to your question."

❧

After leaving the paleskin Colter, Fragrant Grass ducked into an empty lodge to calm down. She had taken a huge risk in approaching him. Her heart was a trapped bird fluttering in her chest. She had turned to the boy Echo in order to speak to the Hawk man. It was crucial that Colter understand her words and that she understand his. She had sworn the boy to secrecy, but he was still just a boy, prone to bragging. What if he told someone what she had done? What if Sly Wolf found out?

No, she must not dwell on such things. The deed was done. The words had been spoken. She had taken the step she had been directed to take. Whatever happened, there was no going back now.

❧

A red-faced Shannon stood at the edge of the open central plaza of the town. Although he thought he knew what lodge Mint lived in, he had barged in on a Mandan family instead. The humiliation left him sweating despite the cold. He had to find Mint. Had to.

A pair of figures walked across the central plaza and stood outside the entrance to the lodge where Captain Clark's group was being entertained. In the gloom of the waning afternoon, Shannon recognized the taller person as the squaw with the cropped hair and white patch and the smaller figure as Echo. For a moment he considered calling the boy over to help him find Mint but changed his mind when Colter emerged from the lodge's tunnel. Shannon slipped into the cover of the closest lodge to observe what transpired.

Why, you hypocrite! Shannon threw his thoughts at Colter. *After all the demeaning things you said about Mint, about squaws, and here you are, letting one stroke your face. Old Man, you're going to hear about this.*

From me.

Hearing someone approaching his hiding place, Shannon moved farther into cover. When next he chanced a look, everyone was gone: Colter, the woman and Echo. Then someone tugged on his sleeve. "What are you do-ing, Friend Shannon?" Echo asked.

"I got turned around," he mumbled, trying to cover his surprise at being discovered spying.

"Your friends are in the lodge over there. Shall I lead you?" Echo said.

Shannon already knew that fact after seeing Colter come out of the lodge but he dutifully followed the boy. He was moving through the entrance tunnel when someone decided to come out that way, and they collided. Tilting his face up to offer an apology, he found himself nose to nose with the one who had haunted his dreams. "Shakoka. Mint."

She frowned at him and tried to brush past.

With fumbling fingers, he pulled the ribbons from his pocket and held them out to her.

Her frown dissolved and she broke into a brilliant smile that momentarily took his breath away. When her hand brushed his in taking possession of the ribbons, his heart skipped two beats. When she beckoned for him to follow her, he did not hesitate.

The next morning Shannon awoke with the scent of Mint in his nostrils and the taste of her sweetening his mouth. The image of her beguiling face lingered in his eyes long after he left her to return to the fort. Mint, beauti-ful Mint. His time with her had been sweet, but all too short. Now his first priority was to get back to Matootonha as soon and often as possible.

While his body went through the familiar motions of roll call and break-fast, his mind combed over the details of the Mandan beauty and his expe-rience with her. Unlike Lisette, Mint was childlike in her lack of modesty and in her affection, a combination he found irresistible. Because other crewmen were also liable to find her tantalizing, his second priority was to keep her as his own private domain.

On this day, he drew no work detail. At any other time, he would have dreaded the empty hours stretching ahead of him. Now, however, he rel-ished the time to savor last night's memories and make plans for future visits. He entered the barracks after muster to find it empty except for Colter who sat cross-legged on his bunk. The man glanced up at him, then went back to his carving.

"You missed the fun yesterday, Old Man," Shannon said. "You should've stayed around."

Colter remained silent.

"Dad blast it! Don't just sit there. Say something!" Shannon demanded.

"Nothin' to say," Colter said.

"What? No lecture about staying away from squaws?"

A shaving curled away from the wood under the blade of Colter's knife.

"I saw you with that woman," Shannon said. "The one with the white streak. I saw how she touched you. She was willing. Why'd you pass that up?"

Colter kept on carving.

"Confound your hide, Old Man. Since when do you get off being so righteous?"

"What you do's your concern. My doin's are mine," Colter stated.

"You got no right to act so high and mighty with me."

"You made your choice, Fuzz. Now leave me to mine."

"I'll leave you all right." He grabbed his things and slammed out the door, his good mood gone. He faced the compound wondering where he would go to pass the rest of the day.

Across the way, the door to the room occupied by the two interpreters and their wives opened, and out came Jesseaume's woman, Mint's twin. Her appearance rooted Shannon to the frozen ground. Longing welled into his loins, dissolving his anger. He had to find a way back to Matootonha, the sooner, the better.

Ordway came through the gates. "Ah, Private Shannon, just the man I wanted to see. McNeal's sick. I need a replacement on water detail. Buckets are in the store room."

The cook had made a career out of shirking water detail, a fact Ordway never seemed to catch on to. Shannon was about to say something before a thought stopped him. Angering the sergeant was not the way to get back to Mint quickly. He swallowed his first words and replaced them with "Yes, Sergeant."

6. *Calling the Buffalo*

C olter gouged another notch on the log next to his bunk. January 7. Dead of winter. Ice two feet thick on the river. Temperatures so low that they shattered the captains' last thermometer. A numbing cold that settled a spirit-smothering lethargy on him. That lethargy ate away at his resolve to not let Ordway get to him and made it impossible to muster the energy to shore that determination back up. He was even too listless to carve.

The door to the barracks opened and Ordway strolled in. "Colter, get your things. You're going to the Mandan town. Meet me at the gates in five minutes."

As soon as the door closed behind the sergeant, the eyes of his barracksmates swung to Colter. "What's goin' on?" Rube asked. "Why you and not me?"

Disregarding the stares and the questions, Colter got up and slowly assembled his gear. What was the sergeant up to now?

When he offered no answers to their questions, the other men went back to whatever they were doing. Not Shannon. "Why are you going over there, Old Man?" he demanded.

"Ask Ordeal."

Echo piped up. "There is a ceremony at my village tonight. In it my people call the buffalo to the river."

Colter relaxed at the explanation. The last time the buffalo came to the river, he downed five, the most of all the crew. No doubt the captains had chosen him to go to the ceremony because of that and not because of any perverse scheme of Ordway's.

He stepped outside into the failing light of the afternoon to find York and Drouillard with Ordway and Jesseaume. Before he had a chance to wonder why York of all the rest of the crew was going to a buffalo-hunting ceremony, Ordway headed out the gate. Colter put aside his thoughts to follow.

Fragrant Grass pressed into the shadows near the entrance of the sacred lodge. After the Hawk Spirit had visited her dreams last night, she had endured a long day with her emotions swinging between excitement and fear. The next few moments would reveal if her dream was truly from the gods or a mere fantasy.

A murmur rippled through the crowd in the lodge. The paleskins had entered the town. Hearing that the Black Giant was in the group, some of the women near her began to gossip about him. "He is a stallion on two legs," one said, holding her hands apart to indicate the size of the giant's male member.

"May he mount many mares this night," another said to a chorus of ribald laughter.

Fragrant Grass closed her ears to such talk. Earlier Mint had confided that she planned to take the Black Giant to her robes next. The thought of her petite sister mating with such a big man might have been laughable if she herself had not experienced terrible pain the first time Strikes Two had entered her with his outsized maleness.

The grim-faced paleskin Second Chief Ordway entered the lodge first. He explained that First Chief Red Hair and First Chief Merry Weather would not be coming to the ceremony. The news clearly disappointed Big White who had enjoyed the deference accorded him because of the paleskin chiefs' frequent attentions.

Next came Jesseaume and Black Giant. While the women gossips continued to speculate about the latter, Fragrant Grass studied Jesseaume and thought about her sister, pretty Kebeka. *How hard it must be to live with such a man in a place as dreary as the paleskins' fort!*

The black-eyed one who looked like a Sioux entered next. She had hoped he would not come. She pressed back against the earth wall. Since refusing him, both Mint and Sly Wolf had treated her as if she had done something wrong.

The one called Colter entered last, and her heartbeat quickened. So, he had come. She had dreamed true and now she must follow the Hawk Spirit's guidance from that dream. She ducked quickly outside and went to prepare for the task ahead.

After the three-mile walk across the river and through the frozen land-scape to the Mandan town, all Colter could think about was getting warm. The lodge they entered was bigger than the ones he had seen on previous visits. It contained none of the usual signs of habitation: no bed platforms along the walls, no woven sacks hanging from the central uprights, no gardening tools piled in the corner. Despite the crush of Mandans, it had the damp feel and smell of a place infrequently used.

A line of men dressed in headdresses and elaborately-painted robes sat apart from the crowd along the wall to the left. Beyond them stretched a row of empty backrests. There was another row of empty seats to the right of the fire.

Little Raven led Colter and the others to the only vacant space left at the front of the packed crowd. Echo wedged himself in beside Colter. "This is the most sacred of our ceremonies, Friend Colter," he confided in excellent English. "If we succeed in bringing the buffalo to us, my people will have enough food to last the winter. If we do not succeed, there will be hunger."

A sharp clapping of hands silenced Echo and the rest of the crowd. Twelve Mandan elders filed solemnly into the lodge. The first eleven carried flat red boards painted with what looked like black hoofprints. Standing these boards on end, the elders created a low wall that stretched from the central fire to the back wall. They then took up the row of backrests on the fire's left.

The twelfth man bore an animal hide. This he carried to the red-board wall where he draped it over a chest-high post. Unfolded, the hide proved to be a beautifully-worked white buffalo robe.

A long silence ensued before the entrance curtain again moved aside, and a group of the town's men entered, accompanied by their wives. Each woman wore a buffalo robe whose edges she held away from her body in a stiff ceremonial way. Sly Wolf and Mint came third in that group, but Fragrant Grass did not appear.

The husbands took the seats to the right of the fire, leaving their wives standing in a line just inside the entrance. At the rear of the lodge, a drum began to beat, and the assembled Mandans broke into song. Their chant had a haunting quality that drew Colter into its rhythms despite his uneasiness.

After the song, the first wife paced to the fire, squatted over her heels and performed a strange waddling walk along the fence of red boards. York leaned toward Colter. "My, my, is that bare skin I see?"

Bare skin it was, for the woman was naked under the robe. Echo whispered, "She walks with the *ptemday*, the buffalo."

The woman reached the end of the wall, raised out of her squat and went to stand behind her husband. Then the next woman repeated the performance, followed by the next and the next until all the wives had rejoined their husbands.

Colter leaned toward Echo. "What's —"

Echo cut him off with a "Shhh" and a nod toward the first elder, who had just risen. In his hand the old one carried a doll, perhaps a foot in length, dressed like a Mandan woman complete with braids of real hair. Holding the doll at arm's length, the old man chanted in a quavering voice as he walked with slow, measured steps to a square of deerskin spread on the packed earth near the fire. He knelt and carefully arranged the doll, face up, on the hide. Finishing the chant, he lifted his face toward the smoke hole and appeared to offer up a silent prayer. Then he positioned himself over the doll and began to imitate copulation.

At that point, Colter's interest turned to foreboding. With Ordway's stare heavy upon him, he sensed there was more to this ceremony than just getting buffalo to show up for a hunt.

After the elder finished the pantomime and returned to his seat, the first of the husbands rose from his backrest, took his wife's hands and delivered a speech to her in a loud formal voice. Then he walked over to the seated elders and delivered a second discourse.

One of the old men rose unsteadily. The husband placed his wife's hand around the old man's medicine bag and she used the bag as a kind of leash to lead the old one outside to the approving murmurs of the watching Mandans.

The second husband repeated the performance of the first, and the second wife left the lodge, leading another elder.

"What just happened? Where are they going?" York whispered to Echo.

"She goes to walk with him."

"What do you mean 'walk'? Where?" York asked.

Echo held a finger to his lips and nodded toward another husband who rose to repeat the performance a third time. This time the chosen elder did not get up. Instead he pointed to Drouillard.

"You must rise and walk with her," Echo urged the hesitant half-breed.

Drouillard looked to Jesseaume, who spoke to him in low urgent French. Drouillard got to his feet then and allowed the third wife to lead him out the lodge tunnel.

By now Colter had a good idea what Echo meant by 'walking the buffalo', and he wanted no part of it. Then again, there was no way out of the lodge before the end of the ceremony.

The next man up was Sly Wolf. He repeated the mysterious performance: delivering one speech to Mint; another to the remaining elders. At the conclusion of his speech, an old Mandan rose, but instead of allowing Mint to clasp his medicine bag, he intercepted her hand and led her over to York.

The slave popped up eagerly and grabbed Mint's hand. "If this means what I think it does, take me away, little lady."

Because Mint barely reached York's chest, she resembled a child leading her father to the jar of rock candy at the general store as she led the slave to the lodge entrance. *Good thing Shannon ain't here to see this*, Colter thought. Then he changed his mind: *Nope, he oughtta be here, find out what he's dealin' with.*

The last husband repeated Sly Wolf's performance. Again an elder rose and guided the man's wife to the crew. Colter kept his gaze focused on the fire to avoid possible eye contact.

His ploy worked. The elder pointed to Ordway, and Colter barely managed to swallow a guffaw of vindication as he watched the sergeant follow the woman outside. Ordway had been caught in a trap of his own devising. Served him right.

Since there were no more couples and no chances to be paired with a squaw, Colter relaxed. All he had to do now was wait for the others to get back, then they could return to the fort.

At that moment the curtain across the tunnel entrance moved aside to reveal Fragrant Grass, wrapped in a buffalo robe that she held away from her body in the manner of the women before her. She walked to Sly Wolf and, eyes downcast, began to whisper to him. The man's face darkened, but he nodded at her, and she glided to the red-board fence. The crowd sucked in a collective breath as she squatted on her haunches.

Colter could not take his eyes off her as she performed the ritual walk. The serenity, the peace in her expression stood in direct contrast to the mix of confused emotions that bubbled in the cauldron of his innards.

When she finished, Sly Wolf got to his feet and approached the remaining elder, the one who had chosen Drouillard. The old man declined but did not motion toward Colter. A look of uncertainty passed between Sly Wolf and Fragrant Grass. She murmured something to him. Sly Wolf glanced at Colter.

Again, she whispered. Colter caught one word: *ptemday*. Buffalo.

Sly Wolf levelled his gaze at Colter and spoke. Echo translated. "He asks that the one marked by the Hawk Spirit walk with this woman."

"Oh, no. Not me," Colter said.

"But you must," Echo pleaded. "If the buffalo do not come, my people and your people will have no meat to eat."

"Weren't my idea to be here and I ain't doin' this. No way," Colter said.

Sly Wolf's gaze narrowed as Colter continued to hesitate. The boy's voice became desperate. "No one refuses. This is a great honor. You must go with her."

Fragrant Grass shifted slightly beside Sly Wolf. Her nervousness touched a chord with Colter. He sensed that she had taken a great risk to do what she had done this night. He did not understand what was at stake for her, but he did recognize the fear lurking behind her eyes.

"Please, Friend Colter," Echo pleaded.

Reluctantly, he rose. Immediately Fragrant Grass turned and ducked through the tunnel. Coming out of the overheated atmosphere of the lodge, Colter's lungs balked at breathing the icy night air. He stopped, racked by shivering. She stopped also.

"T-this ain't r-right," he said, through chattering teeth. *Or was it just the cold that made him stutter?*

She spoke hurriedly, words he did not understand.

"D-durn it all. W-where's that Echo w-when I need him?"

A booming laugh sounded from the direction of the central plaza. York's laugh. The big man appeared with his arm slung across Mint's small shoulder. York looked Fragrant Grass over approvingly. "My, my. Where did you get her, Colter?"

"She ain't mine," he said sourly.

Mint spoke to Fragrant Grass in curt tones. Fragrant Grass neither responded nor looked at her, but Colter felt the tension between the two women and guessed that Fragrant Grass had violated some social rule.

"Hope you enjoy her as much as I enjoyed this little beauty," York said with a wink, following Mint into the ceremonial lodge and leaving Colter alone again with Fragrant Grass.

"I cain't do what you got in mind," He fumbled for the right word to call her and settled on, "ma'am."

As he turned away from her, she grabbed his sleeve. "Col-ter."

The hair rose on the back of his neck and not from the result of the cold. "How do you know my name?"

More figures approached from across the plaza. He had no desire to meet Drouillard or Ordway, so he took her hand and pulled her off to the opening in the picket wall. There he tried to drop her hand, but she clung to his grasp.

"Pshanshaw, no. I cain't."

She looked up at him, a smile slowly dawning on her lips. "You speak my name," she signed.

He nodded, and her smile grew softer. "Come, Col-ter," she said in clear English.

Again, hearing her speak his name dissolved his argument. He watched her squeeze through the opening and walk out into the snowy burying ground. In the hush he could hear the rustle of her buffalo robe brushing the snow as she walked. She stopped on the other side of the closest scaffold and knelt on the snow, facing him.

Colter was torn. He ought to take off now and head back to the fort. He could make up some story to explain why he had come back before the others. Then again, how could he up and leave her here when he perceived that she had broken some social convention in order to be paired with him? He owed her something if only an excuse.

He went to where she knelt in the snow. "I'm goin' back to the fort," he signed, then added a spoken, "Pshanshaw."

She touched his hand and said in a low voice, "Stay, Col-ter."

"Cain't."

She lay back on the snow and opened the buffalo robe to him, exposing her naked flesh to the frigid night air.

"What're you tryin' to do? Freeze?" He stooped to pull the robe shut again.

He had not regained his feet when she threw open the buffalo hide again. "Now don't be like that. I got to go back." As he stooped to cover her once more, the sight of her naked body wilted his resolve.

She grasped his hand and held the free edge of the robe up to him. "Col-ter, come."

"If'n I lay down there, I'll get snow all over you, and you're bound to catch your death, and —"

She touched a finger to his lips. The finger was trembling, and she was shivering violently from the cold, but she kept smiling at him. If he was going to leave, he better do it right now. *Stop lollygaggin' and let the woman wrap up and get warm.*

Her shaking finger moved up to his birthmark. "Hawk Spirit," she said in English through chattering teeth. "Pshanshaw . . . and Col-ter."

Col-ter. With that one word, his resistance evaporated. He stretched out next to her and pulled the robe around both of them.

The buffalo-calling ceremony kept Colter and the others at Matootonha all night. The next morning he deliberately lagged behind the group on the way back to the fort. A welter of strong, conflicting emotions made him shun company. He could not reconcile the fact that he had gone against a lifetime's worth of principle by bedding a squaw — and that he had en-joyed it. Worse, he wanted more. Lots more.

He reached the gates of Fort Mandan to find York surrounded by crew-men, demanding to hear about his overnight adventures. Spotting Shannon among the eager listeners, Colter decided to slide around the group and es-cape to the barracks. He was not ready to face Shannon or tell stories. He had almost skirted the group when Rube grabbed his arm.

"Is it true what York says?" Rube asked. "That it was some kind of fer-tility rite and every one of you got a squaw?"

"That what he said?" Colter hedged.

Someone in the crowd around York called out, "Which squaw'd you get, Beast?" Beast was the nickname the crew had given York after he had convinced the Rees he was a wild creature that the captains usually kept chained in a cage.

"She was a little bitty thing looks just like Jesseaume's woman," York said.

Amid the catcalls, someone called out, "That little thing? Why, you musta split her in half."

Colter glanced over to see Shannon backing toward the barracks, the color leached from his face.

"What about you, Colter?" McNeal asked. "Thought you didn't like brown meat."

He knew he had to come up with an answer or face some ugly ribbing. "It ain't the color of the meat, but the way it tastes. Right, Rube?"

Rube caught the spotlight Colter tossed to him and Colter took the op-portunity to sneak into the barracks. Inside, Shannon lay rigidly on his bunk. His voice was wobbly. "Is it true? Was she York's partner for this, this ritual?"

Colter could not meet the younger man's tortured gaze, and he did not know what to say that would not make matters worse.

Shannon swung his legs off his bunk. "Damn it, Old Man. Tell me!"

"Yes, Fuzz, she was."

Shannon moaned and covered his face with his hands.

"Lord, almighty, Fuzz. What'd you expect? She's a squaw for pity's sake."

The door opened and crewmen crowded into the room, jabbering and laughing. Rube punched Colter in the arm. "Lucked out again, huh, Colter? That squaw with the white streak'll be a real looker once that hair of hers grows out."

Colter took the jibe with a tight smile, then busied himself re-stowing his gear. Shannon grabbed his shoulder and hissed, "Just a squaw, huh. Well, Old Man, I got news for you. So's the one *you* bedded. You who said he'd never crawl into a squaw's robes. Ha! You're nothing but a hypocrite."

Colter stifled the urge to defend himself, to claim he had no choice in the matter. That would have been a lie. He did have a choice. A choice to leave. A choice he had not taken.

"Buffalo! Let's go hunting!" came the shout from the compound.

The little room turned into bedlam as crewmen jostled each other to grab rifles and head off for a hunt. Colter watched the others in astonishment. According to Echo, last night's ceremony was meant to call the buffalo back to the river, to provide meat to see the Mandans through the rest of the winter. And now — just like that — the buffalo showed up.

"You just going to stand there? You, the big-shot hunter?" Shannon said sarcastically.

"I'm goin'," Colter said.

"Good. Maybe you won't come back," Shannon said.

"Oh, I'll be back. You can count on it." Colter slammed the door shut behind him.

In the compound, Fragrant Grass stood with Mint and Jesseaume's squaw in the doorway to the interpreters' room. The sight of her caught Colter by surprise. He had never seen her at the fort before, and seeing her here now preempted every other thought: his self-disgust, his longing, the buffalo hunt, his irritation at Shannon.

Across the heads of the gathering crew, his gaze locked with hers, and he knew what he had to do.

After Colter left Shannon, the barracks continued to reverberate with their exchange. *Why does every conversation between us end in harsh words anymore?* Shannon wondered. *What has happened to our friendship?*

He pondered those questions to the sounds of the crew preparing to leave the fort for the hunt. There was so much noise outside that he almost missed the knock that signalled he had five minutes to get to his post. He pulled on a second pair of moccasins, shrugged on two extra buckskin shirts and a tattered great coat, draped his blanket over his shoulders and let himself out into the compound.

The cold hit him with the force of a blow. By the time he reached the roof, he yearned to be back by the fire. "You sure took your sweet time getting' here, Shannon," Collins, the retiring sentry, complained. "Now I got to run to catch them others."

Shannon was in no mood to carp back. He watched the line of crewmen making their way toward the river. The individuals in the column were recognizable from their strides: Rube, Joe, Drouillard, Colter, Captain Clark, York.

York and Mint. His mind refused to embrace an image of the two of them together. Had bedding York been her idea or her husband's? Was she fickle like Lisette? Was she toying with his heart? Did he mean nothing to her?

He was wrestling with those questions when female voices drew his attention down to the compound. Mint and her twin, Kebeka, Jesseaume's woman, picked up a big bundle from the ground outside the interpreters' hut and carried it inside. Seeing Mint compounded Shannon's sense of betrayal. *Why me? Why me?*

The column of hunters started across the frozen Missouri. One of the men appeared to slip on the ice and twist an ankle. Captain Clark stepped out of the line of march and came back to the hurt man.

Shannon turned away from the drama on the ice. He had problems of his own to ponder. For instance, how to get through the next four hours in the intense cold. He paced the width of the roof, pivoted and stopped.

That was Colter limping back to the fort.

Once inside the gates, Colter's ankle suddenly healed and he walked normally into the interpreters' room. He emerged moments later with Fragrant Grass in tow. The pair hurried to the squad's barracks room and disappeared inside.

It took all Shannon's control not to climb down from his post and storm the room. Colter was the worst kind of hypocrite, stooping to McNeal's level by faking a fall so he could come back and couple with Fragrant Grass. Shannon stomped down hard, dislodging icicles. "Damn your fornicating heart, John Colter!"

"Is there a problem, Shannon?"

He whirled to see Captain Lewis standing in the compound looking up at him. "No, sir, I . . . I was just stamping some feeling back into my feet."

"Then pray, do so a little more softly please."

"Yes, sir. Sorry, sir."

Soon after Lewis let himself back into the captains' quarters, the door to the interpreters' hut opened and out came Mint and Kebeka. Shannon turned away to avoid being seen, but not in time.

He returned a half-hearted wave to Mint's eager one, then pretended to be intent on walking his post. At the far edge of the roof, he knelt to re-tie his moccasins. *What a coward I am*, he thought. *She's just a woman, after all. Maybe I ought to follow Colter's lead and take Mint to the loft when my watch is over. Now there's an idea.*

When he got to his feet to hail Mint, the two Indian sisters were nearly to the river. He would have to yell to get their attention, and he was unprepared to offer another explanation to the captain. Once again, he had blown his chance.

Fragrant Grass drew the moistened porcupine quills between her teeth to flatten them. Putting six more quills into her mouth to soften, she stitched three of the flat ones into place, creating a pattern on the toe-piece of the new moccasin.

The restlessness she had felt since returning to the village from the pale-skins' fort was still with her. It did not help that Sly Wolf would not quit staring at her or that Mint had been unusually quiet all evening. Besides the crackling fire, the only sound in the lodge was the scratch of Mint's awl working holes into the seam of a new pair of leggings for their husband.

Outside, the wind howled, hurling snow in blinding curtains that would disorient anyone foolish enough to challenge the storm. She longed for a place to sort out her jumbled thoughts but it was too early to retire to her bed.

The wind's moans reflected the war her emotions were waging within her. Him Who Sees All had shaken the foundation of her world with the paleskin Colter. Her sense of duty to the dead Strikes Two clashed with her belief that Colter had come to guide her to a new and different life, a life she longed for, yet one she also feared.

She flattened the last six quills and stitched them onto the leather with Sly Wolf's unnerving gaze following her every move. The point of the bone needle broke off on the last quill, pricking her finger, drawing blood. Mint had a new metal needle, a gift from the Black Giant, but asking to use it would mean breaking the stony silence. She decided against it. She rolled the broken needle together with the unfinished moccasin, faked a yawn and nodded her goodnights to her sister and Sly Wolf.

She did not allow herself to relax until she dropped the curtain across the front of her sleeping platform. She tucked away her sewing bundle, then crawled beneath the buffalo robes. The call of the night guard patrolling Matootonha's perimeter drifted through the storm. Tonight, the sound did not reassure her.

She clutched her medicine pouch and offered up a silent prayer, beseeching Him Who Sees All to send her a dream to guide her next steps. Then she curled onto her side to face the earth wall and waited for sleep to come.

The leather of Mint's sleeping couch creaked, followed by murmurs. Fragrant Grass could not make out the exact words, but the strain in her sister's voice and the curtness in Sly Wolf's meant an argument. She covered her ears to shut out the possibility of hearing.

Suddenly, the curtain over her bed jerked aside. Sly Wolf stood silhouetted against the central fire. His lips curled into the sneer that, on him, passed for a smile. "Make room for your husband, Wife."

All that night Fragrant Grass lay rigid with her back to Sly Wolf. His right arm encircled her waist like a vise. She could scarcely breathe. He had pounded his member into her for hours before dropping into an exhausted sleep. She waited for the moment when he would leave her bed and she could get to the river to wash away the loathsome stickiness that oozed between her legs.

He shifted and murmured into her ear, sending shivers along her spine. "You surprised me, Wife. For so long, I have respected the spirit of your first husband. I never suspected that you wished to end your mourning until you came into the medicine lodge to help call our buffalo brothers."

He paused. Her heart raced.

"I was so patient for so long. For nothing." The cold fury in his voice made her suddenly afraid. "Even your sister shows more enthusiasm in coupling. Did your mother not teach you how to please your husband?"

She wanted to block out his criticism, but his voice cut through her efforts.

"Did you just lie there with Strikes Two, showing no more life than a fallen log?" He yanked on her hair and she bit down on her lower lip to keep from crying out.

"You disgust me." He shoved her away from him and rolled off the stretched leather of her sleeping platform. "It is good that your mourning ends. Now I must decide whether to keep you as wife or find you another husband. In either case, I will teach you to be more responsive to a man."

Her stomach fluttered with anguish over the prospect of remarriage. Was it an idle threat, or would he really do such a thing?

He put his mouth against her cheek. "You can let your hair grow now. There is no need to keep cutting it."

He rose. The curtain fell back into place. She tasted bile in her throat. How long had he known?

The plump Sioux woman guarding Hartley began to nod off. Once, twice, three times, her round head fell forward only to jerk back up. The fourth nod, sleep won out. Her chin drooped onto the shelf of her bosom and she began to snore softly.

The preacher continued to scrape hair off the stretched hide until her snores grew in volume and he was certain she was fast asleep. Then he threw down the bone scraper and massaged the aching muscles of his lower back. The squaw's cur — an ugly yellow male of indistinguishable breed — eyed him suspiciously but, for once, refrained from barking.

Back in the Draft when he had been visiting Farley Stuart at home one day, he had happened to pass the kitchen as Jezebel, Stuart's enormous coal-black slave cook, was watching her master through the window. The searing hatred in her expression had left an indelible impression on him.

Now that he was a slave to the Sioux he understood the depths of Jezebel's loathing. The Sioux treated their dogs better than him. The squaws heaped dozens of tasks on him every day, then took delight in beating him when he could not finish them. They would pay for their cruelty and pay dearly. He would see to it.

At a change in the squaw's breathing, he grabbed up the scraper. How he begrudged her the sleep! He had not slept a night through since catching that Indian arrow in his shoulder. The wound had never healed properly, and it throbbed constantly, keeping him from the rest he so desperately craved.

Her snoring regained its volume, and the preacher bent forward to rest his forehead on the ground, easing the strain on his aching back. It was the perfect position to contemplate his dilemma. As much as he longed to run away from the life of agony he had been thrust into, escape was out of the question. He had no weapon and no idea where he was. Was he doomed to die from overwork or malnutrition? Was this all his life would ever amount to?

The yellow cur's ears pricked up at a warbling whistle, the camp guard's signal for intruders. Instantly, the entire village came awake. With the adult men scrambling into their defensive positions, Hartley scuttled out of the tepee before the squaw guard awakened. He bent into a crouch and crowded in behind a young mother carrying a baby on a fur-draped cradle-board. He planned to use her as a shield to scoot inside the safe-keeping tepee with the rest of the women and children.

He had just reached the tepee when a second whistle called off the alert. Women and children, anxious to get back to their lodges, surged out of the opening flap. He had to back up to avoid them, and he tripped over one of the tepee's tether pegs.

He was picking himself up when a group of the camp's braves rode out to meet an approaching party of riders. He edged behind the war chief's lodge to watch and listen, curious to know who would be traveling in such raw weather.

Despite the biting wind, the leader of the newcomers rode with his head bare except for a single eagle feather that pointed to the sky. Several of the men with Lone Feather wore raven-skin headdresses similar to that of the local war chief, the man who had captured Hartley.

The parlay broke up after several minutes, and the newcomers followed the local men into the encampment. Hartley decided he'd better get back to his labors before his absence earned him a beating. But, as he turned, he was intercepted by a doltish warrior named Eagle Claw. Eagle Claw forced him into the war chief's lodge and shoved him unceremoniously into a corner moments before the newcomers and their hosts entered.

The requisite smoking and talking proceeded for a time before the war chief motioned for Hartley to approach. The preacher shuffled forward, trying to make his body as small and inconspicuous as possible.

The war chief indicated for Hartley to kneel in front of Lone Feather, who studied the preacher's face for a long time, then signed for him to lay face down on the ground with his arms outspread.

Hartley was baffled by the strange request, but complied. To his complete surprise, Lone Feather rose and stepped up onto his back. The Sioux was a substantial man and bearing his full weight proved more than the preacher's right-side floating ribs could handle. They snapped with an audible pop.

Hartley yelped with pain. This display of weakness drew a derisive snort from Lone Feather before he casually stepped down from his perch. Two Sioux in raven headdresses pulled the preacher to his feet, dragged him out of the lodge, and boosted him onto a horse. When they slapped the animal into motion, Hartley was beyond noticing.

7. *Slipping Around*

After he satisfied his hunger for Fragrant Grass in the loft and saw her out the gate, Colter began to regret his impulsiveness. He was turning into the kind of man he despised — because of a woman, because of a *squaw*. There was only one way to stop his downward spiral. He resolved to stay away from Fragrant Grass in thought and action.

He turned down two chances to visit Matootonha over the course of the next three weeks and congratulated himself that he was over her. Then, as he was returning to the fort after wood-gathering detail, he thought he saw Fragrant Grass enter the interpreters' hut. That momentary glimpse stopped him in his tracks, forcing the other members of the wood crew to walk around him. When he tried to get his feet to go toward the barracks, they carried him instead to the interpreters' door where the same force that altered his direction caused his hand to tap on the rough wood.

The door opened to reveal the nut-brown face of Charbonneau's pregnant Shoshone wife Sacajawea. A quick glance over the woman's shoulder revealed that his eyes had deceived him. Fragrant Grass was not there. He signed a quick apology and hurried across the frozen ruts of the yard to the barracks.

The familiar smells of smoke, wet leather and unwashed bodies engulfed him as soon as he crossed the threshold. He hoped that his face did not reflect the disappointment he was feeling. He stowed his things and took out his carving.

He had just settled on his bunk when Rube and a young Mandan woman climbed down from the loft. Clutching a handful of trinkets, the woman let herself out the door. Rube strutted to the fire, proud as a banty rooster. The unmistakable smell of sex emanating from him prodded memories in Colter. Memories he could not shunt aside. Memories that quickly grew.

He did not want to acknowledge the fact that his yearning for Fragrant Grass was more powerful than his determination to keep away, but he could not deny it. He had to see her again, and soon. But not here. Somewhere private, away from the fort and the crew. Especially Shannon.

Rube sidled over to Colter's bunk. "Joe's got froze feet from last night's watch. He can't go huntin' tomorrow. You want to fill in for him?"

Colter almost said "no", then he checked himself in time. "Sure, Rube. Much obliged your askin'."

Rube took one step out the door the next morning and turned right around. "It's colder'n a well-digger's backside. Let's stay here where it's warm."

Colter was not about to let cold weather keep him from what he had spent the night planning. "You're imaginin' things, Rube. Ain't that bad. You'll warm up soon's we get goin'."

Rube hung back. "Captain don't want us out when it's so cold. Lead hunter decides."

Ordway did not yet know that he was taking Joe's place and Colter wanted to keep it that way until he was out of range of the fort. He pressed on, "Crew ain't got that much meat left, Rube. What's goin' to happen if'n it gets any colder? I sure don't cotton to short rations. Do you?"

Rube still hesitated. If he checked the storeroom, he would discover that Colter had stretched the truth more than a little.

"I say it ain't that bad out," Colter went on. "I'm goin'. You do what you want." He took off, hoping Rube would stay back and let him get on with things.

Rube didn't. He followed Colter out the gates and along the river for half a mile before asking, "Which way you figure on goin'?" Each word puffed fog in the icy air.

Colter spoke slowly as if he were thinking as he talked rather than speaking the script he had figured out overnight. "Cold as it's been, game's goin' to be scattered. If'n we're goin' to get anythin', reckon we ought to split up. I'll head out that-a-way. What say you go off yonder and meet me back in this here spot 'fore dark?"

Hugging himself for warmth, Rube grunted agreement through chattering teeth. Colter took off toward the north before Rube could change his mind. Even that short stop had stiffened his limbs. It took a mile of moving along before he regained his usual fluidity and felt warmed up enough to pause in the shelter of a pair of leafless elms and peruse his surroundings.

To the east, south and north, the winter-bare trees of the river trench stood like so many skeletal sentinels, silently observing his movements. Five yards to the west lay the frozen Missouri. Across the expanse of ice, ribbons of smoke rose string-straight into the still air from the roof openings of the mound lodges of Matootonha. Far away some creature shrieked, raising gooseflesh on the backs of Colter's hands. He glanced around to make sure he was alone.

Reassured, he moved to the edge of the ice. There he paused again to give his mind one last chance to make a new decisioon. The shriek sounded again. This time he recognized it as the cry of a hunting hawk. He lifted his eyes to see one circling against the dome of the ice-blue sky. As

he watched, the creature tucked its wings and dove down the sky, vanishing beyond the lodges of the Mandan town.

It is a sign, from the Hawk Spirit. Fragrant Grass's phrase popped into
his mind unbidden, and he struck off across the ice.

When Colter pushed through the barracks door the next morning, Rube
popped up off his bunk. "Thank the Maker! We was sure you'd froze to
death last night!"

Shannon kept his back turned while the other men peppered Colter with
questions about how he had survived the previous night. They all pre-
sumed he had gotten himself lost while out hunting. Shannon knew better.
Colter *never* got lost.

"Weren't nothin' to it," Colter said. "Dug me a cave in a drift and curled
there, snug as could be. Somethin' my old partner taught me."

At this, Shannon turned. He could read the lie on Colter's face as clearly
as snow melt, but the other men swallowed it whole. Then York poked his
head in. "Captains want to see you, Colter."

"It be all right for me to catch some grub first?" Colter asked.

"Make it quick," York said.

The door had just shut on the slave when Ordway snatched it open again
and called out men for a water detail. The list included everyone except
Colter and Shannon. Shannon waited until the others had gone to speak.
"You can't lie to save yourself, Old Man."

"You're gettin' real free with your name callin' lately, ain't you, Fuzz?"
Colter said.

"As free as you are getting about fitting your story to whatever suits your
purpose. I used to depend on you to tell the truth. Now all you do is lie."

The door swung open and Ordway waltzed in. "Go on, Shannon. I'd like
to hear what else you have to say about our mutual friend here."

Colter left off tending to his feet to toss a warning glance at Shannon.

"We were having a private conversation," Shannon said. "An argument.
Nothing you'd be interested in."

"Oh, but I'm interested in everything concerning my men, Private. Please
tell me." Ordway's eyes narrowed. "Now!"

Shannon weighed whether to reveal that Colter had sneaked off to Matootonha or to cover for him. He decided in favor of Colter and threw all
the innocence he could muster into his smile. "We were arguing over a
hand sign. Colter claims this here is the sign for 'Sioux'." He held his right
hand across his chest and scissored his fingers. "And I say it's this." His
hands imitated the slithering of a snake. "Which is it, Sergeant?"

The fury of one who knows he has been thwarted flashed through Ordway's eyes. "I say you're both on water duty as of this moment!"

Colter spoke up, "Sorry, Sarge. Captains're expectin' me soon's I get me
somethin' to eat."

Twice blocked, Ordway turned the full force of his malice on Shannon.
"You have one minute to get out the door, Private. Or you'll be on roof

duty the rest of the winter."

The sergeant's departure left the room quiet except for the wheeze of the fire. Shannon wadded up his blanket and flung it against the wall. "God damn it to hell! Water damn duty again!"

He turned to find Colter standing behind him with his hand out. "Thanks, Fuzz."

"You want to thank me? Take my place on the water squad."

"Gotta see the captains, or I would. You just saved me a whole potful of grief. I'm much obliged to you for that." Colter took hold of Shannon's unwilling hand and squeezed it.

"You want to shake? Here." Shannon clamped down hard on Colter's hand.

Instead of returning the squeeze, Colter grinned. "Go on. Squeeze hard as you want. I can take whatever you dish out."

Shannon released the hand. "You heard Ordeal. I got to go, or I'll end up on the roof — with you."

"Ain't so bad up there. Once you get used to it."

"I don't want to get used to it," Shannon yelled over his shoulder as he went out the door.

While clouds of breath-fog wrapped around Shannon's upper body and formed an ice crust on his beard and lashes, tongues of hoarfrost trailed up from the river, licking the front and sides of the fort, creating a curtain too thick for his eyes to penetrate. Under the fog's assault, the fort's walls popped and creaked and crackled, stretching nerves which were already under strain because he could not rely on his sense of sight. Three days of this. When would it ever end?

Thud! Something hit the base of the wall.

His body froze, but his imagination went wild, conjuring a war party of Sioux lurking out in the fog, ready to launch their attack on the sleeping fort.

Over his racing heart, he strained to hear anything that would confirm his fears.

A scratching sound came from off to the right of where he stood. He turned toward the sound and spotted movement. A knee swung over the pickets.

He swung his rifle up. He had only one shot. It had to count.

The knee became a leg.

He waited, gripping the rifle against the quaking in his arms. Whoever claimed the Sioux were stealthy ought to be here now.

An arm reached over the wall. "Don't shoot. It's me," came the urgent whisper as the rest of the body hoisted onto the roof.

"Colter?"

"Shhh, or you'll wake 'em all up."

"Me? You're the one making all the racket," he sputtered.

"Weren't my intention, but fog's slickened up the wall. My foot slipped partways up."

Shannon did not need to ask where Colter had been. There was only one place to go. Matootonha. And in order for Colter to get out of the fort, he had to have the cooperation of Potts, the gate guard last watch. Come to think of it, Colter and Potts had been acting real friendly lately. "I can't believe you'd do this kind of thing, Old Man. It's crazy! You're going to get caught."

"Not if'n you don't say nothin'. Whew! I'm tuckered out. Got to get me some sleep. See you come mornin'." Colter slipped quietly down the ladder and stealthily entered the barracks.

Shannon watched him go, unsure what to make of this unexpected development. It was one thing for a man to take a squaw to the barracks loft. It was quite another to sneak out of the fort without permission for any reason, least of all to see a woman.

Out of the corner of his eye, he thought he saw the door to the sergeants' room move, but when he looked closer, he decided it was only a wisp of fog.

A current of frigid air knifed through the multiple layers of his clothing and started him shivering again. He wrapped his arms across his chest and started moving along the roof walkway with his heart full of dread and his head full of questions for Colter.

Colter smiled down at Fragrant Grass. The black-brown hair of the buffalo hide framed her face perfectly. Her fingers sought his birthmark. She opened her mouth and —

A rude hand shook Colter out of his dream. He opened his eyes to Sergeant Ordway, cunning etched into every line of his face. "Rise and shine, Private. Time to collect your prize."

Colter struggled up on an elbow, shaking his head to clear the dangling dream cobwebs from his mind. "Prize?"

"You're going hunting." The sly look sharpened. "For a week. With Captain Clark. You have a whole twenty minutes to get ready."

Rube sidled over to Colter after the sergeant left. "How'd you luck out? A week out of this hell-hole? Only thing'd be better is a week yonder with my favorite squaw."

Ignoring the chuckles the remark caused, Colter began to gather his things. Ordway's assignments always aimed at one goal — to drive him off the crew. He glanced over at Shannon's sleeping form. Had Fuzz betrayed him, telling the sergeant about his night-time excursions to the Mandan town?

Shannon's eyelids fluttered open. "Did I hear Ordeal, or was it a bad dream?"

"Was him, all right," Colter said.

"Why are you looking at me like that?" Shannon asked.

Colter bent down in order to keep their words private. "What'd you tell him?"

"Ordeal? I wouldn't give him the time of day. You know that."

"He knows, Fuzz. Otherwise he wouldn't be sendin' me out huntin' for a whole damn week. I thought you and me was friends. Why'd you do it?"

"I didn't do anything. If anyone talked, it was Potts."

Colter looked sharply at Shannon, surprised that the younger man had figured out how he was getting out of the fort. Still, he knew better than to suspect Potts who was sneaking off to the Mandan town, too. "Forget it. I got to get goin'."

He pulled a pair of tattered pants over his good ones and stood up to knot the rope belt. He needed to get a message to Fragrant Grass, to let her know where he was going and how long he would be gone. "Where's Echo?"

"Why, you need a Mandan lesson?" Shannon asked sarcastically.

"Cain't a body ask a simple question anymore without you gettin' smart-mouth?"

Shannon backed off. "He went home yesterday. Said he'd come here to-morrow or the next day. You know how Indians are about time."

Colter nodded. Yes, he did know how Indians were about time. Likely Fragrant Grass would not even know he was gone. Rather than risk send-ing her a message, he decided to let the matter lie and head over to Ma-tootonha as soon as he could upon his return from hunting.

"Any particular reason you want him?" Shannon asked.

"No reason. Ain't seen him in a couple of days," Colter lied while he bundled his blankets into a tight roll and lashed the roll with a leather thong.

"What do you mean? He was here yesterday," said Shannon.

"Was he? I don't rightly recall," Colter covered, draping both powder horns and the hunting pouch across his chest and grabbing his rifle and bedroll. "Well, I'm off."

Outside, he ran into Potts. "How'd it go?" Potts asked.

"Think Ordeal found out. He's sendin' me huntin'. For a week."

Potts roundly cursed the sergeant. "She's a looker, that squaw of yours. I wouldn't want to be gone long, neither. Damn Ordeal."

Potts's empathy gave Colter an idea. "I'd be obliged you take a message to her for me."

"How'm I goin' to do that? I cain't say but two words in Mandan. And you don't want me sayin' them to her."

"It's easy. I'll teach you the hand-talk." Slowly Colter drew a series of four signs in the air: Colter returns seven suns.

When Potts tried to imitate the motions, he got only one right, but Colter traced the signs again.

Potts tried and failed a second time.

Out of the corner of his eye, Colter spotted Ordway observing them, but he figured he might as well finish what he had started. With a wink to warn Potts that they were being watched, he shifted to block the sergeant's view of his hands and traced the words a third time.

After botching the last word, Potts finally got the whole message right on his third try. Colter made him repeat the signs three times to make sure he had them. "When're you goin' over next?"

"I was figurin' on tomorrow," said Potts.

"You got two of my rations of rum for deliverin' that there message."

Potts chuckled. "Then I ought to go tonight."

"Just don't get caught and don't forget what I showed you."

"I won't. Not for what you're payin' me."

Ordway started toward them. They parted.

Fragrant Grass positioned the cooking pot in the bed of coals and released the handle. The fire popped, shooting embers and dislodging some of the coals, tipping the pot and splashing soup onto the fire. Amidst the hissing, the air filled with the smell of burned food.

Sly Wolf exploded, "Why, you clumsy woman! Take that kettle from her, Wife."

Mint rushed to do his bidding. Fragrant Grass edged away from the fire, blinking at the tears that came welling into her eyes. Something was terribly wrong. Colter had not come to Matootonha for the last seven nights. Had she displeased him as Sly Wolf kept saying? Was he sick or injured?

Until a week ago, he had come to the village every night since the two of them had called the buffalo together. With him in the lodge, Sly Wolf had to stay out of her robes and sleep with Mint. But, with Colter's absence, Sly Wolf had claimed his rights as her husband, treating her with brutal contempt that left her bruised and afraid. His nightly violations drove her to the river each morning, but even submerging herself into the icy water through a hole hacked in the ice could not wash away the hateful memories of his mistreatment or her dread of another night of forced coupling with a man she despised.

Where was Colter? She was desperate to know, yet unable to go to the fort to find out because Sly Wolf forbade it. She had spent hours over the last three suns, kneeling beside Strikes Two's burial scaffold, pouring prayers into the heavens. To no avail. Him Who Sees All had not spoken. For the last seven nights she had not dreamed. For seven suns the winter skies had been empty of hawks.

Sly Wolf's voice startled her, "He has grown tired of you, my wife. And no wonder. You should be grateful he came here as much as he did. Already the paleskin's medicine makes me, your husband, stronger in the eyes of our people."

At the fire, Mint flinched as if Sly Wolf's words had slapped her. Poor Mint. She had bedded two paleskins, including Black Giant who made her sore for a week, in order to bring honor to the man she adored, only to have him completely ignore her efforts.

Defiance swelled in Fragrant Grass and pushed aside her tears. She turned her back to Sly Wolf and knelt to shuck kernels from some ears of dried corn. He was wrong. Colter wore the sign of her spirit guide. Him Who Sees All had sent him to her. Colter's absence, the lack of dreams —

Him Who Sees All had a reason for everything. He would reveal His plan to her. In time.

Echo darted into the lodge and made straight for Fragrant Grass. "Little Mother, come quickly. Your sister has need of you at the paleskins' fort."

When Fragrant Grass started to rise, Sly Wolf said, "No, you will not go."

"My husband, our sister would not send for help unless she was in trouble. We must go to her," Mint pleaded.

After a long tense silence, he nodded curtly. Fragrant Grass grabbed her pouch of medicines and hurried outside, afraid he would change his mind.

"Come on, Colter. Put your back into it," Ordway said. "Pretend that log's your Mandan squaw and you're plowing her furrow."

Colter bent over the log, shutting his ears to the rest of the foul diatribe. After a week, the sergeant's lewd comments no longer got a rise out of him.

The week of hunting had gone well. They had too much meat to carry back to the fort in one trip so they were building a bunker around the rest to protect it from predators before they headed home.

"On six, ladies!" Ordway bellowed. "One. . ."

On the count of six, Colter strained to lift the log to his waist, adding his grunts to those of the other five men.

"Now to the top. Again, on six!" Ordway yelled. "One . . . two . . . three . . ."

Colter's end of the log shifted suddenly. He reacted by dropping into a squat to counterbalance the force of the log. Before he could get set, however, his knee buckled with a wrenching tear that he felt all the way to his hip. He went down hard with the log atop him, aware that he had perhaps one breath remaining before the weight of the wood crushed the life out of him.

A blur flashed across his field of vision and a shadow covered his face. It took a moment to register that the figure hovering over him was not Death, but Captain Clark who had taken up Colter's position at the end of the log.

"All right, lift!" Clark yelled.

Colter watched with detachment as the log wavered upward, then rolled onto the top of the bunker wall with a crash. The captain dusted his hands and proclaimed in a voice scratchy from strain, "Bravo! Good job, men!" Then, softer, "You all right, Colter?"

"Yes, Captain. I think so anyway." He accepted the captain's hand up. "Thanks, sir."

"No need," Clark said. "You're okay. That's what matters. Now if we can keep the Indians and wolves from getting this meat, we'll all be okay." He turned to the rest of the work party. "Take a ten-minute break, men, then we'll start back to the fort."

The captain bustled away to see about the construction of the sleds that would carry a load of meat to the fort, and Colter tested his knee for damage. He detected no broken bones, only swelling indicating a sprain. With

his week of hunting over, he was determined to go back to Fragrant Grass
as soon as he could. A sprain would slow, but not stop him.

A pelting of snow against his trouser leg heralded Ordway's arrival."Think about her all the time, don't you?"

He had passed beyond the point of watching what he said to the sergeant.
Each exchange had become a skirmish in a war he had no intention of
losing. He plastered a phony smile on his face. "Her who, Sarge?"

"Come the melt, that squaw'll have such a hold on you, you won't be
able to bring yourself to leave her."

"You sound right sure of yourself, Sarge. Goin' to be a real pleasure to
see you eat them words."

"You don't stand a chance, Colter. You're showing all the signs. I'd like
to say I'll miss you when we head west. Only that'd be a lie."

"You ain't goin' to miss a thing, Sarge. Hell, I couldn't let you go on without me. Who else'd you pick on?" He spoke the last sentence slowly and
distinctly, locking eyes with the sergeant. Then Clark called for Ordway and
broke the spell.

Colter limped to his pack, pulled out a strip of hide and set about binding
his swollen knee. Nothing was going to keep him from getting back to
Fragrant Grass. Nothing.

8. *Sacajawea's Baby*

S omeone had placed a deerskin on the floor between the two beds that
crowded the dank, drafty room. The Shoshone girl Sacajawea squatted
over the hide using her elbows to support her weight on the bed behind
her. She looked up at Fragrant Grass's entrance with eyes as wide as a
frightened deer's. Kebeka perched on the other bed, looking even more
helpless and terrified than the laboring Shoshone. Charbonneau's other
woman was nowhere to be seen.

Fragrant Grass pitied the three women for having to live in such a depressing place. She had seen the inside of the room where Colter lived
only once, but that was enough.

The thought of Colter distracted her until a tremor of labor coursed
through Sacajawea who bit down on a piece of rawhide to stifle her cries.
Fragrant Grass turned to Mint. "Kneel behind her and hold her up through
the contractions. Do not let her fall."

Fragrant Grass knelt in front of the laboring woman and assessed her
condition with practiced fingers. Feeling the baby's movement, she sensed
the presence of the spirit of her mother rise up within her, and she relaxed.
Mother was here to guide her hands. Mother, so wise and gentle, yet so
strong.

Another contraction gripped the Shoshone girl. "Hold her," Fragrant
Grass snapped at Mint.

She felt the distended stomach. The baby was at the right angle, but the
Shoshone woman's fear was making her body fight Nature, sapping her

strength. From the looks of her, she had been in labor for a long time already and her strength was ebbing. Something had to be done to relax her.

With the next wave of pain, the Shoshone girl moaned through clenched
teeth. Her eyes began to glaze, a sign that she was close to giving up.

Fragrant Grass grabbed Kebeka's wrist roughly. "Wash her face."

Kebeka whined, "She's going to die. I know it."

Fragrant Grass yanked her sister's arm to get her moving. "Do what I
say!"

Another contraction gripped the young woman, contorting her perspiring
face. The pains were coming faster.

Fragrant Grass closed her eyes and slowed her breathing. She stroked the
leather of her medicine bag in rhythm with each breath until a curtain of
blackness swung across her mind. Gradually the black turned to gray, then
to blue, the color of the Hawk Spirit's home. She waited for the surge of
sensation that was the source of wisdom and knowledge.

By the time she reopened her eyes, she was filled with a profound calm.
She turned to Kebeka. "I need the tail of the rattling serpent."

Kebeka threw up her hands. "That is impossible. The rattling serpents all
sleep during the snow time."

"Go to the paleskin Chief Merry Weather. They say he collects many curious things. He will have the bones," Fragrant Grass said with certainty.

"My husband does not allow me to speak to the paleskin chiefs," Kebeka
declared.

Her sister's limitless supply of excuses ruffled Fragrant Grass's calm. She
blurted out things she never meant to say. "Then find your useless husband
and have him talk to the paleskin chief. Go now, my sister. Do what I say."

Kebeka's face crumpled as she hurried outside to carry out the order.
"You have no right to treat her that way," Mint said after Kebeka left.

Fragrant Grass shrugged off the comment and returned her attention to Sacajawea. Since she could not speak the exhausted woman's harsh-sounding
tongue, she began to sing a Mandan lullaby in an effort to calm the
woman. She sang the song over and over, holding the young woman's
hand through the contractions. Sacajawea's grip weakened a bit more with
each wave of pain. Still, Kebeka did not return.

Where are you, sister? Fragrant Grass thought. *Do not let us down.*

Time passed. Sacajawea's head lolled forward. Mint strained to hold her
upright over the hide. Fragrant Grass continued to sing, struggling to keep
her fear at bay. It had been too long. Had Kebeka been unable to find her
worthless paleskin husband, or had he refused to help? What if Chief
Merry Weather did not have the needed bones?

A new contraction seized the young woman. Too weak to cry out, she
whimpered. The top of the baby's head pressed against the mouth of the
birth opening, then retracted. If Sacajawea did not have the strength to
continue, she and the baby would both be lost.

"I'm so tired," Mint complained.

"Not as tired as she is," Fragrant Grass said, biting back a stronger retort.

Mint's face fell into a pout. Fragrant Grass ran out of patience. "You say you wish to give our husband a son. If you speak true, it is time you learned what that means. Look and learn." She gestured toward the exhausted girl. "This is what awaits you."

She regretted the harsh words as soon as she said them and tried to soften them. "We must think about this girl now, my sister. Not ourselves. Our sister does not return. I must go to the paleskin chief myself. Come for me if something changes."

Fragrant Grass was stiff from kneeling so long. She had to steady herself against one of the beds. She did not know how she would get Chief Merry Weather to understand her need. She only knew she had to try.

The door opened with a rush of cold air. Chief Merry Weather entered, followed by Jesseaume, Kebeka and the black-eyed one called Drouillard.

Birthing was women's work. Mandan men would never enter the birth lodge for fear of destroying their power to hunt. Yet here were three paleskin males, barging in as if they belonged. Their recklessness left Fragrant Grass mute.

She moved aside to allow the paleskin chief to kneel before Sacajawea. She had not learned yet how to read the paleskins' expressions. She could not tell if their chief was repelled or concerned.

Jesseaume elbowed Kebeka out of the way. "What is this about a snake's tail, sister of my wife?" he demanded of Fragrant Grass, puffing out his chest as if to impress Chief Merry Weather who had not learned the language of the Mandan people.

She kept her tone level in spite of her dislike of the slovenly man. "The bones will help the mother relax and bring the baby out."

"How? What do you do to the bones?" he asked.

Fragrant Grass glanced with disbelief at the paleskin chief who was examining the Shoshone woman in the most intimate way. A way no Mandan man, not even a woman's husband, would ever do.

"Answer me, woman."

Jesseaume's haughty tone curtailed her shock. "Grind three bones into a powder. Make a tea with that powder for the girl to drink."

Jesseaume spoke animatedly in the paleskin tongue to Chief Merry Weather who produced from his pocket a section of rattling serpent's tail. Jesseaume broke off three bones and set about pulverizing them on the top of a wooden box with the butt of his knife. "Bring me water, Wife," he ordered Kebeka, then to Fragrant Grass, "How much powder, and how long should it steep?"

She explained, then watched the interpreter make a show out of brewing the tea. Chief Merry Weather missed the whole charade. He remained focused totally on Sacajawea. He sponged her pain-etched face and stroked her hair, murmuring comforting sounds. That a grown man would show such tenderness to a woman in public impressed Fragrant Grass.

Jesseaume imperiously thrust the ladle of tea at her. "See that she drinks this, sister of my wife."

Fragrant Grass took the ladle and knelt next to the paleskin chief. Sacajawea did not seem to recognize her and would not open her mouth.

Crooning baby talk, Fragrant Grass coaxed her into taking a sip before the next contraction. When the pain took hold, Sacajawea's body went rigid in Mint's arms. She clutched the paleskin chief's hand so hard the blood left her knuckles.

The pain passed. From the spreading dullness in the young woman's eyes, Fragrant Grass knew they did not have much time. She forced the rest of the tea on Sacajawea. Her insides churned with uncertainty. Was her memory accurate? Was the tea strong enough?

During the long silence, she felt the black-eyed man's stare. His presence unsettled her so that she jumped when Chief Merry Weather addressed her. She did not need to understand the words to know that he saw through Jesseaume's act and that he was asking her directly how long before the tea worked.

She interrupted Jesseaume's translation employing the same haughty tone as he himself had used. "Tell him it takes —" She hesitated. The paleskins did not measure the day and night in the same way as her people. She scanned the room, seeking something to help explain. Her eyes lit on a tallow candle and she used her thumb and index finger to show an amount of wick to describe how long before the tea would work.

Chief Merry Weather nodded, and, for a long time, no one moved. Even Sacajawea and her unborn baby stayed still.

All at once, the Shoshone woman's eyes shot wide open. She uttered a prolonged moan. Moments later the infant slid into Fragrant Grass's waiting arms. In spite of all the difficulty in separating from his mother, the boy was strong and healthy. He greeted life with a lusty yowl.

Fragrant Grass cradled the baby against her until the afterbirth appeared. She gathered up the mass to be buried later, then cut the navel cord and handed it to Kebeka to put in the new child's medicine bag.

While Mint helped the Shoshone girl onto the bed, Fragrant Grass wiped the baby clean with dried moss, then wrapped him in a soft deerskin and laid him in his mother's arms. Chief Merry Weather bowed his head to her and offered what she knew were words of thanks. She watched him walk out the door, acknowledging that she had never before met such a man.

She was at the entrance to her lodge at Matootonha when she remembered Colter. She had not asked about him while she was at the fort, and Echo, the one person who could tell her, had stayed behind. She turned her face to the night sky and whispered a prayer. "Please tell me what I must do now, Hawk Spirit. I have lost my way."

"Then let me show you, Wife." Sly Wolf came up behind her, grabbed her arm, pulled her through the tunnel straight to her bed.

9. Liberty

"I t's the fort!" Captain Clark exclaimed. "We did it, men! Well done!" Colter straightened up slowly, stiff and weak from the long, cold 30-

mile march, hitched with the others to a crude sled piled to overflowing with frozen meat. The walls of the fort rose black against the white snow and gray clouds of the night sky.

"Leave the sleds here," Clark said. "A double ration of rum to every man of you."

Colter watched in tired amazement as the captain and York hefted a bull elk carcass between them and started for the fort. Earlier, Clark had insisted on taking the lead on the first sled and, along with York, he had broken trail the entire way, showing no trace of the fragile health that had plagued him at the start of the expedition. Indeed, every hardship seemed to make him stronger.

The gates creaked open and out poured the crew, bearing torches, led by Captain Lewis. The men unloaded the rest of the meat and carried it to the storeroom, while the hunters gathered in the compound to receive their rum. "Here's to our success!" Clark toasted and downed his cup in one swallow. "A night's liberty at Matootonha for all of you tomorrow."

Colter's fatigue began to lift. He figured to have to sneak out to see Fragrant Grass. Instead he had official permission.

"Oh, muleshit, what now?" Rube muttered, nodding toward Ordway who was whispering into the captain's ear.

Clark listened, then nodded and announced, "Correction. Half of you will go tomorrow night; the rest, the next. Sergeant Ordway will divide you up accordingly."

"Horseshit!" It was Colter's turn to swear. Ordway would see to it that he went in the second group. That was, if the man did not find a way to block his liberty completely.

"You'll go in the second group," Ordway said, coming to Colter.

Colter mustered his exhausted face muscles into an insincere smile. "Why, thank you, Sarge. I sure can use the rest."

"Oh? If you're that tired, I better have Captain Clark cancel your liberty. Can't have you too tired, can we?"

"Something wrong, Sergeant?" Clark said, coming up behind Ordway.

The captain's unexpected arrival flustered Ordway momentarily, so Colter took the opportunity to jump in. "I was just thankin' the sergeant here for givin' me a night to rest up, so's I'll be ready for the liberty night after tomorrow."

Clark clapped Colter on the shoulder. "Great spirit, Colter! That's what we like about you. Right, Sergeant?"

"Spirit. Yes, sir," Ordway answered, his lips tightening around a forced smile.

"You enjoy yourself over there, Colter. You certainly earned it," Clark said.

"Yes, sir. I will, sir." He looked at Ordway. "Indeed I will."

*

The first contingent of the liberty party headed out for Matootonha. Ordway led the group, a fact that stuck in Colter's craw. He was mulling over the unfairness of the situation when he ran into Potts. "You deliver my message?"

"Said I would, didn't I?" Potts said.

"What'd she say?"

Potts shook his head. "Wouldn'a understood her anyways. First time I did them signs, she give me a kind of strange look, so I did 'em again." He demonstrated. "She caught my drift that time."

Relieved that Potts had remembered the message correctly, Colter slapped him on the back. "Much obliged. Guess I owe you that rum now."

"You're one lucky varmint, Colter. She's a real looker, that one. She and that there twin of hers're about the prettiest squaws in these here parts."

At the word "twin," all Colter's good feeling dissolved. Potts had given the right message to the wrong woman. To Mint, not Fragrant Grass.

"Somethin' wrong, Colter? You be looking mighty pale all of a sudden."

He waved Potts off and made for the latrine, feeling like he had been kicked in the stomach by an enraged stallion. He had witnessed enough interactions between Fragrant Grass and Mint to know that nothing good would come from Potts's mistake. Nothing good – in the form of Sly Wolf. It was critical that he get to Fragrant Grass right away. He had to find out what Potts's error had cost her and figure out how to set things right.

But he couldn't go. Couldn't even sneak out because Ordway was at Matootonha. His long wait to see her just got longer.

Fragrant Grass kept her head bowed over her sewing. According to Echo, the paleskin hunters would come to the village this night. She did not want Sly Wolf and the other men lounging around the fire to see the smile that stole unconsciously across her lips whenever she thought of seeing Colter again. With the riddle of his long absence explained, the awful memories of her recent nights with Sly Wolf lost sway on her emotions, and she allowed herself to again feel hope that her life was changing for the better.

The subject of the paleskins dominated fireside conversation in every lodge in Matootonha these days. Everyone agreed that the strangers possessed great medicine, but no one understood their odd ways. Even Echo who practically lived at the fort did not comprehend all their customs. Everyone had a favorite theory, and exchanging those theories had led to many lively debates like the one going on among Sly Wolf and the other men at the moment.

Since Sly Wolf usually remained on the sidelines rather than risk disagreement that might damage his standing on the council, hearing him speak startled her into glancing up. She was met with a smile from him. The same contemptuous smile as when he invaded her sleeping robes. "I disagree. The paleskins do not have great medicine," he declared. "If they did, why do they hitch themselves to sleds to haul meat? Horses haul meat. Not men possessed of great power."

A storm of comments followed those remarks. Fragrant Grass looked over at Mint for her reaction, but her sister's head was bowed. Since Sly Wolf had deserted her bed to join Fragrant Grass at night, Mint had grown distant and angry. Only Colter's return would repair the situation.

Over the noise of the men's heated discussion, Fragrant Grass heard the signal from the guard at the perimeter wall announcing the arrival of the paleskins. She averted her face so no one would see the joy she could no longer suppress.

Sly Wolf and the others heard the signal, broke off their discussion and went out to meet their guests. Before he left the lodge, Sly Wolf turned to the women. "I will bring them here. Prepare."

How quickly you change your mind, Fragrant Grass silently taunted Sly Wolf as she retrieved a supply of ground sunflower seeds from one of the food caches. She set about making a paste, mixing in a quantity of dried grapes, to form cakes to cook in the fire. Mint surprised her by speaking to her for the first time in a week. "Is your smile for the one with the Hawk Spirit's mark?"

Fragrant Grass could not read her sister's expression so she decided to admit the truth. "Yes."

Mint's expression hardened. "Why are you so cruel to me and to our husband?"

In the face of such an accusation, Fragrant Grass tried to explain. "I must follow where the Hawk Spirit guides me."

"No, you must do what our husband commands and go where he goes. This paleskin has caused you to forget your duty as wife."

Colter had brought back to her life the joy that had died with Strikes Two. The paleskin brought her a peace she had not felt for moons, and he brought her hope. However, she held back her thoughts. Mint did not care about them, anyway. She cared only for Sly Wolf.

"Our husband did not have to take you in, yet he did. You owe him your respect," Mint said

Fragrant Grass hung her head, thinking, *I owe him nothing. Nothing.*

Hoots and hollers heralded the return of the first liberty party from Matootonha the next morning. The moment Rube and Joe came into the barracks, the crewmen who had been left behind peppered them with questions about their experiences. From his seat by the fire, Colter listened closely to the exchanges, alert for any mention of Fragrant Grass. Hearing none, he stared into the flames, anxious for the rest of the day to pass.

Rube plopped down on the box next to him. "There's somethin' you oughtta know." He lowered his voice. "Ordeal tried to buy your woman last night."

Colter shot to his feet, tipping over the box he had been sitting on. "Why that son-of-a-slime!"

"Hold on there," Rube said, righting the box with one hand and pulling Colter down onto it with the other. "I said he tried, but she weren't havin' no part of him. She just up and walked away. Left Ordeal standin' there with a fistful of beads, lookin' the fool."

Colter's anger faded in the face of the image Rube's description painted. Rube went on. "That ain't all. That little squaw, the one looks like Jesseaume's woman, the one Shannon's sweet on — well, no sooner does your woman leave than that one come and took Ordeal's gewgaws and hauled him off to her bed. Somebody oughtta tell Shannon. You want to?"

Colter shook his head. "Be better if'n you did, seein' as how you was there."

Rube sighed. "He ain't goin' to like it, but I suppose I owe him the truth." He got up. "She's quite a gal, that little squaw of yours. Standin' up to Ordeal and all. A good woman's somethin' to hang onto. If I was you, I'd be thinkin' real hard where I belonged come spring — with her or this here crew."

Colter nodded his thanks to Rube, then turned back to the fire. Talking about her made him too restless to sit down. He went to the door and looked outside. Not even noon. Still hours to wait.

Across the way, Ordway came out of the sergeants' room. Colter hailed him and sidled over. "Heard you had a good time last night, Sarge."

The sergeant's momentary delay in responding was not lost on Colter. "Sure did. In fact, I had such a good time, think I'll head back real soon."

Colter made no effort to leave the scorn out of his tone. "Then I wish you good luck, Sarge."

"Keep it, Colter. I don't need it." The sergeant pivoted and headed out the gates.

"Oh, but you do, Sarge," Colter muttered at the man's back. "You do."

Colter watched Fragrant Grass's face as she settled into sleep in the crook of his arm and felt a contentment so deep, so pure that he wished this night would last forever. He smoothed a stray lock of hair off her forehead. In sleep, she smiled and nestled closer.

Pshanshaw. He loved saying the name. Pshanshaw. It sounded like a prayer, like a poem.

Her eyelids fluttered as if she were about to wake. He held his breath. She sighed, sinking deeper into sleep. He smiled tenderly at her. She had told him about coming to the fort to help Charbonneau's wife give birth and about her exchange with Captain Lewis. Like Rube said, she was quite a woman.

That Sergeant Ordway had tried to buy her favors was an affront he would not abide. Somehow, some way he had to find a way to even that score.

Come the melt, she'll have such a hold on you, you won't be able to bring yourself to leave her. Ordway had said that. Gazing at her in sleep, Colter could not deny the hold she had on him even now.

Couldn't let you go on without me. Colter had meant that when he said it to Ordway a few days ago, but now, now he knew that what he really wanted was lying next to him.

Fragrant Grass murmured something in her sleep. He stroked her brow with the tips of his fingers. He had spent his whole life searching for something he had not been able to define, believing he would know it when he saw it. Now here, in the form of a woman — an Indian woman, no less — was the very thing that had eluded him for so long.

He pressed his lips to the skin of her neck and lay back on the buffalo robe, listening to the sound of her even breathing. Yes, he had found her, but soon he would have to leave her. The question was: could he?

Early the next morning Fragrant Grass walked with Colter to the river. She watched until he crossed the ice and reached the other side. On her way back to Matootonha, even the graveyard with its snow-shrouded reminders of grief could not suppress her happiness.

At the lodge, she was surprised to see Mint up already. "Pleasant day, my sister."

Mint whirled. "No, it is not pleasant."

Realizing that the confrontation she wanted to avoid was at hand, Fragrant Grass chose her words carefully. "You have changed, my sister."

"We do not talk of me. We talk of you. Our husband is an important man among the people. His position is our position. Or do you forget that fact?"

Fragrant Grass did not speak, afraid that whatever she said would rile Mint even more.

"After Strikes Two died, my husband took you in. And how do you repay him? You cut your hair in secret." Mint gave her a sharp look. "Did you think he would not tell me of your deceit? First, your hair. Now, this choice of yours." She spat out the words like bad meat. "It is our husband's right to order you to leave this lodge and live without the protection of a man."

The chance was slim that Sly Wolf would risk his hard-won social status by evicting her from the lodge she and her sisters had inherited from their mother. Still, Fragrant Grass did not want to argue. After all, he had already threatened to marry her off.

"And do not think he will consider as husband this paleskin you have chosen. That one has nothing of value to bring to our lodge. Nothing," Mint said.

The venom in her sister's voice made Fragrant Grass wonder just how far Sly Wolf's plans had gone and how much Mint knew of them.

"The snow begins to melt. Soon we must plant the sacred corn," Mint said, leaving the lodge while the threat hung in the air behind her.

Fragrant Grass hugged herself in despair. Melting snow meant that Sly Wolf would be able to travel to other villages to seek a suitor for her. More important, melting snow meant that the ice on the river would break up soon, hastening the day the paleskins — and Colter — would leave.

Despite days of fasting and hours on her knees beside Strikes Two's grave, the Hawk Spirit had remained absent from her dreams. She still did not know the reason Colter had come to her or what action she was supposed to take next. Melting snow meant that she had to have an answer soon or face an uncertain future.

She turned to go to the burial ground. Sly Wolf's voice boomed from the bed platform he shared with Mint at the back of the lodge. "Where is my breakfast, Wife?"

She picked up the empty waterskin. "I go now to fetch water for your tea."

Sly Wolf grunted and let the privacy curtain fall. She ducked outside and hurried directly to the burial yard to pray to the Hawk Spirit. Sly Wolf's breakfast would have to wait.

Colter had not been back at the fort for more than a few minutes when Ordway slapped him with wood detail, which did not get back until late in the afternoon. They arrived just before the return of the men who had been sent downriver to retrieve the meat Captain Clark's hunting party had stock-piled there. The party brought back only a discarded moccasin along with tales of being attacked by a large party of Sioux who stole the meat and burned the log cribs. Although no one was hurt, the stories raised cries for revenge from the listeners. "Let's go after them sons-a-bitches!" Rube yelled.

"Time to show 'em who they're dealin' with once and for all!" shouted Newman.

Captain Clark bellowed over the commotion. "That meat was ours, and we'll go get it back."

Anger changed to shouts of "I'll go!" and "Send me!"

Clark motioned for quiet. "Captain Lewis will lead you out at first light tomorrow." He turned to Ordway. "Sergeant, organize the detail."

When Ordway answered "Yes, sir" to the captain, he was looking straight at Colter.

10. *Sly Wolf's Bargain*

Fragrant Grass gathered her things together with reluctance. For six days, she had enjoyed the serenity of the moon lodge, staying a day longer than necessary in order to avoid going back to her lodge. Now she dared not delay longer. Her monthly flux never lasted more than six days, a fact Sly Wolf would remember.

Outside, she looked toward the paleskins' fort and issued a silent prayer to her spirit guide for Colter's safety while he and the other paleskins searched for the Sioux who had stolen their cache of meat. The Sioux had robbed her of Strikes Two. She prayed that they not harm Colter, too.

She stopped outside the tunnel of her lodge and steeled herself before entering. She had yet to face Sly Wolf over her refusal of the paleskin Second Chief Ordway. The prospect of his anger tempted her to seek out other company, but the sound of weeping from the interior drew her inside. There she found Mint in tears, huddled next to the fire. "What is wrong, my sister?"

"It's all your fault!" Mint wailed.

Fragrant Grass controlled the urge to turn and leave her sister to her anger. Instead, she gathered Mint into a consoling hug. "Please tell me what has made you so sad?"

A new fit of weeping choked Mint's voice. "My courses have started, and I must go to the moon lodge."

"Then let me fix you some tea to ease the cramps," Fragrant Grass said.

Mint wrenched out of her embrace. "Don't you understand? No son grows within me yet. How can I hope to please our husband when I cannot give him a son?"

Fragrant Grass sat back and waited for her sister's fit of weeping to end. She had gone through this with Mint before. No doubt she would have to go through it many times before her sister finally conceived a child. When Mint's sobs reduced to sniffles, she ventured, "I will help you carry your things."

"No!" Mint shrieked and scrambled to her feet. "I do not want your help. You have done a terrible thing. Our husband is furious that you refused the paleskin Second Chief. How dare you bring such shame on us?"

Mint scooped up her belongings and left the lodge. Fragrant Grass decided she was not yet prepared to face Sly Wolf. She fled to the only safe place she knew: Strikes Two's grave.

She spread a worn buffalo robe on the snow at the head of the scaffold, then tilted her face to the cloud-studded heavens and whispered a desperate prayer song to Him Who Sees All. Into her mind's eye came the image of Colter leading her along a trail unlike any she had ever seen. She was not able to turn her head to see what grew along the sides of the path or what lay behind. She could not raise her eyes to see what lay ahead. Her feet did not move, yet she was drawn mysteriously forward, ever forward toward a bend in the path that hid what was before her.

Instinct told her that the vision was the answer to her prayers. Him Who Sees All had sent Colter to lead her into another life, that she must continue to forge ahead on trust. Yet, the idea of another life with an unknown future made her tremble. She dreaded the thought of living among the paleskins like Kebeka, enduring their dreary, drafty lodges and their barbaric habits. She could never be happy with people who seemed to eat only meat and seldom bathed. How could she leave her people, her village and the loved ones who had crossed over the rainbow bridge to become stars?

From the river came a groan, the music of the restless ice, signalling the beginning of the end to winter's hold on the land and the start of a new cycle of life — for the earth and for her. Her gaze roamed slowly over the burial ground and the village. She never considered that she might have to leave this place or her people. Did she have the strength to abandon everything she loved?

Seeking an answer to that question, she lifted her eyes to the sky where a pair of hawks glided on the wind in a joyous spiraling dance. The sight brought an upwelling of joy so intense that her vision blurred with tears.

After a long absence, her spirit guide had returned — with a mate.

In that moment all doubts dissolved. The message was clear. The Hawk Spirit was guiding her footsteps, and it was for her to walk wherever she was led.

Wind moaned around the lodge walls, sending snow sifting down through the smoke hole. Fragrant Grass bent over her sewing. Mint had been gone to the moon lodge for the last five days, yet Sly Wolf had stayed away from her sleeping robes during that time. She wanted to believe that he had finally slaked his desire for her, but experience had taught her that nothing with him was ever that simple.

Across the fire, Sly Wolf put aside his pipe and stretched. "I go to talk with Little Raven."

After he sidled out of the lodge, she sagged against her backrest and exhaled the tension his presence always raised in her. She closed her eyes, glad for a moment of solitude. Too soon, a footfall in the tunnel entrance announced someone's approach. She opened her eyes and set her expression to greet Mint. Instead, it was Big White, husband of her oldest sister and Matootonha's civil leader. "Do not get up, Little Mother," he said, using the people's term of respect for a woman of healing. "I grow weary of my own lodge. May I sit here with you awhile?"

Although custom allowed her to refuse, she could not. Big White was a wise man, charged with keeping order among the people. She guessed that he had come to discuss her refusal to bed the paleskin Second Chief. She was well aware of the gossip in the village about her and knew that defending herself was useless. No one wanted to hear that she had been following the guidance of her spirit protector.

Big White lowered himself to the backrest beside her, filled his pipe with tobacco he had received from the paleskins, lit the pipe with a taper from the fire and leaned back to gaze placidly at the rising smoke. She picked up her neglected sewing and resumed stitching.

After a time, Big White began to speak in a soothing voice. "When first the paleskins brought their war canoes here and asked to build their lodge across the river, I spoke out in council against them. I did not believe that the needs of our people would be served with so many strangers among us."

The chief's words brought back memories from the time of the big sickness, the illness the paleskins called smallpox. The illness wiped out entire families in the villages downriver and left so few survivors that they could no longer defend their towns from the Sioux. Many of that sorry lot had fled upriver to Matootonha for protection. Although those people had the same customs, absorbing so many newcomers caused such chaos that life in the village had yet to return to normal.

"It was your husband, Sly Wolf, who convinced me to welcome the paleskins," Big White continued. "He made me see the advantages of having men with such powerful medicine close by. Not only can we learn about this magic of theirs, but their presence brings us honor in the eyes of other river people. Your husband reminded me that the time to think about tomorrow is today."

Two references to Sly Wolf in one speech made her uneasy. She tilted her head to shield her expression.

"As your husband is wise, so you are wise, Little Mother. Your mother taught you well. You brought great honor to our people when you helped the Shoshone girl who lives at the paleskin fort. Such knowledge is important for our people today and for all the days to come."

He paused as if lost in thought. "Strikes Two was destined to be a great leader. I, too, grieve for him." At his sentiment her throat constricted with sudden sadness. "I see you at his grave, and I know you go there to seek the guidance of your spirit protector. I know you believe that the Hawk Spirit sends the paleskin Colter to you."

He ran his fingers along the stem of the pipe. "My heart tells me that this man Colter is also destined for greatness."

Her sadness ebbed. "You see into my heart and understand my choices, Father," she said, using the people's formal term of respect for the wisest among them.

He laughed, a deep, rich, comforting sound. "Oh, my child, how I wish that were true! There are so many things I do not understand." He turned thoughtful eyes on her. "For instance, I do not understand why you refused the paleskin Second Chief."

She found it impossible to swallow against the constriction in her throat. "The Hawk Spirit —"

"Would never allow you to go against the ways of our people," he broke in and finished the sentence for her. "Just as a man must avoid his wife's mother, a wife must see to the honor of her husband in order for us all to live in harmony. You brought shame upon your husband, Little Mother. Sly Wolf has every reason to cast you out of this lodge."

She could not bear the reproach in the chief's voice. Above all people, she respected his counsel.

"However, again your husband shows his wisdom," Big White went on. "He will not cast you out if you ask for his forgiveness and promise to obey him in all things from now on."

She had no choice. To refuse to accept the First Chief's guidance was to reject her people. Without them, she had nowhere to go. Reluctantly, she said, "I hear you, Father, and I will obey."

Before he left the lodge, Big White said, "Go in peace, Little Mother."

She nodded but knew that, from this moment on, she would never know peace again.

Opening the door of the barracks to the swirling snow, Shannon was sorely tempted to go back to the fire. Twenty crewmen had gone with Captain Lewis to avenge the Sioux raid and that meant he had stood a watch each of the last eleven days. Eleven days of miserable weather. He was sick of it, sick of being cold, sick of watches.

Heaving a sigh of regret for the warmth he was leaving behind, he stepped out into the storm and climbed to the roof. "About damn time you got here!" McNeal said. "Next time I'm your relief, just see how quick I get up here."

"Kiss my butt, McNeal!" Shannon shot back sourly. He had put up with enough of the cook's bitching the last eleven days to last him a lifetime. *Why did I stay behind? Why didn't I volunteer for the search party?* he asked himself for the thousandth time.

He need not have bothered asking. He knew the answer. At the time the news about the Sioux raiders reached the fort, he had been re-reading the Bible. The bloodlust that the prospect of wreaking revenge on the Sioux roused in the other crewmen repelled him and made him choose to stay at the fort rather than join the search party.

It was a choice he regretted before the search party was out of sight. He missed the company of the other men; missed the noise and the bustle of a full fort. Watches, duties and working with Echo to learn signs and Mandan filled less than half the day. The rest of the time he fought a losing battle to keep himself occupied.

Then yesterday, Echo had to stay at Matootonha. Shannon was so bored that he decided to try carving. Colter made whittling look easy. It wasn't. Shannon gave up in disgust after less than an hour, flinging his botched attempt to carve a rabbit into the fire.

He tucked his chin into the top of his greatcoat and paced along the roof walkway. Back and forth, back and forth he paced, mentally counting steps, stopping occasionally to peer into the curtaining snow for anything amiss. Over the moaning wind, the creaks and groans of the restless river ice added to his sense of disorientation caused by the storm.

After a time the snow began to thin, revealing the ghostly shapes of the boats sitting on their supports at the edge of the river. At least the temperature had warmed up enough for it to snow. Warming meant thawing. Enough thawing and they would leave this place. East or west — the direction they went depended on the fate of Captain Lewis and the twenty men with him who were long overdue. If they did not return —

He left the thought incomplete to watch a horse and rider emerge out of the storm. Figuring it was someone from the Mandan town, he whistled down to the man on the gates. After the gate guard waved acknowledgement, he went on with his watch.

He made two circuits of his post before the rider reached the gates. Shannon recognized Sly Wolf's paint horse. Instead of one rider, it carried two: Sly Wolf and Echo. He waved to the boy and watched as Ordway met the pair and took them into the sergeants' room. It struck him as odd that the sergeant did not take them directly to Captain Clark, but, then again, what did he know? He was only a private.

Thirteen days – thirteen days. Colter counted off every step of the way back to the fort with that chant. Once Captain Lewis figured out that they were not going to find any Sioux, he decided to keep the search party out hunting in order to replace the meat the Indians had taken. Thirteen days later the men were finally getting back to the fort. Thirteen days, eighteen crewmen, two sergeants, one captain and a load of meat.

For Colter, thirteen days had been an eternity of torment over his forced separation from Fragrant Grass. A separation he knew had been deliberately engineered by Ordway. Thirteen days had wrung out of him any concern for consequences. When he got back to the fort, nothing, *nothing* would ever again keep him away from Fragrant Grass.

The roof watch spotted the returning men. A cry went up and, soon, everyone who had stayed behind came rushing out to welcome them back.

"Thank God!" gushed Shannon. "I was about to give up on you, Old Man. Here, let me do that." He helped Colter out of the harness of the meat sledge, stepped into it himself and helped pull the load the rest of the way to the storeroom.

While they were unloading the meat, Shannon whispered, "Captain Clark's giving you all liberty tonight. I heard him tell Ordeal as we were coming out to meet you."

Colter snorted. "Means Ordeal'll have everyone goin' but me then, don't it?" He kept to himself his determination to go to Matootonha regardless of what the sergeant did.

He left Shannon and made his way to the barracks room which was in pandemonium over the promised liberty. Shannon came in a few moments later grinning from ear to ear. "You were wrong, Old Man. You do have liberty tonight. I just heard Captain Clark himself say so."

Colter was in no mood for Fuzz's jokes. He continued sorting his gear, setting aside the things that needed mending or cleaning, repacking the rest.

"Did you hear me?" Shannon asked. "I said you were wrong. You got liberty tonight. That is, if you want it."

"He's tellin' you right, Colter," Rube said. "You, me, and Little Brother — we're all goin'."

"Here, take these," Shannon said. "I won 'em in a shoot-off awhile back and I been saving them for something special." He laid a string of the blue beads the Indians prized most in Colter's hands. "They'll look good on her."

That they would. "Thanks, Fuzz."

Colter did not waste any breath joining in the other men's banter on the way to Matootonha. They arrived before it was fully dark. To his delight, they were taken directly to the lodge that Fragrant Grass and Mint shared with Sly Wolf. When he entered, Fragrant Grass was squatting beside the fire, stirring a cook pot. She glanced at him, but gave no other acknowledgement. He did not read anything into her lack of reaction. She was well. That was what counted. He relaxed against the backrest to watch her and savor the delicious smells of whatever she was preparing to serve them. His disappointment at being served by Mint disappeared with the first taste. He had never eaten such good food. Even Ma's cooking could not compare.

As if he read Colter's thoughts, Rube nudged him. "You ought to convince the captains to take her along with us as cook. Get rid of McNeal before one of us gets sick enough of his bitchin' to do somethin' about it."

At any other time Colter would have rejected the idea outright. However, the captains had already decided to take one woman west with them. One with a newborn baby, no less. Why not approach them with the idea of taking Fragrant Grass? She had certainly proved herself useful when she helped deliver Sacajawea's baby.

He was chewing on the idea when Sly Wolf stood up. By now Colter knew enough Mandan to understand him. "Pshanshaw, come here."

She rose and approached Sly Wolf as if her limbs ached. Colter's senses immediately came alert. Something wasn't right.

His state of heightened vigilance got in the way of understanding what Sly Wolf said next. He had to rely on Jesseaume's translation. "Ordway, Second Chief of the paleskins, honors our lodge. He chooses you, my wife, to lie with him this night. Take him to your sleeping robes."

Don't you know when to quit, Sarge? Colter thought. *Tell him 'no,' Pshanshaw. Say it loud. Maybe he'll hear you this time.*

Fragrant Grass stood with her head bowed and her eyes downcast, "Yes, my husband."

"No!" The word erupted out of Colter.

Ordway turned to him with a gloating smile. "You look peaked, Private. Something you ate maybe?"

Fragrant Grass kept her head down, depriving Colter of the chance to see her expression. Anger at being betrayed by the woman he thought he loved flooded through him. His words came out sounding strangled. "Somethin' I swallowed, don't you mean?"

"Hope it passes. I wouldn't want to lose you, Colter," Ordway said.

It was all Colter could do to keep from lunging for the man's throat. "You ain't never goin' to lose me, Sarge. Never!"

"Never's a long time, Colter. A long, long time." Ordway got to his feet, motioned for Fragrant Grass to lead and fell in behind her.

Colter was all too aware of the bulk of the blue beads in his pocket. They had been his surprise for Fragrant Grass. Instead, he got a surprise from her. One that hurt worse than any bullet.

All around him the other men were busy striking deals and heading off with their chosen squaws. He stumbled out through the entrance tunnel, emerging into the clear cold night. The central plaza was deserted. Voices and laughter drifted out from the surrounding lodges. Above him, the stars twinkled across the canopy of the indigo sky like a hundred thousand campfires.

Bratton and a Mandan woman ducked out of the tunnel, almost plowing into him. "Better hurry on up and make your pick, Colter. Best ones're goin' fast."

He started to say "Best one's gone," but stopped himself before the second word. She wasn't best. She had betrayed him. With Ordway.

Leading the paleskin Second Chief to her sleeping platform, Fragrant Grass felt detached from her leaden limbs. Her mind focused on bits of trivial nonsense, like the Second Chief's name. Ordway. According to Echo, the word did not mean anything. What a strange custom, to be called something meaningless. How could any paleskin remember another's name?

At her couch, she lay back on her robes, a stranger in her body. The one called Ordway sat stiffly on the edge of the platform and pulled down the privacy curtain. His breathing sounded labored. His pores exuded a repugnant combination of stale sweat and unwashed flesh.

He mumbled something under his breath. She did not understand the words, but she felt the hostility emanating from the man. Suddenly she was afraid. Sounds from beyond the curtain told her that the lodge was emptying. Ordway lay back and began to stroke himself, whispering something that sounded like a command. She waited tensely, unsure what this strange, repulsive man would do next.

Without warning, he rolled on top of her and drove her legs apart with his knee while jerking her dress up to her waist with one hand and ripping at the buttons on his trousers with the other. His roughness shattered her detachment. Fear gripped her.

He prodded her with his swollen member. She held her breath and waited for the joining which duty had forced her to accept.

The next thing she knew, he groaned and sank on top of her, pinning her to the bed. He lay there a long time with his chest heaving and his face hidden in the buffalo robes. She hesitated before putting a comforting hand on his shoulder.

"No!" he snarled, batting her hand away and catching her across the mouth with a stinging slap.

The shock of the blow numbed her to its pain. The mortification of being struck was too much for her to absorb. Even the Sioux — the hateful, blood-thirsty Sioux — would not strike one another. To do so would be too demeaning, too humiliating.

She was afraid of what he might do if she moved to touch the place where the edge of her teeth had split her lip. Fighting back tears, she lay rigid and waited for him to leave her.

Colter remembered nothing of his walk back to the fort that night. Too shaken to withstand any scrutiny or teasing, when he arrived in the barracks room, he saw that Shannon was the only one present. Thankfully, Shannon was sleeping and did not awaken.

After a wakeful night spent staring at the ceiling above his bunk, Colter rose before dawn and left the room. He slipped noiselessly over the fort's back wall without alerting the sentry and escaped into the woods. He walked south along the river until he got his hurt and anger under control. It took a long time before he could force himself to go back.

By then, York was on watch at the gates. "You're back early."

"Had my fill," he answered, arranging the numb muscles of his face into the pretense of a smile.

In the barracks, the only one of the squad to have returned from Matootonha was Rube Field. "Where'd you disappear to, Colter?"

Colter forced heartiness into his reply. "Disappear? You just weren't lookin'." He went to the hearth and dipped a bowl of gruel from the pot as a way to dodge more questions from Rube.

Shannon sat on his bunk, reading from the Bible. He gave Colter a sharp look but did not say anything until Rube left. "You're a terrible liar, Old Man. I heard you come in last night. What happened?"

The concern in Shannon's face tempted him to answer, but the pain was too sharp; the wounds, too fresh.

"That's right. Be stubborn," Shannon said, placing himself in front of the door. "Well, I can be just as hardheaded as you. You aren't leaving this room until you tell me."

A piercing whistle cut the tension between them, the call to morning assembly. Colter smiled grimly. "After you, Fuzz."

By the time Lewis and Clark came out of their quarters, there were still several holes in the ranks where crewmen had not yet returned from Matootonha. "Sergeant Ordway, call the roll," Captain Lewis said.

No answer.

"Sergeant?" Lewis asked.

Still no answer.

Lewis half-turned to Clark. Clark shrugged. Lewis scowled. "Sergeant Pryor, have the men sound off."

At the odd ring to Colter's "aye," Shannon darted a sideways look at him. Whatever happened last night must have been bad. Colter looked desolate.

After the roll call, Lewis stepped up on the stump. "Today is March 1st. Time to begin our preparations for departure. In place of *Discovery*, we will be building dugouts to carry us upriver. Our first task is to find trees of the proper size. Sergeant Pryor is in charge of that squad. Are there any volunteers?"

After spending the last two boring weeks at the fort, Shannon thrust up his hand. To his surprise, Colter followed suit.

"Two? Is that all?" Lewis said coldly.

The other crewmen shifted uneasily like schoolboys caught staring out the window instead of studying their lessons. The captain's voice took on a biting tone. "I see. Obviously the rest of you have something better to do than get us ready to go. Whatever those important tasks are, rest assured that they will not include any visits to our neighbors, the Mandans, until our dugouts are ready. As of this moment all leaves are cancelled, and, except for work parties, every man of you is confined to this fort."

During a long pause, the captain surveyed each crewman in turn. Under this uncomfortable scrutiny all the men, except McNeal, stepped forward.

"Much better," Lewis said. "Good luck in your search and Godspeed." With that, the captains retired to their quarters and Gass gave the volunteers instructions, then dismissed them.

Shannon grabbed Colter's arm before he could walk away. "Where's Ordeal? Tell me you two didn't get into it. Tell me you didn't do anything stupid."

Colter tried to pull away, but Shannon would not let him do so. "Damn you! Where is he?"

Colter's voice was low and flat. "Last I saw Ordeal, a squaw was leading him to her couch."

"And?"

"And nothin'."

"Out with it, Old Man."

Shannon pinned Colter's arms to his sides and held him in place until Colter said, "The stupidest thing I ever did was think she was any different from every other squaw."

Suddenly Shannon grasped what had happened. He released Colter. "Why, that son-of-a-bitch! So that's what was going on when —"

He did not get to finish. The front gates creaked open, and Ordway strolled into the fort. The instant he saw Colter, the sergeant's lips curled into a malignant smile. Shannon hissed, "That filthy snake."

"No need to get all het up, Fuzz. Old Ordeal done me a favor."

"Bull roar," Shannon snapped.

"I should've listened to you. Them squaws'll raise their skirts for any man with a string of cheap beads."

"Will you pay attention, Colter? It wasn't her fault."

"We ain't talkin' about nobody's fault but mine. Don't get yourself worked up over nothin'. I ain't. Come on, let's go. We got us some trees to find."

Shannon would not budge. "You mean, you'll walk away just like that? Let him get away with what he's done to you?"

"It's done. Over. No sense lookin' back. Man who starts thinkin' with his carrot's apt to run smack dab into the nearest tree. That's what happened to me. The sooner this expedition heads west, the better. I got me a life to get on with."

"This was a set-up. Between Ordeal and Sly Wolf. I know that's what it was."

"I ain't goin' to argue with you, Fuzz. Now step aside, or I'll have to help you move."

Boom! A chunk of river ice broke free from its winter mooring. The sound heralded the start of the spring melt. Soon the ice would be gone, and so would they. Soon Colter would have to leave Fragrant Grass anyway. Perhaps it was better this way.

Reluctantly, Shannon moved aside to let Colter into the barracks.

Gass's squad searched for miles along both sides of the river for five days before they found cottonwoods big enough for dugouts. The stand of trees was located six miles up the Missouri from the fort and a mile and a half inland. There the men set to work felling the trees and hollowing them out.

For the first two days, Shannon kept after Colter to alter his opinion of Fragrant Grass. Colter refused to listen. Shannon hadn't been there. He hadn't seen her accept Ordway. Hadn't endured the pain of betrayal. Shannon finally gave up in frustration.

When another squad came to spell the first at the end of two weeks, Colter opted to stay out with the dugout crew rather than return to the fort with Shannon and the others. By now, the afternoon temperatures had risen into the thirties. The spring melt had begun in earnest. The improved weather, combined with the hard physical activity, moved Colter's mind away from Fragrant Grass's infidelity to thoughts of the future. The sooner they left this place, the sooner he could fulfill his obligation to Captain Lewis and this expedition, the sooner he could even the score with Farley Stuart and get on with his life.

On March 22, two days shy of a month after he left the fort, the crew finished the six dugouts and Captain Clark arrived with a fresh squad to help haul the finished canoes to the river.

The changes in the condition of the Missouri since he had last seen it astonished Colter. In place of the solid surface of ice that he and the others had walked across for nearly four months, a mass of icy water churned free and wild. Aroused from its winter's confinement, it ripped off the bonds of ice, biting off chunks of riverbank and grumbling like something restless and alive.

He helped deposit the first dugout into an ice-free eddy. The canoe floated, and so did all of the other five. Clark addressed the men. "Before we head down to the fort, there's someone we need to recognize. Colter, you were the first to volunteer and you've been out here for nigh on a month. That kind of devotion to the expedition merits a special reward. How about one day's liberty for each week you've slept out here on the ground?"

Aware that all eyes were turned to him, Colter struggled for an answer. Liberty meant nothing to him anymore. The only place to go was Matootonha, which was the last place he ever wanted to see again. "Thanks, Captain, but I'd rather get goin' upriver."

Around him, men muttered "Are you nuts?" and "Send me then."

Clark looked at him. "All the same, a four-day liberty is yours if you want it."

Colter nodded to put an end to the discussion and to acknowledge the captain's gesture. Clark then turned to directing the crew into the new canoes.

Shannon sidled over. "You're wrong, Old Man. So wrong. It's just a matter of days until we leave here. Don't let your stubbornness cost you this chance. Whatever happened, believe me, she is not to blame."

Colter whirled on the younger man. "I don't remember askin' you to butt in."

"For God's sake, Old Man, listen to reason for once in your life. According to Echo, Ordway hit her. Hit her and gave her a black eye."

"That's between her and him. I ain't interested."

Shannon's hands balled into fists. "By Christ, but you're cold-blooded."

"Right kind of blood for this here country, wouldn't you say?"

"Then you're in the right place."

"That I am."

11. *Enslavement*

R ough hands pulled Hartley to his feet. Once his sleep-numbed mind grasped what was happening, his wrists were already bound and he had been dragged outside and shoved onto a horse. When the Indians galloped off, Hartley's mount surged after them, nearly unseating him.

They had reached the southern edge of the arc of tepees before he regained his balance. Beyond the camp perimeter, a group of ten mounted Sioux were gathered in the pre-dawn darkness. Hartley shivered. For the last three months he had been a prisoner and a slave, fighting the camp dogs for scraps of food, scraping hides, hauling water and gathering buffalo chips for fuel, all the while wondering what the Sioux planned to do with him. He guessed that he was about to learn.

Lone Feather sat at the head of the second group of riders on his favorite horse, a sleek black mare who hated everyone but her owner. The Sioux leader scooped up the lead of Hartley's horse and appeared to examine the braided leather. Without warning, he gave voice to an unearthly howl and yanked the lead.

The animal reared. The preacher had no time to dig in his heels. He grabbed for the animal's mane, caught a bit of hair, but immediately lost his grip. He hit the ground, knocking the air from his lungs and jarring fresh bolts of pain from the wounds in his ribs and shoulder. He clenched his jaw against crying out so tightly that one of his teeth came loose.

"You ignorant savage!" Hartley croaked up at Lone Feather who was looking down at him with cruel amusement.

Lone Feather pointed commandingly to the preacher's mount, leaving no doubt that Hartley had better get moving. His wrists were bound, and he failed three times before he regained the horse's back. This time, when the Indians took off, he managed to keep his seat by digging his knees into the animal's sides and hunching low against the cold air rushing past.

Lone Feather rode up alongside him. He pointed at the preacher and said in a voice loud enough to carry over the thunder of the running horses, "You ignorant savage."

At the shock of hearing English coming from the Sioux chief's mouth, Hartley nearly forgot to hang on to the horse's mane.

*

The Sioux rode single-file with Hartley bringing up the rear. He was beyond feeling the aching of his body. He could no longer draw a deep breath for the constant pressure in his chest. The glare of the bright spring sun would not let him open his eyes more than a slit. And he no longer cared where the Sioux were going. All he knew was that, whatever their destination, they were in enough of a hurry to stop only long enough to rest their mounts.

The riders at the front of the group halted now, and one of the lead Sioux climbed up on his horse's back to scan the horizon. Gesturing ahead, he said something to Lone Feather.

Squinting, Hartley picked out what looked like a line of brush at the edge of a snow-patched stretch of prairie in the distance. After more study, he noticed that the arc of brush was too regular to be a natural feature and decided it was an Indian village. Beyond the brush, willows defined the course of a stream, and beyond that, he was sure he saw the glint of sun on water.

His heart began to beat faster. Could it be?

He rubbed his eyes and looked again. Yes, it was! The Ree town where he had stayed before his capture.

He glanced warily at Lone Feather for signs that the Sioux intended to raid the place. The Sioux leader gazed off toward the village, stroking the stock of the preacher's confiscated rifle which rested in a beaded leather case tied to his horse. Hartley had come to hate the red man almost as much as he hated John Colter.

Lone Feather motioned for the group to move forward. Their slow approach indicated that the Sioux intended to talk or trade, rather than scalp and enslave.

As the group drew near to the picket wall, the Arikara Chief Hay and two members of the warrior council came out to meet them. Hay silently exchanged signs with Lone Feather, twice pointing to Hartley.

Two of the Sioux then pulled the preacher off his horse and cut away his bonds. His legs had grown too weak to support him, and he collapsed on the dirty snow. The same pair of Indians hauled him upright and dragged him to Chief Hay's lodge where they dumped him like a bag of refuse inside the entrance and took seats beside the fire.

The women of the lodge served food to the Sioux, bypassing the preacher as if he were not there. Made bold by hunger, Hartley was about to protest his treatment when another person entered the lodge.

"Tabeau," he called out. "It's me, Hartley! Lord, am I glad to see you. These Sioux have been holding me prisoner."

The trader scowled at the preacher before going to sit next to Chief Hay. Once the empty food bowls were cleared, the talking pipe made its way around the assembled men. Then, Lone Feather began to speak. The Sioux leader motioned toward him several times, and the kernel of an idea began to sprout in Hartley's mind: the Sioux were trying to ransom him back to the Rees. That explained why they had kept him alive this long and why Chief Hay and Tabeau both pretended not to recognize him. The one thing he knew for certain about the Rees was that they loved to bargain and that they were better at it than anyone he had ever come up against. Even Farley Stuart.

As the discussions ran on, Hartley's confidence in his assumption grew. Back in the fall, he had convinced the Rees that he was an emissary from President Jefferson, carrying a vital message to the expedition. They believed him enough to send an escort to accompany him to the Mandan villages where the expedition was encamped for the winter. No one had figured on the Sioux attacking that escort and taking him prisoner.

Hartley had had enough to do just to stay alive during his captivity. There was no time to think about John Colter. Now thoughts of Colter and visions of the revenge he would wreak on the man dragged his attention away from the negotiations.

An angry slash of Lone Feather's hand punctuated his discourse and wrenched the preacher out of his thoughts. Anger puckered the corners of the Sioux leader's mouth as his upturned hand sliced across his chest and turned palm down in the sign for no. With one last dark scowl in Hartley's direction, Lone Feather stalked out of the lodge.

Once the Sioux cleared out, a trio of Rees hauled Hartley to his feet and hustled him outside. They thrust him into an abandoned lodge at the outer edge of town and left him. The place reeked of mold and field mice. He waited in the damp darkness, wondering what had transpired.

He did not know how long he sat there before two men entered. "Tabeau! Thank God it's you!"

"Les Tetons, they leave," the trader said gruffly.

"Good riddance," Hartley said. The second man was a stranger. Even in the gloom, his hooded glare made the preacher uneasy. "It was obvious they wanted to ransom me to the Rees. How much did they get?"

"*Rien*," answered Tabeau.

"Nothing? But they left," Hartley said.

"Le Partisan, he was angry."

"What did he have to be angry about? His men ambushed the Ree party I was with and took me captive. The Rees are the ones should be mad. The Rees and me."

Tabeau picked up something from the lodge's littered floor. Balancing it on the end of one filthy finger, he examined it, then popped it into his mouth and chewed it up. It looked to Hartley to be an insect. "The Rees, *oui*, they are angry. But you?"

"I'd like to scalp that Partisan for the way he treated me."

Tabeau grabbed Hartley's collar in a choke hold. "The Rees are angry. I am angry, but *mon ami* here, he is very angry. With you."

"Me?" Hartley squawked.

"You are *un menteur*, a liar," the stranger said, moving in to take over Tabeau's grip on Hartley's collar.

"Who are you?" Hartley asked.

The stranger looked to be constructed from parts of two different men. His upper body was built strong and blocky. From the waist down his hips and legs looked too puny to hold up the rest.

"You know my friend," the man said in a low menacing voice, pushing Hartley against one of the lodge's roof supports with a force that caused more of the earth around the smoke hole to peel off. Debris rained onto the preacher's head.

"Your friend?" he asked, desperately trying to place this man.

The stranger loomed over him like a raptor about to strike. "*Oui, mon ami*, you must know him. You have his canoe."

Hartley gulped. "I-I bought the canoe."

"So you say," the stranger said.

"F-from a riverman. Bonhomme." The stranger's grunt seemed to come from a great depth. Hartley plunged onward, wishing he did not sound so nervous. "His spyglass and river map, too."

"The rifle Partisan carries, it is Bonhomme's." The stranger's statement carried the force of accusation a moment before he plucked Hartley off the floor and heaved him across the lodge, pounced on him and pressed one knee into his throat. "You kill *mon ami* Bonhomme."

"No, I-I didn't," Hartley croaked.

The stranger's savage slap echoed across the empty lodge. "Where you leave his body?"

Hartley struggled to breathe against the choking pressure of the stranger's knee. "He's alive. So help me God he is."

The man's fist plowed into the side of Hartley's skull with a crack that momentarily deafened him. "Where?"

Hartley spilled out as much of a description of the place as he could remember. The strangling weight eased off his throat slightly. "So, you take Bonhomme's things and leave him to die," the stranger said. "You are garbage. I give you back to Le Partisan."

Hartley's heart skipped a beat. The Sioux had no reason to keep him alive now. Going back to them meant sure death. He struggled to keep the panic out of his voice. "I hired Bonhomme in St. Charles to bring me upriver. I have an urgent message to relay to the leaders of the American expedition. Tabeau here kno —"

Another stinging slap across the mouth cut him off. "It is Bonhomme I care about. Not you," the man growled.

Hartley fought to swallow against the man's pressing knee and the lump of fear blocking his throat. "We had an accident down near the Platte. Bonhomme got hurt. His partner — the one without a tongue — Parler . . . You know Parler?"

The stranger nodded, giving Hartley time to concoct a lie. "Parler and me, we flagged down a party of traders. I gave them the rest of my purse so they would take Bonhomme back to St. Louis for help."

He paused to let the stranger contemplate this act of largesse. "I was glad to do it. He was in a bad way."

He took as a good sign the fact that the stranger did not hit him again and hurried on. "Before he left, Bonhomme gave me his rifle, telescope and map. Told me to take them and the canoe. He wanted me to catch the expedition. That's a good man you have for a friend."

After a long hesitation, the stranger rolled up to his feet. Hartley darted a beseeching look at Tabeau. "Now that you know the truth, won't you help me get upriver? I have to reach the expedition before they get any further west. It's a matter of life and death."

Tabeau and the stranger exchanged a look the preacher could not interpret. Hartley talked on, "The captains will be grateful to you for your help, of course. I can assure you of that."

Hartley's hopes expanded with the length of the silence. Enough of the outside earth had fallen away on the far wall to reveal a piece of spring sky. The stranger paced to the gap and stared out. He stood there for a long time. Then, he whirled and kicked Hartley squarely in the face.

The preacher contracted into a groaning ball while explosions of light played on the backs of his eyelids and thunder roared in his ears. Over the roaring, he heard the stranger's hiss. "You lie. To kill you is easy. No, I let you live. For me, you work."

"But the expedition is leaving." Hartley could barely gasp out the words for the pain. "I must —" He flinched away from the stranger's threatening fist.

"Here with me you stay," the man continued. "If Bonhomme he is alive, as you say, he come upriver by summer. For now, you work for me. I am called La Montagne. The Mountain."

"But —"

Montagne's boot smashed into Hartley's groin. "Choose now. Montagne — or Le Partisan."

For a long time, the agony in his crotch and ribs kept Hartley's mouth from forming words. Eventually, one word gasped out. "You."

12. *Sad Farewell*

C aptain Lewis addressed the assembled crew from his stump platform. "With the completion of the dugouts, Captain Clark and I have decided upon a date for our departure. April 7th."

Shannon noted that Colter's cheer rang louder than any of the others.

"Drouillard will lead one last hunting party to lay in meat for our journey. Volunteers?" Lewis asked.

While Colter's hand shot up, Shannon would not look at the captain. The spring thaw had created a restlessness in him; one he had not understood until yesterday when McNeal, as usual, had had a squaw up in the loft. It was when his own body began to respond to the sounds of their activities that he realized he needed the relief that only a trip to the loft or to Matootonha would provide. He could not see himself in the loft — not with his barracks-mates listening in — but Matootonha was different. This morning he awoke determined to find a way over there soon. Someone else could do the hunting this time. He had other, more important things to take care of.

"Who else?" The captain's glance raked the faces of the crew, but no one moved.

Lewis's eyes narrowed. "Since I can guess why no one else seems inclined to come forward, the Mandan town will be off-limits until we leave." He started to step down from the stump, then changed his mind. "And no Mandan women will be allowed inside the fort for that period as well. Dismissed."

Shannon felt as if he had just been slapped. Rube turned angrily to Colter. "You and your volunteerin'! Makin' all the rest of us look bad. What did you and Peckerwood do? Trade attitudes?"

"I'm for gettin' on with this here expedition. Always have been." Colter shoved past them.

Rube watched Colter storm into the barracks. "What's got into him? First he don't take the liberty the captain gives him, then he goes off with Drooler to hunt first chance he gets. What happened to that little squaw he was beddin'?"

If he had not been so upset over the captain's pronouncement, Shannon might have told Rube the story. Instead, he said, "Who cares? Looks like nobody's bedding anything from now on."

Fragrant Grass maneuvered the bullboat into the eddy below Matootonha. Avoiding the thin layer of ice that remained in the shadow of the overhanging bank, she pulled the lightweight craft out of the water and turned it upside down next to the others. Then she bent to retie her moccasins, giving herself time to compose her thoughts before re-entering the town. She had been turned away at the gates of the fort. The paleskin chief Merry Weather would allow Mandan men inside, but not women. She knew from Echo that Colter had gone hunting, but the boy did not know where he had gone or when he would return. This, when she desperately needed to talk with him, to find out why he no longer came to her.

It had been nearly a month since she had taken the paleskin Second Chief Ordway to her bed. Her lip had healed, but the other, deeper wound to her soul remained. During that period, she had not seen Colter and not dreamed of the Hawk Spirit. Not since Strikes Two's death had she felt so abandoned, so lost.

She stood up and pushed the hair out of her face. It was growing fast now that she no longer cut it. By summer it would be almost as long as when Strikes Two rode away from the village never to return.

As she looked toward the imposing pickets, she saw not a barrier to keep enemies out but a wall to trap her inside. The same inexplicable terror she had felt as a child before the Hawk Spirit came to be her guide flooded through her. She could not move.

A figure appeared at the top of the bank. "Hurry, my sister, hurry!" Mint yelled.

The urgency in her sister's tone got Fragrant Grass moving up the path. Mint confronted her at the break in the wall. "Where have you been?"

Before Fragrant Grass could think of a suitable response, Mint went on, "We must pack. Our husband wishes to leave by sun-above."

"Leave? For where?"

"Whatever our husband decides to do, our duty is to obey, not ask questions. Come."

For the next two weeks, Colter and Drouillard ranged far south and east of the fort in search of game. They had horses again to carry the game since the captains had borrowed four horses from the Mandans in exchange for blacksmithing services provided by John Shields. By now the two hunters were so accustomed to each other's habits that they had no need to talk, a situation that Colter preferred.

On the fourteenth night out, they made camp in a clearing within sight of the Missouri. While a slab of elk meat roasted over the fire, Colter stared out at the river. They would return to the fort the next day, and, in three days the crew would leave Fort Mandan to continue west. Although there were only occasional chunks of ice in the current now, the Missouri was running high and swift with runoff, ready to take up the battle against them.

Drouillard's voice, hoarse from two weeks of little use, broke through his reverie. "Why are you here?"

Colter glanced over his shoulder, wondering what the half-breed was getting at, but nothing in Drouillard's expression gave a clue as to his intention. He answered carefully. "To hunt, same as you."

"Why do you not go to Matootonha?" Drouillard asked.

"What business is that of yourn?"

"Why do you not go to see your woman?"

"She's not my anythin'."

Fat from the meat sizzled in the fire. Drouillard watched it for a moment. "You blame her for something she could not help. If she does not obey her husband, she will be — how you say? — vanished."

"You're talkin' gibberish. She ain't goin' to disappear. She —"

Drouillard butted in. "She can no longer live among her people."

"You mean banished. Not vanished."

Drouillard stared at him as if expecting a reply. The look irritated Colter. "What that pack of savages do ain't none of my concern."

He dragged over his pack and took out his carving to curtail further conversation. To his relief, Drouillard let the subject drop. In the restored silence, however, Colter's mind would not let go of the half-breed's words. He had witnessed ostracism back in the Draft. He saw first-hand how quickly peoples' lives could be destroyed because they went against society's rules. The smart ones packed up and moved away to start again in another place. The others . . .

He looked up at Drouillard. "How'd you know all this?"

"I know."

"Then why're you tellin' me now?"

The half-breed tossed three sticks onto the fire before answering. "Three days, we leave."

Colter waited for more, but Drouillard was done talking. He was left to weigh what the half-breed had said against what he had believed about Fragrant Grass. It had never entered his mind that she had been forced to take Ordway to her bed. Forced by the oldest, cruelest of mankind's punishments. He vaguely remembered Shannon trying to tell him something about Sly Wolf coming to the fort to see the sergeant, but he had dismissed it as another of Fuzz's fanciful notions.

Then again, she had turned Ordway down before. Why couldn't she have done so again?

He knew the answer before he asked the question. When you lived in a community, you toed the line or you paid a terrible price. Even so, she had toed the line and paid a price. In the same way the Mandans would have turned their backs on her had she disobeyed, he had abandoned her. A misjudgment that had cost them six precious weeks together.

Lord, only three days left. There was no time to lose. "You asked why I ain't gone to Matootonha? Well, I'm goin' now."

He expected the half-breed to argue. Instead Drouillard nodded. "You go." However, when he turned toward the horses, Drouillard stopped him. "Leave horses here."

"And just how'm I supposed to get across the river? Swim for Christ's sake?"

"Not with a horse and not to swim." Drouillard stabbed a finger toward the river. "The boat."

There, on the bank, resting in the branches of an uprooted tree lay a Mandan bullboat, complete and unharmed.

The moment the flimsy craft was released on the river, the swift current grabbed it and flung it forward with a force that made Colter wonder why he had not waited until morning. Besides the fact that it was too dark even with a quarter moon to see any flotsam the current might be hurling at him, he had never tried to handle a round boat before, let alone one so light.

The Mandans made maneuvering these boats look easy. He quickly found out how difficult it really was. Paddling the usual way caused the boat to spin in the current. Powering his strokes worsened the problem. By the time he figured out that a lighter touch at the paddle and fewer alternating strokes worked best, he had drifted two miles the wrong direction; a distance he had to make up before he was on his way toward his goal.

While he adapted to the quirks of the boat, he put all his senses to work to keep him out of trouble. A dozen close calls later, he pulled even with the site of the fort. Tired from the effort of concentrating and soaked with a combination of riverwater and sweat, he allowed himself a moment's pause to look at the sleeping fort. In three days they would leave this place for the west. "And I have three more miles to go," he muttered.

A shadow cut through the streak of moonlight glittering on the water ahead. He plunged the oar into the river and managed to chop one back-stroke to avoid a sizeable chunk of ice by a fraction of an inch.

The near-collision decided him that he would be better off on foot. He rowed into the east bank, pulled the boat well up above the water line and took off at a trot. He thrashed through the undergrowth and splashed through puddles of melt-water, without regard to how much noise he made.

At the edge of the burial yard outside Matootonha, he stopped to catch his breath. The scattered scaffolds cast eerie shadows in the weak moon-light. The fields on both sides of the cemetery had been cleared of winter debris in preparation for planting. As he started across the burial ground, he heard the bird-like calls of the Mandan night guards, signalling the presence of an intruder. The guard at the opening looked him over care-fully before letting him pass.

Inside the town, the gentle night wind carried the smells of banked fires and spring mold. He made the last turn on the familiar path to Fragrant Grass's lodge and slowed, waiting for the dogs who guarded the entrance to recognize him. Strange. The dogs were not around. *Maybe they're all inside*, he thought.

As custom required, he cleared his throat to announce his arrival before entering. When no one answered, he decided that it was later than he thought and that everyone was asleep. He ducked inside and waited for his eyes to adjust to the darkness. The first thing he noticed was the fire. It had gone out.

He bent to feel the ashes. They were cold. At that point he became aware of a complete absence of sound. No rustling. No snoring. The room was empty.

He was sure he had the right place. Then again, it was easy to get turned around in a town where all the dwellings looked alike and were so crowded together. Outside he rechecked his position. He had the correct lodge, but where were Fragrant Grass and the others?

He lit a brand in the coals under some racks of drying meat and re-entered the lodge. All the cooking vessels were gone. The beds had been stripped of their robes. Gone, too, were the pouches that usually hung on Fragrant Grass's sleeping platform; the bags in which she kept her sewing and supply of medicine plants. Standing in the center of the empty space, he was frozen into inaction, bewildered and heartsick.

Noises from outside cut into his thoughts. "Friend Colter?" Echo poked his head into the room. "They said you had come." He gestured around the now-empty lodge. "They go away."

"Where? When?" Colter urged.

Echo waved vaguely. "To hunt the buffalo. Six lodges go together."

Not getting the answer he wanted, Colter pressed, "When did they go?"

"What is 'when', Friend Colter? I do not understand."

With his patience worn thin by his effort to reach the village, Colter exploded, "Of course you know. When? How long ago? How many days since they left?"

The boy flinched at the harsh words, and Colter knew he had to soften his approach or risk not getting any answers at all. He forced himself to squat down to the boy's height and lower his voice. "Which way'd they go?"

Echo appeared to relax a bit. "Toward the place where the sun rests."

"Good, west. Now how long they been gone?"

"Long?"

"How many sleeps since they left?"

Echo had to think about this for a time before he said, "Many."

A useless answer. He had to restrain himself from shaking the boy.

"Friend Colter will follow her?" Echo asked. "When your brothers leave, you will stay with my people?"

Colter could not answer those questions. Not yet. He pressed. "How many sleeps?"

Echo counted on his fingers and mumbled in Mandan. Colter waited on tenterhooks. His hopes for a reasonable answer — one day, or two — began to fade with each contortion of the boy's expressive face. Brightening, Echo held up his hand, fingers outstretched.

"Five sleeps. Five? You're sure?" Colter asked.

The boy nodded and launched into an explanation of how he arrived at the figure. Tuning him out, Colter thought about the wide, wild country surrounding them. His heart sank. "West" could mean anywhere, and already the trail was five days cold. How could he ever hope to find her? It was impossible. He never would.

"No, by Judas, if anyone can find her, I will!" he muttered, noting the graying of the eastern sky through the smoke hole signaling the arrival of dawn.

"Judas? He is your friend?" Echo asked.

"I'll explain it to you another time." Colter ducked through the entrance. Echo called after him. "May the Hawk Spirit lead you to her."

Colter waved but did not stop. He had things to do that could not wait.

Shannon watched the dawning from his sentry post at the gates of the fort. With only two days to go until they headed upriver, Captain Lewis had relented on his stand about keeping the Mandan women out of the fort. Two days gave him precious little time.

The door to the barracks of Sergeant Gass's squad opened and out came Collins, his relief. Yawning and rubbing the sleep out of his eyes, Collins trudged slowly toward the gates, skirting the still-sleeping crewmen who had abandoned their stifling barracks rooms to live outside until their departure. "Any excitement?" he asked over another yawn.

Shannon shook his head. "Maybe later."

Collins poked him in the ribs and chuckled. "I'm all for lots of that kind of excitement. I'm ripe as a melon in the July sun."

Me, too, Shannon thought, walking away. Collins yelled after him. "Hey, I thought you swore off squaws."

"I did," he tossed over his shoulder as he stepped over a sleeping crewman. The door of his barracks was open and the room looked empty. It wasn't until his eyes had adjusted to the interior gloom that he noticed Colter who was in the process of securing the laces on his bulging pack. "How did you get into the fort?"

"Come over the wall. Don't want to cause no fuss," Colter responded without turning his head to look Shannon's way.

"Drouillard said you'd gone over to Matootonha," Shannon said.

"Come to get some things first."

"You came to get everything, you mean. Want to tell me what you're up to, Old Man?" Shannon asked.

Colter got to his feet and slung the heavy pack onto his back. "She's gone. I'm goin' after her."

"Are you daft? You'll never find her in two days' time. Never."

Colter draped one of his powder horns over his shoulder. "You're right. Two days ain't near long enough. Not with them havin' a five-day head start."

It took a moment for Shannon to comprehend Colter's full meaning. "You can't do this, Old Man."

"Yes, I can and I will."

Shannon grabbed his arm. "Don't."

"Step aside, Fuzz, or I'll walk over you."

"What about your enlistment? What about that man who tried to steal your land?"

"Stand aside."

"Listen! This last week I've been helping Captain Lewis get his specimens and papers ready to go back with the keelboat."

"Outta my way."

Shannon kept talking, desperate to prevent Colter from making a big mistake. "I've seen Captain Clark's map. The one he drew from all the information he got from the natives over the winter."

"That ain't got nothin' to do with me."

"Listen, I said. We're not that far from the Passage. Why not finish what we started, then come back for her? You'll be back before the snow falls, easy."

Colter firmly, but gently, pushed Shannon out of his path. "I cain't leave her, Fuzz. She means too much to me."

Shannon sagged down on his bunk. He knew from the set of Colter's jaw that there was no changing his mind now. "Might as well take my horn, too. It's full."

Colter acknowledged the offer with a nod and handed Shannon his empty spare in return.

"I promise you that the captains won't get a word out of me, either. No one will ever know I talked to you before —" Shannon swallowed against the aching lump expanding in his chest. "Good luck, Old Man. Godspeed."

"Same to you, Fuzz." At the door, Colter turned. "I ain't never met a body like you."

Shannon's voice was thick with emotion. "Same here."

"We had us one hell of an adventure, ain't we? Think on me from time to time."

Shannon could not get his mouth to work so he nodded in reply. How could he not dwell on the man who had become his best friend?

Colter gave a curt wave, stepped out the door and out of Shannon's life.

Colter was in luck. Collins, the gate guard, was dozing; no one was on the roof; and all the men in the compound were still asleep. So there was no one to witness his stop at the fort, no one to see him leave.

Once outside the walls, he loped down to where he had stashed the bull-boat. He flipped it over and squatted beside it to lash down his pack and rifle. Despite how easy his leave-taking had been, his heart was thumping wildly at the enormous decision he had made.

A stick crunching under someone's weight startled him. He rose from his squat to see Ordway step around a tree. "Going somewhere, Colter?"

"Just takin' that liberty Captain Clark give me awhile back." Colter was surprised to hear his voice so level and calm.

"You're too late. She's not there," Ordway said.

"Who, Sarge?"

"Don't play stupid with me, Colter. I know better."

Colter faced Ordway full on. The sergeant no longer had a hold on him. "You know one thing for sure, Sarge: how to hurt them as cain't hurt back. Only a coward hits a woman."

The remark appeared to catch the sergeant off-guard, but he recovered quickly with, "She's not a woman. Not even much of a squaw for that matter."

"Weren't talkin' about her, Sarge. We was talkin' about you — a yeller-belly what beats up on women. Why not try someone your own size for a change? Someone like me."

Ordway's eyes glittered with malice. "Oh, no, Private. You can't goad me into a fight. Not when I'm about to see you float out of my life once and for all. Here I've wasted the winter trying to break you when all it took to get you to desert was some squaw spreading her legs for you."

"I'm takin' liberty, Sarge. I earned it, remember?"

"Save it, Colter. You're deserting. I know it and you know it. Be my guest. Take off. Sooner you're gone, the better. By the time you're missed, it'll be too late to do anything about it."

"Sure, Sarge, you ain't goin' to follow me like the moon's jest a clod in the butter churn."

"There's only one man on this crew the captains would hold up for: Drouillard. You — you're expendable. There's too much riding on the success of this venture to waste a minute on your kind. So go. No one will stop you. No one white, that is. Good-bye and good riddance." He ground around on his heel and strode off toward the fort.

Colter watched him go, filled with equal measures of hope and distrust. Hope that, for once, the man was telling the truth, yet unwilling to take his word for anything ever. "Who cares? If'n they come after me, I'm just takin' liberty," he muttered, sliding the boat into the river.

He paused a moment, listening for sounds that would indicate the sergeant had gone to spread the alarm.

When he heard nothing out of the ordinary, he thought, *Time's a-wastin', Johnny boy. Let's go.* He pushed off, hopped in and began to paddle against the power of the current.

Colter stood at the top of a rise looking down at the mound village with frustration. He had spent the entire morning reconnoitering dozens of the trails that led west from Matootonha. One by one, he followed them. Some led to other villages. Others led east. He eliminated those, then started checking out the others until he thought he had a likely trail that would lead him to Fragrant Grass. Instead it had led him here, to this Hidatsa village set on a bluff above the Knife River. Not the destination a hunting party would choose.

Thwarted, he turned away. Already the sun had fallen far down in the western sky, yet he was no closer to finding her than he had been when he began his search this morning. He opened his pouch to find just five sticks of dried meat. In his haste to leave the fort, he had forgotten about food. Before too long, perhaps tomorrow, he would have to interrupt his search in order to hunt. Now that he was afoot, he had to have food to keep up his energy.

He decided to head back toward Matootonha, thinking he might have time before dark to study more of the skein of outbound trails and find one to follow tomorrow. He headed down the rise away from the Hidatsa town. He was nearly at the bottom when an old animal burrow collapsed under his weight and he went down hard, wrenching his left knee in the process.

He lay on the ground until the pain subsided enough to try standing again. When the knee held under his weight, he tried walking. He found he could limp, but slowly. *If'n I could get me a horse*, he thought. "But you cain't, Johnny-boy, so make the best of it."

Colter smiled grimly at hearing himself speak. Next, he would be answering his own questions. When that happened . . .

Colter awoke during the night to find rain pelting down and his blanket soaked through. Favoring his wrenched knee, he hobbled under a partially-leafed sycamore where he waited out the night hunkered against its trunk.

The expedition was due to leave the following morning. The sudden up-welling of doubt caused by that thought surprised him.

What am I doin' out here? he thought. *As many trails as there be, I could spend all summer chasin' my tail. Maybe I oughtta go back to Matootonha and wait for her.*

"No, sir. That ain't a-goin' to work neither. There ain't no way of knowin' how long I gotta wait, and hangin' around them Mandans uninvited don't sit right."

He smiled grimly to hear himself answer his thoughts. He was already carrying on both sides of a conversation. Not a good sign. *Maybe I should've listened to Fuzz. Gone on, done what I pledged to do, then come back for her this fall.*

He snorted. "Yeah, should have. Bible says 'Make your yea mean yea; and your nay, nay.' Only, now it's too late. Boats're gone and here I sit."

Another thought elbowed its way into his conscience. *Don't be so sure. River's high. They cain't get that far.* "Stupid idea, Johnny boy," he muttered.

He thought for a moment. "No, by God. Not stupid."

Shannon lay awake the entire night, trying to get used to the idea of never seeing Colter again. By dawn's first glimmer, he was no closer to accepting his loss. The first thing he saw on sitting up was Colter's vacant bunk. In their excitement over impending departure, no one else seemed to have noticed the man's absence.

He gave Rube the rest of his breakfast gruel after one mouthful and headed to the captains' quarters to finish helping Captain Lewis catalog specimens. Lewis greeted him with a distracted nod toward the collected plants laid out on the table. Shannon plodded to the bench, opened the cataloguing notebook, and prepared to record names and descriptions as the captain dictated them.

With his thoughts elsewhere, he could not keep his focus on the work. He had to ask the captain to repeat himself. The fourth time, Lewis looked at him. "Are you ailing, Shannon?"

Shannon tried to hide his embarrassment. He had a deep-seated need to confide his secret, to unburden himself of the sorrow that was weighing down his heart, yet he could not bring himself to betray his word or his friend. "No, sir. Excited, I guess."

Lewis smiled tiredly. "For good reason. But, please, keep your mind on this for just awhile longer. We are nearly finished."

The captain's gentleness touched Shannon. For a split second, his tale hovered on the brink of spilling forth. Then Lewis turned away to see to another box of specimens and the spell broke.

Completing their task took until mid-afternoon. The captain closed the lid on the last box and dismissed Shannon to go complete his packing and join the crew assembled at the boats. In the deserted compound, the doors to the empty rooms stood open looking like toothless gaps in a weathered smile. Except for his pack, rifle and pouch, the barracks room was as empty as the others; emptier when he thought back on how much life the room had held for the last four mouths.

Inside, it was a long time before he could bring himself to look at Colter's bunk. When he did, flashes of remembered moments flooded his mind. Learning to like Colter had been hard work, but learning to do without him was proving even harder.

Suddenly he could not stand to be in the room. He scooped together his belongings and hurried outside. He started to leave the door open like the others but could not. He heard the latch catch with a twinge of regret.

York emerged from the captains' room across the compound carrying two crates, one on each shoulder. Lewis followed, pausing to position his tricorne precisely on his freshly-trimmed hair. He spotted Shannon. "Ready to be off, Private?"

Shannon forced a smile. "Ready, sir."

The captain stopped outside the gates to look back at the abandoned fort. "She served us well while we were here. History will remember this place, for I have no doubt that we will do what so many before us have failed to do." He fell into a silence, lost in his thoughts.

For Shannon, the captain's words brought a fresh wave of sadness. Without Colter, he knew he would never have made it this far up the Missouri. Without Colter, how could he go on?

"Shall we?" Lewis said.

Shannon came out of his reverie and fell in behind the captain.

13. *Change of Heart*

The shallow beach below Matootonha's bluff was completely empty of bullboats. It had not occurred to Colter that the Mandans would be using all their boats to cross the river and see the expedition off.

He balanced on his right leg, keeping his weight off his throbbing knee, and scanned the rooftops of the lodges where the Mandans stored the boats they were not using.

The roofs likewise were empty.

The closest Indian village was miles to the north. His only other choice was to get down to the riverbank across from the fort and hope he could attract someone's attention. He chose the latter option.

A quarter mile below Matootonha, the river had chewed away a large chunk of the bank. As he skirted the section, he stepped on a slippery patch of mud. His right foot slid sideways and, in his attempt to right himself, his left foot jammed down on the knob of an exposed root at an angle that tore all the tendons in his ankle.

The pain from this injury was even worse than when he hurt his knee. He gritted his teeth while he wrapped the swelling ankle with a piece of the rawhide torn from the binding around his knee. Then, he pulled himself up, hand over hand, using the trunk of a tree, and gingerly tried a step.

The hurt ankle buckled under him. If he wanted to walk, he had to have a crutch.

The Mandans had picked up all the fallen wood. To get a crutch, he had to knock a branch down from a tree. The only way he saw to do that was to use the stock of his rifle even though doing so went against a lifetime of training to always protect his weapon. Either he got a crutch or he stayed behind while the expedition left.

Steadying himself against the tree, he grasped the rifle by its barrel and swung the stock at the overhanging branches.

The swing missed, and in the process he twisted his knee.

He tried again, launching a second grunting swipe. Again, his effort failed. "Damn you, Johnny! Cain't you do nothin' right?" he chided himself.

Challenged by his own criticism, he made a third attempt. This time the stock connected with a crack that knocked a branch free. He snapped off the thin end to a length that would allow him to lean on it, then he draped his cap over the splintered end to protect his armpit. He refused to examine the rifle. He did not want to know just yet how much the crutch had cost him.

He stumped along, impatient at his slow progress, doing his best to ignore his injuries. After half an hour, the twinging in his ankle became too intense to disregard and he stopped to rest.

He stretched out his throbbing leg and looked out at the racing river while he tried to think up a good explanation for his injuries; something feasible to tell the captains when he got across to the fort. *If you make it across*, came the thought.

"Hellfire, I ain't a-goin' to start thinkin' like that. Time to be movin'." He levered himself to his feet with the crutch. That was when he spotted it.

The river had undermined a tree which had fallen so the top of its canopy lay half-submerged in the channel. A bullboat was caught in the branches on the upstream side. Although he could not tell the boat's condition from his angle and he was uncertain if he would be able to retrieve it given his injuries, he had to try.

Laying aside the crutch, his rifle and pack, he gingerly waded into the river, using the trunk of the fallen tree for support. The water was too murky to see where he was stepping. He had to move by feel and faith. He got to within an arm's reach of the craft when the bottom disappeared.

He grabbed for the dead tree's branches to keep the current from sweeping him downstream and managed to pull himself toward the craft. Slowly, clumsily, he worked it free from a tangle of branches.

One of the uprights in the boat's willow frame had snapped when the river snarled it in the tree. A quick glance showed that the rest of the frame, the buffalo hide, and the lacing were all intact. He decided to chance it.

He wrestled the boat back to the bank. Leaning the crutch against the fallen tree at an angle, he eyeballed the length needed to repair the boat's missing upright, and, issuing a silent prayer that he had guessed right, stomped down hard on the angled crutch with his good foot. The branch snapped off, but at a place below his mark. Cursing his luck, he snatched up the piece anyway and jammed it into the bullboat's frame in place of the broken part.

It was too long and fit at a slant. There was no telling if it would hold against the Missouri's swollen current. He weighed the situation for a moment. Did he want to trust his life to the ill-repaired boat?

Downstream, the crew milled around the expedition's boats, a sure sign that departure was imminent. That decided him. He pried off a length of the fallen tree's bark to serve as a paddle, threw his rifle and pack into the bottom of the boat, and heaved himself over the side.

The current grabbed the boat before he was set and pulled it around. He let the river push the repaired side of the frame away from the brunt of the current, then he focused everything he had on wielding the bark paddle to get himself across the river.

It wasn't until he reached the middle that he noticed the length of branch had worked itself loose from the frame and fallen into the bottom of the boat. River water washed in where the hide covering drooped. He left off paddling to attempt to fit the branch back into place. When he did, a floating log bumped the craft, sending it into a spin.

Dropping the stick he grabbed up the make-shift paddle. Digging hard, he managed to bring the strong side of the frame back around. On his next stroke, the piece of bark fractured in two, leaving him with half a paddle.

He resorted to the only thing he had left. He leaned over the side and began stroking with his right arm, ignoring the pain this action caused in his injured knee and ankle. After three strokes, he shifted over to his left arm.

He was less than a hundred yards from the opposite bank and a quarter mile above the fort when he had to stop for breath. The next moment the boat crashed into something hidden in the murky water. The force of the crash split the hide cover. He had barely enough time to grab his rifle and pack before the boat sank from under him, and he joined the rest of the flotsam hurtling along in the current.

At first, with the shock of being immersed in the cold river, it was all he could do to keep his head above water. Eventually one thought wound its way through the numbness of his brain: the current was sweeping his body out toward the center of the river. He had to reverse that movement if he wanted to make it to the bank.

He dared not let go his rifle or pack, which made kicking and stroking awkward. In the cold water his muscles responded sluggishly, and his arms and legs felt like dead weights.

The action of the river caused his body to bob skyward, giving him a brief glimpse of the fort and the congregation around the boats. "Help!" Instead of a shout, the word came out of his shivering lips like a bleat.

In that moment, part of him wanted to surrender and accept his fate. Yet, the rest of him refused to give up on this crossing, this return that he had fought so hard to make. His next floundering arm movement brought his body a foot closer to the passing bank and into a flow of exceptionally cold water. Those icy, grasping fingers panicked him. With the very last of his strength he lunged for a chunk of wood being carried along in the current.

He missed and plunged beneath the surface, submerging his rifle. While he was still underwater, the current flung him sideways and he lost orientation. It took a moment before he realized that he had stopped moving, that his head was above water and that he was breathing air, not Missouri riverwater. The same current that before had carried him out to the center of the river had swept him into a shallow eddy along the east bank.

Laboring to fill his lungs with precious air, he put his good foot down and found that the eddy was only thigh deep. He struggled to the bank, using his now-ruined rifle for support and collapsed belly-first onto the wet sand.

A boom sounded. The cannon on *Discovery* announcing its departure downriver.

A moment later, the keelboat, carrying the *engagés* with the court-martialed crewmen, Newman and Reed, wheeled into view less than fifty yards beyond him. The sight got him moving again.

He pulled himself up the bank using his rifle as a prop and grabbing vines and branches. There was no room in his mind for his injuries. He had only one thought: *don't get left behind.*

He burst into the clearing below the fort in time to see the last of the dugouts rounding the upstream bend and the crowd of Mandans dispersing in their bullboats toward Matootonha. He sank to the ground in despair. He was too late.

Less than an hour after leaving the fort, Shannon's back and arms already ached from the effort of paddling the dugout against the Missouri's swollen current. He sat in the prow, responsible for keeping an eye out for any trouble that the river might be hurling down on them.

He checked the river ahead, then watched the movements of the other five dugouts and two pirogues of the expedition's flotilla. No problems so far. Just the relentless current and the hollowness inside him created when Colter walked away three days ago.

From behind came McNeal's whine, "I'm not here to row you up this here river, Shannon. And neither is Willard. Get to work."

Willard's voice boomed from the stern. "This is the last time I'm going to say this, McNeal. Shut up!"

Shannon smiled grimly. He had been delighted when Captain Lewis assigned him to the smallest of the dugouts. Because the canoe held only three men, the captains put it in sweep position. Going last meant that, as lookout for the pilot Willard, he had the advantage of observing how the other boats avoided trouble. Even better, the captains put the three sergeants in other boats. That meant he was free of Ordway for most of every day. But, after an hour of McNeal, he was willing to trade any other crewman to get away from the cook's endless bitching.

McNeal's silence was brief. Too soon, he was yammering again. Shannon decided he had to do something to get control before the cook made the rest of the expedition unbearable.

On his next stroke, Shannon deliberately scooped a paddleful of icy water into the cook's face. Choking on the surprise shower, McNeal sputtered curses at Shannon between fits of coughing.

"Good job up there," called Willard.

Shannon twisted around to acknowledge the comment — and froze. A bullboat with a single occupant was following them. *Echo*, he thought, turning forward with a sinking heart. He had tried to mollify the boy with promises that they would return before the snows, but Echo refused to listen. He wanted to go with his paleskin friends as he put it, and now here he was, trying to catch them. Although Shannon felt responsible, he was at his wit's end about how to deal with the situation without crushing the spirit of this youngster who had become like a little brother.

The dugout lurched as if something had bumped into its side. "Make some room up there, you two. We got us a passenger," Willard yelled.

Shannon was not yet ready to deal with the Mandan boy. He was not sure he could keep his temper, so he remained facing forward. He assumed all the grunting and groaning was McNeal's.

"Hello, Fuzz."

Colter? It couldn't be. Shannon whirled around to look.

"Oh, my God! It is you."

Colter made a gesture that spoke of deep exhaustion. "Had some trouble gettin' back from my liberty." He paused as if breathing were an effort. "Echo helped me. Gave me his ma's boat." His eyes darted toward the bullboat tied behind the dugout. "Promised I'd put it off somewhere's he could find it."

Shannon stared at his friend for a long time before he regained the power to speak. His voice came out a whisper. "You and your promises, Old Man. What about — her?"

"Couldn't find her, but like you said: we'll be back."

McNeal's loud complaint cut into the conversation. "Am I the only one who cares that we're fallin' behind? Sarge will. You can be sure about that."

With a questioning look aimed at Shannon, Colter picked up the spare paddle. Shannon nodded, and the cook received another unexpected shower.

"Welcome back," said Shannon.

"Glad to be here," Colter said, smiling wearily. "You cain't know how glad."

Suddenly, he winced, as if from unbearable pain.

"You hurt, Old Man?"

"Nothin' a little hard work won't cure." And, timing his stroke to coincide with those of his three crewmen, Colter dug into the churning waters of the Missouri.

PART 5

SHINING MOUNTAINS, WESTERN SEA

Spring, 1805 to Winter, 1805

*We were now about to penetrate a country at least
two thousand miles in width, on which the foot of
civilized man had never trodden . . ."*
— Meriwether Lewis, April 7, 1805

*(They) might have derived their appelation **Shineing
Mountains** from the sun shin(ing). . . on the snow
which covers them . . .*
— William Clark – July 4, 1805

1. *Bear Fever*

End of April, 1805; Near the Missouri's confluence with the Yellowstone River

"Port!" Willard called urgently from the bow.

Colter's instincts had been honed by three weeks of piloting against the tricky Missouri. He deftly swung the dugout away from the drifting buffalo carcass without taking his eyes off the current ahead. Twenty-one days above Fort Mandan, the river was still brimming with runoff and potential accidents. In the surrounding land, spring reigned, clothing the trees with leaves and blanketing the ground with an explosion of flowers and lush grass.

With bigger game still winter-thin, the crew had turned to eating fish, geese, and beaver. His old partner Zoob had been right about the beaver: the streams feeding into the Missouri teemed with more of the creatures than Colter had ever imagined. Their numbers titillated his imagination and invariably turned his thoughts to Fragrant Grass and the future they would share when he returned to her. They would need a place to settle. Perhaps here.

"Stop that! I'm wet enough without you soakin' me, too. 'Sides, Sarge warned you," McNeal ranted at Shannon, mangling Colter's peace like a saw rips through silk.

Reference to Ordway veered the track of Colter's memories back to the day he caught up with the expedition. His explanation for not being back to the fort at departure was part truth, part deliberate silence. He claimed that an accident on the way back to the fort from his liberty in Matootonha had detained him. That the buffalo boat he was using collided with a submerged tree and sank, throwing him into the river semiconscious, knee wrenched, ankle sprained. All that was mostly true. What he did not say was why he was gone from the fort in the first place.

The captains bought the story and welcomed him back without reservation or punishment. Even his rifle came out of its ordeal in working order, much to his delight. Three weeks had passed since then and the incident had been all but forgotten. Everything seemed to be running smoothly.

Everything except his relationship with Ordway and with himself.

The sergeant took every opportunity to remind him that he knew the whole truth about his supposed liberty and to goad him about Fragrant Grass. "She didn't wait for you before and she won't wait for you now. Or ever. All you are to her is a source of gewgaws. Nothing more."

The barrage acted like a rasp on Colter's conviction that he had made the right decision to continue with the expedition. Each day it got harder and harder to not second-guess himself, to concentrate on getting to the Western Sea and returning to Fragrant Grass before the snows as he had promised.

Willard's head snapped up. "Watch —"

Something hidden below the murky surface of the Missouri slammed into the dugout, sending it into a roll and swallowing the rest of Willard's warning. Instantly, Colter threw his weight toward the high side, countering the momentum of the collision. His actions barely righted the tipsy craft.

"Damn you, Willard!" McNeal yelled. "Watch what you're doin'. You made me piss my drawers."

Colter listened for Shannon to come back with a caustic retort. When none came, he glanced up to see Shannon's head cocked at an odd angle and his bloodless hands gripping the rim of the dugout. *Was bound to happen sometime*, he thought. *Fuzz's been durn lucky he ain't had to go swimmin' so far. He can thank Willard and his sharp eyes for that. Then again, he most likely don't see it as luck. He's got enough to handle just crawlin' into the boat ever' day.*

"How 'bout you watchin' for a change, McNeal, instead of expectin' everyone else to take care of you?" Colter said, answering the cook. "Or maybe you'd rather crawl over the side and take your chances with the river?"

"I can't swim," McNeal said. "Anything happens to me, it's on you. Sarge'll see to that."

Shannon surprised Colter by speaking up. "Don't count on that, McNeal. Something happens to you, the rest of the crew'll likely give the three of us half their pay."

Willard gave the short bark which, for him, served as a laugh. Colter tried to keep the smile out of his voice. "'Less you all want to be out on this here river all durned night, Cook, you best quit your lollygaggin' and work that there oar."

While Shannon and Willard continued to paddle, McNeal sat hunched and unmoving.

"Row or walk, McNeal. Them's your choices," said Colter.

"You can't order me around, Colter," McNeal shot back.

He was tired of both that worn-out refrain and the man. "Headin' in!" and swung the nose of the dugout toward the bank.

McNeal craned around. "You wouldn't dare."

"If'n you ain't paddlin', you're walkin'."

McNeal looked hard at the bank, then reluctantly put his oar in the river. Colter waited to see three good strokes from the cook before turning the canoe back upriver.

When he did, Shannon muttered. "Too bad."

Mint pointed excitedly toward the familiar jut of land bordering the river. "They see us! Our people come out to welcome us home."

Fragrant Grass shaded her eyes against the sun's glare, using her arm to hide the emotion that played across her face. Home at last, back from a journey she thought would never end. She looked to the clouds scudding before the freshening wind and thanked Hawk Spirit for bringing her back to Matootonha, then slipped in a silent plea to be released from Sly Wolf's clutches.

Mint intruded on her reverie. "There is Echo, come to meet us. See how well he rides now. Come, Sister. We must not dawdle and anger our husband." Mint hurried off toward the stream of welcomers.

Fragrant Grass did not follow immediately. She scanned the skies across the river to the south and felt the hope she had nursed since the hunting party turned toward home wither. There was no smoke coming from the paleskins' fort. Colter was gone.

Echo raced his horse up to where she stood. "Little Mother, you return! I watched every day for you."

The boy's enthusiasm brought a smile to lips too long unused to such activity. Echo swung off his mount and came to her, drawing a piece of wood out of his waist pouch. "This is for you. From Friend Colter."

It was a hawk with its wings spread in flight, perfectly carved in miniature from a piece of ash that fit into her palm as if carved for it. Mist obscured her vision. She had trouble keeping her lower lip from trembling. "How long ago?"

The boy nodded solemnly. "Nearly one moon."

Blinking back the welling tears, she ducked her head to hide her disappointment from the boy. It had been fruitless to believe that Colter would wait for her to return from hunting, useless to hope that she would no longer have to put up with Sly Wolf once they returned to Matootonha. But that belief, that hope had been what sustained her in their long absence. Now the paleskins had left and all her dreams of relief were dashed.

As she rubbed the ribbing of wooden feathers on the hawk's wings, another thought wormed its way through her sadness. Yes, Colter had left, but he had thought enough of her to carve this beautiful figure and trust Echo to see that she got it.

The boy touched her hand and whispered, "He said he would return for you before the snows."

She searched the boy's face and found the sincerity and compassion she sought. Then she turned her face to the spreading skies where a hawk rose on a current of air and slid down the sky toward the west. West. It was a sign. She laughed aloud. Echo tossed her a curious look. She did not care, for now she could dare to hope again.

Willard whistled for Colter's attention and pointed toward the other expedition boats drawn up on a mid-stream island. The flotilla had been on
the river less than an hour and no stops were planned until lunch. Regardless, Colter guided them in.

The crewmen from the other boats ringed Captain Clark and Drouillard
who were kneeling beside a huge paw print embedded in the damp sand.
Colter had heard stories about the huge bears that were supposed to roam
the upper Missouri, but he had brushed them off as tall tales until he saw a
necklace strung with four enormous bear claws worn by a Mandan elder at
Matootonha. The image of that claw necklace spun into his mind and stuck
as he gazed down at the track now.

"Rube said he's heard they can run as fast as a horse," Shannon said in a
low, intense voice.

"Doubt that, big as it is," Colter answered.

"How big do you think it was?" Shannon asked.

"More'n five hundred pounds, I reckon."

"Taller than a man?"

Colter studied Shannon and decided he did not like the keenness in the
younger man's expression. "I reckon."

Shannon stared at the track as if mesmerized. "How would you go about
shooting one?"

"I ain't goin' to if'n I can help it."

Shannon stroked his jaw in thought. "I figure a shot in the eye. Put the
ball right into the brain."

Colter distrusted the younger man's tone more than the look on his face.
"If'n you're thinkin' on huntin' one, Fuzz, that there's one damn fool idea.
Bear meat's tough and tastes terrible. 'Bout the only thing them critters is
good for is grease for keepin' off mosquiters. Elk's a sight better eatin' and
one of them ain't a-goin' to turn around and knock your head off if'n you
miss."

Shannon went on stroking his jaw and eyeing the print as if he had not
heard a single word Colter had said.

"Come on, Fuzz. We got to go."

Shannon came to life then, taking hold of Colter's arm and drawing him
away from the others. "I have to get out of the boat, Old Man," he whispered urgently.

"What? You plannin' to walk the rest of the way?"

"That accident yesterday . . . I can't take the dugout anymore. I have to
get into the hunting rotation or I'll —" His grip tightened. "Shooting one
of these bears would be my ticket out of the boat. You did it. Remember?"

Colter glanced at the track and shook his head. "It's way too dangerous.
You got one bullet. One. You miss, you're dead. You. Not the bear."

"But, Old Man, I have to do it."

He pulled out of Shannon's grip. "No sense wastin' more breath on the subject. I ain't about to nerve up my best friend so's he can kill hisself."

"I'm asking you to back me up."

"No way." Colter started to walk off, then reconsidered. "You come along, and we'll figure somethin' else out. Okay?"

"Like what?" Shannon demanded.

He shrugged. He was fresh out of new ideas, but he knew a bad one when he heard it. "Somethin'. Now come on 'less you want to stay here till we come back this way in the fall."

Shannon kicked the dirt, then stalked to the dugout.

A strong headwind sprang up overnight. The prospect of battling it as well as the current for a few miles more progress up the Missouri did nothing for Colter's sagging enthusiasm as he took his place in the dugout's stern the next morning.

They had been underway less than an hour when he failed to negotiate the way through a flurry of flotsam and the canoe flipped, flinging him and the other three crewmen into the river. He resurfaced, rifle somehow to hand, to find a terrified McNeal clinging to the overturned canoe for all he was worth. There was no sign of either Shannon or Willard.

Colter swam over to the boat. "Where're the others?" His voice was breathy from the shock of the cold water.

McNeal babbled something unintelligible, then fell to whimpering. A scan of the bank located Willard crawling out of the river a short way downstream, but still no trace of Shannon. "Where's Fuzz, McNeal?"

Before the last word was out, a clawed hand breached the river's surface five yards off to his right. Shannon's stricken face followed, bobbing up momentarily before sinking back under the water.

Colter pried open the cook's hand and slid his rifle into the man's grasp with a warning to hold onto it, then turned to see where Shannon would reappear next. The hand breached the surface and rose skyward. Shannon's head followed just as a floating island of snagged brush the size of a cabin plowed into it. The collision happened so fast that Colter had no time to react. He watched in helpless horror as the snag rushed downriver, burying his friend under it. He waited breathlessly, hoping against all hope that Shannon would somehow free himself and call out for help.

Nothing of that sort happened. *He's gone. Fuzz is gone* came the thought, but the idea of no more Shannon was too much to wrap the arms of his mind around.

"I can't hold on no more, Colter," McNeal whined. "Help me."

"Don't you dare let go, McNeal. That there's my gun you got in your hand," Colter snarled, suddenly furious that the cook had lived and Shannon —

McNeal snivelled something about Ordway, but kept his hold on the dugout's bottom and the rifle.

Colter trained his eyes on the river for any sign of his friend. There was none, and he finally had to give up and turn to the problem at hand. "We got to get this here boat over to the bank, Cook. You're helpin'. No back-talk, hear? Or you're outta my boat for good."

McNeal moaned.

"Say 'yes', or let go of my boat," Colter said.

The cook choked out a "yes," then, mercifully, kept his mouth shut while doing precious little to help Colter push and heave the upside-down dugout toward the bank. With the current's help, they got close enough to Willard for the big man to lend his strength to hauling the boat up onto the bank.

Willard had also managed to save his rifle and Shannon's. The sight of the second gun made Colter face up to the fact he could no longer deny. Shannon was gone and they might never recover his body. He took the gun from Willard and held it, trying to come to terms with the senselessness of the tragedy.

"Look at this mess!" McNeal demanded. "Now we got to spread all this stuff out to dry. It's all your fault, Colter. You're the worst pilot in this outfit. I'm goin' to tell Sarge to replace you."

Colter's words came out clipped from the effort to rein in his flaring anger. "Willard, you best get him out of here 'fore I throttle him."

"Just try it," McNeal challenged. "Ordeal'd be down your throat so fast —" A yelp cut short the cook's tirade as Willard wrenched his arm behind his back and dragged him out of Colter's reach.

"Wait! It's him! It's Shannon!" shouted the cook, digging in his heels and pointing with his free hand to a pile of flotsam flung up against the shore fifty yards downstream. Among the deep browns and blacks of the water-logged jam was a patch of tan. Could it be?

Colter did not hang around to speculate. He took off at a sprint with Willard hard on his heels. They reached the tangle and began tearing at the debris that blocked access to that small streak of tan. When the last branch was thrown off, there lay Shannon, limp and lifeless.

Together, Colter and Willard pulled the body free and stretched it out on the sand. Colter knelt and took up one of Shannon's hands. Thick calluses covered the once soft palms and dirt was so embedded under the finger-nails that even a day's scrubbing would not remove it. But calluses and dirt would never bother Shannon again. The river he had feared, the river he had braved — the river had finally won. "It weren't supposed to end like this, Fuzz," Colter murmured.

All of a sudden the hand jerked in his grasp. "Fuzz?" Colter breathed, his voice pleading with the Fates.

Willard put a cheek to Shannon's mouth. "By gum, he's breathin'."

Willard flopped Shannon onto his belly, put one hand under his chest and pounded him between the shoulder blades with the other.

The fourth thump produced a wet cough from Shannon, but Willard kept pounding. "There's more. Throw 'er all up, Shannon."

Another burbling cough. Then another stronger one. Then another until the coughing turned to retching.

Colter ignored the bile and riverwater that spewed onto him as he steadied his friend until the gagging tailed off. "Welcome back, Fuzz."

The younger man's eyes opened slowly. "Old Man?"

"Hush," Colter said. "You're all right now."

Fearing that the incident would cause Shannon to reveal his long-held secret, Colter looked over at Willard. "Whyn't you and McNeal bring the dugout up this a-way."

Willard nodded. "Sure thing. Come on, McNeal."

"What about him?" McNeal demanded, thumbing at Colter. "It's his fault. What's he goin' to do to make it up?" A mighty shove from Willard made the cook swallow his complaint with a croak.

Shannon blinked his eyes twice as if struggling to form a thought. "I thought I was dead."

"Well, you ain't, so how about savin' your strength? You're goin' to need it when we go after one of them giant bears. That is, if'n you still want me to back you up."

Recognition awoke in the depths of Shannon's gaze, then turned to resignation. "It's too dangerous. Even for a crack shot like you."

"Then we'll get us three or five or however many men we need to help. Like you said, you got to get off'n this here river."

Shannon rocked his head weakly from side to side. "I don't think it'll work. I'd just be one of a bunch. That won't get me out of the boat."

"Hunt's your idea. That's gotta count for somethin'."

Shannon gazed up at Colter, the flame of life slowly starting to glow again in his eyes. "I hadn't thought about that." He paused. "Could be I get lucky and it's my shot brings it down." He paused again. "Why'd you change your mind, Old Man?"

Colter had not anticipated the question. He stammered around until Shannon stopped him. "That's okay. I know why, and I thank you." He turned to look at the river that had nearly killed him. "There's no way back now, is there? Well, enough talking. Like you're always saying: Time's a-wastin'. Let's get to those Shining Mountains."

*

May 14th dawned summer-hot and swarming with mosquitos. Colter dipped his hat into the river and jammed it back on his head, savoring the delicious shock of the cold water rinsing the sweat from his face and neck. If this gentle-looking country proved so merciless now, what would they face when they reached the mountains?

"There's one!" Shannon pointed excitedly to the mound of grizzled fur half-hidden in the thick vegetation of the nearby bank. He lifted his paddle into the air and wagged it from side to side, signalling the boat ahead. Joe Field wagged back that the signal had been received. As the forward canoe turned toward the bank well above the bear, Colter's misgivings began to rise like a creek after a downpour. "Put us in next to them, Old Man," Shannon ordered.

"Oh, no, you don't," McNeal groused . "I'm not waitin' around while you three go traipsin' off after some killer bear."

Shannon riveted the cook with an icy glare that, for once, dried up the man's complaints and sent him back to rowing.

Upon landing, Shannon took charge, assigning Rube to go with him, Joe Field and Pat Collins to back them up, and Colter and Willard as support to those two. Colter decided he needed to say something. "This don't feel right, Fuzz."

Shannon's tone was heavy with sarcasm. "Then maybe your feeler is off because it couldn't feel any righter to me, Old Man."

"Killin' for killin's sake goes agin' nature."

"So you say."

"So I *know*, Fuzz. There'll be a price to pay. Always is and you ain't near ready to pay it."

"You turnin' coward on me, Old Man?"

Colter stiffened at the implication. "I said I'd back you up and I ain't one to go back on no promise."

"Good," Shannon said. "Then keep your opinions to yourself."

Colter crept through the underbrush and took up a position two hundred yards from where the bear lay dozing in the flattened grass. A hundred yards in front of him, Joe Field and Pat Collins crawled toward their places, and fifty yards farther on, movement in the tall grass showed where Shannon and Rube inched toward their prey.

All of a sudden, the bear snorted and swung to its feet. It tested the air with its sensitive nose, searching for whatever dared disturb its nap. The creature was more than twice the size of any bear Colter had ever seen. It sported a massive shoulder hump, covered with blonde-tipped hair that contrasted with the mink-brown coat of its lower body.

Growing agitated, the bear reared onto its hind legs, giving Colter and the others a good view of what they were up against. It was a good ten feet tall and not happy. *It'll take a dozen balls,* Colter thought. *Maybe two dozen. This is crazy, Fuzz. Back off.*

Before he could complete the thought, Shannon popped up, took aim and rushed the shot. The ball missed, drawing a roar from the bear who dropped onto all fours and charged.

Shannon was slow to react. By the time he did, the bear had closed the gap between them to twenty yards. With the bear coming on, Rube forgot what he was there for and ran for his life.

His defection left Joe and Collins to try to down the enraged creature. Joe shot first with Collins's shot close behind. Both balls plowed into the bear's ribs with no visible effect. If anything, the bear's stride lengthened and the two shooters evacuated their positions, leaving Colter and Willard to cover their retreat.

Colter braced himself, drew a bead and released the hammer, ignoring the powder's explosion, focusing instead on the flight of his ball. It hit square on but failed to slow the bear. Instead the creature let out an earth-rumbling roar and veered Colter's direction.

Colter took off running for the river for all he was worth. He sprinted up a small rise only to find before him a steep bluff that plunged into the river. By now the bear was close enough for him to hear its wheezing and snuffling over the drumming of its footfalls and the hammering of his own heart. He had no time to think. He reacted. As another shot boomed, he jumped, landing in ten feet of water. He came up swimming furiously toward the far bank.

There was a loud splash behind him. The bear had plunged in after him and was hot on his scent.

Colter was near the middle of the river before he heard people yelling his name. Shannon and the other men were waving him back. He looked over his shoulder but saw no bear, so he turned around.

The creature lay sprawled in the three feet of water not far from the bottom of the cliff. Shannon, Rube and the others surrounded it. "It's okay. He's deader'n last night's dinner," Joe Field assured Colter.

Close up, the bear was even bigger and more menacing than his image of it. Rube squatted next to the creature. "By God, Peckerwood, you got him clean through the eye."

While Shannon lapped up the group's praise, Colter dragged himself out of the river and slumped down on a drift log. With the bear dead, the whole dangerous undertaking seemed pointless and wasteful. He was disgusted at himself for taking part. He did not want to see any more of the dead animal or think about what a waste its death was, no matter what the justification.

Shannon strutted over. "How about that, Old Man! Right through the eye. Just like I said I would."

Colter nodded curtly but held his tongue.

"Aren't you going to say something?"

He glanced at Rube and Joe and the others who were attempting to pull the carcass out of the water. "Nothin' to say."

"I shot that monster through the eye and saved your life, and you got nothing to say? Nothing?" Shannon demanded.

Colter turned his tired eyes on the younger man. "You might've got your bear, but you ain't yet paid the price of it."

Shannon drew himself up indignantly. "Sorry I asked."

"Me, too, Fuzz. Me, too," Colter muttered.

2. Babies

Mint had been acting strangely all day, as if she had a secret and wanted Fragrant Grass to guess what it was. After another night with Sly Wolf, Fragrant Grass was in no mood for games. She pretended not to notice her sister and went about her daily business until Mint intercepted her on the way back from fetching water at the river. "Do I not look different to you, my sister?"

Fragrant Grass curbed her irritation. "No."

"But I feel so different. Surely that must show," Mint said petulantly.

Fragrant Grass did not trust herself not to sound impatient. She shook her head rather than say anything she might regret.

"Look closer. Really look," Mint insisted.

"What am I supposed to see?" Fragrant Grass said more sharply than she intended.

Triumph lit Mint's face. "I am with child." She clapped her hands in delight. "It is true. I carry our husband's child." She clutched Fragrant Grass's hand. "Is it a son? I must know. You must tell me."

Her sister's eagerness gave Fragrant Grass pause. What if this child was not a boy? Would Mint try to stop the baby rather than bear Sly Wolf a girl? Stopping a child was not a choice to be made lightly.

"Speak. I must know," Mint pleaded.

"I cannot tell until the baby grows larger," Fragrant Grass hedged.

"My last courses were more than two moons ago. Remember? I used that time in the moon lodge to prepare the hide for our husband's new leggings."

The mention of courses caused Fragrant Grass to think back to her last seclusion. Her own was long overdue, she realized, shifting the pole balancing the two water skins as a way to cover the distress this caused her.

To her relief, Mint was too focused on her own situation to pay attention to anything else. "Have you not noticed my sickness?"

Rather than admit the truth, Fragrant Grass asked softly, "Have you suffered?"

Mint's eyes glistened with tears. "It has been difficult."

Fragrant Grass gathered her sister into her arms.

"Why does it have to be so?" Mint whimpered. "I want to feel joyful. This is a dream come true."

Fragrant Grass stroked her sister's gleaming hair. "This time will pass soon, then the joy will come."

While Mint wept into her shoulder, part of her offered comfort while the rest of her tried to come to terms with her own unhappy discovery. Out of the confusion in her mind rose a prayer: Hawk Spirit, help Your daughter, Fragrant Grass.

Gently, she extricated herself from Mint's hold and brushed the tears from her sister's cheeks. "You do look different. You are even more beautiful."

Before Mint's quavering smile could dissolve into more weeping, Fragrant Grass handed her the pole and waterskins. "I need to check the new corn. Could you carry this back," she added, "Mother?"

Mint blushed with pleasure at that endearment. She took the water and went up the path to the village.

Fragrant Grass headed off in the direction of their garden plot, then veered toward the field of funeral scaffolds in search of the guidance she now desperately needed.

Fragrant Grass lay in her sleeping robes, listening to Sly Wolf preparing to leave on his journey. With food supplies at critical levels and local game scarce, the council yesterday decided to dispatch a hunting party to search for more buffalo. Because of the distance anticipated, the hunters would go without women.

The council had chosen Sly Wolf to lead the hunters, and Mandan custom required that, as leader, he refrain from coupling with either of his wives before the journey. Fragrant Grass had to struggle to hide her relief. In contrast, her sister had wept inconsolably.

She pondered her situation. One image would not leave her mind: the way Sly Wolf had looked at her when Mint announced her pregnancy. Few things that happened in the lodge or the village escaped the man's notice. That look planted a seed of fear in her heart. Fear that he remembered the last time she retired to the moon lodge. Fear that he knew her secret.

Her hands clenched into tight fists. She would never bear a child for him. Never.

She lay rigid until the familiar rustling of the entrance flap announced his departure. She expelled a held breath and rolled onto her side. She willed herself to breathe deeply and slowly and waited for the floating feeling that heralded a connection with her spirit guide.

The feeling did not come and she rolled onto her back in frustration. Nearby the stretched leather of Mint's couch creaked. "Husband?"

Fragrant Grass held her breath. She was not yet ready to face her sister or the day.

"Husband?" Mint repeated.

More creaking. Her sister always made enough noise in getting up to awaken everyone else in the lodge. If you did not get up, she would come to see why, so Fragrant Grass did not have much time. She reached deep into the leather pouch that hung from the bed's post and drew out a bundle. Unwrapping the soft elk hide, she closed her eyes and touched the smoothed wood of Colter's hawk.

A vision of Sly Wolf's unwavering gaze swirled into her head, then dissolved into another image: the interior of the moon lodge. The image sparked an idea. Although it was not the perfect answer to her dilemma, it was one way to put off a decision.

She kissed the carving, rewrapped it and tucked it safely back into the bag underneath the pieces of leather meant for new winter leggings. She pushed aside the bed's privacy curtain and got to her feet with a low groan.

Mint looked up from the fire. "Are you unwell, my sister?"

She grimaced. "I must go to the women's lodge, but I do not wish to leave you alone now that our husband is away."

Mint smiled sympathetically. "I will manage. With him gone, there is little to do." Her smile brightened as she patted her still-flat tummy. "No more moon lodge for me for awhile."

"You are fortunate, my sister." Fragrant Grass turned quickly to gather her things and cover the insincerity. She pulled a pouch from beneath her bed and rolled it with her sewing things into her oldest buffalo robe. The bag held a supply of moss and willow fluff for making absorbent pads. Handling it always brought back the memory of the day her mother had given it to her and escorted her to the moon lodge the first time.

At the fire, Mint handed her a horn-cup of broth. "I will miss you, my sister."

Fragrant Grass squeezed Mint's shoulder, took the cup and made a show of shuffling outside like someone in pain.

3. *Braggart*

T wo nights after the grizzled bear hunt, Shannon was still the center of the crew's attention. With each retelling, he expanded his role in the hunt while diminishing the contributions of the other men, a shift only Colter seemed to notice. In tonight's version Shannon made it sound as if he had singlehandedly brought down the bear. He ended the tale with a flourish of the creature's amputated paw, and Colter turned away in disgust. He never had been able to abide liars. Shannon needed a talking to, and he made up his mind to deliver one after he returned from tomorrow's hunt, after his annoyance had time to mellow.

Ordway strolled over to Shannon and addressed the crew. "We can't waste a sharp-shooter like Shannon here. You're in the hunting rotation, Private. Starting tomorrow."

While a beaming Shannon accepted the congratulations of the crew, Colter followed the sergeant away from the fire. "What do you mean, 'tomorrow'?" he demanded.

"What? No 'sarge' or 'sir,' Colter?" Ordway asked.

"What do you mean 'tomorrow,' Sarge?" Colter repeated, layering the last word with heavy sarcasm.

"That's better," Ordway said. "What don't you understand about 'tomorrow'?"

"Me and Drouillard're goin' out tomorrow."

"You were, but not now. Now it's Shannon and Drouillard. And since we can't leave your boat short-handed, I will be taking Shannon's place whenever he is off hunting." The sergeant started to leave but turned back to Colter. "By the way, rotation's changed now. Shannon's taking your place. Permanently."

Colter would not allow himself to react to the news or Ordway's provocative stare.

"Like I told the captains, the only way to avoid accidents with these dugouts is to keep the best pilots on the river every day. You know the captains. They don't like accidents. Too bad you're such a good pilot, Colter."

Colter's mind spun like a wagon wheel in spring mud. Hunting was his outlet, his haven of peace and solitude, the time he could clear his head and really think. Now that release had been ripped away from him and given to Shannon. Shannon who could get lost on his way to the latrine and who had not yet learned to respect the animals he killed. Shannon had replaced him all because of a once-in-a-lifetime lucky shot that might or might not have come from his rifle.

The sergeant's mouth twitched in victorious amusement, and Colter realized that he had failed to conceal his emotions while his mind churned. Refusing to concede so easily, he plastered a smile on his face and forced his body into a relaxed slouch. "That's the best news these here old ears've heard in a good month, Sarge."

Doubt flickered momentarily behind Ordway's gaze, though his smile did not change.

"Laws, yes. Good news. I been wantin' to get out of rotation for months now. That Drooler, well, he's a piece of work."

Ordway tried and failed to disguise the hint of frustration in his tone. "Don't thank me. Thank Shannon."

Colter shook his head again. "Oh no, Sarge. Got to thank you. You're the one makes all them hard decisions." He strolled away, but the instant his back was to the sergeant, his smile vanished. Damn Ordeal and double damn Shannon!

Over the next two weeks, while Shannon was away hunting and Colter was confined to the dugout, the river grew shallower, swifter, more unpredictable. Jumbles of rocks deposited by the numerous side streams that flowed into the Missouri created obstacles that forced the crew to resort to the tow ropes. Sometimes that meant wading in icy water up to their necks; other times they had to tramp through patches of cactus or across rock falls that sliced through the bottoms of their moccasins and lacerated their feet. Colter cursed Shannon for each obstacle and for every minute he was forced to endure Ordway in the dugout.

His cursing came to nought however, because Shannon not only proved to be a proficient hunter, but he also managed to develop a close camaraderie with Drouillard. About the only good thing to come from the situation was that, with the sergeant in the boat, McNeal shut up and performed like a crew member instead of a prima donna.

Colter was at the end of his tolerance for forced togetherness when the expedition put in for the night at a camp prepared by Shannon and Drouillard on June 1. The whole scene hit him wrong. The racks of drying meat strips. The hides stretched on bent willow frames, curing in the smoke of a small fire. Shannon lounging beside the fire with a self-satisfied smirk on his face. "Glad to see you finally made it, Old Man."

Whether it was that smirk or Shannon's taunting tone, Colter made up his mind to take back what Shannon so unfairly stolen from him.

After supper, Shannon again hogged the spotlight, relating tales about his two weeks of hunting. Colter shut him out until, as usual, Shannon managed to work his way back around to the grizzled bear hunt. Tonight, he exaggerated beyond all sense of proportion making it sound as if he had brought the creature down with a single ball. This made Colter too angry to keep silent any longer. He waylaid Shannon as he was headed for the brush to relieve himself. "Interestin' story, Fuzz. Too bad there ain't a lick of truth to it."

"What do you mean, Old Man? You were there."

"That's just it. Five of us was there, 'sides you, but lately you been forgettin' to mention that, or the fact that there were eight balls in that critter 'sides the one you claim brought it down."

Shannon bristled. "What do you mean 'claim'? That eye shot was mine."

Colter plowed on, his anger fueled by Shannon's arguments. "Then there's the fact that five of us put our lives on the line for your little hunt, and you ain't never said a word of thanks to any of us."

Shannon started to disagree, then stopped. "You're right. I haven't given credit. Thanks for setting me straight, Old Man."

Colter gave a peremptory nod. He was too angry to be soothed so easily.

Shannon swept an arm toward the racks of drying meat. "You see all the game we brought in? Drouillard's amazing at finding the animals, and, when we do, they just stand there and let us shoot them. Easy."

Colter refused to be taken in by Shannon's smile. "Plenty today, nothin' tomorrow. That's the law of huntin'."

Shannon waved him off. "Law? Ha. That's just an old wives' tale. Holds about as much water as calling that grizzled bear a devil or saying that I'd have to pay for killing it. I paid all right. By getting out of the boat and proving I can hunt with the best of 'em. No one'll go hungry if I have anything to do with it."

"You sure got a short memory for someone got hisself lost downriver, Fuzz. Things might be goin' good now. But just you wait. You killed a critter just to be killin' it. That's an account you got to settle. Ain't no way around it."

Shannon tilted his chin. "Look, you've got every right to be angry over how Ordeal handled this rotation thing. I never meant it to happen that way."

Colter was not about to change the subject until he made his point. "Might not be game that disappears on us. Might be we lose somethin' vital, say all our powder. Or could be our luck just plain runs out."

Shannon again tried to lead the discussion in a different direction. "If we run out of anything, let it be this infernal river. We're all sick of it."

"How can you be sick of it? You ain't on it ever'day."

"That's 'cause I'm out hunting to feed the likes of you."

The two men locked stares before Colter threw off his hold and stepped back. "You got a lot to learn yet, Fuzz."

"Don't be so sure," Shannon said scornfully, pushing past him to continue into the brush.

"A whole lot to learn," Colter muttered to himself as the image of Fragrant Grass floated into his head. *Never should have left you, woman,* he thought.

He held onto her image until it faded, then shook his head. "Never," he whispered.

Hartley awoke from his first deep sleep in weeks with his senses alert for hints of danger. The prairie night stretched away from the campsite, black and ominous like the curtain hiding the face of Fate.

From across the ashes of last night's campfire came Montagne's moan. The preacher's tension melted into irritation at being ripped out of sleep by the trader who was sleeping off yesterday's drunk. He listened with right-eous pleasure to the sound of Montagne waking and stumbling into the darkness, followed by the sounds of retching. Yesterday the trader had guzzled enough trade whiskey to down a bull buffalo. He deserved to be sick.

Hartley's satisfaction soon faded. Like it or not, his life depended on Montagne. Other than a vague sense of north and south, he had no idea how to get back to the Rees. More than once on this journey, he had experienced a gripping fear that he would lose his mind if he stared much longer at the horizon yawning in all directions.

The notches on his counting stick told the story. They had left the Rees three weeks ago, headed for an Indian trading fair. Montagne had put him in charge of the string of packhorses with the warning to safeguard the animals and the trade goods or else be sold into slavery to the first Indians who came along. The animals had sensed Hartley's lack of experience and began to test him immediately, jerking him out of the saddle three times before they had gone a mile. He had learned to handle them, but still he was covered from head to toe by the bruises and lacerations caused by their shenanigans.

After more than a week's hard ride, they arrived. The trading fairs happened every summer. Indians from different tribes, even mortal enemies, put aside their differences to pitch their lodges together and spend time bargaining and gambling. After his experiences with the Sioux, the sight of so many Indians all in one place unnerved Hartley. Montagne raced off into the heart of the encampment with a blood-curdling whoop, leaving him to bring in the pack string with his heart in his throat.

The fair turned out to be ten days of nonstop haggling, punctuated with gambling of a ferocity and level of risk that Hartley had never witnessed. With each toss of the marked bones, Indians wagered away their dogs, their horses, their wives, even the clothes off their backs.

None of the half dozen white and half-breed traders in attendance was as astute or successful as Montagne. The trader's stock was made up of just four items: tobacco, woolen blankets, crude hunting knives and whiskey — all irresistible to Indians, especially the whiskey. Montagne used liquor to lower the resistance of his customers. Though he made a show of swallowing huge draughts along with the Indians, in reality he never drank more than a swallow while he was working. The trade whiskey tasted and burned like lye, but that did not stop the savages from downing it in unbelievable amounts. Those it did not level into unconsciousness turned into raving, stumbling lunatics, who committed unbelievable acts of stupidity, everything from burning down their own tepees to trading their children for more firewater.

Hartley's job was to collect and guard the pelts and hides that Montagne traded for, a dangerous job as it turned out. The first day of the gathering, a drunken Brulé warrior cornered him, demanding whiskey and threatening to disembowel him if none were forthcoming. Hartley had no weapon and he barely managed to escape in one piece.

The incident made him realize that he had to have protection. The next day while laying out the piles of trade goods, he filched one of the knives and secreted it in the bundle of traded pelts, praying that Montagne would not notice.

He was wrong. It took the trader just a quick glance over his stock of goods to note the loss. Hartley was choked senseless for his transgression.

When he came to, the knife was gone from its hiding place among the pelts. From that point to the end of the fair, he gave up on the idea of protecting himself and stayed out of Montagne's way. Somehow he managed to survive the rest of the ten days unscathed, though the experience left him drained.

The encampment finally broke up, and the participants scattered. The next day, Montagne spent the day riding lead, chuckling over his various successes, pausing frequently to take long pulls from one of the last jugs of trade whiskey. By the time they stopped for the night, the trader was too drunk to stand up. He passed out on the bare ground. Hartley considered leaving him that way, then changed his mind. If anything happened to the trader, he was lost. He threw a blanket over the snoring man, then rolled into his own and went immediately to sleep.

Montagne now stumbled back to his blanket and fell to his knees with a groan. Hartley's nose wrinkled at the smell of vomit and bad whiskey emanating from the man. He closed his eyes and pretended to be asleep.

He awoke later to find the sun up and the sky clear. He glanced over and saw that Montagne was still under the blanket. He rose creakily to his feet and stepped off to urinate. Returning, he announced, "Sun's up!"

The trader did not move, so he tapped the man's buttock with his foot, then jumped out of reach before Montagne, who hated being touched while sleeping, could grab him.

The trader barely twitched.

Hartley waited. Montagne had throttled him too many times to let down his guard.

When the trader continued to lie still, the preacher warily circled around to the prone man's front side. Montagne's face was flushed, and he was shivering despite the warmth of the day. Stooping, Hartley touched the trader's hand. The skin was too hot to be so dry. This was no hangover.

Emboldened, he shook the trader's shoulder. "Montagne, wake up."

The trader opened his bloodshot eyes. There was a faraway look in them.

"Sun's up. We better get riding," Hartley said.

Moaning, Montagne struggled into a sitting position. Seeing that he could not stand without help, Hartley slung one of the man's hairy arms over his shoulders and lifted him to his feet.

The trader swayed and groaned, "That whiskey, she will kill you."

The man's attempt at humor encouraged Hartley. "I'll collect the string and get 'em loaded."

Montagne managed a weak nod.

By the time Hartley finished, the trader was still flushed and trembling, but he managed to get up on his horse unaided. Hartley swung onto his own mount. *He's not going to make it.* The thought came unbidden into his head and he knew it was the truth. Montagne was dying. *Just let him get me back to the Rees*, he pleaded with God. *Let him hold on that far, then you can have him..*

Montagne kept a personal packhorse separate from the main string. She was a frisky mare that minded only the trader. Hartley had never handled her. Montagne had all he could do to hang onto the saddlehorn, however, so the preacher took up the mare's rope and set off in the lead.

The mare tossed her head, testing his hold and stirring up the orneriness of the other packhorses. Soon his hands were as busy with problems as his mind. The way Montagne looked, he would not last the week it would take to reach the Rees. His only option was to get the trader to tell him the way. That would not be easy. Any question made the man suspicious. It would take a subtler approach to get the information needed.

Hartley spent the morning honing an opening and decided to try it before they stopped for a midday rest. "This country all looks the same. How's a body know where he is?"

"I know," the trader said hoarsely, pressing his arm into his gut and doubling over.

Hartley smiled innocently. "But how?"

Montagne's head sagged onto his chest. Hartley half-expected to see him slide out of the saddle. He didn't, and, after a long interval, he straightened a bit and nodded at the horizon. "The trees, there."

Hartley lifted out of the saddle and squinted into the distance where a darker line etched the prairie grass. "What about the trees?"

"That is a creek. You follow it to a spring. Then turn east —" Montagne's words sputtered off in a contortion of pain. When he spoke again, his voice was raw. "Three days — ride to — to the —" A fit of coughing choked off the rest of his sentence and he toppled off his horse.

Hartley remained in his saddle, enjoying the spectacle of his tormentor sprawled on the ground. He did not bother to get down. Whether Montagne was alive or dead no longer mattered. What did matter was that he, Josiah Hartley, would never again have to endure the man's abuse. The trader's pack string was his now, along with enough supplies and furs to make him rich. All he had to do was get to the Missouri and figure out a way back to St. Louis. How hard could that be?

Squinting toward the faraway line of trees, he started to lose heart. This was such a big country. A man could get lost. A man could die.

Montagne's mare jerked back on her lead unexpectedly, pulling him out of his negative thoughts. In retaliation, he aimed a vicious kick at the tenderest part of her throat. The noise the animal made sounded so much like a human scream that Hartley smiled with satisfaction. At last he was getting somewhere.

4. *Two Forks of the Missouri*

"We got company!" The shout came from the men towing the lead dugout. Colter squinted into the distance where Shannon and Drouillard were making their way down a steep hillside. The pair were supposed to be out for another four days. Their return could only mean trouble.

Ordway hurried off to join the captains, and Colter picked his rifle out of the dugout and took aim on a nearby cactus as if to shoot it in retaliation for all the cactus thorns he had pulled out of his feet the last week. The action took some of the edge off his foul mood. And taking the edge off was all he could do until he reclaimed his place in the hunting rotation. Only then would his discontent dissipate.

"Bet they come onto a whole pack of them giant bears like the one Shannon killed," McNeal speculated.

"Fuzz didn't kill no bear anymore'n you did, and you know it," Colter said loudly enough for others to hear him. "Took six men and nine balls to bring that critter down."

Rube gave Colter a searching look. "So that's the burr's been under your blanket lately, huh?"

"Fuzz's the burr, Rube. Hell, anymore he's a whole prairie full of burrs," Colter groused.

Ordway returned, looking worried. "The river forks up ahead. We'll move up there and let the captains decide how to proceed."

Colter remembered enough from Clark's master map to know that the Missouri was not supposed to split until after a large falls; a falls the expedition had not yet found.

"That mean we get a rest, Sarge?" McNeal asked.

Ordway nodded. "Unless you volunteer to help scout the forks."

"Not me," McNeal said. "Some other fools can scout. I'm restin'."

For once, Colter agreed with the cook.

Hartley slid tiredly out of his saddle. Every rise and gully looked like every other rise and gully in this infernal country. How was a body supposed to find his way anywhere? "Burn in hell, Montagne!"

His shout startled the trader's packhorse. She shied, but he yanked back on her lead with force born of annoyance. The animal whinnied with surprise. For good measure he jerked the lead again. "I ought to shoot you and get it over with."

She snorted and stamped the ground with her front hoof.

"You kick me, you're dead," he warned.

She broke off stamping to blink at him.

For good measure, he whipped her across the nose with the loose ends of the reins, breaking the skin. She tried to evade his second blow but the rawhide lashed her unprotected eye and she squealed worthy of a pig.

"Ha! That'll teach you." He secured the mare's reins to the saddle of his mount and lifted the waterskin to his lips for a drink. The brackish water came from a stream not far from where he had left Montagne's body to rot under the prairie sun two days back.

Lowering the waterskin, he became aware of the silence and emptiness of the surrounding land. Here he was, in possession of a fortune in furs but with no earthly idea when, or even if, he would come to the Missouri. Using the sun as a guide, he had kept heading east, but in country so vast, so empty, a man alone was as vulnerable as a spider-web in a hurricane. Anything could happen. He could run out of water and die of thirst. He could break a leg. He could . . .

One of the horses snuffled, cutting into his thoughts. Standing here and worrying was getting him nowhere. Time to move on. He grabbed the saddle horn, put one foot in the stirrup and pushed off his grounded foot. His free leg was swinging over the saddle when Montagne's mare nudged the rump of his horse. His mount skittered sideways, causing him to lose hold of the pommel and somersault across the saddle. He managed to get his hands out in front of him to break his fall, but he still landed hard, knocking the breath out of his lungs. Dazed, he did not immediately notice the strange new angle to his left arm. Then the pain started and his muddled mind slowly connected it with the jagged piece of bone protruding through the skin of his forearm.

A man can die from a broken bone out here. Who had he heard that from?

He never did put a face with the words because the thought of dying threw him into a panic. He needed to get back on his horse. Needed to get riding. Needed to find help. Or else.

He swiped at the stirrup, but his horse, sensing his panic, pranced out of reach. He gritted his teeth against the pain in his arm and tried to speak normally. "Calm down, you fool plug."

The animal regarded him nervously and edged closer to the frisky mare.

"Damn you! Come here!"

Both horses twitched their ears toward him. The muscles in their haunches rippled, a sign that they were prepared to bolt at the slightest provocation. If that happened, he was lost for sure.

He struggled to his knees, whimpering with the effort to keep from screaming out at the terrible pain in his broken arm. He was forced to remain on his knees until a wave of lightheadedness passed, then, holding the broken arm as steady as possible, he swayed to his feet.

The mare skittered away from him, leading his mount with her.

Hartley spoke through clamped teeth. "There now, good horse. Calm down."

His riding horse nickered softly and eyed the mare which, in turn, eyed the preacher.

It registered on Hartley's pain-soaked brain that the mare was the key to his success or failure. If he could reassure her, he had a chance of regaining control of his horse. "I take back every —"

A fresh assault of pain erupted from his shattered arm, robbing him of breath and words. The world threatened to turn upside down on him. He clamped his eyes shut against an attack of vertigo.

Once the pain subsided, he turned his attention to the mare. Mumbling reassurances to her, he inched forward. She allowed him to approach within a few feet but then she turned tail and trotted off, pulling his horse along with her.

The vertigo returned for a second visit, and he had to cling to the mane of one of the other packhorses to keep from fainting. When the world stopped spinning, he realized that he was leaning against the horse carrying the last of Montagne's trade goods. He managed to work his good hand among the hide coverings and pull out one of the trader's cheap knives along with the one jug of trade whiskey that the drunken Montagne had overlooked.

He uncorked the jug with his teeth and tossed back a slug. The whiskey hit his roiling stomach and threatened to come back up, but he gulped down the bile and focused on the mare, blinking away the gluey film from his eyes until he could see her clearly. *You've pulled your last trick on me*, he thought.

As a boy, his one and only plaything had been a knife. All his youthful practice came into play now as he hurled the knife and caught the animal in the throat.

A gush of arterial blood accompanied her thrashing scream as she tried to throw off the buried weapon. The scent of blood caused Hartley's horse to shy away from her.

The mare bucked and heaved while he watched, enjoying the spectacle of her suffering in spite of his own pain.

After a time the mare's cries grew more desperate and her movements, weaker. Finally she went down on her knees, fell over on her side and heaved one last wheezing breath.

Hartley pointed a trembling finger at his mount. "You cooperate or you're next."

His horse stood as if transfixed by the threat. However, the packhorse the preacher clung to chose that moment to shift its weight. The move pulled him over and he fell to the ground, jarring his broken arm and sending him falling down a long black chute into oblivion.

After breakfast the next morning, two parties left to scout the unexpected forks. Those who remained behind spent the day mending gear and resting. Colter was determined to stay off his sore feet. He cleaned his rifle, then whittled. As far as he was concerned, scouting was useless. Any fool could see that the south fork was too clear to be the Missouri whose muddy course they had been following for nigh onto two thousand miles.

The scouting parties returned around dusk. The captains immediately retired to their tent to discuss their findings with the sergeants. Cruzatte, the expedition's main pilot, came to the fire. "Zee capitaines, zey chose zee south fork."

Colter was sure he heard wrong. "You mean north, don't you, Pilot?"

Cruzatte shook his head. "South, *mon ami*. South."

"Then, by God, they're wrong!" Colter declared. "You told 'em so, right?"

Cruzatte studied the ground without speaking.

"You mean they're in there makin' plans to head up the wrong fork and you didn't say nothin'?"

Shields came to Cruzatte's defense. "Captain Clark reasons that the south fork's clear because it comes from the mountains. Mandans said the Missouri starts in the mountains."

"Ain't them the same Indians what didn't tell us about these here forks?" Colter demanded, drawing murmurs of agreement from several other crewmen.

"Pilot here knows rivers better'n most men know their own privates," Rube joined in. "If he thinks the north fork's the Missouri, I believe him." All around the fire, a few heads nodded in agreement.

"The captains'll listen to you, Pilot," Colter urged, aware that a wrong choice now would likely mean another winter's layover when keeping his promise to get back to Fragrant Grass before winter was what kept him going every day. "You got to speak for all of us. Keep 'em from makin' a mistake."

Shannon spoke up. "Speak for the rest, Pilot. Not for me. If the captains think the south fork is correct, so do I."

"I'm with Shannon," McNeal piped up.

Colter did not add his jeers to those the other men aimed at the pair. Shannon was at it again: going against the rest of the crew. It was the very thing that had caused him so much grief from the time he joined the expedition till the men dragged him off his high horse at McBain's back at Camp Wood

Rube glared at Shannon. "If that's how you want it, Peckerwood." He turned to Cruzatte. "You can speak for all of us, except them two. They stand on their own."

Reluctantly, Cruzatte walked to the captains' tent with Shannon and McNeal in his wake. During the wait that followed, the crew's conversation was subdued and superficial. Colter picked up his whittling, but found his concentration too ragged to work.

Eventually the tent flaps opened and out came Cruzatte, Shannon and McNeal, followed by Drouillard, the two captains and three sergeants. Cruzatte's expression was unreadable while Shannon looked pleased with himself. Lewis addressed the crew. "Pilot has told us of your objections and, though we believe the south fork is correct, we have decided to send a party up both forks to look for the falls the Mandans described as being on the Missouri."

Despite the condition of his feet, Colter was prepared to volunteer for the north-fork party. He did not get the chance because Lewis assigned Cruzatte, Shields, Drouillard, Pryor and two other crewmen to go with him up the north fork and Shannon, York, Rube, Joe and Gass to accompany Clark down the south fork. "Sergeant Ordway will remain in charge here," Lewis said. "We have meat to lay in and baggage to dry, and not much time to do so."

Colter frowned down at his aching feet. Ordeal would see to it that he got every dirty, disagreeable task while the scouts were gone.

Shannon stepped over to him. "I'm surprised at you, Old Man. It's your duty to obey your superiors, not tell them what to do."

"Ain't never wrong to speak up when I see someone makin' a mistake. A mistake like you're makin' right now. Ain't you learned yet not to go agin' the crew?"

"The crew's wrong."

Shannon's supreme self-assurance pushed Colter to the edge of his tolerance. "You think so? What you goin' to do when Pilot and them find the falls on the north fork?"

"That won't happen. Captains are right. *I'm* right."

Colter hated betting and dares, especially after his experiences with McBain, but he could not forgo the opportunity to show Shannon up. "We're friends, Fuzz, but there be times I don't much like you. And this here's one of them times. Once Captain Lewis comes back from findin' them falls, what say you get up in front of ever'one and admit you was flat-out wrong."

"Sounds good, Old Man. Only the falls are on the south fork, and you're the one needs to eat a plate of crow."

"Wanna bet?" Colter stuck out his hand.

Shannon grabbed the hand and gave it a hard shake.

Colter smiled. A dose of public humiliation was just the lesson Shannon needed.

A bolt of agony ripped through Hartley's left arm, shredding the landscape of his dream, and he swam up into consciousness screaming at the shadows flitting around him. It took a moment to realize that the shadows were shapes; shapes that gradually coalesced into a group of Indians standing over him, watching him like hunters waiting for a downed deer to die. "Get away from me!" he warned in a shaky voice.

"Then you are not dead," someone said in perfect English.

Hartley squinted against the bright sky haze. The speaker was a boy around ten or eleven judging from his height and size. "My name is Echo," he said.

Hartley did not know much about Indians, but he did know that war par¬ ties did not bring along boys. *Probably a hunting party*, he thought and relaxed a bit. "Mine's Hartley. I think I broke my arm. Must have blacked out."

Echo turned to the Indians to explain, and the preacher struggled to compose a clear thought out of the fog in his head. That they could readily figure out he was alone worried him.

"That horse is dead," Echo said, pointing to the fly-blown corpse of Montagne's pack mare.

The comment contained a question that Hartley knew he must avoid answering. Indians loved horses. There was no telling what they might do to someone who had deliberately killed one in anger. Hartley grimaced. "I need help."

The boy turned back to the Indians and again they chattered among themselves before Echo addressed Hartley, "We will bind your arm."

"Who's 'we?'"

The boy glanced around the circle. "You pale ones call us Mandans."

The preacher closed his eyes to hide his relief at this stroke of luck. The Mandans were the enemies of the Rees, and they had an insatiable appetite for white man's goods like trade knives and blankets, facts he could turn to his advantage. There was one little problem however. Montagne had been popular with the Rees, and returning to them with the man's trade goods but without the trader was bound to raise dangerous questions. He had to watch what he said to these people. "Where'd you learn English?" he asked the boy.

"I learn your tongue from the paleskin warriors who stay through the snows near my village."

Hartley sucked in a breath. Paleskin warriors could mean only one thing: Lewis and Clark's expedition — and Colter. Surely Echo would remember someone with a birthmark like Colter's. "You speak better than most white folks." He chatted on, waiting for a chance to ask about the man.

The boy's quick smile showed that the remark had scored a direct hit on its intended target.

"Me and my partner were on our way to trade with your people when he took sick and died," Hartley offered.

This prompted another round of discussion among the Mandans. He guessed the leader of the party of Mandans was the one standing slightly apart from the others, listening but not speaking, taking everything in. Even the man's smallish paint horse appeared to defer to him.

Echo motioned toward the south. "We found a dead paleskin."

"That was my friend. I didn't have time to bury him."

Echo cocked his head. "What is this thing — 'bury?'"

The question confused Hartley until he remembered the Rees' graveyard with its funeral scaffolds. If Echo did not know about burying, he reasoned, all the expedition members must have made it through the winter. Unless something happened to Colter before he got to the Mandans, he was still alive.

Another bolt of pain from his injured arm brought Hartley back to the priority of the moment: if he wanted to keep living, he better convince these Mandans to take him to their village. "I have many things to trade with your people," he said. Hearing the underlying desperation in his voice, he modified his tone, "I can pay." The Rees understood the concept. He hoped the Mandans did, too.

After much discussion, Echo turned back to him. "We fix your arm, then you ride with us to Matootonha, our village."

The relieved Hartley nodded, and most of the Mandans walked off, leaving the preacher with their leader and another who wore a beaded pouch slung across his chest. The man with the pouch knelt and began to examine the break. The man's probing brought a fresh assault of pain. The agony was compounded by the Mandan leader's scrutiny. Hartley fought valiantly to keep from showing any reaction, biting his lip against crying out. It wasn't until the two Indians left him alone that the preacher realized his mouth was full of blood. He had bitten through his lip.

Colter was surprised when Sergeant Ordway assigned him to hunt with Willard the next morning. Still, he did know to take off quickly before the sergeant came to his senses and gave him something much worse to do.

Hunting was good, the best in months. Reluctant to end his brief taste of freedom, Colter returned to camp footsore and loaded down with game. He delivered the game to McNeal, then, because his moccasins were in tatters, he endured the cook's chatter while he stripped the hide off an elk. He was carrying the skin to the fire to flesh and stretch when Ordway intercepted him. "Hand that hide over, Colter."

He held the skin out of the sergeant's reach. "Nope."

"Captain Lewis wants all the elk hides."

"He can have 'em if'n he don't expect me to walk nowhere."

"You'll walk all right, even if it's barefoot. Now give it here, and find some deer hide instead." Ordway had to seize the hide. Colter would not give it to him. Deer hide was a waste of time. Elk was the only thing that kept the cactus thorns out of his feet.

"Captain Clark's back!" someone yelled moments before the captain strode into camp, followed by a straggling group of obviously exhausted men. That Shannon dragged in last pleased Colter.

Rube had been part of the south fork scouting party. When Colter caught his eye, he shook his head to indicate that the group had not found the falls. The crew had been right. Colter promptly forgot the forfeited elk hide and his sore feet and hobbled over to Shannon. "Time to pay up on our bet, Fuzz."

Shannon lifted his drooping head to regard Colter through blood-shot eyes. "Captain Lewis isn't back yet. Nothing's proved until then."

"Quit your stallin', Fuzz. You owe me. Pay up."

"I'll pay when — no, *if* I hear Captain Lewis say they found the falls,"

Shannon snapped.

"You want to make a fool of yourself in front of Captain Lewis then? About time he saw what you're really made of, which ain't much."

"It'll be you that looks the fool, Old Man. You. Not me."

"Right sure of yourself like always, huh? Well, enjoy the feelin' 'cause it ain't goin' to last for long."

Shannon muttered something else, but Colter paid no attention. He had heard all he wanted to hear from Shannon until he heard him admit his error.

The prickly pear pad had lodged so firmly in the heel of Colter's foot that it took Willard's knife to pry it loose. Then it was another hour before they extracted the remaining thorns so Colter could walk.

On the long hobble back to camp, he brooded on the elk hide Ordway had taken from him. If he had been wearing elk hide moccasins instead of deer, he would not be limping now.

Upon entering camp, he spotted Cruzatte and Shields from the returning north-fork scouting party. Before he could ask the question, Rube caught his eye and mouthed "No falls."

It was not the answer Colter expected. There had to be falls because the Mandans spoke of them with such awe.

He had not recovered from the news when the captains called for attention. Lewis spoke. "As you all know, neither of the scouting parties located the falls. Nevertheless, Captain Clark and I feel we have enough evidence to show that the south fork is the true Missouri. As is the custom, I have taken the prerogative of naming the north fork Maria's River, in honor of my cousin. Once we have cached the red pirogue and all unnecessary supplies, the expedition will continue up the south fork." He glanced at Clark, then asked, "Are there any questions?"

Silence followed. Colter looked around to see who was going to ask the obvious question. No one did, so he spoke up. "Captain, I ain't been far enough up either fork to say for sure, but from where I stand right this minute, that there north fork looks, smells, feels, and tastes exactly like the river we been followin' all along. What happens if'n you're wrong?"

Lewis replied, addressing the whole crew, rather than just Colter. "Private Colter has raised a valid concern. One many of you share. To answer it, I will lead a small scouting party up the south fork ahead of the boats with the purpose of finding the falls. If, within a reasonable distance, we fail to find the cataract, we will send back word immediately."

Clark added, "So we can turn around and do what you men think we ought to be doing in the first place."

This drew a wary chuckle from a few of the men. Colter was not among them.

"Are we agreed?" Clark asked.

There were a few half-hearted "ayes" from the gathered crewmen.

"What about the rest of you?" Clark prodded.

The remaining men murmured agreement, except for Colter.

"What about you, Colter?" Clark asked pointedly.

Colter studied the ground. He had tried his best to make the captains understand the mistake they were making, but they weren't listening. Weak as it was, they had offered a compromise. Besides, what other choice did he have? "Aye, Captain."

Across the fire, Shannon smirked.

Lewis named off the men for the advance party: Drouillard, Gibson, Goodrich and Joe Field. Colter could not let the fact pass that Shannon was not included. He limped over to chide him. "See you ain't goin' this time, Fuzz." He left unspoken the question of why.

"Our bet's still alive, Old Man."

"Not for long, it ain't. Wish you was goin' along with the captain. As long as you been stallin', it'd be fittin' if'n you was the one to carry back word when the scoutin' party don't find no falls."

The line of Shannon's mouth tightened. "How about we sweeten our wager, Old Man? Say, you get on your knees in front of me when you admit you were wrong *when* we find those falls?"

"Hell of an idea, since it'll be you kneelin' in front of me, Fuzz."

Shannon stuck out his hand. Colter grasped it tightly. Anyone could see the north fork was the right one. Anyone with sense, that is.

Colter put the final knot in the rope holding the last bale of supplies in the dugout. There was still no word from Captain Lewis's advance party. Moments from now the entire expedition would head up the south fork. It was already June 12th. With two months of the traveling season gone, the expedition had yet to catch sight of the Shining Mountains. This was no time to head the wrong way.

He got to his feet and massaged the kinks of frustration out of his lower back while he watched Shannon shovel dirt into a cache. *About time Fuzz got stuck with a dirty job*, he thought.

Down the beach, Clark knelt in the red pirogue, ministering to the ailing Sacajawea. For the last two days, she had suffered from a fever that none of the captain's remedies had been able to break. To Colter, her illness was a strong sign that the captains were making the wrong choice.

The wind flung toward him the fretful cries of Sacajawea's baby, Pomp. The sound unleashed a wave of longing for Fragrant Grass. He squinted up the river. Surely, by now, Lewis had seen enough of the south fork to know he picked wrong. Surely he would send back a scout to head the rest of the expedition the right way, up the north fork.

"What do you see, Old Man: the falls?" said Shannon, strolling over.

Colter pointed toward the north fork. "Falls're up there, and you know it."

Shannon chuckled patronizingly. "Lord, if there's one thing you are, it's stubborn."

Colter narrowed his eyes. "Better stubborn than stupid."

A red flush spread upward from Shannon's neck. Anger clipped his words. "Oh, how I'm going to enjoy seeing you eat those words, Old Man."

"Won't be me doin' the eatin'."

"Speaking of eating, Colter," Ordway said, coming up behind Shannon. "Chew on a midnight watch tonight. Think of it as dessert."

As Ordway strolled away, Colter kicked the dirt. "Dessert."

5. *Hartley Meets Fragrant Grass*

With every stroke of the bone scraper, more hair came free from the staked-down hide and more desperation filled Fragrant Grass's heart. Now when she needed guidance most, the Hawk Spirit would not speak to her. Withdrawing to the moon lodge had bought her some time but no answers. Now that she was back in her own lodge, she faced the problematic task of concealing her pregnancy from her sister.

A shrill whistle split the air and Mint's head snapped up. "Our husband returns! I knew he would come today. In my dream last night, I saw him riding toward home with each horse dragging a travois heaped with meat. Now that he leads the hunts, our village will not go hungry."

The bottom dropped out of Fragrant Grass's stomach. She had learned long ago to trust Mint's dreams. Sly Wolf's return made her situation even more precarious. He was bound to notice her swelling stomach when he next came to her bed. She managed to keep her voice neutral. "You go to meet him. I will prepare the lodge for his arrival."

After Mint hurried off, she slumped against her backrest and focused on the column of sunlight streaming down through the smoke hole. In the silence, she forced herself to dwell on the chance that Sly Wolf would be too tired from his long journey to want her that night. By the time she heard footfalls in the entrance tunnel, she felt composed enough to face him.

He entered first, followed by two warriors, supporting a third man between them. The stranger was a paleskin, dressed in filthy rags. Sticks bound in place with leather thongs braced his left arm, and he appeared unconscious. The man's stench made Fragrant Grass queasy. Regardless, Sly Wolf directed the men to deposit him on the best buffalo robe. "You, Wife, will tend this one's injury," he commanded her.

Fragrant Grass spoke firmly, despite the nausea. "He is filthy. I will bathe him first." Before Sly Wolf could object, she directed the two hunters to carry the man back outside, then grabbed a dipping gourd and a piece of hide for scrubbing the man and ducked after them. At the river, she had the hunters lay the man down, then she waved them away.

Like most of his kind, the man had too much hair — filthy, matted hair — especially on his gaunt face. Even in the open air, his odor turned her stomach.

"Little Mother!" Echo came bounding down the river path, filled with the joy of completing his first hunt with the adult men.

She resisted the impulse to hug him. Such an action was no longer appropriate since he was now considered a man in the eyes of the people. Instead, she smiled as broadly as her churning stomach would allow. "You return, Little Man. Tell me of your journey while I bathe this one."

Echo screwed up his face at the stranger. "How can you stand to touch him? He smells so bad!"

She nodded. "If you talk to me, it will help. Who is he?"

"A trader. He was unconscious when we found him. And lost."

A trader. No wonder Sly Wolf brought him to the lodge, she thought.

Echo grinned slyly. "Could it be, Little Mother, that this one's spirit guide led him to us."

The boy's remark brought back her own dilemma. She looked toward the sky. *Who is this man, Hawk Spirit? Have you brought him here to help me?*

"Here. Let me help you," Echo said, crouching next to the trader.

She gave his arm a restraining pat. "No, Little Man. It is not proper for a warrior to do woman's work. Later you must tell me about the hunt," she said, couching her words carefully, deferring to his new status.

Echo shot to his feet with a glance around to be sure no one had seen him forget himself. "I will tell you many stories, but first I must see to my horse," he said in a voice pitched to adult timbre, then he turned around and strutted away, a chick who would too soon be a rooster.

She looked down at the paleskin again. If the Hawk Spirit had sent this one to guide her, why did he have to smell so awful?

Hartley opened his eyes to a world both familiar and foreign. From the woven-willow frame of the curving walls to the loamy scent that pervaded his nostrils, he recognized an earth lodge similar to the Rees' but different in ways too subtle for him to pick out until his head was clearer. It took a moment to remember that he was with the Mandans somewhere up on the Knife River.

He tried to roll over but discovered that his left forearm was splinted and covered with a malodorous poultice, wrapped with pieces of hide. Slowly, the memories of how he broke his arm drifted into place. Shivering, he became aware that he was completely naked under the buffalo robe.

The privacy curtain moved aside, and a light-skinned squaw peered in at him. "Where am I?" he stammered.

"L-lodge, m-my," she replied in halting English.

Her eyes and smile contained a gentleness of the kind authored by sorrow. Hartley detested papists but could not resist paintings of their saints done by old masters. He loved particularly the faces of those saints. This woman had such a face.

She bent to examine his arm. He saw that what he took at first to be a decoration of gull feathers above her temple was really a patch of white hair. He had always scoffed at the tale of a lost colony of Welshmen living on the upper Missouri. Seeing her, he was not so sure. She had spoken to him in English after all. "I am called Hartley."

She finished her examination before she answered, "M-me Pshanshaw. You say, Fragrant Grass."

Fragrant Grass. An apt name for a comely woman.

Echo bounded through the entrance tunnel and came to perch on the edge of Hartley's sleeping platform. "You are awake. Good."

Although Fragrant Grass moved away, Hartley could not take his eyes off her. Echo noticed this and said, "Little Mother makes your arm well."

So, she's the one responsible for the splints and poultice.

"How do you feel, Friend Hartley? Do you want to talk? I must practice the paleskin tongue." Echo leaned closer. "One day soon I go to the village of Washington to meet Jefferson, the great chief of the paleskins."

"Washington? Whoever gave you that fool notion?"

"What means 'fool notion,' Friend Hartley?"

The preacher waved his free hand to cover the slip of his tongue. "It's — an idea. A good idea."

Echo beamed a smile. "Friend Shannon gives the fool notion to me."

Figuring that Shannon had to be one of the expedition's members, Hartley asked, "I take it he's the one taught you English?"

"Shannon teaches Echo. Echo teaches Shannon — and Colter."

The name popped out so unexpectedly that the preacher sucked in an audible breath. Echo popped off the bed as if he had done something wrong. "You have pain. I must leave."

Now that he was on the verge of learning about the man who had caused him so much misery, it was vital to Hartley that the boy stay. He hastily recovered his lost composure. "No, it's passed now. Please sit back down and tell me more about this trip to Washington. When will you go?"

Echo hesitated, but did as Hartley requested. "Before the snows, when the paleskin warriors return. That is what Friend Colter said."

This time Hartley was prepared to hear the hated name. Before he let himself believe this stroke of fortune, however, he had to be sure. "I knew a man named Colter once. What does this Friend Colter look like?"

Echo indicated Colter's approximate height. "He wears here the mark of the Hawk Spirit." To illustrate, he traced such a shape across his temple and eye with a stubby forefinger.

The knowledge that they were talking about the same Colter and that he would be back here before winter set Hartley's heart hammering against the walls of his chest, while he forced himself to pretend he was trying to match the boy's description to the memory of a face. "It's not the same man, I'm afraid."

Fragrant Grass returned, interrupting their conversation. Hartley took the ladle of broth from her and accidentally brushed her hand, sending an electric tingle up his arm. Again he could not take his eyes off her until she ducked out the lodge entrance.

"Do you wish to know about your horses?" Echo said.

Oh, Lord, the horses. He had forgotten them and the pelts that would make him rich. "Yes, I do. Of course," he said, struggling up on an elbow.

"They are well. I care for them," Echo said proudly.

The preacher sagged back in relief. He closed his eyes and tried to reorganize his scattered thoughts while half-listening to Echo prattle on about the village and the just-completed hunting trip. Only the re-entrance of Fragrant Grass pulled him fully back to the moment.

The boy lowered his voice confidentially. "I am not alone in waiting for the paleskins to return before the snows." Hartley encouraged him to continue with a searching look. "Colter wears the mark of the Hawk Spirit. The Hawk Spirit also guides Little Mother."

Hartley had been with the Rees and then Montagne long enough to understand the importance these Indians put on their guiding spirits. "But how can she wait for Colter? Isn't she married?"

Echo nodded. "She is second wife to Sly Wolf, but she must do what Hawk Spirit asks of her."

The face of a plump squaw appeared at the entrance to the tunnel. She crooked a finger at Echo. The boy hopped off Hartley's bed. "My mother," he explained sheepishly and darted outside.

Hartley was suddenly exhausted. He drew down the privacy curtain and began sorting out what he had just learned. After a time he gave up the effort. The only thing that mattered was that God would soon deliver Colter into his hands. The key to this renewed good fortune was a handsome squaw with a white patch in her blue-black hair. Fragrant Grass. How fitting it would be if Colter died with her name on his cursed lips. That idea curled up in a corner of the preacher's mind and accompanied him into sleep.

Something about the paleskin Hartley made Fragrant Grass wary of him. The man's wounds had healed to the point that he could move freely about the village, yet he rarely ventured outside. Then there was the way he watched her. Inside the lodge, she kept her distance from him, sensing that he was plotting something.

Mint ducked through the tunnel. Fragrant Grass's smile turned to a frown at how pale her sister looked. She helped Mint to a backrest, then shooed the paleskin outside.

Mint sank gratefully against the seat. She had endured three terrible months of pregnancy. The growing baby made her throw up everything she ate, and, with a guest always in the lodge, she did not rest enough. As a consequence, she was too thin. Fragrant Grass worried about her sister's health and that of the baby.

While she sponged Mint's face, a possible solution to one of her problems came to her. She snugged the best buffalo robe around her sister's gaunt form, then dipped a cup of the special tea she had brewed to rebuild Mint's strength. She allowed her sister several sips of the tea before speaking. "I have held my tongue too long, my sister. It is time to speak. It is not good for your baby to have sickness around him."

"The paleskin?" Mint said in a tired voice.

She touched her sister's rounded belly. "You need to rest so he can grow strong."

Mint came instantly alert. "He?"

"The paleskin, Hartley," Fragrant Grass said with what she hoped was the right amount of innocence.

"No, he. My baby. You called my baby 'he.'"

"It is too soon to know yet," she said, hiding her delight that Mint had gobbled the bait so fast.

"Oh, I knew it was a boy," Mint said. "I knew I would give our husband a son."

"If you know this, then you have a duty to make your son strong. You need to rest and eat well to regain your strength."

Mint clutched Fragrant Grass's wrist. "You are so good to me, my sister. I am ashamed of the way I acted toward you when our husband wanted to put you out of our lodge. Sometimes, when I think what my life would be like if he had done that terrible thing, I —" Tears choked off her words.

Fragrant Grass stroked Mint's arm until the sobs subsided. "I need you with me, my sister," Mint said. "I need your wisdom, and my baby needs your knowledge of healing. I will speak with our husband about sending the paleskin to live in another lodge."

Fragrant Grass cradled her sister's head against her breast and smiled up at the circle of sky above the smoke hole. It was done.

6. *The Great Falls*

O ver the next two days, steep bluffs along both banks constricted the river's course. With no place to walk, the towing crews ended up in the cold water, at times up to their chests. While the crew's tempers grew shorter, Sacajawea's condition deteriorated. York made a sling from his fraying shirt and took to carrying the baby in it so the Shoshone woman could rest. The baby cooperated with the arrangement for a time but soon reverted to screaming his displeasure.

By the noon rest stop on June 14, Colter had a crawful of the wailing baby and his surly crewmates. He hobbled away from the others and found a flat rock to stretch out on.

He was just beginning to drift into a snooze when Shannon interrupted his solitude. "We need to talk, Old Man."

The younger man's bedraggled appearance tempered the sarcastic dismissal that leaped automatically to Colter's lips. "Make 'er short."

"I've been thinking about — about the river," Shannon began. "I — this —"

"Spit 'er out, Fuzz. We ain't got all day here."

"This can't be the right way," Shannon blurted.

This astounding admission coming from Shannon brought Colter up to a sitting position. At that very moment Rube called out, "It's Joe!"

Fifty yards upstream the lone figure of Joe Field limped toward them. Rube sprinted past to intercept his brother. Shannon looked after him. "Where are Captain Lewis and Drouillard and all the others?"

While Colter's tired mind tried to frame an answer, Rube shouted, "The falls! They found the falls!"

The change in Shannon was instantaneous. "By the Almighty, the falls! I was right after all. And, Old Man, you were wrong! Wrong, wrong, wrong. Time to pay off."

Colter narrowed his eyes and looked upstream. "I don't see no falls."

"Quit stalling. They're there. Joe says so. So much for your bet."

"Stallin' ain't how you saw it back at the forks. Remember?"

Captain Clark curtailed their argument by calling Colter over to him. The captain greeted him with an assessing look. "According to Meri's message, we'll need to scout and stake a portage route. I want you to help do that."

Colter recognized that this was the captain's way of mending bridges with the crew. "Sure thing, Captain."

Clark clapped him on the shoulder, then turned away to talk to the sergeants. Colter's head was spinning from the sudden turn of events. He wandered down to the boats for his things. Shannon caught him there. "What was that all about?"

Sacajawea was lying in the red pirogue. At the sound of Shannon's voice, her feverish eyes dragged open. Colter shushed him and dragged him off a few yards so they would not disturb her further. "Captain stuck me on a crew to stake out a portage route."

Shannon's eyes blazed with fury. "By God, it's me who deserves —" He stopped himself, and his expression and voice cooled. "Good. The sooner you see the falls, the sooner you get to make a fool of yourself in front of everyone. Everyone and the captains."

He turned on his heel and strode away, leaving Colter with the prospect of paying off on the bet sitting like a peach pit in his gullet.

A mile upstream from the expedition's camp, the staking party reached a creek that would mark the start of the portage. Captain Clark led the men up the steep brushy slope of that drainage and out onto the rolling plains above the river canyon. Colter and Willard followed with a suveyor's chain. Their job: to measure the length of the portage route for the captain's map.

Colter stopped to set his pole partway up the creek, then waited for Willard to pace off a chain-length while he scanned back along the creek and their route so far. He harkened back to the expedition's other portage around the Falls of the Ohio at Clarksville. There they had wagons and horses to carry their baggage. They had known all the difficulties they would face in moving *Discovery* down the falls before they started. Here not only would the men have to carry on their backs tons of the expedition's baggage from the bottom to the top of the falls — a distance he guessed would be at least five miles — but they would know none of the obstacles they would encounter until they ran into them. If this was the way to the Western Sea as so many claimed, folks needed to do some serious rethinking about what they assumed the Passage to be. Getting to the Western Sea by this route was definitely no short, easy undertaking.

He felt the chain tug. Willard stood up the slope, his pole planted and his expression impatient. Colter picked up the pole and resumed his climb, swinging above Willard a rod's distance, then stopping to wait for the man to repeat the process. As he passed, Willard said, "Hear you and Shannon have a bet."

Colter grunted noncommittally. A bet. What had ever possessed him? He had no one to blame but himself for the humbling he would soon face. When would he ever learn not to let his temper get in the way of common sense?

Another tug on the chain set him into motion again. He crested the top of the slope to find Clark who recorded the number of rods up from the creek, then had two other men take the chain for the next leg of the route. While the captain and that pair headed off, Colter waited for Willard to catch his breath. Mopping the sweat off his face, he looked upstream along the river chasm, searching for the rising mist that would indicate a cataract.

Nothing.

Wherever these falls were, the portage was no mere half-day carry the Indians had talked about. "No way in hell."

Willard cocked an eyebrow at him, and Colter felt immediately foolish for thinking out loud again. "Them Indians was wrong. This here carry's five, maybe six miles."

Willard looked off after the retreating figures of the captain and the others. "More."

"Ten or eleven then. What's the difference?"

Willard shook his head. "More." Colter usually found the big man's quiet certainty reassuring. Now it struck him as downright irksome. "How about —" He stopped himself before he could make another wager he would regret. McBain and his constant betting leapt into his mind.

"How about what?" Willard asked.

"How about we get goin' 'fore we have to run to catch up?"

Willard took the lead. The day was hot; the sun, merciless. The plain stretched wide on all sides, bristling with the spiny arms of cactus. Sweat blurred his vision, and Colter went slowly to keep from stepping in the wrong places. He was so intent on picking his way that he nearly bumped into Willard who had stopped to cock his head as if he heard something. When he stopped, Colter heard it too: the roar of falling water.

He had seen many waterfalls, but nothing to match this one. A wall of water three hundred yards wide fell more than eighty feet, part in a sheer drop, part in a crashing course of rapids. The force of the falling water churned up waves twenty feet high at the bottom and created a tremendous frothing backwash that held him transfixed until Willard drew his attention to the rest of the party who were scrambling up the next rise.

He took one last look. Here was the promised falls. He had seen it. Soon as he got back to camp, he would have to face Shannon.

✦

"That's deep enough," Gass said. "You three take a break while you others cart off this last load of dirt."

Shannon was glad to let someone else wrestle the buffalo hide heaped with dirt up the bank. He had done the digging of the cache. Someone else could do the dirt hauling and scattering.

McNeal flopped down next to him. "Well, when's it going to happen?"

"'It' what, McNeal?"

"When's Colter payin' off your bet?"

Shannon's jaw tightened. "He said he had to see the falls with his own eyes first."

"And you let him get away with that? After he made such a big to-do over the wrong fork?"

Shannon scratched at a non-itch under his arm. McNeal's insistence compounded his frustration. He wanted to get things back to normal between himself and Colter as much as he wanted to get back to hunting and leave all this common drudgery to someone else.

McNeal went on. "I sure wouldn't have gone along with that load of horse apples. Not after the grief Colter's handed you these last weeks."

"Well, thank God I'm not you, and you're not me," Shannon snarled.

McNeal huffed away, leaving Shannon to his thoughts. Of all the crew, he alone — McNeal didn't count — had backed the captains' choice of the south fork, yet the captains had not chosen him to help scout the falls. He could have let that slight pass if Captain Clark had not picked Colter to help stake the all-important portage route. Colter who objected when the captains announced their decision to continue up the south fork. For that, the Old Man deserved a reprimand, not the honor of being one of the first to see the falls. Then there was the matter of their bet. McNeal was right. It was high time for Colter to pay off.

"Just the man I want to see." The sound of Captain Lewis's voice startled him. "We need meat. Do you feel up to hunting?"

Shannon's level of frustration and surprise did not allow him to manage more than a mumbled "Yes, sir."

"There are reports of numerous grizzled bear tracks," the captain said. "Keep on your toes, and no heroics. I have all the bearskins I need."

Shannon nodded. Irked as he was at the way the captains handled the situation with Colter, at least they still recognized his skill. He preferred hunting to digging holes and hauling dirt. Receiving his payoff from Colter would have to wait until he got back.

✦

After the first falls came a second, a beautiful twenty-foot drop shaped like a ragged arc. Beyond it came the third, an unbroken curtain of water plunging fifty feet from a quarter-mile curve of ledge to a rock-strewn pool below.

The Missouri occupied a long gash in the spreading plain. Over time, streams and storms had eroded deep gullies in the sides of that gash. In order to ease the work of the portaging crews, Clark swung the route two miles south of the rim, avoiding all but one of these rugged ravines. That one he dubbed "Willow Run."

Impressions of thousands of buffalo hooves pocked the ground over which the staking party moved. The sun had baked the indentations to foot-bruising hardness, giving Colter one more thing to try to avoid treading on. After the third falls, Captain Clark had Colter and Willard take the survey chain again. Keeping count of the chain movements and watching his footing kept Colter so occupied that he did not realize when Willard halted.

Just ahead lay an immense pool. In its center bubbled a spring of clear water, filling the pool to overflowing, disgorging pure icy water into the nearby river. Captain Clark was kneeling beside the pool, head bowed, hands folded.

The sight stirred up in Colter remorse for doubting the captains back at the Maria's. Not only did he owe Shannon for their bet, he also owed the captains an apology.

Clark completed his prayer and rose with a smile, sweeping his arm toward the six-foot cascade beyond the spring. "Meri missed this one."

Willard went for a better look, and Colter decided to seize the chance. "Captain, I got a heap of apologizin' to do. You were —"

"Right?" Clark interrupted. "Well, so were you: to speak up when you thought we were wrong. In honor of that," he nodded to the cascade, "I am calling this 'Colter Falls'."

Words failed Colter. He could not even say thanks.

The captain opened his notebook. "What was the last count?"

Colter was too moved to own a clear thought. He motioned to Willard who provided the information. Clark closed the notebook, stuck it back in his shirt, and walked off, his mind on something else.

Willard looked at Colter. "You ready?"

Colter could not take his eyes off the falls. Off *his* falls. His falls! The idea filled him with a buoyancy that chased away the pain and fatigue of the last few months. He hooted a laugh. "Ready? I ain't never been so ready!"

"What in hell did Captain say to you?" Willard asked.

Colter swept his hand toward the falls. "He said, 'Meri missed this one'."

"That's all?"

There was no need to pat his own back in front of any one else. It was enough that he knew of the captain's honor. "Yep."

Shannon's nose itched, but he dared not scratch it. It had taken all morning to find the game he and Drouillard had been looking for and, now that they had found it, he did not want to chance that it might get away.

The itching grew worse and, with it, came the urge to sneeze. He screwed up his face against the sensation.

At last Drouillard's rifle boomed and the bull elk toppled. The echoes of the shot had barely faded before the half-breed set to work skinning out the carcass. This was the fourth bull elk they had tracked and killed in the last two days. The fourth time Drouillard had taken the skin and left the meat. The fourth time Colter's warning about never wasting the meat you killed had come back on Shannon with full force. He had held his silence for the other three, but, with this creature, his conscience and the memories of the hunger he had experienced after losing his way on the Missouri last fall demanded that he speak out. "We can't just leave the meat like that."

The half-breed continued skinning.

Shannon decided to try a different angle. "It isn't like you to leave good meat to rot."

"Captain Meri orders. I do," Drouillard replied.

Hearing the half-breed use such a term of familiarity for the captain annoyed Shannon. "What makes you think you can disparage the captain that way? He is Captain Lewis. Not Meri."

Drouillard tossed a glance at Shannon. "Why you call Colter 'Old Man' and why he call you 'Fuzz'?"

"Because we're friends. We're equals which you and the captain aren't."

Drouillard did not react to the insult. "If you are friends, why you and Colter argue so much?"

"Because I see things one way, and he sees them another way. That's what makes us friends. But we aren't talking about us. We're talking about you and the captain."

Drouillard rolled the dead elk over. "Friends must respect each other's ways."

"We do respect each other, but it's also my responsibility to point out when he's wrong. Like when he wouldn't go along with the captains' decision on the south fork."

Drouillard freed the last of the skin from the elk's carcass. "How you know that he is wrong and you are right?"

By now the half-breed's attitude and questions had raised Shannon's hackles. "Because I *know*! Now you tell me why we're wasting all this meat."

In one graceful move, the half-breed hefted the rolled-up hide to his shoulder and swept up his rifle. "Captain Meri. He order. I do."

By the time Clark's route-staking group returned, the main body of the expedition had moved upstream to Portage Creek to prepare for the start of the carry. The long trek had wrung out of Colter the euphoria of having one of the five cataracts of the Great Falls named after him. In its place, qualms about facing Shannon again loomed large.

Before starting down the last slope to the expedition's Portage Creek camp, he stopped to collect himself. While the other route-stakers went ahead, he reflected on the difficult struggle they had in store to get around the falls. The staked route stretched from the creek below him to the camp above the upper falls on what they had called White Bear Island, eighteen miles over arduous terrain, more than three times what he had originally estimated. Earlier this morning he had caught his first glimpse of a line of shimmering snow-capped mountains off to the west. Set against the deep blue of a wide cloudless sky, they seemed both as grand as the scalloped bunting decorating some celestial platform and as threatening as a week-long ice-storm.

Camp was littered with preparations for the coming portage. Two crude wagons had been constructed, using rounds cut from a tree trunk, lengths of the mast of the white pirogue for axles, and dugouts for the beds. Each sported a long tongue strung with harnesses for the men who would pull them, reminiscent of the meat sleds he had learned to hate back at Fort Mandan. Baggage and supplies lay everywhere, some bundled for hauling, some sorted to cache, still other things spread out to dry.

Joe Field hailed him, then immediately began grousing about Rube's getting out of all the hard work. "How'd he do that?" Colter replied half-heartedly, glancing around for Shannon.

"Captain sent him and Shields, Peckerwood and Drooler off hunting a couple of days back."

The mention of Shannon got Colter's immediate attention. "Fuzz is gone?"

"That's what I said. Four of 'em. All sandbaggin' no-good dung-rollers. Just look at that heap of stuff we got to haul up past the falls. Damn it all, I'm as good a shot as Rube. I ought to be huntin'."

Colter's mouth relaxed into a smile. No Shannon meant no apology. Could be, as short as his memory was, Fuzz would forget the bet altogether. "Don't that beat all."

Joe looked at him suspiciously. "That's all you got to say?"

"Nope. What's for supper?"

Joe huffed away. Colter was about to head to the fire when the sound of female laughter stopped him. Down at the edge of the water sat Sacajawea, splashing and playing with Pomp, looking as if she had never known a moment's ill health. Captain's medicine must have worked.

The sight lifted Colter's rising spirits even more. Shannon's absence and Sacajawea's recovery — two pieces of unexpected good news.

"Well, well. If it isn't the famous John Colter."

Colter's smile sank at the sound of Ordway's voice. "Famous is one thing I ain't, Sarge."

"It isn't every day a man gets a new falls named after him."

The fiery glint in the sergeant's eye made Colter cautious. "Them falls has been there a long time. They ain't new."

Ordway's lip curled back from his teeth and his voice dropped. "That's quite an honor. One you, of all people, don't deserve."

"If'n you got a gripe, you ought to be talkin' to the captains."

"I have the perfect way to wipe that self-satisfied smile off your face, Colter." He thumbed toward the biggest wagon. "The front harness is reserved just for you."

Colter stared over the top of the wagon until he could get control of the anger that surged up in him. "First the captain. Now you."

The comment seemed to throw Ordway. "The captain and me, what?"

Colter deliberately drawled his words for maximum sarcasm. "I'm just a man doin' my best. Ain't done nothin' special. Not really. But here you go, rewardin' me with first place when there are lots of others deserve it more. McNeal, for instance."

The calculating glint returned to Ordway's glare. "You get just what you deserve, Private."

Colter locked glares with the man. "So do you, Sarge. So do you."

After one day spent hauling bales of expedition supplies on his back from the creekside camp up to the staging area on the plain above the river gorge, Colter took his place in the front harness of the make-shift wagon to begin the long trek across the plains to White Bear camp above the last of the Great Falls. Behind him, also in harness, six other crewmen pulled while two more pushed. Captain Clark went ahead of them, leading the rest of the able-bodied crewmen, all carrying loads of supplies on their backs.

In short order, the wagon crew's good humor vanished and the griping began. As usual, the loudest bellyaching came from McNeal who aimed most of his complaints at Colter.

When the captain called the first rest stop at the top of the descent into Willow Run, Colter stepped gingerly out of the improvised harness, careful not to tread on any cactus, and sat down to rewrap his feet.

"You and your precious feet," McNeal said.

"Damn right they're precious. This here comin' up is one steep draw and I don't cotton to slidin' down it."

McNeal raised his voice for the benefit of everyone. "Why would anyone listen to you, Colter? You're the one didn't know his right river from his left."

The comment drew sniggers from some of the same men who had agreed with Colter about the north fork. Men who had not had the guts to speak up against the captains' decision when he alone had. He shrugged off the comment and laughter and continued to attend to his feet. The others could go lame for all he cared.

The descent into Willow Run quickly turned into a nightmare. Near the top, one wheel of the wagon collapsed, then another. With no level ground and no wood available for repairs, the wagon crew had to rope the wagon bed and its load to the bottom. Colter lost both moccasins in the process. That forced him into foregoing a rest at the bottom to search for his foot-wrappings.

Following the wagon's dragmarks upslope, he came upon the pieces of the second wheel. He had fallen when it broke and figured that had to be where he lost his moccasins.

He examined every inch of ground around the area but did not find the vital leather strips. If he did not find those moccasins, he would end up too crippled to walk, a fate he did not relish. The success of the expedition hinged on this portage. The success of the expedition and his timely return to Fragrant Grass.

McNeal stepped out from behind a clump of low brush. "Lose something, Mr. Know-It-All?"

"Yep. Them." Colter pointed to the cook's feet which were clad in his lost buffalo-hide wrappings.

"Finder's keepers," the cook said. "Here, take these. Looks like you need 'em." He tossed down his old ripped-up moccasins.

The man's chuckle touched a flame to the fuse of the resentment that had been building up in Colter for days. He lunged at the cook, hitting him hard and tackling him to the ground. He scrambled up, ready to punch the sass out of the man. The cook did not move. He was out cold.

"Finder's keepers," Colter said, mocking the cook while stripping off the purloined moccasins and putting them back on his own feet where they belonged. By the time he finished, McNeal still had not moved. *Playin' possum again*, he thought, heading back to the bottom of the drainage.

The crew had felled a small tree and cut and mounted four new wheels to the wagon's undercarriage by the time he arrived. He helped lift the dug-out-turned-wagonbed onto the undercarriage and reluctantly climbed back into his harness.

"Where's McNeal?" Sergeant Pryor asked.

Colter craned around. The cook was nowhere to be seen. *Why, that no good shit-eater.*

"McNeal!" bellowed Pryor.

No reply.

"Anyone seen the cook?" the sergeant asked.

Colter pointed up the slope. "Last I seen, he was up there."

Pryor scowled as if he wished McNeal were someone else's problem. "Better show me."

The cook still lay where Colter had left him. The sergeant looked him over. "Something knocked him out, looks like."

Colter decided to fess up. "We had us a little tussle."

"Confound it, Colter," Pryor said. "I expect better out of you. McNeal's all mouth and penis. You know that. Now what do I do with him? He can't pull in this condition."

Colter bit back a defense of his actions. The sergeant wasn't an angry sort. No need to rile him more.

Pryor looked from Colter to the cook and back. "Hellfire, we need everyone fit to carry, and here you give him an excuse to sandbag the rest of the portage."

Colter felt downright foolish. With the cook out of the harness, it would be that much harder for him and the rest of the wagon crew to pull their load out of this ravine.

Pryor sighed. "Well, come on and help me get him down to the bottom. Nothing to do but leave him there till he can find his own way back to the lower camp."

Colter took hold of McNeal's feet. As he lifted, he could have sworn he saw the cook smile.

Why'd I ever leave you? The question swirled around the picture of Fragrant Grass that Colter held in his mind to help him forget the pain of the wagon harness cutting into the flesh of his chest and shoulders. One painful step at a time, he strained against the load of baggage. With every step diminishing his strength, he held fast to her image to keep himself going.

Crack! Something gave and he was dragged back into the man in harness behind him. They tumbled together to the ground, tangled in their leather traces.

They had company on the ground. The wagon tongue had broken, felling the pullers and the pushers both. Dusk was well-advanced. Soon it would be dark, and darkness in this country meant bears; grizzled bears; lots of them from the tracks he had seen around the end-of-portage camp above the last falls.

"This is as far as I go," Rube announced, curling onto his side and falling instantly asleep.

Three other pullers followed Rube's lead. Instead of getting the men up and going again, Sergeant Pryor sagged against the broken-down wagon and stared dully at the ground. "Camp's about half a mile," Colter offered.

Pryor wagged his head wearily.

"Lots of them grizzled bears hereabouts. Best be near a fire," Colter said louder.

The sergeant shrugged.

"Them bears ain't nothin' to fool with."

"We heard you, Colter," someone growled. "Now shut up and leave us sleep."

"Fine-a-ree," he muttered, pulling off the harness and getting to his feet. "Don't never say I didn't warn you."

Finally Pryor spoke up. "Where're you going, Colter?"

"Findin' me a fire, Sarge. Tired ain't no excuse for chancin' one of them grizzled bears."

"Take a load with you. Please."

Ordway would have said "That's an order," not "please." Commanding without seeming to was a trait Pryor shared with his dead cousin Floyd. Remembering Floyd, Colter turned back, picked up a bundle and hobbled painfully off toward White Bear camp.

Colter arrived at White Bear camp to bad news. Scavenging animals had made off with all the meat he and the staking party had laid in. No meat meant no dinner, no breakfast and a long, hungry walk back to the lower camp the next day, dragging the empty, repaired wagon.

For the second carry, Captain Lewis, Charbonneau, Pomp and the recovering Sacajawea went ahead of the portagers, leaving Ordway at Portage Creek camp in charge of McNeal and the other crewmen too ill or injured to participate in the carry. Overnight, the wind had come up, and, throughout the morning, bruise-colored clouds piled up on the peaks to the west, streaming out like pennants caught on pikes. By noon, the cloud cover had spread eastward across the Missouri's canyon and the plain, hanging low over the men struggling with the loaded wagons. Around two o'clock, lightning slashed through the cloud layer and unleashed a downpour that sent Colter and the others diving for cover under the wagonbed, the only shelter available in the wide-open country.

From this scant cover, Colter stared numbly at the pelting rain and slashing lightning. Under the onslaught, the sunbaked earth quickly melted into an ooze that would mire the wagons and sabotage every foothold once they got going again. The realization that all he could do was wait out the storm drove his flagging spirits even lower.

While the storm raged, one by one the other men drifted into sleep. He closed his weary eyes and willed to mind the comforting image of Fragrant Grass. Slowly a face coalesced: a mouth with its gentle, upward tilt; the cheekbones high and proud; shining eyes and . . .

Before his imagination could fill in the white patch above her forehead, the image blurred.

Another flare of lightning illuminated the inside of his eyelids, all but erasing the image, but he persisted, keeping his eyes shut, waiting for the vision to return.

Slowly, her face began to take shape. Then, for the second time, it blurred away and faded before being fully realized.

The rain beat down. A man twitched in his sleep. Colter willed his mind to bring up the memory of her face a third time. It would not come.

Beneath the fury of the storm, he groaned, glad that the roar of the weather hid his despair. Fragrant Grass's image had sustained him through all the miles and hardships since leaving Fort Mandan. If he could not conjure up her face, if he did not have that to lean on, how could he ever hope to go on? "Don't leave me now," he whispered.

Another sleeper stirred, jostling his elbow. He held himself motionless against a surge of anguish and peered up at the sieving clouds. What was he doing here when everything he wanted — his heart, his dreams, and his future — was back at the Mandans?

He knew the answer before he asked the question. It was the same reason he had waited so long to leave Virginia when all the other trappers he knew had gone west: John Colter was a man of honor.

Honor and keeping his word were the guiding principles of his life. Holding to his promises had seldom been easy, but he had never gone back on his word in all his twenty-nine years. Now here he was, caught between two promises — one to see the expedition through and the other to get back to the woman he loved before winter. He could not accomplish either one of those promises without breaking the other. He was trapped by his own good intentions. And he was bound to let someone down. Someone and himself.

⭐

Back at Portage Camp two days later, still weighed down by the corner his personal code of honor had forced him into, Colter ate his breakfast without tasting it, then trudged dejectedly to the heaps of baggage and equipment remaining to be portaged. He picked up a box containing Captain Lewis's specimens and was turning to load it on the make-shift wagon when Ordway yelled, "Not that, Colter. All that goes back. That over there goes with us." He indicated a heap next to the white pirogue.

Colter did not care what he hauled at that point. He put down the box of specimens and gathered up another from the indicated stack. It wasn't until he was on the climb out of Willow Run later that afternoon that what the sergeant had said registered. "All that goes back."

'All that' referred to the boxes and barrels containing the captains journals and collected specimens and "back" could only mean downriver. And that explained why the white pirogue had not been portaged with the dugouts and the red pirogue.

Of course. It all made sense. The captains were concerned about how late in the summer it was getting and they had decided to send their reports and findings downriver to St. Louis before the Missouri became impassable.

In the space of a heartbeat he saw the way out of his dilemma, the way to keep his promises to Fragrant Grass *and* to the expedition. The white pirogue needed a pilot. A good one. Him. And just to make sure he got that assignment, he would go straight to Captain Clark and ask for the job the minute he got to the upper camp. Ordeal had deprived him of his rightful spot in the hunting rotation because he was such a good pilot. Now he would use that same endorsement as the ticket to send him on his way back to the woman he loved.

The idea put a spring back into his step. "What's got into you?" groused Rube.

Colter answered with a chuckle. He was on his way home.

⭐

Buoyed by this planned change of fortune, Colter reached the upper camp well in advance of the other portagers. Except for McNeal cooking, the camp looked deserted. He dropped his load and made straight for the captains' tent. York ducked out the flaps to meet him. "Master's sick," he murmured, indicating that the captain was having problems with his stomach again. "He just got to sleep. You need to see him, best wait till morning."

Colter stifled his impatience and nodded. York squeezed his shoulder in gratitude and re-entered the tent. Frustrated, Colter hobbled to the fire to see about some food.

McNeal was slicing meat off a shoulder of buffalo and hanging the strips on racks to dry. To see the man doing the kind of critical but tedious job he usually squirmed out of pleased Colter. "You run outta excuses for once or wouldn't nobody listen to you no more?" he taunted.

McNeal gave him a withering look.

"Glad to see you enjoyin' yourself so much," Colter jibed. He bent over to cut off a chunk of the haunch roasting over the fire. In retaliation for his ridicule or just out of orneriness, McNeal nudged the center log of the pile in the fire, unseating the whole pyramid and sending up a blanket of sparks and ash, covering Colter and the meat he intended to eat.

Colter reacted to the stunt by leaping across the fire and snatching McNeal by the hair. He cocked his fist back, ready to pound the vinegar out of the man.

"Go on, hit me, Big Shot," the cook challenged.

Colter remembered then that Captain Clark lay a few yards away and he released the cook. The pleasure of throttling McNeal was not worth possibly damaging his chances to pilot the white pirogue downriver.

McNeal scuttled out of reach. "What's wrong, Colter? Lost your nerve?"

Slowly, deliberately, Colter unsheathed his knife and lifted it to eye level. The cook's stubborn expression faltered. "You wouldn't."

Colter turned the blade so that sunlight reflected off the well-honed edge into the cook's eyes. McNeal's expression slid from uncertainty to fear, and he slunk back to his work.

Colter sat down to scrape ash off his piece of haunch and ponder the trip back. The captains would likely send two men downriver rather than just one. Unfortunately, of all the crew, McNeal was the logical choice because he was so useless. Outside of his ability to cook, McNeal was a thorn in everybody's side. He had been since he signed on. His departure would be popular with the crew and the sergeants.

The idea of being thrown together with McNeal for the long run down the river gave Colter pause. Such a journey would be dangerous enough with someone he trusted. Somehow he had to affect the captain's choice, to convince them to send Willard or Potts or even Shannon, if it came to that.

The arrival of the rest of the portagers suspended his speculation. He watched them trudge in, the strain of three carries obvious in their bowed backs and hang-dog expressions. He had known some of them for nearly two years now. Together they had gone farther up the Missouri than any other Americans, and, in doing so, they had discovered unknown animals and seen sights no one else knew existed. Together they had weathered storms and bears and the Sioux and the moody, fickle Missouri.

Once he left, he would probably never again cross paths with the likes of York, Joe Field, Potts, Willard, Rube and Shannon. And, with Shannon gone hunting, he would not be able to say goodbye. That he would regret.

He had never met anyone like Shannon before. Someone who could make him laugh one minute, and the next minute, cause his blood to boil. This time tomorrow or the next day it would be Shannon's blood boiling, when he learned that he had left without paying off on their bet.

Joe sagged to the ground next to him. "What's got you smiling?"

"Gas," he replied.

The sun was well up when Colter awoke the next morning. His bladder was too full to ignore. He hurried into the brush to relieve himself as fast as his stiff muscles would allow, then, putting aside his usual morning appetite, he headed directly for the captains' tent.

The tent was empty.

A search located Captain Clark, York and three crewmen lowering boxes into a cache dug into the side of the hill a hundred yards beyond the portage trail. He hung back until they finished. No one needed to know his plan until the assignment was his.

Captain Clark looked so wan that Colter decided to get straight to the point when he had the captain to himself. "Since you and Captain Lewis are plannin' to send back the white pirogue, I'm volunteerin' to take her for you. Them records is important. You need someone can get 'em back safe. For that, I'm your man." He cringed at the last sentence the moment he heard himself say it. Unlike other men, he had never been one to hum his own tune.

The captain shook his head. "That was our plan a few days ago. Not now. This last portage changed my mind. We can't afford to let able-bodied men go."

Like a crystal mirror shattered by a tossed rock, those few words brought Colter's whole beautiful idea crashing to his feet. He was incapable of keeping the surprise and disillusionment off his face.

Clark continued, "You were going to pilot her back, Colter. Before we changed our minds."

Instead of comforting or reassuring him, the remark drove the blade of frustration ever deeper into his soul. To know he had come so close to going back was the unkindest cut of all.

"We need you with us, Colter," Clark said. "You have shown your mettle time and again."

He was too empty to speak or meet the captain's eyes. Whatever mettle he might have had left him, replaced by a numbing futility.

"Are you still with us?" Clark asked gently.

He swallowed. His spirit had already left this place to fly to Fragrant Grass ahead of his body. Now his body was trapped. There was no way to leave. Yet, here was the captain, asking him to call his spirit back, to force it to return to a place it did not want to be.

Clark's voice fell. "Colter, I need to hear your answer."

Colter lifted his eyes to the eastern horizon, to the direction he longed to go, the direction now blocked for him by circumstance. His words rang with all the bitterness he felt. "I'm here, ain't I?"

The captain's face softened. "Yes, thank God, you are."

What God, Colter thought. *Ain't no God. Ain't no hope. Ain't nothin' but this bloody river under a sky that gives a body blisters one minute, goose-*

flesh, the next. I come all this way. For what? To get myself into a place I cain't never leave? To finally find a woman to love only to leave her behind? What kind of fool decision did I think I was makin' when I come on instead of waitin' for her? Why? Where's the sense in anythin'?

Questions tore at his heart. Questions of a man stripped of hope.

The captain shielded his eyes against the sun advancing across a cloudless sky the color of a robin's egg. "And thank God for a clear day. Maybe we can finish the carry in two more trips and be on our way day after tomorrow. We leave in half an hour."

Colter wandered back to camp in a dispirited fog. There was no reason to hurry. They had spent three months getting here. No telling how much longer it would take to reach the Western Sea. One thing he did know, however: In order to reach the ocean from this point, they had to find a way through the mountains. Mountains high enough that even now, the end of June, they wore mantles of snow. In order to cross the mountains, they had to have horses. In order to have horses, they had to find the Shoshones. Yet in three months they had not seen so much as one other human being.

No, there was no reason to hurry for anything now. Fate had intervened. It was now clearly impossible to keep his promise to Fragrant Grass. Would she wait for him?

7. *Little Mother*

F ragrant Grass dug at the thistles invading the patch of new corn with a hoe fashioned from the shoulder blade of a buffalo. As she bent to yank a particularly stubborn weed, a shaft of pain shot upwards from her abdomen. She gasped, dropped the hoe and pressed her hands into her midsection.

The pain passed in moments. She wiped the cold sweat from her forehead and darted a glance toward Mint. Luckily, her sister was gossiping with women in the neighboring garden plot and had not noticed the incident. Relieved, she plodded to the waterskin for a drink.

Three days ago, the paleskin Hartley moved from their lodge into Big White's. With Hartley gone, she had hoped that Hawk Spirit would return to bring guidance about her pregnancy. That had not happened, and with every passing day, the child grew within her and, with it, the chance that someone would become aware of her condition. When that happened, her course would be set, and she would be forced to live out her days as Sly Wolf's second wife, cooking meals, making clothes and bearing children for a man she despised. The idea sickened her.

From the direction of the village came a shout. Echo dashed across the field to her. "Little Mother, Sly Wolf sends me to tell you to prepare to receive Black Cat from Rooptahe."

Mint immediately broke off her gossiping to join them. "Black Cat? But he is still in mourning."

"Yet he comes to see Little Mother," Echo said slyly before sprinting away to join the boys swimming races on the river.

Mint looked after him. "With his wife dead, Black Cat will seek another. A match between him and a woman from Matootonha would bind our village to his. Our husband says that such a bond grows more critical every year as the Sioux become bolder."

Afraid of where the line of talk was leading, Fragrant Grass stooped to collect her seed pouch. Could it be that Sly Wolf was at last making good on his threat to send her from their lodge? Such was his right; one she had dismissed because of the harm it might do to his standing in the village. However, marrying her to another man, especially one as respected as Black Cat, would increase the reputation he had so carefully and relentlessly honed over the years. She shivered.

"A match between you and Black Cat would be good for our village, our clan, and our husband," Mint said.

Fragrant Grass checked the sharp rebuke she wanted to throw back at her sister and drew herself up tall. She had carried on, hiding her condition, and so she would continue to forge her way, hiding her desperation until Hawk Spirit came to lead her along another path. She handed Mint the hoe. "I must see to our guest."

Hartley carefully set aside the looking-glass and strings of glass beads before rewrapping the rest of his trinkets and tucking them away. Over Big White's protests, he had moved into an abandoned lodge two days ago rather than risk offending the chief by continuing to turn aside the attentions of the man's oldest daughter. He had his sights set on other game. Game he would hunt tonight.

Outside, he threaded his way through the narrow passages between the other earth dwellings. He was a common sight to the Mandans by now. No one gave him a second glance.

The walk gave him time to go over the routine he had learned from watching Montagne. Indians never rushed into things. Tonight was the first step, and he had to do it right. That meant putting aside his impatience and slowing way down.

Sly Wolf's lodge sat in the prestigious section of Matootonha at the edge of the central ceremonial area. The door flap had been pulled back in deference to the night's heat. He stepped to the side of the opening, coughed and mentally counted to twenty-five before entering, in order to give the occupants time to prepare for guests.

Sly Wolf waved him to the place of honor near the fire, and Mint brought him a platter of roast venison and green corn. Hungry as he was, he let the food sit while Sly Wolf prepared a welcoming pipe. He did not pick up his platter until after the requisite smoking. He was chewing the first bite when Fragrant Grass entered the lodge. Seeing her heightened his appetite, but he forced himself to eat slowly. To bolt the food would have been a breach of Mandan hospitality and a fatal misstep that could sabotage his careful planning.

He laid aside the empty dish, regretting that he had not brought Echo along to translate. Too late for that now. He launched into his prepared speech, using hand-talk. When he reached the key moment, he pulled the looking-glass out of his pocket and laid it on his host's sitting robe with great ceremony.

Sly Wolf ignored it and Hartley began to perspire. Had he made an error? He signed some more and carefully laid three of the bead strings side by side across the mirror.

This time the Mandan looked at the items presented and spoke the one word Hartley had come to hear: Pshanshaw, Mandan for sweet-smelling grass.

Fragrant Grass started at the sound of her name. She rose uncertainly and approached the fire. She was three paces from Hartley when her step faltered and a quizzical expression spread across her handsome face. Then she winced and bent over as if with a stomach-ache.

Sly Wolf spoke harshly and too rapidly for the preacher to decipher. She straightened with obvious effort and wobbled the last three steps to the fire.

Sly Wolf spoke crossly and pointed at her legs. Blood had traced glistening trails down the tawny skin of both legs.

She nodded and immediately crumpled like a rag doll to the dirt floor.

Mint rushed to the aid of her fallen sister, and Sly Wolf signed to Hartley, "This wife sick. Take my other woman."

Hartley signed back, "I want only one woman. Her!" He pointed to the prone Fragrant Grass. When he reached for the mirror and beads, Sly Wolf stopped his hand. "You come another time."

"No. This woman. Now."

Sly Wolf growled at Mint. She shot back a reply in a voice choked with anger and worry. Face darkening, Sly Wolf indicated for Hartley to remove the goods.

The preacher gathered the trinkets while struggling to contain his own fury. The squaw might have the others fooled, but not him. He saw through her and her little tricks. She could not turn him aside this easily. After all he had been through to get this far, he would not give up until he got what he wanted. He would come back again and again until she was his. By God, nothing was going to stop him now.

*

Fragrant Grass awoke with a sense of dread. She could delay no longer. This day she must leave the isolation lodge.

Her miscarriage had saved her from the anguish of bearing a child for Sly Wolf. She had spent her days in the isolation lodge singing her thanks to Hawk Spirit for that miracle. Singing because her elation would not let her remain silent, would not let her regret the child who would never be. Now, however, joy gave way to dread as she steeled herself to face returning to her lodge, and Sly Wolf.

Though she was not obliged to, she paused outside her lodge and coughed to warn those inside of her coming. The moment she entered, Mint jumped up and ducked outside without a glance or a word. Sly Wolf settled unblinking eyes on her face. "Sit," he commanded, omitting any softening words such as "my wife" or even "woman."

She sat before him, shoving her trembling hands into her sleeves. "Explain the baby," he demanded.

"I, I did not know," she stammered.

His strong fingers grasped her forearm. "You lie."

"No, no, I —"

"Silence, woman! I want the truth. Explain why you thought you could hide your condition from me."

When she did not answer, Sly Wolf twisted her wrist until she winced. "Why did you go to the moon lodge when you had no need?"

Denial was useless. He knew. She saw it in his eyes.

He dragged her to him. "Everyone has heard you singing your happiness to Hawk Spirit. A woman who will not bear children for her husband does not deserve his protection." With that threat, he flung her away and prepared his pipe.

Secretly rubbing her wrist, she tried to sort out her options if he ordered her out of the lodge. By the time he drew his first puff, she decided that, difficult as it would be, she could survive on her own until Colter returned. The decision gave her the courage to glance at him. The cruel set to his mouth made her wish she had not looked.

"No, woman. Sending you away would not repay me for all the effort and trouble you have caused me. For that, I deserve a reward."

Fragrant Grass found it suddenly hard to breathe. As far as she knew, Black Cat from nearby Rooptahe had shown no further interest in her. What could Sly Wolf mean?

"Fetch the paleskin trader and Echo to me," he said. "Where you spend the rest of this day is of no concern to me as long as I do not have to look on you. You disgust me."

She hurried away from the lodge, throwing her silent pleas toward the clouds. *No, Hawk Spirit. Not the paleskin Hartley. No.*

8. *Eating Crow*

T wo days later, every crewman who could still walk joined in the last carry from the lower camp. By noon, the sun had baked the mud from the preceding days' rain into bruising ruts. Colter bent under his burden, too disillusioned to think beyond his next footfall.

He was hobbled from miles of portaging and did not reach the river bank opposite the end-of-portage camp on White Bear Island until dusk. Moments after he had slumped down to rest before proceeding to wade across to the camp, a familiar figure hailed him from the island. "About damn time, Old Man," Shannon said.

With Shannon off hunting the last ten days, Colter had put him and their bet out of his mind. Now that respite had ended. He had a debt to pay. Better get on with it. He stepped into the river and immediately lost his balance, falling onto his hands and knees in the swift, icy water.

"Don't you dare drown before I get my pay-off," Shannon yelled through cupped hands.

Colter picked himself out of the water, shifted his load for better balance and splashed to the island. Shannon greeted him with, "What? No smile for your friend?", but made no move to relieve him of his burden even though he had not carried a single load the entire portage.

Colter pushed past him and deposited his burden with the other baggage. Shannon shook his head at the heaps of bundles and boxes around them. "There are some compensations for being a hunter."

Colter was too done in to parry the remark with the scorn it deserved. "Let's get 'er over with," he said tiredly.

Shannon swept an arm toward the fire. "After you."

Barely half the porters had reached the camp. Most were too exhausted from the carry to walk the few steps from the baggage pile to the fire. The few who managed to get to the fire found meat aplenty, though chewing more than a bite or two was beyond the capacity of most of them. Colter trudged into the midst of these men and knelt stiffly in front of Shannon. He dragged in a deep breath. "You were right about the south fork and I was wrong . . . Shannon." To regain his feet, Colter had to push himself off the ground.

With a glance around at the crew, none of whom had paid the least attention to Colter's apology, the satisfied smile slipped off Shannon's face. "Nobody heard you. Do it again, louder."

"Nope."

Shannon grabbed his arm. "I said, do it again louder."

"Let go, Fuzz."

"Not until you do what I say."

"Bet's paid. Now let me eat."

He tried to skirt Shannon, but the younger mand caught him and threw him down. He banged his head on a rock in the fall. Sergeant Gass rushed over. "All right. What's the problem?"

"He tripped," Shannon lied, sounding contrite.

All Colter wanted was food and sleep, not more grief. "Cain't a body get some grub around here?"

The sergeant gave Shannon a withering look before walking away. When he was out of earshot, Shannon said, "You cheated me, Old Man. I expected better out of you."

Shannon's stubborn insistence hit Colter exactly wrong. Suddenly the prospect of the leaden days that stretched ahead drained him of all desire to eat, to breathe, to go on living. "Too bad," he muttered.

9. *Experiment*

S hannon learned the reason why Drouillard had gathered so many elk hides the morning after their return to White Bear Island. That discovery erased his indignation over leaving so much meat to rot, replacing it with a new level of respect for Captain Lewis's foresightedness. Among his early preparations for the expedition, the captain had designed a portable boat with a collapsible iron frame. The bull elk hides that Shannon and Drouillard had collected would be formed into a skin to fit over that frame.

He and Drouillard had collected the biggest portion of the twenty-eight hides gathered whereas thirty-two were needed. Once he understood the situation, he regretted that he had not applied himself more vigorously to the hunt. In recompense, he threw himself into the task of scraping the hair off the hides to prepare them for forming the cover for the boat frame.

Hide-scraping was boring work. His thoughts often turned to Colter and their bet. He felt cheated. The man's public apology had been totally inadequate. The idea was for Colter to be humiliated. But the crew had been too worn out to be their usual mocking selves. Their apathy had denied him his moment of vindication. That wasn't fair.

He was washing up at the river at dusk on July 5th, his mind on his indignation, when Rube approached him. "What's wrong with Colter, Peckerwood?"

Given his thoughts, Shannon had to choose his words carefully. "Didn't know anything was wrong."

"Better open your eyes then. Somethin's real wrong. He's been actin' right peculiar since the portage ended. For three days he was mad as one of them giant bears. No one'd go near him. Now it's like — well, you best take a look-see for yourself."

Shannon wanted nothing to do with Colter. "He and I aren't on speaking terms these days."

Rube gave him a long look. "That's too bad. Looks to me like talkin's what he needs. And you're about the only one he's likely to open up to."

As Rube wandered back to the fire, Shannon remembered the conversation he had had with Drouillard about his friendship with Colter. One thing in particular had been bothering him: How was it possible for a friendship to be based on bickering?

He glanced toward Colter. Because of the shadows cast by the fire and the angle of the man's face, he could not decipher Colter's expression. He didn't need to. The man's empty idle hands spoke volumes.

Those inactive hands decided Shannon to put aside questions of who was right and who was wrong and find out what was troubling Colter. He gathered himself to that purpose and walked over to his friend.

Colter did not look up when he plopped down. "Ordeal's sending me off to hunt tomorrow. Said I can choose my partner. Want to come along?" Shannon asked.

Colter kept staring at the ground.

"You need a break, Old Man. The routine's getting to you."

Colter gave no sign that he heard.

"You look sick. Want me to go tell Captain Clark you're ailing?" Shannon asked.

This drew a weary shake of the other man's head.

"Confound it, Old Man. What's wrong. Talk to me."

Colter's voice was nearly inaudible. "Nothin' to say. Nothin' to . . ." His words trailed off as if he had lost interest in what he had to say.

Shannon noticed that the soles of Colter's moccasins were worn through in at least three places. In all the time he had known the man, he had never known him to neglect his feet. "I'll fetch the captain."

Colter looked at him for the first time. "Don't."

The plea in his gaze stopped Shannon. "Then tell me what's wrong."

Colter's mouth worked for a time before any sound came out. "She — I — lied."

"You're not making sense. Who lied?"

Shannon had to strain to hear. "Me. I ain't goin' to get back to her in time."

Fragrant Grass. He should have guessed she was the issue. Fragrant Grass and the excessive importance Colter placed on keeping his word. "What do you mean? The worst is behind us. We've passed the falls now. Captain Lewis's boat'll be ready in a day or two, and we'll be on our way again, doing what a whole lot of other men have failed at: We're going to find the Northwest Passage. Think of it. We'll all be heroes!"

He paused to experience the thrill of his own words. "All we have to do is cross the mountains, and we're there. Imagine. The Western Sea. After that we turn around and head home. You'll be back to a certain pretty squaw in no time."

"Ain't goin' to be that easy."

"Of course it is. You aren't giving up on us, are you?"

The question was meant to provoke a response, and it worked. Colter's voice rose a notch. "We been travellin' three months, Fuzz. Three months without seein' another soul."

"That's good! The Teton Sioux were trouble enough. We don't need the Blackfeet or Atsinas mucking up our passage on this leg of the journey."

"We need Shoshones, though."

"Janey'll lead us to them," Shannon said, using the crew's nickname for Sacajawea.

The short spurt of energy deserted Colter. His shoulders slumped. "Ain't enough time."

"Poppycock! We have a good four months left to travel. Plenty of time to get to the Sea and back to the Mandans. So snap out of it."

Colter shook his head and fell silent. Shannon threw up his hands in frustration and got to his feet. Why bother? When the Old Man made up his mind, nothing could change it but the course of events. The captains had been right about everything so far. That was good enough for him. Soon enough Colter would see that for himself and snap out of his dejection. Until then, he would mind his own business.

The collapsible iron boat, *Experiment*, took four days to build with better than half that time spent trying to seal the seams between the hides used to cover the iron frame. When, after all their efforts, it floated, the crew cheered wildly. Colter did not join them. All told, they had spent twenty-three days at the Great Falls of the Missouri. Twenty-three long, frustrating days when all he could think about was the chance he had missed.

Ordway's low voice slashed across his train of thought. "You're looking peaked, Private. You catch some kind of strange disease rolling around in that squaw's filthy robes?"

After days of lethargy, a small spark of anger flared within Colter before he could check his response. "Only filth ever was in her robes was you, Sarge."

The last few words were whisked away by a tremendous blast of wind that swept down on the camp. The force of the blast tumbled Colter to his knees as a cloudburst deluged the island.

He scrambled into a copse of willows for shelter only to find Shannon already there. "Move over. Gimme some room!" He had to yell to be heard over the storm's fury.

Shannon looked primed to refuse but slid over. Colter crawled in and, for the next hour, the two sat side by side without talking or acknowledging each other's presence.

When the storm began to abate, Shannon nudged Colter. "I miss our arguments."

Colter looked sideways at Shannon. "You do, huh? Maybe that's 'cause you like to argue more'n anyone I ever seen."

"I don't like to argue. I need to. With you. How else am I ever going to learn anything?"

"That's some kind of bullroar you're shovelin' today, Fuzz. And I ain't in the mood for it."

"I'm not lying. I'm telling you God's own truth, Old Man. I miss having you bite me back. I can't know how you feel right now. I don't have anyone waiting for me downriver, but it's got to be hell to be way out here when she's back there."

The younger man's empathy disarmed Colter. He could not come up with a response before Shannon went on.

"But, for God's sake, Old Man, it's not the end of the world. You'll be with her soon enough. Snap out of it, will you? Hey! Where do you think you're going?"

"Away from you." Colter crawled out from the copse and hobbled into the tangle of woods beyond the camp. Neither Shannon nor anyone else on this infernal quest could ever understand how he felt, how important Fragrant Grass was to him, how trapped he felt not knowing when he would see her again. Not a blessed soul. He was all alone in his pain.

The storm took its time spending its fury. He limped into camp to find crewmen gathered on the banks of the river, gawking at Captain Lewis's iron boat. *Experiment* lay in the river, flooded to the gunwales, a victim of the storm. The seams between the elk hides — the ones that had given the crew so many problems — had failed. Repairing it meant more delay, more time lost.

"Haul her out and let's go to work!" Captain Clark ordered.

"No, Will," Lewis intervened. "We've wasted enough time. Some experiments never work. This was one of them. Better we build two more dugouts."

"Dugouts take trees, Meri and there aren't any, in case you haven't noticed," Clark said impatiently.

Shannon barged into the captains' conversation. "Sir, I know where there are trees south and west of here."

"Sure that's not northeast, Shannon?" McNeal jeered, bringing snickers from the crew.

Clark's glare cut off the ridicule. "You're sure about the location, Private?"

"Shannon, he is right," Drouillard said, stepping in. "South and west. A walk of eight miles *peut-être*. I see them, *aussi*. They are small, but they will do for dugouts."

"Sergeant Ordway, form a party. Shannon here will lead you," Clark asked.

Confidence restored, Shannon boomed, "Yes, sir."

It took six days to prepare two new dugouts, each barely three feet wide, and, after a month's delay at the Great Falls, the expedition again set off up the Missouri. Two days later, they entered a gorge whose sheer walls constricted the river into a deep channel. With no banks to walk on for towing and with the river too deep to consider wading, the crew had to resort to oars and setting-poles to propel their unstable craft forward.

Soaring mid-July temperatures combined with the swift current and a punishing headwind to quickly deplete the crew's energy. Colter was ready to drop when a shrill whistle echoed off the walls of the canyon, the signal for a rest stop. The spot chosen for the halt was a strip of rocks and sand cupped by a bend in the river. Opposite this little beach, the river surged against the base of a monolithic cliff, throwing up waves that danced with rainbows. Colter was too tired and down to care.

He slumped onto the first vacant spot of sand, grateful to have an immobile surface under him. Someone tossed a piece of cold roast venison into his lap. He stared at it, unable to find the will to lift it to his mouth. He shoved the meat aside and stretched out for a nap.

He had just drifted into sleep when the scrunch of sand announced he had company. He cracked open one eyelid to see Shannon looking gray and worried. Shannon fell onto his knees and said in a barely audible voice, "You have to help me, Colter."

That he had called him "Colter", not "Old Man" kept his slitted eye open. Shannon's right hand began to twitch. Fear strained his voice. "The river — I c-can't d-do it. I-I c-can't g-go on." He grabbed the twitching hand with his left and forced it down into his lap. "W-what am I g-going to d-do?" His voice was as close to a wail as a whisper could be.

Colter let his eye close again. "You're goin' to go on."

The sand rasped under Shannon's shifting weight. "This is no joke, Colter. I'm in real trouble."

"Ain't no joke, Fuzz," Colter said tiredly. "You got no choice. You got to go on."

"But I can't. Don't you see?"

The refrain acted like a needle piercing a tender membrane deep within Colter. Time to hand back to Shannon some of his own advice. He rolled up on one elbow. "Listen up, Fuzz, 'cause I'm only goin' to say this once. You can sit here and rot, or you can go on. Either way, I'll give you the same advice you give me back at White Bear Island: Snap out of it."

Shannon's head jerked back and his jaw tightened. "Well, I never!" He got up and moved away from Colter, kicking sand on the cold venison.

"Peckerwood, wake up!" Shannon clung to Rube's voice like a lifeline and struggled to free himself from the quicksand of the awful dream. "If you got to cry and carry on like a woman," Rube groused, "for Christ's sake, do it somewhere else so's the rest of us can get some shut-eye."

Shannon rolled onto his back, grateful to be in the crowded tent, free from the grip of the nightmare that hung like cobwebs on the fringes of his consciousness. In a few hours he would face another day in the canyon. The thought sent a chill up his spine and he drew his blanket more tightly around his body.

The farther they progressed upriver, the closer together the walls of the canyon grew and the deeper the water compressed between them. Yesterday they had abandoned the setting-poles and relied strictly on paddles for propulsion. With every stroke, he was forced to lean out over that mass of green swirling liquid where death waited impatiently to claim him. Every stroke eroded his courage and amplified his fear. He did not know how he made it through each day. Whenever they stopped for camp, he was the last to leave the dugout, staying put until he could trust the support of his quivering legs. As he grew weaker, he came to understand how fragile, how insignificant he was compared to the tenacious, expectant river. Would today be the day it claimed him?

Colter rolled over in his sleep, jabbing a knee into Shannon's thigh. The jab brought to mind their exchange of three days ago. *Snap out of it.* Coming from the one man he considered his best friend, the man he had turned to for consolation, the words still stung.

He crawled out of the tent. There would be no more sleep for him tonight.

10. *Searching for Shoshones*

"Oh, my Lord! Would you take a gander at that, Rube?" exclaimed Joe Field from the front of the dugout. "We're out of that God-awful gorge. The other boats're puttin' in up ahead. See, there. The captains're up the rise, checkin' things out."

Rube shaded his eyes against the glare of the water under the afternoon sun. "Let's hope they find us some horses. Ain't that right, Colter?"

From the stern, Colter stared at the figures of the captains on the hill who were scanning for the elusive Shoshones with their telescope. Since leaving Fort Mandan, the expedition had not encountered a single human being. It was as if God had given animals and birds supremacy over this wide, sprawling land and demoted humans to the level of passers-through or complete strangers.

Rube craned around. "Still not talkin', huh, Colter?"

"Lay off him, Rube, and get back to paddlin', or we'll miss the stop," Joe said.

A few minutes later they landed their dugout at the end of the line of expedition boats. Colter stayed beside the river for a time in order to study the broad valley that sloped away upstream. He did not like what he saw. The Missouri continued to flow south and east, splintering into many channels. All those channels meant more delays every time they had to search out the main one.

The two captains strode down the hill. A glance at their faces announced that they had not spotted any Shoshones.

"I'm taking a party ahead to scout for Indians. Any volunteers?" Clark asked.

Shannon's hand did not go up with the others. He sat with his forehead resting on his drawn-up knees. He never once looked up while the captain picked Joe Field, Potts and York for his party.

"Back to the boats!" Ordway yelled.

While the groaning, muttering crew picked themselves up and headed for the boats, Shannon stayed where he was. Before Ordway could jump on him, Colter hobbled over. "Come on, Fuzz. Time to leave."

No response.

"Fuzz?"

When Shannon finally looked up, his eyes were dull and he appeared to have aged ten years in a week. Bending stiffly, Colter held out his hand. "Come on."

Shannon stared at the hand before he accepted it with a weak grasp. Colter held on until he was sure Shannon could stand on his own.

"So tired," Shannon murmured.

The younger man's depleted condition stirred Colter's pity. "Yep, but you been hangin' on, ain't you?"

"Hangin' on," Shannon repeated in a weary voice, drained of all flavor.

Colter gave his arm an encouraging squeeze. "Good goin', Fuzz."

The words acted like a potion on Shannon. His stance steadied. His chin rose slowly and a bit of brightness began to return to his eyes. He looked at Colter as if he saw him for the first time. "You're right, Old Man. That *was* good going."

Captain Clark's group rejoined the main body three days later after failing to find Shoshones. Clark refused to give up and asked for another group of volunteers to make a second search. This time only three hands went up, a reflection of the crew's sinking morale. The captain quickly chose those three, Rube, Robert Frazer and Charbonneau, plus Joe who decided to go along with his brother, and off they went. In their wake, Captain Lewis shuffled the boat crews. In place of the two Fields, Colter drew Potts and McNeal.

He got down to the dugout to find the cook, who had done nothing more strenuous in the last four days than roasting some meat, bending Potts's ear unmercifully. Potts had been with Clark's first scouting party, and he was clearly tuckered out. He shot Colter a pleading glance.

"Give it a rest, McNeal," Colter said.

The cook went right on talking, never missing a beat

"I said, give it a rest," he repeated.

When the cook continued to ignore him, he caught McNeal's gesturing hand and stuck an oar in it. "You got the prow."

That got the cook's attention. "To hell with you, Colter. I'm sittin' where I always sit. In the middle."

"Nope. You're in the prow." Colter bent to untie the dugout's painter.

"I don't have to listen to you," McNeal fumed.

Colter slowly straightened up. "Oh, yes, you do. You got no choice. None. Ain't no other boat'll have you."

The cook's head, with its mantle of filthy matted hair, swiveled left and right, taking in the truth of Colter's statement.

"Ordeal put you in my boat, cook. So you cain't go cryin' to him, can you? I'd say you're stuck. Now get in or stay here, your choice."

McNeal uttered not a peep as he climbed into the canoe and settled in the prow.

The cook was still quiet, still in the prow two days later when the boats broke out of a swell of hills into a low-slung landscape of sage, grass, willows and wild rose bushes, scattered with cottonwoods. In short order, the Missouri split into two forks, then, a short way upstream, below a gray knob of limestone, the westernmost fork again split into two. The Mandans had said that Shoshones frequented this Three Forks area. However, the place proved as devoid of humans as everywhere else they had looked.

Ahead and on both sides of the river, the land stretched wide, rising to dark bands of timber that skirted rounded peaks dappled with lingering patches of snow. Colter's sharp eyes picked out signs of beaver and otter everywhere he looked. His trapper's instincts sprang to life.

However, the expedition needed two-legged, not four-legged, creatures, and they needed them soon. It was nearing the end of July and already there had been muttering among the crewmen about turning for home. A note from Captain Clark impaled on a stick thrust into the marshy ground saying that he and the scouts had gone up the western fork to investigate the source of some smoke did nothing to quell the crew's growing discontent. That night there was little idle conversation to break the tension of waiting for word from the scouting party.

It wasn't until the next afternoon that Clark and his band reappeared. At the sight of the limping captain being supported into camp, the crew's level of alarm surged. Before anyone could ask the key question, Clark answered it. "We didn't find them."

York took charge of his ailing master, and a grim-faced Captain Lewis gave orders to lay over the next two days before hurrying off to see about his co-leader. Colter watched Sacajawea struggle to lead her hobbling husband to the willow shelter she had built for her family. According to York, Three Forks was where Hidatsa raiders had stolen her from her Shoshone band and turned her into a slave. Yet, this place did not appear to affect her. He wondered why. Was it that she did not remember, or did she, as an Indian, attach no importance to places?

And what about Fragrant Grass? How would she react when he took her away from Matootonha?

While he pondered those questions, Rube and Joe joined the crew at the fire. With the captain and sergeants occupied elsewhere, the crew was free to talk as long as they kept the level of their conversation low.

"What're we facin' up yonder?" Potts asked.

Rube glanced around the ring of anxious faces. Colter had never seen him look so discouraged. "We got us one bitch of a pull. Channels goin' every which way, snakin' all over the country. No tellin' which one's the real Missouri."

"Any sign of the Shoshones?" someone else asked.

Joe answered with a weary "Nary a blessed one."

The crew sank into silence while they absorbed these two essential facts. McNeal's whining voice broke the spell. "Like I been sayin', why wear ourselves out tryin' to find the Indians? We ought to stay in one place. Wait for them to come to us."

The remark brought murmured jeers along with a couple of nods.

"West fork is Captain Clark's choice from here," Rube said. "Way she zigzags, we'll be pullin' four miles for every one we make south."

Shannon leaped up. "South? The mountains we have to cross are west, not south. Why keep on the river when we can cache the dugouts and walk?"

Among the murmurs of approval, Potts said quietly, "Shannon's right. We're wastin' precious time. I say we take a vote."

Colter got up to leave. "Where are you going, Old Man?" Shannon challenged.

"Away."

"What's your vote?" Potts asked.

"Ain't votin'," Colter said.

"What's that mean, Colter?" asked Rube.

"Means I'm followin' captains' orders."

He looked hard at Shannon before walking down to the river. He stalked along the bank until he no longer heard the crew's voices. He looked beyond the racing river to the patches of unmelted snow on the peaks in the distance, glowing with an eerie intensity in the fading light of the late afternoon. Where snow lingered late, it fell early — and deep. Such snow was bound to block them if they put off crossing the mountains much longer. If they got blocked, they would be forced to wait out the winter.

But where would they wait?

Not here. Not with those mountains so close. At the first sign of winter, the game that seemed so abundant now would head for lower ground. One man or two might have a chance to survive the winter here in this high valley. A crew of thirty-three, never. McNeal was dead wrong. They could not stay in one place. Not this late in the year. Whether west or south or back the way they came, they had to move.

Rocks crunched under someone's tread. He turned to see Shannon coming his way. He had only a moment to brace himself against the demands he was sure the younger man had come to make. Instead Shannon surprised him with, "Thanks, Old Man."

"What for?" Colter asked warily.

"For setting me straight back there. Don't know what got into me. No, that's wrong. I do know. I let my . . . my problem with water get in the way of good sense."

"'Twere a surprise to hear you goin' agin' the captains."

Shannon's voice fell. "It's this river. Times out there I think I'll lose my mind." There was no artifice in the gaze he turned to Colter. "It was my fear speaking. Not me."

"Happens."

"The crew can't agree. Thank God and John Colter for that. I never would have been able to deliver an ultimatum to Captain Lewis. What was I thinking?"

"Like you just said, you weren't thinkin'."

Shannon held out his hand. "Looks like you saved me again. Thanks."

"Don't say that no more, Fuzz. Don't. It be wearin' on me somethin' awful. It ain't natural you bein' so agreeable. Say somethin' contrary, or don't say nothin'. Argue. Tell me off. Get on your high horse. Do somethin', anythin' that proves the old Fuzz is still inside that there bag of skin of yourn."

Shannon drew back. "Damn it! Here I came to thank you and you act like I insulted you. Confound you, Colter, sometimes I'd like to punch you in the mouth."

Laughter erupted out of Colter, the first he had experienced in weeks.

The bafflement on Shannon's face made him laugh harder. Then Shannon started to chuckle.

Colter's laughter turned to guffaws and he clapped Shannon on the shoulder.

Shannon's chuckles grew into full-fledged laughter and he clapped Colter on the other shoulder. And there they stood, face to face, laughing until they were all laughed out.

All the laughter in Colter died as soon as the expedition left Three Forks. Rube's predictions about what they would encounter on the Jefferson fork proved painfully accurate. The river twisted and turned every which way so miles of walking every day yielded precious little forward progress. To add to that difficulty, thick brush along the banks and increasing numbers of shoals and rapids forced the crews to spend all day wading in the icy water.

When August 1st passed without any sign of Shoshones, the captains sent out yet another search party. Those men rejoined the crew on August 7th to report — no Shoshones. Talk among the crewmen shifted from speculation about *whether* the captains would turn back to *when*.

Then, on August 8, Sacajawea recognized a rock that resembled a swimming beaver as a landmark her people used in their yearly trips east to hunt buffalo, and Lewis announced he would make yet another attempt to hunt for the elusive Shoshones. He singled out Drouillard, Shields and McNeal to accompany him.

Shannon grumbled to Colter, "McNeal wouldn't recognize a Shoshone if he stepped on one. Be just like him to miss our only chance to make contact."

"If'n there's a two-legged female, Shoshone or not, anywhere about, McNeal'll find 'em all right," Colter said.

Shannon fell to brooding. When he spoke again, his voice was low and hesitant. "We're running out of river, Old Man. What if we don't find the Indians? What then?"

Colter glanced toward the captains' tent where the two leaders were deep in conversation. What were they talking about: trying to cross the mountains on foot or turning back?

"If we turn back, I'll have to go home," Shannon said. "I'll have to face Father. I'll . . ."

The events at the Great Falls had dashed all Colter's thoughts of turning back this year. Now a new tendril of hope began to sprout in their place. "Don't do no good to think such 'fore it happens." He spoke as much to himself as to Shannon. For all the good it did.

11. *Murderous Intent*

C olter splashed across the icy river and quickly discovered that his feet were in worse shape than he believed. "Damn it all," he muttered, cursing this latest stroke of rotten luck, coming just when he had been assigned to hunt, to get away from the boats for the first time in over a month. Shannon was waiting for him on the opposite bank. "I gotta go slow, Fuzz. Ain't no sense you waitin' on me all day. Let's split up."

Shannon stared at Colter as if waiting for more.

"You gone deaf? I said let's split up."

"I was waiting for the rest of it."

"Rest of what, damn it?" Colter snapped.

"For you to tell me not to get lost. Everyone else says it. Why not you?"

"Well, I ain't goin' to say it. Way you been traipsin' all over, you're bound to know your way 'round by now."

Shannon grinned, showing the gap in his front teeth. "Thanks for the vote of confidence. See you back at camp tonight, Old Man."

After he left, Colter took stock of the surrounding country. Willows and brush and an occasional low tree marked the wild serpentine course of the river. Standing in the middle of all that emptiness, he considered the enormous distance they had come, the remoteness of their position and the plentiful signs of high altitude that belied the low rise of the hills ringing the valley. If the captains were going to turn back, they'd better be doing it soon.

The notion of going back held him in its grip for many minutes before he headed off at an angle to Shannon to eliminate the possibility of mistaking his hunting partner for a deer. A quarter of a mile later he sensed something following him. He stopped to check but saw nothing. He shook his head ruefully. *I been on the river too long. My senses is playin' tricks on me.*

A mile beyond, he came across a fresh set of tracks. He squatted and examined the prints of two small deer. "Small's better'n nothin'," he muttered, rising to his feet.

Off to the left, a rifle boomed. A ball whizzed past his ear, and he dove for the dirt. After the shock cleared, it occurred to him that Shannon must have circled back and mistaken him for game.

He was on the verge of calling out when he checked himself. What if it wasn't Shannon? Could be another hunter. A Shoshone or . . .? He listened for the sounds that would confirm the shooter was coming to see what he downed.

If it were a Shoshone, he could try to make contact, or . . . or he could stay hidden and let the Indian go on about his way. After all, no one need know, especially if Captain Lewis's scouting party failed to find Indians and the captains opted for the only rational choice, which was to turn back.

The snapping sounds of something, or someone, moving through brush came from the direction of the shot. Colter scrambled into a crouch and caught a glimpse of something tan making for the river. As far as he could tell, there was only one creature, though whether two-legged or four-, he could not make out.

While he tried to decide whether to let go whatever or whoever it was or go after it, it occurred to him that, in this remote place, the Indians would not have guns. Which meant that the shot had to come from Shannon. After all the hunting he had done, Fuzz ought to know that you always checked up on where your shot had gone so you never wounded some critter and left it to die in agony.

Tonight he would set Fuzz straight on that matter. For right now, he had some hunting to do.

Goodrich had drawn cooking duties in McNeal's absence. He frowned at the small deer Colter brought in. "That's it?"

"Weren't much out there," Colter said. The regret in his voice stemmed from how quickly his day of freedom had passed rather than the sparseness of his take.

Goodrich heaved a sigh. "Well, it's better than nothing which is what all the others found." He eased the carcass off Colter's shoulders and set to skinning it out.

"Fuzz's back then?" Colter asked.

Without looking up from his work, Goodrich cocked his head toward the opposite side of camp. "Yonder."

Hobbling that direction, Colter nearly bumped into Ordway coming out of the sergeants' tent. The sergeant's eyes widened at the sight of him, and he turned and hurried away.

Shannon lay napping with his head atop his pack. "Right fine shootin', Fuzz," Colter said loudly, waking him.

Shannon cracked one eye open. "What shooting? I never got off one shot all day. Might as well have pulled the bloody boat for all I accomplished."

Colter scanned the younger man's face for any sign of a lie but found none. If the shot hadn't been Shannon's or an Indian's, then whose?

Shannon yawned. "Hope you did better. I'm hungrier'n a bull moose."

The words were only background noise to the roaring that filled Colter's ears as he stared toward the sergeants' tent and struggled to grasp a truth his mind did not want to hold.

Shannon shifted and squirmed, searching for a comfortable sitting position. The night was cold; too cold for the middle of August. Even so, his restlessness did not stem from the cold; rather from how long it was taking Captain Clark and the sergeants to retire to the captains' tent to discuss the day's progress. Why was it taking them so blasted long to eat?

He and the other crewmen huddled around three small fires of green willow that produced more smoke than heat. No one spoke. No one had to. The crew's discontent had finally come to a head. Tonight Rube and Joe would deliver the crew's ultimatum to the captain: Orders or not, this was as far up the Missouri as they intended to go.

Clark rose. Shannon tensed. For the first time in his life, he was about to go against his superiors, to become part of a mutiny, and he was flooded with doubt. Quitting now meant the end of his dream of returning home a hero. He would be just another of the scores of men who had tried — and failed — to find the Passage. Quitting also meant the end of his dream of a military career. He could never expect anyone to follow orders when he himself had chosen not to do so.

Instead of going to his tent, Clark came to stand next to Shannon. Afraid that the captain had read his thoughts, Shannon held himself still, staring at the ground, every nerve screwed tight with anxiety over what the captain wanted from him.

"You all know it's been six days since we heard from the scouting party," Clark said, addressing the whole crew. "Hard as it is, we have to assume that something has happened to them." He paused. "Meri wanted this expedition to succeed more than anything. It could be he gave his life to that end.

"Time grows short and we now have a difficult decision to make. If Meri were here, we could celebrate his 31st birthday in two days. However, it now appears that a memorial will be more fitting." The captain's right hand rose and fell disconsolately though his voice remained strong.

"The way the river's shoaling, we can't be far from the Missouri's headwaters. I know how tired you all are, how much frustration and hardship you have endured. For that and for your steadfastness, I thank you." He looked slowly around the gathering of crewmen, making eye contact with every one, ending with Shannon who felt the captain's gaze knifing to his soul.

"I thank you and I ask for one last sacrifice," Clark said. "I ask that you continue up to the river's source, as a tribute to our missing comrades. The decision is up to you, but whatever course you choose, by rights, ought to be unanimous."

He motioned the sergeants to follow him out of camp, giving the crew the freedom to talk openly. Rube was the first man to speak. "Whatever's happened to Captain Lewis's group could be waitin' for us. I say we turn around right now."

That brought a chorus of agreement from everyone except Colter and Shannon. "Cat got your tongue, Peckerwood?" Rube asked caustically.

Shannon started to flush under the scrutiny of the other men. What had been so clear this afternoon now seemed fraught with consequences beyond his reckoning. He needed time to think. Time the other men were in no mood to give him.

"Come on, Shannon. Where're your guts? Stand with us, or agin' us," Rube said, :but stand somewhere."

Shannon looked at Colter, hoping for some support. Instead the man's eyes and face were unreadable.

"Come on, Shannon! You're with us, or you're with Colter. Which is it?" Rube demanded.

Colter spit into the dirt. "Dividin' up way out here's just plain stupid. Ain't you all never heard of compromise? Captain's just lost his friend and we lost us some friends too. But you galoots is only thinkin' about your own miserable hides." He glared at Rube as if daring him to contradict. "Captain asked us to honor Captain Lewis. In my book there ain't no man deserves honorin' more. What do you say, Rube?"

Under Colter's withering gaze, some of the obstinacy left Rube's face. "Captain's birthday is in two days. How about we go ahead till then?" When no one answered him, Rube's tone turned hostile. "All right, what if I say it like this? Anyone with a different idea best speak up now."

No one spoke. "Okay, it's agreed. I'll go tell the captain."

Colter wasn't done. "What if we come across some of Janey's folks 'fore then? You still goin' to stop in two days?"

The dark flush mottling Rube's cheeks was visible even in the dim light of the weak fire. Combined with Colter's stubbornness, the sight prompted Shannon to end his silence. "Or what if we find Captain Lewis and the others?"

"Hell'll freeze over first," someone muttered, earning angry glares for both Rube and Colter.

"Two more days and we turn back," Rube said. "Unless we find Captain Lewis or some Shoshones, in which case we keep going. Does that cover it for you, Colter?"

Colter nodded.

"Shannon?"

Shannon hesitated. He wanted to ask what would happen if Lewis had not found the Shoshones, but one look at Colter warned him that this was not the time for more questions. He nodded.

Rube turned to the group. "Time to vote. If you go along with what I said, raise your right hand."

Shannon watched hands go up around the campfire, and it occurred to him that the scouting party could just be lost. Didn't the other men understand that, if they turned downriver in two days, they might be abandoning their comrades in this hostile, unforgiving land? How could he live with himself if he voted for such a possibility?

"Shannon?" Rube demanded.

With two dozen pairs of eyes drilling into his body, he had to make a decision. Reluctantly, he raised his right hand.

The lines on Rube's face eased. "Good. It's settled. Little Brother, go fetch the captain."

While they waited for Clark to return, Shannon could not stay still. He had voted with the other men, but the longer he sat there, the less certain he felt about his choice. This new country devoured time and men, yet in a mere two days they might be leaving to a certain death one of the finest leaders he had ever known. He was about to voice his uncertainty to Colter when Clark and the sergeants reappeared.

Rube relayed the crew's offer to the captain. Clark listened intently, then turned to the crew. "Two days it is. Thank you." He turned to walk to his tent.

Shannon got up to follow, but Colter restrained him. "No, Fuzz. Let 'er be."

When Shannon protested and tried to pull away, Colter pulled him back to the ground. "Now you listen and you listen good. You voted with the rest of us, and the captain got the unanimous answer he was askin' for. That's the end of it. I ain't goin' to let you go off half-cocked. Captain don't need that. And you don't need that."

Shannon saw Colter's point. Like it or not, he was one of the crew. Like it or not, he had voted with them. He ceased struggling. Colter released him. He studied Shannon for a moment. "I take back what I said awhile back. You *are* learnin'."

For the next two days, the crews struggled upriver, walking five miles of river for every one mile of forward progress, hauling the loaded dugouts over dozens of shoals in water so cold it numbed their limbs and their minds. The tribulations compounded Shannon's equivocation over turning back. Whenever he glanced up, he prayed to see Captain Lewis and the scouting party, or a band of Shoshones — anything human instead of the yawning expanse of scrub-covered country that lay in wait to swallow the rest of the expedition if they gave it the chance. However his prayers went unanswered.

The morning of August 17 dawned clear. The mountains ringing the plain through which they travelled stood sharp-edged against a cornflower blue sky. The good weather bolstered the crew's spirits, already heightened by the prospect of heading downriver the next day.

Shannon tolerated the laughter and horseplay of the other crewmen of his dugout until a playful push from Potts sent him sprawling face-first into the shallow water. He surged out of the river and threw himself at the prankster, but Potts pinned his arms before he could land a punch. "Whoa there, Shannon. I was just funnin' you. Where's your sense of humor? Hell, we be headin' home tomorrow."

Realizing he had overreacted, Shannon said, "I got to piss."

"Go on then. The rest of us can use a breather," Potts said.

Shannon pushed his way into the brush until he was well away from the others. As far as the eye could see, sagebrush swayed in the wind, the only moving shapes. No Captain Lewis, no Drouillard, no Shoshones. Nothing.

Sadness replaced his anger. After coming so far and enduring so much, tomorrow they would turn back, and there was nothing he could do about it. Only God had the power to change reality.

He lifted his face to the sky. "Dear God, I don't want. . ." No, he would not whine to God. Not when Captain Lewis and the three men with him needed all the Divine help they could get. He started over. "Dear God, Captain Lewis is a fine man. Please watch over him wherever he is. And help me to accept whatever comes. Amen."

He kept his eyes shut until his edginess began to subside. Then an unfamiliar sound made him strain to hear a repetition.

Something moved in the distance. Something besides sagebrush. As he stared at it, that something became figures, became men on horses. Men with headdresses, galloping toward the river!

He jammed fingers into his mouth to whistle an alert to the men back on the river when something familiar about the lead rider stopped him. He tensed, waiting for the group to draw closer.

It was Drouillard! He whooped before it occurred to him to wonder why the half-breed had on an Indian feather bonnet. The answer that popped to mind dried up his spit.

He had to swallow three times before he could whistle. Then he turned tail and raced back to the dugout.

12. *Miracle!*

S hannon's whistle threw the dugout crews into chaos. Colter dropped the towrope and dived for cover. A moment later Shannon crashed through the brush yelling, "Drouillard! Indians! Attack!"

Ordway grabbed Shannon. "Drouillard?"

"In headdress," Shannon gasped.

"A headdress? Captain!" Ordway yelled.

Clark splashed over and, after a quick conference with Ordway, he directed the crew into defensive positions with the warning against firing a shot without his explicit command.

Sweat from the day's summer heat and the tension of waiting trickled into Colter's eyes. He had to blink constantly to keep his vision clear. Every time he closed his eyes, images from last night's dream returned. Blurred images of Fragrant Grass that made him believe something had happened to her, that she needed him. The dream swept away his long-held resistance to thinking about turning back. He had to get back to her. Now.

"Here they come," the captain said in a collected voice. "Remember: shoot only on my command."

Colter's ears picked up the beat of horses' hooves moments before the riders burst out of the brush. Drouillard was in the lead on a rangy roan. He wore a feathered headdress and fringed deerskin leggings. His companions were all Indians, riding sleek, well-tended horses.

"These Shoshones, they do not believe you are not Blackfeet out to trick them," Drouillard explained. "This feather bonnet they make me wear to make from me a target."

"Thank God you're safe," Clark said. "Where's Meri?"

Drouillard motioned up the river. "The capitaine and the others, they wait for us beyond."

Shoshones. Captain Lewis. Colter struggled to take in the facts. The impossible had happened. The missing Shoshones had been found. Tomorrow the crew would be going on, not heading back. For the second time the seeds of hope of a quick return to the Mandans had been ripped from the soil of his heart before they had the chance to flower.

He was blind to the scene playing out before him until Sacajawea began to hop up and down, sucking her fingers and jabbering excitedly in Hidatsa. Drouillard turned to the astonished captain. "She say these are her people. People she ate with."

"You mean, her band?" Clark asked incredulously.

When Drouillard nodded, the captain shouted, "By God, it's a miracle!"

There was a long pause while the information sank in, then the cheering began with Shannon's cheers loudest of all. Colter could not speak. He was overcome by the same feeling he had experienced with the old Sioux back when he was tracking the lost Shannon. The feeling that some force was at work in his life. A force beyond his comprehension or power to resist was pulling him ever westward, clearing away each and every obstacle that barred his way toward that goal.

"The sergeants will post a guard here," Clark announced. "The rest of us will go meet our saviors." He clapped his hands. "Come on, men. Let's get moving. We've got the Passage to find!"

The men gathered their things and started to move to the dugouts. Colter walked through a daze until Ordway planted himself in his path. "You weren't cheering, Colter. Since you haven't run off before now, maybe this'll change your mind."

Colter looked the sergeant square in the eye. "Was that what you was plannin' on tellin' the captains after you shot me: that I'd run off?"

Ordway's expression shifted, but he covered the change with a snarl. "It's written all over your face, Colter. You were counting on going back. Only, there's no going back. Not now. Now instead of that little squaw, there're two things you can look forward to every day: me and the worst duties I can scrounge up to give you."

"Only a fool counts on anythin' out here, Sarge."

Clark's hail curtailed their exchange. "I'm not finished with you, Colter. Not by a long shot," Ordway said, hurrying off to join the captain.

Colter watched him go. There was only one thing that could make a man so hateful. That thing was fear. Fear that something he did not want others to know — some dark secret — would be uncovered and that he would be reviled for it. "Whatever you're hidin', Sarge, I'm goin' to find it and I'm goin' to let everyone know about it. Hell or high water, that there's a promise."

The expedition found Captain Lewis, Shields, McNeal, and the rest of the Shoshone hunting party a few miles upriver. Lewis met them wearing a tippet made from ermine skins. The captains shared an emotional reunion, then began the drawn-out process of meeting the chiefs and other important men of the Shoshone band. Lewis spoke in English to Labiche who translated into French for Charbonneau who relayed the information to Sacajawea in Hidatsa, leaving her to speak to the Shoshones in their tongue.

Shannon paid close attention to the proceedings in order to be able to make sketches when he could get to his journal later on. The emotions playing across Sacajawea's face particularly absorbed him. He had never seen her so animated, so happy. Then again, it wasn't everyday a woman got reunited with people she thought were lost to her forever.

In the midst of relaying a bit of translation, Sacajawea suddenly broke into a wail and tossed her blanket over the head of the Shoshone Chief Cameahwait.

"What's going on here?" the astonished Lewis demanded. "Charbonneau? Labiche?"

Charbonneau tried to pull his wife away from the chief, but she resisted, tracing frantic signs to accompany her choked words. Drouillard answered the question. "This man is her brother."

"Her brother?" gasped Clark.

The Shoshone chief lost his reserve and embraced his sister, sharing her tears. Shannon was awestruck. First they had found Shoshones just hours before the expedition was to turn downriver. Then the Shoshones they found turned out to be Janey's own band. Now they discovered that the band's leader was her brother. No rational person could attribute such amazing coincidences to mere luck.

It took some time before the captains recovered their equilibrium enough to continue. "According to Cameahwait and the elders, there are two ways to cross the mountains," Lewis said. "First is a trail completely lacking in game that the Pierced-Nose Indians use when they come east to hunt buffalo. Second is a river north of their main village. Both lie over that saddle." He swept an arm to show the way. "They say that river joins a bigger one further to the west and leads out to what they call the stinking water. An apt way to describe the ocean, don't you think, Will?"

Clark returned Lewis's grin. "We'd best check out the river right away."

Shannon thrust his hand into the air with all the passion of a man whose most cherished dream was only a step away from coming true. The Passage was just over the ridge — he was sure he could smell ocean brine on the wind.

Clark quickly called out five names for the scouting party, picking Colter, but not Shannon. Shannon turned slowly away. He had battled the river, blisters, mosquitos, hunger, pox and hydrophobia — for what? To be denied the chance to discover the Passage? To see Colter waltz into the history books? Colter who openly questioned the existence of the Passage when he himself believed in it with all his heart and always had?

He did not need to ask why this was happening. He knew why. Since way back at Clarksville, Captain Clark had held a grudge against him. And nothing he had done — none of the sacrifices or extra duties he had taken on — nothing had changed the captain's opinion of him.

The injustice of the situation was more than he could abide. He found Colter sitting in one of the dugouts, elbows resting on his knees, chin resting on his hands. "Why d'you bother?" Shannon demanded.

Colter looked up. "You talkin' to me?"

"Don't play dumb, Old Man. Admit it. You stuck up your hand back there out of orneriness, so I wouldn't get picked."

"If'n you want to go so much, ask Captain. It don't matter to me one way or t'other whether I go."

In the face of Colter's indifference, the steam went out of Shannon's argument. "What's the use? Captain never has liked me. I've come all this way for nothing."

"What on earth are you moanin' about?" Colter asked irritably.

"The Passage. My dream."

Colter slowly shook his head. "One river don't make no Passage. Nor one mountain pass. Nor one portage. Besides, we ain't discovered nothin'. Body can't find somethin' what ain't lost. Indians're all over this here country, in case you ain't noticed. They know where they are. It's us who been wanderin' around confused."

Shannon knew his lower lip was trembling, but he forged on. "All this way I've dreamed of discovering the Passage. Every stretch of deep water, every time I froze up." His voice cracked. "That dream's what pulled me through. And just when that dream's about to come true," he reached up as if to pluck a handful of air, "it gets snatched out of my hands. This whole trip was for nothing. I'm a failure."

Colter looked into Shannon's eyes. "A failure would'a quit back at Camp Wood. A failure would'a never stood agin' the crew. You done so twice since the Mandans, and both times you was right."

"If I can't be there to find the Passage, it was all for nothing," Shannon insisted.

Colter stood up and jammed his hands in his pockets. "Durn it all, Fuzz! Get it through your thick skull: this here route ain't no Passage. Not unless someone figures out how to chop off a couple thousand feet of them Shining Mountains and straighten all the kinks out of this here river. Unless they do, this route ain't no good to no one 'ceptin' the curious. Besides, we ain't discoverin' nothin'. We're out here stumblin' around like fools when we ought to be home raisin' families."

"There you go again, telling me how stubborn I am. I got news for you, Old Man. You're as stubborn as they come. For all this means to you, you should've stayed back at the Mandans."

"You got that right, Fuzz," Colter said.

Shannon heard the despair in the man's voice, but he shrugged it off. Since Colter had not tried to hear him out, he would hand him that same favor in return.

Rube cut into Shannon's brooding. "Hope we find us a few deer. I'm so hungry, hell, you're startin' to look tasty. 'Sides, Captain sure could use the help."

Shannon held his peace. Talking about food aggravated the hollow ache in his stomach. Talking about Captain Lewis reminded him that the captain had given to the Shoshones the only game the expedition hunters had bagged since leaving the Missouri. Although he understood intellectually that the captain was trying to overcome the Indians' reluctance to part with their horses, that did not help his stomach feel any less empty.

"Still not talkin', huh?" Rube said. "You and Colter fight again? I swear you two are worse than my ma and pa for argu. . ." He interrupted himself and signaled for Shannon's silence. Pointing to a thicket ahead, he mouthed "Mine" and crept toward it with his rifle positioned for a quick shot.

Shannon watched him without interest. While he was stuck behind with the main part of the expedition, Colter was off with Captain Clark discovering the last piece of the route joining the Mississippi with the Western Sea, the water link that was the Northwest Passage. True, he too would see that river, but he would not be the first. Only the first counted. No one cared who came in second.

Rube's rifle boomed. "Got him!"

Shannon heaved a sigh and trudged to help. The fallen deer was so scrawny that it was hardly worth the effort or the powder to kill it.

The two men took turns carrying the carcass the seven miles back to where Lewis and the others were still camped with Cameahwait and the Shoshone hunting party. When they arrived, hungry Indians mobbed them until Lewis stepped in. "Keep one hindquarter for the crew and give the rest to our benefactors."

Shannon stared incredulously at the captain. What was the man thinking? There were twenty-one crewmen in camp. Twenty-one hungry crewmen. One hindquarter would barely flavor the water to make enough soup to feed that many men.

The Indians pounced on their portion of the animal, ripping meat from the bones in a frenzy and cramming it into their mouths raw. Shannon watched in horror. If they were so hungry, why did they choose to live in this barren mountain fastness? Then again, they owned horses and horses were edible, so why didn't they eat them?

One of the Shoshones yelped and thrust a bloody hand into the air. In it was the deer's heart. With another cry, the man sank his teeth into the purplish, dripping mass.

Shannon stumbled away. Suddenly, he had lost his appetite.

The Indians were right about the river route west. That river, which Clark named Lewis's River, was much too wild and turbulent to be passable. That left the expedition one option for crossing the mountains: the route the Shoshones called The Hungry Trail of the Pierced-Nose People. For that, the crew had to have horses. That news was contained in the note from Clark to Lewis that Colter was carrying back to the Shoshone village located on the Lemhi River.

Once he got used to the peculiar hitching gait of the horse he was riding, he found himself thinking about Blaze and Zoob and Stuart's Draft, of Ma and Pa and the farm. One after another, old memories played across the field of his mind. Their images overlaid the passing countryside like wisps of smoke blown across a window.

With the images came a vague longing. Over the course of the day, that longing grew more specific, eventually turning into a feeling that he was adrift, belonging nowhere, heading toward some unknown destination, driven forward by a series of near-misses and coincidences. In this state he was unaware of the shadow crossing the sun or of Toby, his Shoshone guide, reining to a stop until the motion of his own horse ceased.

The Shoshone pointed to a lightning-struck pine across the foaming river. A magnificent hawk was on the topmost blackened limb. The bird leaped skyward, swooped low over the water, rose into the clear air beyond the two men, then screamed, wheeled, and dipped so close to Colter that he could make out the individual ribs in the feathers of the bird's outstretched wings. Using the air currents, the hawk swung three tight circles over the river, rising higher with each one. On the last turn, it sang out its triumph in three bursts and soared away over the western ridge of the mountains.

Toby spoke then, accompanying the Shoshone words with signs. He pointed to Colter's temple. "Your brother comes to guide you. Three times he blesses you with his shadow. Three times he calls out for you to follow."

After Toby kicked his horse into motion, Colter did not follow immediately. Here was yet another sign of the force that was directing him ever westward, but directing him toward what? When he had stumbled onto the old Sioux warrior in the abandoned camp during his hunt for the lost Shannon, he felt — no, he *knew* — that the old one had been waiting for him. The moment his eyes met Fragrant Grass's across the water that separated *Discovery* from that Missouri island, he knew she too was waiting for him. Now the appearance of yet another hawk, guiding him over the mountains. No matter how much he wanted to be back with Fragrant Grass, no matter how disturbing the dreams about her, the signs continued to lead him on. Willing or not, with or without understanding why, he must continue what he had begun.

Captain Lewis scanned the scrawled words on the note that Colter handed him. For a fraction of a second, deep lines scored the usually determined smoothness of his face, giving Colter a rare glimpse of the physical toll the expedition was taking on its leader. "If you are a praying man, Colter, you might ask the Almighty to intervene," Lewis said softly. "These Shoshones know we are desperate for their horses and their prices are climbing. I just hope that some brave does not start asking for rifles and ammunition." His hand swept a despairing gesture. "If we are to take the trail, not the river, we will need more than the fifteen horses we have now. Probably thirty. I'd best get started."

No sooner had the captain walked away than Shannon took his place. "Tell me about the Passage, Old Man. I have to know." His tone echoed the network of tension lines around his mouth.

"Indians was right, Fuzz. The river ain't it. A dugout wouldn't last two minutes in them rapids."

Shannon blinked slowly as if coming out of a dream. "So you didn't find the Passage. There's still a chance."

"If you call the worst trail you ever seen a chance, then yep."

"The Passage." Shannon spoke the phrase with awe.

The young Shoshone lad who had been shadowing Colter since he arrived at the village the previous day joined them. He carried the thick piece of pine that Colter had been shaping while he waited for Captain Lewis and the main party to cross the pass and move down to the permanent Shoshone village on the Lemhi.

"What's that?" Shannon asked disinterestedly. "You haven't carved since the Great Falls. What made you start again?"

Colter was unprepared to discuss the realization the appearance of that hawk yesterday had prompted, but he had to say something or put up with Shannon's endless pestering. "'Cause you ain't seen me whittlin', don't mean I ain't been doin' some."

"You've come back to yourself, Old Man," Shannon said.

"Back? I ain't gone nowheres," he challenged.

"Since we buried that last cache at Great Falls, you've been as low as I've ever seen you. I haven't had a decent argument with you till . . . till now." Shannon ruffled the Shoshone boy's hair. "Who's your friend here?"

"Not Looks Away. Fittin' name, that. I ain't made a move the last two days without him followin'. He's partial to my whittlin'."

Shannon's stomach growled. "Lord, I'm hungry! Captain Lewis better be planning on letting us eat one of the horses he traded for. He's been giving the Indians all the meat the hunters have brought in."

"You wouldn't be sayin' such if'n you'd had to do any carryin' back at the Falls. Horses are more precious than gold. They ain't for eatin'. Not if we're headin' out on that there trail."

"I did my share at the Falls, Old Man," Shannon shot back.

"Huntin' ain't work. Not like carryin'."

"It is too work. Hard work."

Colter snorted. "You ain't seen hard work till we start haulin' everythin' over them mountains yonder."

"Nothing's worse than getting into that dugout every damn day."

"You don't know how bad it can get, Fuzz."

"And you do, right?"

"Yep."

"Seems to me you think you know everything, Old Man."

"I know some things."

"What? Only some?" Shannon scoffed.

"Don't know why you're so het up, or why we're even talkin'." He motioned at the Shoshone boy. "Come on, young'un. Let's go 'fore Fuzz here splits a gut." He led the boy away, ignoring Shannon's demands to "come back here and have this out right now."

The haggling over horses stretched through two days, then three, then four. Colter passed the time at a spot next to the river, working on his new carving. Not Looks Away stayed by his side during that time, silently o b-serving every gouge and cut. Whenever Colter got up to stretch his legs, he gave the boy the piece to hold. It pleased him to watch Not Looks Away run his stubby fingers over the surfaces and angles of the wooden horse as if memorizing them.

Toward noon on the fourth day of trading, the boy was called away by one of the Shoshones bargaining with Lewis. It was the first time the youngster had left his side voluntarily and Colter was curious to know the reason. The lad scampered off to the field where the Shoshones kept their large horse herd and returned minutes later leading a handsome black gelding. Captain Lewis came forward and took charge of the horse.

Twenty-two, Colter thought, upping his mental tally of horses the captain had procured, eight less than the number the expedition needed to cross the mountains. He looked to the sky. August had just two more days to run. How much longer did they dare linger, trying to get more horses? More critical, how much longer would the Shoshones be willing to put off heading east for their autumn buffalo hunt, taking their horses with them?

He smoothed the last rough spot on the horse's mane to finish the carv-ing just before the boy rejoined him. He handed him the piece and began to whet his knife. The boy studied the carving, then reverently placed it on the ground next to Colter and ran off.

Moments later, Captain Lewis left the trading circle and came to where Colter was seated. The captain rolled his cramped shoulders and stared across the river at the heavily-timbered slope on the other side. Twice his hand strayed up to swipe his brow, then dropped back to his side as if it acted on its own separate instruction. After a long silence, Colter ventured, "Tradin's hard work. Anythin' I can do to help, Captain?"

"Not unless you can come up with eight more horses." Lewis's voice was heavy with discouragement. Absentmindedly, he picked up the carv-ing. "I see you have put your time to good use, Colter."

Seeing the captain holding the horse figure gave Colter an idea. "There more horses where that last black one come from?"

"Wolf Nose has the biggest string and the best horses from what I have seen, but that was the only one he would trade. In the process he also ma n-aged to double the prices the Shoshones are asking."

At the bitter edge in the captain's voice, Colter forged ahead. "If'n them's the horses you want, Captain, you're holdin' the way to get 'em." He explained about Not Looks Away's interest in the carving. "Wolf Nose is the young'un's pa and 'less I miss my guess, the lad's gone off to get ol' Wolf Nose to trade for it."

The captain ran his hand along the flanks of the wooden horse. "I'm wil-ling to try anything, Colter. Wish me luck."

Shannon had just finished his sketch of the Shoshone traders when Captain Lewis returned to the circle bearing Colter's carving. It took less than ten minutes of haggling for the captain to wangle four more sleek horses from the wily Wolf Nose in exchange for the carving. Shannon watched with growing resentment as the Shoshone handed the wooden figure to his son, the youngster who had taken such a liking to Colter. The lad whooped with delight and ran to show off his treasure to the other Shoshone children.

Shannon's envy expanded even more to see the warmth of the thanks Colter got from the captain for his contribution to the expedition's cause. He fumbled at the pages of his journal until he found the one he wanted. He ripped it out and took it to the captain.

"What's this, Shannon?" Lewis asked.

Shannon withheld his answer. He wanted the captain to recognize the man in the drawing without prompting.

"Cameahwait, of course. An excellent likeness," the captain said.

"Perhaps you can use it for the trading, sir?" Shannon said. "It ought to bring four more horses, Or even five." He made no effort to hide his pride.

"We shall see," the captain said, turning back to the circle.

The ensuing bargaining took the better part of an hour and yielded three horses from Cameahwait himself, bringing the expedition's total herd to twenty-nine. Despite the captain's thanks, Shannon was disappointed that his offering had not bettered Colter's. He was not up to conversation when Colter sidled over. "Good job, Fuzz. That there's the best picture I seen you draw yet."

"It was worth more. Captain didn't try hard enough."

"Captain's 'bout worn to a nub. Ain't many could do what he's done with what little we got to trade."

"He should have pushed for five horses. That picture was worth at least that."

Colter cocked an eyebrow. "That all you care about: bestin' me?"

"That has nothing to do with how I feel," Shannon lied.

"It don't, huh?"

"This is about what's right and fair."

"This here weren't no contest. This was about gettin' the horses we need and we got 'em. If'n you had any sense, you'd know that."

"I didn't ask for your opinion, Colter."

"You got 'er anyways. I oughtta charge you for it. Only, that won't do no good, seein' as how you still owe me for the whore."

"She wasn't —" Shannon nearly choked, swallowing the rest of the sentence. Colter was doing it again. Goading him into behaving like he was the know-nothing he had been back at the start of the expedition. If he were going to see this journey through to the end, he had to keep control over his temper. Starting now, he would do exactly that. "I'll pay you the minute I have any money to hand."

"Sure you will," Colter said. "And ice don't melt in hell."

13. *The Hungry Trail of the Pierced-Nose People*

T he expedition left Cameahwait's village the next day to head north to
join the Nez Perce trail which would, they hoped, lead them through
the mountains to the west. The Shoshones called the mountains the Bitterroots after the plants they harvested for food. The Shoshones again sent
Toby along to guide them. Now that the chance to discover the Passage
had been restored to him, Shannon was determined not to miss any opportunities to distinguish himself during this momentous mountain crossing and have his name go down in the history books. To that end, he resolved to stay as close to Captain Lewis as possible.

The gray packhorse assigned to him had different ideas, however. The
horse tested him at every opportunity that first day. By the time the crew
halted for the night, he was worn out. He slept deeply and awoke stiff and
sore, not at all eager for a second long day spent grappling with the willful
packhorse while scrambling to hold his position at the front of the line of
march.

After breakfast, Toby struck off straight upslope. At the top, he immediately headed down into a deep valley, across a sizable creek and up the
other side, scaling a hillside so thickly wooded that Shannon and the others
at the front were forced to hack a trail for those following. The effort
sapped his reserves of energy, and he began to lag behind the leaders despite his best efforts to keep up. He was relieved when the captains
stopped to consult with their Shoshone guide. The slow process of translation gave him time to rest before pressing onward. He was not so relieved
when he heard that there was a series of marshes in their path up ahead.
The wind had a wintry bite to it and slopping around in muck was the last
thing he needed or wanted.

The column began to move out before Shannon was ready. Rube took the
forward position, forcing him into second place. For a change, the gray
horse seemed content to follow and let him concentrate on keeping his
place in the line of march.

He had not gone far when the ground grew spongy, then boggy. With so
much water to support it, the brush had grown so thick that it blocked his
view of Toby and Rube in the lead. He did not want to risk getting lost and
pressed forward only to find himself shin-deep in ooze. The gray chose
that opportunity to plant itself. "Confound your bloody hide!" Shannon
yelled, yanking at the lead so hard that he pulled it out of his own grasp.

Free of Shannon's restraint, the gray sloshed after Toby and Rube, leaving Shannon to figure out how to extricate himself from the mire. Pushing
against the slushy mess, he slogged along in pursuit.

The first bog gave way to a second, then a third, then so many more that he
lost count. The gray led him through each one, keeping well out of his reach.

The chain of bogs came to an end at the foot of a steep slope. The morning's mist had long since turned to rain, and the rain had soaked Shannon
through, turning the slope dangerously slippery. Lunging up the incline,

the gray immediately began to struggle for footing. Shannon managed to catch up to the horse and reclaim the lead rope. "No more out of you. Hear?"

The horse found its stance and allowed Shannon to lead on. The higher they climbed, the steeper the incline. Finally, Shannon was forced to drop the rope so he could use his hands to help him climb. The feistiness seemed to have gone out of the gray. It followed docilely along behind him.

At one point, Shannon stopped to catch his breath. Toby and Rube were making their sliding way up the slope that stretched above as far as he could see while the rest of the crewmen and horses were strung out to the edge of the farthest bog. Suddenly the rain-soaked earth gave way beneath the hooves of his packhorse. The frightened animal plunged sideways in a desperate attempt to keep its balance, causing more of the unstable soil to peel away. The horses' legs went out from under it and it began to slide down the hill, neighing in terror.

Shannon made a wild swipe for the trailing lead rope and dislodged the rock he was standing on. The next thing he knew, he, too, was sliding down the grade after the gray horse.

With the crew's shouts of "Falling!" "Watch out!" "Move off!" ringing off the surrounding hills, Shannon clawed at the gooey earth, trying to arrest his fall. His efforts only served to rotate his body so he was sliding head first. Mud flew up into his face, blinding him. He did not see the rock outcrop until he bounced over it. The change in momentum pulled his legs around so his body was across the incline but did little to slacken the pace of his slide.

Then his legs collided with something — he supposed it was a clump of brush or perhaps another outcrop of rock — that slowed his descent, allowing him to gain purchase on a trailing vine. His grasp and the vine held and he slid to a stop with his heart beating a tattoo against the walls of his chest.

"Gol-durn, Fuzz. Watch where you're goin'. You like to took us all out."

Shannon shook enough of the mud off of his face to see Colter standing just uphill from him, covered from forehead to toenails with mud and bits of vegetation. "Was it you I hit?"

"Somebody had to get in your way or you'd be down in yonder gully with your horse."

Shannon groaned with the effort to move.

"Them legs goin' to hold you?" Colter asked, offering him a hand up. "If'n they will, we best be headin' back up. Got us a far piece to climb yet."

"What about my horse?" Shannon asked. "We can't just leave it and the load."

Colter glanced down the steep slope into the remote ravine where the gray had ended up. "It'd take us all day to get down there and back. It's for the captains to say now what we oughtta do about that there critter."

Shannon looked down the ravine. The horse's frantic cries tore at his heart.

What if it had broken a leg? How could he leave it to suffer after what had happened Lump?

"Won't do no good to fret. It ain't your decision, Fuzz. It's the captains'. Come on 'fore we get left." Colter struck off up the hill.

Shannon gave one last look down the ravine. "Don't let it suffer, God. Please." Then he started to climb after Colter on trembling legs.

The captains decided the load packed on the lost horse was too critical to abandon. Over Shannon's protests, they chose Colter and McNeal to go back after the supplies and to rescue the horse if they could.

The march of the previous three days had wrung all the bitching out of McNeal. He lagged behind from the start which suited Colter just fine. The cook also refused to go down into the ravine once they reached it. Colter didn't object. Dealing with the situation would be easier without the cook's ineptness.

Leading his nervous packhorse, he started the precarious descent into the ravine, picking each step carefully and making sure his foot was set before committing to the next one. He had to stop frequently to coax the jittery horse along.

Halfway down, he caught a glimpse of gray hide amongst the thick brush, and stopped to study the slope for the best way down to that place.

"Colter! It's rainin'," came McNeal's demanding shout from above.

"What do you want me to do about it?" Colter muttered.

Shouts of "Colter, damn you! I'm getting' soaked" followed him the rest of the way down to the gray. The horse lay on its side with its load miraculously intact. The animal's hide was scratched and matted from its fall, but its legs looked sound.

The animal tried to get up at his approach but could not because of the way its load had shifted. Colter moved cautiously forward, murmuring softly to keep the horse from lashing out at him. When he was close enough, he laid a tentative hand on the animal's neck, ready to pull away if the horse tried to nip him.

It didn't. Rather, it closed its eyes and allowed Colter to slice through the straps securing the load. The bundles fell away, revealing only minor scrapes and cuts along the horse's body, not broken ribs that would have doomed it. "Think you can stand?" he asked.

The horse opened an eye, but made no attempt to move.

Colter ran his hand gingerly along the animal's side, feeling for an indication of internal injury. All of a sudden, the horse sank its teeth into his sleeve, ripping off a chunk of cuff. Startled, Colter cursed and fell back on his tailbone. The sudden movement caused his skittish packhorse to shy and he had to fight to hold it back.

"If'n you can bite, you can get up, you fool plug!"

The gray heaved to its feet and surveyed Colter with a baleful look. It limped a bit but it could still walk.

"I shoulda known you'd try somethin' like that there," Colter said. "I got a horse back home knows the same trick."

He kept a wary eye on the gray while he secured the load of baggage onto his packhorse. Then he started back up the ravine, leading his horse and letting the gray limp along at its own pace. To make the climb easier on all three of them, he made long traverses, using the whole face of the slope, zigzagging his way to the top.

When he reached the crest, McNeal scrambled to his feet. "Sweet Jesus, Colter, you brought me a horse to ride."

"Nope. Critter's lame."

"Lame or not, I ain't about to walk when I can ride."

Colter was too done in to care. Let the cook learn the hard way.

McNeal no sooner laid a hand on its mane than the gray lashed out a hoof, catching him squarely on the shinbone. McNeal yipped and grabbed at his lower leg. "It's broke! My leg's broke!"

"Like hell it is. That'll teach you to go agin what I say," Colter said, pulling his horse into motion and grabbing up the gray's lead.

"Where are you goin'?" McNeal cried.

Colter kept walking. "Back."

"But I'm hurt. You gotta help me."

"I don't gotta do nothin'."

"Damn you, Colter!"

Colter glanced wearily around. What a time to have two gimps on his hands. One was ornery as all get out; the other, a whining good-for-nothing bag of air. Lord only knew how far they would have to go to catch up with the others. The way they were going, they would be lucky to make it to camp before dark. Things couldn't get much worse.

Something floated past his eye. Something solid and fluffy. He groaned. Things had just gotten worse. The rain had changed to snow.

Retrieving the gray packhorse and its load proved to be the one bright spot in the hard four days that followed. The weather alternated between snow and freezing rain. The route alternated between steep ascents and seemingly steeper descents. While streams abounded, game did not. After they exhausted their supply of flour, the crew scrounged for whatever berries they could find.

Hunger weakened everyone, hitting Ordway especially hard. Colter took grim pleasure in seeing the man who tried to shoot him being slung onto a horse because he was too weak to walk.

Finally, on September 8, the expedition crossed into the most beautiful valley Colter had ever seen. To the west a wall of mountains rose high, high into the bluest, widest sky imaginable. Their pristine peaks stood like Divine sentinels over an expanse of waving grasses and stands of pines. The floor of the valley, called the Valley of the Bitterroots by the Indians, was braided with ribbons of shining water. All along the front of the mountains, creeks tumbled out of the thick forest that stretched like a wide velvet band along the skirts of the peaks where they brushed the valley floor.

The sight of those creeks quickened Colter's pulse. A trapper could live out his days here in peace and ease. He had always wanted a home of his own. He had searched years for one, and at last he knew he had found it. The streams and the peaks and the lush growth of the valley belonged here and so did John Colter.

He stepped out of the line of march to study the scene before him. This beautiful place was perfect for Fragrant Grass and their children.

Children. Family. Suddenly those words took on heightened significance.

His packhorse side-stepped to allow another to pass, carrying Ordway slumped over the horse's neck. Colter pitched his voice loud enough for the man alone to hear. "Serves you right, you bastard." Ordway looked up at Colter dully, then closed his eyes and dropped his head, tucking his chin back into his chest.

A short distance behind the sergeant came Shannon who gestured toward the glittering peaks. "Up and over and we're there."

"I doubt it," Colter replied.

Shannon's smile slipped. "Doubt what?"

"Ain't goin' to be near that easy."

"Lord, Old Man, don't you ever get tired of naysaying everything?"

"Got my opinion. You got yours."

"Then we'll see who's right. Again." Shannon shoved past, leaving Colter's good mood diluted. The crossing from the Shoshone village to this valley had been the most difficult passage of the expedition's journey so far, yet the Indians did not consider it important enough to give the trail a name. Whatever they were about to face on the Hungry Trail of the Pierced-Nose People had to be something bad. Real bad.

Once the crew established their Bitterroot Valley camp, the captain declared a five-day layover. They sent out hunters to lay in meat for the mountain crossing, then turned their attention to trading with the valley Indians for fresh horses, using those animals that had been injured during the trek from the Shoshones, including the gray that Colter had rescued. Their experiences with the Shoshones stood the captains in good stead and they succeeded in bringing the expedition's remuda to forty, including three mares and their new-born colts.

The march west began on September 11 under overcast skies. Shannon was assigned to ride a mare and lead her week-old colt. The antics of the frisky young horse matched his own high spirits. He rolled into his blanket that night, elated by the certainty that he was on the brink of becoming one of the world's greatest explorers.

That elation was still with him the next morning when he awoke to find that there had been a frost overnight. Yet, nothing — not weather nor Indians nor even God Himself — could keep him or the expedition from keeping their appointment with destiny.

He and Colter drew the assignment that day of hunting ahead of the main body. When Colter greeted him with a snarled, "Where you been?" Shannon checked a come-back and waved for the man to ride on. He was not going to let anything spoil his mood or his hunting.

He fell in behind Colter and rode along content with the silence of his own thoughts. After an hour Colter reined his horse to a stop. "You see anythin'?"

Shannon would not admit that he had been lost in contemplation of the future, paying no attention to his surroundings. "No. You?"

"Nothin," Colter said.

"Maybe we ought to cross the creek," Shannon suggested.

"Rube and Joe're over there. We best stick to this side." Colter went thoughtful for a time. "This ain't good, Fuzz. I ain't seen a game trail since we left the valley. Nary a one."

Shannon sat quietly, still wrapped in a private vision of future fame. "There ain't nothin' to smile about, Fuzz," Colter chided.

Looking for a way to draw the man's attention away from him, Shannon pointed to a stand of trees. "Wonder what could have happened to those trees? Looks like the bark's been stripped off. You think it was a storm?"

"'Tweren't no storm. Was folks cuttin' it off to eat."

"You mean a horse or a deer, don't you? People don't eat wood."

"No, I mean folks. Hungry ones like you and me're likely to be 'fore this crossin's over."

"Just listen to you. All you ever talk about is how bad things are and how much worse they're going to get."

"Least I ain't moonin' over some fancy notion that ain't got no chance in hell of bein' real."

"Jealous that I *have* dreams? Dreams are what got me here and they'll keep me going."

"Then you better be dreamin' up some dinner 'cause that's all you'll be eatin' tonight." Colter swung off his mount and walked to one of the untouched pines. He cut loose a section of bark, then freed the slippery inner membrane and sliced it into strips.

"What the hell are you doing?" Shannon asked.

"Chewin' on this here takes away hunger cramps," Colter answered.

"Go on and waste time if you want. I'm going on," Shannon said.

Colter didn't answer.

Shannon picked up the reins. "Come on, Mama, Baby. Let's leave him to his stubbornness."

"You ought not do that, Fuzz," Colter said.

Shannon pulled back on the reins. "Damn it all! How many miles do I have to go till you and everyone else forget that I got lost once?!"

"I ain't talkin' about gettin' lost. I'm talkin' 'bout them critters."

"What about them? Ye gods, can't I do anything right in your eyes, Old Man?"

"Givin' them critters names . . . It's goin' to hurt you, is all."

"Names? Hurt? What is this: some kind of riddle?"

"If'n we don't find us some game, that there little one is goin' to be dinner soon. Maybe the mare, too."

"God, you're despicable."

Colter tossed him a hard look. "Don't rightly know the name you just called me, but since we're friends, I reckon it weren't no cuss word."

"Shit!" Shannon yanked the mare's head around and kicked her flanks to set her in motion. Colter had an uncanny way of always riling him. Some friend – negative, pessimistic, bull-headed.

He patted the mare's smooth neck. "They're not touching you, Mama. Or Baby, either. Anyone who tries will have to answer to me."

The mare's ears flicked out. Baby lifted his small head, a miniature of the mare's, and gave Shannon a trusting look that penetrated to his soul.

Colter watched Toby examine the ground ahead with growing apprehension. The Indian's black hair was shot through with silver. He wore it pulled into two braids that hung down his back outside his deerskin shirt, leaving to plain view the lines of intense concentration scoring his face.

Finally, the Shoshone guide straightened up and conferred with the captains, Drouillard, Sacajawea and Charbonneau. Colter pressed a palm against his midsection. Lord, he was hungry! He would give just about anything — even his carving knife — for one rib of venison. The meat they had laid in at their valley camp had run out two days ago. Two days of difficult going and bitter cold that had quickly worn down his and everyone else's reserves of strength.

From down the line of crewmen came a muffled voice. "Forget the damn trail. Let's find us some damn meat 'fore we all starve." McNeal. The man never stopped grousing.

The huddle went on. Colter's stomach cramps grew more intense. He reached into his pouch for a strip of pine bark. His fingers counted just three pieces left, and he chose to wait. There was no telling how hungry they would get before they got across these mountains. That was, if they got across.

At last the discussion broke up. The captains motioned to the sergeants and gave them instructions to relay to their squads. "Move out!" Gass yelled.

McNeal groused, "Hell! We need to eat, not walk."

Colter shut out the cook's complaints and took up the lead of his horse. The whole crew was afoot now. Afoot and hungry.

At the head of the column, Toby struck out along the creek, rather than turning upslope where Colter's instincts told him they ought to go. He threw a thought toward the guide, *I hope to God you know what you're a-doin'*, then fell in behind the line of march, forcing aside his feelings, doing his duty.

Shannon blinked three times before he realized that the mist he was seeing was not a problem with his eyes, but rather thick, clinging fog, lying like a shroud across their ridge-top camp. His head was still muzzy with sleep, and it took a moment for him to realize that his blanket had not bleached out overnight, but that it was covered with snow. Six inches of snow. And it took still another moment to remember that he was hunting today with Rube.

Since leaving the valley four days ago, hunters had brought in only two small rabbits. Two rabbits to feed thirty-three hungry people. If they could not find meat today . . .

He closed his eyes again to squelch the thought and said a silent prayer that he would find game today. "For their sakes, dear God. Amen." He didn't have to say who "they" were. God would know he meant Mama and Baby.

Tossing aside the blanket, he rose gingerly and stretched his sore muscles. The awful climb up to the ridge yesterday had taken its toll on everyone, but miraculously no men or horses had been lost. He shook the snow off the blanket and was tucking it into his kit when the stomach cramps hit, doubling him over. The cramps passed eventually, taking with them his train of thought. A shake of his head helped him catch hold of a thread of his last idea, Hanging onto it, he plodded slowly over to where Colter sat, head hanging and shoulders slumping.

Colter lifted his head slowly. His face was gaunt and gray with fatigue. "Hope you brung me some grub, Fuzz."

"Tonight for sure. Me and Rube are hunting today."

Colter shook his head. "Cain't bring back what ain't there. Best you take this here along." He held out one of the bark strips.

"No thanks. You keep it. There is one thing you can do for me though. Trade me horses for today." He lowered his voice. "This snow will be too much for Ba — the colt."

"All right. Just bring mine back in one piece, hear?"

Shannon managed a tired grin. "Same for you, hear?"

14. *Food from a Baby*

Persistent fog made the difficult task of hunting even harder. Shannon and Rube were both exhausted and hungry. They had to stop frequently, though they dared not pause for long because of the freezing wind assaulting the ridge and bringing down on their heads the heavy snow that had piled up on branches overnight. They searched for hours without finding a single track. More than once Shannon regretted not taking Colter's bark strip to quell his hunger pangs.

As the day began to wane without any sign of game, Shannon spotted a faint track and followed it to find a lone rabbit, its fur already white except for an irregular brown patch on its rump. He took aim and dropped the hammer with a whispered "For Baby."

The sound of the explosion reverberated through the forest fastness. The rabbit dropped. Instead of joy, a feeling of futility filled Shannon. One scrawny rabbit was hardly worth the powder.

Rube came running. "Lordy, is that all?" He picked up the thin carcass. "Well, at least we're comin' back with somethin'."

By the time they reached the others, Shannon was shivering so much that it took three tries before he succeeded in wrapping his blanket around him. He did not remember falling asleep until terrible screams brought him awake to find Colter restraining him. "Don't look, Fuzz."

The sound ceased abruptly, and a sudden realization pierced through the veil of his grogginess. "Baby?"

"Warned you," Colter said.

Though Shannon's mouth worked, his mind would not supply any words. Frantic neighing filled the eerie silence, followed by shouts of "Whoa!" and "Hold her!" On the far side of the camp, Mama fought against the efforts of half a dozen crewmen to keep her from the dead colt.

"Mama!" Shannon cried.

Colter pinned him to the ground. "It's done. Best you stay out of it."

"No, I have to go to her. I have to do something."

Colter torqued Shannon's wrist behind his back. "Ain't nothin' to do. The colt's food, Fuzz. 'Tweren't meant to be no pet."

Held in Colter's iron grip, Shannon looked helplessly toward the crazed mare. This tragedy was all his fault. He had failed in his responsibility to the two dumb creatures entrusted to his care. Failed utterly and completely.

"You won't feel near so bad once you eat," said Colter.

"You think I could eat any of . . ." Shannon could not bring himself to say "Baby," not in the same breath with the idea of food. "No way can I eat that, not if it was the last edible thing on the face of the earth." He brushed aside Colter's hand and stumbled away from the camp, from the struggling mare, from everything. He stumbled along, blinded by tears that he could no longer hold back.

Another day of icy wind and snow flurries, of steep climbs and dangerous descents, of falls and injuries to men and horses, of hunters returning to camp empty-handed. Another colt killed for dinner. Another night of bellies screaming to be filled with meat instead of thin, watery soup. Through it all, Shannon doggedly led the mare who tried again and again to break free of his control. Colter tried to talk him into letting him handle the horse, but Shannon would not hear of it.

That night Colter was too tired to fall asleep immediately. Fatigue and lack of food dulled his mind. Thoughts formed slowly, faded quickly. He had never seen a stretch of mountains like this; an endless fabric of precipitous ridges scored by deep valleys and water courses covered by lush forests yet utterly devoid of the wildlife that might sustain human life. It had been a week since they left the Bitterroot Valley to follow the Hungry Trail of the Pierced-Nose People. A week since crewmen and the horses alike had had enough to eat. A week of the most difficult terrain imaginable. With the harsh toll this mountain crossing was extracting from them, unless they found enough game or an end to this crossing soon, horses — and men — would begin to die.

He peered blearily up at the cloud-obscured night sky. Was this what the hawk had guided him west for: to die?

Something brushed his shoulder blade, catching him by surprise. A hand cupped his mouth to prevent him from crying out. Captain Clark stooped so as to whisper next to Colter's ear: "Tomorrow I'm going to take a small group on ahead. Either we'll find game or the end of this trail. I want you to come with me."

If he had been sent west to die, Colter figured he had two choices: he could wait for the summons to arrive, or he could go out to meet death face on. He knew before he completed the thought which one he would choose. "I'm with you, Captain."

Clark patted his shoulder. "Get a little more rest, then. We'll be on our way at first light." With that, he was gone as stealthily as he had appeared.

A raging thirst woke Shannon. The act of sitting up made him dizzy to the point of nausea. He scooped snow into his mouth to take away the awful taste of stale saliva. The snow reawakened the hunger creature scrabbling at his guts. It no longer mattered whether he moved or remained still. Both states aggravated the cramps. He needed something to eat. Anything. And he needed it now.

He fumbled open his pack and took out his journal. Opening to the back, he ripped the corner off a page with his teeth and swallowed it.

His stomach rejected the unchewed paper, gagging him. Desperately, he ripped off another piece and forced himself to chew it into pulp before swallowing.

His stomach lurched, but accepted the masticated lump.

Another bite, more chewing, then swallowing. And another. And another until he had consumed the entire page. Gradually, the cramps subsided.

By now the rest of the camp was coming awake. He made sure no one was watching before tearing out another page. He had found a way to help himself. It was up to the others to find their own solutions.

He was tucking the folded page into his shirt for later consumption when an angry Sergeant Ordway came to find him. "You hobble your mare last night, Shannon?"

Shannon's head was too muddled to remember much about last night other than that it had happened.

"I thought so," Ordway said. "By God, you're getting more useless as the days go by, Private. McNeal!" The cook scuttled over. "Shannon's mare took off. Find her and catch up with us when you can."

The sergeant's unfair criticism had raised Shannon's hackles, but assigning the good-for-nothing cook to find his horse was more than he could stand. "She's my charge, Sergeant. I'll go."

"Oh, no. You're caused enough problems already," Ordway said.

Shannon would not be dismissed. "I happen to know where she went."

"Where?" demanded the sergeant.

"I'll say when you give me permission to go after her," Shannon answered.

Ordway's face darkened, but he relented. "Then both of you go. We don't need anyone lost. Now where is she?"

Shannon let the insinuation pass without reaction. "Back to our last camp."

"Ah, Sarge, what's he know? I don't need him. He'll just slow me down," McNeal said.

Shannon kept his cool in the face of the cook's slur. "She tried to bolt that direction a dozen times yesterday."

"It's a long way, Shannon. You better be right or you two won't make it back to camp tonight," Ordway said.

After the sergeant left, the cook glared at Shannon. "You better make damn sure you don't get lost, Shannon. I'm not lookin' for you."

Shannon lacked the energy for the scornful laugh that rose as a retort. He tucked his journal away in his pack. By the time he got to his feet, he regretted volunteering to go after Mama. Then he reminded himself of the circumstances. He could do it. He would do it. This was for Baby.

Soon after Colter left camp with Captain Clark's scouting party, the weather closed in. A driving wind pelted them with sleet and knifed through their soggy buckskins as if they did not exist. The cold robbed Colter's legs of strength and his feet grew so numb that he had to watch where he placed them.

The only one the weather did not seem to affect was the captain. Clark pushed forward, breaking trail for Colter and the other five crewmen.

Late that afternoon Colter was halfway up a steep ridge when he stumbled and fell. His leg muscles were twitching so much that they would not support his efforts to get up. *I'll just lay here*, he thought. *Rest up a bit 'fore I go on.*

He was not aware he had fallen asleep until he jerked awake sometime later. From the amount of sleet layering his clothing, he realized that he had been lying there a considerable time. He got slowly to his feet and stood swaying, waiting for the stars to quit zinging off the insides of his eyeballs.

The other men of the scouting party were above him, moving slowly if at all. He could just make out a faint track ascending to the crest of the ridge. He heaved a sigh and started climbing. Grasping ice-encrusted brush with his hands and clawing at the frozen soil to pull himself up, he reached a place below the ridge crest when another bout of lightheadedness forced him to stop. He had been hungry for so long now that his stomach no longer complained with cramps. Now he had to contend with a persistent, dull headache and dizziness.

He felt for the last remaining strip of pine bark in his pouch. Every cell in his body screamed to be fed, but every instinct told him to wait, that things were bound to get worse. Reluctantly he left the bark tucked away and rubbed the spots out of his eyes before starting up the last bit of incline to the top of the ridge.

Thirty feet beyond the crest, Captain Clark was on his knees with his arms wrapped across his midsection. It hit Colter that the captain's stomach problems had returned in the worst possible place at the worst possible time. He wobbled down to the captain as quickly as his shaky legs and numb feet allowed.

When he was within a foot of Clark, the captain lifted his face to reveal tear-glazed eyes. His voice was a low, hoarse whisper. "If you're a praying man, Colter, give thanks to the Almighty, for He has delivered us."

Colter glanced around but saw nothing to justify the captain's words. He was considering how to respond when Clark pointed. "We're across. Look."

In the distance the trees gave way to a broad sloping prairie. "It's still a far piece, Captain."

Some of the hope faded from Clark's face. "We have to get there. Have to find game. We've come too far —"

The doubt in the captain's voice cut through Colter's pessimism. Through all their trials, Clark had never shown uncertainty. Until that moment, Colter did not realize how much he had depended on the man's steadiness, his unshakable belief in their success, his energy and his example. He forced into his voice a lightness he did not feel. "Another twenty or thirty miles ain't nothin' after what we been through, Captain."

Clark's mouth stayed set in a grim line. "There's no food and we need to make camp for the others."

"This here looks as good a spot as any for the night." Colter pulled out of his pack the remnants of an old moccasin. "Got this here to boil up for some soup. Cain't speak for the taste, but it's somethin'. Then tomorrow I'll find us some meat, or my name ain't John Colter."

The captain stared at the tan patch of prairie in the distance for a long time. When he looked at Colter, his face and mouth had softened. "Back at Louisville when that sheriff tried to take you into custody, I was against Meri's coming to your defense. But, thank God, he did. And thank God for you and the way you always come through, Colter."

Colter was too flustered by the impassioned praise to know what to say. The captain rescued him by turning away to search for wood. "At least we'll have a fire going for the others."

Shannon was hungry and weak, but he was also determined to salvage something from the colt's tragic end. He drove himself relentlessly through the day's sleet and wind to arrive at the previous day's campsite by dusk. There was the mare standing over the spot where her colt had been butchered.

Her maternal grief stirred Shannon. He hugged her neck and whispered words of comfort in a voice roughened with restrained sorrow.

"Je-sus Kee-Rist, Shannon," McNeal groused. "It's just a damn horse."

Shannon was beyond caring what the cook or anyone else thought. He continued to stroke the mare's neck, giving her what consolation he could.

"Forget the horse and help me get a fire goin'," McNeal demanded.

Shannon ignored the man until the smoke from the wet wood of the fire brought him around to the fact that he was shivering. Reluctantly he left the mare for the inadequate warmth of the fire. McNeal was on his knees, searching for something on the ground. Shannon was too tired to ask what he was doing. He closed his eyes and tried not to think about how hungry and cold he was.

McNeal straightened up suddenly. "This place is cursed. I can't even find no bug to eat." He threw his head back and yelled, "Food!"

Shannon closed his eyes again, hoping the lack of a reaction would silence McNeal.

"Damn it all! I ain't goin' to starve! Not when there's meat on the hoof right here," the cook said.

At the sound of a rifle hammer being thumbed back, Shannon shot up and barreled into the cook with a strength he did not know he possessed. The rifle fired so close to his ear that the sparks singed his beard and the explosion momentarily deafened him.

McNeal worked himself free of Shannon's hold and commenced to reload his rifle. "You ain't stoppin' me!"

The cook's voice was muffled by the ringing in Shannon's ears like echoes down a long hallway, but Shannon grappled the weapon out of the man's grasp and rolled over so it was underneath his body. "You killed her colt. You won't kill her!" he bellowed against the roaring in his ears.

"Damn you, Shannon!" McNeal shouted. "She's food. We're hungry. Either she dies or we do."

"No!"

Furious, McNeal pounced on Shannon, trying to wrestle him off the rifle while Shannon fought to keep the gun underneath him. As his strength ebbed, he had a flash of clarity. He grasped the cook's powder horn and gave it a yank, snapping the worn strap. He then shoved the horn down his pants along with his own. "*Touché!*"

"Give it back, Shannon."

"No! There'll be no horse-killing. Not here. Not tonight. Now you'd best get out of my sight. Or else."

For a long moment the cook did not move, then slowly he turned and trudged into the darkness. Shannon watched after him to be sure the man was not trying some trick, then he went to the mare.

Stooping for her lead, he nearly blacked out. Somehow his fingers found her mane, and he managed to hold himself upright until the world stopped spinning. The mare eyed him and nickered. Shannon sensed in that soft sound the mare's thanks for saving her life, and a bit of his guilt over Baby's death eased.

He led her to the fire and settled onto the half-frozen ground. He drew out the folded page he had torn from his journal that morning and stared at it, thinking about food. He had eaten so many meals without paying attention to what was on his plate. Time and again he had mouthed the meal blessing, unconscious of the words or their meaning. He had ignored the outstretched hands of hungry beggars, despising them for their neediness. Until this expedition, hunger had been just another word; a condition shared by the lazy and the luckless. Now twice in one year, he had experienced the depths of hunger. Starvation was no longer a word or idea. It defined his very existence.

The mare nudged his shoulder.

"Not you, Mama. No matter how hungry I get, you aren't food." He ripped off a corner of the page and began to chew.

"Zoob!" Colter whirled toward the familiar figure of his old partner. "By God, you're a . . ." The words died on his lips as the image merged with the trees, the snow, the silence.

Not Zoob. Colter closed his eyes and leaned against a tree. He was hallucinating. He longed to sit down, to rest, but he did not dare for he might not be able to get up again.

The numbness in his feet from yesterday had climbed to his knees, and his spit tasted rank from the old moccasin they boiled into soup to eat last night. Trying to spit out the vile taste was useless. He could no longer work up enough moisture.

He reached into his pouch and fumbled out the last strip of pine bark. He chewed each bit slowly, making it last, stretching out the moment when it was all gone and there was no more standing between him and the triumph of hunger over his life. Then he levered himself away from the tree and waited for the earth to stop tilting before plodding off again, one short heavy step after another. He had to keep his eyes on the ground now because he could no longer depend on his unfeeling feet to plant themselves.

It took a long while for comprehension to dawn on him. The ground around him had lost its layer of snow. In fact, it was muddy and tracked. Tracked with the hooves of . . . horses!

Figuring the tracks were another figment of his imagination, he squeezed his eyes shut, then took another look. The tracks were real. He looked ahead. "My Lord," he croaked through cracked lips.

Standing not three feet away, placidly munching on a patch of tan grass, was the creator of those tracks. A buckskin horse with spots dappling its rump and legs.

Colter mumbled, "You ain't there," and blinked twice.

The horse remained, although it left off cropping grass to return his stare.

"Oh, Johnny-boy, you done crossed the line this time," he muttered to himself. "You got to pull yourself together 'fore Captain and the others get here."

He lifted his hand to rub his bleary eyes, and the horse shied back. Its movement revealed a frayed length of leather rope dangling from its neck.

Colter's hunger-dulled mind then registered that he and the horse were on the edge of a gentle slope of autumn-yellowed grass. He glanced behind him at the snow-draped peaks they had struggled to cross. "My God, we're here, ain't we?"

The horse's ears swiveled back.

"We're here, and we're hungry. And you're food." He set about loading his rifle, but his hands were shaking and would not cooperate. His jerky movements caused the horse to become alert and suspicious.

Colter was all too aware of how much this animal meant to him and the rest of the expedition. He left off loading his gun and laid the weapon down before moving cautiously forward, murmuring, "No need to be scairt. Good horse."

The animal eyed him warily, but did not retreat further.

"There now. I'm a-goin' to reach for your rope." He swiped at the broken lead, but the animal pranced away. It took all Colter's control to check his frustration and keep his voice soft and reassuring.

He caught the rope on the second try and wrapped it twice around his hand so as not to lose hold. In his wobbly state, he decided to sit down and wait for the captain and the others to catch up before trying to dispatch the horse.

Time passed. The numbness rose into his thighs, then into his hips. "Better find the others whilst I can still move."

He had not taken more than four steps when Clark limped out of the trees, leading two other crewmen. "Any o' you up for some dinner?" Colter asked.

Clark gasped, but then, looking at the frayed lead, shook his head. "Wish it was dinner, Colter, but that animal belongs to somebody and we have to return it."

Colter exploded in disbelief. "Return it? Where? This here's food. And we're starvin'."

"It belongs to Indians," Clark said. "We have to give it back."

Colter managed to lower his voice a trifle. "We got to eat — and soon, or there ain't goin' to be a soul left to find them Indians."

The captain glanced from Colter to the horse to the other men of the scouting party. His face mirrored the internal battle his conscience was waging. "Better make it quick, then. I'll start a fire."

Colter led the horse off a few yards, unwrapped the rope and stood on it while he loaded his rifle. That done, he stepped back three paces.

The horse bent to crop some grass. "That's it. One last bite," he coaxed.

When the horse lifted its head to chew, he thumbed back the hammer and took aim. "Good horse. There'll be lots of grass for you in heaven," he said and fired.

Shannon kept McNeal's powder horn until they rejoined the main party. They arrived too late to get any of the thin soup of boiled-down bits of tallow candles that had served as the crew's only meal that day. Shannon went to sleep hungry and woke up hungrier. He quelled some of his craving with part of another journal page, then, leading Mama, he joined the ragged queue of marchers.

One step, then a rest. Another step, another rest. As the day wore on, his steps got shorter; his rests, longer; his stomach, more insistent. He tried to remember the last time he had eaten his fill. He decided it was back on the Jefferson. That led him to remember all the elk he and Drouillard had killed. All that meat, left to rot when they needed it so badly now.

He did not remember falling until one man — or was it two? — pulled him back to his feet. At one point he gave up trying to walk up the steep slope and got down on his knees to crawl. Soon crawling became too much and he sprawled out on his stomach. Though he had stopped moving, the world around him whirled and spun too fast for him to ever again stand upright in it. He clung weakly to the ground, fearing that he would be flung into the heavens if he let go.

Gradually he stopped caring what became of him and relaxed his grip. The trail from Ohio had been long and difficult. He had come a long way, but now he had reached the end of the line.

He rolled onto his back for one last look at the sky. Dying under the open sky was for the wild, the unattached, the dispossessed. Which had he become? When had he changed? Why hadn't he noticed that change? How much of his life had he lived without noticing?

Mama pushed her wet nose against his cheek. Shannon brushed it away. She evaded his hand and snuffled in his ear. He tried to say "Go away, girl," but speaking was beyond him.

With another snuffle, the mare moved off, pulling her lead rope out of his fingers. In the quiet that followed her departure, he let out a long breath and surrendered to the earth beneath him. There were worse ways to die than this. *I'm ready, Lord. Take me now.*

Clark insisted that most of the horsemeat be saved for the main party. Colter's small portion took the worst edge off his hunger but left him far from satisfied. He helped secure the left-over meat to a tree limb, out of the reach of predators, then forged on with the rest of the scouting party to locate the Indians the horse had belonged to.

The next day they reached a village of thirty lodges constructed of mats woven from withes. The lodges belonged to a band of Pierced-Nose, or Nez Perce, people who had come to the high meadows to harvest the roots of the camas lily, one of their staple foods.

Holding a heaping platter of salmon fish and roasted roots almost undid Colter's control. Such delicious smells! So much food just for him! He lit into the meal like the starving man he was, shoving fistfuls of roots and the orange-colored fish into his mouth as fast as he could chew and swallow. He finished the first helping and passed the empty platter back for seconds. Then thirds.

When everyone had eaten, Clark dispatched Joe Field to retrieve the horsemeat and carry it back along the trail to the main party. Then he assigned Colter and Rube and three others to hunt while he led the rest of the scouting party to a neighboring village that, according to their hosts, lay on a navigable river flowing to the west.

With his stomach full for the first time since before meeting the Shoshones, Colter had the energy to think about what they had gone through the last eleven days. Riding along, he revelled in the songs of the birds who flitted through the trees around him. They were the first birds he had seen since leaving the beautiful Bitterroot Valley on the east side of the mountains. "All them preachers got it wrong." He aimed his comments to Rube following. "Hell ain't all fire and it ain't down below, neither. Hell's them mountains we just crossed."

When Rube didn't answer, Colter craned around to find the trail behind him empty. He retraced his steps and found Rube down on all fours, vomiting into the dirt and groaning about dying. While Colter was trying to decide what to do for Rube, his own guts erupted and his half-digested meal geysered from his mouth.

He was still heaving when another lower pain gripped him. He managed to rip apart the knot at his waist and drop his pants just in time.

He wasn't done squatting before another wave of nausea brought up more of the Nez Perce meal. He was spitting left-over bits of pink fish out of his mouth when the thought occurred to him: *We ain't outta hell yet.*

🦅

With Echo standing lookout at the lodge entrance, Fragrant Grass listened to the laughter and boisterous talk of the wedding party as it threaded its way among the lodges of Matootonha.

The noise level dipped as the group reached the plaza area and waited for the groom to step to the front. Then the sounds picked up again.

Echo ducked inside. "He comes."

Sly Wolf nodded smugly to Mint. "Prepare her, Wife." He strode outside to greet the groom.

Mint looked at Fragrant Grass. "Your new husband comes, my sister."

Fragrant Grass stared blankly at the wall.

"This is a good match," Mint said, drawing a comb through her sister's shining hair for the last time. "Good for you. Good for all of us."

Still, Fragrant Grass did not move.

Mint touched her arm. "I do not want you to go from this lodge, but you must."

Fragrant Grass turned to face her. "Yes, I must."

At the resignation in her voice, Echo ran out of the lodge. He would hide himself in a secret place where no one would see how sad he was, where he did not have to see Little Mother marry someone she did not want to marry because she must obey and keep the ways of the people.

🦅

"Shannon, wake up!" Hands jostled him into a sitting position.

He decided not to open his eyes until he heard the unmistakable voice of

God, the only one he intended to obey.

"Wake up, damn you!"

Cursing. There wouldn't be cursing in Heaven. God wouldn't allow it. This was Heaven, right? Oh, no! It couldn't be. He squeezed his eyes tighter.

Gradually he became aware of the wonderful aroma of roasting meat. Immediately he went on the alert, certain that this was the Devil's trickery. His thoughts flew back to the exemplary life he had led for so long, until, in a moment of weakness, he had given in to Sarah Cooper's temptations. Ever since that night, he had been on the path to Hell. Yet until now, he had given no thought to the consequences of his actions.

The smell grew stronger, more persistent. His voice was low and faltering. "Get t-thee away, S-satan."

"Satan? You'll wish I was him if you don't crack those eyes open now and eat something."

The meat's perfume overwhelmed Shannon's resolve. He was so hungry, so tired of being hungry. He might as well accept reality. He had no call to assume he was headed for Heaven after all the commandments he had broken. Envying others, lying, committing adultery, even killing a man.

"Shannon," the voice commanded.

Steeling himself for his first glimpse of an eternity in Hell, he opened his eyes to see — Sergeant Ordway instead of Lucifer. *Same difference.* "About time you opened those baby blues of yours! If you want anything to eat, better come along."

"You mean, I'm not . . . not in, in Hell?"

Ordway snorted. "We're all still in Hell, Private, but at least we got some horsemeat to eat for a change."

At the mention of a horse, Shannon cried "No" and struggled to his feet. The sergeant grabbed him in time to keep him from toppling off his stance. "Just where do you think you're going?" Ordway demanded.

"Butchers! Sadists! Why do you have to kill everything I love?"

Ordway pulled him into a tight hold. "Whoa there, Shannon. What are you babbling about?"

"My mare. Why did you have to kill her? Wasn't her colt enough?"

"No one killed anything except a stray Indian horse. Your mare's over there."

Sure enough, there Mama stood, munching grass at the edge of a broad patch of tree-dotted prairie. When he was satisfied that she was safe, he allowed Ordway to lead him to the fire and cut a chunk off the roasting horse's haunch for him. He eyed the meat suspiciously. How did he know all these people weren't the Evil One using familiar disguises, waiting to steal his soul when he let down his guard?

Someone, or something, that looked like McNeal tossed a cleaned bone into the fire and held out a hand to Shannon. "You don't want the meat, I'll take 'er off your hands."

There were strings of meat hanging from the rotting stumps of McNeal's front teeth as he belched loudly, filling Shannon's nostrils with an odor so charnel that he held his breath rather than having to smell more of it.

That smell proved to Shannon that he was still very much alive. He snubbed the cook's outstretched hand and bit into the meat. Instantly a rush of awful-tasting saliva surged into his mouth. He spit the bite into his hand and hawked into the dirt to clear away the vile taste, then put the meat back into his mouth.

This time the full taste of the meat was his to savor. Nothing had ever tasted so good, so sweet. That was when he noticed Joe Field. Joe and Rube had both gone with Captain Clark to scout the trail. "You can thank Colter for the meat," Joe said, responding to his surprised look. "He found the horse. Shot it, too."

A lump formed in Shannon's throat. Once again Colter had saved his life. Not only his, but the lives of every person on the expedition, including Ordway's. The meat hit his empty stomach and the digestive juices began to flow, making audible noises. To Shannon, it was the sweetest music he'd ever heard. Food had never tasted so good.

15. *Last Leg*

S hannon hugged Mama's neck one last time, then sadly turned away. The forelocks of the expedition's thirty-eight surviving horses had been shorn and their rumps branded so they could be identified if and when the crew returned to the Nez Perce to claim them. Five new dugouts lay on the riverbank ready for tomorrow's departure down the west-flowing Kooskooskee, the beginning of the last leg of their journey to the Western Sea. It also marked the moment when Shannon had to face the bitter truth. Whether or not the Kooskooskee led them out to the Western Sea, the route the expedition had followed was not the Northwest Passage. Not the easy "up and over" that would make commerce between the Western Sea and the Mississippi viable. He stared dejectedly at the river. He had come all this way, endured all this pain and hardship, for nothing.

Colter announced his arrival with "Been lookin' for you, Fuzz."

"Well, here I am," Shannon said dispiritedly.

"I'm thinkin' you oughtta be in one of the big boats tomorrow," Colter said.

Shannon could not work up the interest to answer.

"You still pukin'?"

Shannon shrugged.

"Then spit 'er out, Fuzz. If'n you ain't pukin', what's eatin' on you?"

"What are we doing here?" Shannon asked in a low voice.

"Last I checked, we was headin' to the Pacific Ocean."

"Why bother?" Shannon said sadly. "This isn't the Passage."

"Good Lord. You back to that? Hell, ain't you been listenin' to what I been tellin' you? There ain't no Passage. None. You know why?" He jabbed a thumb at the wall of mountains, piercing the sky to the east.

"They 'bout done us all in and it might still be we got to go over 'em to get home." He sighed. "But that's for later. For now we got us an ocean to find and, if'n you want to be in one of the big boats, I'll fix it up for you."

Shannon's complete belief in the existence of the Passage had fueled his dreams for too long to lay them aside now. It would take time for that belief to die and the truth to prevail. Meanwhile, he owed his friend an answer. "Might as well stay with you."

"You sure?"

"I'm sure."

"Then you got to keep on your toes. This here river's a wild one."

Shannon heard the warning and nodded absently. What difference did it make what dugout he rode in? He would have to face deep water every day of the journey to the Western Sea, to do battle with terror, and for what? He picked up a pebble and heaved it at the Kooskooskee. Damn this river! Damn this expedition! Damn his own soul!

Colter spotted the tell-tale ripple on the surface of the water ahead, indicating boulders lying just below the surface. Boulders could do terrible damange to tipsy wooden dugouts. He raised his voice over the sound of the rushing Kooskooskee, "Starboard."

To his satisfaction, Willard and Shannon reacted like a well-rehearsed team, wielding their paddles in unison, allowing the scout dugout to slide around the obstacle. The fourth person in the canoe was a passenger: Toby, the Shoshone guide. He sat tensely between Shannon and Colter, never taking his eyes off the wild writhing river.

As the canoe skimmed past the ripple, Colter experienced a thrill of delight. Delight in the river and the beautiful country it passed through. Delight in the performance of this small scout canoe he had convinced the captains to build. Delight in Willard and Shannon whom he had hand-picked, with the captains' permission, to be his crew.

"Old Man!" Shannon pointed up the river before them. "We got a swimmer."

Craning around, Colter spotted Pat Gass's dark head bobbing in the foaming tongue of white water. Above Gass, the sergeant's upside down dugout was hung up against a pillar of rock, being pounded by the intractable current. Baggage and the heads of the other crewmen of that canoe dotted the calmer water above that rapid.

"Backpaddle!" he yelled, positioning his oar to keep the nose of the dugout straight while the current carried Gass down to it. "Fuzz, slap down your paddle so's he can see it."

Shannon did and the sergeant caught the oar as the current swept him along. Then Willard caught Gass and held onto him while Colter turned the dugout into the nearest eddy. Gass's feet found the bottom, but the shock of being immersed in the ice cold water had set him to shivering so violently that it took Willard and Shannon both to help him to the bank. They dumped him there and turned back to using their paddles to scoop in baggage and floating crewmen.

Colter hauled the dugout onto the rocky shore and signed for Toby to wait with the recovering sergeant. He left Shannon and Willard to worry about baggage and swimmers and went after the overturned canoe that the force of the current had just kicked free of the mid-stream rock. They could afford to lose supplies, but not a boat.

He splashed out to the fringe of the rapids, icy water rising up to his calves, then to his knees, then to his thighs and made a lunge for the loose boat as the rapids flung it past him. He managed to catch it and hold onto it long enough to tug it into the calmer water of the eddy.

Pat Gass had recovered enough to come help him pull it onto the bank. "Lord, would you look at that crack. I thought I had her in line to miss the rock on the right."

"You cleared that one, Sarge. This here hit's to port," Colter said.

The observation was meant to reassure Gass; instead it provoked him. "I told the captains we're pushing too hard. What's the all-fired hurry?"

Colter didn't bother to respond. They both knew they were racing Winter. With October a third gone already, the priority was speed over caution.

He and the sergeant watched the next expedition boat negotiate the rapid. The crew made it through without mishap and pulled into the eddy. In it were Captain Clark, Sergeant Ordway, Sacajawea and Pomp, Charbonneau, Cruzatte and three other crewmen. "Nice work, Gass. Enjoy the swim?" Ordway mocked in a muttered undertone as he walked past Gass.

The glare of hatred that passed between the two sergeants was not lost on Colter.

"Colter, wasn't Toby with you?" Clark asked.

"Sure was," Colter replied.

"Where is he, then?"

A scan of the area showed no trace of the Shoshone. "Last I saw he was pulling his kit out of the dugout and heading off that-a-way," Gass said, pointing up the Kooskooskee "Didn't think it meant anything, though."

The captain looked upriver. The set of his shoulders echoed his annoyance. "Just like that, huh? Well, I suppose we ought to be thankful he stayed around this long." As quickly as his mood darkened, it brightened again. "Sergeant Ordway, it's time to move some folks around. Pick someone from our dugout to take Toby's spot. Sergeant Gass, let's have a look at your boat."

After the others moved off, Ordway turned to Colter. "Well, well. I finally get to break up your cozy little gang. Got to admit though, that scout boat of yours was a good idea. Wish I'd thought of it."

This time Colter was ready for Ordway. "Didn't think scoutin' was your strong point, Sarge. After all, the captains send Gass and Pryor out to hunt and scout and such, but never you. Why is that, you think?"

The smile slid off Ordway's face. "You'll have to ask them that question."

"Now that there's a good idea, Sarge."

"Think so? Here's another one, Colter: You get Charbonneau."

The announcement caught him by surprise. He had taken for granted that Ordway would elect to be the one to move into the scout canoe. But Charbonneau? Next to McNeal, Charbonneau ranked as the most useless man in the company. Lazy, surly and cowardly, Charbonneau was the cook without a lick of talent. The only worthwhile things he had accomplished so far were marrying Sacajawea and fathering Pomp. Colter managed to keep his voice level. "Charbonneau and who else?"

Ordway smirked. "Oh, that ought to be enough — for now."

Over the next two days, the country through which the Kooskooskee flowed changed remarkably. Trees thinned into grasslands. The terrain flattened. The weather remained sunny, but a piercing headwind buffeted Colter and his crew at every turn and stop. For stop they did — again and again — because Charbonneau claimed he needed to relieve himself approximately every fifteen minutes.

The wind was especially fierce by the time they pulled in for the sixth time on the second day and the Frenchman scuttled off into the sagebrush. After ten minutes, Shannon threw his paddle into the bottom of the canoe. "Where the hell is he? Let's leave him, Old Man! No one'll miss the son-of-a-bitch. *Arrêtez*, I have to sheet," he hissed in a falsetto, aping the Frenchman. "No one has to crap that much."

Colter squinted against the sun's glare. He felt the same way, but, like it or not, Charbonneau was his responsibility. "Hold your horses, Fuzz. He'll be along."

While Shannon continued to mutter under his breath, Willard sat quietly in the bow. He was the only one of them that Charbonneau did not grate on. *Thank God for Willard*, Colter thought. Time and again, the man had compensated for Charbonneau's blunders and saved them from accidents through sheer strength and cunning.

Charbonneau was hopeless with a paddle and even worse in a crisis. He could not even be trusted to do something as simple as securing the dugout's painter.

A few moments later the Frenchman stepped out of the brush, still hitching up his pants. Crusted patches dotted his filthy leather shirt and pants where he had wiped his fingers after picking his nose, the only skill he excelled at. The man's lollygagging pushed Colter's patience to the limit. "*Vite*, Frenchy!"

Charbonneau scowled and sauntered to the dugout where he picked up his paddle as if it were something unclean and climbed in without acknowledging the time he had cost them. By the time they got back out to the main current the next dugout came barreling past. The man in the bow signalled to ask if they needed help.

When Colter had to wave them on, his patience for Charbonneau's antics ran out. There would be no more stops for the Frenchman. Scout boats were supposed to run first, not second.

By now he did not need to see river obstacles to sense their presence, and Shannon and Willard anticipated each command before he spoke it. He gave himself to the task of getting back in the lead. He was so focused that he did not hear Charbonneau speak until the man bellowed, "To sheet, I must!"

"That's too damn bad. We stopped for you all we're goin' to stop today," Colter shouted.

Shannon cheered. "Hooray! It's about bloody time, Old Man!"

"Stop *maintenant!*" Charbonneau demanded.

"No stop *maintenant*," Colter growled.

The Frenchman grabbed the sides of the dugout and set it to rocking. *Like a brat who don't get his way,* Colter thought. *Well, here's how you stop that.* He slammed his paddle down on the back of the man's hand. Charbonneau yelped and grabbed his bruised hand. "My hand. My hand."

"You had your last stop back yonder, Frenchy. You need to shit, do it in your drawers," said Colter.

Charbonneau hunched over, muttering in a mixture of Hidatsa and French.

"Good, now maybe we can get back in the lead where we're supposed to be," Colter said for the benefit of Shannon and Willard.

The next thing he knew the Frenchman was on his feet with his pants down around his ankles, exposing a fish-belly white posterior which he thrust out over the side of the dugout. Charbonneau's sudden movement upset the delicate balance of the canoe, and in the blink of an eyes, the craft capsized, flipping Colter into the river The next moment an arm snaked around his neck. "For you, a geeft!" Charbonneau mashed a fistful of something brown and runny into his face.

Colter grabbed for the man's shirt, but, just then, the overturned dugout struck him in the back of the head and he felt himself losing consciousness.

Shannon stared at the water surging past him in horror. One minute he had been in the dugout; the next minute he was immersed in the river. Why? How?

The questions parted the curtain of fear for a moment and he remembered what had happened. It was Charbonneau's fault. Charbonneau had deliberately caused the dugout to roll. That understanding stirred a fury up in him, displacing some of his fright.

He glanced around in time to see the overturned scout canoe slam into the back of Colter's skull. Then he saw Charbonneau grab the disoriented Colter and shove his head underwater, holding it there.

"Hey!" Shannon yelled. "Stop that, you French bastard!"

The words were barely out of his mouth when Willard came from out of nowhere to overpower the Frenchman and pull Colter and the capsized canoe out of the river.

By the time Shannon got out to the bank, Colter lay stretched on the sand, bedraggled, eyes closed. Some brown substance caked his forehead and clung to his brows and beard. To Shannon's eyes, he looked dead.

"He'll come around," Willard reassured him.

Charbonneau gained the bank then and declared proudly. "Now, I go to sheet."

It was the wrong thing to say. Willard pounced on the Frenchman, shoving him back into the river and pummeling him in the face and chest with his mighty fists. The Frenchman's resistance was as futile and feeble as everything else he did.

Shannon was enjoying the action when Colter struggled up on one elbow. "Stop 'em."

"Why? It's about time Frenchy got what's coming to him," Shannon answered.

"Willard'll take him apart. You got to stop 'em."

"Good for Willard."

"For God's sake, Fuzz, look at Willard's face. He's gone outta his head."

Colter was right. Instead of the usual self-contained expression, the big man's face was a murderous mask. "Go, Fuzz!" Colter urged.

Unsure how to go about pulling Willard off, Shannon waded into the river. He never knew how he got drawn into the fray, but he was punched and kicked, even bitten, though he did not know by whom and despite all attempts to extricate himself, he seemed glued to the center of the battle.

Then, suddenly, the attack broke off and he came up out of the shallows to find Willard pinning Charbonneau's head and shoulders to the riverbottom.

It took a moment to understand that this was no ordinary fight. Willard was out to kill Charbonneau. "Willard, no!"

The big man did not give off his murderous intention, so Shannon leaped on his back. When that didn't dislodge Willard's hold, he dug his hands into the man's beard and yanked with all his might.

Willard bellowed in pain and let up on Charbonneau. He reached around and peeled Shannon off his back like a dirty shirt, then clamped his massive hands around his throat in a stranglehold. Shannon struggled to free himself, to no avail. *I'm going to die,* he thought as consciousness began to fade.

He was on the verge of blacking out when the gripping hands suddenly let go of his throat. Shannon fell to his knees in the river, clutching his bruised neck. Willard stood over him, flexing and relaxing, flexing and relaxing his huge hands. The murderous glaze had gone from his eyes and his face had relaxed back into its normal placid angles.

Colter moved out from behind Willard, gingerly rubbing the back of his skull. "Anyone asks, we been takin' us a rest stop."

Shannon looked over at the mewling, sputtering Charbonneau. "Yeah, and what about him? What's he goin' to say?"

"He don't matter as long as us three agree." Colter looked at Willard. "We're havin' a rest stop, right, Willard?"

Willard didn't respond.

"Nothin' happened. Huh, Willard?"

The big man's head jerked up, as if he suddenly awoke. "You say some-thing?"

"Asked if you was ready to get a move on," Colter said.

Willard nodded. "Give the word."

"I'm givin' it."

Willard looked around at the loose gear bobbing in the current and scattered among the rocks downstream. "How'd all our stuff get scattered out like that?"

"You mean you don't remember?" Shannon asked.

Colter's gesture cut him off. "Hit us a little bump's all. Come on. Let's gather her up and get back on the move."

Willard stepped past Charbonneau and set about gathering in their loose baggage. Shannon looked at Colter in amazement. "What happened?"

"Just like I said: nothin'."

Willard's beating put an end to Charbonneau's demands for stops. Whenever they did put in, the Frenchman scuttled away from the big man's reach and stayed scarce until it was time to get back on the river.

The Kooskooskee carried the expedition into increasingly arid country. At one point another large river came in from the south. Thereafter, the merged rivers flowed into a section of low bluffs lining both banks. Through gaps in those bluffs, Colter caught glimpses of the empty scablands that stretched without limit to the horizon in all directions.

With the change in the land came a change in the native people of the area. Instead of skin or earth lodges, they lived in communal longhouses, simple rectangles fifteen to sixty feet in length, constructed from a frame of forked timbers topped by ridge poles angled to vent smoke from interior fires. The roof and walls were formed by rush mats laid over this frame.

Along with the permanent villages scattered along the river were numerous empty ones that would be occupied by a large temporary population during the salmon migrations. Rows of racks used for drying fish stood outside every longhouse.

Besides the different way they lived, the natives dressed differently, although undressed described their customs better. Except for leather thongs around their waists and an occasional necklace or bracelet, the river people — men and women — rarely bothered with clothing.

On October 14, the merged river joined a much larger one which, by Captain Clark's calculation, was the Columbia, the river that would at last carry them out to the Western Sea. The captains declared a lay-over at the confluence to celebrate.

Colter had little to do once he had cleaned his rifle and put his gear in order so he started the carving of a swimming salmon. Given the windrows of rotting fish carcasses along the riverbanks, the remnant of the just-completed migration, he found the work grimly satisfying. Less than a month ago, none of them had ever seen a salmon. Now that was all they ate — and all they smelled.

The wisp of another, better odor momentarily overlaid the stench of rotting fish. *Thank God for them Indian dogs*, he thought, glancing at the meat roasting over the cooking fire. The captains had traded for some dogs at a Sokulk village the previous day. Most of the crew, Colter included, welcomed the change in their diet. Shannon was the exception. He went hungry rather than partake of the meat.

The October sun sank below the western horizon, whipping up the cold wind that had been beating at the camp all day. The cooking fire sputtered under a gust, an uneasy reminder that the expedition now had to trade for fuel as well as food, doubling the rate of depletion of their trade goods.

Colter held the roughed-out wooden fish up for inspection and recalled the carving he had left behind for Fragrant Grass. A hawk in flight. What would happen when he did not return before winter as he had promised? On the heels of that question came the feeling that she was in some kind of difficulty, that he ought to be there.

He snapped apart that chain of thought before it worked him into a frenzy. He was where he was at that moment because he had made a choice to come ahead rather than stay at the Mandans. Second-guessing that decision now served no purpose except to worry him when his mind needed to be on keeping his spirits up for the push out to the ocean.

"Meat's done!" came McNeal's call.

Crewmen rushed the fire. Colter held back. He leaned toward Shannon. "You better be eatin' tonight."

"Mind your own business, Old Man."

"I am. You're in my boat, and tomorrow we're back on the river. I don't want you passin' out or some other fool thing 'cause you didn't eat out of sheer mule-headedness."

"I'll eat when there's something I want to eat."

Colter gave up on Shannon and took his place in the line. McNeal was up to his usual tricks and tried to short Colter's portion. Colter returned the favor, grabbing one of the two dog legs off the cook's plate with a loud "Much obliged." He left McNeal spluttering complaints and returned to his place. Draping the blanket across his shoulders against the chill, he savored the juicy meat and picked the bones clean. The food was good, but it wasn't enough. He was still hungry.

While he was wondering what else there might be to eat, Shannon rose and went to get his portion. He returned to his place, carrying the dog meat, avoiding Colter's eyes. Seated, he lifted a roasted rib to his mouth and nibbled tentatively. Colter leaned toward him in anticipation. If Fuzz was too squeamish to eat dog, he would be glad to take it off his hands.

"What do you think you're doing?" Shannon demanded.

"You don't like dog, remember? No sense wastin' it," Colter answered.

"You told me to eat and I'm eating. Okay?"

Colter eyed the rib in Shannon's hand hungrily. Of all the times for Fuzz to change his mind. "Fine-a-ree," he muttered, tossing the picked-over bones into the rocks.

16. *Around Celilo Falls–Portage*

T he expedition set out on the Columbia River on October 18th. The river turned immediately west, running through basalt cliffs that grew steadily in height where the river had cut through ancient lava flows. As the river grew bigger, the dugout crews had to contend with treacherous whirlpools on top of snarling rapids.

Whenever they stopped at native villages to trade for food and fuel, the Indians warned of the "timm" they would encounter if they kept going. No one knew what "timm" meant until October 22 when they reached the spectacular twenty-foot cascade called Celilo Falls, according to Captain Clark's old map. Here the force of the plunging water filled the air with thunder and a cloud of cold mist that obscured the foaming water at the bottom.

Dozens of native longhouses crowded the banks around the falls. It took a sizeable portion of the expedition's dwindling stock of trade goods to convince the resident Indians to show them the usual portage route around the falls. The portage trail, however, proved to be a narrow, crumbling rock ledge hard beside the falls, much too precarious to accommodate the cumbersome dugouts. Either they had to find another way to move the boats, or they would have to abandon them and continue their journey on foot. No one relished the latter option.

Now that he was on the Columbia, Colter was impatient to get to the Western Sea and find a comfortable place to sit out the winter. Waiting for the captains to decide what to do about the portage stretched his impatience thin. He tried whittling to pass time, but quit because he was too keyed up. He did not want to risk a slip that would ruin the graceful swimming salmon emerging from the block of wood.

Finally, the captains worked out an alternate idea for portaging the boats. They would rope the dubouts one by one down a lower cascade beyond the main falls. They directed all the sick and injured crewmen to move camp to the bottom of the rapid below the falls by way of the precarious Indian portage route. Then they ordered the able-bodied into the dugouts. With Charbonneau claiming illness, Captain Clark took the Frenchman's place in the scout canoe. "Cross to the south side," he ordered.

Colter ruddered the boat across the current. Because they were so close to the top of the falls, he needed all his skill and instinct to guide them through the tricky cross-currents. Concentration elbowed his impatience aside.

"Put in there." Clark pointed to an abandoned native fishing camp. The place was piled with debris and reeked with the stench of rotting fish remains, but it was relatively flat for hauling the heavy, awkward dugout across.

On the captain's count, the four lifted the scout canoe out of the water. "Take a minute to find the right position for hauling her," Clark said. "We don't want to stop once we start moving."

It took a good deal of shifting before Colter found the right spot on his shoulder to rest the stern. Willard and Shannon made similar adjustments forward. Then the captain cheered "On-on!" and they set off across the former Indian camp, juggling the boat.

They had not gone five paces when Willard bellowed "Je-sus!" and began swatting at his clothing with his free hand. The big man's movements caused the heavy dugout to dip and lurch on the shoulders of the others.

"Fleas!" cried Shannon, who also set to slapping wildly at the arm of his shirt.

Then Colter's skin came alive. From his ankles and calves to his hips and chest; from his toes to the top of his head, his body was under attack. There were so many fleas biting so many places that he forgot the canoe to defend himself.

After he let go, the others did, too, and the scout canoe crashed onto the rocks. Colter could not move his hands fast enough, could not pound himself hard enough to rid himself of the voracious creatures. Desperate for relief from the stinging bites, he stripped off his flea-infested shirt and flung it down beside the dugout.

"Colter, we have to keep moving — only way out — Clark gasped between swats.

Colter knew the captain was right. They had to keep moving, but the fleas would not let up.

"Colter. *Now!* Go. Move."

He managed a nod between swats at the fleas swarming on his neck and started moving toward the other side of the camp.

"Your shirt, Colter. We can't leave it here," gasped the captain who was rallying Shannon and Willard to help with the boat.

Colter did not want to pick up the infested garment, but it was the only one he had and he needed it. He hooked it with one finger and heaved it into the dugout without interrupting his counterattack on the feasting fleas.

"All right now, count of three," the captain yelled. "One — two — three — Move!" The urgency in the captain's voice was palpable.

The four took off scrambling over the rocky beach. Willard caught a toe on a large stone and cursed loudly. His tone reminded Colter of the beating the big man had given Charbonneau. *Not now, Lord. Don't let him throw another fit.*

"Almost there," Clark rasped.

The river lay twenty yards off. To Colter, the distance seemed a mile as he fought to keep hold of the lurching load.

"Hell with it. Forget the boat. Run!" Clark yelled.

Colter and the other two needed no more urging. They dropped the boat and sprinted for the nearest water. Colter made a running dive into the river and stayed underwater as long as he had breath, banking that the fleas would run out of air before he did. When he broke the surface, Willard and the captain were rinsing off their fleas, too intent to notice Shannon standing up to his waist in the river, staring fixedly at the river.

Colter swam over to him. Shannon's eyes were wide and unblinking. Colter grabbed his wrist. "Fuzz, look at me.

"It's back," Shannon whispered.

"Look at me, not the water." Shannon's gaze stuttered to Colter's face. "Now you're goin' to sit."

"No, I —"

Colter jerked him down into the shallows and forced his head underwater. Shannon came up spluttering. "Damn you, Old Man. That was uncalled for."

Colter pointed to a swirl of fleas that had washed out of Shannon's hair. "Got them critters outta your hair, didn't it?" He lowered his voice. "Captain ain't noticed your problem."

"I don't care if he did notice."

"Yes, you do, Fuzz. We got us a long time together yet. And we still got to get home."

Shannon started to say something, then stopped. "You're right as — Ouch!" He swatted at his right ear.

"Duck your head. Drown them critters."

To Colter's great surprise and satisfaction, Shannon did exactly that without a moment's hesitation.

Once all the dugouts had been carried across the abandoned Indian camp, the flea-harried crews had to make a run down the swift narrow channel to the side of Celilo Falls. That channel ended at the top of a second snarling cascade that hurled down a chasm gouged out of of crumbling basaltic rock. It was the captains' plan to rope the boats down this shorter maelstrom one by one. The plan called for two groups of crewmen to scale the steep, mist-slippery cliffs, one on either side of the chasm, and maneuver each dugout down the abyss by means of elk-hide ropes.

Shannon was assigned to the roping crew on the south side. He was still reeling from the effects of the hydrophobia he had suffered earlier and each step on the unstable rock–knowing what would happen if he fell–was a trial.

The crewmen took up positions along both sides of the falls. Shannon was barely in position when the man above him whistled, the signal that the first boat was approaching the top of the cascade. As he relayed the signal to the man below him, his gaze strayed to the angry churning tumble of river beneath him and his heart leaped into his throat.

He was not set when the first boat dropped over the edge of the cascade. The force of the water pounding against the boat transmitted along the rope and he could not hold on. He tried valiantly to reassert his grip but the leather was wet and too slick to grasp. His attempts to hold it only succeeded in stripping flesh from his palms.

When eventually he did get a hold on the rope, the vibrations of the tremendous waves of the falling water thrashing against the dugout's wooden hull and jerking the rope every which way, lacerated his already throbbing hands.

Grimacing with pain, he allowed himself a quick glance downward to see how much farther the boat had to go until he could ease up. It was the wrong thing to do. A thick mist obscured the boat but not his imagination. He was hit by a terror so strong, so stupefying that his lungs constricted and his heartbeat speeded up until he felt he was being strangled.

Without warning, the upthrust of rock anchoring his front foot snapped off. His foot kicked out and he fell on his hip and he began sliding down the precipitous rock face.

Clawing frantically for purchase, his fingers caught a ledge of rock and slowed him enough to jam his other hand into a fissure. The rock grabbed and held his hand, arresting his fall but savagely torquing his captive wrist.

Dangling as he was, it took some time before he was calm enough to become aware of shouting. He had not been the only one to fall. At least two others had lost their footing. With three men out of action, the other men on the his side of the falls had lost control of the rope. With one side of the dugout unrestrained, the north side rope crew could not hang on. The loose dugout plunged into the maw of the river which tossed it end over end down the lower third of the falls, then spit it out into the rapids at the bottom. The current then carried the battered boat onto a downstream island where a group of natives pounced upon it, claiming possession.

Frantic, Shannon found footing and worked his hand free, then collapsed on the jagged crumbling rock, completely drained. With his fright ebbing, he was heartsick over the loss of the dugout. He had been in on enough of the captains' trading sessions with these usurious Columbia River Indians to know that they would demand a ransom for the return of the canoe. He had only himself to blame. If he had set himself better, he would never have fallen and the other men would not have fallen and the canoe would not now be in Indian hands.

The roar of the falling water covered Colter's approach until he was directly above Shannon. Colter had to yell to be heard. "The others're gatherin' up top. You comin'?"

Shannon's legs were in no shape to carry him anywhere, and he needed to collect his wits before he had to face the inevitable recriminations from the other crewmen. He waved for Colter to go on without him.

Colter ignored the wave and squatted gingerly, moving with the caution of a man who is leery of heights. "Be better for you if'n you went along with the captains. We got to get that boat back. It's either that or walk. Better for you, too."

Shannon reacted to the indictment in Colter's tone. "It's not my fault the bloody rock gave way."

Colter looked hard at him. "Best you face what you done and don't hide behind some lame excuse, Fuzz."

They both knew Colter was talking about his fear of water, but Shannon refused to talk about it. To talk about it was to admit his failings and force him into dealing with the issue in ways he was not prepared for. Not yet. "Go get the boat if you want. I got to sit awhile yet."

"Suit yourself."

A flea chose that moment to bite Shannon on the tenderest part of his body. He refused out of pride to swat the perpetrator until Colter was out of sight.

"Where d'you think you're goin'?" Joe Field demanded of Colter while keeping a wary eye on the trading circle where the captains and Ordway were attempting to win the expedition's canoe back from its salvagers. The captain had chosen Joe, Rube and Colter to accompany them to the Indian village below the falls to attempt to win back the wayward dugout.

"To drown me a whole lotta bugs," Colter answered, splashing into the river fully clothed.

"Come on back here 'fore you get us in trouble," Rube urged.

Colter was not about to sit back and let himself be stripped of flesh by the local flea population. Even Ordway's worst punishment was worth the risk for ridding himself of the torment. He dove headfirst into the river and remained submerged until he ran out of air. He resurfaced for breath and dived back down, swimming away from the cloud of pests the water had rinsed off him. He emerged from the river ten yards downstream, shivering but grateful to be momentarily free of the biting irritants if only for a moment or two.

As he was trudging back to the Field brothers, a drawn-up Indian canoe caught his eye. It was of a design he had never seen before. Shaped out of some type of enormous tree, it tapered gracefully on both ends with an unusually wide midsection where the wood had been scraped thin then strengthened with crossbars. It took only a glance to recognize the superiority of the design. The concave shape of the bow and stern would deflect waves. The wider body would give paddlers more room to move as well as providing more cargo space. A thinner hull meant less mass to move on water and land. The crossbars would allow for easier lifting.

As he ran his fingers over the carved figure that graced the bow, absorbing through touch the art of the men who had created such a beautiful thing, a shout came from the direction of the longhouses. He turned to see a native racing toward him, gesticulating and yelling in an angry voice. He had never seen such an ugly man. The Indian's head slanted severely from the end of his nose to the top of his cranium as if some great fist had pounded his forehead flat and shoved all the features of his face down several inches. The back of his head had likewise been flattened so that his skull came to a rounded point.

Colter side-stepped the charging man and raised his hands to show he meant no harm. The Indian ignored the gesture and shoved him away from the boats, then shadowed him back to Rube and Joe.

"Told you there'd be trouble," Rube said.

Colter nodded absently. His mind was on the new canoe. Its design solved every failing inherent in the expedition's dugouts. It was roomier and lighter and built to shrug off the kind of high water that would swamp the dugouts. The pilot in him longed to have one, but the realist in him knew there was no chance the captains would be willing to spend any of the expedition's precious trade goods for a new boat when food and fuel were proving so costly.

The bargaining for the salvaged dugout ended. Lewis and Clark stood up, looking grim and tired. Ordway beckoned Colter and the Fields over. "Well, we got her back. Now it's for you three to see the boat gets back up to camp."

"What are we supposed to do when we get there, Sarge?" Joe asked.

"You stay with the boat and don't let it out of your sight. Not for an instant. Understand?" Ordway said.

Joe opened his mouth to ask another question, but Rube's elbow in the ribs warned him off. Rube waited until the sergeant was out of hearing range to rasp, "For God's sake, Little Brother, when're you goin' to learn to shut up? One more question, we'd all be back on them rocks ropin' more damn boats down the falls. Right, Colter?"

Colter didn't answer. He was studying the captains, debating whether to tell them about the native canoe or hold his peace.

"Come on, Coal-Tar," Rube drawled. "We got us a break for once. Time to loaf."

Coal-Tar. The despised name pushed Colter into a decision. He strode over to Captain Clark who was more a boatman than Captain Lewis, and, disregarding Ordway's glares, he described the canoe he had seen and explained how it could help them. "If there's any way at all, Captain, gettin' that there boat'd be the smartest move you could make."

"So that's what the fracas was all about," Clark said. "Point the canoe out to me."

Colter did, and the captain walked over to get a closer look. "I see what you mean," Clark said. "And I wish we could. Only, we don't have the means to get it. Not now. You better get back to your task."

Rube was nervously watching the natives when Colter rejoined them. "Let's get out of here before they decide they didn't like the captains' deal."

They slid the reclaimed dugout into the water. Colter shoved them off, then leaped into the stern to guide the craft to the camp. He cast one last longing look over his shoulder at the beautiful Indian canoe. He wished now that he had never seen it, never known what he might have had.

"Leave somethin' behind?" Joe asked.

"Sure did," Colter said under his breath.

When the last boat was through the falls and secure, Shannon sank down among the mist-covered rocks, completely wrung out. He watched the other crewmen through bleary eyes as they picked their way down the slope toward the expedition's camp at the bottom of the cascade while he took out his kerchief to swab the sweat off his face.

R-rip. The thinning fabric tore, rendering the kerchief all but useless. There were no replacements for kerchiefs. This one would have to serve him the rest of the journey. *The rest of the journey.* The phrase conjured visions of all the deep angry water he would have to face until they reached the Western Sea. There would be no more respites. Every day he would have to face up to his fear; fear that, until the last few days, he thought he had conquered. He had not conquered anything. That was clear.

He was making his way cautiously down the treacherous incline toward camp when something red among the rocks stopped him. It proved to be another kerchief, the same color and pattern as his torn one. That would make it Willard's, if he remembered correctly. He noted that the cloth was still sound before jamming it into his pocket and continuing on.

Beyond the bottom of the falls, he came upon Willard crouched beside the river. Unaware that he had pulled out his own torn kerchief, he held it out to the big man. "Is this yours? I found it in the rocks."

Willard turned stiffly toward him but did not reach for the proffered cloth. The peculiar look on his face put Shannon on guard. "I'll lay it down here, okay?" He put the kerchief down and turned to go.

"It's ruint. You did it," Willard growled, springing at the half-turned Shannon and sending him sprawling onto the rocks. The next thing Shannon knew, Willard had clamped a vise-like arm around his neck. He struggled against the hold, trying to gasp out an explanation. "Mistake . . Yours . . . my pocket."

Willard grunted like a rooting pig and increased the pressure of his hold.

"Mistake," Shannon croaked.

"Torn! Ruint!" Willard growled.

The menace in the big man's voice compounded Shannon's desperation. "No!" he rasped, shoving at Willard's arm, trying to ease the pressure on his windpipe.

"Think you're so smart. Bah!" Willard pressed a knee into the small of Shannon's back, escalating the strangling effect of his armlock. Shannon's pleas turned to squeaks.

"Willard! Let him be!" Colter yelled.

"He ripped it," Willard snarled.

"Damn you, Willard, let up!" Colter bellowed, taking hold of the man's arm and pulling it away enough for Shannon to gasp out a weak "Help."

"Give off, damn you!" Colter kicked Willard hard in the shins.

Willard yelped and let go, and Shannon crumpled to the ground, heaving for breath.

Willard made a move for Shannon, but Colter slapped him across the face.

Shannon expected the slap to turn the big man against Colter. Instead, Willard's face and body relaxed as if he had just awakened in a strange place.

"You know what set him off, Fuzz?" asked Colter in a low voice, keeping his eyes on the big man.

Shannon drew Willard's kerchief out of his pocket and held it out for Colter who took it and placed it into the big man's fist. Willard stared at it with puzzlement. "How'd he get my bandana?"

"You tell him, Fuzz."

"I found it up in the rocks. You must have dropped it during the pull."

"Then I owe you thanks," Willard said.

"Thanks?" Shannon exploded. "That's all you have to say after what you just did?"

Colter stepped between them. "Willard, you go on over to camp. Fuzz and me got some talkin' to do. We'll be along in a minute, anybody asks."

"You can't let him go, Old Man. He —"

"Go on, Willard. We'll see you back to camp."

Shannon stared after the retreating man in disbelief, but Colter's glare held him mute until Willard was well out of earshot. "That man's a killer and you let him go!" Shannon exclaimed.

Colter dusted off his pantleg. "That weren't Willard come after you."

"Of course it was! You saw him. He was out to kill me." He rubbed the shoulder Willard had wrenched for emphasis.

Colter shook his head and picked Shannon's ruined kerchief off the rocks. "Weren't him."

Shannon snatched it away. "That man's a menace. We need to report him before he hurts somebody."

"What good'll that do?"

"Captains ought to know what that man's capable of."

"So's they can do what?"

Shannon was about to say "Lock him up" when he realized how ridiculous the suggestion was. Something had to be done, but what? "They need to know about him. It's up to them what they do with the information."

"Ain't no one needs to know nothin' 'cause there ain't nothin' to know and nothin' to be done except to keep goin' and make sure he don't get touched off no more. He's the strongest, steadiest rower in the crew. He don't never let me down. I cain't do without him. Not now. Not after comin' all this far, countin' on him." Colter turned to leave. "You comin'?"

"Later," Shannon grunted. Colter shrugged and walked off. Shannon put his fingers through the rip in the kerchief. This half-rotten rag had nearly cost his life. Twice now some small thing had sent Willard into a murderous rage. Only luck had saved him just now and Charbonneau back on the Kooskooskee. Luck and Colter. He had a duty to tell the captains about the man, to warn them what they were facing.

Then again, Colter had a point. What could the captains do, even if they knew about Willard?

Ordway showed up while he was considering this question. "Captain Lewis sent me out looking for you, Shannon. He wants to see you right away."

Despite his experience with the sergeant at Camp Wood, Shannon decided on the spur of the moment to tell him about Willard, to see what he would advise. Ordway listened intently to the recitation. At the end he said, "Willard's my responsibility. You let me handle it." He made to leave, then looked back at Shannon. "Thanks."

Thanks? From Sergeant Ordeal? Shannon did not know whether to be delighted or suspicious. Bending to scratch the flea bites on his bare ankles, he decided to accept the sergeant's gratitude for what it was: confirmation that he had done his duty. That and nothing more.

Colter wedged his body into a cleft in the rocks in an effort to get out of the chill wind sweeping down the river. The day had presented him with two dilemmas; one, frustrating; the other, worrisome.

The thought of the sleek Indian canoe would not leave him alone. With the real thing out of reach, he decided to carve a replica out of a knot of driftwood he found on the way to camp after subduing Willard.

Willard was his second problem, the worrisome one. He had come to rely on the big man's strength and steadiness in the bow of the scout canoe. The three of them — Willard, Shannon and himself — had melded into the kind of cohesive unit that acted from one mind, able to compensate for the river's tricks and the failings of even a Charbonneau.

He understood — or at least he thought he did — Willard's attack on the Frenchman. Lord knew Charbonneau deserved a good thrashing. But Willard's going after Shannon earlier, that was a whole different thing.

Captains ought to know what that man's doin'. He agreed with Shannon that this was one for the captains. However, he also agreed with his own response: *So's they can do what?* What could they do? What could anybody do but hope to be around to stop the man when he went berserk?

A commotion at the other end of camp drew him out of his musings. A boat pulled in next to the expedition's dugouts. He did a double-take. It was the Indian canoe, the one that he could not get out of his mind, with Captain Lewis in the bow and Drouillard in the stern.

Colter set aside his carving and hurried to see what was going on. Clark met him with a broad smile. "You and your good ideas, Colter. Now this Chinook canoe belongs to us. Meri and I changed our minds, captains' prerogative."

Lewis came up to them. "According to George, she handles exactly like you said, Colter."

"We had to trade the scouting dugout, however," Clark said. "First thing in the morning, you and your crew need to paddle it down to the Indian village.

"We will have to shift crews and baggage," Lewis said.

"Sergeants can do that in the morning, Meri," Clark replied.

Colter turned away, feeling worse after the ebb of elation at learning the expedition now had one of the beautiful canoes. "Sergeants" meant Ordway, and anytime that one shifted crews and baggage, he saw to it that Colter ended up worse off for the change. He had no illusions. It was only a matter of time till Ordway figured out a way to replace him as pilot.

Lewis went on. "On second thought, things are working fine the way they are. There is no reason to change. Colter?"

Colter turned back to the captain. "Sir?"

"You take the new boat. Same crew, same load."

"Yes, sir!"

Colter settled down next to Shannon. "We got us a new boat, Fuzz. Wait'll you see her. No more wet feet. She's a beaut. Captain traded off the scout dugout for her."

While Colter described the new boat, Shannon watched Ordway updating the orderly book by the light of the guttering fire. Why had he told the sergeant, of all people, about Willard? When Colter found out what he'd done, he would be furious.

Colter paused. Shannon grunted as if he had been listening, and Colter took off again, lauding the new boat's superiority over their old dugout. Shannon stopped listening after a few words. He owed it to Colter to admit what he had done. After all, but for Colter, Willard would have choked the life out of him. But how? Where could he begin? How could he explain the impulse to entrust Ordway with such sensitive information?

He realized that Colter had stopped talking and was staring at him. "It's been a long day. I'm done in," Shannon explained.

"Better take care of that shoulder you got wrenched," Colter said sympathetically.

Shannon reached up to rub it. "I will."

Colter leaned down and tapped Shannon's other shoulder. "It's this one, Fuzz."

Colter rousted out Shannon and Willard early to take the scout dugout down to the Indian village. He left Charbonneau to sleep rather than introduce early discord into the day when he would pilot the Chinook canoe for the first time.

He was back at camp and setting ropes into the new boat when Charbonneau finally appeared at the pile of baggage to be loaded into the new canoe. The Frenchman tried one load after another, discarding each, until he found a half-empty box. This he carried down to the Chinook dugout, dumping it on the sand.

"Oh, no, you don't, Frenchy! Put 'er *in* the boat," Colter demanded.

"You do eet," the Frenchman shot back over a rounded shoulder.

Colter was on his feet in an instant, grabbing the Frenchman's arm, twisting it behind his back, and frog-marching him to the dropped box. "No, you useless bag of skin! *You* do eet!" He shoved the Frenchman's face down toward the box and booted him in the rear.

Charbonneau stumbled and fell. As he regained his feet, he was muttering. "You got somethin' else to say, Frenchie?" Colter demanded.

Charbonneau straightened up and hawked spit into the dirt at Colter's feet. "Colter ees *merde*."

Colter took one menacing step forward, and Charbonneau retreated a pace. "You load 'er now 'fore I really get mad."

As the muttering Frenchman bent to do as he was told, Willard came down to the beach. The big man hefted two loads from the baggage and carried them to Cruzatte's canoe. "You got the wrong boat, Willard," Colter called out. "Over here."

"No, he's right, Colter," said Ordway, coming from the opposite direction. "He's on Cruzatte's crew from now on. I'll be riding with you in his place."

Colter crooked a challenging smile at the sergeant. "You will, huh? You picked a good day to make a change. That's for sure. Hear tell we got us a wild one today. Ridin' up front, you'll see 'er all first. That oughtta get your blood up."

Out of the corner of his eye, he saw Shannon come up short when he spotted Ordway beside the boat. The look on his face prompted Colter to recall that Fuzz and Ordeal had walked into camp together yesterday after the incident with Willard. It didn't take a detective to guess that Shannon had told Ordway about Willard. That explained the big man's shift to Cruzatte's crew.

The sergeant tossed a shrewd look at Shannon. "Sorry to spoil your fun, Colter, but it won't be me riding up front. Private Shannon here will have that honor. After all, he has the experience. I'll row in his spot."

Shannon's mouth gaped. "Me? In front?"

Colter looked straight at Shannon. Fuzz had been warned to keep quiet about Willard; yet, he hadn't listened, so now he would get what he deserved: the chance to be the first one to face whatever this big, treacherous river decided to throw at them. That ought to teach him if anything would. "Fine-a-ree, Fuzz up front, Sarge behind, and Frenchy and me in the back. Might as well get her loaded quick so's we can see what's down the way. I'm ready for a wild ride. Huh, Fuzz?"

Shannon blanched as he climbed unsteadily into the bow of the new canoe.

17. *Big Water*

T he bow swung abruptly to port, narrowly skirting a half-submerged snag. "Got them eyes closed again, Fuzz?" Colter yelled from the stern.

Though Shannon knew the jibe was deserved, the words stung. Defending himself against Colter was useless until he could get a grip on the fear that had him so rattled about riding in the bow.

Above the slap of wind-whipped waves against the thin hull of the Chinook canoe, his ears picked up another sound: the ominous throb of falling water. His intestines turned to water.

"I'm puttin' in ahead so's we can scout that there roar," Colter shouted.

A stop. Thank the Lord! With solid ground underfoot, he could catch his breath and settle down a little.

As soon as the nose of the canoe scraped into the sand, Colter and Ordway jumped out to go view whatever was in front of them, leaving Shannon and Charbonneau alone to secure the boat. The Frenchman stretched out on the bank and immediately began to snore. Shannon tied off the painter, then found himself a protected spot out of the wind where he could sit with his back to the river. There he drank in huge gulps of air, filling lungs freed for the moment from the constriction of fear.

By the time the other expedition boats put in, he was breathing and feeling easier. Another falls meant another portage. Another portage meant time to figure out how to get himself moved to another boat, away from Colter and Ordway, away from manning the bow of the lead canoe. Enlivened by the prospect of bettering his situation, Shannon joined the rest of the crew to meet those returning from scouting the river ahead. Of that group, only Colter did not look grim. Instead, excitement animated his face.

Captain Clark described what they faced. The entire sprawling river squeezed through a fifty-foot-wide gap between rock promontories. The thought that they would have to portage again only a day after working themselves to exhaustion at Celilo Falls brought a chorus of groans from the crew.

Clark held up his hands to restore order. "We've decided to try something different here. Our two best pilots, Cruzatte and Colter, believe this is a compression rapid. They say we can run the boats through rather than having to carry or rope them. That means two men in each boat, with the five pilots picking who they want as their seconds. The rest of us will lighten the boats' loads and carry the excess down below."

The crew broke into a buzz. Shannon did not join in. He guessed what was coming, and his blood ran cold at the prospect. He did not have long to wait for Colter to sidle over. "You got a front row seat, Fuzz, 'cause you earned it."

Shannon shoved his hands into his pockets so Colter could not see them twitch. "You don't think I can do it. But I can. I will."

Colter leaned toward him, his eyes ablaze. "You better, 'cause this here's big water. Bigger than anythin' you seen yet. Just the thing to teach you not to flap them lips of yourn."

"The bigger, the better," Shannon said defiantly.

The Chinook canoe had been relieved of two-thirds of its load when Shannon climbed into it. Faced with the rushing river, his false courage drained away. He looked after the crew straggling over the rocks with their loads. Among them was Ordway. He would never, never trust the man again.

"Whenever you're ready, Colter!" Captain Clark called out.

Colter acknowledged the captain with a wave. "Ready, Fuzz?" he taunted.

Shannon forced bravado into his voice. "Ready."

"Then I'll shove 'er out."

Shannon scarcely had hold of his paddle when the current grabbed the boat and swept it toward a solid massif of black rock. As they moved closer, the wall of rock loomed overhead like a figure in a nightmare. Closer still, he noticed a narrow cleft in the approaching rock. From where he sat the fissure looked like the eye of a beading needle, far too narrow to allow the whole huge Columbia to pass through. The roar grew louder with each downstream yard gained. His hands clutched the paddle, the only solid thing available.

Colter shouted through cupped hands, "There be two big waves. Only way through 'em is head on. If you don't do nothin' else, remember to keep paddlin'."

Shannon could not take his eyes off the sight ahead. Gone were thoughts of Willard and the sergeant, even Colter. For him, the only realities were the river and the moment and the terror.

The current quickened. The water's surface began to boil. Rock walls closed in, deafening him with thunder.

Without knowing how, he managed to jam his paddle down and pull once, then twice.

Suddenly the water in front of the canoe erupted into a churning mass of grayish foam. Waves converged from all directions, striking the boat, soaking him and making him forget where he was and why. He looked down at the paddle. What was he supposed to do with it?

Another wave crashed over the bow, sending frigid water sluicing over his head. Over the throbbing drum beat of the water, he heard Colter's faint cry of "Dig!" Though his mind seemed frozen, his body responded by reaching out and thrusting the head of the paddle toward the water.

In the split second before wood and river connected, a wall collapsed within him, releasing the full force of the fear he had withheld all morning, and paralyzing his arms.

He was held in the grip of that fear while a succession of waves burst over him one after another, leaving him shivering violently and gasping for breath. The next instant a vertical wall of water rose up in front of the boat. The nose of the canoe tilted toward the sky, throwing him backward.

He knew that if he wanted to save himself, he had to let go the paddle and grab the sides, but his hands were incapable of any movement.

From the stern of the canoe came the unmistakable sound of a whoop. Colter was actually enjoying this!

The nose of the canoe arced over, and the boat slid down, down, aimed straight into a yawning void. A strangled "No!" ripped out of his guts, eclipsed by the roar around them.

The next instant the bow slammed into the hole, flinging him against the bow. Clutching the paddle with one hand, he wrapped his arms around the carved bowpiece.

"Heads up!" Colter's yell came just as the nose of the boat started up another higher wall of seething water. This time the boat lay at an angle across the face of the wave. It was Shannon's responsibility to straighten out the nose. If he didn't, the wave would dump the boat over on its side and throw them both out. He knew he had to act, but he could not get his body to cooperate. The only thing it seemed capable of doing was to cling to the bowpiece.

Water from the rising wave poured over the side, drenching him and filling the canoe. For the first time he noticed a smell to the river, a mixture of moss and minerals, of soil and sweat, of salmon, deer and death. That scent evoked the words he had earlier thrown at Colter: *I can and I will.*

"Yes," he gasped, and at the sound of his own voice, he began to move, taking up the paddle, and, with eyes clamped shut against the sight of all that tumbling, churning water, driving it down into the swirling water

The water met his paddle and pulled back against his effort. He hung on, however, and jammed another stroke.

I can and I will. He felt, rather than saw, the canoe's nose reach its zenith and slide into a descent.

I can and I will. He powered another stroke and another, forcing aside all fear and fighting the river for his life.

The river was ferocious and his arms grew leaden from paddling against it, but he would not stop, would not surrender. Plunging and pulling, muscles burning, he drove himself on. *I can and I will. I can and I will.* The phrase rolled like a chant through his mind as he struggled to continue.

"You can stop now, Fuzz."

It took a moment before it registered that Colter's voice sounded normal, that the thundering had softened. Still, Shannon kept stroking, head down, eyes closed, every fiber of his being concentrated on the battle he was fighting.

"I said stop, Fuzz."

The command caused him to raise his chin and open his eyes to the sight of water placid as a forest pool at dawn.

"You can put that there paddle down now," Colter said.

Shannon stared at the piece of wood gripped in his hand. He watched his fingers unwrap their grasp, heard the paddle clatter into the bottom of the boat.

"Looks like we got us an audience," Colter said.

On the bank ahead stood a village of twenty Indian longhouses. The natives from the settlement lined the shore along with the portaging crewmen who were cheering wildly.

"Too much excitement. I'm tuckered out. Let's put in," Colter said.

Shannon turned stiffly. His voice wobbled in concert with his knees, but he was still determined to speak. "I said I'd do it, and I did."

Colter gave him a long look. "That you did, Fuzz. Eyes shut and hangin' onto the bow. You looked just like someone who'd go to Ordeal when he oughtta know better."

Eager crewmen surrounded the canoe, preventing Shannon's reply. The crowd parted to allow Captain Lewis through. "Good job, Colter!"

Shannon hung back, waiting his turn to receive the captain's praise. Instead, the next boat started through the narrows and Captain Lewis and the others turned to watch its run. Shannon did not have time to dwell on being ignored. The sight of the dugout tossed about on enormous waves of crashing water like a stick of wood made him back out of the crush of crewmen.

In an effort to blot out the comments and actions going on behind him, he focused on the native village. Its twenty-one longhouses were cloaked with wood planks rather than woven mats. In front of these structures rose a dozen pyramids of woven baskets, holding fish meal, seven below and five above. More fascinating, however, were the people. The skulls of every adult and child had been flattened to such an extreme degree that his artistic curiosity overcame his hesitation. He pulled out his journal and set to sketching the people and the town.

By the time he finished his fourth drawing, he became aware of someone watching him. He raised his eyes to find a small brown boy studying him and the drawings. "Ah, you're wondering what I'm doing, right? Here." He held the journal out to the boy.

The boy tensed but did not flee.

"I know you want to see," Shannon coaxed, pushing the book closer.

The boy reached out one tentative hand.

"That's right."

Suddenly the boy's interest fled and so did he. "You better run, you little weasel." The words belonged to Colter who came up behind Shannon. "Good thing I showed up, Fuzz. If'n he got hold of your book, it'd be a goner. These here Wishrams'll steal you blind."

"That a fact? And just how would you know?" Shannon said scornfully.

"Joe for one. His mouth-harp's gone. And Rube would've lost his knife if he hadn't been quick. If'n I was you, I'd keep my things close to hand."

"Well, you're not me, are you?" Shannon shot back.

"No, I ain't, but I'd still watch my things and keep away from that there young'un."

After Colter's departure, Shannon looked around but did not spot the boy. The Old Man had done it again. Ruined a moment that might never repeat. Confound his interfering hide!

Shannon was about to slam shut his journal when something among the crowd of Wishrams strolling back into their longhouses caught his eye. A woman carried a baby with its head bound between two slabs of wood jointed into a "V." Shoving aside the questions that came to mind, he fell to sketching.

Although the baby and its mother disappeared before he finished, he completed the drawing from memory. Then he studied the result. Why would someone do such a thing to a baby? What earthly purpose did it serve?

A sneeze interrupted his thinking. The little boy was back, sitting two feet away. "You're back. Good. What do you think of this?" He positioned the journal so the boy could see the sketch of the baby.

The boy looked at him suspiciously.

"Here. Take it. Go on." Shannon pushed the book toward him.

The boy took a hesitant step forward.

"That's right. Come on. I won't hurt you."

The boy took another step and another, then stopped as if afraid. Shannon held the book steady and waited, praying no one would show up before he had won the boy's confidence.

Cautiously the boy reached out his hand to grasp the book. Shannon sat still and waited.

The boy grasped the book. "That's it. Now have a look." Shannon gave an encouraging wave.

The boy pulled the journal close, turning it this way and that, studying the picture, feeling the paper. A smile began to play around his mouth.

Shannon pointed at the journal. "Book."

The boy managed to get out a "K" sound. "Book," Shannon repeated.

"Book," the boy said.

"Good. Excellent. Now, Shannon." He pointed to himself.

The boy mimicked the move, pointing to himself and saying something incomprehensible. Shannon shook his head and pointed to himself again. "No, me, Shannon."

"Shon-er," came the response.

"Shannon."

The boy looked down at the book as if taking in the unfamiliar sounds, then looked up. "Book."

"Yes, that's a book. Me, Shann —"

The boy took off running, clutching the journal like a prize. Shannon leaped up. "Come back here!"

The boy ducked into one of the longhouses. Furious, Shannon reached for his rifle to give chase but discovered that another Indian had hold of its stock. He kicked, catching the would-be thief on the knuckles. The native let out a yip, let go the rifle and slunk off.

With the attention of the rest of the natives on the dugouts running the falls, no one noticed the little altercation, so Shannon decided to go after his book.

He found the boy hunkered down between empty fish-meal baskets, leafing through the stolen journal. He skirted around behind the boy's hiding place and crept up without the youngster hearing him. He snatched the book cleanly away. "Book," he declared triumphantly. "Shannon book."

The youngster lunged out of his hiding place and vanished into the crowd. The journal fell open to a sketch of the village. Shannon now found the picture and the people revolting instead of interesting. He wanted to tear out all the sketches he had done of this place and its inhabitants. Wanted to erase the memory so it would not sully all the good memories he had of the other Indian tribes the expedition had visited. Before now, Partisan and the Teton Sioux were the only exceptions to a string of successful Indian encounters for the crew. Now . . .

He closed the journal and tucked it into his shirt where no light-fingered native could get it. From now on, he would mind his things. He would trust Indians again when they gave him a reason to do so. Not before.

18. *Ain't Worth Squat*

F orty miles below the Columbia Narrows, the river and land again changed dramatically. In the space of a few days, the expedition went from an arid land of few trees into one of rain, mist and huge fog-draped Douglas firs, red cedars, spruce and hemlocks. Below a cataract called the Cascades, they encountered the first evidence of tidal surge. Dealing with daily fluctuations in the river's ebb and flow added to the pilots' challenge.

October gave way to November. November advanced one wet day after another. Fog gave way to a howling wind that whipped the river into white caps and drove straight down on the boats, slowing the crew's progress to a crawl until it stopped them cold below a cliff-sided promontory. Captain Clark named the promontory Cape Dismal for its forebidding aspect against the perpetually cloudy skies. No one knew how far the ocean was, even though the air was thick with brine and sea-mist.

For five straight days the expedition tried to round the point only to be beaten back by screaming wind and lashing waves. For five nights the crew camped on a narrow shingle between the river and a cliff too steep and brushy to scale. By now, all the tents had rotted from the constant damp. For shelter the crewmen draped old elkhides over their heads and huddled into their blankets, catching whatever sleep they could while crouched in the rocks.

On the morning of November 10th, Shannon awoke feeling awful. His head and muscles ached. His nose was running and he could not stop shivering. He used the shreds of his rotted kerchief to blow his nose and surveyed the shingle camp through rheumy eyes.

Miserable-looking crewmen crowded the narrow rock-strewn space. Rain had darkened their drooping buckskins to the color of wet bark. Despair and hunger etched every face. The shrieking wind had long ago robbed everyone of the desire to talk, or even to grumble.

Colter was the only man up and moving. He came in Shannon's direction carrying two steaming cups. "This ought to help what's ailin' you." He held one of the cups out.

A sneeze seized Shannon before he could take it. At the same time the wind snatched the remnants of his kerchief out of his hand and sailed it into the river. He watched dully, lacking the energy to utter a curse.

Colter shoved a piece of rag into Shannon's hand along with the cup. "Here's mine. Now drink up your breakfast 'fore she's cold."

Shannon took a sip. Watery gruel. Again.

Colter settled down next to him. "Wind's dropped."

"Like hell it has." Shannon caught a surprise sneeze in Colter's rag. "Same for the rain in case you haven't noticed."

"Guess I best find someone else then."

Shannon repositioned the piece of soaked elk hide across his head. "If you're talking about getting back on that river today, that's a good guess."

"Captains want me to give 'er another try."

Shannon blew his nose. "They ought to be heading us back up river. Getting around this Point's impossible. As far as I'm concerned we found the ocean and it's nothing to write home about."

Colter gave Shannon a hard look. "Ain't you forgettin' somethin'?"

Shannon sneezed twice. "Since I've sneezed out half my brains already this morning, it's a wonder I remember my own name."

Colter looked back out at the river. "A man who forgets his promises ain't —"

"Ain't worth squat," Shannon interjected crossly. "Lord, what I wouldn't give to be under a roof next to a fire right now."

"Sergeant Floyd ain't never goin' to see another roof or another fire," Colter said quietly.

A series of sneezes left Shannon out of breath and aching in a dozen new places. Sergeant Floyd. The name came from a past so remote from this moment and place that he had trouble dredging up memories of the grief he had felt over Floyd's death and of the graveside promise he had made. "Floyd's lucky not to be here. I can't keep a promise if we can't get to the ocean, can I?"

Colter rose. "Cain't get there sittin' here. That's for sure."

"Try your buddy Willard."

Shannon sniffed and watched Colter move down the shingle of rocks to Willard, saw him talking earnestly to the big man and watched Willard nod and accompany Colter over to Rube and Joe. Then Shannon fell into a sneezing fit that ripped a hole through the elk hide he had draped over his head. He muttered every swear word he knew. Didn't the captains recognize the futility of hanging around here any longer?

He blew his nose hard, trying to unclog it enough to breathe. The attempt only served to gouge a hole in the rag Colter had lent him. That was the speck of sand that tumbled the pile for Shannon.

He levered himself to his feet and picked his way across the slippery snag of driftwood to where Colter squatted with Rube, Joe and Willard. He did not wait for an opening, "Okay, I'll go, Old Man, but we have to leave now before I change my mind."

"Hey, you hold on there, Peckerwood. I was just about to say I'd go," Rube protested.

Colter patted Rube on the shoulder and popped to his feet. "I got a crew now, Rube, and the tide's turnin'." He jerked his head toward Willard and Shannon. "Come on, you two. Time's a-wastin'."

🐦

Colter squinted ahead at the river's churning surface. Now that the Chinook canoe was away from the scant shelter of the headland, the wind jammed against them like an invisible hand, determined to stop them. He corrected the angle of the nose according to the course he had plotted in his head, then tucked his chin down and poured all his energy into paddling. For his plan to work, they had to get far enough out from the promontory in order for the river's flow and the receding tide to pull them around the Cape.

The sound of sneezing came to him over the sound of the wind. Shannon had turned out to be a lot sicker than he realized. He had to hope that the younger man would not give out before they reached the critical point. This was their best chance — maybe their only chance — to clear the obstacle that had stymied the expedition for five days. As low as morale and the food supplies were, the success or failure of the whole venture rested on this try.

A fresh blast of wind caught the canoe broadside, flinging up a sheet of spray. Colter scanned their course again. He was relieved to see that they were on target and that the projected point of turning was closer than he anticipated.

Shannon sneezed three times in rapid succession, interrupting his rowing cadence. *Maybe I should've picked Rube*, Colter thought.

In the prow, Willard rowed strongly, steadily. In contrast to Shannon's erratic strokes, he never missed a beat. His strength never flagged.

Despite the cold wind, Colter was sweating. His eyes burned from lack of sleep. His muscles burned from lack of food and rest. But he forced himself onward. He was not ready to accept defeat. Not until he and the river had one last rematch.

He glanced back at the promontory, forbidding in its drapery of gray mist, dark green foliage and wet-black rock. The river writhed around the Cape's base like a pack of vicious dogs bent on disemboweling a treed wildcat. The headland stood like the keeper of some other-worldly portal, determined to bar entrance to anyone unwilling to match wits with it.

The turning point was just ahead. He counted strokes: one . . . two . . . three, then shouted, "Ready about." A gust of wind flung his words back at him. Too breathless for another shout, he had to hope Willard and Shannon heard him.

He ruddered his paddle for the turn. For a moment their forward progress stopped. The wind and the river tugged at them from competing directions. Willard and Shannon lost synchronization.

Colter dared not lift his paddle before the nose was lined up. Waves dashed over the sides of the wallowing canoe and the wind pushed against the craft, fighting the turn.

Just as he was beginning to doubt success, Shannon craned around. There was a grayish undertone to the skin of his frightened face. Colter mouthed, "Dig!" praying his face did not give away his own trepidation.

Shannon turned forward and reapplied himself to his paddle. One faltering stroke. A second stronger one. A third, stronger still. By the fourth, he was back in cadence with Willard.

Slowly the nose inched around. Colter held his paddle steady until he judged they had reached the right angle, then he too joined the rowing, shifting his paddle to the opposite side of the craft to compensate for the new angle of the wind and current.

They were making good progress when Shannon suffered a prolonged sneezing attack and left off stroking. With one-third of their strength missing, the canoe's momentum slowed. Although Colter redoubled his efforts, port was his weak side and his muscles were already straining. The shore looked impossibly far away. He cursed himself for going with Shannon when he could have taken a healthy Rube.

Then a new sensation registered on his awareness. Although Shannon was still out of action, it felt as if a third oarsmen was rowing. It took a moment to realize that the help was coming from the tidal flow which was pulling them around the point in its rush back to the sea. He had guessed right. As a reward, he eased off rowing.

Relaxing proved a mistake. With nothing to balance Willard's strong strokes, the canoe's nose swung back toward the center of the river. Before Colter could correct the problem, Shannon reacted. He plunged his paddle back into the river before he had proper hold on it. Immediately the strong wind ripped the paddle out of his grasp and flung it into the ocean-bound tidal current.

Shannon cast Colter a stricken look. For the rest of the ride, he would be dead weight, worse than useless. *Should'a waited for Rube*, Colter thought irritably, bending to his paddle and mentally commanding his straining muscles to work harder.

Should'a waited. I knowed better. Reproach fueled his strokes, and, for a time, blocked out the burning sensation in his arms and shoulders. The burning turned to aching, then to torment. Still he rowed on, propelled by one concern: if they didn't make it now, no one else would try again and the expedition would turn back without reaching the goal they had come so far to achieve.

"Old Man, look!" The insistent voice brought Colter out of his self-imposed fog. "Look! We're here. You can stop rowing," Shannon said.

A broad sweep of sand led up to the perfect site for a camp in the protection of some enormous trees. They had made it around Cape Dismal.

◢

Shannon settled himself on the spongy ground. A gust of wind whipped through the canopy of trees above him, showering raindrops down upon his bare head. He hunched forward, resting his feverish brow atop drawn-up knees. He ached from his toes to his eyebrows, and he could not stop shivering. Still, they had made it around the headland. The only thing that kept him from stretching out and going straight to sleep was the rejuvenating vision of ocean whitecaps he was sure he saw in the distance.

With his mind elsewhere, he ignored the desultory conversation of Colter and Willard until he heard Colter swear. "Thunder-gol-durnation! That ain't no ocean we're seein' out yonder. It's still this bloody river. This here's another gol-blasted bay!"

Closer observation confirmed Colter's statement. If they had not yet reached the ocean, would they ever reach it?

A long silence hung over the three tired men, broken only by the drip-drip of rain off the surrounding foliage. Then Colter spoke, "Tide's turnin'. It'll carry us back if'n we catch it right now."

For the first time since leaving the east side of the promontory, Willard spoke, "I can't go." Shannon looked warily at the big man, unsure what to expect from the declaration. Despite Willard's two wild outbursts, the man was always ready to take on a challenge. He never complained, never wore out.

"My shoulder hurts something awful. I can't make 'er back just yet," Willard said.

Colter's shoulders slumped forward, and, for a time, he studied the wet sand at his feet. A distracting ringing began to sound in Shannon's stuffed-up ears, adding to the affliction of his running nose and fever-racked body.

Colter lifted his chin. "Then the two of you will have to stay here till the rest of us get back."

"Hold on, Old Man," Shannon demanded. "I'm not staying here." His voice sounded far away to his stuffed-up ears.

"Wind and tide'll carry me back same way as we come," Colter said. "Tomorrow I can lead the others over here."

The ringing in Shannon's ears grew louder. "No way are you leaving me here."

"It's damn hard to row without a paddle, Fuzz."

Shannon looked at Willard, but the big man did not offer up his oar, and Shannon knew better than to presume to take it.

As Colter headed out onto the river, Shannon was suddenly afraid. What if Willard went berserk again and attacked him? He could be dead before this day was out.

"You're sick, Shannon. Why'd you come?" Willard asked.

Aware that he had to avoid giving the big man any provocation that might lead to one of his fits, Shannon gulped back the sneeze that threatened to come and forced lightness into his tone. "Had to keep you company."

But the big man didn't seem to hear the flip remark. His eyes were locked onto something behind Shannon's back. "Oh, oh," Willard murmured.

Shannon turned to see what had made Willard say that and saw a group of native men materializing out of a riot of ferns and tangled bracken on the western edge of the clearing. He managed to control a gasp of surprise and realized too late that his rifle and Willard's were both leaning against a tree well out of reach. Neither of them could get to their weapons without making a move the newcomers might take as the signal to put to use the spears and arrows bristling from their hands.

Willard's low voice filtered through the growing roar in Shannon's ears. "They got just one gun amongst the twenty of 'em. Looks to be an old fowling piece."

The odds did nothing to keep a cold sweat from forming at Shannon's hairline. One of the Indians came forward and addressed them with what sounded like an order spoken through mush. "What's he say?" Willard asked.

"How would I know?" Shannon said crossly. "I don't speak his language."

The Indian spoke again, his voice louder, his face clouding.

"Oh, oh. He's gettin' mad," Willard said.

"Confound it! I'm not blind, but I still don't know what he's saying."

This time it was Willard's face that darkened. Shannon realized he had better do something and do it fast. He signed back the only thing that occurred to him.

"What'd you say, Shannon? He don't look happy," Willard said.

Before Shannon could explain what he had said, the native began to speak and sign simultaneously. Shannon replied in signs, translating for Willard. "They're Chinooks. He wants to know where we came from. I'm telling him from upriver."

"Jesus! Don't do that. They might attack the others."

"Why don't you talk to him then, if you don't like how I'm handling it?"

"No, you talk," Willard said. "Just get us out of this."

Two of the Chinooks wore knitted wool watch caps, the kind American and European merchant sailors wore. The caps brought to mind stories Shannon had heard of attacks made on the crews of trading vessels exploring the Columbia and surrounding territory. The Indians' spokesman signed some more. "He says he'll lead us to the ocean," Shannon translated.

"No way," Willard said. "I don't trust no pointy-headed savages. See how they're checkin' out our rifles."

Shannon made the signs and the Indian spokesman traced his reply. Shannon had to swallow to keep his voice steady. "They want to camp with us tonight."

"Sure they do, so they can steal our guns. Well, they ain't gettin' mine. Not without a fight," Willard said.

The big man moved to pick up his rifle. Shannon had no choice but to follow suit, expecting at any moment to feel the sharp thud of an arrowhead pounding into his heart. To his surprise, the Chinooks did not move.

Shannon glanced sideways at Willard whose face was edged with irritation. That emotion had begun to twist the big man's features, the first sign of a building explosion. There was no telling what might happen if he had a fit now. Shannon struggled to figure a way out of the situation, but his fever-soaked brain did not want to work. Meanwhile, the natives shifted restively, waiting for a reply.

Needing to say something to break the stalemate, Shannon signed, "I thanked him for the invitation and accepted their offer to be their guests tonight."

"You what?" Willard thundered. "You want to get us killed?"

Fighting down another sneeze and growing weary of the criticism, he swung on the big man. "Hey, if you don't like the way I'm handling this, you come up with something better."

Watching Willard's face turn from red to purple, it hit Shannon that he had just blown up at the one man more dangerous to his life and limbs than the natives. However, the purple began to fade from Willard's face as soon as it appeared and his voice turned querulous. "Why guests?"

"Every Indian tribe we've come across so far has strict taboos against harming a guest."

"You mean, you're playin' a hunch?"

"Do you have a better idea?" Shannon asked in exasperation.

Willard held up his hands in acquiescence. Shannon took two wheezing breaths to calm himself before he turned back toward the natives. To be sure the Indian spokesman got his point, he repeated, "We are honored to be your guests tonight."

The man's reaction was hard to decipher. He waved for the sniffling Shannon and Willard to follow him and his band into the forest. Doubt flooded over Shannon as he fell in behind the slope-headed Chinook. His observations about the way Indians treated guests applied to those tribes the expedition had encountered before they reached the Columbia River. From thievery to lying and double-dealing, so far the natives who lived along the Columbia had proved false every assumption of goodness he had ascribed to Indians.

"We're surrounded. This is suicide," Willard grumbled, hugging his rifle to him.

"This is the best chance we have, so shut up!" Shannon warned. He was all too aware of the armed Indians silently bringing up the rear, the rotting vegetation and foreboding gloom of the surrounding forest. What if he was wrong?

The forest gave onto a small clearing. Quickly, silently, the Chinooks built the most substantial fire Shannon and Willard had seen in weeks. Despite his misgivings about their hosts' intentions, Shannon huddled close to the blaze, grateful for its warmth and the chance to dry out.

After a meal of roasted fish and cakes made of wapato root, the Chinook leader stood up and stretched expansively. Under his breath Willard murmured, "They can't get our rifles if we sleep on them."

"No, it's better if one of us keeps watch."

"That figures," Willard grumbled.

"What's that supposed to mean?" Shannon demanded, checking a sneeze.

"Means that figures," Willard snapped.

This time it was Shannon who backed off. "I'll take first watch."

"You do that." Willard stretched out with his head on the butt of his rifle and tilted his cap over his eyes.

Shannon blew his nose and pretended to turn in as well, laying his rifle next to him, his hand gripping the barrel. He closed his eyes to wait until the Indians dropped off so he could assume his watch.

The next thing he knew, Willard was shaking his shoulder and urgently whispering his name. Shannon struggled to sit up. It hurt to swallow and his head felt packed with cotton. There was a painful pressure behind his eyes and he could not remember where he was.

"Some watch you kept, Shannon. Now they got both our guns," Willard said. "You got us into this. Now get us out."

Shannon was set to argue when the Chinook leader swaggered over. Mustering all the dignity he could manage, Shannon rose to face the man whose cruel mouth now sported a crafty smile. "We demand the return of our rifles," Shannon said.

"Use your hands," Willard hissed.

Shannon repeated his demand in signs. The leader held out his empty palms, then gestured toward his men implying their innocence also.

"Don't toy with me," Shannon muttered, slashing the air with another demand for the return of their weapons.

This time the leader signed a curt denial.

The man's manner insulted Shannon into action. In a move perfected in militia drills, he grabbed the nearest Chinook, wrested the man's war club out of his hands and locked him into a choke hold.

The Chinook leader shrugged and started to walk away. Furious, Shannon raised the club over the man's head. "Stop or he's dead!"

The leader halted. His smile vanished, replaced by a cunning scowl, as he set to loading his fowling piece.

"Now you done it, Shannon," Willard said.

"Unless you got a way out, Willard, shut up!" he shot back, frantic to figure a way out of their mess.

"Now what?" Willard said to Shannon's signs.

"I'm telling them that if they don't return our guns by noon, a group of white men will come from upriver and put them all to death."

"Noon?" Willard exploded. "For all you know, the crew might never get here."

Shannon needed help, not criticism, but arguing with the big man in front of the Chinooks was not a wise move. They might not understand the words, but they could read the flaring emotions and hear the fear in their voices. With great difficulty he checked his anger and lowered his voice. "I bought us some time. If you think you can do better, be my guest."

He let go his captive, and, still clutching the war club, walked off to blow his nose and collect himself. The Indians went into a huddle around their leader. Between watching them jabber and darting glances at the river, his uncertainty increased with every passing minute. Noon could not be that far off. What if Colter had failed to make it back to the others? After all, he had been alone in the canoe; anything could have happened.

Willard drew in a sudden breath. "Sunshine."

The shroud of clouds had parted to reveal brilliant sun at its apex. Noon was here. Between the cold clogging his head and the fever ravaging his body, the men and objects around Shannon began to take on a surreal quality. He was trying to shake off the effects of the temporary hallucination when the huddle of Indians parted and the Chinooks looked toward the eastern side of the clearing.

"Someone's comin'," whispered Willard.

Shannon shifted his grip on the war club, determined to take out as many Indians as he could if they rushed him. The ground around him seemed to undulate in time with the throbbing inside his skull. He strained for sounds, dreading to hear the incomprehensible babble that would mean Chinook reinforcements.

"Oh, my God," Willard gasped. "It's them."

Captain Lewis strode out of the woods, illuminated by a column of sunlight. Drouillard, Rube and Joe were on his heels.

A huge sneeze exploded out of Shannon. Wiping his nose on his sleeve, he marched over to the Chinook leader, fixed him in an imperious gaze and began to sign. Immediately the Indian barked at one of his followers who vanished to reappear moments later with the missing rifles. Shannon continued to sign, paying no attention to the guns.

"For Christ's sake, Shannon, we got our guns. What more do you want?" Willard said.

"I'm telling these pilfering slope-heads that we'll put to death anyone who steals anything at all from us again. Anything."

"You cain't say that," Willard continued.

Shannon turned away from the deflated Indian leader, gathered up the rifles, and carried Willard's to him. "I can and I just did. As of now, they're on notice."

"That ain't your place and you know it."

"It's our rifles they stole. Any chance I get to throw the fear of God into these thieving vermin, I'll take. Now keep your mouth shut about what's happened. I'll do all the talking. All of it, hear?"

"Talk all you want, Shannon. Only leave me out of your conversation. You're plumb crazy!"

Shannon watched Willard stalk angrily away to greet the captain, regretting that he had made an enemy of the man. *Well, that couldn't be helped,* he reminded himself and turned to meet the men who had just saved his hide.

19. *Ocian in Sight. Oh, the Joy!*

— An entry in Captain Clark's journal

Once the whole expedition made it around Cape Dismal, Captain Clark surmised from his maps that they had entered the eastern end of

Baker's Bay and that the difficult promontory had already been named Point Ellice by previous Columbia explorers. Those same maps showed the Western Sea close enough to walk to. Colter was one of the few men to join the captain to make the walk and confirm that the map was right. Shannon joined the small group at the last minute, and Colter decided to drop back to walk with him. He was curious to learn what had happened to Shannon and Willard the night they had camped with the Chinooks. Something had happened, he was sure of it, because there was now a distinct coolness between the two men.

Shannon greeted his arrival with, "What are you doing here?"

"Cain't a body want some company without gettin' snapped at?"

Shannon blew his nose. "I'm not up to much talking."

"Me, neither." Colter didn't probe. Shannon was not one to keep quiet for long. He would open up soon enough.

Shannon motioned for Colter to take the lead, and they walked along to the accompaniment of the younger man's snuffling and wheezing. With his mind free to wander, the image of Fragrant Grass spun into Colter's thoughts. An image he did not recognize as memory. She was alone inside her lodge, dressed in an elaborately-painted hide dress the color of flesh. Her hair was plaited into two sections, braided with strips of gray fur and strings of blue beads. Her head was bent as she studied something in her hand. That something was the hawk carving he had left for her.

A man with an indistinct face and blurred body moved out of the corner of the image to stand before her. The man spoke, words too muffled to understand. Fragrant Grass nodded and wrapped the hawk carving in a piece of doeskin. As she bent to tuck the small bundle into a hanging pouch, there was a finality about her movements, a finality that made Colter's blood run cold. She rose to her feet, brushed the back of her hand across her eyes and —

Just as he was about to see her face, the face he had not been able to summon up for weeks now, the scene faded. He was unaware that he had stopped walking until Shannon touched his arm. "You see a ghost?"

He refused to admit what he had seen, to himself or Shannon. "I was just thinkin' about what's next, now we made 'er all the way out here."

"I expect the captains will try to find a trading ship to restock our trade goods supply. Then we'll settle in for the winter," Shannon said.

Colter looked around at the riot of damp, dripping vegetation. "We best hope this ain't the place they choose, then. This here weather'd crack a body's sanity in a month."

Shannon wiped his nose on his sleeve. "I don't care where we stay just so it's dry."

Dry. The word formed the seed of a plan that began to take root in Colter's thoughts until shouts from the top of the slope interrupted. The rest of the group was cresting the ridge. "Come on, Fuzz. We're missin' out on all the fun."

A fit of coughing cut short whatever Shannon started to say. He waved

Colter to continue on.

Colter stopped short of the crest to wait for Shannon. The two of them had shared the whole journey thus far in tandem. They would share the first view of their final goal the same way.

The view from the top anchored them in awe. The whole world beyond where they stood was filled with water. More water than either of them had ever imagined. Water that flowed from all the rivers the expedition had travelled and all the rivers beyond those. Moving, heaving, restless water too vast and deep for men to know. Vaster than all the land they had just crossed.

Here that land ended. Land wilder than a drunken dream, more majestic than a palace. Land devoid of expectation, yet pregnant with every possibility. A place for dreamers and seekers, for those forever pulled to see what lies over the next rise.

Both of them had paid a heavy price to get to this place, but, in that one timeless moment, wonder erased all thoughts of the cost. Standing on the edge of the world, Colter understood why he had been drawn West across the continent. He had left the Draft to find a place of temporary refuge. Instead, he had found a woman to love and a place where they could belong together. Along the way, he had found himself.

Laughter drifted up from Captain Clark and York who were racing across a rock-strewn beach below toward the surf. "You ready to do some wadin', Fuzz?"

Shannon gulped. "It's deep, isn't it?"

"We ain't goin' in far. I'm wet enough already."

A blast of wind struck them. Between chattering teeth, Shannon said in a strong voice, "Damn right, I'm ready."

Descending the slope on the ocean side was worse than climbing it from the land side. With every step, tangled thorn bushes clutched at Shannon's clothing, tearing the rotting hide and lacerating his skin. In making sure he kept his footing, he forgot to be worried about what awaited him at the bottom.

The slope ended at a shelf of tossed-up driftwood and slippery rocks sprinkled with coarse sand. Colter walked out to a stony point scoured by waves. "Come on, Fuzz."

There's no need to be nervous. It's just like a riverbank, Shannon told himself over and over as he walked slowly out to his friend.

Colter swept his arm in a wide arc. "The Western Sea, Fuzz. We made 'er."

Shannon could not move, could not look away from the ebb and flow of the water. The wash of the surf combined with the wind to muffle out all other noises. The smell of brine saturated his nostrils and lungs, filling his mouth with its taste. His heartbeat faltered. Only Colter's solid presence kept him from being overwhelmed by the sensations.

"The others're are headin' off north. You'd best be quick 'bout wadin',"

Colter warned.

Shannon remained rooted.

Colter walked out into the water until the ocean lapped over his knees. "Floyd should'a seen this."

The mention of the dead sergeant reminded Shannon of his grave-side promise. Struggling not to panic, he took one tentative step toward the breakers. Then a second step. Then a third.

On the fourth step the advancing wash caused him to hesitate. The ocean was rising up, reaching out her hand to grab him, to drag him into her arms, into her depths. She knew his fear and that made her want him for her own. She would embrace him. She would suck the air out of his lungs and crush the life out of his limbs.

Surf washed over his worn moccasins, shocking him out of his vision. As it lapped at his ankles, then receded, leaving his feet wet but free, he could feel Colter's eyes on him. Two more steps, he coaxed himself. *I'll go to the water, not wait for the sea to come to me.*

One foot, then the other splashed into the foam-flecked water. The surf flowed around his calves, then sloughed away, leaving him upright and safe, alive and free. He had been wrong. The ocean had not claimed him. He had faced it and won!

A feeling of triumph brought a lump to his throat. He raised his head, presenting his face to the wind, savoring this victory over a lifetime of fear.

At that exact moment, a sizeable wave crashed into him, wetting him to the waist and ripping a yelp of surprise out of him. The sound broke the moment's spell.

Elation surged through his bloodstream. He had done it! He was really here! Now he could go home to his parents, to his father with his head held high. Passage or not, he had done something that only this small handful of Americans could claim. With the Western Sea foaming around his legs, he spread his hands in a salute to the arching clouds. "Here's to Sergeant Charles Floyd and the Western Sea. Here's to the Corps of Discovery."

Colter stretched his hands up, too. "Amen to that, Fuzz. Amen."

It was no use. No matter where Shannon positioned his body, the gale drove rain between the drift logs he and Colter had wrestled into a pile to form a shelter. Would this infernal storm never end?

Beside him, Colter worked away at his latest carving, oblivious of the storm outside. He sucked constantly at the toothpick stuck in the corner of his mouth. The sound of that sucking set Shannon's teeth on edge. It had been nine days since he first saw the Western Sea and two days since a gale pinned the expedition down after crossing to the south side of the Columbia. For two days, he had been crammed shoulder to shoulder with Colter, crouched under a tumble of wet wood in a space barely wide enough for one man. Two days of enduring a wrenching cough so painful he feared it would crack his ribs. Two days of putting up with Colter's toothpick sucking. "Stop that!" he snapped.

Colter's knife jerked. "Durn it, Fuzz. You 'bout ruint my piece."

Shannon grabbed the toothpick out of the man's mouth and flung it into the rocks. "You're driving me crazy with that — *achoo!*"

Colter swiped a hand across his face. "Durn it! I hate bein' sneezed on!" With a look that dared Shannon to complain, he picked up another sliver of wood, stuck it into the corner of his mouth and sucked away.

A sudden cramp gripped Shannon's bowels, checking his anger, propelling him out into the storm. He had to lean into the wind to keep from being toppled as he scrambled to the upper end of the rocky spit away from where the expedition was pinned down. The force of the pelting rain stung the places where his skin was exposed.

He could not get his belt unknotted before his bowels evacuated into his trousers. The storm whipped away his anguished groan.

Humiliation forced a decision. He had to find a way to affect where the expedition would winter over. He had to find a way to convince the captains to move upriver to a drier climate where they could find game to replace the diet of fish and roots that had turned his bowels and everyone else's to soup.

He stripped off his pants and, in the process, poked a hole in the right rump. He stared at the hole in exasperation. It was bad enough to never be dry, but with water sloshing in unimpeded onto his bare buttocks . . . While he rinsed the mess out of his pants, he sifted through ways to sway the captains' decision. By the time he pulled the wet trousers back on, he had settled on a course of action.

Colter glanced up at his return. "Good trip?"

"We got to get off this coast," Shannon said.

"That's what I been sayin' for the last three weeks."

"All you've done is talk, but talk doesn't get the job done."

Colter snorted derisively. "Way you smell, ain't no one gonna listen to you. Have a little accident, did ya?"

Shannon shrugged off the question. "If the captains can't make up their minds about where to settle for the winter, we need to help them."

"If you mean, like me and some others tried to do back at the Maria's, forget it. I ain't fool enough to go agin' the captains no more. No way."

"You don't have to do anything, Old Man, except stand behind me when it comes time to count who's for heading upriver instead of staying on the coast."

Colter laid aside his carving. "That there cold's affectin' your mind, Fuzz. You're forgettin' yourself. You ain't gone agin' the captains this whole trip. Not at the Maria's. Nor at Three Forks."

Shannon banged his fist against a log for emphasis. "I'm not going against anything. Captains haven't made a decision. I'll help them make the choice the crew wants."

"How do you know what the crew wants?"

"I'm going to find out by talking to them. I figure that's better than rotting in this hole with you."

"What about those don't agree with you?"

"It won't be hard to convince them to our way. Any fool can see what a few months here would be like."

"One thing about you, Fuzz. You're right sure of yourself," Colter said. "Well, good luck."

"That I won't need."

Colter went back to concentrating on his carving. "Don't be so sure."

Shannon dismissed him with a disdainful wave of his hand and hurried off to begin his mission.

20. *Gumption*

S hannon spent most of two days moving from one group of crewmen to the next, talking up the notion of standing together to convince the captains to spend the winter in the drier regions upriver rather than remaining on the coast. By the end of the second day, he had talked to everyone and had promises from most of the crew to back him. Two of the hold-outs he expected: McNeal and Willard; but two others troubled him. Rube and Joe would not budge from their stand that it was the captains' decision where they stayed the winter. Not the crew's.

On the night of November 29, he returned to the log cave he shared with Colter worn out and more than a little disheartened after spending hours trying to change the brothers' minds. He replied to Colter's greeting with a weary grunt, then fell into an exhausted slumber leaned up against the logs. That night he dreamed he was lying between white sheets atop the feather mattress in his room at home with the smells of his mother's biscuits drifting up from the kitchen below.

The next morning he awoke to an alteration in the usual sounds outside. The wind had dropped, creating a quiet his ears were not used to.

"Glad to see you're still livin'," Colter said.

Shifting painfully, Shannon groaned. His back was stiff from sleeping upright again and his bladder was full to bursting. Before he untangled his limbs to crawl outside, a pair of legs appeared at the opening to the little cave. Captain Lewis bent to peer in.

Seeing the very man he had been rallying the crew to sway flustered Shannon. He did not know whether to scramble outside or stay where he was.

The captain addressed Colter. "Are you up for an adventure, Colter?"

"Anythin'd be better'n sittin', Captain."

"Good. Get your things. We'll take the Chinook canoe."

The captain made to stand and Shannon blurted out, "I want to go, too, sir."

"Only healthy men, Shannon."

"I'm well, Captain. Cold's gone."

Colter shot Shannon an incredulous look.

"I plan to move fast. You sure you can keep up?" the captain asked.

"Positive, sir."

"Very well, then. Be ready to leave in five minutes." The captain splashed away.

"Cold's gone? Positive, sir?" aped Colter. "What're you thinkin' of, Fuzz? This ain't gonna be no picnic."

"This is my chance to get Captain Lewis aside to present our case. I can't *not* go. There might not be another opportunity. You want to spend the winter here?"

"How're you fixin' to hide that there cold of yourn?"

"I'll figure something out. I have to."

"Got to hand it to you. You got gumption."

Shannon's shoulders squared. Gumption. That was just the word to describe the new Shannon. The one that had faced starvation not once, but twice, and survived. The one that had shot the grizzled bear. The one who had faced down the Chinooks to get their stolen rifles back. Yes, George Shannon had gumption. More of it than anyone realized. And now he would get the chance to show what he was made of by convincing Captain Lewis to take them to a habitable place to wait out the winter. Gumption.

Captain Lewis's adventure turned out to be a scouting expedition composed of the captain, Drouillard, Labiche, Rube, Colter and Shannon. Instead of heading out to the ocean to search for a trading vessel as Colter expected, the captain ordered them to explore a river that flowed into the Columbia from the south. That task proved more easily ordered than accomplished. First they had to ferret out the main channel from among the dozens of possibilities that laced the river's mouth. Then, as pilot of the Chinook canoe, Colter had to feel his way along the winding course while keeping them from dead-ending in the many marshy areas overgrown with brush and small trees.

Once on the river, it became apparent that the captain and Drouillard were looking for something. Colter viewed their mysterious search with a mixture of curiosity and disquiet. He was too preoccupied to pay much attention to how Shannon managed to mask the symptoms of his cold.

The river's exploration stretched into six wearing days without Shannon approaching the captain. Then on December 4th, Drouillard called out, "*Capitaine, voilà.*" He pointed toward a rounded hill rising thirty feet above the high-water mark ahead.

"Put in, Colter," Lewis ordered.

The canoe nosed into the marshy grass at the bottom of the hill. The captain and the half-breed leaped out and scrambled up the incline. Once they were out of earshot, Rube broke a three-day silence. "Don't know about you three, but I'm goin' to find out once and for all what them two been lookin' for."

Labiche responded. "*Moi aussi,*" and the two headed off in pursuit of the captain and Drouillard.

Colter looked at Shannon. "What about you?"

Shannon sneezed three times in rapid succession, bending forward to muffle the sounds in his lap. "What about me what?" he sniffled.

"When you goin' to do what you came along for?"

Shannon took pains to mask the sound of blowing his nose. "When the time's right."

"Seems to me you've had lots of right times the last six days. Maybe you ain't got gumption after all."

"Now you wait just one minute."

"Waitin's all I been doin'. What happened to all that big talk o' yourn?"

"Nothing's happened to it. You'll see. Once Captain Lewis hears the crew is behind me on this he'll —"

"I will what, Shannon?"

Neither Colter nor Shannon had heard the captain's approach. Shannon's mouth moved but only a sneeze came out.

"Bless you," said Lewis. "I thought you were over that cold."

Shannon still did not speak, and the captain turned to Colter. "Since Shannon seems to have lost his voice, you tell me what you two were discussing."

Colter looked at Shannon, who would not meet his eyes.

"Well, Colter?" Lewis demanded.

Colter lifted his chin. The task had fallen to him. "Time we settled for the winter, Captain. Crew wants to go upriver where it's drier."

Lewis glanced at Shannon who blew his nose noisily. "You speak for all the crew?"

"Fuzz. . . I mean Shannon here, he does."

Lewis turned back to Shannon. "What has gotten into you today?"

"I . . . I don't know, sir," Shannon stuttered.

The captain dismissed that subject with a wave. "Never mind that. Answer my question."

"What question, sir?" asked Shannon.

The captain's voice was too soft. "Does all the crew want to go upriver for the winter?"

Shannon darted a frantic glance at Colter. He had lost his nerve. Either Colter stepped in or they would lose the only chance they were likely to get to make their case. "All but a few, Captain," Colter said.

"How few?" demanded Lewis.

"Three, maybe four."

"The rest of you will be disappointed, then." Lewis pointed up to the crest of the hill where Drouillard stood. "We will stay here for the winter."

"They ain't no game, sir. What're we goin' to eat for four months?" Colter argued.

Lewis swept an arm toward the half-breed. "George and I found numerous elk tracks up there just now."

Shannon recovered. "Excellent choice for a fort site, Captain. Best one I've seen so far."

Colter could not believe the drivel pouring out of Shannon's mouth.

There was irony in the captain's voice. "Glad you approve, Shannon. We will leave two men here to hunt while the rest of us go back for the others."

Colter had to speak up. "Might be tracks, sir, but whatever critters live hereabouts ain't goin' to be worth much. Not in this wet, they ain't."

Lewis turned a cold stare on Colter. "That will remain to be seen, Private."

Colter was not about to give up so easily. He kept pressing. "Food's one thing, but, hell, Captain, they ain't nothin' here. How we expect to get along without Indians to trade with? And the ocean's way over yonder if'n you're lookin' for a ship. At least upriver it's dry and there's game for sure."

"He doesn't speak for me, sir," Shannon chimed in. "Request permission to stay behind to hunt."

Lewis nodded. "Good. Drouillard will stay with you. Good luck to you both." He walked up the hill to the half-breed, leaving Colter with Shannon.

"Why, you chiselin' heap of shit!" Colter shoved Shannon. "You'll talk to the captain, eh? You'll get us upriver, eh?"

"Let me alone, Old Man," Shannon demanded.

"I'll leave you alone. For good."

"What does that mean?"

"Means I'm throwin' you away once and for all."

"But we're friends," Shannon said.

"Oh, no, we ain't. Not after what you just done."

"But I didn't do anything."

"No? From my angle you sold out me and the rest of the crew rather than stand up to the captain. You're a coward, Shannon. Worse than Frenchy. I don't brook with no cowards. Now get out of my way or get run over."

Shannon stepped aside and Colter shoved past him without a look or a regret.

PART 6

CLATSOP WINTER

Winter, 1805 – 1806

Rained verry hard . . .
— William Clark's weather diary entry,
January, 1806

1. *Rot*

End of December, 1805 — Fort Clatsop

T he ceaseless coastal rain rotted everything: wood, clothing, moccasins, meat, men's souls. Shannon endured a fresh downpour while he
waited dejectedly beside a downed elk for the sounds that would herald the
arrival of Drouillard with the dugout to carry them back to the newly-
finished Fort Clatsop. It had rained every day but one since the crew
reached the coast. In less than a month, he had lost his appetite for hunting.
He and every one else had come to loathe this place, the rain, the chilling
damp, the rot.

He shifted his weight to scratch a nagging itch in his crotch. His movement caused the rain pooled on the brim of his hat to flood down his neck.
"Damn!" he muttered.

The sound of his own voice after days spent in silence prompted an up-
welling of such loneliness that, for the first time since his falling out with
Colter, he allowed himself to admit how much he missed the man's friendship.

After Colter had called him a coward, he had spent an exhausting month
running away from that word and all that it implied. Now he had nowhere
else to run, and nothing left to do but face the truth. He had let Colter and
the rest of the crew down. He was . . . a coward.

For comfort, he stroked the coarse hair on the dead elk's muzzle. Tomorrow was January 1, New Year's Day, 1806. Instead of a feast, the members of the crew would be lucky to get one decent serving of meat apiece
from this woefully thin animal. Another failure, compliments of George
Shannon.

The Chinook canoe nosed into sight. Shannon rose slowly on damp-
stiffened legs that made him feel sixty years old instead of not-quite
twenty. Drouillard grunted a greeting and waited for him to load his kill
next to the half-breed's take of two wild turkeys.

They came out of the protection of the creek an hour later to find another
gale blowing up the Columbia. Before they could get turned upstream, the
strong wind grabbed hold of the canoe and nearly drove them into a massive tangle of driftwood until they could regain control. From that point to
the mouth of the Netul River, the stream that led to the new fort, Shannon's whole focus was on getting back to Ft. Clatsop in one piece.

It wasn't until they were back in the shelter of the hulking cedars that
grew along the Netul's banks that his thoughts could shift back to his lost
friendship with Colter. Although he wracked his brain for some way to
mend the breach between them, the canoe reached the boat landing below

Fort Clatsop before he had come up with any solution.

He had just lifted the elk carcass out of the canoe when Colter emerged from the nearby lean-to that served as one of the fort's two latrines. Their eyes met. The hostility in Colter's gaze made Shannon turn away.

He stayed at the dugout, pretending to fiddle with the canoe's tie-down lines until both Colter and Drouillard had entered the fort, then he slumped down on a rotting stump. He desperately needed someone to talk to, to confide in, to argue with. Especially that. His arguments with Colter had kept him on his toes. Sometimes they had even made him change his mind. Always, he learned something. Without Colter to disagree with, he felt stagnant and uninspired. "I need you, Old Man," he whispered.

Speaking his heart called to mind something he had noticed in Colter's look. Beneath the animosity, there was something else. Something deeper. Something troubled. Enough time had passed since the expedition reached the ocean for the elation of that accomplishment to be overshadowed by thoughts of returning home. In Colter's case, home meant Fragrant Grass.

Suddenly, out of the muddle of Shannon's thoughts, an idea took shape. An idea that could prove to be the solution to his problem. With more enthusiasm than he had felt for days, he slung the dead elk across his shoulders and started for the fort.

🦅

Fort Clatsop was built in a square, fifty feet to a side. Two rows of rooms faced each other across a twenty-foot-wide compound. The row on the west side held four rooms with the largest assigned to the captains. Charbonneau, Sacajawea and Pomp occupied one of the smaller rooms bracketing the captains'. The other was the sergeants' orderly room with the small room on the north end set aside for smoking and storing meat.

Three equal-sized rooms along the east wall housed eight crewmen each. Sharpened pickets walled the north end of the compound. A small gate set into that wall gave access to a freshwater spring and the second latrine. The main gate faced the boat landing to the south.

Colter was standing his post in the little guard shack built into the wall outside the captains' room. He hated everything about the fort and its surroundings: the perpetual cloud cover, the never-ending drizzle, the sight and smell of rotting things, the sudden drenching downpours, the riotous foliage and looming oversized trees, the boredom of waiting for winter to end. The monotony of Fort Clatsop made the three months to the end of March seem an eternity away. Exacerbating the situation, at least five times a week, he had some miserable outside duty, thanks to Ordway.

Colter poked his head out from beneath the overhanging roof. Clouds the color of dirty towels cloaked the sky again, weighing on all the crew, causing every man to drag through his tasks and withdraw increasingly into lethargy.

Potts emerged from the middle barracks room and glanced up at the leaden sky before padding through the mud and puddles to the guard post.

Potts relieved him, and Colter sloshed across the compound to his barracks. For the last four hours he had done no more than stand in one place, looking out at the rain, yet he felt as tired as if he had walked thirty miles.

Inside the room the stench of unwashed bodies, damp hide and smoke from fires built with wet wood overpowered the smell of the new-sawn wood of the walls. For a change the room was empty except for Collins and Gibson who sat on opposite sides of the small central fireplace, staring morosely into the flames, lost in their own worlds.

As Colter threw his hat onto his bunk, he noticed a lump under the ragged blanket. That lump turned out to be a scroll of tanned hide. He unrolled it to find a portrait of Fragrant Grass.

His heart knotted at the sight of her precious face before he could wonder where the picture came from. The rendering was exquisite. He could not take his eyes off her likeness. *How'd I ever leave you?* In the echo of that old question, the feeling spawned from his recurring dream of the last month hardened into the belief that something had happened to her in his absence. Something terrible.

He had to put the picture down until the paralyzing sense of powerlessness it raised in him passed. Once he regained equilibrium, he recognized the drawing as Shannon's handiwork.

The door opened and Rube entered. Colter thrust the picture behind him just before Rube reached the next bunk. "Ordeal's sendin' me huntin'. Again," Rube said, stuffing his pack without enthusiasm. "What Shannon brought back yesterday ain't gonna feed Pomp, let alone the rest of us so now I got to step in. Damn Peckerwood's hide." He finished and slammed back out the door in a temper.

Shannon this and Shannon that. Wherever there was a problem, you could count on Shannon being the root cause. Shannon was responsible for condemning the crew to living — if anyone could call it that — out the winter in this god-forsaken place.

Colter re-rolled the picture and tossed it on Shannon's bunk. Much as he liked the picture, he refused to keep it. Forgiving Shannon required a saint, and a saint he wasn't.

*

McNeal stopped just inside the fort's gates and turned to Shannon. "I'm goin' to let you in on a secret."

After a miserable day of gathering wood with the cook, Shannon had had plenty of the man and his endless tales of sexual conquest. "Not interested," Shannon said.

McNeal went on anyway. "You know that Clatsop village about two miles that-a-way?" He thumbed toward the west. "Last week I saw a couple of young fillies ripe for the pickin'. I tell you, lookin' at them, my pecker got so hard I like to broke it climbin' into the dugout."

"You don't say," Shannon said sourly.

McNeal neighed a laugh and punched Shannon's shoulder. "You're a stitch, Shannon. Come on over to my barracks. They're savin' extra grub for me. We can talk some more."

"Some other time." Shannon headed for his barracks as fast as his tired legs could drag him. He let himself into the little room, slammed the door shut behind him and slumped against it, exhausted from the day's accumulated tension. For him, wood-gathering was the worst duty at Fort Clatsop, but doing it with McNeal was pure hell.

"Welcome back, Peckerwood."

Shannon pushed himself away from the door and acknowledged Joe with a nod. Then he remembered. Before he left that morning, he had put the drawing of Fragrant Grass under Colter's blanket as a surprise, figuring to give the man all day to accept the idea that he was trying to make amends.

A quick scan of the room located Colter seated behind Joe at the fire, engrossed in his carving. Nettled at being ignored by the man he was trying to appease, Shannon went to his bunk to find the familiar roll of hide atop his blanket. He stared at it in dismay. It had never occurred to him that Colter might refuse it.

Joe came up behind him and thrust into his hands a bowl containing three pieces of gray-tinged meat floating in a watery broth. "Saved you some stew."

Shannon tried to hand the bowl back. "Not hungry."

Joe refused to take the bowl. "That's your problem."

Shannon looked from the food to the rolled hide to Colter beside the fire. Nothing was going the way he planned.

Colter raised his head, glaced briefly his direction, then went back to his carving, leaving Shannon feeling as insignificant as a pile of sawdust.

"That's it!" He picked up the picture and slammed back outside. The drizzle had abated for the moment. He stopped in the middle of the muddy compound, trying to decide what to do next.

McNeal came out of the next barracks room, opened his trousers, and proceeded to urinate into the nearest puddle. Shannon watched, appalled at the man's blatant disregard of the captains' strict orders to use the latrines.

McNeal was tucking himself back into his pants when he noticed Shannon. "What you got there?"

Impulsively Shannon handed him the bowl of food.

McNeal snatched it greedily and pointed at the rolled hide. "That for me, too?"

Why not? Where else was he going to use it? Shannon handed the picture to the cook. Balancing the bowl in the crook of his arm, McNeal examined the drawing in the weak light coming through the cracked door. His eyes flicked warily up to Shannon's. "This here's Colter's squaw."

Rain began pelting down in earnest. "It's just a picture. Use it or throw it away. Whichever." Shannon turned his back on the cook and splashed down to the boat landing, mindless of the puddles. He had failed to make amends with Colter. He did not intend to try again.

Shannon lay motionless on his bunk until the door closed behind Rube who had the dawn watch. Then he shifted cautiously toward the edge of the bunk to minimize the creaking of the leather straps that made up the frame. His objective was to avoid company, even if that meant getting up long before anyone else.

He tied on his ever-damp moccasins, draped a blanket around his shoulders and crept to the door, opening it slowly so as to make no noise, and closing it behind him with the same care. He gave a curt nod to Rube in the guard post and let himself out the narrow door in the rear stockade wall. Only when he was outside the fort and alone did he breathe freely. He had never overcome the discomfort of relieving himself in the presence of others. Getting up early to visit the latrine had become as critical to him as food. He considered losing a little sleep to have this time to empty his bowels in private was well worth the price.

He stepped across the clearing past the spring, luxuriating in the moment of rare solitude and his body's growing urgency. This latrine was fifty yards farther from the fort than the one near the boat landing. Most of the crew frequented the latter. For that very reason, he preferred this one.

It had been three days since Colter refused his attempt to mend their rift, and the rejection still stung. He made up his mind not to tell anyone what had transpired or to let anyone see how it bothered him. Only McNeal knew anything, but that posed no problem since the rest of the crew either avoided the cook or ignored his blathering.

The latrine's low roof required him to duck to enter. Good, it was empty. He untied his pants and squatted over the trench with his back to the entrance for additional privacy. No sooner had he set himself than he heard McNeal's familiar voice, "So this is where you get off to every mornin'."

The cook strolled in and squatted down next to Shannon. "Figured you'd want to hear what you done for me." He chuckled. "Yes, sir. Thanks to you, I cracked me a right fine teacup last night."

With the need to void his bowels approaching urgent proportions, Shannon was condemned to stay where he was. "Teacup? What are you talking about?"

"That picture you give me, it got me one of them young Clatsop squaws I was tellin' you about."

"You talk about so many women, you need to refresh my memory," Shannon said disdainfully.

"I swear, Shannon, smart as you are, sometimes you be thick as a tree."

Before Shannon could answer, a shadow darkened the lean-to's opening. Colter peered in. "I'll wait," he said.

Colter's presence rattled Shannon. He made to leave, but the cook tugged at his shirt. "Let me tell you the best part. It's not ever' day a man gets him a fresh one. If'n you know what I mean."

Shannon felt a flush spreading across his face despite his best efforts to curtail it. "Let go of me, McNeal."

"Her mama stood right there and watched us."

Shannon pried off the cook's hand. "How disgusting."

"No, not a-tall. It was excitin', if'n you know what I mean." The cook dragged the tip of his tongue across his lower lip.

"I don't want to hear anymore."

McNeal followed Shannon outside. "Yes, sir. Her mama stood right there. Kept one eye on us and the other on that picture of Colter's squaw."

Shannon held out his hands in supplication to Colter. "It's not what you think."

"Was, too. That there picture of your squaw got me a young'un to break in, Colter," McNeal bragged.

Colter's right hook caught the cook on the jaw. McNeal yowled as a blackened tooth with a bloody root flew out of his mouth, bounced off Shannon's forearm and dropped into the mud.

The commotion brought Ordway and Pryor from the fort. While Pryor led the complaining cook away, Ordway slammed Colter against the lean-to wall with a force that made Shannon wince. "Two weeks inside'll take the fight out of you, Private."

Colter glared defiantly at the sergeant but stopped short of talking back to the man. As he was being hauled off, Colter's malevolent stare left no doubt that he would loosen a couple of Shannon's teeth, given the chance.

Alone again, Shannon took stock and decided he was blameless. After all, it was Colter who refused his gift which gave him the right to dispose of it however he saw fit. He wasn't responsible for what McNeal had done with it. His conscience was clear. Colter's anger was misplaced at best. He had done nothing wrong. Nothing. He ground the cook's tooth into the dirt with his heel.

Colter walked in front of Ordway, feeling grim satisfaction. In hitting McNeal, he went against a life-long principle of never throwing the first punch, but how good it felt when his fist plowed into the repugnant cook's face! And how he longed to do the same to Shannon for desecrating Fragrant Grass's image in such a despicable way.

Upon reaching the back wall of the fort, Ordway ordered him to brace against the picket wall. "You deserve two years, Colter. Not two weeks. If I were captain —"

"Which you ain't," Colter shot back.

"I'd have you hung." The sergeant took a short step back, and his face took on a studied look. "Only, then you'd miss out on the punishment you really deserve. The one you'll get any day now." He made a show of straightening his worn uniform. "Ship's liable to show up at any time."

"You finally run outta squaw beads, Sarge?" Colter asked sarcastically.

"You're a pilot. How long do you guess it'll take to get back to Washington — by ship?"

Colter could see where this was leading and shot back, "No time a-tall, seein' as how there ain't no ship. Even if there was one, ain't goin' to be room for this whole crew, let alone one man. Passage on a ship costs money, Sarge, or ain't you heard?"

Triumph flashed into Ordway's hooded eyes. "We might be short of a lot, Private, but money to pay for the crew getting back to Washington on a ship is no problem. Not when Captain Lewis carries a letter of credit against the U.S. Treasury for whatever that passage might cost. A letter signed by the President himself."

Colter's mind raced through the implications of this new information for his return to Fragrant Grass. Ordway peered into his face. "Why, Private, did something I said upset you?"

It was all Colter could do to keep from jamming his clenched fist into that leering face. He managed to keep his voice level. "It's just gas, Sarge."

"Sure, it is. Inside. March."

The day after the altercation at the latrine, Shannon had no assigned duties. All week he had looked forward to spending the entire day inside the barracks, sitting next to the fire, drying his clothing, getting thoroughly warm, and relaxing. Instead, he had to put up with Colter's constant glare tracking his every move. He was willing to talk, to argue about what happened, but Colter refused to talk, preferring a hostile silence.

The situation soon drove Shannon outside where the compound was its usual mire of mud and, also as usual, it was cold and raining. "Damn your eyes, John Colter," he muttered in the direction of the depressing layer of clouds.

"Shannon!" McNeal splashed over before he could duck back inside. The cook grabbed his arm and held him fast. "Has Colter gone stir-crazy yet? Can't happen soon enough to suit me." Every "s" forced spittle through the new vacancy in the cook's front teeth. "Listen," McNeal dropped his voice to a conspiratorial rasp. "I'm headin' over to that Clatsop town tonight. How about you come along? We can have us a real good time together. if'n you know what I mean." He jabbed a bony elbow into Shannon's ribs.

York's hail from the open doorway of the captains' quarters across the way saved Shannon from answering. He pulled out of the cook's grasp and hurried across the compound.

"Captain Meri is feeling poorly today. He asked if you'd do some work for him," York explained.

"Of course," said Shannon. Inside the captains' room, a fitful fire blazed in the wall fireplace. Captain Clark hunched over a table set along one wall, studying his ever-present maps, oblivious of everything else. Lewis lay sleeping on one of the two beds.

York led Shannon to a second table and told him to copy verbatim the contents of the captain's journal into another notebook. Since anything beat having to be out in the rain or enduring Colter's pique, Shannon settled down to work.

Except for places where the captain's scrawl required interpretation, the work was mindless, and Shannon's interest in the task soon dwindled. While his hand continued to copy the endless boring details that made up the record of their westward journey, his mind wandered along a path that led him to consider how his life had changed for the worse in a little over a month and the part he had played in those changes.

His reverie was broken when Captain Lewis threw off his blanket and sat up. With his hair awry, his clothing rumpled, his face pale and drawn, the captain looked more unkempt than Shannon had ever seen him. While York tended him, Shannon kept his eyes averted to give the captain some privacy. However, the interruption had broken his concentration, and, after several mistakes, he said to no one in particular, "I've done all I can today, so I'll be going."

When no one objected, he got up from the table and quietly let himself out the door. He was surprised to find that it was dark. This day had passed faster than any other day since the expedition arrived on the coast. He decided to wander out to the latrine to prolong the return to his barracks and Colter's bitterness.

He had just reached the lean-to when a hand clamped over his mouth. "Listen, I got news," McNeal said, showering Shannon with spit. "But just for your ears, since you're my friend."

The filthy hand released him and Shannon snapped, "What now, McNeal?"

"Use that kinda tone and I'll keep it to myself."

"It's been a long day and I'm all done in," Shannon said, softening his tone a bit.

McNeal accepted the shift in Shannon's attitude and lowered his voice. "We're sailin' home, soon as a ship comes."

Shannon drew back in horror. "What?"

"Heard it from Sarge himself. Captain Lewis stayed out here close to the coast because he's lookin' for a ship to take us home. He's got some letter from Old Tom Jefferson hisself that'll pay our passage."

A ship . . . on the ocean . . . the deep, dark, endless ocean. It couldn't be true. Shannon was unaware that his head was wagging until McNeal said, "What do you mean, no? I give it to you just the way I heard it, and I figure news like this oughtta be worth somethin' real special in return."

Dread — the kind deep water raised in him--drained Shannon of the ability to think or speak or move. Yes, he had followed the Missouri, the Kooskooskee and the Columbia. He had waded into the Western Sea, but crossing that huge, deep, rolling ocean. . . he could never, never do that.

"Well, what's it gonna be?" McNeal demanded. "What're you gonna do for me, seein' as how I brung you good news?"

Good news? The cook's revelations had been the worst possible news. He put the cook off with a shaky "Tomorrow," stumbled back to the fort, and slipped into his barracks before McNeal could catch up with him.

Since it was late, all the men were back from their details. Only Colter took notice of his arrival. Shannon stood with his back to the door, feeling the hard-packed earthen floor beneath his feet. *The ocean. No! I can't. What am I going to do?*

His eyes darted around the crowded room. Someone had to help him.

The only someone who knew of his weakness.

He wedged his way through the crowded bunks to Colter's. "Old Man."

Colter's chin whipped up, and he held Shannon in an unyielding gaze. "Don't you never call me that no more. And don't bother talkin'. I ain't interested in anythin' you got to say. Git outta my sight."

Shannon desperately needed for Colter to understand. "There's going to be a ship," he rasped through his fear. "One that'll take us back home."

Colter's voice was low and menacing. "A ship, huh? Guess you got a real problem then, don't you?"

Suddenly the room was too small and too close for Shannon. The atmosphere felt like a noose, choking the life out of him. He had to get back outside, had to get a breath, had to put a wall between himself and Colter's malevolent glower.

He paused before opening the door. He had kept his fear of water a secret from everyone but Colter all the way from St. Louis. No matter what happened, no one else must find out. No one, especially McNeal, who might be outside the door at this very moment.

To his relief, however, the compound was empty. There was no sign of McNeal. Relieved, Shannon looked around, searching for a place to think, a place where no one would consider looking for him. His eyes fell on the meat room.

Although a saltworks had recently been established over on the coast, the men assigned to that detail had produced only enough salt to flavor the crew's food, not preserve it. Without salt, fresh meat spoiled quickly. As a result, the meat room stank worse than an abattoir. No one went near it without good reason, making it the perfect refuge.

He pushed open the door and disappeared inside.

2. A Ticket Home

A shout of "Sunshine!" awoke Colter at dawn. Overnight the perennial cloud cover had broken. Eager for a rare day of sun, the other men of his company quickly vacated their cramped room to go off to their assigned details, leaving him alone to get through this, the last day of his confinement. By now he was sick of carving. That left him with the choice of thinking or worrying or pacing the narrow aisle between bunks to pass the time. Back and forth, back and forth, he plodded, trying to grasp the thread of a thought that had been hanging just out of reach for the last week. A thought connected to the reason why taking a ship back to Washington made no sense.

The door opened and in shuffled Shannon, stooping as if the very air weighed him down.

As Colter watched Shannon plod to his bunk, the thought he had been trying to capture crystalized. Back at the Great Falls, the captains had decided to cache all their specimens and field notes, rather than send a boat back to St. Louis. Since Lewis and Clark would never allow all that vital

research to be lost, that meant that someone — probably a small party —
had to go back by land. "That's it!" He was unaware that he had spoken
until surprised by the sound of his own voice.

"Ah, shut up," growled Shannon.

Colter's racing thoughts blotted out the comment. He had to make sure
he was among those going back overland. He had the ideal qualification as
the pilot of the Chinook canoe, the most reliable craft in the expedition's
fleet. Colter regarded the boat as his own, a sense of ownership that the
captains and the other crewmen deferred to.

As he exulted in the first optimistic moment he had experienced in
months, the door banged open to admit the arguing Field brothers. Seeing
Colter, they abruptly stopped talking. Then Joe blurted, "Blame him, Colter. He's the one lost it."

"Durn you, Little Brother," Rube warned. "Quit tryin' to weasel outta
this one. You was the last one out of the boat. Last one out ties her off."

"Weren't my fault, Colter," Joe declared. "Bet one of them Chinooks
stole her. You know how they are."

Rube pointed an accusing finger at his brother. "Don't blame the Indians,
Little Brother. You let Colter's boat drift off. Time you fessed up."

Colter's mind could absorb only one fact: The Chinook canoe had been
his ticket back to Fragrant Grass. Without it. . .

⬥

The specter of an ocean return turned Shannon's entire world upside
down. His life became a nightmare, fueled by the knowledge that he would
never survive an ocean voyage, that stepping aboard a ship was as good a
suicide.

For the next three weeks he spent every day copying the captains' journals, all too aware that he was doing so to provide a second copy in case
the first books were lost during their return. Lost. He dared not dwell on
the word and the horrifying images it raised. Every day he worked to put
forward a false front of normalcy, aware that his mask could slip at any
moment, revealing him as the imposter, the weakling he really was.

By February 1 his nerves were shredded and his state showed in the
mistakes he made on every page he copied. He left the captains' quarters
weighed down by the sense that he had betrayed the leaders' trust in him.
He was barely aware of the rain lashing his face until McNeal planted
himself in his path. "Tonight, Shannon."

The last thing he needed at the moment was one of the cook's schemes to
sneak out to one of the local Indian villages. He had never gone with
McNeal. He intended never to go with him. He never gave the man any
encouragement, but still the cook persisted by inviting him. "It's raining,"
Shannon observed.

"That's good. Ain't no one goin' to suspect us then. Besides, rain's good
for these squaws hereabouts. Gets their blood up."

"Not tonight, McNeal."

The cook grabbed his arm. "Not so fast, Shannon. Whether you come or not, I need me some tradin' material."

"No."

"Yes, Shannon. Or else."

Something in the cook's tone stopped Shannon. "What do you mean by that?"

"Or else I'll tell the captains about your little problem. The one you been tryin' to hide all these months."

Shannon drew back, repulsed by the man's breath and the cruelty in his twisted smile. "Problem? You're dreaming, McNeal."

"Am I? Ain't nobody can keep a secret from me. Nobody. Not even you."

All the fight ebbed out of Shannon. It was true. One way or another McNeal managed to know everything about everybody. "All right. One picture. But that's all. One."

McNeal let go of his arm. "That's plenty as long as it's as good as that last one. Got my eye on a sweet little thing. She's got these two —"

Shannon stormed into his barracks before he had to hear more.

Colter waited with the gathered crew for their assignments. With so many men sick, there was a good chance Ordeal would be forced to let him leave the fort for a change. Weeks of hanging around the place had him primed for anything that got him outside the walls, including wood-gathering. He would even settle for a day of hunting with Shannon if it meant not having to think about the lost Chinook canoe and how that loss had hurt his chances of getting back to Fragrant Grass this year.

Ordway stepped out of the orderly room. He named off assignments, leaving Colter's to the end. "You get to clean the meat room, Private. Captain wants it nice and tidy."

Shannon had been paired with McNeal to hunt. Colter watched them leave together through the front gates before turning toward the meat room. Even with the door shut, the smell of death and decay coming from it made his gorge rise. He was steeling himself for the task ahead when voices drew his attention to the front gate in time to see a man stagger into the fort and immediately crumple into the mud. The gate guard, Hugh Hall, yelled for the captains, then knelt beside the fallen man.

Colter ran to lend a hand. He scarcely recognized Willard who had been at the coastal salt camp with two other crewmen for the last six weeks. In that time the big man had lost so much weight that his skin hung off his frame like a too-large suit.

Hall and Colter had Willard back up on his feet by the time Clark, York and Ordway arrived. Willard spoke with great effort. "Captain, we got trouble."

"Were you attacked?" Clark asked.

"Nothin' like that. It's just that . . . that we're all three sick. Bratton, he can't hardly move. Somethin's wrong with his back." He swallowed with obvious difficulty. "We need someone to spell us awhile."

Colter spoke up. "Send me, Captain."

Clark glanced at Ordway. "Sergeant?"

Ordway surprised Colter by agreeing. "You'll have to walk, Colter. We don't have a canoe to spare," Clark said.

At this point, Colter would crawl to get away from the fort, if that was what it took. He hurried off to gather his things.

The closer Shannon got to the fort, the slower he walked. The slower he walked, the more hopeless he felt. He had spent all of yesterday searching for game without coming across a single track. He had gone so far he had not been able to make it back to the fort, and he had been forced to bivouac overnight in the hollow of a rotten tree without even his tattered blanket for warmth. Now here it was nearly noon and he had nothing, nothing to show for his efforts. To make matters worse, he would have to endure the needling of the crew for his overnight absence when teasing was the last thing he wanted to deal with.

The emaciated Willard was standing guard on the front gates. His placid expression changed to a dark frown at Shannon's empty hands.

Shannon sloshed across the muddy compound to his barracks, glad that no one was about. For a change the room was empty. Or so he thought until he saw the blanket on his bunk moving. The cause was McNeal and an Indian woman.

"Off my bunk, McNeal," he said crossly.

One of the cook's hands snaked out from under the blanket to wave him away. The gesture hit Shannon exactly wrong. He ripped away the blanket and dragged the cook and the Indian woman onto the floor.

The squaw looked warily at Shannon. She was missing both her front teeth and Shannon guessed that the scars on her bare thighs were venereal. He jerked his chin toward the door, and she scuttled out of the room.

"Damn you, Shannon! I was about there."

"Get out!"

The cook struggled to his feet, pulling up the pants that were puddled around his ankles. "Now just one minute here. I got my rights. You weren't nowhere around."

"Out!"

"No, by God! I ain't leavin'. I got a right to stay and do as I please."

"Not on my bunk, you don't."

"By God —"

Shannon's left hook caught the cook in the mouth and another of the man's blackened teeth found its way onto the dirt floor. "Out!" Shannon ordered.

McNeal's lisp was twice as pronounced with two front teeth missing. "I'll go to the captains, tell 'em about your little problem."

From outside came the call for assembly. "Good," said McNeal. "I'll tell the captains now so's them and all the crew can see what happens to them what crosses me." McNeal swaggered out the door.

With the cook about to reveal his long-held secret, Shannon's temporary fury sank back into a well of despondency. Suddenly he was exhausted. He cast a longing look toward his bunk before heading out to muster.

Since it was afternoon, there were gaps in ranks where the hunters and wood-gatherers normally stood. A harried-looking Captain Lewis came out of his quarters and climbed atop a stump to address the assembled men. "It is the end of February. Time to begin preparations for our homeward journey."

Shannon braced for the bad news that a ship had arrived.

"Captain Clark and I have decided that —"

A tic began to work under Shannon's left eye.

"— since no ship has arrived, we will — return by land on April 1st. Your sergeants will hand out assignments for those preparations. Dismissed."

Shannon was trying to absorb the captain's announcement when McNeal nudged him. "Wanna come along, hear me tell the captains about you?"

Shannon looked down his nose at the cook. "What problem, McNeal?"

McNeal's mouth twisted with rage. "I'm warnin' you, Shannon. This here's the end of you."

"Go ahead. Tell your story to whoever'll listen. We both know who the captains'll believe though, don't we?" Shannon turned on his heel and walked away from the fuming cook. Freed now from the possibility of a sea voyage, he felt as if a huge weight had fallen from his shoulders. He felt lighter and freer than he had in months. Once more, life was sweet, and there was a new bounce in his step.

Colter dumped an armload of wood on the pile, then straightened to massage his tired back muscles. When he came to the salt camp two weeks ago, he was not prepared for the miserable conditions he found. The two remaining crewmen were too hobbled by pain in their legs and arms to move around, and the hut they had built for shelter and sleeping gave scant protection from the incessant cold wind sweeping in from the ocean. As a consequence, they had been able to produce little useable salt for the fort.

He immediately relocated the hut to take advantage of a sheltering sand dune and took over those tasks that required the most movement — procuring wood for the fires and hauling buckets of seawater up from the ocean — leaving the fire-tending and salt-boiling to the two weaker crewmen.

The Clatsop Indians from the nearby village kept a daily vigil on the camp from the top of a massive drift log that had been driven onto the sand by a past storm. Draped in their rain-shedding capes and conical hats and oblivious of the rain and stiff wind, they seemed insatiably curious about the activities of the strangers in their midst.

As Colter looked over these people now, one of them rose and started back toward their village. He himself had done some watching, observing the Clatsops building one of their excellent canoes. From what he had seen, the departing Indian was in charge of the construction.

He eyed the pile of fire wood. There was enough there to free him up for a couple of hours though he would have to hustle to catch back up later.

"Oh, oh, we got company," Bratton wheezed, curtailing Colter's plans. A straggling line of men, with Ordway in the lead, were approaching the camp along the beach to the north.

"Help me get up, will you, Colter?" Bratton asked.

Colter gave the man a hand up, then held him steady until he could balance on his own. Bratton was in sorry shape and his condition was deteriorating daily. Whatever the approaching detail's mission, Colter owed it to the man to convince Ordway to take him back to the fort.

Ordway arrived first and started issuing orders immediately. "Colter, douse that fire. You two, stack the kettles over here."

"Mind tellin' us what's goin' on?" Colter asked.

Ordway turned toward him. "You mean, 'what's going on, *sergeant*, don't you?"

Colter gritted his teeth. He wanted an answer, not an argument. "Yes, *sergeant*."

"We're dismantling the operation and taking the equipment, the salt and you three back to the fort." He thwarted further conversation by walking away.

Rube joined Colter. "Sarge tell you the news? We're headin' back east-ways April 1st."

So a ship had come at last. How had he missed seeing it sail past? "When'd it arrive?"

Rube drew back a little. "It? What are you talkin' about?"

Colter was only half-listening. His mind was on learning how to build a canoe to replace the one Rube and Joe had lost. April 1st gave him only a month. If he had to go back to the fort now, he would never learn the last critical steps in the building process. Appealing to Ordway to stay would be worse than useless. The sergeant would find a way to subvert his intentions. His only hope lay in convincing the captains that he had a workable plan and that they needed to allow him to carry it out.

He was unaware that the sergeant replaced Rube at his side until Ordway spoke. "Ah, so Rube told you. Too bad. I wanted to break the news to you personally."

The sergeant glanced toward the men gathering up the equipment and hammering the last casks of salt closed. "We're returning overland, in case you're wondering."

He brushed a piece of leaf off his shoulder. "That is, most of us are. Captain Lewis still wants to get word of our accomplishments to the President as quickly as possible. So a few men will be left behind here on the coast with copies of the captains' diaries to wait for a ship."

Colter was immediately wary of the casualness of Ordway's tone. The sergeant continued. "When Captain asked me who I'd choose to stay," his lips parted, "guess whose name popped up first?"

"Mine, of course. Who was second?"

"Surely you know, Colter."

"Just wanted to hear it from you direct, Sarge."

"All right then. Your best friend. Shannon."

On the way across the compound, Shannon's mind was clear and his resolve, strong. When presented with McNeal's accusations, he would speak to his record on the expedition and claim the cook's story was a fabrication. That was his plan until the door to the captains' room shut behind him, and he was left alone to face Captain Lewis. "I think you know why you are here, Shannon. What do you have to say for yourself?"

In the ensuing silence with the captain's gaze leveled on his face, every word, every thread of what he had so carefully rehearsed deserted Shannon.

"Well?" the captain said.

The door opened, admitting Colter with a rush of damp air. "Beggin' the captain's pardon, sir, but this cain't wait. Sarge brung me back too soon. Them Indians over to the coast are carvin' them a canoe. They're about done, and I got to watch the last bit of the buildin' so's we can make one to replace the one Rube and Joe lost."

Lewis did not suffer interruptions and his tone made that clear. "The answer is no."

"But, captain, I —"

"No, Colter."

Still, Colter pressed. "At least tell me if what Sarge says is true. You plannin' to leave me and Shannon behind to wait for a ship whilst the rest of you head back?"

Shannon stared at Colter in stunned disbelief. *Stay behind? Wait for a ship?*

"That is the current plan," Lewis said coldly.

"Captain, that don't make no sense at all. I'm the best boat-handler you got. Sarge, he's had a bone to pick with me since way back at Kaskaskia."

An abrupt movement of the captain's hand cut Colter short. "You have made your point, Private. You are dismissed."

Colter seemed ready to press his argument further but wisely left. Shannon's heart felt as big and hard as a fist in his chest. He had come in here believing he was exempt from an ocean voyage, only to discover he was not. He had to think fast. Had to come up with a reason why he shouldn't be left behind. But his mind was a muddle, incapable of forming a single cohesive thought.

"Where was I?" the captain said, looking with annoyance at the papers scattered across the table in front of him.

Shannon edged out the door and ran across the compound and out the gates. In his blind rush, he nearly collided with a group of Indians hauling baskets of fish to trade at the fort. He ran down to the boat landing where the river cut off his escape.

As he stood on the river's edge, frantically searching for something to reassure him, one fact wormed its way through the mire of his anguish. There was no way out of here. The captains held his life in their hands. They could order him onto a ship. They could order him to wait on this god-forsaken coast for as long as it took. And there was nothing, nothing he could do about it.

Colter awoke to a crash, followed by a loud "Horseshit!" Rube glared at the mess he had made trying to get the fire going. In the expedition's two years the man still had no patience or skill when it came to starting a fire. Joe was the fire-builder in that family and usually took over such duties, but he was down sick along with everyone else in the barracks except Rube, Colter and Shannon.

Colter rolled wearily off his bunk, figuring he'd better help Rube before the man hurt himself or set the fort afire. The fire had just caught when Shannon came back in from the latrine and started gathering his things for another day of hunting. Colter considered laying into Shannon about the poor game he had been bringing back but decided that sarcasm took more energy than he had to spare.

He stared into the smoking fire. By the notches he had scratched into the log next to his bed, today was March 17th. Fourteen more days to April 1st, the day of departure. Departure for everyone else, that was. Instead of thinking out his argument beforehand, he had acted impulsively, barged in on Captain Lewis, interrupted the captain's conversation with Shannon, and blurted out whatever came to mind, gutting any chance he might have had to be included in the return party. Oh, how Ordway must have laughed over that one!

Ordway. Once Colter returned from the salt camp, the sergeant had kept him on an even tighter leash than ever. The imposed restrictions were doubly hard after the freedom Colter had enjoyed at the camp. If that wasn't bad enough, Ordway had the uncanny knack of choosing Colter's most vulnerable moments to make comments to keep him on edge. What if a ship never came? How could a handful of men hope to survive among the surly coastal natives, let alone make it back to St. Louis alive? How was he ever going to get back to Fragrant Grass? And when?

Colter glanced up as Shannon let himself out. Fuzz looked sick, too. There was an unhealthy pallor to his skin, and he had lost so much weight that he had to gather the waist of his stained hide trousers and cinch them tightly in place with a piece of frayed rope to keep them from sliding completely off his lips.

Colter turned back to the fire and to thoughts of the Indian canoe under construction at the Clatsop village near the abandoned salt camp. This was his one chance to learn the secrets of how they built such superior vessels, yet here he sat, twiddling his thumbs because he had acted like a bull on a rampage with Captain Lewis.

The door creaked open and Ordway poked his head inside. "Get your gear, Colter. You're hunting with Shannon."

Once the sergeant slammed the door, Colter got slowly to his feet, not at all sure he wanted to pay the price of spending the whole day with Shannon for a little freedom. As he draped his hunting pouch over his shoulder, an idea struck him. He needed something to change Captain Lewis's mind, and he knew just the thing, something that had worked once and might just work again.

Shannon knelt in the bow of the canoe, acutely aware of Colter's eyes on his back. They had not been in such close proximity for weeks, and the closeness forced him to acknowledge his guilt in tearing apart their friendship. They rowed up the Netul to the Columbia, then west to the mouth of the Skipanon River. By the time they turned south into that stream, his remorse had built into an internal storm that made it impossible to hold back the words he had been suppressing for so long. "We have to talk, Old Man."

Colter did not disagree which encouraged Shannon to forge on. "You have every right to be angry with me."

Still nothing from Colter.

Now that he had begun, Shannon knew he had to get it all out while the Old Man was in a position where he had to listen. "It comes down to one fact: I can't stand up to Captain Lewis. Not even when —" He gulped air to steady his shaking voice. "— when it means an ocean voyage that I — I know I won't live through."

He choked on the words and had to pause to regain control. The only sound from Colter was the soft splash of his paddle. Shannon knew his courage would fail if he turned to look at the man so he remained facing forward and waded into a subject he had never before broached. "I'm on this expedition because of my father. I wanted more than anything to go to West Point. But he refused to let me apply. Then when I tried to go around him, he found out and packed me off to Philadelphia to study the law. And I let him."

He paused to remember that painful episode. "That first night on the way to Philadelphia, Father arranged for me to stay with his friend Moonbeam O'Toole. It was O'Toole who let slip to Father that I had gone ahead and applied for West Point over his objections. He felt so bad about letting me down that he urged me to forget Father's plans for me and instead head to Kentucky where a friend of his was organizing an expedition to explore for the Passage. That friend was Captain Lewis. It was O'Toole's recommendation that got me on the crew.

"All those letters you saw me writing back at Camp Wood, they were to my mother and I didn't send and of them until we started up the Missouri. I never wrote to Father because I couldn't bring myself to admit to him what I'd done."

Colter spoke for the first time. "Put in ahead."

Put in ahead. That was all. Nothing to indicate that he heard or cared about anything Shannon said. Undeterred, Shannon forged on, determined to finish what he had started. "What happened to me that day Captain Lewis chose the site for the fort, when I couldn't tell him that the crew all wanted to move back upriver, is part and parcel of that same weakness in me, Old Man. If there were some way I could change what happened, I would — but I can't."

The nose of the canoe bumped the bank. He hopped out and faced Colter for the first time. "All I can do is apologize, and ask for your forgiveness."

Colter backstroked away from the bank and swung upstream.

"Wait! Where are you going? What about my apology?" Shannon yelled.

"You hunt. I'll be back 'fore dark," Colter said, rowing up the stream, leaving Shannon to doubt whether the man had heard a single word he said.

3. *Tit-for-Tat*

T wo miles above the place where he dropped Shannon, Colter secured the dugout to the bank, grabbed up his heavy pack and struck off for the Clatsop village near the old salt camp. He made a wide circle around the village in order to look over the Indian canoes prior to making his presence known.

Even the worst of the Indian boats was superior to any of the expedition's remaining dugouts, but one in particular grabbed his fancy. About the same size as the lost Chinook canoe, it had a V-shaped bottom to slice through rough water; for repelling waves, higher, more radically curved sides than the lost canoe. Despite the dents and scratches of hard use, it was still solid.

He was tempted to run his hand along the side when the village dogs caught his scent and set up a racket that brought the Clatsops pouring out of their longhouses. Colter remained where he was and waited to be welcomed by Chief Comowool and the town's other important men before advancing closer. He glanced over toward the canoe under construction and saw that it was done and ready to be launched. Now he would never know how the craft were built.

Comowool welcomed him and invited him into the longhouse. Inside, four fireplaces were spaced at equal intervals along the floor while shelves built along both sides of the room provided sleeping platforms with space underneath for storing personal possessions. Finely-woven mats covered the floor and walls and animal skins provided the interior decoration as well as clothing for the inhabitants.

Surrounded by curious Clatsops, Colter became acutely aware of the precarious position he had put himself in. Not only had he come alone, but no one knew where he was either. He forced aside such thoughts and turned his attention to the purpose that had brought him here.

Once the ritual of smoking and greeting was completed, it was time to reveal the reason for his visit. He carefully opened his pack and removed one of his carvings, placing it on the trading mat. He did the same with the second, then the third and fourth.

This last was a carving of a roosting eagle. Comowool ignored the first three and picked up the eagle. He looked it over carefully, weighed it, then set it back down. When he did not reach for any of the other pieces, doubts began to nibble at the hem of Colter's idea. Had he come all this way for nothing?

He drew out his last piece, his finest carving, the figure of a racing buffalo. It stood two-and-a-half feet high and was as close to life-like as anything he had ever done. He had captured the flowing movements of the running animal with a skill that thrilled him every time he looked at it. He set it next to the other four.

Comowool took his time picking it up and examining it, making comments in the strange Chinookan tongue and passing it to his subchief. From that one, the carving made it all the way around the council circle until Comowool placed it back on the mat.

Encouraged by their interest, Colter signed that he wished to trade for one of their canoes. The chief cocked an eyebrow and motioned him outside to the line of canoes. "Which one?" the chief signed.

Colter pointed to the chosen boat.

Comowool nodded gravely. "Then that is what I want from you for it," he signed, pointing to Colter's rifle.

Colter signed back emphatically. "The carvings are what I have to trade. Not this."

Comowool glanced back at the Clatsops looking on. "What am I to do with your carvings? What use are they to me?"

Colter signed, "You look at them and touch them."

This drew laughter from the gathered Indians. Comowool again demanded the rifle.

"No trade," Colter slashed and pushed through the crowd to the longhouse where he scooped the carvings back into his pack and stalked out of the village.

A group of chattering Clatsops followed him nearly to the river before turning back to their village. He continued on, smarting over his failure. He was swinging the pack into the boat when he realized that it felt lighter than it should. He ripped it open.

The running buffalo carving was gone.

After spending the day sulking over Colter's failure to listen to his apology, Shannon was seething with indignation by the time the man finally returned to pick him up. He had no game to show for his efforts, but then neither did Colter. Without a word, he got into the canoe, picked up his paddle, and off they went.

It took some time for him to rise out of his own pique enough to pick up on Colter's mood. The man's dander was up about something more than the lack of game. Just what had Colter been up to all day?

That question rolled around his head until they were nearly back to the fort and the answer hit him: Colter hadn't been hunting at all, unless you called diddling a Clatsop squaw hunting.

That realization struck with the force of a match to lamp oil. He twisted around to glare at Colter. "And you dared call me a liar! You! You're the liar. You're the traitor."

"Put that there paddle in the water and shut up," Colter ordered. "I ain't in no mood to listen to you."

"No, by God! Put in. I'll walk rather than be in the same boat with the likes of you."

"I ain't doin' no such thing, so you best be paddlin'."

Shannon pointed an accusatory finger and imitated Colter's way of talking. "Tell her I'll be back before the snows." He snorted and fell into his normal voice. "I hope for her sake she didn't listen. To think that I believed you were a man of your word. Ha! What are you planning to tell this new squaw when we leave?"

"What new squaw?" Colter said testily.

"The one you bedded today. She must be something for you to try to get Captain Lewis to send you back to the salt camp." He grabbed the sides of the dugout and pushed himself to his knees. "So much for what your word means. For what it's always meant."

His movements caused the boat to rock dangerously, but all he cared about was having it out with Colter once and for all.

Instead of rising to Shannon's challenge, Colter started to chuckle, a low mirthless sound that grew steadily in volume and intensity. Laughter was the last thing Shannon expected and he slumped back on his heels, baffled by the strange reaction.

Eventually Colter got control of himself enough to speak. "It ain't no squaw I been after so you can put that there notion out of your head right now."

Colter's reaction punched the wind out of the sails of Shannon's argument and he turned back to his oar. When they put in at the boat landing below the fort, a group of crewmen were gathered around an Indian canoe Shannon had never seen before. Rube came over to help drag the dugout out of the water. He nodded toward the new boat. "That there puts us one step closer to leavin'. Drooler traded for her somewheres up north."

To Shannon, the canoe looked like a copy of the lost Chinook canoe, and that reminded him that he would not be leaving with the others. He was on the verge of falling back into a funk when Colter swore. "Them thievin' goddamned red-skins. They ain't goin' to get away with this." He stomped up to the fort.

Rube looked to Shannon for an explanation. Shannon shrugged. If Rube wanted to find out what was going on, he could ask Colter himself. He himself had had enough of the man for one day. Perhaps forever.

No duties the next day meant that Colter had all day to work up a lather over the Clatsops' treachery and the loss of his prized carving. To compound his bitterness, Drouillard got a hero's treatment from the crew for procuring a native canoe for their return journey. It stuck in Colter's craw that the half-breed had succeeded where he had failed.

He was slumped beside the smoking fire, mired in frustration when Rube bounded through the door. "Captains just gave the word. Ordeal's takin' a detail out to find a tree. You comin'?"

"I'm restin'," he muttered. The tree would be for a fifth and final dugout. As soon as it was done, the crew would head home.

Rube slammed back out, leaving Colter more frustrated than ever. If he had been able to stay at the salt camp, he would know how the Indians built their canoes and could use those techniques to build a boat worthy of the trouble, a boat that could withstand everything the Columbia had to dish out, rather than making do with an unstable, unreliable dugout. If only he had . . .

An idea stopped his thoughts cold. There was another way to get an Indian canoe and get back at the thieving Clatsops. Why hadn't he thought of it before?

Sadistic. That word came to mind every time Shannon looked at Ordway. Only a sadist would assign a man, condemned to remain behind when the expedition headed home, to the detail charged with locating the tree that would become the final dugout needed for that journey.

Suddenly the room felt stifling. Shannon shoved his portion of stringy elk meat at Rube and escaped out the door. On the way out, he heard Rube say, "I swear Peckerwood's got the weakest durn stomach on him." *Your stomach would be weak too if you were facing what's in store for me*, Shannon thought.

Outside, the all-day drizzle had come to an end and stars were winking through small tears in the cloud cover. Across the compound the door to the captains' room opened. A rectangle of candle glow fell briefly across the mud and standing puddles before York closed the door behind him. Bereft, Shannon watched the black man splash to the back gate with a bucket and duck through the low opening to draw water from the spring. A small voice in Shannon's head whispered, "Don't just stand there, George. Do something."

Before he could take a step, a crewman left the barracks next door and made his way to the roofed sentry shed outside the captains' room to re-lieve the other guard. There was vigor in the voices of both men. The same heartiness that echoed in the conversations coming from all the rooms of the fort. Vitality that expanded as the date for departure drew closer.

Of course, he thought. *They're all going home.*

Home. How very far away it seemed. How he missed his home and his family. How he longed to be there again. Only, he would never see it again. Not for a long time, if ever.

No, that wasn't going to happen. He splashed across the compound and pounded on the captains' door.

Lewis opened to his knock. Before his courage failed, Shannon blurted, "Don't leave me behind to wait for a ship, Captain. Please don't."

"Why, George, whatever gave you that idea?" Lewis said.

"You did, sir. The night Colter came back from the salt works."

"Oh, yes. Well, we have changed our plans. Waiting for a ship is too chancy. The whole company leaves here April 1st."

Clark's voice came from the interior of the room, "If not before."

"All of us?" Shannon asked.

"Yes, Shannon. All of us. Now, is that everything?"

Overcome with relief, Shannon did not mind that he stammered. "Y-yes, sir. Goodnight, sir."

After the captain closed the door, Shannon stood still, processing the news. York came up behind him. "You need to see the captains, Shannon?"

"N-no. That's okay. I . . ." His hands fluttered in an attempt to finish his sentence.

York stepped around him and let himself into the room. Shannon turned toward his barracks, savoring the sensation of having been pulled out of the jaws of a nightmare. *Colter,* he thought. *Colter doesn't know about the change in the captains' plans. I'd better tell him.*

He hurried across the compound and re-entered his barracks to find the room half-empty. Colter wasn't there. Neither were Rube nor Joe nor Willard. Now where could they have gone?

Colter knelt in the stern of the dugout, straining to separate the sounds that would mean trouble from the usual night noises. Willard in the bow and Rube and Joe between rowed carefully, trusting him to pilot them safely to the Clatsop village and back again. It was a clear night, only the fourth one in the last three months. A half-moon hung in the night sky, its shadowed features tracking their progress.

Colter had not counted on a moon. He kept glancing at it, hoping for cloud cover. The closer they got to the village, the more doubts assailed him. Were the four of them enough? What if the dogs started barking and woke up the Clatsops? What if the Clatsops caught them? And if they did manage to take a canoe, would the captains still leave him behind to wait for a ship despite all his efforts?

His thoughts were interrupted by the sight of two downed cedars, toppled by some long-ago wind. The top of one of the trees lay buried in the silt at the bottom of the river while its massive ball of roots loomed over the huge hole the tree had ripped in the earth. In the dark those roots looked like so many snakes frozen in a mid-air dance. The second tree lay across the first, forming an "X". It was the landmark he was looking for.

He gave a low hoot, the signal to put into the bank. His three companions obeyed in a way that lifted his flagging confidence a notch. On the bank, the four of them huddled. "You got them bones, Rube?" Colter whispered.

Rube touched his shirt. "Right here."

"Then you go along first," Colter said to Rube. "Remember: throw 'em far as you can away from the longhouse and the boats. Then get on back here quick."

Rube nodded stiffly.

"Joe, you stay with the dugout."

"No way," came Joe's too-loud objection.

Colter clamped a warning hand over Joe's mouth. Joe pried the hand loose and said in a lowered voice, "I didn't come all this way to wait at no boat."

"What if we need him?" Rube asked, backing up his brother.

"Okay, but remember this ain't no fight. We're here after one thing. We get it, we leave. Hear?"

There were three murmurs of assent. "And we don't get caught neither," Colter said.

Again three murmurs. "No more talkin' till we're done. Rube, you take off."

Rube hurried out along the river bank in a crouch. Colter watched until the man disappeared around a low hillock, then signaled for Joe and Willard to follow and took off toward the village.

There was a faint path along the bank used by the Clatsops to get to the bogs where they harvested wapato roots. Yet even with the path, it was impossible to move without making noise. With every crack and snap of vegetation, Colter's stomach knotted a little tighter. Then one of the pair behind him stumbled, a noise too loud not to be heard.

Colter froze, holding his breath, waiting for discovery.

For a long time, nothing stirred, then came a single yip from a dog. Joe touched Colter's arm and mimed a throwing motion.

Colter nodded. Rube was doing his job. Colter motioned the others forward.

They circled the village and hunkered down behind a mound of vegetation at the edge of the beach south of the Indian camp. The Clatsops had moved their canoes to a sand spit directly below the longhouse just off the mouth of a creek. Had they done so because they expected an attack? Were they lying in wait?

Colter jumped at Willard's touch. The big man pointed out an overturned canoe resting on a raised platform built at the edge of the surrounding forest a few yards farther south. From his stay at the salt camp, Colter knew that the canoe covered the body of its deceased owner, the Clatsop version of the Mandan funeral scaffold. And that explained why the other boats had been moved up this way.

It occurred to him to take the burial canoe and be done with it. He quickly decided against that idea. He would take the boat he came to get, the boat the Clatsops had traded away when they took his carving.

With his heart pounding at the danger he was leading them all into, he beckoned Joe and Willard to follow and stepped out of the cover of the brush.

A dog barked, an odd muffled sound. Rube was still at work with his supply of bones.

Colter did not pause. He kept moving for lack of a better option. Then, up ahead he spotted the figure of a man, moving among the canoes. At first he thought it was Rube, but then the man climbed into one of the beached craft and Colter realized it was a Clatsop. Immediately he waved Willard and Joe into cover behind a rotting cedar log.

The Indian was perched on the crossbar of one of the boats, his head thrown back, face lifted toward the moon. Colter's heart jumped into his throat. What if Rube decided not to head on back to the rendezvous point? What if he mistook this Clatsop for one of them and got nabbed?

The Indian continued to gaze at the moon. The few bones they had brought would not hold the dogs much longer.

Minutes passed. Joe nudged him impatiently. Colter ignored it.

More precious minutes passed. Colter weighed staying in cover versus rushing the Clatsop.

Joe's elbow dug into his side, but before Colter could return the favor, the Indian stood up, yawned and ambled back to the longhouse.

He counted to fifty after the man entered the dwelling, then broke cover and raced to the boats. Time was now as critical as silence. As he looked for the right canoe, Joe grabbed his shoulder and pointed at the closest one. Colter brushed off the hand and went on looking for the small canoe, the one he felt he was owed.

It was on the far end. As they moved toward it, Willard stubbed his toe on a rock protruding from the sand. His curse set the camp dogs to barking furiously.

They were too close to their goal to stop now. Colter picked up one end of the canoe and, with little help from Joe, slid it into the creek. He knew from his time at the salt camp that the creek would lead them back to the rendezvous point. Joe and Willard leaped aboard, and Colter began paddling hard up the stream toward the river where they had stashed the dugout. They were nearly around the bend above the village when the first Clatsop shouts went up. "Dig!" Colter yelled, breaking his silence.

Neither Joe nor Willard argued. They understood the consequences of failure.

Drawing close to where they had left the dugout, Colter turned them into the bank, praying that Rube was there and ready to make a run for it.

There was no one standing in the shadow of the fallen cedar. *Oh, God, what now?*

"There!" Joe said, pointing upriver.

Sure enough, Rube was already in the dugout, paddling toward the fort for all he was worth. However the dugout was heavy and Colter doubted that Rube could keep up the pace. They should put in so Willard or Joe could join him.

"He's okay," Joe urged. "Keep goin'."

Colter glanced over his shoulder, afraid to see a phalanx of Clatsop canoes in pursuit. Instead, there was no one after them. Surprised, but elated, he dug even harder with his paddle.

The Clatsops had his carving. He had their canoe. Now they were even.

Now that an ocean voyage no longer hung over his head like the sword of Damocles, Shannon enjoyed his best night's sleep since arriving on the coast. At dawn's first light he snapped awake, ready to savor every precious moment of the day ahead. Rising from his blanket, he noted the four empty bunks: Colter's, Rube's, Joe's and Willard's. None of them had watches last night, so where were they? It didn't take much to guess the answer.

Outside, he filled his lungs with the damp air and stretched luxuriously. A bubble of laughter rose into his throat. The old George Shannon would have run to the captains to report the missing men, but not the George Shannon who had been reborn overnight. A satisfying rumble in his lower regions hurried him out the back gate to the latrine. He smiled gratefully at the sight of the empty lean-to. An auspicious start to a wonderful day. He unknotted the rope that held up his pants and squatted over the trench.

At the sound of voices in the forest beyond the lean-to, he peeked around the wall to see the four absentees. He pulled his head back and strained to overhear their discussion.

The men stopped on the other side of the latrine wall. "Willard, you first," Colter said. "Then Joe, then Rube."

One set of feet crunched toward the fort followed by the sound of the gate opening and closing. The same sounds repeated a second time. Then a third. Shannon was waiting for a fourth repetition when Colter walked into the latrine. He showed no surprise at finding Shannon there. "Gotta squat. Move over."

"Hard night?" Shannon asked, layering his tone with as much scorn as he could muster, given his compromised position.

Colter settled himself over the trench. "Had me some business."

"Same squaw or are you tired of her yet?"

"Think what you want. I ain't about to explain nothin' to the likes of you."

With the conversation heading the same fruitless direction as all the other exchanges bettwen them since arriving on the coast, Shannon tried another tack. He was sick of the enmity between them and desperate to reclaim Colter's friendship. "I've tried to apologize, but you won't listen."

"Nothin' you say is worth hearin'."

"Old Man, please. Hear me out."

"Don't never call me that there name again."

"Please listen. I've changed. I really have. I can, and will, stand up for myself. Even to Captain Lewis."

Colter snorted. "Sure you will."

"When we go back —"

"I ain't listenin'." Colter stormed out of the lean-to before Shannon could tell him about the change in the captains' plans, before he could tell him that the two of them were not going to be left behind to wait for a ship.

Stymied and distraught, Shannon stared out at the endlessly dripping forest. "What do I have to do?" he moaned.

The leather hinges of the barracks door creaked despite Colter's best efforts to quiet his entry. He was in luck. No one stirred. Rube, Joe and Willard were all on their bunks, sleeping off their night's labors though they would not have long to rest before the sergeants rousted everyone out for the day's details.

He settled onto his bunk, too keyed up from the night's activity to either sleep or lie down. They had hidden the Clatsop canoe along the Netul upstream from the fort. Now it was up to him to figure a way to explain the development to the captains. Except for that stray Nez Perce horse he found on the Weippe Prairie at the end of their starvation mountain crossing, the captains had stuck fast to their principle of never taking anything from the Indians without paying for it. Although he viewed his actions as completely justifiable, he needed to convince the captains to see things the same way. That was bound to be difficult since the captains favored Chief Comowool and his band of Clatsops over the other Indian bands within proximity of the fort.

Colter was in the process of sorting through possibilities when Ordway entered the barracks, followed by Shannon. *Fuzz done it again. Went straight to Ordeal about us bein' gone all night. He ain't changed one lick. Well, this time I'm ready for 'em both.*

He pushed past the surprised sergeant and bounded across the compound. The door to the captains' room was open, Captain Lewis was sleeping and Clark working on his maps at the crude table. With Ordway hot on his heels, Colter did not stand on ceremony. "Captain Clark?"

Clark left his maps and came outside, closing the door on the sleeping Lewis. "What is it, Colter?"

"Sir, I got important news," Colter said.

Ordway arrived then. "Captain, this man was AWOL last night."

"Got a good reason, Captain," Colter countered.

"And not just him," Ordway said. "There were three others with him, sir."

"I can explain, Captain," Colter said.

Clark motioned the sergeant to silence and nodded for Colter to proceed.

"We got us a canoe, Captain. A good Indian one."

"Got one how, Colter?" Clark asked warily.

Colter heaved in a breath. "We took it."

Ordway butted in. "Stealing from the natives and AWOL. By his own admission. Which will it be, sir: Firing squad or hanging?"

Colter hurried on, wedging his words in front of anything the sergeant might say. "It was a trade, Captain."

"A trade for what, Colter?"

"A carving. My best one. That runnin' buffalo you seen me workin' on all winter."

The captain stared, saying nothing. That look combined with desperation to loosen Colter's tongue. He raced through an explanation about how the carving came to be taken.

"Taking that canoe was not a trade, Colter. It's retaliation," Clark said.

"No, Captain, durn it. I went there to trade and one of them took my best carvin' whilst I was dickerin' for a boat. Old Comowool, he wanted my rifle and I weren't never goin' to do that so I picked up my things and left. Didn't notice the carvin' was gone till I got back to the dugout. Since they took what I was offerin', it's only fair I get what I went there for."

The captain's expression remained inflexible, but he also continued to refuse to hear Ordway out. Colter knew he had to do something fast or lose whatever slim chance he had to press his case for returning overland with the main party. "My God, Captain. I got you the canoe you need to leave this damn mud-bog. How can you not want it? You want to stay here any longer'n you have to?"

Clark's reply was low enough to be nearly inaudible. "Dear Lord, no."

"Then keep her, and let me pilot her. I'm the best pilot you got, next to Cruzatte. Don't leave me behind to wait for some ship might never come."

Clark looked at him in confusion. "Leave you? Where did you get that idea?"

"Sarge here told me."

The captain turned an iron gaze on Ordway. "Is that true, Sergeant?"

Ordway's whole body tensed under the captain's scrutiny. "I don't recall, sir."

Clark's gaze on Ordway continued unabated.

"I remember, sir," Colter said.

Clark's eyes remained fixed on the sergeant's face. "I believe you, Colter. No, you won't stay behind. Everyone goes back. And, as for the canoe, keep it out of sight. We don't want the Clatsops to find it. Not now."

Relief made Colter giddy. "They ain't about to, Captain."

The sergeant tried to interject a comment, but Clark's warning hand shut him up. Clark scanned the muddy compound through narrowed eyes. "We have all the boats we need now. There's no sense waiting here. We leave in four days. Spread the word, Sergeant." He let himself back into his room.

The moment the door shut behind him, Colter met Ordway's anger-clotted face with a smile. "Better do what Captain said, Sarge. Looks of things, he ain't too happy with you right now."

He ambled to the gates, feeling better than he had in months. In just four days he would be on his way to Fragrant Grass. Four days! Because he had taken a risk and pulled it off. Then again, part of the reason he did what he did was that he thought he was about to be left behind to wait for a ship. A belief that came from Ordeal, who else?

At the gates, he turned to look back at the treacherous sergeant. The man had made his life a living hell for far too long. No more. The sergeant had lost his one advantage: fear. What was more, they both knew it. That gave Colter an edge he had never had and a whole return trip to hone that edge to a razor-sharpness.

News of Colter's exploits raced like wild-fire through the crew. When the other crewmen began to treat Colter special, Shannon refused to join in, refused to talk to or about the man. He knew better. Colter was a lot of things, but hero wasn't one of them.

For the next three days, he got his fill of Colter-worship on the details he was assigned to. He also tried several times to convince Colter that he had not been the source of Ordway's information about their absence that night. Every time, Colter shut him down with, "I ain't listenin'." Finally, Shannon gave up.

Now the boats were packed except for some last-minute things of the captains. Shannon grew tired of hanging around the landing stage waiting out some last-minute delay, and decided to walk off his restlessness. He wandered around the fort to the back latrine. A corner of its roof had already rotted through, the result of three months in this miserable climate. The sight brought up a string of memories from their stay in this place. Every memory was colored in gray, the shade of the clouds that perennially blanketed the sky.

A shout from the canoes warned him that the boats were set to depart. He tapped the lean-to wall in goodbye and started toward the river.

At the sound of a crack, he turned to see the lean-to collapse in a heap onto the brimming latrine trench. He smiled grimly and continued on his way. It was definitely time to leave.

PART 7

THE RETURN

Spring, 1806 — Fall, 1806

Every body seems anxious to be in motion, convinced that we have not now any time to delay if the calculation is to reach the United States this seaon; this we are detirmined to accomplish if within the compass of human power.

— Meriwether Lewis, June, 1806

1. *Heading Home*

End of March, 1806 — on the Lower Columbia

T he Columbia's surging run-off pounded the expedition dugouts, battering the crews and forcing one delay after another. The Clatsop canoe cut easily through all but the highest, roughest waves, so the delays of the other boats further aggravated Colter's patience which was already worn thin from having to put up with Charbonneau and McNeal as crew in his canoe. Now that he was finally on his way back to Fragrant Grass, the power controlling the universe, the one that had spurred him to reach the Western Sea, seemed unwilling to let him leave.

Although most of the river Indians were still living in their winter lodges — small excavated caverns eight feet deep, roofed with timbers and earth — some had moved back into their bark-covered longhouses. This was true at the Cathlamet village where Colter put in to wait for the other boats to catch up so the captains could trade for food. No sooner had they landed than one of the Indians separated from the crowd and came over to the Clatsop canoe. From the man's profile Colter recognized him as the Indian who had been outside staring at the moon at Comowool's village the night he and his companions took the boat. Furthermore, he guessed from the man's manner that the Indian either owned the boat or knew who did.

"Trouble?" Willard murmured.

"'Fraid so," Colter answered. "Find me that spare elk hide. Quick."

Willard wedged his strong fingers under the cords that held the boat's baggage in place and extricated the hide.

"Turn the boat 'round and be ready to push 'er out quick when you see me signal." Colter plastered on a smile and walked up to the native. He went through an expansive signed greeting, then pressed the hide into the man's hands. "Much obliged."

He whirled toward the canoe and used his body to shield his signal to Willard to shove off. "Go!" he ordered in a low tense voice as he leaped into the stern.

"What're you doin', Colter? We're supposed to stop. Captains gotta get us some vittles," McNeal complained.

"Paddle 'less you want to swim," he shot back. "Same for you, Frenchy."

Charbonneau muttered something that sounded like an Hidatsa curse.

"Shut up, Frenchy," Willard growled from the bow, his words ominous with menace. The Frenchman's sullen expression shrivelled like a frost-struck apple and, without another mumble, he applied himself to his oar.

"Wave 'em off back there," Colter told Rube.

"What's wrong?" Rube asked.

"Later," Colter said, putting everything he had into paddling in order to put a long span of river between them and the gaping Indian on the bank.

By the time the expedition turned against the flow of the Columbia, Shannon remembered why he hated dugouts. Even Labiche's superb piloting skill could not compensate for the boat's inherent instability in the high, churning water. Still, he would rather take his chances in the dugout than lower himself to ask Colter for a place in the stolen canoe.

To take his mind off the violent river, he set his sights on the approaching Cathlamet village and their forthcoming rest stop. Colter's canoe was already beached. Just a few more minutes till he was standing on solid ground again. Potts broke into his thought. "Scout boat's pullin' out again. Rube's wavin' us off. Must be trouble."

"Then we go!" Labiche ordered. "*Vite. Vite.*"

With his destination denied, Shannon kept going by sheer force of will until at last Labiche yelled, "Pull in." Shannon was incensed to learn that the reason for Colter's hasty departure from the Cathlamet village was that the stolen Clatsop canoe had been recognized. Then, instead of chastising Colter for creating the potentially dangerous situation for the crew by the theft, the captains praised the man for quick-thinking in buying the Indian off with one of their last elk-hides. He had an entirely different opinion and was not about to let it go unvoiced. He pulled Colter aside. "It'd serve you right if that Indian comes after *his* boat."

"You itchin' for a fight, are you?"

"You're no hero, Colter. You're a thief. Because of you, we could be attacked tonight. We could all die, and you'd be to blame."

"You and Sarge Ordeal must be gettin' to be good friends. You're startin' to sound like him."

Shannon threw a punch at Colter's gut, but Colter proved faster, grabbing Shannon's hand and twisting it painfully behind his back. "Gotta be quicker'n that, Shannon. A lot quicker."

"God damn you, Colter."

Colter's expression turned to mock horror. "What's this? George Shannon takin' the Lord's name in vain? Oh, my." He released Shannon with a shove. "'Let him who is without sin cast the first stone.' Ain't that what the Bible says?"

Fuming, Shannon made to follow Colter when someone grabbed his shoulder and spun him around. Ordway's eyes glimmered maliciously. "Why, Shannon. I didn't know you had it in you. Temper, temper. By the power vested in me by our esteemed captains, I hereby reward your show of aggression with guard duty midnight to dawn tonight. Oh, and reassignment to Colter's canoe, starting tomorrow. It's high time the two of you kissed and made up."

Shannon managed to hold back his angry response until the sergeant moved off. By then he was near to choking on his need to vent his spleen and to pour out his misery. Only, who would listen to him? Who cared about him and his problems?

In that moment the full realization of his position hit him. He was all alone and friendless, in the unfairest of situations. The realization extinguished the fire within him and left him with a hollowness far worse than his anger.

Tired as he was, Colter couldn't sleep. Now that he had the Clatsop canoe, he was not about to lose it.

Night passed slowly. He started at every small sound. He did not relax his vigil until streaks of light gray were showing at the seam of the eastern horizon. He didn't realize he had fallen asleep until someone grabbed his shoulder. "Good news, Colter! The Indian canoe's still ours!" Rube crowed.

Joe scratched his sleep-tousled hair and yawned. "Bet them Indians never tried to come after us, the lazy sons-a-bitches."

The mood at breakfast was buoyant. Afterward, Colter ambled down to oversee the loading of his canoe. "Where you want this?" The question came from Shannon and referred to his pack and gear.

"You got the wrong boat. Yours is over yonder," Colter said, indicating the dugout.

"I got the right boat. Now where's this go?"

Colter flung a stone at the river. "You ain't ridin' with me."

"Tell that to Ordeal. Now answer my question, damn it."

Colter glanced toward the watching sergeant. What kind of stunt was Ordway pulling now? "Whose place you takin'?" he asked warily.

Shannon jerked his chin toward Charbonneau.

Colter cast another look at Ordway. To be rid of the Frenchman more than made up for having to put up with Shannon. Was the sergeant getting soft? He pointed to the prow. "Put your gear up there. And make durn sure them knots is tight. You lose it, you swim for it. Them's my rules."

Shannon set to work without a word of sass. Mystified, Colter shrugged and bent to continue tying down the day's load.

The Cascades from the downstream side were a sobering sight. Above the narrow gap in the obsidian rock face that the river had to squeeze through — the gap the boats had shot through three months before — the mile-wide Columbia brimmed with spring run-off and ran twenty feet over its previous level. The river roared with aggravation at being forced to wedge through the narrow opening, drowning out all attempts at conversation. The conditions dictated portaging the expedition's baggage around the falls, a grueling seven-mile trek, and roping the boats one by one up through the maelstrom with the one remaining elk-hide rope.

To make the situation more difficult, the area around the falls teemed with short-tempered natives chafing at the wait for the spring salmon run to begin. Churlish Indians watched every move the crew made.

After a scant breakfast the morning of April 10th, the captains divided the crew into three groups. The first, under Ordway, would portage the baggage and supplies. Under Clark, the second group would move the boats through the falls while the injured and sick, under Lewis's direction, would guard baggage at both ends of the carry. While the men were sorting themselves out, a scowling Indian swaggered up to the captains, and, with slashing hand signs, demanded payment for use of the portage trail.

With the rumble of the falls as a backdrop, a silent signal passed from Lewis to Clark to York before Lewis faced the native and traced out a reply. "We come in peace to travel back to our village beyond the far mountains."

Brusquely, the Indian repeated his demand of a toll for passage, and the ring of natives began pressing in around the crew.

Lewis did not miss a beat. "We bring gifts to you, his red children, from the Great Chief who lives beyond the mountains in the village of Washington." He swept an arm toward York who passed to his master a half-dozen parchment certificates and Indian medals, three of the few remaining strings of beads and an iron cooking pot. Colter recognized the pot as McNeal's favorite. With these items, Clark conducted a hasty making-chiefs ceremony, thrusting certificates, medals and beads into the hands of various Indians.

Lewis himself presented the Indian spokesman with a medal, two strings of beads and the pot, then grabbed the man's hand and pumped it.

That was the signal for the portagers to move out. Colter took up what was nearest to hand — two casks, one of gunpowder; the other of shot — and fell into line behind Shannon.

Heavy mist coated the portage trail. Keeping his footing while balancing the unequal loads required his total attention. He was a third of the way from the top of the Upper Cascade and five paces behind Shannon when a sizeable rock tumbled onto the path a fraction of an inch from his leading foot.

The next instant a fist-sized rock struck Shannon in the temple, causing him to drop his load.

A third rock, larger than the other two, just missed hitting Colter When he looked up, a trio of native men were crouched on a ledge, their hands filled with rocks ready to be hurled. He and Shannon were in an exposed position that did not allow for retaliation or cover. Their only choice was to get out of the line of fire as fast as possible. "Come on, Fuzz. We gotta get out of here," he urged.

Shannon's head was bleeding. "Not 'til I settle the score," he said, uncapping his powder horn. "I'm going to teach those three not to throw rocks." He filled the pan of his rifle, then spit a ball down the barrel.

A glance down the trail showed Ordway and the other carriers a good three hundred yards behind. Another rock caught Colter in the elbow, and he lost his grip on the heavier cask of shot. The keg fell onto the sloping path, tipped, and started to roll toward the lip of the chasm.

Shannon flung aside his rifle to grab the cask in the nick of time. "For God's sake, Old Man, we can't afford to lose shot."

Before Colter had the chance to correct Shannon for calling him "Old Man," two more stones thudded down, missing them by scant fractions of an inch. Shannon hefted the shot cask and, screaming curses at the Indians, hustled up the trail, forgetting his rifle in his rush.

Dodging two more rocks, Colter scooped up the forgotten weapon and rushed after Shannon.

Shannon did not remember his rifle until he reached the top of the Upper Cascade.

"Lookin' for somethin'?" Colter came up, cradling his gun. When he reached for it, Colter refused to give it up. "That temper of yourn's makin' you downright stupid. Wonder what Captain Lewis'd do to someone what shot an Indian?"

"All the time I spent with the captain, I know him a whole lot better than you do, Colter," Shannon said. "First and foremost, he's a pragmatist. Someone needs to stop those Indians before they hurt one of the crew."

"And you're that someone, right? You shoot an Indian, Captain'll have your hide."

Their bickering was interrupted by a screeching cry from McNeal. "Captain! Your dog!"

While the crew were engaged in other activities, the three Indians had taken advantage of their preoccupation, tied a rope around Seaman's neck and were leading him away. Shannon recognized two of the men as rock-throwers.

"Shannon, Colter, McNeal, after them," Lewis snarled. "Shoot if you have to. Just get him back."

Shannon wrested his rifle away from Colter, threw the man a contemptuous look and raced off after the animal and its captors. Righteous anger deadened the pain from his rock-wound, drove his pursuit and fueled his determination to get Seaman back and put an end to the treachery of these light-fingered natives. He quickly gained ground on the thieves. Within range for a sure shot, he halted and jammed his rifle into his shoulder.

"Shannon, don't!" came Colter's breathless yell, overlaid with the captain's shouts of "Seaman! Seaman!"

Shannon steadied himself and took aim on the Indian holding the dog's lead and dropped the hammer. At the same instant Colter slapped the barrel of the rifle, sending the ball slamming into a boulder beyond the Indians instead of its intended target.

"Damn your hide, Colter! I had him in my sights."

He grabbed for his powder horn to reload and found Colter's hand wrapped around it. "You ain't shootin' nobody, Shannon. Not over no damn dog."

"Captain gave the order."

In one quick move, Colter's yank broke the thong holding the horn on Shannon's body and his throw sailed it into the rocks. "Ain't no man goin' to die for no dog. Not while I'm around," Colter said, then stuck two fingers in his mouth and shrilled a whistle.

The huge dog skidded to a stop with a force that nearly pulled the arm of the native holding the rope out of its socket.

Colter whistled again.

This time Seaman's great head turned expectantly toward them.

Meanwhile, Shannon remembered his priming horn. He one-shotted the pan, spit a ball down the barrel and jammed back the hammer. He swung the rifle up and took aim on the thief holding the rope. This was one shot he was not going to miss.

"Seaman, come!" Colter shouted through cupped hands.

The dog gave a booming bark, and the Indian dropped the lead. Seaman barked again and bounded toward Colter.

Shannon had to hold his shot until the animal cleared out of his line of fire. He was about to drop the hammer when Seaman plowed into him, toppling him and knocking the rifle out of his hands, then pinning him and licking his face. "Get him off me!"

"Nope," Colter said, picking up the fallen rifle and walking off.

"Bring that back here!" Shannon yelled.

Colter kept walking, passing McNeal who came dragging up the trail to where Shannon lay. "Need some help?" the cook asked.

"Give me that," Shannon pulled McNeal's rifle out of his grasp. He loaded the gun and took aim on the retreating thieves.

"What're you doin'?" McNeal demanded.

"Getting even." Instead of a spark, a boom, and a ball flying toward the target, the rifle's hammer came down with a dull click.

One glance at the firing mechanism explained why. Rust and grit and caked dirt spoke to months of neglect. He flung it back at McNeal. "You and your filth! Get out of here before I jam that thing down your throat."

"Just try it, Shannon. Sarge'll —"

"He's not here, McNeal. It's just you and me. And if you don't leave right now, there'll just be me standing. I guarantee it."

The cook started to argue, then thought better of it and took off, moving faster than Shannon had ever seen him move. He found no satisfaction in the sight. Colter had ruined everything. Again. The man was getting to be a real pain in the behind. Something had to be done, and he needed to figure out what.

With secret reservations, Colter accepted Captain Lewis's thanks for rescuing the dog. In truth, he had acted out of the purely selfish need to save his own skin. If Shannon had shot an Indian, the crew would certainly have been massacred. He had not pushed himself to the limit to get to the coast and then endured a miserable winter at Fort Clatsop to die before he had the chance to fulfill his ambitions to get back to Fragrant Grass, to even the score with Farley Stuart and then to establish a home for his new family in the Shining Mountains.

So he was not prepared when the captain sent six crewmen out to round up all the natives looking down on the camp from the surrounding rocks and march them back at gunpoint. Once the natives were assembled, the irate Lewis addressed them while Drouillard signed the words. "We come as friends, yet you treat us as enemies, throwing rocks at us and stealing my dog. Your actions anger us, who have been sent to you in peace by the Great Chief in Washington. We will not be treated this way. If any one of you touches or harasses me or any of my men or tries to take anything that belongs to us, you will be shot."

Colter's jaw dropped in disbelief. What was the captain thinking? There were hundreds of Indians living here at the Cascades. Hundreds against a crew reduced by hunger and injury to no more than two dozen healthy men. In anyone's book, those weren't odds to test.

The captain ordered the natives out of the expedition's camp without giving them a chance to reply. All of them went but one man. His outraged gaze swept slowly over the crew before he wheeled and strode off with the purposeful gait of someone who plans to return with reinforcements.

Over the next two days the captain's threat kept the river Indians at a distance but also increased the number who gathered to watch the crew's movements. In the tension-saturated environment the crew completed the portage and succeeded in dragging all but one dugout through the falls to the upper camp, leaving that one to wait until the following day.

With everyone primed to leave the Cascades and its menacing residents, Colter and the other portagers rousted out early the third day to help the roping crew move the last dugout. The effort came to failure when the elk-hide rope snapped under the strain, dropping the dugout into the thrashing river which quickly pounded it into firewood.

The dejected ropers reached camp to find that the captains had gone to try to trade for another boat. To trade with the very people they had threatened with death three days before.

With nothing to do but wait and wonder what the crew would do if the captains failed to secure a replacement boat, Colter was too keyed up to sit. He prowled the campsite like a caged bobcat. He was so preoccupied that he did not immediately spot the pair of Indians intently observing Shannon. The pair were part of the trio who had tried to steal Seaman.

Shannon was sketching on the outer edge of the campsite. From his frequent glances toward the Indian pair, Colter gathered that they were the subject of his drawing. After a few moments, Shannon put down the charcoal and held the book away from him as if to inspect his work. Apparently satisfied, he yawned, set the journal down on a nearby rock, and strolled over to his pack. The studied casualness of his movements put Colter on alert.

When one of the Indians crept toward the journal, Colter was ready. He planted himself between Shannon and the book. "Oh, no, you don't."

Shannon craned around, trying to hide the fact that he had his rifle to hand. "Clear out, Colter!"

"Nope." Colter signed for the Indian to back off. The native froze but did not retreat.

"Move. He's mine," Shannon hissed.

Colter repeated his warning to the Indian with an emphatic "Git!" That got the native moving in the right direction. Colter retrieved the journal and held it out to Shannon. "You lose this?"

Angry red blotches mottled Shannon's face. "Why, you interfering son-of-a-roach!"

Colter tossed the book at Shannon who let it fall to keep his rifle trained on Colter's chest. "Put 'er down, Shannon."

"No."

"Down, Fuzz." Colter had not spoken that nickname for a long time, Hearing it come out of his mouth surprised him and pulled Shannon back to his senses enough to lower the rifle.

Colter's mouth was dry, sanding his voice. "You ain't no killer. Now don't forget your durn book."

When he turned to walk away, he spotted two Indian canoes landing at the camp. In them were Drouillard, Clark, Lewis and Cruzatte. Just when they needed a miracle, somehow, some way, the captains had worked one, procuring the boats the expedition needed to continue on upriver. How they had done so registered a moment later. Neither man now wore his red officer's jacket.

For Shannon, the next four days proved to be the worst of the expedition. Worse than the humiliating episode at McBain's. Worse than enduring pox treatments a second time. Worse than getting lost on last fall's starvation mountain crossing. Spending each day an arm's reach from Colter was worse than all of those.

While he struggled to swallow the fact that he had been ready to shoot Indians and to kill the man who had once been his best friend, his rowing suffered. As a result, Colter nagged him unmercifully while they were on the river, and, at rest stops and camps, the scout-boat crew snubbed him.

On April 17, the expedition reached the Long Narrows. Weighing the distance they had come against that left to travel to St. Louis, the captains decided to attempt trading for horses to carry them overland, hoping to speed up the trip. Captain Clark took on the task and used the scout canoe to carry him to a village on the south bank. Thanks to Colter, Shannon got moved into the captain's dugout to make room in Colter's for Clark.

Shannon quickly discovered that he had traded one problem for another. The proximity of Captain Lewis was at least as distracting to his concentration as Colter's. Although the captain did not berate him for his many mistakes, Shannon sensed the man's disapproval. The harder he tried, the worse he did. The worse he did, the more he doubted himself. The more he doubted himself, the harder he tried, the worse he did.

After Clark had been gone for two hours, Lewis ordered the expedition boats to cross to the south bank. To make the crossing, the captain switched Shannon to the less-critical middle rowing position and took the bow himself. So close to Long Narrows, the river was even more turbulent and full of debris than normal. While executing a turn to avoid a jumble of drift logs, Shannon hooked his paddle on a snag and lost his hold on it.

Another snag, this one the size of a small island, had broken loose from an upstream eddy and was hurtling toward them with unbelievable speed. All the oarless Shannon could to do was watch the lethal object bear down on them.

They avoided the snag by a twig's width, and, within five minutes, they arrived at the other bank well in advance of the other boats. Lewis craned around to look at Shannon. "Is something amiss, Private?"

"Lost my paddle, sir," Shannon answered in a tension-roughened voice.

"There are no more paddles, Capitaine," Labiche growled. "No more."

The captain stared stonily at Shannon, his silence as loud as a shout.

"Make camp here, Capitaine?" Labiche asked, indicating the rocky point set below some bluff-top longhouses.

Lewis shrugged wearily. "Might as well. It is late."

"You want I go with you to trade?" Labiche asked.

Lewis glanced downriver. The wind swept back his hair and the rays of the late afternoon sun highlighted the deep furrows of worry etched around his eyes. The sight aggravated Shannon's feelings of inadequacy. He lowered his head and struggled to keep the lump of discouragement in his chest from rising into his throat.

"Bring the pack of goods," Lewis said to Labiche before turning back to Shannon. "Tell Sergeant Pryor to set up camp. Can you remember that, Shannon, or do I have to write it down?"

Shannon managed a head-hanging nod in the face of the captain's sarcasm. He found it hard to look up when the next boat arrived, but he relayed the captain's order to Pryor who directed the crew to set camp.

Temperatures dropped with the setting sun. With no food or fuel, small groups of crew huddled together among the rocks for warmth. Shannon sat by himself wrapped in his thin, ragged blanket without a single companion to share his misery. In no time, he was chilled to the bone, and his stomach clawed to be fed. Hunching against his drawn-up knees, he heard someone mutter, "God, what I wouldn't give for a bonfire."

Into Shannon's mind flashed an image of the annual harvest bonfire back home. Every fall neighbors heaped up dead corn stalks and squash vines and set fire to the pile at moonrise. He had always loved that spectacle. A lump formed in his throat at the memory.

"Be one long night without a fire," another man said.

"Another one, you mean," a third corrected.

"Shut up. Captain's comin'," warned a fourth.

The sun was down but the lingering glow from the surrounding rocks provided enough light to reveal that the captain and Labiche had brought back food but no wood. Shannon was close enough to hear Ordway ask, "What'll we do for a cooking fire, Captain?"

"Chop up both dugouts," Lewis growled.

"Sir?" the sergeant said.

"The Indians, they laugh when we try to trade the dugouts," Labiche explained. "They say, 'Why trade? Them you must leave here to go up-river.'"

"What we will leave here is a pile of ashes," Lewis declared. "Nothing more. Build us a fire, Sergeant."

While Ordway called out names of men to carry out the captain's order, Shannon studied Lewis. Clark had not yet returned. No one knew if he had horses. If he didn't, burning two boats would put twelve men afoot, carrying whatever baggage would not fit in the other boats. Such a brash action made absolutely no sense in light of the need to get to the Nez Perce to retrieve their horses before the Indians took off for their spring hunts. "Not right," Shannon whispered.

Lewis turned. "You say something, Shannon?"

Under the captain's narrowed gaze, Shannon's small bit of resolve vanished. He had no right to question anyone, especially the captains. "No, sir." The words came out high-pitched, the voice of an adolescent.

Two long days of trading at every Indian village on the south bank below the Narrows yielded only three scrawny horses, hardly enough to handle the baggage from one of the canoes let alone the sick and the lame among the crew. Colter's frustration grew along with his opinion that the river Indians were taking unfair advantage of the expedition's plight. That opinion hardened into conviction as he tried to choke down his portion of that night's dinner: dried salmon meal mixed with icy river water. Without fuel, they were not able to cook. He gave up on the food and held out his cup to any takers. "I ain't hungry."

Shivering from the biting night wind, Rube took the cup and balanced it on his bent knee. "Sure could use a fire."

Colter checked to make sure Clark was out of earshot before speaking aloud the thoughts that had been rattling around his head all day. "If'n them Indians won't trade fair, we oughtta take us what we need."

"Say the word," Joe said.

"Okay, come on."

Colter got to his feet to find his ankle in Rube's grasp. "No way, Colter. A boat's one thing. It don't make noise. Horses do."

"Who's goin' to hear?" He cocked his chin toward the nearby Indian village. "Wind's blowin' t'other way from them longhouses. We'll be gone 'fore they know anythin's missin'."

"Come on, Rube. Leastwise we'll warm up some," Joe urged.

"You sit back down, Little Brother. We cain't afford to get caught," Rube insisted.

Colter glanced around. "Captain and the rest ain't payin' no heed to us and Willard's standin' guard. Cain't get no better odds'n that."

"Let's leave Rube here if'n he don't want to come," Joe said.

His brother's eagerness got Rube up. "All right, I'm in."

The three left the shelter of the rocks and strolled to the boundary of the camp as if they intended to take a walk. "Halt! Who goes there?" demanded Willard in a hoarse whisper.

Colter whispered back, "It's us, goin' over yonder to get us some more horses."

"You don't want to do that," Willard warned.

"We sure do," Colter said. We'll —"

"You'll what, Colter?" Clark stepped out from behind a tumble of boulders, knotting the cord holding up his pants.

Colter made an instantaneous decision. "Bring back the horses we need, Captain."

"Oh, no, you don't" Clark said.

"Sure. We'll get 'em just like we us got the canoe," Colter said.

"No, Colter. That is not how this expedition acts," Clark said firmly.

Colter wanted to argue that the expedition would not be here now if they hadn't taken what they needed, that these river Indians were natural-born thieves who had stolen God-knew-what from the expedition, so it was only fitting to take something back. He wanted to argue that, but something underlying the captain's tone stopped him. "Yes, sir."

"What?" erupted Rube.

Colter stomped down hard on Rube's foot to shut him up. Rube yelped with surprise and pain.

"'Yes, sir' what, Colter?" Clark demanded.

"Yes, sir, we won't be takin' no horses."

Clark nodded. "Then I'll hold you to that."

After the captain had walked off, Rube sputtered, "What kind of argument was that, Colter?"

"Cain't argue with somebody won't listen."

"You weren't about to cross him, you mean," Rube fumed. "Next time you got some big idea for making yourself a hero, Colter, leave me out. Hear? And stay off'n my feet, too."

"Me, too," echoed Joe, supporting his limping brother back to the shelter of the rocks.

"Why'd you tell the captain what you were up to," Willard said. "You should'a lied."

"Lyin' so's I could steal?"

"Least you could have gone after them horses."

"What? Risk my hide so Captain could give 'em back tomorrow?"

"He wouldn't do that."

"You heard him. Give 'em back is just what he'd do. So why go out and do somethin' that I know's goin' to get undone?"

"Don't get mad at me," Willard said defensively. "Weren't my fault you backed down."

"Why not? You and every other galoot on this here crew's always pointin' the finger and criticizin'. Amongst the lot of you, you ain't had one good idea since we left Camp Wood."

"And I suppose you have?"

"Who got us around Point Ellice when everyone was givin' up? And who stole the Clatsop canoe?"

"You *and* me, Colter. Both times. That's the trouble with you. You forget who helped you out. You and Shannon. You're both right there ready to take the glory but not to share it. Like Rube said, next time you get a bright idea, don't come to me." Willard spun on his heel and went back to his post.

Colter stood staring at the man's back, furious at being dressed down by three men he had considered friends and smarting from the captain's treatment. Suddenly his world seemed all out of whack.

2. *Where Am I?*

Through the hard-won efforts of the captains and all the iron cooking pots, save one per mess, the expedition's horse herd grew to nine by the time they left Celilo Falls on April 21. Their baggage was parceled out among the horses and two of the five remaining canoes. Colter and Potts rowed one of these and four other pairs of crewmen managed the other boats while the rest of the men were divided into three details: one to lead the packhorses; another to march ahead of the herd; and the third to bring up the rear.

Shannon drew the first detail. He was assigned to lead a nervous filly who viewed his every move with alarm. He tried coaxing her, singing to her, petting her, but nothing calmed her. Finally, in exasperation, he decided to use force instead of gentleness.

The next time she shied away from him, he gave her lead a vigorous yank. The move startled the horse and it reared, slashing the air with her hooves.

"Down! Stop!" Shannon ordered, jerking the lead again.

Tthe animal seemed to reconsider her lack of cooperation. "That's better," Shannon said just as a hoof caught him on the brow, felling him before he knew what hit him.

"Whoa up! They're wavin' us in," Potts called from the bow.

"Hellfire!" Colter muttered, ruddering them toward the bank. "We just got started. What in tarnation's the hold-up this time?"

Ordway met them on the bank. "You got a passenger. Rube, Joe, move those three bales over to Labiche's boat. You two," he waved over the two crewmen carrying the unconscious Shannon, "lay him out in here."

The addition of Shannon made for a tight fit in the scout canoe. The top of his rag-bandaged head wedged against Colter's thighs. His toes jammed into Potts's rear. "What's with him?" Potts asked.

"He tangled with his horse. And lost," Ordway said. The smile he turned on Colter was full of spite. "Figured you'd want him in your boat, since you and him are such good friends."

Colter had lost his taste for sparring with Ordway. "Can we go now, Sarge?"

Ordway seemed disappointed that Colter did not rise to the bait. He dropped the smile. "You're to stay no more than five lengths ahead of the next boat, Colter. Captains' orders."

Five lengths meant holding to a snail's pace when every sinew of his body wanted to paddle until he ran out of river, but he kept his reply to a nod and backed the canoe into the river.

"What are we supposed to do with him?" Potts asked, nodding over his shoulder at Shannon.

"Damned if I know," Colter answered.

A sensation of pain drifted into Shannon's awareness. The feeling was coming from his spine where something — in fact several somethings — were pressing into his flesh in tender spots. Surrounding the sensation was the sound of water splashing, mixed with animal-like grunts and panting.

Where am I?

A search of his memory produced no answer to the question. At a stab of pain in his forehead, he attempted to raise his hand to that spot. His arm would not respond. A niggling worry crept into the peaceful vagueness of his mind. *Something's wrong with me.*

From the direction of his feet, someone called out, "Port."

Port? That was a boating term. Boats? Why would he be anywhere near boats? A small puddle was plenty enough water for him, thank you.

He tried to open his eyes, but the lids felt glued together. Another voice, this one above and behind his head, said, "Hellfire, Potts, we just missed that there log. You got to watch better'n that."

Missed what? Watch what? Who is Potts?

With enormous effort, Shannon managed to raise one lid a slit before it slid down again. In that brief instant he glimpsed the sky stretching above him and the figure of a man positioned at the top of his head, wielding a paddle. The man had a purplish-red mark spreading from cheek to brow across one eye. It was the kind of facial feature no one could possibly forget, yet he could summon up no recollection of the man.

The first man, the one named Potts, spoke again. "Confound it, Colter! I'm watchin' as best I can. How'd you like to trade places, see what it's like up here for a change, huh?"

The man above Shannon — Colter — replied. "How'd you like to be walkin' behind Ordeal all day? You can, you know. Just say the word." He spat out the word "Ordeal" like a bite of rotten apple.

Shannon knew what an "ordeal" was, but he could not feature it being something to walk behind. Where was he? What was happening?

"A few more horses," Potts said, "and both of us are goin' to be out of this here boat."

"A few more horses," Colter said, "and we'll be ridin', not walkin'. That suits me just fine."

"Cain't be too soon for this child," Potts said. "I got a gutful of fightin' this here Columbia. Give me the Missouri any day."

Shannon recognized the names as rivers, but he had to work to recall their geographic placement. He seemed to remember that the Missouri emptied into the Mississippi above the frontier settlement of St. Louis, and that, above St. Louis, it wound north and west into wild, unexplored territory. No one knew exactly where it went or how far it stretched though there was speculation that it linked up with the Western Sea.

The name "Western Sea" led to his mind recalling that the Columbia also emptied into that great Western ocean. Potts had said they were on the Columbia. Yet that couldn't possibly be, could it?

When he tried to speak, it felt as though his tongue filled his entire mouth. Eventually, he got his eyes open. The sun was so bright, it hurt to look. He swallowed, which also hurt, but he had to speak, had to get some answers. His first words came out muffled and run-together.

"What say?" Potts asked.

The one called Colter peered down at Shannon. "Looks like Sleepin' Beauty finally woke up."

Shannon's lips did not easily form the words he had to say. "Where am I?" came out as "Whamy."

Potts craned around to look at him. "Welcome back to the world, Peckerwood."

When Shannon tried to lift his head, the world tilted and began to spin out from under him. Spears of pain attacked the inside of his skull. He lay flat, eyes shut, praying for the spinning and the pain to recede.

"Good thing you're awake," Potts said. "Captains have been worried about you."

Captains? What captains? "Where . . . am . . . I?"

"In the bottom of my canoe, takin' up space," Colter said.

"Starboard!" Potts shouted.

The surface on which Shannon lay pivoted suddenly, followed by a high-pitched scraping noise next to his left ear. "Damn this blasted river!" Colter said.

"W-what river? W-where?" Shannon managed to croak.

Colter's face hardened. "You know damn good and well where you are."

Potts intervened. "Go easy on him, Colter. I seen this kind of thing before. A conk on the noggin makes a man forget stuff. Happened to my brother. Horse kicked him, too."

Colter scowled down at Shannon. "What's your name?"

"George Shannon."

"What's mine?"

"Colter."

Colter looked back at Potts. "There ain't nothin' wrong with his memory, Potts."

Shannon struggled back up to an elbow. The movement increased the throbbing in his temple. His mouth filled with bile. He choked back its sour taste and stammered, "He called you 'Colter.' T-that's how I know your name. P-please tell me where we are. I c-can't remember."

Colter's expression remained skeptical. Potts answered. "We be on the Columbia River, a day and a half above Celilo Falls."

"But that, that can't be," Shannon said.

"He's fakin'," Colter said impatiently.

"Could be the truth, Colter." Potts addressed Shannon. "What's the last thing you remember?"

Shannon racked his brain and came up with one memory: he was sitting opposite Parson Cooper at the Parson's desk, watching him press his signet ring into the hot wax sealing a parchment envelope. "This ought to reach Washington in a month," the Parson had said. "Figuring another month for a reply, you should have your acceptance to West Point in plenty of time to break the news to your father before you have to leave for New York."

Shannon haltingly related the scene to the two men. When neither Potts nor Colter said anything, he blurted, "How can I possibly be on the Columbia River when I'm supposed to be at West Point?"

Potts spoke quietly. "You don't remember the expedition?"

"The what?"

"Or Camp Wood or the Teton Sioux or the Mandans or the Great Falls?" Potts asked.

"What are you talking about?"

Over his prone body, the two men exchanged a pregnant look. "What do we do?" asked Potts.

"*We* don't do nothin', 'cept put in and wait for the captains."

By now, a growing anxiety had shunted aside all Shannon's vagueness. "What captains?"

Colter glanced down at him. "You'll see."

While Shannon waited with Colter and Potts for the captains, whoever they were, to arrive, the hammering pain in his forehead kept him from bringing to bear any logic on what was happening to him. He remained at the mercy of his emotions which swerved between utter bewilderment and angry disavowal that he could be somewhere and not know how he got there.

At last a ragged group of men and horses came into view and Shannon pushed himself up to his feet with difficulty. One glimpse at their disorderly ranks and dirty, hirsute appearance raised his hackles. If these captains were of the military variety, they would get a piece of his mind when they showed up. As the son of his father and a lieutenant in the best militia unit in all the new State of Ohio, he could not — no, he *would* not let pass such a breach of basic military discipline.

One of the men broke away from the front of the trudging column. The man's red hair was filthy and matted and much too long for a proper military appearance. The man clasped Shannon's surprised hand. "Praise God, you're okay, Private Shannon."

Private? I'm no private. Father promoted me to lieutenant a good six months ago.

"Well, what have you got to say?" the red-haired man asked.

"Who are you?" Shannon demanded, freeing his hand from the man's grimy clutches.

The man threw back his head and howled a laugh. Shannon turned to Colter. "Why is he laughing? Who is he?"

Colter cast him a strange look. "That's Captain Clark."

"Captain?"

Colter ignored the question and addressed the red-haired man. "Shannon here claims he don't remember the expedition, Captain."

Clark's laughter tailed off. Colter continued, "Claims he don't know me, or you, or anyone else."

"I don't claim anything," Shannon protested. "That word implies lying when I'm telling the truth."

Clark eyed Shannon. "What do you remember?"

Shannon described the scene in the Parson's study.

"What day is it?" asked the captain.

"It should be June 6th," said Shannon a little uncertainly.

"What year?"

His uncertainty vanished. "1803, of course."

The group clustering around them all started talking at once. The discussions were cut short by a wave of Clark's hand, the only sign of discipline Shannon had witnessed so far. "Do you know where you are now?" Clark asked.

Shannon glanced around in confusion, then nodded toward Colter. "He says we are on the Columbia River, but that can't possibly be."

"And why is that, Shannon?" Clark asked.

"Because, according to Father, the Columbia is west of a chain of mountains that no one has yet found, let alone crossed."

This set off the unkempt men around them again. This time the captain did not interrupt the chatter. Shannon raised his voice to compensate. "What is going on?"

Clark motioned for quiet. "Let me assure you of two things, Shannon." He indicated the river flowing by. "First, that is indeed the Columbia River. Second, someone has most definitely found those mountains. Found and crossed them. Those someones are us. All of us, including you."

A cheer went up from the ragtag mob. Shannon remained in its midst more confused than ever.

Another man stepped forward. Despite the filthy, patched hide clothing he wore, he carried himself like a true military man, the first Shannon had seen so far. He unwound the rags from Shannon's head and examined the wound. "You are healing nicely, Shannon. Undoubtedly your memory will return in time. Until it does, it is best for someone to keep an eye on you so you don't re-injure yourself."

Shannon shook his head. "But I don't need —"

"Colter, he's your charge."

Although Colter offered no argument, his face clearly showed his lack of enthusiasm for the assignment. Shannon had to wait for the group around them to disperse before asking him, "Who was that?"

Colter whipped toward him. "You don't fool me, Shannon. Stop your playactin' 'fore you cause us all a lot of grief. You ain't worth the space you take up or the air you breathe."

After Colter stomped off, Shannon turned a slow circle, desperate to figure out what had happened to him. After many anxious minutes, it came to him that he was dreaming. The most vivid, most upsetting dream ever, no doubt brought on by the momentous steps he had taken that very day. Never before had he gone against his father's wishes, by applying for an appointment to West Point.

Immediately he relaxed. Soon he would wake up and everything would be as it had been before he went to sleep, familiar and comforting. All he had to do was wait till morning.

Colter had no doubt that Shannon was lying and set out to prove it the next day. As soon as he and Potts and Shannon were out on the water away from the others, he started in. "You catch a look at them two horses Captain Lewis traded for last night, Shannon? One of them's the spittin' image of old Lump."

"What's a lump?" Shannon asked crossly.

"Don't tell me you forgot old Lump? He was your favorite."

Shannon craned around. "I don't know who you're talking about."

Colter aimed his next question at Potts in the bow. "You thought about what you're goin' to do when you get to Saint Lou?"

"Been thinkin' about it ever since we left," Potts said.

"I'll bet you have. There's some fine fillies in that town. Ain't that right, Shannon?"

"I wouldn't know," Shannon shot back.

In spite of the younger man's snappishness, Colter kept his tone light and bantering. "You think she's in St. Lou now? Or do you think she stayed in St. Charles?"

"Are you talking to Potts or me?" Shannon asked.

"You, of course. You're the one emptied his purse *and* mine on Lisette."

Shannon showed absolutely no reaction to the name or the implication. Potts shot Colter a shrugging glance. Colter glared at the younger man's back. There was no way Shannon could keep up his ruse much longer. He wasn't that clever. He would slip up and, when he did, the little game he had been playing would come to an abrupt end.

Eventually the captains succeeded in trading for enough horses to accommodate all the baggage plus a few spares for carrying ailing and injured crewmen and, on April 25, the expedition left the river and struck out across country. Shannon lay down to sleep each night with the prayer that he would wake up to normality. But each morning his hopes were dashed when he awoke to find himself still caught in the web of the terrible nightmare. He was forced to concede that he was not imagining his circumstances. He had wandered into a reality far worse than a bad dream, and he had no idea how that had happened.

The full impact of this realization hit home as he rode through a desolate treeless expanse of wind-scoured country on April 27. It took all the rigid discipline of years of militia drills to maintain his composure while he adjusted to the idea and tried to figure out what to do next. He made up his mind to start by reconstructing the steps that had led him to be on this "expedition."

Over yet another appallingly poor meal of some repulsive fishy-tasting mush, he perused the men of the crew. What a miserable lot they were! Dirty, hairy, surly, undisciplined, coarse. Something dramatic must have happened to force him to join such a disreputable group. If only he could remember.

A man settled down beside him. The cook. Cupping a hand over his nose to block the atrocious stench of the man, Shannon wondered how to move away from him without causing offense.

The cook extended a hand his direction. "Name's McNeal. I cook."

Seeing no way to refuse the man's hand, Shannon grasped it gingerly, then immediately dropped it.

"I feel for what you're goin' through, Shannon. Got to be mighty strange not rememberin' the last couple of years," McNeal said.

The man's compassion tempered Shannon's initial visceral reaction to him. No one else had displayed such understanding. Most were indifferent to his situation. Others, like Colter, were openly hostile or contemptuous.

McNeal motioned toward the setting sun. "This country gives me the fantods. Be glad when we get to the Nay Percies."

Shannon lowered his defenses enough to allow a question. "What's that?"

"Beg your pardon. I plumb forgot that you don't remember. Them are the Indians what live east of here on the Kooskooskee River. Nice folks. They kept our horses over the winter. Captains're nervous they might up and leave, go off to hunt buffalo before we get on over there. Ain't no way to get back across them Shinin' Mountains without them horses."

Shannon listened closely for any clues that might mean something to him, that might provide a string to allow him to pull a chain of memories to mind. Though he strained for the familiar, he did not find it.

"Like I said, them Nay Percies're nice folks," McNeal continued. "Any one of 'em would give the shirt off'n his back if you asked for it. Not like them red-skinned pirates we just left back there on the Columbia."

"What did they do?"

McNeal launched into a litany of the Columbia Indians' offenses against the expedition. Shannon listened intently, adding more pieces to the reconstruction he was building in his head of the events of this journey he found himself on. As he did so, an idea began to take form.

At the end of his spiel, the cook cocked an eyebrow at him. "That help you any?"

"More than you know," Shannon answered, meaning it.

"Anythin' else I can do, all you got to do is ask. Okay?"

This time Shannon did not mind the grubby hand the cook laid on his shoulder. "Since you ask, there is something. Would you be willing to tell me about the expedition?"

"How far back?"

"From the beginning."

"You were already signed on 'fore I joined up," McNeal said.

"Then I'll find another way to fill in those blanks. Will you help me with as much as you know?"

McNeal's forehead, the little Shannon could see under the bird's nest of his matted hair, creased in thought. "That'll take a lot of tellin'."

"It doesn't have to be all at once. We can go your pace, however long that takes."

The cook's eyes narrowed slightly. "You remember how to draw?"

"Of course, but what does that matter?"

"Where I come from, if one man helps another, that other helps him back."

"So, what are you asking?"

"From time to time I want you to draw me a picture or two. I help you. You help me. Deal?"

What were a few drawings compared to figuring out how he got here so he could figure out how to get back? "Deal."

"Shake." McNeal stuck out his filthy hand again.

This time Shannon shook it firmly and without hesitation.

After two nights of watching McNeal and Shannon together — McNeal talking and Shannon listening raptly — Colter's curiosity got the better of him. He sidled over to the pair and settled himself down beside them to listen. McNeal interrupted his discourse. "What do you want?"

"Came to hear what you two're jawin' about."

"That's none of your business," Shannon said.

"Accordin' to Captain Lewis, everythin' you do's my business."

"Go away, Colter. We ain't invited you," McNeal said.

"Don't need no invitation. Captain give me a job to do, and I'm doin' it."

Shannon dismissed him with a haughty wave. "Go on, McNeal. Ignore him."

Scowling at Colter, the cook picked up his narrative, a rambling discourse about the winter they spent at Fort Mandan. It did not take much
listening to figure out that McNeal was relating the events of the expedition in a way that cast the cook as the hero of every happening. When
Colter couldn't take anymore, he blurted, "That there's the biggest pile of
bull-diddle I ever heard."

"You callin' me a liar?" McNeal bristled.

"You said it, McNeal," Colter replied.

Shannon swung toward Colter. "This is a private conversation, and you
aren't included."

Colter got to his feet. "Don't know what you're tryin' to do, Shannon,
but you picked the wrong man if'n you want the truth."

"Butt out, Colter," Shannon said.

"Fine-a-ree."

On April 30th, the expedition arrived at the spot where they needed to
cross the Columbia in order to continue their journey to the Kooskooskee.
In return for the local Walla-Wallas' help in ferrying their horses and supplies across the river, the captains agreed to stay long enough for the Indians to hold a celebration in the expedition's honor.

When Captain Lewis asked Shannon to accompany him to that celebration to make sketches, Shannon jumped at the chance. He had thumbed
through his journal countless times in hopes that something — a word or a
picture — would trigger remembrance, but nothing had struck a responsive
chord. Perhaps being among natives would jog his recall.

The first thing he noticed upon entering the village was the open counte-
nances and ingenuous smiles of the Walla-Wallas so unlike the surly Indians the expedition had encountered downriver. The melodic lilt of their
language captured his ear while his eyes drank in the charming disorder of
the busy village preoccupied with preparations for the coming celebration.
The grassy smell of the nearby river combined with smoke from the many
cooking fires and the scent of roasting meat, filling his lungs and making
him glad he came.

He had just settled down to sketch when McNeal grabbed his shoulder.
"Glad I found you, Shannon. See that little gal yonder, the one squattin'
t'other side of the fire?" He pointed to one of a group of Walla-Walla
women grouped around a nearby cooking pot.

Shannon had been trying not to look at that particular woman and her
naked breasts. She was as comely a female as he had seen since . . . since
his last memory of home, although he could not pin down exactly how he
knew that. His throat felt oddly constricted. "Yes."

"Draw me a picture of her," the cook said in a low intense voice.

Shannon wanted to say that he could not possibly presume to impose on
the woman's modesty for such a purpose, but before he could get out the
words, McNeal challenged, "Don't tell me you're backin' down on our
deal?"

Shannon managed a soft "no."

"Then get to work. Sooner you get her done, sooner I have my fun."

The cook wandered off, and Shannon set to work. After a couple of false starts, he found his rhythm. While everything else faded into the background, the woman ceased to be a whole object, a solid figure, and became a series of lines, curves and planes to set down on paper with his charcoal.

He had barely finished when McNeal snatched the book away, ripped out the page and made a beeline for the woman. Shannon watched the exchange of hand motions between her and the cook, wishing he could understand what was being said. Finally the woman accepted the picture. The cook smiled the smile of a bird-eating cat, and the two of them went into a longhouse. The predatory nature of the cook's coarse laugh and the leering way he looked at the woman troubled Shannon. He pushed himself to his feet, intending to go after the cook and retrieve the drawing when Colter sauntered out of the shadows. "Won't do no good to chase after 'em. You shoulda said no when you had the chance."

"No one asked your opinion," Shannon said.

"Ain't no opinion. It's a fact. McNeal'll bed anythin' that'll cooperate and most likely some that won't. And you're helpin' him. That ain't somethin' to be proud of neither, in case you're wonderin', you bein' without your memory and all."

"I don't have to listen to you and I won't," Shannon said, storming away. He had taken McNeal's many tales of sexual conquests of native women as so much harmless bragging. He had borne those accounts with a clenched jaw, prompting the cook to move on to another subject as soon as he could interject a word. After all, he had been around enough of his father's old friends to know how crude grown men could be. He was willing to put up with just about anything from McNeal if it meant getting that one image, that one word or phrase that would lead to reclaiming his lost memory.

As he strode away from Colter, the lascivious tone of McNeal's laughter haunted him. Its echoes grew louder and louder until they blocked out all other sound. Unable to withstand the idea that he had abetted the cook in fornication, he covered his ears with his hands. He had to find a way out of his agreement with the cook, but how?

Eventually he circled back to the spot where he had left Colter. His journal lay on the ground. Stooping to retrieve it, he realized he held in his hand the answer to his dilemma. Without the journal, he had no paper. Without paper, he could not make drawings for the cook to put to sinful uses.

He strode to the river, stopping at the edge. By the light of one of the celebration torches, he regarded the book. Its drawings and descriptions teased him with the secrets they refused to divulge. By destroying it, he was also destroying his only physical link to the past two years, yet he could not keep it if it meant that he continued to subsidize the cook's wrongful liaisons.

He was about to fling the journal into the rushing water when he heard
Captain Lewis's commanding voice, "What do you think you're doing,
Shannon?"

The question froze Shannon's arm and his ability to think.

"Speak up, Private!"

Shannon had learned long ago that he could never lie and get away with
it. "I was throwing the book into the river, sir."

"I specifically asked you to record your impressions of tonight's events
on paper, did I not?"

"Yes, sir."

"How do you intend to carry out my request without your journal?"

"I f-forgot, sir."

"You forgot what, Private?" Lewis demanded.

Shannon was unprepared for the sudden sorrow that welled up into his
chest, damping his voice to a hoarse whisper. "Two . . . two years of my
life, Captain."

The change in Lewis from icy to warm, from superior to fellow human
was instantaneous. Immediately, sympathy replaced the frost in his tone.
He gently took the book from Shannon. "All the more reason for you to
hold on to this. Your memory will return. Just give it time. Now come,
let's go to this little party, shall we?"

Shannon could not trust his voice. Mutely, he took the journal and followed the captain back to the village and the celebration.

The captain's unexpected support acted to restore Shannon's equilibrium
during the feast. By the time the Walla-Walla drums began to throb, signaling the start of the night's dancing, he was completely caught up in the
festive atmosphere. He made sketch after sketch of the dancers and the
surrounding audience, capturing images on the pages of his journal as
quickly as his hand could move.

He was in the process of drawing a trio of Indian elders when the tempo
of the drums slowed and a line of young women draped in elegant feather-
covered shawls shuffled into the firelight. Immediately he left off the unfinished portrait and turned to a new page to sketch this new spectacle. He
was so involved that he did not realize he had an audience until McNeal
said, "You draw real good, Shannon."

Overlaying the cook's normal foul odor, Shannon detected a muskiness
that teased at the scrap of a memory.

McNeal grinned knowingly. "That's woman you smell. Best perfume
there is." McNeal leaned closer. "Place is crawlin' with squaws ripe for the
pickin'. You best be gettin' yourself one 'fore the other men start heatin' up.
If'n you know what I mean."

Shannon gave the cook his most indignant frown. "No, thank you."

McNeal raised a placating palm. "Just thought you'd want to know."

"I'll do my own thinking, thank you," Shannon snapped.

The cook wagged his head docilely but did not move away. Shannon went back to sketching.

There was a lull in the dancing, and he was about to get up to stretch his cramped legs when two of the feather-shawled women strolled by. The natural grace of their movements caught his artist's eye. He quickly turned to a new page to try to capture on paper those elusive qualities.

"Great job, Shannon! Either one of those two gals'll do to cure my itch. Hand it over," McNeal demanded.

Shannon slammed the journal shut and stood up. "You can be sure they will never see it."

"Now you hold on here. You and me, we had a deal."

Shannon drew himself to full height. "I do not, I *will* not deal in sin."

"Why I oughtta —"

"You ought to leave before you give them," he jabbed a thumb toward the captains, "a reason to convene a court-martial."

McNeal's face swivelled from Shannon to the captains and back again three times.

"Leave, McNeal," Shannon said.

"No man goes back on a deal with me," the cook hissed.

"I said leave." Shannon put into his voice all the coldness and command-force he had learned from hearing his father lead the militia.

With a scalding glare, McNeal finally sulked off.

Once the cook had gone, Shannon resumed his seat and reopened his journal, intending to make more sketches before the evening ended. Instead, he found that the exchange with the cook had soured his enthusiasm for the task. He laid the book in his lap and turned his attention to the renewed dancing. A huge bonfire backlit the movements of the dancers. He basked in the fire's warmth while enjoying the prodigious leaps and whirling antics of York.

York. The black man was one of the many gaping holes in his picture of the expedition. There were so many unanswered questions. A whole list of questions, beginning with how he came to be on the expedition and what had happened to his plan to go to West Point. The weight of those questions prompted him to abandon the festivities and head back toward the expedition's camp. He was well out of the range of the firelight when a fallen branch cracked under someone's tread.

He was turning in the direction of the sound when a figure leaped at him out of the darkness. He went down hard, throwing up his arms and flexing his knees in an attempt to ward off the attack. As the man slammed down on top of him, Shannon's elbow caught him in the face. There was a "mmmph" of surprise.

Shannon took advantage of the momentary opening to wriggle out from under the attacker and roll to his feet. His eyes, adjusting to the darkness, found the cook writhing on the ground, cradling his nose and whimpering.

"Damn you, Shannon! You broke my nose! Now I owe you for it and another tooth."

Another tooth? It had never occurred to him to ask about the two-tooth gap in the cook's front teeth. If McNeal blamed him for only one of those, who had knocked out the other?

McNeal's face was contorted and splotched with blood. "You're a joke, Shannon. A sorry damned joke."

The curse pushed Shannon beyond the limit of what he was willing to take from the vulgar cook. He aimed a kick at the unprotected place between the cook's legs. McNeal's yowl sounded over the throbbing of the drums in the distance. Shannon smiled. McNeal would think twice before he tried anything again. The man's slovenly demeanor turned his stomach, but the unprovoked attack could have ended his own life. Revenge felt good.

Once the expedition left the Walla-Wallas, they quickly reached the river, named after Captain Lewis, seven miles below its confluence with the Kooskooskee. The elation at their progress was shortlived. The spring salmon run had not yet reached this far upriver and the natives' food stocks were either depleted or nearly so. As the expedition pressed on up the Kooskooskee in search of Twisted Hair's band and the horses they needed to re-cross the mountains, groups of Indians attached themselves to the crew in hopes of obtaining food. With their own thirty-three mouths to feed, plus Seaman, there was no food to spare, and the situation grew dicier the farther east they moved.

Hope of relief came when they learned that Twisted Hair's village was just upriver. The captains called an immediate halt to the march and sent out pairs of men to scour the countryside for game in preparation for the reunion with the Nez Perce and their precious herd of horses. To Shannon's dismay, he found himself teamed to hunt with Colter.

Since his confrontation with McNeal back at the Walla-Wallas, he was aware of a deep reservoir of anger lying just beneath the surface of his emotions. Anger that could erupt at any time with little provocation. The last thing he wanted was to spend an entire day with the one man who steadfastly refused to believe he had lost his memory and who seemed bent on proving him a fraud.

Colter took the lead riding out of camp, an act that Shannon viewed as presumptuous and arrogant, and typical of someone of Colter's intractable character. He spent the morning growing more and more disgruntled at being forced to spend his time looking at the back end of Colter's horse.

He was working up to a confrontation when his horse suddenly stepped in a hole, pitching him over her head. He landed hard, then bounced up and went after the dazed horse with a stout stick. "Stupid, clumsy animal!" he yelled, ramming the splintered end of the branch into the creature's chest until it broke in two.

The horse reared up in defense.

He ducked the thrashing hooves, picked up another fatter piece of wood and prepared to launch a swing at the creature's tender underbelly. Before he could, a rifle boomed, its ball peppering the side of his face with chips of tree bark. "Hey, what're you doing?" he yelled at Colter.

Colter ripped the stick out of his grasp and threw him face first into the dirt. Shannon came up sputtering in fury. "This is my horse and my score to settle. Butt out!"

In one quick move Colter pinned him to the ground and torqued one leg up in a way that left Shannon completely immobilized. "The only stupid, clumsy critter here is you, Shannon."

Somehow Colter had gotten hold of his rifle. Shannon made a swipe for it and missed. "Damn you! Give it here," he fumed in frustration, unable to extricate himself from the man's hold.

Colter dangled the rifle out of his reach. "This here rifle's the only one you got."

"Yeah, so give it back," Shannon yelled.

"What, so's you can whip up on that critter some more? How about I take you over there so's she can beat on you awhile?"

"She already did, damn it!"

"No, by God! You did that! You! You like to split her neckhide. I say you earned a few kicks more'n the one you already got from her."

Colter's words knifed through Shannon's anger. "That's what happened to me? That's how I lost my memory? That horse kicked me?"

Colter relaxed his hold on Shannon's leg. "It was more like your fool head run into her hoof. You goin' to behave now, or do I have to sit on you all durned day?"

Try as he would, Shannon could remember nothing of such an incident. "You can get up," Colter said, and rose. Holding the rifle in one hand, he offered the other hand to help Shannon up. Shannon was too ashamed at how easily he had been subdued to accept help. He got up under his own power and reached for his rifle. Colter pulled it away. "Better I keep 'er."

"I can't hunt without it."

"I'll do the huntin'. You can hold the horses, if'n yours'll let you near her, that is."

"Confound it, Colter! You're proved your point. Now give me my rifle."

"Nope. Not till you simmer down from the rollin' boil you been stewin' in all week."

Shannon made a lunge for his gun, but Colter sidestepped him easily.

"Better mount up," Colter said. "Time's a-wastin'." He swung up on his horse and prodded it into motion.

The anger drained out of Shannon, leaving him empty and tired. Once his life had made sense. Then in some cruel cosmic joke he had been robbed of time and memory. Now nothing made sense. He wondered if it ever would. He lifted his eyes to the tops of the surrounding trees. "Why?"

The trees answered with a mournful sigh.

After his set-to with Shannon, Colter turned his full attention to the task of bringing meat back to camp. Although he searched the rest of the day, he picked up no sign of game, not even a rabbit track for all the good such a small animal would do with so many hungry bellies to fill. The afternoon was waning when he decided to try a different route back to camp. His mount seemed to sense his decision and turned in the intended direction before Colter could pull on the reins. It was exactly the kind of anticipation Blaze used to surprise him with, and his thoughts swung to the horse he had left with his cousin Quent back at Maysville. Blaze had been such a fine animal, such a good friend.

As if he could read minds, the stallion under Colter nodded its head. Again, it put Colter in mind of Blaze's uncanny mind-reading ability. "We better stop here."

The horse drew up before Colter could finish the sentence.

While he waited to be certain that Shannon, who was dragging behind, saw that he had changed direction, Colter considered other ways this new horse resembled Blaze, turning from feisty and disagreeable when on its own to cooperative the moment Colter got on his back. Like Blaze, the stallion swung his left front foot out to the side when he walked. As Shannon rode into view, Colter reached down to stroke the animal's neck. "Come on, Blaze."

He smiled at himself for the slip of the tongue. Zoob always poked fun at him for talking to Blaze like a person. He lifted his gaze to the distant peaks with their glistening mantles of snow. Zoob should have lived to see this country. Together they could have . . .

He did not allow the thought to finish. Zoob was dead. Period. No amount of wishful thinking would change that fact.

While he watched, upper-level winds began to herd clumps of clouds against the distant peaks, collecting them there like ewes in a pen until they blotted out the sun. "Snow tonight," he muttered. "Pray it's light. We come too far to get stopped now."

The horse did not react.

"Guess I can't expect you to be Blaze now, can I? Suppose I ought to call you somethin' though. How about . . . Blazer. For your temper?"

The horse looked around at him and passed gas.

Colter prodded the animal into motion. "That mean you agree?"

The stallion snorted and stopped short, nearly unseating Colter. It was one of Blaze's favorite tricks. "Okay, Blazer it is."

🦅

Spurred on by the lack of game and the difficulty of obtaining food through trade, the captains set a relentless pace up the Kooskooskee until, at last, they located Twisted Hair's band. Since coming into Nez Perce country, they had heard rumors that Twisted Hair's people had starved and otherwise mistreated the expedition's horses. Anxious to see if those rumors were true, the captains made short work of the formalities, then asked to see the herd.

The tension of waiting for the horses to be rounded up scarcely touched Shannon. He was immersed in problems no one else could understand, struggling with the loss of so much of his history and trying to reconcile himself to that loss.

"Here they come," Rube said from his spot next to Shannon.

On the slope above the Nez Perce village, horses poured out from among the trees like an undulating shadow, flowing across the bright green spring grass. Bareback-mounted Nez Perce rode alongside the herd, driving them forward with whoops and brandished strips of colored cloth.

Rube poked Shannon's arm. "What a sight, huh?"

Shannon grunted a response. Little mattered to him except the missing months of his life.

The horses thundered into the village, guided into a brush and branch corral by the front riders who swung expertly aside at the gates. After the holding pen was secured behind the stragglers, the crew surged forward to view the horses, carrying Shannon along with them.

He found a place to stand along a brushy section of the enclosure. With his mind on his problem, he paid no attention to the horse watching him until the animal bumped the back of his hand with its nose. "Be glad she remembered you and didn't take a bite outta your hand," said Colter from inside the pen, coming up to pat the horse's neck.

Shannon pulled his arm back. "She looks docile enough. I doubt she would do such a thing."

Colter circled the horse, looking her over, then swung over the branch rail and landed at Shannon's side. "She's a bit thin, but it ain't nothin' a week of sweet grass won't fix. She's in foal, too. Good news, huh?"

"Whatever you say," Shannon said drily.

Colter gave him the once over. "All this fakin' is workin' a toll on you, ain't it?"

Shannon stiffened at the accusation.

"You ought to forget about soldierin' when you get home. Try playactin' instead. Hell, look at all the experience you're gettin' here." He leaned toward Shannon. "Only plays end, Shannon. All of 'em. Even this here one you been workin' so hard at." He dusted his hands and walked off.

Shannon stared after him, despising every muscle in the man's lanky body, wishing he had the energy to poke a hole in the man's inflated self-importance.

Inside the enclosure the mare nickered. The sound plucked a familiar chord in Shannon. He turned to study the horse. Deep within him, something stirred. Something familiar. The faintest glow of a single ember of hope that two year's worth of memories had not been completely destroyed.

3. *Stymied*

T he day after their arrival at Twisted Hair's village, the crew awakened to eight inches of fresh snow. After the joy of discovering that their horse herd was intact and generally healthy, the snow put a damper on everyone's spirits, especially Colter's. He spent an anxious couple of hours, dreading that the change in the weather would cause yet another delay in the homeward journey, before the captains ordered camp struck to continue on to Broken Arm's village.

That village rested on a shelf set into a curve of the Kooskooskee twenty feet above the level of the river. An arc of close-growing cedars on the upstream side of the shelf provided protection from the cold wind that perpetually swept down the canyon. Snow lay deep and sparkling less than half a day's march above the Nez Perce lodges and the crew's talk began to mix complaints about lack of food with worries about crossing the mountains still swathed in their winter coats of snow.

Colter shut his ears to such talk. His desire to forge on, to keep going eastward, to get back to Fragrant Grass had grown into a need. A need bordering on compulsion. He was ready to do whatever it took to see that the expedition did not stop now.

The day after their arrival at Broken Arm's village, May 11, the captains conducted their first formal council with the Nez Perce. The council used up the last of the expedition's supply of trade goods which meant that there was nothing left to pay for a guide across the mountains.

As he watched the signed talk, sensations from their last crossing came flooding back to Colter. The bitter taste of the inner bark of the pine tree. The feeling of being deserted by every other form of animal life and that they would never escape from the web of deep canyons and brooding mountain fastnesses. The hunger and desperation beyond anything he had ever experienced. And that was on a clear, if barely discernible, trail with Toby guiding them. It was true that Toby had lost the way occasionally; regardless, he had led them out of those mountains and not a single man had died on the crossing.

But now the tables had turned. The crew was weak from hunger, the route lay buried in snow, and they were on their own to find the way. The odds for success were even lower than the chances that he and Ordway would ever become friends.

Colter had been paying little attention to the parley until the sweep of Broken Arm's expressive hands captured his full attention. He waited for Drouillard's translation to make certain he understood the signs correctly: the Nez Perces had volunteered to supply guides to the expedition.

Before his spirits could launch into flight however, Broken Arm traced more signs to say that the Indians would not venture into the mountains until the snow had melted enough to make the journey possible. By their reckoning, that would be at least another month.

Faced with the choice between going ahead without a guide and waiting a month trying to keep alive on sparse game, Colter's head chose waiting, but his heart chose forging on. His heart sank when Captain Lewis instructed Drouillard, "Tell the chief that we accept his offer and will wait for one month."

One month. How would he ever manage to last it out?

The expedition needed a temporary camp while they waited for the snows to melt in the upper elevations. For that, the captains chose the site of an abandoned pit lodge far enough away from Broken Arm's village to hold the promise, if not the fact, of plentiful hunting.

The pit lodge was a three-foot-deep circular depression, thirty-feet in diameter. Over it, the crew erected a low roof of wood covered with brush. To Colter, it looked like a root cellar, smelled like a root cellar, felt like a root cellar. Despite the frequent snowfalls, he opted to sleep under the open sky.

Beside the lodge, the crew built two corrals for the expedition's remuda. The next task was to separate the mares from the stallions. That was the detail Colter drew.

He was in the main corral closing the gate behind the last mare when one of the stallions became agitated. The horse, a deep roan with a nasty temper that had been trouble since they got him from the Walla-Wallas, charged Colter, butting him into the fence, pinning him there.

With everyone else working the mares, he had to handle the situation alone. He swatted at the roan's rump in an effort to get him to move. The horse responded by leaning more heavily into him, pressing his back into the prickly logs and making it hard to breathe.

"Durn fool horse, move it!" Colter slapped at its rump to no effect.

There was a sharp snort from the other side of the roan. Another horse was challenging the stallion. Pressed against the fence, Colter could not make out which one. The roan responded with a snort of his own and more pressure against Colter.

Colter swiped off his cap and used it to swat the horse's head, drawing a guttural bear-like sound from it.

With a sharp whinny, the challenger reared up and slashed at the roan's ribs with his hooves. "Blazer!" Colter called out as a hoof struck the lower part of the roan's front leg.

The roan neighed in protest and stepped away from Colter to face its attacker. Freed from the horse's crushing weight, Colter scrambled over the fence out of harm's way.

The sound of battling horses drew a handful of crewmen to join him at the corral fence.

Angered by Blazer's blow, the roan reared and raked a hoof across Blazer's muzzle. Blazer cried out in pain and the sound got Colter moving.

He vaulted back into the corral and got behind the roan. Armed with nothing but his hands and quick reflexes, he grabbed the horse's tail and yanked back on it as hard as he could.

The surprised roan broke off the attack on Blazer and kicked backward.

Colter anticipated the kick and, still hanging onto the tail, leaped to the side.

The roan did not cotton to having his tail tweaked. He whipped his head around and sank teeth into the sagging rear of Colter's rawhide trousers. The seat ripped free as he swung to the side, and one of the roan's lashing hooves caught him in the shin, knocking his leg out from under him.

Knowing the the furious horse was liable to trample him if he stayed on the ground, Colter gritted his teeth against the pain shooting up his leg and scrabbled out of the way. He had just reached the fence when a loop of newly-made rope dropped over the roan's head, encircling the red neck, jerking tight. On the other end of the rope, Drouillard.

In the space of two breaths, the half-breed had the roan subdued and two men had hold of Blazer while the rest of the stallions milled in a nervous clump at the other side of the enclosure.

Clark rushed up. "Anyone hurt?"

Colter added his "no" to the others' replies.

"Well, those two stallions just made up my mind." Clark waved a trio of young Nez Perce braves into the corral. One took the roan's lasso from Drouillard and the other two took up places on either side of the animal. One of them drew a knife; the other concealed behind his back a glowing taper recently taken from the fire. They moved with such speed and deftness that their work was done and the three Indians had leaped clear before the roan could react.

As the horse squealed its dismay, one of the Nez Perce held up the bloody sack of the horse's testicles. Colter had no problem with the idea of castrating the stallions, but he did not want anyone else touching Blazer. He appealed to the captain. "Let me do that one there, Captain," he said, pointing to the restrained animal.

Clark nodded. "Very well."

Colter started into the corral but his injured leg collapsed under his weight before he had taken two steps.

"You said you weren't hurt, Colter," Clark said.

"I ain't," Colter said.

Clark waved to Drouillard and two other crewmen. "You three finish the rest of the stallions while I see to Colter's leg."

Colter was rolling his pantleg over the bruise when an unearthly scream rent the air. He turned in time to see Drouillard dance away from Blazer, holding a blood-drenched knife.

Bright red blood pulsed down the inside of the horse's back legs. Drouillard had botched the castration. Now the horse would die, a swift but agonizing death.

Colter forgot his injury and the captain, staggered into the enclosure and hurled himself at the half-breed. Drouillard went down on his backside, dropping the knife. Colter grabbed it up and glared down into Drouillard's emotionless, fearless, remorseless eyes. "You filthy 'breed. You deserve to die for what you done to my horse."

"Colter, drop it!" Clark bellowed.

Drouillard's voice was completely calm. "We eat horses, Colter."

"Why, you —"

As Colter lunged for Drouillard, a foot connected with his wrist and the knife flew out of his grasp across the corral. Captain Clark dragged Colter away from Drouillard, shoved a rifle into his hands and turned him toward the shrieking Blazer. "For God's sake, man, put that animal out of its misery."

Blazer was on its knees, the crimson pool beneath its hindquarters spreading while its tortured cries grew steadily weaker.

A knot of grief rose into Colter's throat and stuck there. Such a waste. Such a crime.

Some of the anger left the captain's tone, replaced by the strains of a plea. "If you care for that horse, shoot it, Colter."

Colter could not swallow against the knot in his throat. Slowly, he raised the butt of the rifle to his shoulder. He was unaware that his hands were shaking until the captain's hand cupped his shoulder. "Steady."

The understanding in the captain's voice and the strength in his touch calmed the raging tides of emotion in Colter. He took aim on a spot behind Blazer's ear.

"That's it. Now shoot," Clark said.

The hammer fell. The rifle boomed and a ball pierced the proud brain. Blazer's cries ceased abruptly and the horse collapsed onto its side. Colter lowered the rifle and limped to the animal's body.

"Such a waste," the captain muttered, echoing Colter's own thoughts.

"Goddamn that Drooler."

Clark's hand on his shoulder restrained him. "The horse is dead, Colter. Now let it go."

"Just how'm I supposed to do that, Captain? How? You tell me."

"The same way you've done everything else on this journey, Colter. You do it."

"Is that an order, sir?" he said bitterly.

"Do you really need an order?"

Colter was too enraged to reply.

"It's still a long, long way home. Too long to nurse a grudge," Clark said.

Colter stared at the lifeless carcass at his feet for a long time before lifting his gaze to the deep snow blanketing the peaks encircling the camp. Zoob, Pa, Ma, Rachel, Stuart's Draft, Blaze, and now Blazer. His life had become nothing but a string of losses. How many more did he have to endure before he began to win something? How much love could a man lose before he would never let himself love again? How many questions did a man have to ask before God gave him some answers?

When the terrible screams started, Shannon was standing beside the mare's corral. He whirled toward the stallions' enclosure to see Drouillard darting away from Colter's horse, the one Colter called Blazer. The animal's head was cocked at a strange angle. The cords in its neck were pulled taut. And it cried out in a way that pierced Shannon's soul. He clamped his hands over his ears, but he could not block out the sounds. "Dear God, please make it stop," he whispered.

While the plea stirred the shadow of another memory that would not be coaxed forward, the wounded stallion's cries whipped the mares into a frenzy. Shannon moved over to offer comfort to Mama. He had no idea why he called her that. Only that it seemed right.

The mare pressed her velvety muzzle into his outstretched hand. With his other hand he stroked her forehead and crooned comforting noises against her neck.

The cries from the other enclosure began to weaken, but their effect on Shannon did not diminish. "Please, someone, help that poor creature," he whispered against Mama's hide.

A rifle boomed, its report reverberating off the surrounding hills. By the time the echoes faded, the terrible cries had ceased. Shannon laid his forehead against the mare's muzzle. "Thank God."

At the mare's soft nicker, a scene swam up to the surface of Shannon's mind: Mama standing over a wobbly new-born colt. He looked into the mare's eyes. "You had a colt?"

With a toss of her head, she jerked away from his hold and backed out of reach where she eyed him accusingly. He was stunned. "Oh, my God, I remember. I really remember."

She turned and trotted to the opposite side of the corral. Her movements pulled out memories of other screams. The screams of a dying colt. Mama's colt.

Using a smoothed branch as a crutch, Colter hobbled to a sunny spot at the back of the converted pit lodge that he and the rest of the crew had dubbed the Root Cellar. He settled onto the box and listened to Sergeant Pryor's barked instructions to the day's wood detail. *Least I ain't got no details till this here leg of mine heals up*, he thought with grim satisfaction.

Rube and Joe waved at him as they headed off to hunt. He could not return the wave. Just breathing seemed to take all the effort he had the last few days, thanks to a deep and growing lethargy.

Ordway came around the side of the lodge. "So, there you are." The tip of the sergeant's nose was a dark purple-red from constant exposure to the cold.

Colter would have pointed out that this was the very same place he had been sitting since he got kicked in the leg. He would have but that took more effort than he wanted to waste.

"Captains have to go down to Broken Arm's village, and they're taking both Sacajawea and Charbonneau. You get to watch Pomp," the sergeant said.

"What am I s'posed to do? I don't know nothin' about babies," Colter said sourly.

"Guess you'll learn, won't you? Janey's in with the kid now. Ask her to show you what to do."

Ordway moved off, leaving Colter to stare morosely at the melt water oozing into the sergeant's footprints. He needed peace. He needed to be left alone, not to be saddled with some squalling nuisance. Slowly he levered himself up and limped to the little dome-shaped shelter of branches, brush and earth that housed the Charbonneau family.

Sacajawea turned at his approach and motioned that the baby was asleep, then she handed him a leather-wrapped bundle filled with clumps of dried moss. Colter had no clue what he was supposed to do with the stuff. His puzzlement drew a rare smile from Sacajawea and reminded him how very young she was. Using signs and pantomime, she explained that the moss was for diapering Pomp and that Colter was to save the dirty moss so she could rinse it out later. Their exchange was curtailed by Charbonneau who lumbered up to the hut, barked to her in Hidatsa, then stalked away. Immediately her face lost its smile and youth. She glanced worriedly back at Pomp.

Suddenly Colter felt the need to reassure her. He signed that Pomp was in good hands and that she need not worry.

She nodded uncertainly and hurried off to join the captains, York, Charbonneau, Shannon and Drouillard for the ride to the Nez Perce village. Colter watched Drouillard ride away. *We eat horses.* From deep within the shadows of his apathy, the half-breed's words caused a small spark began to ignite and begin to glow. The spark of retaliation.

A baby's mewling reminded Colter of the duty he had just taken on. Slow as he was to move, by the time he got down to his knees, the baby's cries had grown to wails. "Hush up there," Colter muttered.

His words had no effect on the unhappy baby so he raised his voice a notch. "Quiet."

The wails grew louder.

"Attention!"

The cries stopped abruptly and that success gratified Colter. "Now, that weren't so hard, were it?"

Pomp immediately began to wail. Colter threw off the verbal approach in favor of scooping up the disconsolate child. It was the first time he had held Pomp and the sturdiness of the small body surprised him.

The baby's cries trailed off, and Colter found himself the object of examination by two bright round eyes. "Hello."

Pomp began to whimper.

"Oh, Lordy. Now what?"

McNeal's snorted chuckle sounded behind him. "Kid's hungry."

"What do I feed him?"

"Pull out a tit, why don't you?" The cook cackled at the joke.

The baby's whimpers turned into choked sobs. "Look what you done now, McNeal. Get outta here," Colter said disgustedly.

"And what if I don't? You plannin' to shoot me?" McNeal challenged.

Colter hugged the child to his chest in order to pull out his knife. He lifted the well-honed blade to the cook's eye level. "Shootin'd be too easy. 'Sides, I got other ideas for you, McNeal. I figure some night you're goin' to feel a little tickle around that there carrot you're so proud of. Figure you'll reach down to scratch that itch, only there ain't goin' to be nothin' left to scratch."

"You wouldn't!"

Colter glared steadily at the cook who made a strangled sound and hurried away, leaving him alone to deal with Pomp. By now, the little one had forgotten why he was crying and began to explore Colter's face with tiny fingers and assorted gurgles and smacks. When Pomp's fingers found Colter's birthmark, his little face crinkled into a question.

"It's a bird," Colter said.

"Bhhh," the child repeated.

"Bird," Colter said, drawing the word out.

"Bird."

The baby said the word so clearly and distinctly that Colter went on, "A hawk bird." He flapped his free arm and pointed to the sky.

This time the child mimicked the actions and the word.

Colter pressed Pomp's finger to his chest. "Me Colter."

"Colter," the little one said seriously.

Then he held the finger to Pomp's chest. "And you're —"

"Pomp," the child exclaimed, giggling so infectiously that Colter found himself grinning, despite how foolish he felt nursemaiding a baby. He set Pomp on the ground, then spent the next eight hours limping after him, keeping him out of harm's way.

By the time the captains' group returned, Colter was exhausted. He turned the child over to Sacajawea with a whole new appreciation for how well she managed to juggle her responsibilities as translator, diplomat, wife, and mother.

Broken Arm and the elders of the Nez Perce village came out to greet the captains' group, then led them into the band's communal longhouse. Shannon entered the building, invigorated by the slice of memory Mama had helped restore to him. He settled onto the floor next to the Field brothers and turned to studying the rough-hewn planks and slabs of bark that formed the frame of the fifty-foot-long building, looking for clues that might uncover more of his missing two years.

The outer walls of the building slanted toward each other meeting at a point above the center of the raised ten-foot-wide floor. Two dozen rock-lined hearths, one for each family, were sunken into the floor. The only other sources of light in the interior besides these fires were smokeholes set into the peak of the roof.

While he waited for his eyes to adjust to the dimness, he sensed many people crowding the small space. He felt their eyes probing him and moved closer to the outer wall. Over everything hung the pervasive odor of smoke from wood too wet to burn completely.

When his eyes had adapted, he found himself seated across from a young Nez Perce woman. Her open, level gaze disconcerted him and he felt himself blushing. To counter his embarrassment, he took out his charcoal and began to sketch the village elders grouped around the next hearth.

He finished the drawing with a dash of charcoal shadow under the chief's hatchet-shaped nose, and someone tittered. The young woman had moved up beside him without his being aware of her. Her nearness disturbed him and he shifted away as unobtrusively as possible.

She said something.

"What?"

She mimed a big nose and pointed to the chief in the completed drawing, her laugh a clear flowing ripple of delight. That laugh combined with the scent of her to make him acutely aware of a stirring in his loins. When he squirmed to hide that stirring, his elbow brushed against her. "Pardon me."

She rested three fingers on his forearm and murmured something in a low, urgent voice.

" I-I don't . . . can't understand you," he stammered.

She leaned closer and her voice fell to a whisper.

He started to sweat. The stirring in his loins became a major movement. "I wish I could figure out what you're saying," he said helplessly.

She laughed, low and throaty, exacerbating his condition. He tried to look away, but she cupped his cheek with one hand and turned his face toward her. Then she aped drawing and pointed to herself.

"You want me to draw you?" he asked, miming his words.

She nodded and arranged herself into a stiff pose, her lively face set into a solemn mask. "No, no," he said, motioning for her to sit and smile naturally. Looking doubtful, she did as he asked, and he set to work, hoping the act of sketching would subdue his body's longings.

It had quite another effect as he became aware of another stirring, this one in the recesses of his mind. This woman acted as if she knew him. Knew him in ways he was certain he did not want to contemplate . . . or remember.

All of a sudden he needed to get away from her and the idea.

He closed the journal and got to his feet, holding the book in front of his erection. There was a pause in the talking between the captains and the Nez Perce elders as they turned to see what he was doing. He had to climb across Drouillard and York to the only vacant space to sit, bumping his head on the low roof. Once seated, he kept his head turned away from the woman so he would not be tempted to look at her. There were *some* memories he would be better off without.

4. *Blood Feud*

B y May 25th, Colter's leg had healed enough for him to draw a duty. He could scarcely believe his ears when Ordway called him out to hunt. Then the reason for the sergeant's unexpected beneficence became clear: he was paired with Drouillard. Colter longed to get out of camp, but not with the man who had killed his favorite horse.

He roped the first mare handy and joined Drouillard at the edge of camp.

Colter noted that the half-breed had chosen the roan that had been involved in the fight with Blazer, the one that had led to that horse's death. The half-breed looked over Colter's choice of horses. "She is no good."

A quick glance showed that Drouillard was right — the horse was a poor choice — but there was no way he was going to admit that. "She'll do. Time's a-wastin'. Let's go."

"You pick another horse," Drouillard insisted.

"I got this one, and I'm stickin' with her."

"No."

"Yes."

"Then you will walk." Drouillard mounted his horse and headed out of camp. Colter followed, taking grim satisfaction in scoring one round against this man he so despised.

At the end of his water-hauling detail, Shannon hurried up to where the expedition's horses were feeding, scattered across a broad meadow. The animals moved restlessly, their necks bent to the ground, noses searching hungrily for grass to fill their winter-shrunken bellies.

He paused at the edge of the meadow to take in the image of the herd and decided that he would bring his journal and sketch the scene the next day. Then he went looking for Mama, wishing he had a lump of sugar to surprise her with. He located the dappled mare who was Mama's usual companion, but he could not find his horse.

Potts, the herd guard, came riding over. "If you're lookin' for that mare you fancy, Colter took her this mornin'. Went huntin' with Drouillard."

"But she's a pack horse, and she needs rest," Shannon said.

"That didn't bother Colter none. He's been settin' too much to think clear."

Shannon turned away with a bad feeling in his gut. Colter and Drouillard and *his* horse. Not a good combination. *Dear God, please don't let anything happen to Mama.*

Drouillard set a faster pace than usual. Before long, Colter's injured leg began to ache, and the mare began to falter. Colter could ignore his own pain, but he would not abuse a horse. "Pull up!" he called toward the half-breed before sliding off the mare's back.

He examined each of her hooves but found neither cuts nor embedded stones to explain her limp. During his examination, he discovered he had chosen the mare Shannon favored, the one Fuzz called "Mama." He brushed a hand across the animal's prominent ribcage. "Fool critter, we need to fatten you up quick. We got us a long trip ahead."

"*Allez!*" Drouillard yelled, motioning for Colter to catch up rather than riding back to see what the problem was.

Colter realized he had put himself in a major pickle. On the one hand, the mare belonged back with the herd, eating and resting, not hauling his bulk all over these hills. On the other hand, if he continued to ride her, he would wear her down to the point where she might never recover fully. He was bull-headed, but, when it came to animals, he could not be cruel. His conscience would never allow that.

"*Allez!*" Drouillard yelled again.

Colter ignored the shout and stroked the horse, wondering how he could turn back and still save face with Drouillard.

Finally Drouillard rode back to him. "I tell you at camp she is no good."

Colter glared at the half-breed. "It's you ain't no good, Drooler. You're the horse-killer."

"We eat horses, Colter."

The words acted like an explosive charge, ripping apart Colter's lethargy and igniting within him a fireball of red-hot fury. He grabbed for the half-breed, pulling him off the roan and piling on top of him. Drouillard fought off his hold and bounced to his feet. Colter launched a violent kick at the man's right kneecap, but the half-breed countered with his own kick in the exact spot where the roan's hoof had caught Colter on the shin a week earlier.

The pain exploded in his leg, nearly causing Colter to black out. By the time the stars cleared from his vision, the half-breed was back on the roan, his face completely composed, his body relaxed and confident. "Be damned, you miserable 'breed," Colter snarled.

The roan pawed the ground with the restless energy of an animal unused to standing still. "No hunting for you today, Colter," Drouillard said. "Go back."

"Wait just one minute there, Mr. High and Mighty. You're the lead. You gotta get me back."

Drouillard clicked the roan into motion.

"Stop, damn you!"

The half-breed drew the roan even with the mare and yanked Colter's rifle from the loop attaching it to the leather riding pad. It hit Colter that the half-breed was going to shoot him, with his own rifle. Miles from camp with no witnesses, Drouillard could claim it was an accident, and no one, especially the captains, would doubt him.

"Go ahead. Shoot me, you lyin', murderin' son-of-a-bitch. You might fool them others, but you're the one's got to live with his conscience, if'n you got one."

"You think I want to shoot you," Drouillard said calmly.

"Don't toy with me. Get it over with and be done."

"I think it is you who wish to shoot me. Since I wish to live, I leave your rifle there." Drouillard gestured with the barrel of the rifle toward the top of the saddle ahead. He urged the roan into motion, and Colter pulled himself painfully to his feet. With his leg throbbing mightily, he used the mare to hold himself upright while he watched the half-breed ride up the slope. At the crest, Drouillard leaned Colter's rifle against a pile of rocks, then disappeared over the crest without a backward look.

"Damn your Shawnee hide!" Colter yelled at the man's back.

Every five minutes Shannon looked up, hoping to see Colter and Mama riding into camp. Those hopes did not come to fruition, but, around noon, a group of Nez Perce riders did show up. Among them was the young woman who had caused his disturbing reaction a week ago. Shannon ducked toward the crew latrine rather than face her. Ordway intercepted him on the way. "Potts is sick, and McNeal needs a fill-in. You're it."

Shannon looked longingly down the route to safety.

"Well, Shannon, what're you waiting for? A written invitation?"

The arrival of unexpected guests had thrown McNeal into a frenzy. "Skin out them three rabbits and get 'em over the fire fast," he snapped at Shannon without looking up from plucking a thin grouse.

Shannon set to work. While preparing the rabbits, he kept an eye out for both Mama's return and the Nez Perce woman. "Tarnation, Shannon," McNeal yelled. "Get crackin' or the captains'll have both our hides!"

In his distraction, Shannon's knife slipped and sliced his knuckles. Blood welled out of the cut so quickly he could not keep it from dripping onto the rabbits. McNeal hurried over and grabbed the half-skinned creatures from him. "Instead of helpin', you're ruinin' the meat. Get the hell out of here."

Glad to get away, Shannon was packing snow onto the wound when another hand gripped his arm. A young female hand, belonging to the young Nez Perce woman.

He jerked away from her touch. She flung a few curt words of Nez Perce at him and turned away. Sensing that he had unintentionally offended her, he hastened to speak. "I didn't mean to be so rude. I'm sorry."

She hesitated, then gestured for him to follow her. She led him to the river and directed him to plunge his hand into the clear cold water. The flow of blood stopped immediately. When he looked up to thank her, she was gone.

Unwilling to acknowledge disappointment, he rubbed the wet hand against his trousers and trudged back to camp. He had not gone far when he caught sight of something moving erratically in the shadows of the thick forested slope behind the camp. His first thought was of a wounded or sick animal, stumbling through its final misery.

Then as the thing came closer to camp, it became two things, a horse and a man leading it, Mama and Colter, both limping. The horse was covered in lather and faltering badly. Her head hung down so far her nose nearly scraped the ground. He ran forward to throw his arms around her neck. "Oh, my good God, what's he done to you?"

"What I done is walk her all the way back here so the wolves wouldn't get her," Colter groused.

"Why'd you take her? Of all the horses? You wore her out. Oh, Lord. Just look at her."

"Look at her is all I done for eight damn miles."

"Then you should have done something."

"I did. A lot more'n you would'a done."

By now, several of the crew had come to see what was going on. Among them was Ordway. "Where's Drouillard?" he demanded.

"Horse and me both pulled up lame. He went on," Colter answered.

Shannon studied Colter. His artist's eye picked up on the tension around the man's eyes. Tension that said Colter was hiding something. He guessed that that something concerned the half-breed. Everyone knew about the bad blood between Colter and Drouillard. Had that feud finally boiled over? If so, where was Drouillard? What was it that Colter wasn't saying?

Ordway thumbed toward Mama. "That horse is done for. Shannon, take her to McNeal."

"No!" Shannon put himself in front of the mare, ready to take on any one who dared touch her. "She'll be fine. She just needs rest."

"Step aside, Private," Ordway growled.

"No, I won't let you touch her."

Lewis showed up, trailing the group of visiting Nez Perce. "Our guests here want to look our horses over. Is there a problem, Sergeant?"

The hollow feeling like the one Shannon used to get whenever he dared to disagree with his father began to spread upward from his stomach when he heard Ordway answer, "Shannon here is refusing my order, sir."

"Shannon?" the captain asked, turning to him.

With sweat beading his forehead, Shannon's resolve to protect Mama began to dissolve. Just then, the young Nez Perce woman stepped forward. She walked a slow circuit around the mare, then signed to the captain. Lewis answered back and the two of them carried on a lengthy conversation that ended when each of the parties tapped one balled fist into the open palm of their other hand, the sign for a bargain struck.

"Step aside, Shannon," Lewis said. "She just bought the horse."

"She what?" he blurted.

"Move, Private!" Ordway threatened.

The command and the captain's glare overcame Shannon's reluctance. He moved. The Nez Perce woman gently lifted the horse's head and blew into her nostrils. Then she tapped the mare on the neck and walked off. The exhausted horse trudged after her without the need for a lead rope.

Lewis dismissed everyone but Shannon. Instead of the storm Shannon expected to break over him, the captain's voice was calm. Too calm. "It isn't often that we get a bargain when we trade with these natives. Today we did. You just witnessed the most lop-sided trade of our entire journey: two strong spotted Nez Perce geldings for that broken-down mare. Also, I have never, until today, bargained with a woman. I am having trouble accepting that both of these unusual circumstances would happen at once. Perhaps you can fill me in."

Shannon discarded every answer that came to mind but held onto the single fact that, even if they were starving, the Nez Perce would never eat their horses. Never. Mama was now safe, and that was all that mattered.

"Yes, Shannon?"

"I don't understand any of this, sir."

"You are certain of that?"

Certain was the one thing he could never be. Not until his memory returned. *If* it ever did. All he could do was tell the captain the truth. "I don't know who the woman is, or why she did what she did, if that's what you mean, sir."

"Very well," Lewis said after a long pause. "Resume your duties."

Shannon saluted.

"Saluting isn't necessary, Shannon."

"I-I forgot, sir."

Down in the camp, the Nez Perce were about to leave. The young woman was in the middle of the group, riding double behind an older man that Shannon recognized as a subchief of Broken Arm's band. From her resemblance to the man, Shannon guessed she was his daughter. She held a long lead rope that was draped around Mama's neck. He felt he owed the horse one last goodbye, but he could not bring himself to move. A moment later, the mare limped out of sight and out of his life forever.

When Drouillard rode in with two deer slung across the roan's back, the rest of the crew mobbed the half-breed, celebrating his success. Even the captains joined in the scene.

Colter stayed back. Even if he were at the point of starving to death and the half-breed had the only food left on earth, he wouldn't thank Drouillard. Not until the man expressed remorse for Blazer's death.

The crew's elation was so loud that he did not hear the child crying right away. He hobbled over to the little shelter. "Janey, what's wrong with Pomp?"

Sacajawea peered out. Her eyes were puffy and red-rimmed. She murmured something in Shoshone, then ducked back inside. Colter squatted down and in the dim light, saw that the side of Pomp's little neck was swollen to the size of a piglet's bladder. Sacajawea reached out to touch her child but jerked her hand away when Pomp started to wail.

Colter had seen such a growth on one of his now-dead siblings and it rattled him to the core. He could hardly speak for the tightness in his throat. "I'll go get the captain."

She nodded without taking her eyes off her child.

It was not until he had gone ten steps that he realized she understood what he said.

After two days of enduring the crew's teasing about his part in the horse trade with the young Nez Perce woman, Shannon jumped at the chance to get away from the camp even though it meant accompanying Colter on a wild goose chase. Colter had convinced the captains that a hot poultice made from wild onions would reduce the swollen growth on the neck of Sacajawea's child. Shannon had come to doubt everything Colter said, but he was willing to go along to get away from all the lewd remarks he had

had to put up with.

Besides the Nez perce woman, the crew teased him unmercifully about some woman named Lisette. Whoever she was, Lisette was a woman of easy virtue. That was clear from the coarseness of the comments. But he knew enough about himself to be certain he would never, ever consort with such a woman no matter what the other men claimed. He did not need to reclaim his missing memories to know those two facts.

At the crest of a low ridge a few miles from camp and a mile after separating from Colter, he paused to enjoy the sweet silence. Here there was no one to snicker at him, no one to suggest that he had participated in wanton and sinful acts. Here it was just him and a pretty creek leaping along its rocky bed in its rush toward the Kooskooskee a mile or so down the drainage.

While standing atop the ridge, it occurred to Shannon to wonder why he no longer got lost or turned around. Since the day he took his first baby steps, he had had trouble with directions. Now, however, he knew with gut-level certainty where he was in relation to the camp, the river, and Colter. Why?

Frustrated by his lack of answers to so many disturbing questions, he struck off along the creek, poking half-heartedly in the boggy places for wild onions. As he walked, more disturbing questions began to circulate around in his brain. Why was a woman, a new mother with an infant, along on a military expedition? How did he come to be part of such an endeavor? What experiences were contained in the two-year gap in his memory?

He had learned not to ask the other crewmen such questions since asking invariably resulted in his becoming the butt of some private joke. It was, he decided, better to not know something than to put up with more cruel ribbing from men who had no idea how painful losing a big chunk of their lives could be.

An unexpected sound brought him up short. At first he thought it was the wind. Then he decided it was someone singing. He ducked behind a screen of wild rose bushes and stole in the direction of the sound, circling around a tangle of thorn bushes to a spot where he could see but not be seen.

The creek here slid three feet down the slick face of a rock into a pool that was deep and wide enough to swim in. And that was exactly what a brown-skinned woman was doing. She crossed to the little cascade, put down her feet and rose out of the water. It was the young Nez Perce woman, and she was naked.

She bent to allow the little fall of water to flow over her head, then she straightened, smoothed the wet mass of hair back from her face and laughed, a rich full-bodied sound of pure pleasure. The sight of her riveted Shannon. He had never seen a woman's naked breasts. Or . . . had he? For the second time, something dim and forgotten stirred inside him.

A branch cracked behind him. He whirled to see Colter glaring at him. "Now ain't that a sight. A baby's back at camp wastin' away whilst you're out here spyin' on a naked squaw instead of lookin' for what you come for."

He jabbed an angry finger toward the far end of the pool and a stand of wild onions Shannon had not noticed. "Open your fool eyes for once," he growled, brushing past Shannon and hobbling down the rocks to the pool. The woman watched, but made no attempt to cover herself while Colter waded into the onion patch and yanked up two handfuls, nodded, then limped off in the direction of camp.

Her scrutiny then turned on Shannon. There was no hostility in her stare, and no friendliness. He glanced around for a way to cross the creek without tangling with the thorn bushes and spotted three exposed rocks at the lip of the little cascade that would serve as stepping-stones. He moved to them, anxious to be away from her intrusive gaze.

In his hurry, he neglected to test his steps before committing his weight. The second stone spurted out from under his foot and pitched him down the little falls into the pond. The water his fall kicked up splashed the woman. "I'm so sorry," he muttered, picking himself up.

She did not say a word, just stared while he climbed out of the pool. It was only as he was walking away that he heard her laugh again.

Colter sat on the ground, cutting hides into strips that would be braided into ropes for lashing baggage onto the horses once the expedition finally got going again. Rube and Joe sat across from him, performing the same task and arguing. He knew from experience that asking them to shut up was useless. They would only gang up on him when, right now, he had all he could do to stay calm while little Pomp lay desperately ill a few yards away.

He glanced toward the brush hut. Captain Clark had been in the hut with Sacajawea and the baby most of the morning. The wild onion poultices had had two days to work. Surely they had had some effect by now.

As if in response to his thoughts, the captain crawled out, swiped a hand across his brow and, seeing Colter watching, shook his head sadly.

Colter bowed his head. He had been so sure the poultice would work. Ma had used wild onions to cure his younger brother Joey of a similar condition a year before the smallpox took him.

"Now what?" Rube asked in a gentle voice.

Colter was fresh out of ideas, and that felt worse than any pain he had felt since Zoob had died in his arms.

"Why you askin' him, Rube?" Joe asked. "Kid's just a half-breed."

Colter's head jerked up and he drilled the brothers with his glare. "If'n I was you two, I'd find me some place else to be and damn quick."

Neither man dawdled. They picked up their work and moved off across camp. A weak mewling from Charbonneau's hut wrenched at Colter's heart. He ought to move too, away from Pomp's distress. He ought to, but he couldn't. The only thing he had left to give the sick child was his closeness, and that he intended to give no matter how much it hurt.

Shannon recognized Broken Arm's village through the gap in the trees. "Why didn't you tell me we were coming here?" he called to Drouillard in the lead. "I thought we were out to hunt."

"You did not ask," Drouillard said.

At the edge of the village, Shannon was left with the horses while Drouillard entered the longhouse. The encampment bustled with activity. The annual salmon run had finally reached the upper Kooskooskee. Besides the racks filled with drying fish, the Nez Perce had built dozens of the low brush huts they preferred to use as dwellings over the hot summer months.

Shannon looked around warily. After two embarrassing encounters, he had no wish to see the young Nez Perce woman again. The village children spied him then and crowded around, chattering, giggling, pointing, hemming him in. His edginess increased under their barrage, and his smile grew strained.

All of a sudden she was there, the one he had come to name "Bold Laughing Woman." After shooing away the children, she gave Shannon the once-over. As the silence stretched, he heard himself say, "Thank you, ma'am."

She said something back, signing along with her words.

"I-I'm sorry. I don't understand."

His stammered answer appeared to irritate her. She ceased talking but continued to spank the air with her hands. "Dear God, what is she trying to say?" he muttered to himself.

"She asks why you not come for her before today." Drouillard's quiet voic7e came from behind him. "She say she tires of waiting."

Shannon glanced at the package in the half-breed's hand, then at the man's impassive face. "Lord, Drooler, something tells me I know her, but I don't remember. Do I know her?"

The half-breed's tone hardened. "Why do you call me that name?"

"What name? What did I say?"

"Drooler."

The irritation underlying the half-breed's words was unmistakable. "I don't know where that came from. Really."

More signs from the woman interrupted the men's exchange. "She say she wait too long for you to come for her. She wait no more."

Bold Laughing Woman spun on her heel and strode away, leaving Shannon to stare after her in bewilderment. She had given him an ultimatum. Only, he had no idea what she expected from him.

By the time he came back to his senses, Drouillard was riding away. Shannon gave one final glance at the Nez Perce lodge and added Bold Laughing Woman to the questions on his mental list, then he took out after the half-breed.

As soon as they rode into camp, Drouillard tossed the roan's reins at

Shannon and headed off to the captains with the mysterious package. That left Shannon with the task of tending the horses. He returned from the task to find Captain Clark, stooped beside the fire, filtering foul-smelling yellowish liquid through a strip of muslin, while Drouillard watched. "What's he doing?" Shannon asked the half-breed.

"He strain hot bear grease."

Getting a straight answer for a change prompted Shannon to ask a second question. "What for?"

Drouillard glanced toward Charbonneau's brush hut. "Onions, they do not work. Bear grease, it fix Pomp."

The caustic remark was spoken just loudly enough to reach Colter who sat nearby stripping out a hide. Seeing the line of Colter's mouth harden, Shannon decided to change the subject. "I took care of your horse." Without even a grunt of acknowledgement, the half-breed got up and walked off.

"Some thanks, huh?" Colter said to Shannon. "Next time let that son-of-a-whore see to his own damned horse."

Shannon chose not to respond. Instead he asked, "How's the . . . Pomp?"

Colter appeared to slump into himself. "Who knows."

"You look like you've given up," Shannon said, trying to keep the conversation going.

Colter snapped back. "Well, I ain't. You're imaginin' things again."

Shannon heard the desperation underneath the harsh words, revealing the depth of the older man's concern over the sick child. Enmeshed as he was in filling the gaping hole in his history, Shannon empathized. He lowered his voice. "How's your leg?"

"Been better." Colter stared moodily into the little fire. A succession of emotions played across the man's face until Shannon grew uncomfortable watching. He felt as if he were invading Colter's privacy and looked away.

Before he could think of anything to say to fill the space between them, Colter spoke, "You gettin' involved with that little squaw?"

The question jogged Shannon back to a question of his own. "I have to know, Colter. Do I know her? You know, from before?"

"Know her how?" Colter asked.

Shannon shifted, nervously searching for the right words and landing on the Biblical ones. "Have I committed, you know, adultery with her?"

Colter shrugged. "Last time through here weren't none of us in shape to look twice at no squaws. We was starvin'. You can be glad you forgot that part anyway. You fancy her?"

"I . . . she . . ."

"Either you do or you don't. Which is it?"

Shannon gulped out a "yes."

"Then what's stoppin' you?"

"Adultery is a *sin*."

Colter spit into the dirt. "So's cursin', lyin' and killin'. You done all them things already, includin' beddin' women. Ain't one more sin goin' to matter much for you, I reckon."

Clark yelled for Colter who was up and hobbling to Charbonneau's hut before Shannon had time to absorb what the man had said. *Killing? I killed someone? Oh, my Lord, no. That can't be true. Please let it be a lie.*

5. *Pomp's Peril*

C olter glanced up from slicing an elk haunch for drying to see Sacajawea plodding past on her way to the nearby creek to wash out some of Pomp's used moss diapers. Her back was rounded from worry and her skin was gray from exhaustion. He gave her a smile of encouragement, but she looked right through him. This was not a smiling time for either of them. The baby was not getting any better despite all their efforts to help.

Colter watched her squat at the water's edge. How did she bear up day after day under the burden of caring for a churlish brute of a husband and a desperately ill infant, plus all duties the captains heaped on her? She was so young to shoulder such heavy responsibilities.

Pomp's weak cries issued from inside the hut. With Sacajawea too far away to hear, Colter flung aside his scraper and hurried over to see to the baby.

The ugly abscess on the infant's neck looked even worse under a coating of the bear grease Drouillard had brought back from the Nez Perce village. Desperate to offer what comfort he could, Colter reached out to touch one of the baby's fever-mottled cheeks. Pomp's small brown hand clasped his thumb. Colter placed his other hand under the baby's for support. "That's right, young'un, hold on tight."

Rather than comforting, Colter's actions upset the infant whose weak cries rose to weak wails, bringing his frightened mother on the run. As Colter moved aside to give her access to the child, his ears picked up on a change in the timbre of Pomp's cries, a change for the worse. *Not Pomp, dear God. Not the baby.*

He drifted away from camp to a spot where the creek bank swung around a tumble of boulders. He sat down on the ground and stared into the faces of the rocks, engulfed by a sense of loss and failure. Why, after all the hardship they had lived through, did sickness strike the weakest of them, a child who had not lived long enough to hurt anyone or to learn what life was all about? Was everyone he cared for doomed to early death? Did that mean his love was lethal? Was he doomed to withold his love, to remain alone for the span of his life, because Fate would strike down whoever that love touched?

It was with a heavy heart that he returned to camp many hours later. The place was deserted except for Drouillard who lounged beside the fire. A full rack of meat drying by the fire reminded him of the task he had left undone.

"That there your doin'?" he asked Drouillard, nodding at the tiers of drying meat.

The half-breed grunted.

"Then I owe you my thanks for finishin' up for me. I left my knife somewheres hereabouts. You seen it?"

Drouillard pointed to where the knife lay. It was coated with dried blood and bits of flesh. Colter picked it up and turned to the river with the aim of washing it. Drouillard's words stopped him. "You leave meat to spoil."

Colter glanced toward the drying racks. "What're you talkin' about? Looks fine to me."

"There is your meat." Drouillard stabbed a finger at some charred lumps in the fire, the remains of the haunch Colter had been working on.

"Believe me, it weren't intentional. I was seein' to the young'un."

With no warning Drouillard leaped to his feet and barreled into Colter, sending him crashing into the Root Cellar. The force of impact caved in some of the roof and wedged him between two of the supporting timbers. Before he could extricate himself, the half-breed pressed a knife against his ribs, angled upward toward his heart. Murder glinted in the man's black eyes.

"Cut me and you got a lot of explainin' to do to the captains," Colter said breathlessly.

"What I tell them, they believe," Drouillard said.

"What you tryin' to prove, Drooler?"

"My name is Drouillard." The undisguised hatred in the half-breed's tone chilled Colter's blood while the knife's tip pierced through the hide of his hunting shirt and dug into the flesh of his side.

"Weren't my aim to let no meat go bad, but the baby's dyin' and I went off awhile to sort things out."

"Why do you care? The baby is a half-breed."

Colter had nearly come to blows with Joe for saying the same thing a few days back. Now the tables were turned and Drouillard had the upper hand. Drouillard, the half-breed.

"Half-breed," Drouillard snarled. "Such an ugly name for something people cannot help. You and the Mandan woman, your children will be half-breeds. Will you love your children, or will you hate them because the blood of two races mixes in their veins?"

That unacknowledged truth hit Colter with the force of a hammer blow.

"In your eyes I see that you hear my words," Drouillard said.

Colter managed a croaked "Yes, I hear."

The half-breed pulled away the knife and stepped back. With quaking legs, Colter extricated himself from the bashed-in roof and faced his nemesis. "I was wrong. About the meat and you. I'm sorry, Drouillard."

Drouillard hissed something in French and looked toward the interpreter's hut where Sacajawea's tear-streaked face pulled back from the entrace. That she had witnessed the altercation meant nothing to Colter. Drouillard had given him too much gristle to chew on for that.

"You're *askin'* for work?" asked McNeal skeptically.

"It's better than sitting around doing nothing," Shannon said, though escaping his thoughts was the real reason he had asked the cook if he could help out with the meal. He had moved beyond denying he had killed a man during the two years he could no longer remember. Now he had wandered onto the treacherous ground of trying to embrace that possibility. After all, why would Colter, even as antagonistic as he was, lie about such a thing?

The cook jabbed his knife toward a quail. "Yank out them feathers, then gut it and get it on the fire. And mind it don't burn. It's the captains' supper."

Shannon made short work of preparing the bird, skewering the carcass on a stick and positioning it over the bed of coals to roast. He sat down intending to watch it cook, but his thoughts drifted back to his conversation with Colter, and soon he was too perturbed to sit still.

"Shannon!" McNeal's yell brought him out of his stupor into an awareness that he had wandered away from the fire and the roasting quail. "Where do you think you're goin'? You wanted to work. Get on back here and finish what you started."

Shannon returned to the fire, feeling foolish.

"What's wrong with you anymore, Shannon?" the cook asked with his face taking on a lascivious leer. "You needin' some of Captain's pox medicine again?"

Shannon thought to ask about the reference to pox medicine. Instead, he heard himself speak the question that had haunted him for the last six days. "Who'd I kill?"

The cook leaned back to study him. "You mean, you don't remember?"

"If I did, I wouldn't be asking," he said sharply.

McNeal held out his hands in a placating gesture. "No need gettin' all het up. It's just hard to imagine forgettin' somethin' so important." He lowered himself onto the ground and patted the place beside him. "You best be sittin' down when I tell you."

Shannon did not completely trust the cook's sudden solicitude, but he went along. McNeal stared into the distance as if recalling the details of the incident in question.

"He was a bad one," McNeal began, his gaze shifting to Shannon. "Partisan was his name. A Teton Sioux chief. That one deserved dyin', he did. And you took care of that. Only one problem. We got to go back through there to get to St. Lou. Partisan's people ain't about to let us pass through their territory without a fight. Likely some of us ain't goin' to make it home."

The idea that, through committing the mortal sin of taking another man's life, he might condemn innocent men to death — men he knew — appalled Shannon. "Oh, my Lord."

McNeal's upper lip twitched. "That's right. You best be prayin'. You got us into a real pickle."

Colter welcomed the chance to get out of camp. True, chasing down four horses that had wandered away from the expedition's herd would test his gimpy leg, but it would also remove him from proximity to Pomp's worsening condition.

Before leaving camp, he looked in on Sacajawea and the boy. It took only a glance at the baby to recognize that the end was near. *Make it quick and merciful,* he wished silently, hurrying away to round up strays.

The loose horses had wandered a surprising distance. It was deep dusk when Colter and the others returned them to the main herd. He lingered with the animals, steeling himself for the bad news he was sure awaited him in camp. Little Pomp. He would never forget the feel of the child's fingers exploring his face, or the piping voice saying his name, or the little one's delighted laughter when something pleased him.

Captain Clark got up from the fire and came forward to meet him. *Here it comes,* Colter thought, bracing himself for the bad news.

The captain clutched his upper arms. His voice was raspy. "Our boy has made it."

It was the last thing Colter expected to hear and he did not know what to say. Clark's face creased into a grin. "You hear me? Pomp's going to live."

Live? He's goin' to live?

"Come, see for yourself." The captain pulled him over to the brush hut. "Janey, Colter's back."

The woman who peered out looked completely different from the one he had left behind that morning. Her back was straight and there was a hint of sparkle in her dark eyes. The captain helped her rise to her feet. Smiling tiredly, she put a blanket-wrapped bundle in Colter's arms.

There lay Pomp, a healthy pink coming back into his drawn little cheeks, the glassiness in his wide-open eyes replaced by a glimmer of restored life. Colter touched the boy's cheek. The fever was gone.

Pomp grabbed one of Colter's fingers and held on tightly. "Hawk," he said, the word clear and precise, his little voice strong. "Hawk, Colter."

Colter was overcome by a flood of suppressed feelings. He threw back his head and laughed aloud for the pure joy of life.

6. *Laughing Water*

I t had taken all night for the shock of McNeal's revelation to sink in and now Shannon wandered to the fire in a haze of remorse. He arrived at the same time as Sacajawea who was carrying her baby. The crew broke into wild applause upon seeing the child alive and recovering from his illness. The baby looked around at the men, trying to decide whether to laugh or cry. Then his focus landed on Colter and his round face crinkled into a wide smile. He held out his little brown arms and piped, "Hawk, Colter."

Colter swept the boy out of his mother's arms and began to waltz around in circles. Man and child shared such obvious joy that Shannon's mood darkened even more. He had always thought he would have children someday. But now, there was a good chance he would never have that experience. Not after the battle the expedition would have with the Teton Sioux.

Colter stooped to let Pomp stand, then, holding the wobbly child's hands, he launched into a merry hornpipe accompanied by the syncopated clapping of the crew. All at once, an idea slammed into Shannon's mind. An idea of such force and clarity that he knew in his heart it had come from the Almighty. His missing memory might never return. So instead of moping over it, he must make more memories. In the time he had left to live, he must embrace every experience that came his way. Every experience, beginning with Bold Laughing Woman.

Colter's impromptu jig ended, and he returned Pomp to the drawn, but broadly smiling Sacajawea. She wrapped her arms around her son, kissed his cheek and smoothed his wayward hair with a tenderness that deeply moved Shannon. Captain Lewis then stepped into the center of the ring of crewmen. All talking ceased, and the air turned electric with expectation.

"Tomorrow, we leave here," the captain announced. "We will move east to the prairie where we first met the Nez Perce last year. We will stay there five days to lay in enough meat to see us across the mountains. Your sergeants will give you your assignments."

After a long boring month of waiting, the news set the crew buzzing. Amidst the clamor, Shannon realized that he had delayed almost too long. If he did not find a way to Broken Arm's village right away, he would miss out on the experience of Bold Laughing Woman entirely.

Ordway's squad gathered around their sergeant. "We're still missing three horses. Shannon and Colter, you scout the area around that big creek just this side of Broken Arm's village."

The beating of his heart kept Shannon from hearing the rest of the assignments. He had just drawn the best of all possible duties. Now all he had to do was get separated from Colter and make for the Nez Perce village.

It wasn't until they later reached the pool where he had seen her bathing that he realized the flaw in his thinking. He did not know signs or the Nez Perce language. How could he ever hope to communicate with her?

Colter glanced back over his shoulder. "See anythin'?"

"You sure this is the right way?" Shannon asked, trying to cover his flustered state.

"*You're* askin' me if'n *I'm* lost?" Colter shot back.

Shannon had taken enough ribbing about two weeks of wandering lost up the Missouri in front of the boats — an event he had zero recollection of — that he had to choke back the impulse to let his umbrage at the sarcasm show. "I meant, are we that close to Broken Arm's village? Already, I mean?"

Colter reined his horse to a stop and turned to face Shannon. "You been with her yet?"

Though he could feel his face flushing at the thought of what he intended to do, Shannon threw himself on Colter's mercy. "I need some help, Colter. I want to go to her, but I don't know how to talk to her."

Colter glanced up the creek, then back at him. "Guess them fool horses'll just have to fend for theirselves."

"You'll help me?"

"If'n you'll let me by, I will."

Shannon maneuvered his horse out of the path of Colter's mount and fell in behind him, not quite sure what he was getting himself into.

"Busy place," Colter said when they had reached the outskirts of Broken Arm's encampment. Women in hide dresses pounded roots and gossiped while other women moved about their lodges, cleaning, cooking, sewing and tending babies. Here and there clumps of men lounged in the shade, smoking pipes and talking. Naked children and barking dogs cavorted around a pond formed by a bend in the river, and a group of older boys held an impromptu horserace in the nearby meadow for an audience of admiring girls. The wind off the grassy slope carried the fragrances of spring flowers.

"You ready?" Colter asked.

Shannon gulped at the panic tightening his chest. "Maybe this isn't such a good idea."

Colter turned on him. "Land sakes, Shannon. Make up your fool mind."

"I . . . she . . . we . . . what do I do?"

Colter's expression softened. "So that's it. Well, I cain't help you there. You got to figure that out by yourself." He looked toward the village. "Indians got different ways of dealin' with these here things. Easier ways. Likely she'll know what to do. Then again, some things just come natural."

Instead of helping, Colter's words knotted Shannon's guts even tighter. He dismounted and followed the man into the village, sweating more than the day's mild temperature demanded. Colter stopped in front of a group of Nez Perce men and began to sign. At one point, he turned to Shannon. "What's her name?"

"I-I don't know."

"How'd you expect me to ask for her then?"

"She's the one who traded for Mama. Does that help?"

Colter's hands traced the words. One of the elders replied. "Her name's Laughing Water," Colter said, his eyes still reading the Indian's signs. "And it looks like you're clean out of luck. She's gone to the moon lodge."

Shannon's panic faded into disappointment that he might be thwarted after he had come this far, but somehow it sparked renewed determination to see through what he had started. "How far is this moon place? Can I get there before dark?"

Colter cocked his chin toward a copse of trees up the river. "It be just up yonder, but you and me cain't go there."

"Maybe you won't, but I will."

Colter grabbed Shannon's shoulder. "Oh, no, you don't. That ain't their way, and seein' as how we're here in their town, their way's all we got.

Hear?"

Shannon made to evade Colter's hold and failed. "You want to get us all in trouble, man? She's on her courses. You ain't goin' to see her. Period."

Shannon had only a vague idea of what a woman's courses were since such things were never openly discussed and all his knowledge came from the whispered speculations of the boys he had grown up with. "Why didn't you say so in the first place?" he said, resorting to curtness to cover his embarrassment.

Colter appeared to check his come-back. "This feller's her mother's brother. Want to leave a message for her with him?"

What could he say that would not offend her, or embarrass himself? Shannon declined.

"He says she ought to be back soon," Colter said.

"I said no, Colter. Let it go at that."

Colter tossed him a calculating look, then signed to the elder.

"Can we go now?" Shannon asked.

"Anytime you're ready," Colter said. "Horses're what we really come for."

They rode along in silence for the better part of an hour before Colter spoke. "What'd you bring to give her?"

"You're looking at him," Shannon answered snidely.

"Durn good thing for us both she weren't there then. No tellin' who's toes you'd be steppin' on with that there attitude."

Colter's patronizing manner was wearing thin. "Attitude? You make it sound like I tried to get us in trouble when trouble's the last thing I want."

"All I'm sayin' is that, with these here Indians, a man's got to pay for his privileges. You want her, you got to give her somethin' in return. Hope you held somethin' back, beads or such that'd please a woman, 'cause there ain't much else left for such tradin' that I know of."

"Even if I had something, what good would it do? We move camp to-morrow."

Colter stopped his mount and stared back at Shannon. "So? What's a few miles? We got horses now."

"No, today was my only chance."

Colter kept his eyes focused on Shannon's face while he moved his mount up next to Shannon's.

"What're you staring at, Colter? Move on. We got work to do."

"I'm lookin' at your head. Ain't never seen one so durn hard. Sure your pa weren't a mule?"

"My father is the finest man I know."

"And no doubt the stubbornest critter on two feet. Next to you, that is."

The truth of the statement shut Shannon up.

"Good. About time you shut that yap of yourn. I told you before a man cain't learn nothin' whilst he's yakkin'. You listen to me, hear? When, not if, but when you go see her, you give her this here." He took Shannon's hand and closed his fingers around an object. It was a palm-sized replica of a swimming salmon, beautifully carved from a piece of equally beautiful wood.

"I can't take this, Colter."

"Oh yes, you can. Time you started makin' some new memories to take back home with you."

Shannon looked at the carving a long time before slipping it into his pocket. Later he would find some way to get it back to Colter, but for now there was no sense continuing an argument that was going nowhere.

While the summer heat had already settled over the Root Cellar by the time the expedition abandoned it on June 10th, spring had just begun to touch the high tree-rimmed prairie the Nez Perce called the Weippe where the expedition was to lay over for five days preparing for the mountain crossing. There, camas lilies bloomed in wild profusion, giving the vast expanse of wind-kissed grass and flowers the appearance of a series of rippling sun-kissed ponds.

Colter had little chance to enjoy the spectacle. Now that he was about to clear the last obstacle on his journey back to Fragrant Grass, he threw himself completely into the task of hunting the meat they needed for the journey over the mountains. For three days he returned with the most game of any of the other hunters. Despite his efforts, the day before their scheduled departure, another problem cropped up, one he could not solve: the promised Nez Perce guides had not shown up.

To add to his worries, Potts, his assigned hunting partner, turned up at breakfast too sick to go out. Figuring that Ordway would use this as an excuse to make him sit around camp all day or worse — assign him to help McNeal — Colter lit out before the sergeant knew about Potts. He had something more pressing than hunting to do. Something he needed to find out.

When he got back to camp that night, the Nez Perce guides had still not materialized. He went to the captains and found them both writing in their journals by the light of a single candle stub.

When they looked up at his approach, Colter was struck by how much both men had aged in the bare three years he had known them. It occurred to him to wonder how he himself had fared, until he remembered his mission. "I know them guides ain't showed up yet, captain, but that ain't no reason to wait around. As far as I rode 'er, that there trail's prett' near clear."

"How far did you go?" Clark asked.

"Ten, twelve miles."

The captains exchanged a glance, then Captain Lewis asked, "We'll need someone to scout for us. You up for that?"

Colter had not thought that far ahead but his "yes" was firm and determined.

"Good, we will leave tomorrow as scheduled with you and Drouillard riding ahead."

The pair went back to their writing and Colter walked to the fire. Although he was pleased to be finally moving the right direction again after so much sitting, he was not so sure he wanted to be thrown together with Drouillard. He had made an enemy of the half-breed. There was no telling when or where the man might strike out at him. The pressure of scouting was enough without having to watch his back.

"We leaving tomorrow? Without guides?" Shannon asked as he got to the fire.

"Captains think we can find the trail without them Indians."

"Can we?" Shannon asked.

"Reckon so, near as I can tell."

"Then, here." Shannon held out the salmon carving.

"Keep it. You might need it."

"I don't want it. It's yours." Shannon tried to force it into his hand.

"Look, Fuzz —"

"What did you call me?"

Colter was as surprised to hear himself say the name, which he had struck from his vocabulary back on the coast, as by the vehemence in Shannon's question. "Called you Fuzz. Same thing I been callin' you since we met. Don't tell me you don't remember."

"I wish there was something, anything I could remember," Shannon said longingly. "Take this back, will you?"

Colter took the carving. "We was good friends most of the way out here. 'Fuzz' was the name I give you a long time back."

"Why?"

"Your beard weren't more'n peach fuzz."

"Not that. You said 'we was friends.' What happened that we aren't anymore?"

Colter looked down at the wooden fish. How could he explain that time on the coast, the awful weather, his own sense of powerlessness at not being able to keep his promise to the woman he loved, the captains' decision to stay the winter in that godforsaken place because Shannon had betrayed him and the rest of the crew? "That there's a real long story."

"Then tell it. I'll listen as long as you can talk."

"Ain't no way I'll try. Too much of it depends on what you were thinkin' at the time and that's somethin' I cain't speak to. Maybe you'll remember someday."

Shannon snorted. "Yeah, right. I'll remember everything. Someday. I'll remember about you and Partisan. Right." Angrily he stalked away.

Colter looked after him mystified. *You and Partisan? What in tarnation was he talkin' about?*

The first day out from the Weippe Prairie, the trail proved easy enough to follow despite places where the remaining snow covered it. Colter kept a cautious eye on Drouillard, but the man mostly ranged ahead, completely ignoring him. Between them, they managed to mark the route and rejoin the crew for a sparse supper.

When they reached the limit of the previous day's marking the next morning, the path was no longer clear. Drouillard pointed up the draw to the right. "You look that way."

Something in the man's tone set Colter's senses on the alert. He watched Drouillard branch off to the left. The 'breed was up to something. He was sure of it. He prodded his horse into motion, deciding to keep to the high ground and maintain a lookout for whatever Drouillard might try to pull.

Near the top of the draw, Colter's horse plunged through the snow's crust. He had to dismount to help the animal extricate itself. The snow here was still eight to ten feet deep, except for pockets around rocks and tree trunks where the sun's reflected heat had melted craters. Colter hated sunpockets. He had lost two good packhorses to broken legs because of them.

His mount struggled out of its dilemma only to break through the crust a second time. Unnerved by its plight, the horse floundered wildly, causing Colter to lose hold of his rifle. The gun immediately slid down into a four-foot deep sunpocket. "Hellfire!" he muttered, scooting after it.

He was reaching for the weapon when a shadow fell across the depression. He looked up to see Drouillard outlined against the gray sky. The moment of reckoning had finally come.

"You find it?" Drouillard said.

"Yeah, here," he raised the rifle as defiantly as the narrow confines of the hole would allow.

"No. The trail. You find it?"

Colter shook his head, his eyes glued to the half-breed's face, his body tensed for the man's next move.

"Then it is no use."

Colter was not about to go quietly. "You ain't got no call to do this, you know."

Drouillard shrugged. "If we the trail cannot find, the captains we must tell. Come." He moved beyond Colter's line of sight.

Sure that it was a trick, that Drouillard was waiting for him to climb out of the hole unaware that he was about to be shot, Colter crouched low and loaded his rifle. Then taking a moment to collect himself, he scrambled out of the sunpocket and whipped his rifle up to shooting position and took aim, praying he had guessed right about where the half-breed had positioned himself.

Drouillard was not there or anywhere else close. Instead, he was tramping down to the bottom of the draw where his horse stood waiting.

Colter drew a bead on the man's back. Drouillard had been a thorn in his side for too long. It would be so easy to . . .

Drouillard reached the roan and swung onto its back. He waved up at Colter to follow, then turned his horse and began to ride off, all as if he did not see or care about the rifle aimed his direction.

Colter lowered the gun. What was he thinking? He could never shoot a man in the back. He could never shoot a man. Period. Not even Ordway.

Not unless his life was in danger. He was letting these mountains, all the delays, the waiting, get to him when what he ought to be concentrating on was getting back to Fragrant Grass in one piece.

He turned toward his horse.

The animal was not there.

It was halfway down the slope, making its way to the bottom of the draw where Drouillard and the roan had just been. "Shit!" he said, turning a slow circle in the crusted snow before going after his mount. Here it was past the middle of June and the snow still lay winter-deep, hiding the trail that they must follow. The mountains had won again.

Shannon had been delighted when the captains ordered the expedition to turn back to the Weippe Prairie, but two day's ride had wrung all that emotion out of him. His legs ached from the effort of gripping the horse's sides during the arduous descent to the Prairie, and, after riding all morning with Drouillard back to Broken Arm's encampment, his private parts were numb. The closer they rode toward the Kooskooskee, the day's heat increased and the number of voracious mosquitos grew into thick oppressive clouds.

Drouillard rode along maddeningly unconcerned about either the heat or the bugs. Shannon tried for a time to engage the half-breed in conversation to take his mind off his discomfort but soon gave up. The man's occasional grunts were not enough to sustain a dialogue.

Shannon felt for the small lump in the bottom of the pouch slung across his chest. The wooden salmon. Colter had pressed it into his hand before Shannon and the half-breed left the crew back up on the Lolo, the name the Nez Perce gave to the trail over the mountains. "Good luck. With her and the guides," Colter had said.

That Colter, who had, according to Rube, a woman waiting for him among the Mandans on the upper Missouri, would think to help him at such a difficult time had touched Shannon and he had taken the carving. "We'll come back with those Nez Perce guides and get on our way again. You can count on that."

You can count on that. The phrase that rang so well when he said it to Colter now sounded like so much hot air. What on earth could he and Drouillard hope to accomplish? It was obvious that the Nez Perce had no intention of fulfilling their promise to provide guides to lead the expedition through the mountains.

A shout from the Nez Perce camp down the slope signalled that the camp guards had spotted their approach. The next moment a mosquito flew up Shannon's nostril. Instantly, his eyes teared and he blew his nose into his palm. That was when he realized that someone else was riding beside him. Laughing Water, the woman he had called Bold Laughing Woman.

She winked at him, then loped off to catch up to Drouillard at the village outskirts. Shannon arrived to find the half-breed in signed conversation with Broken Arm, encircled by a crowd of curious Nez Perce. Laughing

Water was nowhere to be seen.

The crowd parted to allow Shannon to join Drouillard. He stood to the right and a little behind the half-breed and tried to act as if he understood hand talk. At one point Drouillard turned to him. "Hold out your rifle."

He did and the Indians conferred, then one of them, a younger man with a protruding chin and wildly bushing eyebrows, tried to take the gun. Shannon jerked it away.

"Give it him to hold," Drouillard growled.

Shannon yielded the gun hesitantly. The Indian peered into the barrel, sniffed the pan, and rubbed the stock, then passed it to a second Indian to examine and on around the circle of Nez Perce.

Shannon reached out to reclaim it.

"No," Drouillard said in a low voice.

"Why? It's my gun."

The half-breed shot him a look of warning, and Shannon dropped his hands. He waited uneasily while Drouillard and Broken Arm continued their incomprehensible discussion.

After a time the half-breed and the Nez Perce chief clasped hands, and Drouillard nodded for Shannon to take back his gun. "The guides, they come back with us tomorrow."

Tomorrow? That gave him only today — and tonight. "I helped you, now you help me," Shannon said. Drouillard cocked an eyebrow at him. He hurried on before his shaky courage failed. "There's a woman. The one who rode in with you. Her name is Laughing Water."

The half-breed shook his head. "With her, I cannot help you."

"Now look here, Drooler —"

Anger puckered Drouillard's neutral expression. "My name is Drouillard!"

The abrupt change in the man shook Shannon. His words poured out in a wild tumble. "Drouillard, please, I need your help. I have to . . . to be with her. This is my last chance."

"With her you have no chance."

"If you're talking about having nothing to give her, that's not true. I brought this." He pulled out the carving.

Drouillard ignored it. "You must have horses to take a Nez Perce woman to wife."

"Wife? But the other men, all their stories about squaws, how did they get those women?"

"The husbands of those women, they give their wives to other men. It is an act of friendship. That is their way to show welcome."

Shannon struggled to check his growing desperation. "But she said she was waiting for me."

"She has no husband. To have her, you must marry her. To marry her, you must pay many horses to her family. Where do you go, Shannon?"

"Back" was the only word Shannon could get out around the taste of disappointment in his mouth.

"No, you stay. For the guides, we must wait," Drouillard said.

Shannon spun around. "No. You stay. I'm going back now." He got on his horse and rode away from the village, holding himself rigid against this final crushing blow to his illusions.

His body was too weary and sore for him to hold a ramrod posture for long. He made it into the trees above the village before slumping over the horse's neck. He shuddered and let the reins drop. The horse could go where it wanted. Nothing mattered except getting away from the village. And her.

The horse carried them into the Nez Perce horse herd which was strung out across a large grassy meadow. Shannon realized that it was getting on toward sundown, too late for him to ride back to the camp on the Weippe Prairie. What to do for the night?

He did not see the person watching him from the shadows of a stand of sugar pines until a lissome figure moved into a shaft of remaining sunshine. Laughing Water.

Surprise did not prevent him from sliding off the horse and reaching into his pouch for the carving. He did not know how he was going to talk to her or what he was going to say, but he did know he was not going to pass up this chance.

He was five feet from her when something bumped his arm. A horse's nose. "Mama!" The mare acknowledged her name with a soft snuffle and tug on his pouch. "Afraid you're out of luck, girl. I don't have any treats for you. I didn't think I'd see you again."

The disappointed mare turned to the woman who stroked the horse's muzzle. "Mama," Laughing Water said distinctly, watching Shannon as she spoke.

"Why, yes, that's right. Mama. That's what I called her."

"Mama," Laughing Water murmured into the mare's neck. Then she spoke to Shannon in her own tongue.

He did not question how he knew she was commenting on how much the mare's health had improved since she had taken over her care. "She's lucky you have her," he said. "Mama's a good horse. She's been through a lot. Thank you for all you've done for her."

The woman nodded as if she also understood.

"I wish I hadn't waited so long to come back. Maybe, I mean, you and I . . . we could have, could have . . ." The thought dribbled off unfinished. A silence settled between them. He shifted on his feet, not knowing how to go on.

Then she extended a cupped palm toward him. That reminded him of the carving. He handed it to her. She examined it closely, then pointed to him as if to ask if he had made it.

"No, not me. One of the others. Colter, he carved it for me to give to you."

She looked at the figure again. The hint of a smile blossomed on her face, rising from her mouth to her eyes like the summer sun rises into a clear sky, transforming her attractive face into a thing of incandescent beauty. Watching her, Shannon longed to touch that face, to wrap her in his arms, to hold her, but uncertainty about how she would react rooted him in place.

She pointed at him. "Sha-On."

It was his turn to smile. "Shannon. How did you know?"

"Shannon," she repeated.

"Exactly right. Yes."

"Shannon," she said proudly.

"Laughing Water. Whoever named you chose well."

She nodded, then turned as if to leave.

"Stop. Don't go. Please."

She looked back at him with a bemused expression. Before he could think himself out of doing so, he hurried to her side. "Won't you stay?"

She glanced around the little cove of trees as if considering his request. He touched her arm. She did not pull away.

His hand closed around her forearm. She let it.

He pulled her toward him. She came.

He guided her arms around his waist, then put his arms around her. She leaned into him.

At that point, his courage faltered. He did not have a clue what to do next. She looked up at him. There was a wicked gleam in her eye. A gleam that banished his doubts. He gathered her up in his arms and carried her deeper into the ring of trees where he discovered a freshly-made bed of pine needles. The gleam in her eyes grew brighter. "Why, you little devil," he murmured.

She wriggled out of his grasp and knelt on the pine-needle mound.

"I thought you had to be married before —"

She shook her head to silence him and patted the mounded needles.

Was Drouillard wrong, or had he lied? Or was he, George Shannon, about to commit some grievous error, an insult to Nez Perce customs that would bring that whole proud nation down on the heads of the expedition?

"Shannon," she whispered.

"Ah, hell, why not?" He moved toward her then, forgetting all the taboos, lost in the moment.

Something roused Shannon out of a deep sleep. From the sun's position through the overhanging bows he realized that morning was already well advanced. Then his ears caught the sound of men calling and whistling.

When he moved to get up, he discovered that there was a weight on his left arm. A head. The head of a sleeping woman. The head of Laughing Water.

She stirred in her sleep and rested a hand on his chest. He experienced a rush of tenderness at the sight of the dusky skin of her bare shoulder. Gently he pulled the hide she had supplied for their pine-needle bed over her. Colter had been right. He had known what to do. Even better, so had she.

The memory of their night together brought up a satisfied sigh.

The men's voices ranged closer. Tenderly lifting her head with his right hand, he slipped his arm out from beneath her and placed her hand on the depression where he had lain. After pulling on his trousers and moccasins, he crept out of the hidden copse to investigate the source of the noise.

The herd of Nez Perce horses were clumped together in the nearest corner of the grassy field while Nez Perce braves cut out a few mounts. Ten yards from Shannon's position one brave held the leads of a trio of the Indians' prized spotted horses, the ones they called Appaloosas.

He located his own horse among the milling animals. A moment later, a hand grasped his biceps. Laughing Water's hand. She was naked except for the thick tangle of hair the color of a raven's wing, tumbling to her hips and covering her breasts. She motioned him back to their hidden bed.

He was about to follow when the sight of Drouillard stopped him. The half-breed was leading his roan up the slope from the village, accompanied by Broken Arm and four other Nez Perce men. Shannon touched a finger to Laughing Water's lips, warning her to keep quiet.

She glanced at the herd and the men, and her eyes took on the same crafty glint of the previous evening. Shannon was torn over what to do. He had been so wrapped up in exploring the delights of this woman that he had put Drouillard and their mission out of his mind.

A sudden wrenching sadness accompanied the knowledge that the horses the Nez Perce were picking out of their herd were for the guides that would lead the expedition over the mountains. The time had come for him to leave.

From the copse came her whisper, "Shannon."

Judging that he had a few minutes before Drouillard and the group reached the horses, he crawled back to her. From their bed of pine needles, she offered him her hand. He could not take it. "I have to go."

Her smile faded. Abruptly, she rolled up to her knees and reached for her leather dress. Distressed that he had caused this sudden change in her, Shannon stammered, "I don't want to."

She stood to smooth the dress down over her hips and thighs, then pulled her long hair back and caught it in a leather thong which she knotted at the nape of her neck. He watched her movements with an aching heart. What had been such a magical experience in the dark seemed, in the bright light of morning, to be unwise, if not altogether wrong. Had he taken unfair advantage of her innocent eagerness only to leave her now to suffer unknown consequences alone?

She stooped to retrieve the discarded sleeping hide, shook it, and folded it. Tormented by her silence and matter-of-fact manner, he blurted out, "I won't forget you."

She gave him a penetrating look, then said something curt in Nez Perce and ducked out of the hidden nook.

He looked after her for a time, then, heaving a frustrated sigh, he looked around for the length of cord that held up his pants. Spotting it half-covered by the pine needles, he squatted to retrieve it. The scent of her clung to their bed and stopped him before he could rise.

An image floated into his head. The image of a woman in a room. He knew the woman — she was Lisette — and he knew the room. It was her room above the tavern in St. Charles.

The clarity of the memory startled him and he had to sit back on his heels to get a grip on himself. The memory was real. He was absolutely certain of that. As certain as he was that she was what polite society called a "soiled dove" and that he had lost his head over her. But how could he ever have stooped to such depths of depravity?

He lingered in the question until noise beyond the copse wormed into his consciousness. It was time to leave this place of magic. Time to step out into the meadow in front of Drouillard and all the Nez Perces, claim his horse from among the Nez Perce herd, and ride away. Away from the Kooskooskee and the Nez Perce. Away from Laughing Water.

All those things were now memories. His memories. He ducked out of the copse, straightened his back and strode into the meadow.

7. *Memories Through the Mist*

S hannon reined up his horse, slid off its back and led the tired animal to the creek to drink its fill beside the other horses. Then he plodded up the stream a short way, knelt and scooped handful after handful of the cold clear water into his mouth. His thirst quenched, he splashed creek water into his face and over his head, hoping the cold would penetrate the gloom that had settled over his spirit since leaving that Nez Perce meadow the previous morning.

The exquisite pleasure he shared with Laughing Water had been dampened by the reclaimed memory of Lisette. The effect was to solidify the conviction that he was no longer the upright, God-fearing man he had been before he left Ohio. That conviction had sprouted from the seed of self-doubt planted when Colter had told him that he had lied, cursed, womanized and killed. Then McNeal had watered the seed by telling him that he had killed Partisan. But it had taken the memory of Lisette to germinate that seed. Now within Shannon grew a strangling vine of torment that threatened to choke the life out of him unless he could find the vine's roots and yank it up out of his soul once and for all.

In his dark mood he nestled against a fallen log and studied his traveling companions from a distance. Drouillard and the three Nez Perce guides were sprawled in the shade, catching a rest before pushing on to rejoin the main body of the expedition. It struck him how much Drouillard resembled the three Indian guides. Only his clothing set him apart.

One of the Nez Perce men bore a resemblance to Laughing Water. That man turned to Drouillard now and signed, "Before we begin this journey, we must ask the gods to give us good weather."

Drouillard signed back a response, but Shannon was not watching. He had known what the Indian said! He had understood the signs! But how was such a thing possible?

He had not completely digested his discovery when Drouillard rose and motioned for everyone to get mounted. Shannon got up slowly. By the time he was on his horse, he had made a decision. At least for now, he would keep to himself the fact that he could read signs. Such a skill was bound to come in handy, especially when they got to Teton Sioux territory. Between now and then, he would continue to try to piece together more of the picture of his life. Maybe it would turn out prettier than it now appeared. It was a small hope, but he clung to it as his only connection to sanity.

Colter took the expedition's first retreat hard. He felt doubly responsible. Not only had he brashly assured the captains that the trail was cleared off enough to follow without native guides, but also he had been entrusted with scouting out the way, a duty he had failed in. The third blow came when the captains sent Shannon with Drouillard to ride back to Broken Arm's band to procure the promised guides. Shannon, instead of him.

In a desolate mood, the last thing Colter needed was the foot race the captains ordered the sergeants to organize to keep the men occupied. As such, participation was not voluntary.

He drew a match against Goodrich, a wiry man from Sergeant Pryor's squad with a six-inch bow between his knees when he stood feet together. Despite over two years of traveling in the same expedition, Colter had exchanged less than ten words with the man. He figured to get the race over with, then wander off to brood in private.

As he stepped to the line marked in the dirt, Pomp broke away from Sacajawea and scampered to him. The toddler hugged Colter's knees, gurgling, "Colter, Colter." Colter could not resist the pure joy on the little one's round face. He picked him up and returned the hug. Sacajawea reclaimed the baby with a shy smile and carted him back to a scowling Charbonneau.

Colter then nodded his readiness at Goodrich who spit into the dirt between them. "Get set!" Pryor yelled.

Colter set his feet.

"Go!"

As Colter lunged forward, Goodrich yelled "Foul!"

"Come on back, Colter," Pryor said.

Colter was sure he had not fouled, but he returned to the line anyway.

He was off again on Pryor's second "Go!" Again, Goodrich claimed "Foul!" Again the sergeant called him back.

This time he faced his opponent who had yet to move from his original position. "Are you plannin' to stand there or are you goin' to move sometime this year?"

"I'll move when you stop cheating," Goodrich said.

Colter checked an angry response and faced the finish line before he did something he might regret.

Goodrich slapped his arm. "You hear me? I called you a cheat."

"You don't want to hear what I'll call you if'n you don't take off this time," Colter said in a low voice.

Goodrich took a swing at him. Colter blocked it and countered. Before he could get in another punch, the sergeants had them separated. Gass pulled Goodrich back while Ordway and Charbonneau restrained Colter.

"They're back!" someone shouted. Everyone's attention swung to the five riders and three empty horses that had just broken out of the trees rimming the meadow beyond the camp. Gass released Goodrich who immediately scuttled away. Gass and Ordway hurried forward with the captains to meet the newcomers. The rest of the crowd surged after them.

Instead of releasing Colter, Charbonneau wrenched his arm behind his back with spiteful force, making him wince. "Zee squaw, she ees mine," he warned in breath fouler than McNeal's.

"She ain't no slave. She don't belong to nobody but herself," Colter said.

The Frenchman torqued his arm painfully. "You weell stay away from her, or to me you weell answer." He gave the arm one last wrench and shoved Colter onto his knees.

Colter popped up and started after the Frenchman, but York pulled him back. "Whatever you're planning to do to him, he's not worth the bother or the price you'd pay."

He knew that the black man was right, knew that Charbonneau's jealousy had no merit. However, he also knew that the Frenchman was unpredictable, cowardly and stupid, a dangerous combination.

"Are you cooled off, or do I have to hold onto you awhile longer?" York asked.

Colter shrugged out of the man's hold. "I'm cooled."

York eyed him skeptically, then turned to look at the crowd around the new arrivals. "Looks like Drouillard worked more magic."

Colter nodded curtly. He did not know what to say or think about Drouillard anymore, not since the half-breed had had the perfect opportunity to shoot him five days back and didn't. Why? The question had haunted Colter every waking minute since.

York went off to join his master and Colter skirted the crowd to find Shannon, who was unloading his horse in the meadow away from the others. "Good work, bringin' us some guides. Now maybe we can get on home."

Shannon grunted.

"Suppose you had a good time, huh?"

"If you call it that."

Colter detected the haunted look in Shannon's eyes. "Too bad for you we got to leave so soon," he said.

Shannon looked away as if ashamed to be read so easily. "I remembered something. Lisette in St. Charles. But that's all. There was nothing to connect it to anything else."

He directed his tormented gaze toward the trees. His voice dropped. "How did you ever leave Fragrant Grass?"

Colter's eyes locked onto his. "You remember her then."

Shannon bowed his head. "A few snatches. Enough to know you could have stayed there."

Now it was Colter's turn to look out at the trees. "I lived my whole life by one rule: when I make a promise, I keep it."

"You don't sound very sure about that."

"Lookin' back I realize I been so busy makin' good on my word that there ain't been much room left for what I want."

"Sounds like you've made a decision."

Colter riveted on Shannon's face. "Damn right. From now on, I'm goin' to be mighty particular what promises I make. They're goin' to be my promises for what I want, not what somebody else thinks I ought to be doin'. That's somethin' for you to remember, too."

His words brought up the memory of Shannon's betrayal back at Clatsop. All the anger toward Shannon that Colter thought he had shunted away came flooding back with it. He turned to leave.

"What aren't you telling me, Old Man?"

Colter whirled to face Shannon. "What did you call me?"

"Old Man. Why? Something wrong with that?"

"There's only one way you'd know to call me that. What ain't you tellin' me?"

Shannon looked at him uncomprehendingly. "I-I don't know how I know to call you that. It just feels right."

Suddenly everything snapped into focus for Colter. "Why you lyin' sack of hog guts! You been playactin' all along. Makin' me believe you don't know what a weasel you been."

"No, I —"

"Don't waste your stinkin' breath, Shannon. I ain't buyin' no more of your lies. None. Understand?" He stomped away before his anger got the better of him. He had enough problems already. He did not need to add another to the pile. Not when he was about to cross the last physical barrier separating him from Fragrant Grass.

Squinting ahead, Shannon suppressed a groan. The trail continued steadily downward for as far as he could see, and his legs were already screaming for relief from the strain of trying to keep the make-shift saddle from sliding up onto the horse's neck. To make matters worse, his horse was starting to limp, and its uneven gait jarred his stiff joints with even more force.

"Six clear days, Little Brother. No snow. No rain. No nothin' but sunshine." The conversation between the Fields riding just ahead drifted back to Shannon.

"I told you them guides knew what they was doin' when they set fire to them pine trees as a prayer to their spirits," Rube said.

"You said no such thing, Rube. You were complainin' about them wastin' good wood," Joe carped.

Instead of bickering back, Rube barked a laugh and pointed. "By God, they done it! Lookee there."

Shannon followed Rube's point toward some mist rising among the trees ahead.

"Same hot springs we passed goin' west last fall," Rube crowed. "Means we got less than a day out to Traveler's Rest."

"It means a bath!" whooped Joe over the exclamations of the other men who recognized the landmark.

Ten minutes later Shannon was immersed in a large pool of steaming water along with the captains, the sergeants, the Nez Perce guides and the rest of the crew. When the hot water grew uncomfortable, he crawled up on a rock where he could cool off but still keep his sore legs immersed. From his perch, he watched the crew celebrating the fact that they had completed in six days the crossing that had taken eleven days last year.

Rather than work up more frustration by trying to dredge up memories of that first crossing, Shannon turned his attention to the conversation between the three Nez Perce guides and the captains. He was relishing his new-found ability to understand the hand-signs, but then Colter raised up out of the pool and lifted Pomp to his shoulders, blocking his view. The little one clapped his hands and laughed the infectiously delighted laugh of a child who is seeing his world from a new angle. Sacajawea crouched at the side of the pool, beaming at her son's happiness.

As he took in the scene, Shannon's ill-feelings toward Colter began to shift. Although he did not know what had happened between them to destroy the friendship everyone said they had had, he decided this was a good time to try to set things right again.

He lowered himself into the pool and waded over to the man. Smiling, he held out his hands to the happily burbling Pomp. Instead of sharing the baby with him, Colter drew back a step. "What do you think you're doin'?"

"Thought I'd join in the fun."

"Think again, Shannon. Fakers ain't invited."

Shannon felt his smile slipping. "You're wrong about me, Colter."

"Look who's callin' who wrong?"

Sensing the eyes of every member of the expedition swing toward him, Shannon splashed out of the pool. He had had enough hot water, enough humiliation, enough Colter. From now on, they were enemies. Period.

Captain Lewis set another box of plant specimens on the make-shift table next to the two that already rested in front of Shannon. "There, that ought to keep you busy enough until I get back. Any questions?"

Shannon tried to push his tired lips into something resembling a smile. "No, sir."

"Then I'll be off."

Shannon looked after the captain whose jaunty stride mocked his own deep fatigue. The dream had come again last night. The same dream as the last three nights since the expedition got to Traveler's Rest. In it, he was out hunting. He downed a buck with a magnificent rack of antlers only to discover, when he approached the carcass, that it wasn't a deer but a man, lying face down on the ground. Try as he would, he could not roll the body over to find out who the man was. The dream invariably ended with a scream lodged in his throat and no possibility of more sleep.

Shannon turned his attention back to the work before him. Why bother cataloguing the captain's specimens knowing that the Teton Sioux were waiting to avenge Partisan's death? Vengeance Shannon had brought down upon them all in a fateful moment he no longer remembered. He yearned to know what he had forgotten, longed to ask all the questions he had stored up. However, memories and answers would not change what had been done. All he could affect now was this moment and all the moments he had left to live.

The image of his father's disapproving frown descended like an ominous shadow over his thoughts. The image spoke. *If you caused the problem, George, it's up to you to solve it.*

"How? By telling the Teton Sioux I'm sorry I killed their chief?" Shannon muttered.

Instead of rebuking him for daring to talk back, his father's image leaned persuasively forward. *You can do better than that, George. Think.*

"Oh, shut up, Father." Shannon heaved himself up. In the process, Captain Lewis's leather portfolio slipped off the rough planks that served as the table. It hit the ground, casting loose a piece of parchment.

Cursing his clumsiness, Shannon stooped to retrieve the page, hoping that it was undamaged. Immediately the words "Teton Sioux" written in the captain's spidery scrawl drew his eyes. He was fully aware that reading the page was a breach of the captain's confidence, and he quickly stuck it back among the others.

Before he released it, however, some perverse impulse made him pull it out again and read it. The letter was addressed to a trader living among the Mandans. The captain asked the man to intercede with the Teton Sioux on the expedition's behalf by convincing the Sioux to accept a peace-offering. That peace-offering was the crew's horse herd that a detachment under Sergeant Pryor would drive back to the Mandans ahead of the main party as soon as the crew reached the Missouri River.

As he read, it dawned on Shannon that he held in his hands the solution to his need to vindicate himself for killing Partisan. He resolved to get himself into Pryor's detachment. To do so, he must be extra careful to hide the fact that he had violated the captain's trust by prying. He slid the letter back into the portfolio and whispered to the mental image of his father. "What do you think, Father?"

The image nodded. *Now you're thinking, George.*

Colter guided his horse off the trail to let the other riders pass while he surveyed the valley. The Valley of the Bitterroots was even more beautiful and inviting than it had been the previous year, strengthening his conviction that this was where he and Fragrant Grass would make their home and raise their children.

Their children. Half white, half Mandan. Half-breeds, like Pomp, like Zoob, like Drouillard. Neither white enough nor Indian enough to be accepted by either society, they would always live at the bottom of the social barrel unless . . .

He slapped his thigh. "No, by God! Her and me'll be out here where things're different. Ain't no one way out here goin' to give a holy hoot who your ma and pa was."

At that moment another horse and rider moved past. Goodrich, the man he never got to race back at the Weippe. The man's inquiring glance irked Colter. "This here's a private conversation, Goodrich. Skedaddle."

The man's gaze shifted, searching for whoever Colter was talking to. He had to suppress a smile at the man's gullibility. "We ain't talkin' to you so git along."

Still searching for the second party to the conversation, Goodrich rode off, and Colter turned his attention back to the scenery and his plans for the future. By the time he reached camp late that afternoon, he was brimming with the energy that comes from glimpsing a wonderful tomorrow.

As he climbed off his horse, he spotted Pomp toddling along beside Sacajawea. Whistling, he squatted down and held his arms out to the little one.

"Colter!" Pomp squealed. He started toward Colter, but his mother scooped him into her arms and hurried off without an explanation.

Colter dropped his arms. He knew immediately what was going on: Charbonneau could not keep him from playing with Pomp, so he had laid down the law to Sacajawea. Damn.

8. *The Split*

Six days later on July 8th, Captain Clark led the main body of the crew to Camp Fortunate, the place where they had cached their dugouts and non-essential supplies after locating the Shoshones the previous fall. A small group led by Captain Lewis had split off from the main party at Traveler's Rest in order to explore the upper reaches of the Maria's River. They planned to catch up with the expedition at the Maria's-Missouri confluence. Those men missed the impromptu celebration that resulted after the Shoshone caches were found intact.

Enlivened by his first taste of rum since the previous fall, Colter joined in the applause when Cruzatte pulled out his fiddle and launched into a reel. York immediately swung Pomp up onto his shoulder and began a spinning, leaping dance. The delighted child giggled and waved his little arms in time to the men's clapping.

The next tune another crewman danced with Pomp. Since Traveler's Rest, Colter had deliberately kept away from Sacajawea and the baby so as not to bring down more grief on their heads from Charbonneau. Spotting the Frenchman among those encouraging the dancers, Colter figured the man's pique had run its course, and, the next tune, he stepped into the dance circle. Pomp came into his arms with a piped, "Spin me, Colter."

With the child on his shoulder, he turned circle after circle, first right, then left, moving in time to the music. The youngster laughed and swayed. "Faster, Colter. Faster."

Colter closed his eyes and gave in to the music, reveling in the feel of the small trusting body resting on his shoulder, the child's joyful crowing, and a sense of well-being that came from knowing that the worst was behind him and he would soon be reunited with his love.

The music ended and another man stepped up to claim Pomp. Winded and a little dizzy, Colter pushed to the rear of the ring of spectators to catch his breath and bearings. A hand clutched his shoulder.

Charbonneau's mouth was twisted into a snarl and his eyes were glittering slits. He held Sacajawea hard in the grip of his other hand. "You I warn last time, Colter. Thees ees my woman. Pomp ees my son. Away from them you weel stay, or off I cut their noses. Make them ugly like peegs. Comprendez?"

Only a coward like Charbonneau would threaten those who could not fight back. Only a brute would disfigure his family in the cause of his own petty jealousy. A brute and a coward, Charbonneau had proved he was both too often for Colter to risk injury to two people he cared for.

"From her you stay away," Charbonneau growled.

Colter pulled out of the man's grip. "That I will, but let me warn you, Frenchy. If I ever, *ever* find out that you hurt Janey or Pomp, you'll answer to me."

"Of you I have no fear," the Frenchman said haughtily.

"Then you're as stupid as you are gutless. Because, believe me, you hurt them, I'll make you wish you was dead instead of just yeller. You got my word on that."

Sacajawea spoke urgently to her husband. Charbonneau darted a glance over his shoulder. Captain Clark was looking their way. Colter stepped into the opening. "Captain ain't lookin' too happy, I'd say. Wonder what he'd do if'n I told him about this here little talk of ours."

A muscle in the Frenchman's jaw twitched.

"Captain's mighty fond of Janey. Cain't say he feels the same about you, though. Fact is some of us've been wonderin' when he'll cut you loose now we're on our way back."

Doubt flickered in Charbonneau's piggish eyes. Colter kept pushing. "If'n it was me, I'd think real hard 'fore I did somethin' might turn the captain agin' me. Maybe you ain't never seen the captain in a temper, but I have. You lay a hand on Janey or Pomp, he's liable to let you take your chances with the Blackfeet. That is, if'n he don't set you up in front of a firin' squad. Seems to me just 'bout every man on the crew'd volunteer for that there duty. Me for sure."

"He cannot do that." There was major uncertainty in the Frenchman's voice.

"Oh, yes, he can. This here's U.S. territory now, and he acts for the President. Yessir, I'd sure be careful what I did from now on if'n I was inside your miserable hide."

Charbonneau grunted something under his breath and hauled his wife away. After they left, Colter started to regret his brashness. Threats were only words. They might work to keep Sacajawea and Pomp safe. Then again, they might not. If Charbonneau was anything, he was unpredictable.

Since he seemed to be the focus of the Frenchman's jealousy, he had to make a point of keeping out of their way. There was only one sure way to do that. When they reached Three Forks in a few days, the party would divide into two groups. Clark would lead one eastward to explore the Yellowstone as an alternate to the Missouri for a route west. The second group, under Ordway, would trace their westbound route back to the Great Falls and the Maria's to pick up Captain Lewis's group, dig up the records and specimens cached last year, then move down the Missouri to reunite with Clark's group at the Missouri-Yellowstone confluence.

Colter had thought to go with Clark's group, given the bad blood between him and Ordway. Now, though, Charbonneau's threat to harm Janey and Pomp had changed his mind. Clark's fondness for Pomp meant the captain would take Charbonneau and his family in his group. That left Colter with one option.

Like it of not, he would go back the way they came. With Ordway's detachment.

Colter and the rest of the main party reached Three Forks five days later. The crew went to work sorting the remaining baggage into two piles, one for Clark's group to take back on the Yellowstone; the other for Ordway's detachment following the original Missouri route. That done, it was time for the party to split up.

Colter watched the captain boost Sacajawea onto her horse and hand Pomp up to her. The sight tugged at his heart. He longed to hold the child one last time, to hear Pomp pipe his name, but he dared not arouse Charbonneau's irrational jealousy. He turned away sadly to find Shannon watching him.

Since leaving the Shoshone cache site, Shannon had developed a sudden, suspicious interest in the expedition's horse herd. "What're you lookin' at?" Colter growled.

"Just wanted to say 'So long'," Shannon answered.

"Then say it and be gone."

"The way you're acting, why bother?" Shannon said crossly.

"Good question."

At Pryor's whistle, Shannon swung onto his mount, and the Yellowstone detachment moved off. Colter turned away from Shannon to watch after the child who had brought joy into even the dullest days. Tarnation, he was going to miss the little tyke. Damn that Charbonneau!

"My, what a touching sight," sneered Ordway, coming to stand at Colter's side. "Private Colter all long-faced over a half-breed whelp."

Colter checked his reaction in favor of a bland question. "Where do you want me, Sarge?"

Ordway's mouth curled cruelly. "Why, in the last dugout with me, of course. We have so much to catch up on, you and me."

Colter kept his eyes and tone level. "Bow or stern?"

Ordway tapped his nose with a crooked finger as if considering his answer. "The bow, I think. Where I can watch you better. You don't mind, do you?"

After months of turning himself into one of the best river pilots among the crew, of course he minded, but he would never give Ordway the satisfaction of admitting so. "Makes no nevermind to me, Sarge. Just so's we're movin'."

Ordway cocked an eyebrow as if he had more to say. Instead he nodded, turned to his waiting detachment and bellowed, "All right, ladies. Time to go!"

Shannon kept a close watch on the spotted horse as it moved through the remuda. "You better keep moving," he warned the animal, fingering the edges of the fresh rip in the arm of his leather shirt. The horse had come from the Nez Perce. One of the their Appaloosas, it was the horse Colter had ridden across the mountains. Since Three Forks, the horse had grown steadily more ornery. *Just like Colter*, Shannon thought. Also like Colter, it bestowed most of its nastiness on Shannon.

Clark's group had reached the Yellowstone River three days back. Ever since, they had ridden along her banks, searching in vain for trees to build dugouts. Whoever heard of a river without trees? Until they found trees, Shannon was stuck. He did not like being stuck.

Gibson wandered out to where Shannon stood watch on the herd. "Sarge's sending me out to hunt," he explained. "He said you'd give me a good horse."

Shannon did not hesitate. He pointed at the Appaloosa. "Take that one."

Gibson wagged his head vigorously. "Oh, no. He's a handful. I want one won't give me no trouble."

"You asked for a horse, and you got one. Now take it or go afoot."

Gibson scowled at Shannon, then, harness in hand, marched out to the spotted horse. Shannon waited, ready to enjoy seeing the horse make a fool out of someone else for a change. Instead, the animal docilely allowed Gibson to slip on the harness and lead it away.

Shannon could not believe his eyes. He watched the pair until they were out of sight, sure the cantankerous creature would act up, but nothing happened. He stood with hands on hips, feeling early morning cold nipping his bare skin through the new hole in his shirt sleeve.

The farther upriver they went, the smaller and sparser the vegetation. Without dugouts, his plan to save the expedition from slaughter at the hands of the Teton Sioux was hopelessly stalled. "What's the use?" he muttered.

From the back of his mind came the echo of his father's voice. *No one likes a quitter, Son. And I did not raise you to be one.*

"Yeah, well, you didn't raise me to be or to do a lot of things, did you?" he muttered. In his mind's eye, he saw himself facing his father and saying for once what he really thought. "Come to think of it, Father, most of what you taught me has been less than useless. So save your breath. I'm not listening anymore."

With that, the image of himself slammed out of his father's study, leaving the man with his mouth agape, unable to speak for the first time in all the years Shannon had known him.

Ordway's voice broke the morning's silence. "They'll be half-breeds."

With his thoughts somewhere else, Colter responded, "What say?"

"The children you get on that squaw of yours. They'll be half-breeds. Only place they'll be able to live in peace is with the Mandans. Whites won't want them. That's for sure."

Colter had been waiting five days for Ordway to come at him, and because, thanks to Drouillard, he had already come to terms with the issue of what his off-spring with Fragrant Grass would be, he was ready. His experienced pilot's eyes picked up the telltale signs of a debris jam-up lying directly in the path of their dugout half a mile downstream. If anyone else had been at the rudder, he would have spoken up. However, the sergeant had shown again and again the last five days that he had his own ideas about piloting, and Colter had long since given up trying to correct the man's incompetence. Instead, he quietly braced himself for the coming accident.

The sergeant went on. "We got a-ways yet to the Mandans. Could be you'll come to your senses before then. But I'd be willing to lay odds it won't make a difference what you do one way or another. The way things work with these savages, she's probably got one baby at her teat and another one in her belly."

Colter kept his face forward and his mouth shut. The jam ahead grew larger as they drew closer.

"Some other man's babies, Colter. Not yours. She didn't wait. They never do. She's an Indian after all."

Colter dipped his paddle and studied the current that was pulling them inexorably into the obstruction.

"Hey, what's that?" Ordway asked.

"What's what, Sarge?" he responded.

"Oh, my G —" A loud thud cut off Ordway's words, followed by the sickening sound of splintering wood as the dugout rammed the floating mass. At the moment of impact, Colter slipped over the side into the river, holding his rifle over his head and clutching the pack of his personal gear to his chest.

While the overturned canoe lodged on the snag pile, the sergeant surfaced a few yards away from it, coughing up river water and thrashing his arms uselessly. Colter positioned himself in a tongue of current that would carry him to the bank, leaving Ordway on his own.

The weight of the dugout shifted the balance of the snag and, creaking and popping, the mass of debris started to split apart. Ordway spluttered over the noise, "The boat, Colter. We have to save it and the captain's specimens."

"Hellfire!" Colter muttered, as he side-stroked across the current, reluctantly responding to Ordway's appeal to intercept the canoe as it swung free of the jam. Most of the bales of baggage were soaked and there were two cracks in the bow. Nothing a little air-drying and a bit of caulk couldn't fix.

Ordway reached the boat a moment later. He flung an arm over its side and glared across at Colter. "Thanks for the warning."

Colter could not keep the satisfaction out of his voice. "You're the pilot, Sarge."

"Damn your eyes, Colter."

"Oh, oh. Hear that?" Colter said, cocking his head as if to listen harder. "Sounds like falls to me. Big falls."

Uncertainty flickered in the sergeant's eyes as he strained to hear. Colter continued, "Gotta be the Great Falls, Sarge. Unless you plan to ride over 'em, we best be makin' for that island up yonder."

For once, Ordway let Colter take control. He followed Colter's lead, adjusting their course and doing his share of the kicking to put them in line with the island. A second after Colter's feet hit the river bottom, the current carried the canoe's nose into the mud and muck at the upper end of the island.

The other members of the detachment were already there. They helped drag him, Ordway and the boat up onto the pebbly beach. Sergeant Gass was among them. He answered the question before Colter had the chance to ask it. "Captain Lewis left us here when a thievin' bunch of Indians made off with all but four of the horses. Only Captain, Drouillard, Rube and Joe went on up north."

Observing Ordway's negative reaction to the presence of a second sergeant, Colter pitched his voice loud enough for everyone to hear. "Captain left you in charge then?"

Gass nodded. "Till he comes back anyway."

"And when will that be?" Ordway asked, looking straight at Colter.

"Your guess is as good as mine," Gass said. "All I know is that Captain ordered us to wait for him at the Maria's joining until August 5. If he's not back then, we're to head on downriver without him."

Colter had not put up with Ordway for the last six days or dunked himself in the Missouri to delay his return to Fragrant Grass for another three weeks just to wait for Captain Lewis to satisfy his curiosity about some other fool river. There was *no* way through the Shining Mountains — no river, no easy trail — and whatever the captain was trying to prove by following the Maria's was not going to change that fact.

Lewis's putting Gass in charge over Ordway gave him a rare advantage for once, and he knew he had to press that advantage while it lasted. He deliberately unlocked gazes with Ordway to address Gass. "Well, Sarge, seein' as how you're in charge, what do you want us to do now?"

Gass had been a private before he became sergeant, and he had never lost his sense of irony over the position he now occupied and how he could thwart Ordway's drive to be first among the three sergeants. That irony was evident in his smile. "You can start by patching up your boat. Then we need some water hauled up to the fire."

He focused on Ordway. "That ought to keep both of you busy until dinnertime."

He waved the other crewmen to follow him up to the camp, leaving Colter alone with the sergeant. "Ain't that somethin' about them horses?" Colter said. "Too bad for Gass and them others that they had to stay behind." When Ordway's hands balled into fists, Colter had to tilt his face to hide his smile. "Yep, just too damn bad."

Another day of following the Yellowstone. Another day of driving the horses. Another day without finding a single useable tree. Shannon arrived at the creek where the detachment was to camp that night, worn out and despairing of ever being able to carry out his plan. To add to his troubles, the critical voice of his father had grown so loud it shouted down any clear thinking.

He was on his knees tying the hobble rope around the legs of his mount when Windsor grabbed his shoulder and yanked him roughly to his feet. "Gibson's not here. So help me if anythin's happened to him 'cause of that horse you give him, I'll skin the hide off'n your bones and hang it up for the crows to pick at."

The murderous look in Windsor's eye reinforced the threat. Windsor and Gibson had been tight friends throughout the expedition. So Shannon was relieved to see the man in question riding into camp at that very moment. "Calm down. There he is."

Windsor gave Shannon one last look of warning, then dashed off to meet his friend. Gibson rode at an angle that threatened to unseat him from the Appaloosa's back. Blood caked the man's pants around one thigh.

The sight of blood made Shannon regret assigning the man the spotted horse that morning. Wounds deep enough to cause so much blood were serious business. What if Gibson lost that leg, or, worse, his life?

He joined the group gathered around the injured man. Clark examined the wound, then announced, "Leg's bad. He'll have to stay off it. Means we have to improvise." He motioned to Pryor. "Take four men and cut down the two biggest trees you can find. We'll carve them out as best we can and lash them together as a raft."

Pryor tapped Windsor and three other crewmen for the squad and went off to carry out the order. The captain opened the medicine box that York had brought and tended to the wound while Gibson lay moaning, barely conscious.

Despite feeling responsibility for Gibson's condition, Shannon decided not to waste the rare moment of privacy. He waited impatiently for an opening. "May I ask you something, sir?"

Captain Clark grunted, which Shannon took for assent. "What'll we do with the horses once we have dugouts?"

Discouragement lined the captain's face. "Why are you asking, Shannon?"

Shannon feigned innocence. "I've become attached to some of the animals, sir."

The captain glanced up from his work. "Then you'll want to go with Sergeant Pryor's detachment, driving the herd overland."

Shannon continued playing out the role he had practiced. "Overland to where, sir?"

"To the Mandan villages. The horses will be used to pacify the Sioux."

Shannon had difficulty controlling the relief that rose to his face. "In that event, I want that assignment, Captain." He turned to leave, delighted that things had turned out exactly according to the way he had visualized it.

"Shannon."

He turned slowly, on guard that the captain had seen through his subterfuge. Clark pointed to the Appaloosa. "Under no circumstances is anyone to ride that horse again. Understand?"

Shannon swallowed hard. "Yes, sir."

9. *Phantom Thieves*

S hannon walked a circuit around the horses grazing on the grassy plain at the edge of the group's camp. It was his last night watch before his journey of redemption began. A few yards away, the Yellowstone gurgled and swashed as if talking itself into continuing its journey to join the Missouri. The sky above hung star-flung and bewitchingly beautiful. Too beautiful to ignore, given that there was no hint of danger, nothing to watch for.

He settled himself on a little mound that afforded a view of most of the herd and tilted his face to the magnificent scene overhead. In the stillness his thoughts traced back over the events of the last three days.

After searching more than five miles up the Yellowstone, Pryor's detail had located two trees of sufficient size to hollow out a pair of dugouts, twenty-eight feet long, sixteen inches deep and sixteen to twenty-four inches wide. These had been lashed together with cross-ties to make a raft. That raft now lay at the river's edge, ready to carry Captain Clark's detachment down the river just after daybreak. Once they left, Pryor, Shannon and one other man yet to be named would then drive this precious herd of horses east to the Mandans.

With his shining hour so near at hand, Shannon was slow to pick up an unusual sound. He listened, tightening his grip on his rifle.

When the sound repeated, he relaxed. It was just the troublesome Appaloosa again, blowing through its nose.

In the east, a paling of the deep indigo canopy announced the approach of dawn. He shifted, moving against the nervous energy that had collected in his muscles since his talk with Captain Clark three days before. A pair of equine snuffles conjured in his mind the image of a bare-chested, bronzed Indian atop the Appaloosa. The vision wavered and his own image replaced the Indian, riding tall and proud, in complete control of the expedition's remuda as he led them down a slope toward a town of close-set, earth-walled lodges enclosed by a picket wall.

The village had a familiar quality to it, as if he had once been there. He shrugged wistfully. If only he could remember something more than occasional, unrelated fragments. If only his mind could grasp the string of a thought that would pull to him everything he had lost. If only.

Heaving a sigh, he got to his feet and dusted off his butt. The dome of the sky to the east now showed pink, shading into light blue in the west. Soon the sun would appear and the day would begin. His day.

He wandered over to the spotted horse. For once, the animal allowed him to approach and to touch it without so much as a quiver. Strange. He tentatively stroked the horse's smooth flank. The animal moved into his touch.

Shannon was encouraged by the change in the animal's temperament. "Good horse." The words froze on his tongue.

When he had sat down, there had been two dozen horses grazing with the Appaloosa. Now there were none. He stumbled around the spotted horse and frantically scanned the plain, unwilling to accept what his eyes told him: At least half the herd was gone.

He ran for Pryor. Together they woke Clark with the bad news. Inside the captain's bedraggled hide tent under his unwavering gaze, Shannon related what had happened.

"Thank you, Shannon. You're dismissed," Clark said, tossing a "stay here" look at the sergeant.

Shannon ducked out into the fledgling morning. He felt as if Fate had dealt him a blow from which he would never recover when Windsor confronted him. "What kind of fairy tale did you make up for this one, Shannon? How's a man explain that twenty-five horses just, poof, vanished? Magic? Witches?"

Before Shannon could get out an answer, the captain and Pryor came out of the tent. "Windsor, go with Sergeant Pryor and Shannon to drive the remaining horses overland," Clark said. "The rest of you men eat up. We're leaving."

After the captain went back into his tent, Windsor said, "You ain't off the hook yet, Shannon. Captain's not stupid, and horses don't just walk off by theirselves. One thing's for sure, whether it was Blackfeet or Atsinas got 'em, they'll be back for the rest. When they do, you best be awake. I ain't about to lose my hair 'cause of you. Understand?"

"I was awake," Shannon declared angrily.

"Like hell. You ain't never been awake." Windsor pushed past him, leaving Shannon to get used to the fact that his road to redemption had already developed a major pothole.

Among the horses stolen were the herd's leaders. With them gone, Pryor, Windsor and Shannon had their hands full moving the remaining animals in the desired direction. It took most of the morning to stop going in circles and start making progress eastward.

Once they got underway, Shannon's spirits began to brighten. They had not lost all the horses. They still had half the herd to mollify the Sioux.

With its gray-streaked mane and tail flowing in the breeze, the spotted horse came up even with his mount. Encouraged by this show of companionableness by the fickle animal, Shannon allowed himself to consider that things might not turn out as badly as he earlier feared.

All of a sudden the Appaloosa's ears laid back, and it whirled away from the rest of the herd at a full-out gallop, taking five horses with it. Shannon immediately saw the problem: a mass of buffalo were grazing on the plain to the south, exactly where the horses were heading.

A sentinel bull among the buffalo spotted the horses bearing down and alerted his companions. The great creatures wheeled as one entity and thundered off the opposite direction. That was when Shannon's horse decided to join the chase. Nothing Shannon tried could stop his mount or alter its direction.

Then, with no warning, the horse veered and Shannon went flying. He slammed down on the summer-hard ground with an explosion of lights and an audible "whoosh." Hoofbeats bore down upon him from behind, but his muscles would not obey his mind's command to move.

A blur crossed between him and the sun. Windsor's voice cut through the humming in his ears. "What the hell are you doin'? These here horses are trained to hunt buffs, for Christ sake. You cain't get 'em so close. I got a mind to ride right over top of you, Shannon. Pay you back for what you did to Gibson. And I ought to shoot that there spotted horse 'fore we lose the rest of the herd."

Biting back the moans his jarred bones urged on him, Shannon pulled himself up to a stooping stance and faced Windsor. "Don't even try it." The words came out in a register as high as a woman's.

Windsor chuckled humorlessly. "Or what?" he said in a falsetto. "You goin' to whup me with your petticoat?

Shannon forced his voice into a deeper range. "So help me, Windsor."

Pryor yelled for them to get after the loose horses. Windsor sneered and bowed to Shannon. "Come along, darlin'. You're being called."

Shannon managed to remount his horse and catch up but could scarcely hold himself upright for the pain that racked his body. Pryor and Windsor had the herd stopped by the time he caught up. "Don't get down, Shannon," the sergeant said. "We're heading back to the river. Got to find the captain and get us some help."

"Why? I'm all right."

"You better be. The most help Captain's liable to spare is one more man. We'll be damn lucky to get that."

The sergeant and Windsor took up positions on the perimeter of the herd. Shannon sucked in a breath and forced himself to sit a little taller.

"Ready?" Pryor asked.

"Ready," he lied.

Captain Clark listened patiently to Sergeant Pryor's story about the horse stampede, then assigned one extra man, Hugh Hall, to the horse-herding detail. The addition of a fourth man freed one man of the detachment from standing watch each night. The second night after resuming their eastward journey that privilege fell to Shannon.

He was enjoying a deep sleep when a rifle shot jerked him awake.

"Get up! They're gone!" Hall yelled.

Shannon staggered to his feet. "Oh, no!" he gasped. The horses were gone. *All* of them, including the ornery Appaloosa.

Hall pointed southwest. "Tracks lead off yonder."

Barely awake, Shannon grabbed up his pouch and rifle.

"What're you doing, Shannon," Pryor demanded.

"Going after them," Shannon said without stopping.

"Come back here," the sergeant said.

Shannon was not about to waste another breath or another second of precious time arguing. Those horses were his and no one, *no* one was going to take them away. Not without a fight.

The thieves had made no effort to hide their trail. Driven by blinding anger, Shannon stumped along until the injuries from his recent fall forced him to slow his pace. Finally the pain in his ribs became too much to ignore. He had to stop, and Pryor caught up to him. "I'm not quitting until I get those horses back," Shannon wheezed.

"No, Shannon. This is as far as we go. Those horses are long gone. We're heading back to the river. All of us. We'll be damn lucky to make it before dark, late as it is."

Shannon attempted to push past, but Pryor stopped him. "Enough heroics, Private. We're all going back together if I have to hog-tie you. I lost a cousin on this expedition. I won't lose anyone else if I can help it."

Pryor's words unbarred the door to another cell of Shannon's memory, freeing a stream of images of Sergeant Floyd. With the images, another missing piece of the puzzle of the past two years of his life snapped into place.

"We're just four men alone on foot now," Pryor said. "If we all want to stay alive, we have to work together, watch each other's backsides."

Shannon glanced toward Hall and Windsor trudging toward them in the near distance. "The only reason either of those two would watch my back, Sarge, is to take aim at it before shooting. I'll take my chances with the Indians, thank you."

He wrenched his arm out of the sergeant's grip only to have Pryor pull a loaded pistol from the waistband of his pants, cock the hammer and press it into his breastbone. "You're not going anywhere but back to the river with the rest of us. Got that?"

"You don't expect me to believe you'd shoot me, do you, Sarge?" Shannon said. "You just said you wouldn't lose another man."

Pryor's voice was low and challenging. "So I did, but how do you know I told the truth?" The hardness in the sergeant's eyes matched that of the pistol barrel pressed into his chest. "I have all of us to think about, Shannon. If that means getting just three of us back alive, so be it. Your choice."

Shannon looked at the line of horse tracks leading off into the vastness beyond them. Those horses were his best chance to save himself and the expedition. Such a chance was not likely to come again.

The sergeant gave the pistol a jab. "So, what'll it be, Shannon? A bullet or cooperation?"

Shannon turned away from the tracks. "Let's go."

"Not so fast. I don't want you taking off on me. Stick out your arms."

He did and the sergeant bound them with a stout leather thong that he secured to his own wrist.

"But I can't shoot like this," Shannon protested.

"That's the whole idea," Pryor said. "We've got a lot of ground to cover and not much daylight left. You best come along unless you want me to drag you."

Shannon went.

🦅

Windsor slung his grimy bedroll into the dirt. "Not one bloody tree anywhere. Now what'll we do? Walk home?"

Pryor, Hall and Shannon stared morosely at the riverbank before them. There were lots of willows, for all the good they would do. Their plight drew only an occasional stare from the dozens of buffalo grazing around them. The sound of the animals ripping up grass underscored the deep silence of the place.

"There gotta be trees upstream," Hall suggested.

"That's going the wrong direction," Shannon said snappishly. He was thoroughly miffed at being dragged along on a lead by Pryor like some kind of fractious farm-animal.

The sergeant shifted his grip on the pistol, keeping it aimed Shannon's direction. "No trees means no boats. We got to keep looking."

"You look like you need a break, Sarge. How about we split up? You two go on ahead, and I'll keep an eye on Shannon, bring up the rear,"

Windsor said with a little too much enthusiasm to suit Shannon. With his hands tied, he had no way to defend himself if Windsor or Hall decided to take out their frustrations over their desperate situation on him.

Pryor agreed and transferred the thong leash and the pistol to Windsor and struck off upstream with Hall. When the pair were out of earshot, Windsor started in. "Why, don't this beat all? Me guardin' the man what got us into this here mess." He weighed the pistol, testing its balance. "Hope this here thing don't go off. Accidentally, I mean. Be a shame to have to leave you out here all by your lonesome 'cause there ain't no way for us to haul around a wounded man."

The sight of the grazing buffalo caused a plan to coalesce in Shannon's mind. A plan attached to a memory that would get them out of their fix. He still had his rifle. Pryor had made him carry it, awkward as it was, with his hands bound together. He pushed it toward Windsor. "Load this. Hurry."

"Oh, no. I ain't smart, but I ain't stupid neither."

"Come on. I know how to get us out of here."

Windsor eyed him. "How do I know you ain't goin' to shoot me?"

"Good God, man! Stop wasting time. Load the damn gun."

Hesitantly, Windsor reached for the rifle, then took his sweet time loading it.

"Now, give it here and step aside," Shannon said.

Before Windsor had time to object, Shannon grabbed the gun, jammed it against his shoulder and fired. Startled, Windsor dived for the dirt, then came up spluttering, "You, you tried t-to k-kill me."

"If I'd been aiming for you, you'd be dead. You're not, but it is." He pointed behind the man to where a buffalo bull had fallen in its tracks.

Shannon dragged the stunned Windsor along by the lead to check out the shot. Perfect. Smack in the center of the left eye. The sound of the shot brought the sergeant and Hall running back.

Shannon pointed his bound hands toward the dead animal. "Here's your boat, Sarge. All we have to do is skin it and stretch the hide over a willow frame and we have a Mandan bullboat."

The sergeant's eyes narrowed. "I thought you couldn't remember anything. How'd you know about them?"

Shannon was about to answer when Hall jumped in. "What say we get crackin' and get the hell out of here?"

"You're right," Pryor said. "Where do we start?"

Three pairs of eyes turned toward Shannon. "We need two boats. I'll shoot another buff while you three skin this one out and build two frames.

"Sounds like a plan," Pryor said. "Hope you remember how to do the frames."

Shannon didn't have to rely on his memory. He had a detailed sketch of a bullboat in his journal, including notes on how the frame was put together. Since losing all memory of the expedition back on the Columbia, he had often studied that picture, hoping it would prompt remembering. Every time he had closed the book in frustration — until a few moments ago, that was. "Sure do," he answered.

10. *Second Attempt*

With so little baggage left, Colter and the other men made short work of the portage around the Great Falls. They then dug up the cache at Portage Creek and found the white pirogue intact. This eliminated the need to move the remaining dugouts, except for the scout canoe and the two smallest ones, around the falls and allowed the detachment to head downriver to the Maria's confluence on July 28th. Instead of making Colter pilot of the white pirogue where he logically belonged, Ordway put him in the bow of the two-man sweep dugout.

Now that the portage lay behind them, Colter no longer cared or wondered at what the sergeant did. Nothing lay between him and Matootonha now but a long stretch of river. And one possible delay, at the Maria's.

If Captain Lewis's party was not there, he and the others might have to wait ten days, until August 5. Even then, there was no guarantee that they would head downriver. Given the power struggle between Ordway and Gass, there was liable to be a disagreement over leaving which could turn into a stand-off and an even longer delay.

By now Colter's need to get back to Fragrant Grass was acute. He doubted he could wait even ten days before he did something rash like taking this little dugout and heading downriver alone.

Ordway's voice knifed into his thoughts. "Turning in." The nose of the dugout swung toward the bank. A glance showed no other boats had pulled up. Why were they stopping?

Ordway answered Colter's unspoken question. "Spotted an elk up aways. Fresh meat for dinner."

Elk were hard to miss. Colter took his failure to not see the one the sergeant spotted as a sign that he needed to pay more attention to his surroundings and spend less time lost in thought.

Together, they dragged the canoe up on the wet sand and loaded their rifles. Ordway pointed the direction and struck off in the lead. After fifty yards, he signaled Colter to angle off to the right. Deducing from the sergeant's movements that the elk was in the draw ahead, Colter crept toward an opening in the brush that figured to give him clearance for a shot.

The draw was empty. Turning to locate the sergeant, Colter found himself looking down the barrel of a rifle aimed at his gut. "Where's the elk, Sarge?"

"What elk?" Ordway answered.

There was a strange set to the man's jaw. Determination? Restrained rage? Withheld mirth? Colter could not decipher which until it hit him. Ordway was hunting and he was the prey.

"Lay down your gun, Colter." There was no bantering or sarcasm in Ordway's tone. No inflection at all. Rather, the chill of inevitability, the calm of finality.

While Colter placed his rifle on the ground, his mind grappled with the precariousness of his situation. They were the last boat. The sergeant could kill him and dump his gutted body in the river, then claim he had simply disappeared while they were hunting. Of all the crew, only the captains might question Ordway's story, but neither of them was around. By the time Captain Lewis returned, Colter would be dead and likely forgotten in the rush to get down the Missouri. Ordway had picked the perfect spot, the perfect time, and he had not seen it coming.

He could not take his eyes off the dark circle at the end of the sergeant's rifle barrel. His mind had lost the ability to paste together cohesive thoughts.

"What, no smart-ass comment?" Ordway said, with emotion finally seeping into his voice. "Tell you what, Colter. How about I give you a choice? Heart, gut or pecker. Pick your shot."

"Why not do it up right, Sarge? Shoot me in the back. Here I'll turn around so's you got a clean shot."

"Oh, no, Colter. I want to see your face. I want to enjoy seeing the life drain out of you. I want to be sure you're good and dead and that you'll never see that squaw again."

As the venom seeped into Ordway's voice, Colter pressed for time. "That why you slugged her, Sarge? 'Cause you hate me?"

Surprise flashed across Ordway's face but before he could speak, four riders burst into the draw. "Captain Lewis!" Ordway gasped, lowering his rifle.

If the captain was surprised to find two of his crewmen in that particular place, he gave no sign. "Where's camp?" he asked tightly.

"No camp, Captain," the sergeant said. "The other boats are downstream about a mile. Is there trouble?"

"Blackfeet. You two get back to your boat and get down to the others fast. Tell them to be ready to launch the minute we get there."

Before Ordway could get out a "Yes, sir," Lewis, Drouillard, Rube and Joe galloped off.

"You heard him, Colter. Come on!" Ordway took off toward the dugout.

Colter slowly picked up his rifle. At Fort Clatsop, he had lost his fear of Ordway. He figured then there was nothing else the sergeant could do to him. He had been wrong. He thought the Great Falls was the last obstacle on his way to Fragrant Grass. Wrong again. Now he had Blackfeet *and* Ordway to worry about. Which would get him first?

Colter and Ordway had just put in with the other boats at the expedition's former camp at the Maria's confluence when Captain Lewis's group thundered in. The captain's voice was rigid with tension. "Get that cache up now, Gass! Ordway, you and Colter stash what they dig up wherever there's room in the boats. Move!"

Infected with the captain's urgency, the crew rushed to dig up the cache. While Drouillard set the horses loose, Rube and Joe came to help carry the unearthed bundles to the boats. This gave Colter the chance to ask Rube what happened. "We had a little run-in with some Blackfeet. Captain shot one."

A sharp crack startled Colter. He whirled around, expecting to see a party of attacking Blackfeet. Instead, Windsor held up a section of the red pirogue's gunwale. "She's rotted clean through, Captain," Gass said.

Nervously, Colter scanned the surrounding country for signs of Indians. Doing without the red pirogue meant cramming all the cached baggage into the already-burdened boats. It also meant fitting an additional man into each one.

It took a moment for Colter to fully absorb the significance of this last fact. No longer would there be only two men in the sweep dugout. He turned to look at Sergeant Ordway. The sergeant had missed his best chance to do him in. Like Sacajawea's reunion with her brother, the coincidence of Captain Lewis's showing up at exactly the right place at exactly the right time was not lost on Colter. The mysterious force was still with him, still guiding his life, still clearing his path, still . . .

"Why're you lookin' so strange? You spot Indians?" Rube asked.

At his friend's haggard appearance, Colter composed his voice to sound nonchalant. "Nope, thank the Lord."

"Well, they're out there and we'd better get a move on. Captain says to put all his papers and specimens in the white pirogue. And he says you're to be pilot."

Colter gaped at Rube, not quite sure he had heard right. "Me?"

"You, unless you want to stay with Ordeal, of course."

It was another turn of luck in his direction. He took a box of specimens from Rube and lugged it to the white pirogue, to *his* boat.

11. *Back from the Shadows*

T he two bullboats went together quickly. Then it was time for Shannon, Windsor, Hall, and Pryor to head off in pursuit of Captain Clark and the rest of their detachment. It was also time for Shannon to face the problem he had been pushing into the background since they had reached the Yellowstone.

He knew for certain that he had been terrified of deep water for as long as he could remember. He also knew that he had no choice but to get into a bullboat with Windsor and face that fear. That was the only option he had left if he ever intended to see his family again. It was also his sworn duty to do everything in his power to see that his companions made it back alive.

Jaw clenched, he waded into the river and held the tipsy boat while Windsor climbed aboard. Then, with a ragged breath, he pushed off and splashed into the boat, prepared for the usual paralyzing terror to seize him. Whether he won the battle with that fear or lost it, either way he would have given it his best. The way Father had taught him was the way it would be.

Only, the fear did not come.

At first he was surprised, then bewildered. What could have changed something so ingrained, so deep-seated? He was sure the answer lay within the tangle of memories that remained lost to him.

For the next week he and Windsor maneuvered the fickle little craft down the Yellowstone. Sometimes they led the second boat. Other times they followed. Always the issue of how he could have lost his fear of water bedeviled Shannon's thoughts. His efforts to remember what would not be remembered gave him headaches. Usually dipping his hat full of river-water and sluicing it over his head helped. However one bright, hot afternoon — August 2nd by his calculation — the pain grew so intense he had to ask Windsor to put in.

"You look awful," his companion said. "Why didn't you say somethin' sooner?"

"I just did," he murmured.

"You hunker on down. I'll get us in, okay?"

Shannon nodded gratefully and sank onto his bottom, shutting his eyes against the painful pulsing behind them. The pain magnified every sound: the rush of the wind, Windsor's heavy breathing, the splash of the man's paddle.

Involved in his own discomfort, he did not immediately realize there was more noise surrounding him than one man and one paddle could possibly make. Opening his eyes a crack, he took in two facts. First, the left river-bank had come alive with a herd of buffalo that had decided to swim the river. Second, Windsor had not seen the herd and was steering the bullboat directly into it.

Shannon yelled, "Back up!" and started backpaddling for all he was worth.

It wasn't enough.

The animals were upon them in an instant. Shannon held his paddle poised, unsure of what to do. On the other side of the boat, a terrified Windsor held up his own paddle like a scepter. One of the beasts had stepped on the paddle's head, snapping it off and leaving him with a use-less length of handle.

Suddenly the boat bounced upward and tilted, ejecting both men. Shannon came down across the shoulders of one of the swimming buffalo.

The displeased creature snorted and tossed him off. Shannon grabbed wildly for a handhold that would save him from falling under a hundred flailing hooves, and he managed to latch onto the hide of another beast.

No sooner had his fingers found purchase than they began to slip. The next thing he knew, he was wedged between two swimming beasts with his head and shoulders in the river and his feet in the air.

Struggling to raise his head high enough to catch a breath, he sucked in riverwater with the air and that set him to coughing. One of the wedging buffalo eyed him balefully and swam away from its partner, freeing Shannon who plunged headfirst into the river. Instinctively, he put out an arm to cushion his fall. The instant his hand sank into the silt at the bottom of the river, another buffalo rammed him from behind, knocking him into a somersault. A thought flashed through his mind: he had hit the bank, then something hard and heavy struck the back of his skull. And all thought was erased as the screen of his mind went blank.

After leaving the Maria's, Colter and the rest of Captain Lewis's group pressed down the Missouri. Running from the Blackfeet meant no rest stops, no hunting, no fires. As much as possible, they stayed to the south side of the river. As pilot of the white pirogue, Colter drove himself hard. He had been rescued from Ordway's bullet for some purpose, and he intended to abet the forces of the Universe in whatever that purpose might be.

Wary that Ordway might try again to kill him, Colter stuck close to other crewmen whenever they were off the river. In this cause he was aided by Lewis's order to post triple watches every night against the Blackfeet threat.

On the morning of the fifth day, he came awake to the smell of fire. He whipped to his feet, knife drawn. Instead of attacking Indians, he found the captain squatted next to a small fire, tending the spitted fish that sizzled over the coals.

"Good morning, Colter," the captain said, flashing his first smile since the Maria's. "It appears that we have outrun the Blackfeet. Hope you are hungry. The river has surely yielded up her bounty this morning."

The aroma of the roasting fish made Colter forget everything but his empty stomach. "Take two. There are plenty for everyone," Lewis said.

While Colter devoured his first helping, the rest of the crew roused and came to the fire. When they were all assembled, the captain spoke. "With the Blackfeet no longer a threat, we can resume a normal routine. The first order of business is to rearrange baggage and men to free up the two smaller dugouts for hunting. That way two pairs of hunters can move ahead every day and keep us supplied with meat down to the Yellowstone.

"Sergeant Ordway will be in charge of assigning those hunters. From now on, he will also leave a signal whenever the main body passes one of the hunting canoes. This signal." He held up a stick tied with a strip of canvas. "When you hunters find this in the bottom of your boat, it means that we have gone ahead of you and you are to come on. Do you all understand that?"

Every head nodded. "Very well then. Take your time with breakfast. We are out of danger."

"We still got Ordeal," the man sitting next to Colter muttered under his breath. The skin of John Collins's high aristocratic forehead was blistered from the sun. He sat with his lanky legs tucked underneath him Indian style.

"That we do," Colter said. During the portage of the Great Falls, Colter and Collins had discovered that they shared the same intense dislike of McNeal, Goodrich, and Ordway.

"I sure was glad I didn't draw Ordway's company at Camp Wood," Collins said. "I had a gutful of him back at Kaskaskia. Suppose I ought to be charitable toward a man who lost his wife, but it's right hard to forgive how he treated that young'un of his."

Intrigued, Colter asked, "What'd he do?"

Collins glanced around to be sure no one was listening before he answered. "Why, he give away his own flesh and blood. Just like that. A dog or horse, I can understand, but a baby not even two months old and his own son to boot? No sir, that's not right. I don't care who he is. A man's got a sacred obligation to his own. But not Ordeal. Oh no, he had his sights set on this here expedition, and no baby was gettin' in his way. No sir."

The order came to break camp and load the canoes. Colter took his time getting to his feet. He walked over to the fire and dropped the picked-clean fish skeleton on top of the coals. Long ago he had sensed that Ordway was hiding something and he had been right. All he had to do now was figure out how to use that information against the man.

The first sensation to enter Shannon's awareness was an intense stinging in his right forearm. The next was a cacophony of buzzes and low drones. He cracked open one eye. Thousands of flying things — black flies, sweat bees, mosquitos, and horse flies — swarmed around his prone body, waiting for a chance to land and share in the blood feast they had found.

He lifted one hand to swat at them and found it crusted with blood and mud. Touching a tender spot on his forehead, he discovered a huge knot also caked in dried blood and mud.

Memories swarmed back. Buffalo. Hundreds of them, swimming across the Missouri. The bullboat crashing into them, flipping. Being carried along wedged between two of the swimming beasts. Then gagging on riverwater, falling and somersaulting. Then . . . nothing.

He knew he ought to be dead, yet he was alive. With enormous effort and a long pause for the stars to clear from his vision, he managed to rise into a sitting position.

He was alone in a sandy hollow among waist-high sagebrush. The river lay fifteen yards to his right. The wet sand of the bank was pock-marked with the tracks of thousands of buffalo. Leading up to where he sat was a wide scuff mark such as a heavy sack dragged through the dirt would leave.

Wait a minute. Where's Windsor? The boat? He staggered to his feet.

A short distance downstream, he spotted Windsor, helping Pryor and Hugh Hall extricate the bullboat from a tangle of flotsam and river reeds. Hall caught sight of Shannon and waved.

He waved back to show that he was all right even if that was not exactly how he felt, then he made his wobbly way to the edge of the water, squatted and scrubbed the crusted muck from his face, arms, and hands. The effort brought on another bout of dizziness. He decided to sit down and let the others come to him.

While he was sitting there staring out at the meandering river, it dawned on him with a rush: the yawning gaps in his memory of the expedition had filled in. It was as if in the last hour his memory had been darned by an expert seamstress. He remembered how he and Colter had fallen out. Right on the heels of that memory came the image of the man he had killed. A gambler named McBain, *not* Chief Partisan of the Teton Sioux. McNeal had lied to him. "Why, that worthless bucket of mule piss," he hissed.

In a temper he pushed himself to his feet and stormed toward his three companions. He waved off their inquiries about his condition and examined the bullboat. The thong tying one portion of the hide to the upper willow crosspieces was missing, but that was the only obvious damage.

"Let's make camp here," Pryor suggested. "You can rest up, Shannon."

"I'm okay. Let's go on. We don't need to get any further behind than we are," Shannon insisted, stripping off the string anchoring his moccasin to his foot and using it to connect the hide to the boat frame.

"That's a nasty knot you got there on your head. You sure?" Pryor asked.

"Positive," Shannon said, growing angrier by the second over the lie the cook had told him. A lie that made him volunteer for this detachment. A lie that had put his life in jeopardy. Damn McNeal!

"We'll go on then." Pryor gave Shannon one last glance before trudging away with Hall toward their boat which was beached thirty yards downstream.

"Why're you starin' at me like that? Weren't my fault," Windsor said after they were alone.

The man's whining sounded too much like McNeal's. "Just shut up."

"But, I need —"

"Shut up now if you know what's good for you."

"Since when do you get off orderin' me around?" Windsor bridled.

Shannon flipped the boat over and waded it into the river.

"Shannon?" Windsor said, a hint of panic creeping into his voice.

Shannon looked back at the man on the bank. "Shut up or stay there."

"The captains'll have your hide for leavin' me."

"That won't help you much, will it?"

Windsor splashed into the bullboat without another word.

Colter dumped the body of the deer into the little dugout on top of Collins's kill, then squatted beside the lapping river to wash the dust and blood off his arms. It had been a good day all around. Clear and sunny but not too warm. The kind of day that made a man glad to be alive.

Collins was perched on a downed log, chewing on a grass stem. "Might as well sit a spell, Colter," Collins said. "There weren't no passin' signal. Means they ain't been by here yet."

Colter shook his head. "That can't be right. We ain't gone that far from camp for them to be takin' so long to get down here. That signal stick don't weigh that much. Wind must've blew it into the river."

Collins spit a piece of grass into the dirt. "That hasn't happened yet, has it?"

Colter shrugged.

"Then I reckon it didn't happened today, neither," Collins continued. "Somethin' mighta happened at the camp, kept 'em from comin' on. Might as well unload. We'll need to stand watches tonight, make sure varmints don't make off with our take tonight."

Colter watched his companion haul the deer carcass toward a small clearing. He wanted to argue, to go on now that they were daily drawing closer to the Mandans, but Captain Lewis had made it clear: stay put if you don't find the passing sign.

"Well, Johnny boy. Guess you're campin' here tonight," he muttered.

12. *The Purloined Signal*

The closer the Yellowstone carried Shannon's bullboat toward the Missouri confluence, the more determined he grew to resuscitate his friendship with Colter. And he figured he had the ideal way to do so in McNeal. To Colter, the cook belonged in the same class as Ordway and Charbonneau. It wouldn't take much effort to enlist him in a scheme to extract revenge on McNeal for the anguish the man's lies about Partisan had caused.

Recognizing the day-dreamy look stealing yet again over Windsor's face, he yelled, "Hard port!"

Windsor jerked out of his reverie, nearly tumbling out of the boat in his haste to respond. The man's thrashing made Shannon laugh. "Relax, Windsor. I was just checking to see if you were awake."

He tuned out Windsor's angry response to take in the passing scenery. The area of the confluence was even more beautiful than his newly-reclaimed memories of it. The widening Yellowstone wound around numerous small islands thick with trees and lush vegetation that most certainly teemed with game. Even the river, spangled with August sun, looked her peaceful best.

Windsor pointed his dripping paddle ahead. "Sarge is going in."

Shannon recognized the place the other bullboat was putting into. "Can you believe it? We're back where we started. See, yonder's last year's camp."

"Where is everybody?" Windsor asked. "Captain Clark's group should be here by now. You don't think anythin's happened to 'em, do you?"

Shannon did not have a chance to respond, because the dugout was suddenly engulfed in an enormous cloud of ravenous mosquitos. He and Windsor landed, swatting and swiping at the thirsty pests, and floundered up to the deserted campsite.

"They left this," Pryor said, handing Shannon a slip of paper, between slaps and stabs at the mosquito cloud around his head. "They tied that note to this here tree with this." He dangled a strip of red cloth that had long ago faded to pink.

Shannon recognized York's old sash, and he could not mistake Clark's familiar handwriting on the paper. *Bad mosquitos. Went on.*

"Best you put that note back up, Shannon, and get on out of here before these blood-suckers call in reinforcements," Pryor said, sprinting for his boat.

Shannon glanced at the note. It did not mention Captain Lewis's party, or Colter. Then again, why should it? Surely, Clark's group and Lewis's had reunited and were waiting for them downriver.

He started to fold the note back into the sash, then stopped, deciding it would make an excellent souvenir. A peace-offering for Colter. A reminder of all they had endured together on this journey of discovery. He tucked the slip of paper into his shirt where it would stay dry, then he flung down the worn-out sash and made a dash for the bullboat.

Colter tossed down his knife and heaved the half-carved piece of wood into the fire. "That's it! You stay if'n you want, Collins, but I'm leavin'. And I'm doin' it right now."

"Sit down, Colter. It's only been three days. They'll be along," Collins said patiently.

Colter was full up with waiting and with Collins's boundless, nettling forbearance. "Ain't no way they're behind us. Not after this long. I'm leavin' 'fore they get so far ahead we cain't never catch 'em."

"Oh, no, you don't. You can't leave without me, and I ain't goin' till I see that there sign."

"Watch me." Colter gathered his few possessions and half the remaining deer meat and strode down to the dugout where he proceeded to lash everything down.

"Colter, don't. What you're doin's not right," Collins pleaded.

Colter placed his rifle into the boat and picked up the canoe's nose. "If you're comin', you best be for hurryin'."

Collins's hands clenched into fists of indecision. Colter shoved the canoe off the bank into the reedy shallows.

"You wouldn't leave me here," Collins argued.

Colter let his glare serve as his answer.

Reluctantly, Collins gathered his things and the rest of the meat, kicked dirt over the little fire, and plodded to the canoe. "We're disobeyin' orders, you know."

Colter motioned for him to put his things in the boat.

"There was no signal," Collins insisted.

Colter turned to face his partner. "If'n you're comin' with me, I don't want to hear no more 'bout that damned signal. Not one word, or you can stay right here by yourself and wait till hell freezes over.

"All right," Collins muttered, clambering into the bow.

For the next five hours they rowed steadily downstream. Scanning the river for danger and the bank for signs of the main party absorbed all Colter's attention. For his part, Collins kept quiet though his paddling was less than enthusiastic.

Day began to wane without a sign of the others. Colter knew that he needed to find some evidence that Captain Lewis's party had passed this way, or he was not likely to get Collins to cooperate in the morning. That would force him into another ultimatum when he was not at all sure he could actually leave the man behind even to get to Fragrant Grass sooner.

The sun had sunk behind the low ridge to the west when Collins pulled in his paddle. "This here's far enough, Colter. Time to stop. Because of your bull-headedness, the others're even farther behind us now."

Colter pretended not to hear.

"Don't ignore me, Colter. I said stop."

"Half hour more," Colter said.

"No way. They're *not* ahead of us — and you know it."

Colter's warning hand-slash cut Collins off. He turned the boat toward something he thought he saw on the bank. He left his companion to tie off the dugout and went to investigate. From the remains of a campfire, he scooped up ashes and held them out to Collins. "Told you they was out front. At least two days, cold as these here are."

Collins folded his arms over his chest. "What's a fire prove? Could be anybody's. Blackfeet maybe."

Colter scanned the ground for more evidence. Three paces from the cold fire, he found some. Collins peered into Colter's extended hand. "A lump of pitch. So what?"

"It's wax. The end of a candle. Far as I seen, ain't no Indians figured out how to make candles yet."

Collins fingered the object doubtfully.

"Lick it, if'n you don't believe me," Colter said. "If'n it ain't tallow, I'll eat the damn thing."

Collins closed his palm around the lump. "But what happened to the signal?" he asked lamely.

Colter gazed downriver at the deepening dusk. "That's somethin' I intend to find out."

Upon leaving the Yellowstone-Missouri confluence, Shannon and his three companions faced a river twice as big and difficult as the Yellowstone they had grown used to. To make things more difficult, they hit a spate of nasty weather over the next two days that forced them off the river for hours at a time. The third day, a prolonged squall pinned them down most of the day.

The squall had not blown itself out when Shannon refused to stay put any longer. "I'm leaving and I'm going now."

None of the other three answered him.

"Okay, then I'll go alone."

"Durn it, Shannon. Hold your horses. What's the all-fired hurry?" Hall complained. "Cain't nobody move on the river in weather like this."

"I can and I will!" Shannon said. "You coming with me, Windsor?"

Windsor's confidence in the fragile bullboat was shaky at best, but he pushed himself to his feet and followed Shannon down to the river. Pryor and Hall fell in behind with their bullboat.

Driven by a strong trailing wind, the little boat gave them a wild ride over the next couple of hours. More than once big waves threatened to flip the boat. Still, Shannon paddled doggedly on.

"Shan-non-look." The bouncing action of the bullboat on the waves jostled Windsor's voice into syllables.

Shannon followed the man's point to see men on the bank. Men he knew. They had found the rest of the expedition.

His initial elation faded when he realized that the only boat in evidence was Captain Clark's dugout raft. Where was Captain Lewis's party?

Once Shannon and his three companions had been reunited with Captain Clark's group, it fell to Sergeant Pryor to recount the travails of the horse-herding squad. "The bullboats were Shannon's idea, or we'd still be out there somewhere on foot," Pryor explained.

Shannon received the credit with little relish. He had taken the note Captain Clark had left at the Yellowstone confluence. Taken it as a souvenir. Now there was no way to alert those in Captain Lewis's party that the rest of the expedition had gone on beyond the agreed-upon meeting place. It had never crossed his mind that anyone could possibly be behind his little group, and now the lives of everyone in the trailing group — Lewis, Rube, Joe, Colter and the rest — were in jeopardy.

He knew he ought to say something, knew he ought to admit his mistake, knew he . . .

"Meri's group will be along any day when they get the note I left," Clark said. "Meantime, the mosquitos aren't nearly as bad here as at the confluence."

Shannon forced himself to speak. "Sir, I think someone needs to go back upriver and wait, just in case. Request permission to be that person."

"Now that we've come this far, we'll all stick together and wait here at least for a few more days. Request denied," Clark said with a gentle smile on his face.

The group began to filter back to the camp which was set up away from the river in a thicket of elms. Shannon did not join in. He slipped a hand into his shirt and clutched the scrap of journal paper he had carried there for the last three days. Oh, God, why had he taken it? Why didn't he tie it back up as Sergeant Pryor directed? Why?

Windsor tapped his elbow. "What was that all about, Shannon? Wantin' to go back upriver? You leave somethin' back there?"

No, something I should have left. That's what Shannon wanted to say, only his mouth refused to form the words.

Windsor's hand cupped his shoulder. "It's Colter you're worried about, ain't it? About time you two patched things up. It's a shame to let some fool argument get in the way of friendship. You two got too much in common to be enemies."

The mention of Colter buried Shannon's speech beneath an avalanche of regret at the harm his latest bit of impulsiveness would bring. How could he ever justify such a thoughtless act to himself or anyone else?

"Come on up to the fire and eat somethin'. It'll help you feel better anyways," Windsor urged. Taking his hand out of his shirt, Shannon allowed himself to be led up to the fire, allowed himself to pretend that everything would work out for the best if he kept quiet.

⋌

It didn't take long for Collins to start doubting Colter's explanation for the piece of wax found at the riverside camp. By the time they had waited out a storm the next day, Collins had convinced himself that the wax had been left by fur-traders circling south from the French-held regions to the north. The day after that, the man went back to insisting that Colter was wrong, that Captain Lewis and the others were still behind them, that they had been attacked by Blackfeet and would now perish because of Colter's decision to continue downriver when they should have stayed put.

To add fuel to his arguments, they found no other evidence — no campfires or campsites — to prove that any other party was traveling the river ahead of them.

Between piloting the dugout around snags and keeping Collins going, Colter was at his wit's end when the man stopped paddling and sat up. "Is that the Yellowstone up yonder? Why, it sure is. There's our old camp." He pointed toward an island, then turned accusingly toward Colter. "And nobody's there."

The island was empty. No men, no boats, nothing. But Colter had come too far to change his mind. The others were in front of them. They had to be. "I'm turnin' in. There's bound to be a message."

"Don't let me stop you," Collins answered sarcastically.

Ten yards out, an enormous swarm of mosquitos descended on them. Collins threw down his paddle, tossed a hide over his head, and refused to row. Colter had no choice. If he wanted to land, he would have to do it under his own power, bugs or not.

The boat's nose bumped the bank, but Collins stayed wrapped in the hide. "You go look. I ain't budgin'," he said.

Colter clambered out and headed up the bank, windmilling his arms to give himself a bit of bug-free air to breathe. Through a curtain of insects intent on siphoning off all his blood, he made a quick survey of the campsite, searching for any message that might have been stuck on a stick or tied to a tree trunk.

Nothing.

Swatting and slapping, he paced around the site, looking for anything that would show that all or part of the expedition had passed this way. The dirt was littered with moccasin tracks, but it was impossible to know if they had been made by Indians or someone else. Other than that, there was a fire pit filled with cold ashes and a few discarded animal bones. There was nothing to tell him who had built the fires or gnawed on those bones.

In frustration, he turned back to the canoe. He had gone only a couple of paces when his eye spotted something in the sand. Scrawled letters. *Gone downriver.*

Colter forgot the bugs. "They been here! They're downriver."

"Why don't I believe you?" Collins responded, his voice muffled by the hide.

"Come look for yourself," Colter snapped, spitting three mosquitos out of his mouth and slapping at those attacking his forehead.

Collins left the dugout and plodded up the bank clutching the hide. He peeked out at the message, then immediately closed the gap. "Nice try, Colter. Didn't know you could write." He turned back to the boat.

Colter grasped the edge of the hide and yanked it off Collins. "If'n you don't believe me then give me back my deerskin."

Collins made a swipe for the hide and, in whipping it away, Colter lost his grip on it. The hide went flying across the clearing where it wrapped around on a tree trunk before sliding to the ground.

While Collins dashed over to reclaim his protection, Colter picked something up off the ground. "What about this here?"

"I ain't fallin' for any more of your tricks, Colter," Collins said, wrapping the skin across his face and head.

"This here's York's sash. The one he was wearin' back at Three Forks. Take a look, if'n you don't believe me."

Collins opened the hide a slit, then quickly reclosed it. This time he changed his tune. "All right. You win. Let's go."

Another powerful squall forced yet another delay on Colter and Collins. They sat side by side in the inadquate shelter of a prickly blackberry thicket, sharing the deerhide for cover. Colter stared morosely out at the driving rain and the frothing river. His mood had been up and down the emotional scale so many times the last few days that all he felt now was numb. The closer he got to Fragrant Grass, the more trouble they seemed to run into.

Collins tugged on his side of the shared hide. "Bet you'll be glad to see that little sprout of Janey's again."

Colter grunted noncommittally. Since Three Forks, he had not allowed himself to think of Pomp.

"What about Shannon?" Collins asked.

"What about him?" Colter said flatly.

Collins cast an appraising look sideways. "You still cartin' around a grudge? Lord, man, we're about home. Time to let it go. What if he didn't make it? You give any thought to that?"

Colter snorted. "If'n there's one thing this here world's got way too much of, it's advice nobody asked for."

"You think I'm talkin' off the top of my head, but I ain't. A few years back my brother and me had an argument and I stomped off, swearin' I'd never speak to him again. You know what? I never did. Later on that same day a tree he was fellin' came down wrong. Crushed him. I was the one found his body."

Collins paused as if to allow the remembered image to pass. "Just like that, he was gone. Just like that, it was too late to set things to rights again."

He fingered a tuft of grass. "He was a year older than me. That made him someone I'd known my whole life. All the times we shared together — all the jokes, the quarrels, the long talks and quiet times — died with him. Now I'm the only one left to remember them or him. It hurts to be the one got left behind."

The wind howled, pelting the rain harder against the sheltering hide. Collins cocked his head as if hearing a voice. "When Captain Lewis first put you and Shannon together, I figured you'd be at each other's throats in a week. Figured wrong, didn't I? Took awhile but you two turned out friends."

Colter couldn't let this pass. "Friends like Judas and Jesus."

Collins wagged his head. "You don't get it, do you? It was Captain Lewis's decision that kept us out on the coast all winter. He was bound and determined to wait for a ship and nothin' nobody could say would've changed his mind. Not Captain Clark, not you, not me, not Shannon. Stayin' mad at Shannon makes about as much sense as tryin' to milk one of them grizzled bears."

Collins fell silent, allowing Colter to absorb the truth of the words.

"You and Shannon'd be good partners after we get back," Collins said.

"Partners?" Colter said, flicking at the dip where the hide drooped between their heads to displace the water pooled there. "We cain't be together two minutes without arguin'."

"That's why you'd make good partners. Arguin' keeps a body honest," Collins said.

Collin's words brought up memories of all the near-battles he and Zoob fought over the course of their long partnership. Arguments that invariably brought them closer together rather than driving them apart. Just as Zoob had been one constant, inseparable fact for more than half his life, Colter could not separate Shannon from everything he had seen, heard, felt, smelled and tasted since before the expedition left Maysville. Like it or not, Shannon was a part of him, and he was a part of Shannon.

What if Shannon hadn't made it back with Captain Clark's detachment? Collins's question brought up an image of the cemetery back at the Draft. Zoob, Pa, and Ma — all gone now. Three mounds of words not said, of business not finished.

"Storm's lettin' up. Think we oughtta give 'er a try?" Collins asked, pulling Colter back from images of death, back to the moment.

Colter tossed off the wet hide and rose. Shannon was one question. Ordway, another. And Fragrant Grass, yet another. He intended to answer all those questions. And soon.

The next two days passed in an agony of indecision for Shannon. At least three times he made up his mind to tell Captain Clark about taking the note, but every time his courage failed him before he reached the captain's makeshift tent.

By mid-morning of the third day, the burden of his actions became too much to bear. He had to admit his mistake. Now it wasn't a question of courage. It was a question of pain. He was walking toward the captain's tent when someone yelled, "We got company!"

A canoe with two occupants nosed into the little landing stage below the expedition's camp. One glance doused Shannon's hopes. The pair were strangers, not the advance guard of Lewis's group.

Along with the other crewmen, he gathered around the newcomers. They were American trappers, Joseph Dickson and Forest Hancock. They looked around at Shannon and the others with astonishment. "Ever'one down to St. Lou thinks you all are dead," Dickson said.

Dead. The word sent a frisson of fear down Shannon's spine as Clark answered the newcomers. "And it's a surprise to us to find two Americans so far upriver this soon."

The two men exchanged a cautious look before Dickson answered, "Here tell there's beaver fair leapin' outta the streams out yonder. We wanted to see such a sight for ourselves."

"We'd be much obliged for any information you could give us about the river and the country we'll be travelin' through," Hancock added.

"How about the Blackfeet and the grizz? Want to know about them, too?" one of the crew offered, sparking a gale of crew laughter. The trappers smiled tentatively. Someone else chimed in, "Shannon here's the expert on grizz. He can tell you all you need to know."

The remark and so many gazes swiveling toward him caught Shannon by surprise. Captain Clark pre-empted the awkward moment. "Let me get my map."

As the captain went off to his tent, Shannon saw his chance and ran after him. "Captain, there's a problem, sir." He shoved the slip of paper into the captain's hand.

Clark glanced at it, then looked at Shannon. "I see."

Shannon's words tumbled out in a rush. "I have to go back upriver, sir. Because of me, Captain Lewis and the others don't know to come on."

Clark turned the note over in his work-roughened palm. "Why didn't you show it to me before?"

It required enormous effort to meet the captain's gaze and to force words past the fear jamming his throat. "I was afraid to admit what I'd done."

The captain handed the note back to him and ducked into the tent. "Sir?" Shannon said uncertainly.

"No, Private."

"But, sir, Captain Lewis and the others, who'll tell them about, about us?"

Clark re-emerged with the rolled map under his arm. "That's a good question, Shannon." With that, he returned to the trappers.

A faint curl of smoke rising above the trees around the next bend caught Colter's alert eye. He turned the nose toward the middle of the river to keep as much water between the dugout he shared with Collins and the bank until they could round the bend and see whose fire it was. The last thing he wanted this close to the Mandans was a run-in with a Teton Sioux raiding party.

Collins's chin snapped up. "It's Captain Lewis and them!"

It was indeed. The boats from Captain Lewis's detachment were lined up side by side on the bank next to an unfamiliar canoe. Colter swung the dugout toward the bank and landed them ten yards below the other boats. Rube was the first to reach them. "'Bout damned time you two showed up. Where you been?"

Collins tossed Colter a shame-faced look. "We got company?" Colter asked.

"Couple of trappers, headed upriver," Rube answered. "Accordin' to them, Captain Clark's camped just down a-ways." He lowered his voice. "Only we got a problem. Captain Lewis got shot."

Colter was on his way to the captain before Rube's sentence was finished. Lewis lay on his stomach in the bottom of the white pirogue, a swath of bandage covering his buttocks. His voice was raspy with pain. "Colter, thank God, you're safe."

The captain's wound wasn't fatal, but he was obviously in no condition to bring up the subject of the missing passing signal. Instead, Colter turned his glare on Ordway. The sergeant had played his last trick on John Colter.

"I want to hear what happened to the two of you, but I am afraid that will have to wait until," Lewis's face contorted, "until we find Will."

Colter kept his eyes riveted on the sergeant. "No problem, Captain. Not much to tell. When you're able's soon enough."

Grimacing, Lewis shifted on his elbows. "Sergeant Ordway, get us moving." He cocked his head toward the two strangers. "Best of luck with your endeavors, gentlemen."

As Colter walked down to the dugout, one of the newcomers stuck out his hand. "Name's Joe Dickson. This here's Forest Hancock."

"John Colter." He shook the hand absently, his mind still on Ordway and the missing passing signal that had cost him so much time.

"That's quite a mark you got on your face," Hancock said.

It took Colter a second to figure out that the man was talking about his birthmark. It had been out of his mind for so long that he had almost forgotten it.

"If you don't mind me sayin' so," Dickson said, "you got the look of a trapper."

"Should have. Been trappin' most of my life."

"Is what they're sayin' true?" Hancock asked eagerly. "That the streams out yonder're chock full of beavers?"

Colter watched the white pirogue launch while he answered. "That where you're headed?"

"Why you askin'?" Dickson said with enough suspicion that Colter decided there was no point in continuing the conversation. He started to leave.

Hancock stopped him. "What Joe means is, we might be interested in takin' on a partner. Say, someone who could show us the best places to go. Someone like yourself, say."

Colter brushed off the man's hand. "You got the right idea, but the wrong man. Now I got to go. Good luck."

When he reached the dugout, Collins asked, "What did you say to those two? The way they're tearin' down their camp, you'd think the Sioux was after 'em."

Colter shrugged. "They got a long way to go. Guess they figure they best get movin', same as us. Come on."

They shoved off. When they reached the current, Collins glanced back over his shoulder. "Where'd you say they were goin'?"

"Shinin' Mountains, they said."

"Either they're mixed up or they changed their minds."

Colter looked back to see Collins was right. The two trappers were following them.

13. *Settling Accounts*

S hannon kept his head down, pretending to devote his full attention to slicing up the buffalo shoulder while ignoring the hostile glances of the other crewmen. Word that he had taken the captain's note from the confluence had spread like a rash. Now the men blamed him for delaying Lewis's detachment and holding up their return to St. Louis.

"It's Captain Lewis!" came the shout.

The camp became instant bedlam. Captain Clark burst out of his tent and ran down to the water, splashing out to meet the white pirogue. Shannon abandoned his task and climbed onto a log to better see the other boats as they rounded the upstream bend. Two boats, then three, then four. Colter wasn't in any of them. Shannon's heart sank.

The fourth boat had just landed when a fifth small dugout hove into view with Colter in the stern. Behind them came the canoe containing the two trappers, Dickson and Hancock. Shannon wondered why the two trappers had returned, but the sight of Captain Lewis being lifted out of the white pirogue and carried to the shade of an awning pushed the thought out of mind.

"What happened?" Shannon asked, waylaying Rube on his way up from the pirogue.

"Huntin' accident," Rube said. "Flesh wound's all, but he's in a heap of pain. Could've been a lot worse though if'n them Blackfeet'd ever caught up with us."

The comment drew other crewmen who crowded around Rube, peppering him with questions, forcing Shannon to the periphery. He listened until the questions and answers began to repeat, then turned away.

"Why, Shannon, fancy meeting you here. Thought you'd be at the Mandans already."

McNeal's nasal voice ignited a long-smoldering spark inside Shannon. His doubled fist caught the cook square in the midsection and folded the man in half. "That was for Partisan, and this is for me," Shannon hissed, jamming his knee upward into the cook's crotch.

McNeal's agonized screams brought Pryor on the run. "For God's sake, Shannon. We got enough trouble already."

"There's no trouble here, Sarge," Shannon answered. "We were just settling a score."

"He's out to kill me!" cried McNeal.

"Try harder next time, will you?" the sergeant murmured to Shannon, walking away.

Smiling grimly, Shannon left the cook to his pain and marched to the riverbank to meet Colter. He helped pull in the dugout, then drew Clark's note from his pocket and held it out to Colter. "This is for you."

Colter made no move to take it. "What's that?"

"Another mistake I made."

Colter took it and read it, then pulled a length of faded red fabric out of his pouch. "Good thing you left one and took t'other, or Collins and me'd still be sittin' up on the Yellowstone gettin' et up by bugs and waitin' for hell to freeze over."

Facing this man he had so wronged and betrayed filled Shannon with profound shame. "Like I said, my mistake. I'm sorry."

"Ain't no harm done, Fuzz."

The old nickname stopped Shannon. "What did you call me?"

"Fuzz. Though that name don't hardly fit you no more, what with all that there hair growin' out your chin and ears."

Colter's bantering tone encouraged Shannon. "I've done a lot of stupid things where your friendship's concerned."

"Fuzz —"

"No, let me finish."

"No, you let me finish."

"Confound it, Old Man. You're always interrupting me."

"That's 'cause you never get to the point."

Shannon began to defend himself until Colter's grin stopped him. "I'm doing it again, aren't I? Here you just get back and I'm arguing with you."

"Feels good, don't it?" Colter said. "I got to say I missed you, Fuzz."

"Me, too, Old Man." Shannon felt too good to care that his voice caught.

"Come on, let's eat," Colter said. "Got a heap to catch you up on."

He walked with Colter to the fire, filled a cup with stew, then settled down next to his friend, feeling better than he had in weeks. While Colter told his story, Shannon found himself losing the thread and falling into the welcome rhythms of the man's voice and all the memories it called forth.

"There we was —" Colter stopped and the smile disappeared from his voice and manner. Shannon looked around to see Ordway heading down to the boats. "That son-of-a-swamprat," Colter said venomously. "You sit tight. I got somethin' to take care of. Be right back."

Ordway squatted at the edge of the water, drinking from his cupped palm. At the sound of Colter's footsteps, he whirled around, then got slowly to his feet. "Glad you caught up, Colter." Something — fear or relief or anger — tinged the bravado in his voice.

"Sure you are, Sarge. What'd you tell Captain?" He pitched his voice to the sergeant's register. "'I put that passing signal in the dugout myself, sir. Just like you said to do. Wind must've blown it into the river. It was a gusty day, remember?'"

Colter dropped back into his own voice. "That how it went, Sarge?"

Across the dark space between them, Colter sensed the cruel smile curling the corners of Ordway's mouth. "Damn close, Colter."

"Truth is you never left the signal. You never intended to. What'd you do? Toss it overboard when no one was lookin', or hide it in the weeds whilst you were pissin'?"

"You do have an imagination, Colter."

"So do you, Sarge. It'd take a powerful one for a man to turn his back on his own baby." Across the gloom, Colter felt Ordway go rigid. "How's a body do such a thing — toss away his own flesh and blood like old boots that don't fit no more? 'Out you go. I got other things to do 'sides be your pa.' That how it went for you?"

Against the backdrop of the river, the shadow that was Ordway shifted slightly.

"I wonder how it feels to be a baby whose pa don't want him no more?" Colter went on. "Whose pa wants to go gallivantin' so bad he's willin' to turn his back on his own motherless child?"

The sergeant's breath came in strangling gasps. "Lies!"

The campfire flared up, illuminating Ordway's face. "Are they? Then why're you lookin' like you seen a haint?"

"It wasn't like that. I couldn't care for him."

"Don't tell me, Sarge. I ain't the one you owe explainin'. Tell your son. If'n he'll listen."

Ordway's mouth contorted and his voice turned pleading. "Ruthie died and left us alone. I didn't know what to do."

"Now who's lyin'? You wanted him outta the way so's you could join this here expedition. Did you tell the captains you had a baby?"

"I . . . they . . ." A pistol Colter had not noticed before slipped out of the sergeant's grip and thudded to the ground at his feet. Ordway stared down as if wondering how it got there.

Colter pressed his advantage. "Do they know?"

Ordway's mouth worked but nothing came out. Slowly he dropped onto his knees next to the discarded pistol. Colter picked up the gun and heaved it into the river, then looked down at the sergeant. "Seein' as how you didn't tell 'em, maybe I ought to. What d'you think?"

A low keening sound emanated from the sergeant, then, "No, please." The word came out as a sob.

"Then you best be stayin' away from me from now on."

Colter took Ordway's muffled answer as assent and started to walk away, then stopped and turned back. "One more thing, Sarge. I ain't the only one knows about you. Anythin' happens to me, you can be sure that you and the Army'll be partin' company. What'll you do then? Bust sod?"

He shook his head. "Nope, you ain't no farmer. Come to think of it, you ain't much of a man, neither." With that, he walked back to camp.

Shannon came to his feet when he saw Colter step into the circle of firelight. But, before he could intercept him, the two trappers Dickson and Hancock headed Colter off and guided him to the darkest corner of the camp to talk. Shannon sat back down and observed the conversation.

The trappers' interest in Colter made him uneasy. It was obvious that they wanted something from Colter, but he could not figure out what.

Eventually the conversation broke up and Colter made his way back to the fire. "What was that all about?" Shannon asked, trying to mask the disquiet of his thoughts with nonchalance.

Colter settled down next to Shannon. "Wanted me to partner up with 'em. Go back upriver and show 'em where to trap. Offered me a full stake of the take."

Shannon's mouth went dry. "Are you going?"

"Yes. But not now and not with them two. I got somethin' to see to down at the Mandans."

Relief relaxed Shannon, gentling his voice. "It's been a long time since you saw her, Old Man."

Colter's eyes took on a far-away look. "A real long time."

Only later, when Shannon was about to drift into sleep, did he realize that he forgot to ask Colter what happened between him and Ordway.

14. *Heartbreak*

When the pirogue in the lead made for the sand landing stage below the Mandan village of Rooptahe, Colter swore under his breath. Why bother stopping at Rooptahe when Matootonha — and Fragrant Grass — were just downriver?

As the expedition boats landed, Mandans streamed out of the town, crowding the path to the beach and spreading along the edge of the bluff. Colter scanned the throng, hoping for some reason that she might be at the town visiting and that he might spot the familiar white-streaked hair, the long-dreamed-of face. No luck.

There were so many people on the little shingle of beach that he had to stand in the river, waiting for space to wedge onto the sand. While he waited, he heard Shannon call to him, "Old Man, look who's here."

Shannon pushed through the crowd leading a young Indian man. Colter stared at the Mandan without recognition until Shannon said, "It's Echo."

Despite his frustration over his delayed reunion with Fragrant Grass, Colter managed a smile. "By God, so it is. You done growed up on us, boy."

Echo came forward, a flush prominent on the newly-adult contours of his face. "Thank you, Friend Colter."

Shannon saved Colter from having to make more conversation by pulling Echo away to greet Rube and Joe. In the respite, Colter gazed longingly downriver. It was only another mile to Matootonha, to Fragrant Grass, but there was no telling how long it would be before they could make that short journey. Unless he could figure something else out, he would be stuck here until then.

A brown hand grasped his forearm. The earlier flush had left Echo's face, making him look younger and more cunning. He beckoned for Colter to follow him.

They threaded their way through the milling Mandans to the top of the bluff. Echo led him along the picket wall to a side entrance into the town, then through the tightly-spaced mound lodges and across the open central plaza to a lodge that fronted it. Echo halted outside the entrance. "Wait here, Friend Colter." Then he ducked inside.

Colter had been to Rooptahe only twice during their winter's stay at Fort Mandan. He did not recognize the lodge. With all the Mandans out welcoming the expedition, the town had an eerie deserted feeling that made him edgy to be moving again. The thick walls of the lodge muted the voices within to low murmurings. What was Echo doing and what was taking him so long?

When the boy reappeared at the tunnel entrance, his face was alive with a mixture of excitement and nervousness. "There is not much time. You must come out when you hear this sound." He imitated the cooing of a dove with the perfection of a born mimic. "You must leave then. To be here now is dangerous. For both of you."

Impatient to discover what all the fuss was about, Colter agreed and ducked inside. In contrast to the bright day outside, the interior of the lodge was dark. His eyes were not completely adjusted when a female voice said, "You return."

He did not need to see to recognize the voice he had carried in memory for over a year and a half. Fragrant Grass lay on a pallet next to the small central fire, looking more beautiful than the image Colter had carried in his head for so long. Seeing her made his breath catch and took away his ability to stammer anything except "Yes."

She lapsed into Mandan and signs, asking him to come closer so she could see him. He rounded the fire and approached the pallet, watching her closely for clues as to why she was abed here in Rooptahe rather than Matootonha. His examination revealed nothing.

Her hand drew out signs. "You are well?"

Before he could answer, a mewling sounded from the other side of her. She moved aside the edge of the hide covering her to reveal a tiny baby. Cradling the child in the crook of her arm, and murmuring to it, she pulled down the top of her shirt and guided the infant to an exposed nipple.

Colter watched in stunned disbelief. The baby could not be more than a few days old. To fill the yawning silence, he asked, "Is it . . . a girl?"

The eyes Fragrant Grass turned to Colter glistened with maternal tenderness. "A boy. A son," she said in halting English, smoothing the silky black down on the baby's head.

Colter wanted so much to touch her, to hold her, to breathe in the scent of her. He wanted to tell her how much he missed her, that he never should have left her. He wanted to tell her about the Western Sea where the land ended and the water stretched beyond imagination. He wanted to tell her about the Shining Mountains and the beautiful valley home he had found for them there. He wanted to do all these things, yet how could he when, here she was, suckling the son of . . .

"I live here now," she signed. "I am wife to Black Cat, chief of this village. This is his son."

Wife? No, that could not be! He said he would be back, and he always kept his word.

"My husband is a good man," she said.

The baby pulled away from her breast and she placed him gently on the robes beside her. She looked back at Colter wistfully. "You did not come before the snows."

Colter's voice sounded strained through the confused mix of emotions churning within him. "I wanted to, believe me, but we was stuck somewheres else."

The baby began to fuss and she bent to soothe him. As Colter watched, it slowly sank in that this woman he loved, this woman that he wanted to marry and take to the Shining Mountains, was now the wife of a Mandan chief and the mother of that man's child.

The sound of her voice brought him out of his musings. "Rooptahe is a good place. I am happy here."

From outside the lodge came the coo of a dove. Echo's signal.

With great effort, moving against the shock and disappointment that weighted his limbs, Colter knelt beside her and cupped her cheek. "I got to say somethin' I ain't never said to no one before, not even my Ma. I love you, Pshanshaw. Love you more than I got words to tell. I want you to always be happy. I want —"

She touched a finger across his lips to silence him. "I wish the same for you, Colter. Now, go." There was finality in her voice.

Another dove coo, this one more urgent.

With the heart in his chest as heavy as the air in the lodge from all that remained unsaid, Colter got to his feet and turned toward the entrance, but his feet would not move.

Another coo.

"Go," she whispered.

He looked back at her, but her head was bent again to her child, denying him a last look at the face that had warmed his soul for seventeen months. He stumbled back outside to find Echo, visibly distraught.

"They come. No one must see you here or there will be much trouble. Go." He pointed to the narrow path between Fragrant Grass's lodge and the next.

Colter lurched away from Echo, from the lodge, from Fragrant Grass. In the course of a few minutes his world had turned upside down, pouring all his dreams into a bottomless black pit of regret and leaving him empty, a cup drained of tomorrow. She had been his future, his destiny. Now she was the wife of another man, the mother of that one's child, the member of a community where she was respected, where she was happy. He had no right to expect her to turn her back on those choices, no call to ask her to leave her home, her life. To him, she was as dead as Zoob and Pa and Ma.

Yet he could no more erase the vision of her and the home he had planned for them in the Valley of the Bitterroots than he could erase any of the memories crowding his mind. Only death could still those images. As long as he lived, he was doomed to remember and to mourn what might have been.

He stumbled onward, blind to everything but his own pain, until he found himself on the outer edge of Rooptahe. Here the villagers had placed their graveyard on the top of the river bluff. He zigzagged among the scaffolds to the edge of the bluff where the land fell twenty feet down to a narrow secondary channel of the threading Missouri.

Colter stood on the edge, hating the river that had drawn him away seventeen months ago. That same river now stopped him when he wanted to keep walking, to get away from this place, this pain.

He glared up at the fleecy, scudding clouds. He had been so sure of his dreams, so sure that the forces that drove him to the western edge of the continent sanctioned his dreams and would conspire to make them come true. He had never given a thought to the alternatives. Why should he? He was so sure. So very sure.

Now that his future lay in ashes, he had no direction and no anchor. He was adrift, a tangle of raw nerves, caught in a current bound for nowhere. Without Fragrant Grass, life had no meaning. There was no reason to stay here and little reason to go downriver. Even heading back to the Bitterroot Valley had lost its appeal. He was a man without a reason to live or a place to be.

It took a long time for his turmoil to ebb. He turned away from the bluff to find himself between two scaffolds, one recent, the other near collapse from age. The odor of decaying flesh still clung to the newer one. From the corners of the platform hung the weapons of a warrior: a spear, a bow, an arrow quiver and a shield, their paint and feathers still bright, as yet untouched by the elements.

Atop the older platform bleached bones showed through rents in the weather-rotted hides that had once wrapped the body. Around it lay the possessions of a Mandan woman: a hoe fashioned from a buffalo shoulder bone, leather bags of corn seeds, beaded parfleches, three rusted cooking pots and two skinning knives. One of the knives was steel and fine enough to have cost three horses in trade. Colter picked the knife up and tested the edge with his thumb. Despite the passage of time, it was still sharp enough to skin out a deer.

"Well, well, we meet again."

Colter started, dropped the knife, and whirled to see a thin man with a heavy beard and a lopsided stance step around the end of the decaying platform. "First time we met was in a graveyard," the newcomer said.

Something about the stranger's voice was familiar, but Colter could not dredge up a name to attach to it.

"Can't place me? Here, I'll come closer." The man walked into the space between the two scaffolds. Still, only the man's voice was familiar.

"You know me all right. Look hard, Colter. Use those keen eyes of yours."

Something in the man's gaze sparked recognition. "Oh, my God. Hartley."

The instant he said the name, the stranger lunged at him, throwing him into the newer scaffold. Colter's head slammed into the upper crossbar. The force of the blow buckled his knees, but he managed to grab the dangling shield and stay on his feet. His reactions had been honed by weeks of piloting small boats on the Missouri, and he managed to feint away from the slash of Hartley's drawn knife.

Instead, the thrust sliced through the strap attaching the shield to the scaffold. Without support, Colter went down, tumbling under the platform. He scrambled to his knees only to have the barrel of Hartley's pistol jammed beneath his ear. He froze.

"I've waited a long, long time for this moment, Colter. Waited to watch you die."

"Stuart must be offerin' a lot for you to come all this way, Preacher."

Hartley croaked what passed for a laugh. "This is all for me now, Colter. For my pleasure. Not for Farley Stuart."

"What's a preacher doin' talkin' about killin'?"

"I stopped believing in God a long time ago."

Colter had only his hands for defesne. He made a desperate grab for Hartley's straggling beard, digging his fingers into the tangles of hair and yanking down hard. The preacher fell forward and Colter's bended knee caught him in the throat.

Gagging, Hartley dropped the pistol. Colter immediately grabbed it, staggered to his feet, and heaved the weapon over the bluff into the river.

"Now we got even odds. Get up, Hartley. Let's finish this once and for all." He backed away three paces to give the man room to rise.

Coughing and spitting, Hartley tried to get to his feet, but his lopsidedness threw him off-balance and he grabbed for the closest scaffold to steady himself.

Though Hartley had been his mortal enemy, Colter's natural compassion overcame his hatred. "Watch out!" he yelled, too late.

The old platform gave way, caving in on the preacher and burying him under a load of cooking pots, hoes, seeds and other tools of domesticity.

Colter stared at the rubble, waiting for the preacher to rise up out of it. When Hartley did not move, Colter prodded an exposed hand with his foot. "Preacher?"

No sound. No movement.

Colter lifted the hand, then let it drop. It flopped to the ground, lifeless.

Using his shoulder as a lever, he managed to move part of the surprisingly heavy mass off the preacher's upper body. There, buried to the hilt in Hartley's chest, was the dead woman's steel knife. Hartley had met his end at the hands of a ghost.

15. *Away On a Gust of Wind*

S hannon glanced up when Colter wandered back in from wherever he had been all afternoon, but, between snatching bites of roasted buffalo hump and fielding questions from Echo and a group of the boy's friends, he was too busy to do more than nod the man's direction. The youngsters were eager to learn about the land to the west, and, now that his memory was whole again, he was more than happy to tell them everything.

At one point a pretty young woman came to replenish his food platter. Shannon paused in his narrative to admire her. At the same time he noted that Colter was again huddled with the two trappers. The sight prompted the same uneasy feelings he had experienced earlier. He decided he did not like the pair, but Echo interrupted his thoughts, reminding him about a story he had promised earlier to tell, the story of the beached whale he had seen while at Fort Clatsop.

In the midst of his tale, Shannon noticed that Colter had moved over to talk with the captains. From his position he had a clear view of only one participant in the conversation. Ordway's face was a study in barely-controlled fury. What was going on?

He was unaware that he had stopped talking until Echo said, "Friend Shannon?"

With difficulty, Shannon dragged his attention back to his listeners. "Sorry. Where was I?"

"There was a giant fish on the sand."

Before he could restart his narrative, movement at the captains' circle reclaimed Shannon's attention. Colter and the two captains rose and Colter shook each man's hand in turn. When he turned to head down to the boats,

Shannon could no longer contain his curiosity. "I'll be back," he assured Echo and the rest of the group and took off after his friend.

He caught Colter at the top of the path down to the river. "All right, Old Man. What's going on?"

"I'm leavin'."

"We all are tomorrow. What were you saying to the captains?"

"They give me a discharge. I be headin' back upriver tomorrow with them two trappers."

The news was too much for Shannon to take in immediately. "What about Fragrant Grass?"

"Thought Echo would'a told you."

"Told me what?"

"She's married. To the chief of this here town. And as of a few days back, she's a mother."

"No," Shannon blurted in astonishment.

"Yep."

"But she's your woman."

Colter faced Shannon squarely for the first time. "She's Black Cat's woman and the mother of his son, Fuzz." His voice dropped into a muted register. "She says she's happy here."

Colter looked away, his throat working, his eyes clouded. "How can I ask her to leave happiness? That's somethin' I been chasin' my whole life. For all the chasin' I done, I ain't never caught much neither. I ain't got nothin' to offer her that she ain't already got."

"What about that man, that Stuart character back in Virginia?"

The ghost of a mirthless smile played around Colter's mouth. "Virginie and Farley Stuart done seen the last of John Colter."

"What about your wages, the land you're to get?"

"Captains said they'd save 'em for me for when I want 'em."

"Then what about me?" Shannon exploded.

Colter gave him a long look before he answered. "You'll do just fine, and so will I."

"But we're friends, Old Man."

"And always will be. You know that, don't you?"

Shannon knew his voice would break if he tried to answer. Even his nod felt brittle.

"I ain't never felt like I belonged no place before, Fuzz, 'cept out in them Shinin' Mountains. I been lookin' my whole life for a home. Now I found me one, and, though it won't be as good without Fragrant Grass along, I'm headin' for it, just like you be headin' home to Ohio where you belong."

Shannon had to try twice before he found his voice. "Tomorrow?"

"Yep."

"What about Ordeal?"

"I'm a civilian now. Ordeal ain't got no hold on me no more." He looked ready to add something else but didn't. He slapped Shannon on the shoulder and continued on down to the boats.

Shannon stood for a long time, thinking about Colter, about all the two of them had been through together the last couple of years. The two of them had crossed a continent together. They had walked into the Western Sea together. They had faced starvation and storms, raging rivers and treacherous Indians together. They had bickered. They had fought. Yet, through it all, their friendship had taken root and flourished. He could not imagine what his life would be like without Colter. Maybe he ought to turn back West, too.

No, exploring the West had been an adventure, but his home and his heart belonged in settled places, attending to civilized pursuits. Too distraught for conversation, he headed down to the boats but stopped when he saw Colter laughing with the two trappers.

Colter saw him and waved. "Fuzz! Come on down and meet my new partners."

The request was beyond him at that moment. He waved the man off and veered onto a faint trail leading toward the Rooptahe graveyard.

"Fuzz?" Colter called behind him.

"Say he's your friend?" one of the trappers asked.

Colter answered, "Best one I ever knowed."

The next day broke bright with late summer sunshine. By now the whole crew had learned of Colter's discharge. They greeted his arrival at the breakfast fire with congratulations, friendly jibes and more than a little envy that, for him, their long journey was over.

He accepted their reactions with mixed emotions. He had meant what he told Shannon, that he felt he had at last found a home in the Shining Mountains. What he had not said was that all his mental pictures of the place included Fragrant Grass. Yet today he would leave for that imagined home, and she would remain here with Black Cat and the son she had borne to that man. That was the only thought in his mind as he accepted a bowl of steaming corn cakes from the Mandan woman tending the pot.

He had just taken a seat on the ground when Echo appeared, brimming with questions about Colter's destination. He did his best to answer the questions between bites of breakfast. He was describing the Shining Mountains when two young Indian boys ran into the gathering, gesticulating and sputtering in Mandan.

Echo listened, then explained, "Someone has been killed in the graveyard. One of the graves collapsed." Colter knew all too well who it was before Echo said in disbelief, "It is Friend Hartley."

Colter had many questions about the preacher's stay among the Mandans, but he chose to leave them unasked.

"He was a good man," Echo said sadly. "He was my friend as are you and Friend Shannon."

The youth's words prompted Colter to remember that he had not seen Shannon since the previous evening. Before he could go in search of his friend, Dickson and Hancock showed up. "Time's a-wastin', Colter,"

Dickson said.

Hearing the phrase he had used so often on himself throughout his life, Colter chuckled and handed Echo his empty bowl. "Time to go, young'un."

"Take me with you, Friend Colter," Echo pleaded, clinging to his wrist.

"Cain't do that," Colter said. "Maybe next time."

"You will come back?" Echo asked.

"Will you be here?"

"Oh, yes. Where else can I be?"

Colter ruffled the youth's thick hair. "Then I'll be back for sure."

Echo followed Colter and the two trappers to the captains. "I'll be leavin' now, captains," Colter said.

Clark rose from beside Lewis's pallet and reached for Colter's hand. "Good luck, Colter."

"Thank you, sir."

Because Lewis was still suffering from his wound, Colter squatted down next to the bed. "And thank you, sir. For everything."

Lewis grasped his hand. "Make a name for yourself, John."

Colter did not know what to say. He was not after fame. A new life, a new start, yes, but not fame. Not John Colter. He kept his thoughts to himself and nodded.

"And may we meet again some day," Lewis said.

"I hope so, sir," Colter said, getting back to his feet. "Goodbye, Captains. We had us quite an adventure. I ain't about to forget none of it." There was so much more to say to these two extraordinary men who had led them all so far and so well, but he chose to salute and leave rather than stammer around for the right words to say all that was in his heart.

Surrounded by crewmen, he and the two trappers made their way down to the boats. Shannon was standing beside the trappers' canoe. His eyes were heavy with sadness, but his chin had a purposeful set. He came forward with his hand outstretched.

Colter nodded toward that hand. "What's that, Fuzz?"

"My way of wishing you good luck, Old Man."

Colter shook his head. "Nope."

That stopped Shannon in his tracks. "What do you mean: nope?"

"The only luck I'll accept from you is this." He gathered the surprised Shannon into an embrace and whispered, "You watch them women, hear?"

"What women?"

"All of 'em. When it comes to females, Fuzz, you got no more sense than a turnip."

Shannon broke the embrace in a huff. "Now, that's not fair."

Colter doubled over laughing.

"What's so funny?" Shannon demanded.

"You. Just when I'm startin' to know which of your strings to pull, I got to leave you. Sure am goin' to miss arguin' with you, Fuzz."

Shannon's anger melted into understanding. "Confound you, Old Man."

"Same to you." Colter turned to the two trappers. "Let's head out."

Colter helped them slide the canoe into the water and held the stern while they climbed in. Then he turned for one last look at the assembled crowd.

She stood at the top of the bluff, her baby cradled across her body in a sling of soft hide. As he looked at her, she pointed to the sky where a lone hawk circled above the crest of the trees.

He nodded toward her, turning aside his regrets in order to remember how she looked at that moment, then he shoved off and hopped into the boat.

As he dipped his paddle into the Missouri, the hawk banked on a current of air and wheeled toward the west. Toward the Shining Mountains and the Western Sea.

AFTERTHOUGHTS

JOHN COLTER'S partnership with Dickson and Hancock took them to the Three Forks region of the upper Missouri, where they had a falling out after only six weeks and dissolved their business arrangement. Colter continued his life as a trapper, and in 1807, he joined Manuel Lisa on the Big Horn River.

In 1809, Colter and former expedition member John Potts started trapping in Blackfeet country, but the Blackfeet did not take kindly to this incursion. They killed Potts outright, then stripped Colter naked and made him run for his life. Colter outran the Blackfeet, narrowly escaping death. He killed one of his pursuers with the man's own spear. Eleven days later, he staggered into Fort Raymond, barely alive, having survived on roots and bark. After several deadly encounters with the Blackfeet, he left the West forever.

With his earnings, he bought a plot of land in Missouri and built a cabin on it. He married a woman known only to history as "Sally" and had a son. He died in 1813 of jaundice.

Colter is widely acknowledged as the first white man to see what is now Yellowstone Park. For years, it was known as 'Colter's Hell,' because of the tales he told about the geothermal springs and shooting geysers.

GEORGE SHANNON returned to the west in 1807 with a party led by Ensign Nathaniel Pryor, which attempted to return Chief Shahaka to his home among the Mandans. Shot in the leg by the Arikaras, Shannon suffered severely, until the leg was amputated in St. Charles, Missouri. In 1813, by an act of Congress, he received a pension for the loss of his leg. That same year, he married Ruth Snowden Price of Lexington, Kentucky. Shannon refused an offer from Clark to go into the fur business, electing to study the law, instead, at the Transylvania University of Kentucky, and later at Philadelphia. He began his law practice in Lexington, Kentucky in 1818 and was elected to the Kentucky House of Representatives in 1820 and 1822. After his Kentucky years, he practiced law in Missouri, and was a senator from Missouri for a time, then returned to the law. In 1836, aged forty-nine, he died abruptly in court at Palmyra, Missouri, and is buried in that city.

Shannon was honored by the creation of a geographic legacy. when a tributary to the Yellowstone River in Montana was named "Shannon's Creek" by Captain Clark.

JOSEPH AND REUBEN FIELD (their name is sometimes spelled "Fields') were discharged on October 10, 1806. Upon completion of the mission, Lewis wrote that Joseph and Reuben Field were: "Two of the most active and enterprising young men who accompanied us. It was their peculiar fate to have been engaged in all the most dangerous and difficult scenes of the voyage, in which they uniformly acquited themselves with much honor."

Clark recommended Reuben for a lieutenancy in the army, but he declined. Although he had a warrant for land in Missouri as a reward for his part in the expedition, Reuben returned to Kentucky to live. In 1808, in Indiana, he married Mary Myrtle. Reuben died in late 1822 in Jefferson County, Kentucky.

Joseph led a small party which explored the lower Yellowstone. After the expedition, he received a warrant for land located in Franklin County, Missouri. William Clark noted that he was "dead by 1825-28."

PATRICK GASS served in the War of 1812 and participated in several major campaigns. He lost an eye at Fort Independence in 1815 and was discharged with full pension that same month. At the age of 60, he married Maria Hamilton, aged twenty. They had six children. The last surviving member of the expedition, he died in 1870, at nearly 99 years of age.

Gass was the first to publish a journal of the expedition in 1807 and is credited with giving it the name 'Corps of Discovery.'

JOHN ORDWAY received double pay, on Lewis's recommendation, as did most of the men in the Corps. After purchasing the land warrants of his fellow expedition members, William Werner and Jean Baptiste La Page, Ordway went with Captain Lewis to show off a group of Indians to the President in Washington. He returned to New Hampshire, then in 1809, he returned to Missouri and settled near New Madrid. The owner of extensive lands, he was prosperous, having two plantations of peach and apple orchards. He and his wife Gracy died in Missouri about 1817. They had no survivors.

GEORGE DROUILLARD lived for a few years at Cape Girardeau, Missouri after the expedition. Following a return trip to the Rocky Mountains, he contributed numerous topographical details to Clark's map of the Northwest. In 1810, he was with the Manuel Lisa party when he was killed by the Blackfeet Indians, not far from where he had had an encounter with these same Indians during the expedition, when he accompanied Captain Lewis on the exploration of the upper Maria's River.

MERIWETHER LEWIS returned to a hero's welcome, but his lifelong bout with depression finally conquered him. Receiving double pay for his service with the expedition ($1,228), a warrant for 1,600 acres of land in Missouri, and being named governor of the Territory of Upper Louisiana in 1807 were not enough to overcome his malady. Failures in attempting to publish his and Clark's journals, two unsuccessful romances, increasing consumption of alcohol, and his year of delay in taking up his governor's post put him at odds with President Jefferson.

When he finally arrived to assume his appointment, St. Louis was overrun with opportunists, land speculators, ruthless traders, and Native Americans, all vying for larger and larger shares of the pie.

Unable to cope with all this, Lewis fled St. Louis in March, 1809 for Washington to plead his case before the new administration. En route, while staying in a roadhouse along the infamous Natchez Trace, Lewis purportedly took his own life by shooting himself first in the forehead, then in the breast. It was deemed a suicide, despite the multiple fatal wounds, because he had attempted suicide twice before. He was buried next to the tavern, and today the site is marked by a monument that was erected in his honor in 1846.

WILLIAM CLARK spent the rest of his years in exemplary fashion, a direct contrast to that of Meriwether Lewis. He served as Governor of the Misouri Territory from 1813, until it became a state in 1820. He was defeated for the governorship, but having attained the rank of Brigadier General, he continued serving his country as Superintendent of Indian Affairs.

Native Americans, traders, and trappers all respected Clark and regularly contributed knowledge to his map of the American West, which he updated constantly.

Clark died of natural causes in September 1838.

Chapter One from

MISSION

The Birth of California,
The Death of a Nation

MARGARET WYMAN

I

TWO WORLDS

Fall, 1767 — Fall, 1768

Chapter 1 — Late Summer, 1767

*The Kumeyaay Desert Village of Hawi in
the Great Desert east of what is now San Diego*

Web lay in a pit on a mat of deer grass and desert mallow spread over heated stones. A similar mat of grass and mallow covered her and the other initiate, Mishtai, her best friend. She was able to ignore the dust the dancers kicked up, but the persistent itch on her lower back tested her control. She bit her lip against the urge to move. The priest had precisely positioned two crescent-shaped stones on her abdomen just above her budding pubic thatch. Any movement might shift the stones before the ceremony ended. A lifetime of criticism awaited the girl who could not withstand the temporary discomfort of the roasting pit during her three-day passage from childhood to womanhood.

Out of the corner of her eye, Web watched her friend Mishtai. The two girls had begun their monthly courses on the same day, the day of the last *hellyach-temur* full moon. While Web and Mishtai had gone into seclusion to prepare themselves for the responsibility that went with their new power to bring forth life, their parents had sent out runners inviting the scattered members of their respective *sh'mulq* sibs to come to Hawi for the girls' initiation ceremony. During their seclusion, Web and Mishtai had spent hours exchanging confidences. As the first members of their sibs began to arrive, they had made a solemn pact to help each other through the ordeal ahead of them in whatever way they could.

The itching on Web's back intensified. *No,* Web thought. *I will not give in to you. I will not move. I have not come this far or endured this much to fail now.*

To keep her mind off the torment, she turned her attention to the crowd dancing around the sand pit. Some of the dancers had traveled many days to reach Hawi in time. So many had come that their numbers strained the resources of the small village.

While Web watched the dancing, the girl Amul pushed through the crowd and came to stand at the pit to smirk down at the two girls. Despite the mesh ceremonial cap that hid her face, Web stared back, matching her nemesis' mocking smile. For as far back as she could remember Amul had been the bane of her existence, teasing her, calling her "Slime-Frog" and making slurping noises that caused the other children to laugh at her, always careful to hide her cruelty from the adults.

After a time, Amul tired of her staring and disappeared into the crowd. The moment she was gone, Web's itching reasserted itself. In order to ignore it, she narrowed her eyes to slits to concentrate on the weave of the mesh that had protected her face and head from the swarming spring flies during her time in the pit.

Her mother had woven the ceremonial cap from juncus grass, spending hours wrapping and stitching to create a piece every bit as beautiful as the baskets she made to trade. Woven into the coils was a unique design of frogs and ducks. The animals had been sacred to their *sh'mulq* since the dawn of time when First Ancestor had seen fit to give certain women of her mother's line webbed hands–hands like Web's–where flaps of skin grew up to the first joints of each finger. Web had been named for her hands. Before her, the last one so endowed was her mother's grandmother. Yet, despite the many stories of Great-Grandmother's abilities as a healer and maker of baskets so beautiful that even the warlike Quechan people came under the flag of truce to Hawi to trade for them and despite her mother's exhortations to be proud of her hands, Amul's teasing and the stares she drew whenever the people of Hawi traveled to other Kumeyaay villages made Web self-conscious of her hands.

One of the elders of her father's sib now stepped out of the group dancing a shuffling circle around the pit and launched into a harangue about the responsibilities the roasting girls must assume as adult members of the Hawi band. Web tried hard to be attentive, but she was too tired and uncomfortable to absorb much. *So many must-nots. So much to remember. How can I ever live up to the expectations of my parents and my band?*

The delectable perfume of roasting *haakwal* lizard, her favorite, assailed her nostrils. In the last three days she had been allowed to eat only a cup of *shawii* acorn mush at those times she had been allowed to leave the pit so that the cooling rocks could be replaced with hot ones. Now that her monthly courses had begun, she must not eat meat or fish or salt for at least one moon; longer if she intended to follow the tradition of the women of her mother's sh'mulq. She knew her mother expected a longer period of absten-tion, but at that moment, Web could not imagine another hour with-out a taste of *haakwal*, let alone a full moon cycle.

Steady pressure against her right arm broke through her thoughts. Mishtai had given into the exhaustion of three days without sleep.

"Mishtai," Web hissed softly without moving her lips. "Wake up."

Her friend did not respond.

Cognizant of the consequences to Mishtai if someone caught her sleeping, Web checked to be sure no one was paying attention before inching her covered hand slowly toward her friend, praying no one would notice the barely perceptible ripple in the layer of grass.

At that moment, the dancers parted to reveal Amul watching her with unblinking eyes. The sight stopped Web's hand. Pact or not, she refused to give Amul the pleasure of being the one to catch her breaking the rules of initiation.

Suddenly Mishtai snorted and jerked upright, convulsing the entire covering of grass. Instantly the presiding shaman leaped to the side of the pit and launched into a tirade aimed at the offending girl. Disgust painted the faces of the members of Mishtai's extended family, standing with her dismayed parents.

Throughout the harangue, Mishtai kept her eyes lowered and barely breathed. After the priest finished and the adults went back to their dancing, she murmured a hurt, "You promised" to Web.

Web could think of nothing to say that would satisfy the embarrassed Mishtai, especially with Amul still watching her every move. She kept her eyes on the lengthening shadow of the closest 'aanall mesquite. The roasting would end at sunset. This close to the end, perhaps the adults would not hold Mishtai's slip against her for long. Perhaps she could claim she too had nodded off momentarily. Would a lie help, or make the situation worse?

She hoped the right answer would come to her before they were lifted out of the pit for the last time.

After what seemed an eternity, the singing stopped, leaving a gap of deafening silence. The priest signaled the girls' mothers and aunts forward. While the women rolled back the pit covering, Web leaned toward Mishtai and whispered, "I didn't see you until it was too late."

"Don't lie," Mishtai said coldly. "I can always tell when you don't speak the truth."

"But, I–"

Her mother's touch cut off Web's protest. Mother and two aunts helped her out of the pit. "Oh, my daughter, you have made me so proud. Now you are a woman," her mother said, removing the basket cap and smoothing Web's long hair. Prior to the ceremony, she had cut her daughter's bangs just above her eyebrows in the style of the adult women of the people. Now she cupped Web's cheek and gave her a tremulous smile full of the emotion she did not voice.

"Not quite yet, my sister," said Web's aunt, Button Cactus. "We must first give her the tattoo marks of a woman and then the priest will lead her to the holy place."

"The marking will hurt, my child, but you must not cry out," her mother whispered. "Remember what I have taught you."

Web nodded, sucked in a breath to steel herself against the pain to come and allowed her mother's sisters to lead her to a small boulder. Button Cactus, as the eldest, waved for Web to sit, then took charge. After a quick glance at the prickly-pear cactus thorns, laid out in a row next to the sticks of charcoal, Web closed her eyes, took several deep breaths and retreated to the quiet place within her as her mother had taught. She was only partially aware of the thorns puncturing the skin of her chin and of charcoal being rubbed into the wounds until her mother announced, "Stand, child."

Web came out of her trance to find her mother draping a *hekwiir* blanket of twisted rabbit skins over her shoulders. "Remember how I showed you to hold it?" her mother asked.

Despite the throbbing pain in her chin, Web grasped the edges of the drape together at the neck so that both hands were hidden inside the folds of the *hekwiir*.

Her mother smiled, and the aunts placed garlands made of pliable yucca on her head, then stepped away, leaving her standing by herself. Suddenly she was uneasy about what she would soon witness. Besides making the pact to help each other through the roasting, she and Mishtai had spent endless hours wondering over what the priest would show them in this final stage of their initiation. Was it a hole so deep that it led to the back side of the sky? Or a deep pool in whose depths they would be able to see into the spirit world? Or something even more terrifying?

Suddenly she was not at all sure she wanted to become an adult, burdened with responsibilities and cares. Her chin throbbed from the recent assault of thorns and charcoal. She had one last step to complete her initiation into womanhood. No woman in either parental sib had ever failed any of the ordeals of her initiation, yet her leaden legs refused to move.

"Go, child. The priest awaits," her mother urged.

Web swallowed against the cottony feel in her throat. *I do not want this*, she wanted to scream.

"Daughter?" The exasperation in her mother's tone got Web's feet moving.

Mishtai was already with the priest. She side-stepped away from Web.

An assistant stepped forward to help the priest wrap strips of hide around the girls' eyes as blindfolds. Then the priest command-ed, "Come."

Already light-headed from hunger, fatigue and pain, Web stum-bled along, blindly following the faint crunch of the priest's steps in the sand. Her senses told her that he led them out from the village toward the hot-springs. Sulfurous smells a short while later confirmed her guess as the little party followed the foot path around the steaming water and headed up the rising pan toward the boundary beyond which ordinary Kumeyaay did not pass. The jumbled rocks that lay beyond that boundary were sacred, reserved for those who possessed the power to enter the world of Spirits. When Web tried to stop, the priest's assistant prodded her to keep moving.

At the edge of the rocks, the branch of a creosote bush caught at Web's ankle. She stumbled and would have fallen if the assistant had not caught her and restored her to her feet. She wanted to turn back, away from the land of Spirits into the land of mortals, but the assistant's grip remained on her arm, guiding her over the rock-strewn path.

On and on they went until Web's legs turned rubbery. She was close to fainting when the priest's voice intoned, "Stop."

The assistant stripped off her blindfold, and the shaman command-ed, "Look. There."

Web blinked to adjust to the flickering light of the firebrand the priest carried.

"Behold Mother Goddess," the priest thundered. "Behold Her sacred Self. Look you well upon Her for it is from Her that you gain the power to bring forth life. From this moment you, Web, and you, Mishtai, are no longer children. Now you are women."

While the priest's voice boomed off the wall of boulders before them, relating all that would be expected of her now that she was a woman, Web observed, confused by what she saw. An enor-mous rock formation rose up before her. An odd formation that looked like a double-yoked egg.

She waited for the priest to explain, to tell her what she was supposed to see, but he had fallen silent. She continued to stare, then suddenly it hit her. Not an egg, the rocks formed the flower petals that a woman–that Web herself–carried tucked between her legs. The two lips that kiss each child as it leaves its mother to join the world, and the door through which a baby passes into life.

With that realization, power seemed to pour forth from the rocks, glit-tering with the afterglow of Sun. That power washed over her, engulfing her like the wind that precedes the life-giving rains. Awestruck, she nudged Mishtai. "Do you see it, my sister?" she whispered over the sound of the shaman's chanting.

"Do not call me sister. You are no longer my friend," Mishtai hissed.

"Silence!" the priest's assistant ordered.

Under his glare, Mishtai seemed to shrink while Web bit back the urge to defend herself.

The priest finished his song and waved his sacred staff toward the rock formation. "The Mother Goddess shows Herself to you now so that you may bear many strong sons and daughters. Look you and think about the man who will be your husband."

Husband.

In one word, Web's awe for the Mother Goddess and her concern about Mishtai vanished, leaving in her innards a void that had no bottom. She had been so intent on performing her role in the initiation ceremony cor-rectly that she had not thought beyond it. Now that the rites had reached their conclusion, the future yawned before her like a deep, pitch-black cave. She was now a woman. Womanhood meant marriage. Children. And keeping a husband happy.

When she had five summers, her parents had betrothed her to Shadow Dancer, a boy of seven summers, son of the renowned *wekuseyaay* rattle-snake shaman, Casts No Shadow. Casts No Shadow and Shadow Dancer lived in the village of Nipaguay over the mountains in the fertile valley of the river that ran into the *'ehaasilth* ocean far to the west. The betrothal had brought her parents great honor and many wonderful gifts from the *wekuseyaay* and his band. Nipaguay controlled some of the richest planting and hunting land and the best fishing areas along the coast. Web's marriage would tie Nipaguay to Hawi. For the people of Hawi, it meant reserves of food should they face another starving time, and reinforcements should the Quechan people decide to wage war again.

In the eight years since her betrothal, Web had seen Shadow Dancer only once: four years ago, when the winter rains did not come for the fifth straight year and the desert refused to bloom, the hungry people of Hawi undertook the long dangerous journey to the coast for food, and there she had set eyes upon her future husband. He was a tall boy with an intense gaze who seemed to be constantly asking questions about everyone and everything around him. Since the time, she had dreamed about him occasionally, but the dreams were the fantasies of a mere girl. Now the reality hit her with the force of a blow.

Marriage to Shadow Dancer meant leaving Hawi and everyone she loved, forever. Why had she never thought of that before?

A great sadness welled up from the pit of her stomach. She ducked her head and blinked back the tears that threatened to betray her. She must not cry. Whatever happened, she must make her parents proud.

Beside her, Mishtai sniffed. Deep in her own misery, Web ignored her friend and looked again upon the Mother Goddess through the mist of her unshed tears. The force flowing from the rocks changed from an engulfing wave to the tenderest of caresses as if the Spirits of the rocks, as if the Mother Goddess Herself, felt Web's fear and wanted to reassure her.

Web had no time to absorb the sensation. The priest repositioned her blindfold, and her world again went dark.

"You are now women. Come. We will return to the village," the priest said, pebbles clattering under his sandaled steps.

Before she could take a step, a small hand gripped Web's arm. "I hope you will leave Hawi soon," Mishtai said. "You are no friend of mine." Releasing her grip, she stumbled off, leaving Web to return with the assistant priest.

Quick Order Form
Shining Mountains, Western Sea
by Margaret (Peggy) Wyman

Name:		
Address:		
City:	State:	Zip
Telephone:	Email:	

Copies		X $21.95 per copy	
Sales tax: Please add 7.75% for products shipped to California addresses			
Order Sub Total			
	Shipping (see below)		
Order Total			
Special Instructions:			

Shipping	
US Media Mail (6 days):	Add $3.00 per book
U.S. Priority Mail (2 days):	Add $5.00 per book

Toll-Free: 866-IDPUBCO (437-8226)
FAX orders: 909-659-4950. Send this form.
Email orders: ipc@tazland.net
Postal orders: Idyllwild Publishing Co., P.O. Box 355, Idyllwild, CA 92549

Quick Order Form
Shining Mountains, Western Sea
by Margaret (Peggy) Wyman

Name:			
Address:			
City:		State:	Zip
Telephone:		Email:	

Copies		X $21.95 per copy	
Sales tax: Please add 7.75% for products shipped to California addresses			
Order Sub Total			
		Shipping (see below)	
Order Total			
Special Instructions:			

Shipping	
US Media Mail (6 days):	Add $3.00 per book
U.S. Priority Mail (2 days):	Add $5.00 per book

Toll-Free: 866-IDPUBCO (437-8226)
FAX orders: 909-659-4920. Send this form.
Email orders: ipc@tazland.net
Postal orders: Idyllwild Publishing Co., P.O. Box 355, Idyllwild, CA 92549